Books by Michael R. Ellis

Apollo Rises
Chief Page
The Bonifacio Strait

NEA MAKRI

Michael R. Ellis
U.S. NAVY RETIRED

AuthorHouse™
1663 Liberty Drive
Bloomington, IN 47403
www.authorhouse.com
Phone: 1-800-839-8640

This book is a work of fiction. People, places, events, and situations are the product of the author's imagination. Any resemblance to actual persons, living or dead, or historical events, is purely coincidental.

© 2011 Michael R. Ellis U.S. NAVY RETIRED. All rights reserved.

No part of this book may be reproduced, stored in a retrieval system, or transmitted by any means without the written permission of the author.

First published by AuthorHouse   6/17/2011

ISBN: 978-1-4520-1051-9 (sc)
ISBN: 978-1-4520-1052-6 (e)

Printed in the United States of America

Any people depicted in stock imagery provided by Thinkstock are models, and such images are being used for illustrative purposes only.
Certain stock imagery © Thinkstock.

This book is printed on acid-free paper.

Because of the dynamic nature of the Internet, any web addresses or links contained in this book may have changed since publication and may no longer be valid. The views expressed in this work are solely those of the author and do not necessarily reflect the views of the publisher, and the publisher hereby disclaims any responsibility for them.

For
Red

Acknowledgment

Nea Makri front cover illustration by Joel Roberson

Notes and Quotes

A Few Notes

In response to suggestions from my non-navy readers, I have included a *glossary of navy terms* and a *table of the navy rank* structure at the end of this book.

I welcome comments from my readers. I use your comments to improve my writing with the intention to improve your reading pleasure. See publisher website for my email address.

Some Quotes Applicable to the Story

"Truth is incontrovertible, malice may attack it and ignorance may deride it, but, in the end, there it is."
- **Sir Winston Churchill**

"It ain't what you don't know that gets you into trouble. Its what you know for sure that just ain't so."
- **Mark Twain**

"Communism is the riddle of history solved, and it knows itself to be this solution."
- **Karl Marx**

"There is no greater evil than those who crusade to destroy the American Republic."
- **Rigney Michael Page**

Introduction

During the early years of the twentieth century, the United States Navy established a network of communications stations around the world. This communications network provided support to America's deployed navy and was crucial to America's victory against Germany and Japan during World War II.

The threat of Soviet aggression after World War II required the United States to deploy navy ships overseas for extended periods. To support overseas deployed ships, dozens of overseas Naval Communications Stations were added to the worldwide network. By the late 1960s, these Naval Communications Stations and U.S. warships were networked via high-frequency, inline encryption radio teletype circuits.

Each Naval Communications Station had at least two geographical locations—a transmitter site and a receiver site. Geographic separation was necessary, so that the powerful transmitters did not interfere with radio receiver operations.

Many Naval Communications Stations were remote and, therefore, categorized as sea duty. Those Naval Communications Stations and those U.S. Navy flagships permanently stationed overseas provided a means whereby a navy radioman could serve his whole career overseas and seldom step foot in the United States. Occasionally, this environment created an American military expatriate.

Prologue

Email dated March 19, 2003
From
Larry "Charmer" Webb

I served at NAVCOMMSTA Greece from 1966 to 1968. It was a small base located on the north side of the Aegean coastal town of Nea Makri. I was only nineteen when I arrived, and I had never been outside the United States before. My running mates and I consider our time in Greece to be the best time of our youth. We were young, brash and adventurous. All of Greece was open to us, and we daringly explored the country and enjoyed its cultural treats.

We arrived at NAVCOMMSTA Greece during January 1966, immediately following Radioman School at Bainbridge Naval Training Center. Three radiomen from my class were lucky enough to get orders to Greece. Everyone else in our class went to ships in Norfolk, Charleston, and Mayport.

The NAVCOMMSTA main gate was on the west end of the base along the Marathon Road. When we arrived at the main gate, I was astonished by the minimal security protecting the base. Two sentries stood guard at the main gate. One sentry was a U.S. Navy SK3, and the other sentry was a Greek sailor. Although they wore .45 caliber automatics, they just did not appear as threats to possible intruders. If the enemy wanted to penetrate the base, all they needed to do was straddle over the fence anywhere around the perimeter. I later learned that the minimal security was intentional so that the American navy presented a non-intrusive and non-aggressive presence.

As I went through the check-in process, I discovered the rough and simple conditions of the base. The base had been in existence for less than three years. The base had one single-lane, crudely constructed road that ran from the main gate, through the support area, through the receiver antenna field, and stopped at the communications trailers compound near the east end of the base. No road existed beyond the communications trailers compound, only a sandy path that led past the firing range to the beach. The enlisted barracks, admin building, BOQ, and galley were on the west end of the base near the main gate. Those buildings were all single story, pea-green colored prefabs. I was just an RMSN—E3. So I was housed in the four-wing junior enlisted barracks. Everyone in the junior enlisted barracks lived in four-man cubicles. Each sailor had one metal locker to call his own. Sailors sometimes argued longevity rights when cubicles had less than four sailors and empty lockers were up for grabs.

Within a few days or reporting aboard, I was assigned to a watch section in the communications trailers. Each trailer was the size of an eighteen-wheeler trailer. The trailers were connected together and doorways led from one trailer to the other. The interior of the communications trailers was packed full of modern teletype machines and state-of-the-art radio equipment. The air-conditioned, lowered ceiling, fake-wood paneled décor provided a comfortable work environment. I was assigned to the top secret NAVCOMOPNET trailer, also known as HI-COMM trailer. HI-COMM operations included circuits with aircraft carriers, cruisers, and other type flagships. I was initially assigned as XRA teletype broadcast operator.

Although barracks living sucked, working hours were fantastic. We worked a 3-3-3-72 watch rotation. We stood three eight-hour day-watches, followed by twenty-four hours off. Then, we worked three eight-hour mid-watches, followed by twenty-four hours off. Then, we worked three eight-hour eve-watches, followed by 72 hours off.

When there were not enough hours between watches to go on liberty, we would drink beer in the makeshift enlisted club located in the northeast wing of the barracks. The club, which was open between 1030 and 2300, was always packed with off-watch sailors who drank and played cards, dice, and a few board games. Those watch standers assigned to cubicles close to the club continuously complained about the noise, because some watch standers were always attempting to sleep between watches. On paydays, the gambling sharks descended on the club and thousands of dollars changed hands in large crap games and in dice games called *ship, captain, and crew*.

When my first 72 arrived, some radiomen from my watch section invited me to join them on a trip to Athens. They told me to pack a liberty bag, because we would spend a couple of nights at a hotel. We took the base liberty bus which was an express to-and-from Athens city center. The bus drop-off and pick-up was always Zonar's Restaurant, one block from Syntagma square. Because of the dollar and drachma exchange rate, the hotel, which catered to Greeks and not tourists, cost less than ten dollars a night. Our hotel, Syntagma Square, Plaka, and the Acropolis were all within walking distance of each other.

During our hotel stay in Athens, we spent mornings at the cafés on Syntagma. During the afternoons we roamed the Acropolis and the Parthenon. At night, we prowled the nightclubs of Plaka for female companionship.

I discovered during those early excursions into Athens that it was difficult to pick up women during the mornings and afternoons; they were more interested in touring than embracing male advances. So, I started going into Athens by myself and going on the tours. I purchased some books on Athens history. After several months, I gained sufficient knowledge of the city and its history to impress woman tourists, and they became more willing to accept my companionship.

An interesting incident occurred in Nea Makri on May Day 1966. I grew up being taught that not all in the world considered America as the best place to live, and that many people in the world did not believe the *American way* is the best way. America had enemies devoted to destroying us. Every year on May Day, the Greek Communist Party marched from Marathon to Athens and protested capitalism and cheered communism. The Marathon

Road ran by the main gate. The Greek army bivouacked on the base for a few days before and after the May Day march. I was outside watching the march, and I was bewildered that many of their protest signs were in English. They shouted anti-American slogans in English as they paused near the main gate. But, they did not get belligerent or out of control, and they moved on.

As the 1966 summer season approached, Northern European tourists flooded into the Aegean coastal town of Nea Makri. My running mates and I spent less time in Athens and more time in the town of Nea Makri. Our favorite spot was *The Blue Lights* restaurant on Nea Makri beach. We called it *The Blue Lights* because we didn't know the Greek name and the restaurant had blue neon lights all around it. Unlike the women tourists in Athens, the European women who spent summer vacations in Nea Makri were all about fun, recreation, and erotic pleasures.

Near the end of summer 1966, my running mates and I were ready to expand our adventures beyond Athens and Nea Makri. Three of us went together and bought a deteriorating 1956 Chevy convertible from a transferring Seabee chief. We spent a month repairing her; then, we were ready to discover the rest of Greece.

We toured the Greek mainland and the islands during the fall and winter when rates were cheaper. By December 1966 we had driven all over Greece from Thessalonica to Patras to Sparta.

I don't remember if it was late 1966 or early 1967 when the Club Zeus opened on base. The opening of Club Zeus was a welcome event that closed the enlisted club in the barracks. Club Zeus was in its own building along the south fence, just across the base road from the admin building. The new club had a bar, dance floor, stage, small grill, and later a swimming pool was built next to the club. Live bands played in the club, which enticed sailors to bring their girlfriends and wives for nights of entertainment.

During early January 1967, our Greek island travel plans were quashed when the communications department went from a four section rotation to a three section rotation of 2-2-48 with twelve-hour watches, which really sucked! During the previous year, many radiomen transferred and were not replaced, as evidenced by drastic reduction in barrack's occupancy. The communications officer explained that with the build up of troops in Vietnam more radiomen were being assigned to Vietnam and other WESTPAC commands. He attempted to motivate us by telling us that every time we thought how tough we had it, we should think about how tough sailors in Vietnam had it. It was a valid point, but our morale sank anyway. As morale got worse, communications operating errors increased. As errors increased, chiefs and officers ramped up with negative motivation actions like EMI, snap barracks inspections, and unscheduled seabag inspections. The more errors increased, the more the punishment increased. As a result, morale got even worse and processing errors increased drastically. To punish us further, we shifted from the three section rotation to a two-section, port and starboard, watch rotation of twelve-hours-on and twelve-hours-off; the justification being that we needed more radiomen on watch to reduce processing errors. But, yes, you guessed it. Processing errors continued to increase. We became resigned and deadened to the barrage of punishments. We coined a standard protest response to each new punishment: *"It could be worse; I could be sent to NAVCOMMSTA Greece."*

During the spring of 1967, a bloodless coup d'état led by a group of Greek colonels took over the Greek government. We were all ordered to stay on the base until the Greek government gave permission for us to do otherwise. Fortunately, *the colonels*—also called *The Junta*—were pro American, and we were allowed to continue our journeys off base in the same manner as before.

About the same time of the coup, we heard that a female lieutenant commander would be assigned as executive officer. No woman had ever been stationed at Nea Makri before. We were told she was part of a new program to assign women to remote overseas duty stations. Rumors and innuendo ran rampant as to what this female XO would do to make our lives even more miserable. We knew she had never served at sea; therefore, her leadership ability was in doubt. We heard that we would be required to hang frilly curtains in the barracks and would be required to paint the barracks pink during our off time. When Lieutenant Commander Blakely reported aboard, we were all stunned by her beauty, which reinforced our perceptions that she was just a U.S. Navy showpiece for equal opportunity.

Two weeks after the new XO reported aboard, we went to a 2-2-2-96 four section, eight-hour watch rotation. Senior Chief Hallford explained the conditions for the four section watch rotation. He told us that during the 2-2-2 we would work many extra hours during the peak message traffic periods, and our performance would be evaluated by the number of mistakes we made and evaluated by average message handling times. Senior chief said that if we reduced processing errors and operated within DOD message handling times our reward would be hassle-free, uninterrupted 96 hours off between watch strings—no personnel inspections; no barracks inspections; no required training and meetings. However, each of us would be held individually responsible for keeping the barracks neat and clean and for keeping our uniforms and appearance within regulations. Senior chief said violations to any of the conditions would put the four section watch rotation in jeopardy.

We struggled to maintain a four section watch rotation. Something unusual happened; well, unusual according to the lifers. The junior sailors were policing themselves to stay within the conditions of the four section watches. In the communications trailers, error rates were posted by individual's name, and message handling times were posted by watch sections. The junior sailors would pressure their peers to improve performance. When a junior sailor was in need of a haircut or his uniform was in need of improvement, his peers would force him to get a haircut and fix his uniform. When a barracks cubicle became messy, junior sailors would urge the residents to tidy-up. If a common area in the barracks became cluttered with trash, junior sailors would take care of it without prompting from seniors.

We discovered later that the entire four section plan was ordered by the new XO. We learned that she had been the Communications Department Head at her last command—NAVCOMMSTA Norfolk, and she was experienced in NAVCOMMSTA operations. Just when we were convinced that the navy really sucks and all chiefs and officers blow, a female officer arrived and gave the old salts a lesson in leadership. Our morale improved, and respect for the XO increased.

Shortly after going back to four sections, my friends and I advanced to second class petty officers, and we were ordered to move into the petty officers' barracks. My friend *Toot*—his nickname—suggested that we rent a house on the beach and move off base. So, *Toot, Sniper, Frenchie,* and I moved into a four bedroom, two-story house just two doors away from the sand of the Nea Makri beach.

All my running mates had nicknames. My friend, *Toot*, coined my nickname, *Charmer*. He said he labeled me *Charmer* because I was polite, persuasive, and witty. There were others with nicknames like *Big Louie, Dancing Bear, Bagpipes, Bullseye,* and *The Professor*. For some of them, I cannot remember their real names, and for all of them, I don't remember the origins of their nicknames.

Toot was a babe magnet. He was a tall, good looking surfer from Southern California. During our first summer in the house, *Toot* offered the house to female tourists from northern Europe as a place to change clothes for the beach.

As more women funneled through our house to and from the beach, our house became a constant party with a mix of male and female Greeks, Germans, Norwegians, Swiss, and Brits. Many were drawn in by the American music and American liquor. We didn't stock American beer, because it was substandard compared to the German and Dutch beers that we purchased on the local market. All beer was served at room temperature, because that is how Europeans drink it. We didn't keep the kitchen stocked, but we made three or four food-runs per day to *Sam's Souvlaki*.

Everything on the local market was cheap compared to costs in the States. Back then, the exchange rate was 30 drachma to the dollar.

Those Europeans were excellent guests; they were wild partiers, but they were cooperative and never got out of control. And they were more than willing to contribute to our party fund which was in a large jar on the bar. Because my roommates and I worked different watch rotations, one or more of us were always in the house. During that first summer in the house, seldom did any of us spend the night in our beds alone.

One incident nearly sent us back to a two section watch rotation. When the USS *Liberty* was attacked by the Israelis, message traffic volume increased by fifty percent for several days. NAVCOMMSTA Greece was accused by higher navy commands of mishandling USS *Liberty* messages. It was like the Navy was saying errors made by NAVCOMMSTA Greece were the reason the Navy responded slowly to the USS *Liberty*'s initial attack reports. For more that two weeks, demands for explanations and punishment dumped down on our commanding officer. However, the CO sent several messages to Washington stating that no judgments should be made regarding his command's actions and no punishment should be awarded until the investigation was complete.

One week later, an investigation team arrived. Anyway, to make a long story short, the investigation proved with facts taken from logs and teletype record monitors that NAVCOMMSTA Greece was not at fault. As a matter of fact, all the messages we were accused of mishandling were sent to us in error in the first place. So, NAVCOMMSTA Greece was absolved of wrong doing, and we stayed in four sections.

When the summer season of 1967 ended, the town of Nea Makri settled down to its off-season calm. We went back to prowling the Plaka, Syntagma Square, and the Acropolis, and we again toured the Greek Islands via car ferry.

As we transited from 1967 into 1968, morale was up, reenlistments were up, and some sailors who had previously declared they would *"never ship-over in this fucked-up navy"* re-enlisted with incentives to extend their tours in Nea Makri.

Then, during the spring of 1968 we got a new commanding officer, Commander Caldwell. He immediately made changes that sent morale to the depths of hell. My enlistment was up in July 1968, and I had been thinking of extending my enlistment to stay in Nea Makri for another year. Fortunately, I had not signed the papers, and I decided not to extend my enlistment. I figured that as long as the navy allowed officers like Commander Caldwell to command, I would not spend one minute more than my initial obligation.

During early July 1968, I departed Nea Makri. Before departing, we all promised to write, but we didn't, and memories of the best years of my youth faded. I went through discharge processing in Norfolk. After the navy, I used the GI Bill and went to college and earned a degree in business management.

Because of the internet, I am now reconnecting with *Toot*, *Sniper*, *Frenchie*, and many others. They have sent me emails about the events in Nea Makri following my departure. Appears the summer and autumn of 1968 was full of unusual and interesting incidents. I'm sorry I missed it!

There is discussion of a NAVCOMMSTA Greece reunion. I plan to attend, and I hope to see all of you there.

Regards,
Charmer

Chapter 1

Spring 1968 - Athens, Greece

Ray walks along the flat stone streets of Plaka. He enjoys the variety of smells and sounds in the pleasant evening air. The aroma of grilling lamb meat at souvlaki stands causes his mouth to water. The sounds of traditional Greek music emanating from various Greek clubs lend authenticity to the Athens experience. A first time visitor may find the streets that are lined with white-washed buildings and red tile roofs indistinguishable from each other. However, for Ray, each street is unique. Each street hosts shops and sidewalk vendors that differentiate one street from the other. During the past twenty years, he patronized all of Plaka's nightclubs, cafés, and restaurants.

He smiles contentedly as he passes each sidewalk café and hears conversations in different languages. Many of the street vendors are interesting attractions in themselves, because of their unusual products and their expertise at haggling price, usually emotionally with waving hands.

I could walk Plaka blindfolded and know where I am at all times.

Plaka draws thousands of tourists during spring and summer. In recent years, Plaka became a haven for American hippies. During semester break, students from many nations visit Plaka and create a center of multicultural excitement.

Many shop owners and employees of Plaka's establishments know Ray as a frequent visitor over the last twenty years. They also know that in recent years, Ray works at the United States Navy Station at Nea Makri, which is ten miles east of Athens on the other side of the peninsula. As Ray passes those with familiar faces, they smile and exchange greetings.

Occasionally, Ray looks up toward the top of the Acropolis where the Parthenon stands illumined by floodlights, as if the Parthenon emanates ancient enlightenment over the entire city.

The Plaka, built on the slopes of the Acropolis, dates back to the earliest days of the city. Plaka is Ray's most favorite spot in the world. He first discovered Plaka during a port visit by his U.S. Navy destroyer back in the summer of 1949. He had been in the navy for ten years then. That port visit was his first experience in Athens. If it is possible to fall in love with a place, then Ray fell in love with Plaka. Plaka provides him with an escape from the daily and mundane routine of navy life. He loves the Greek culture and the Greek people. Ray studies the Greek language, and he becomes more proficient with each passing year.

On most evenings when he walks the streets of Plaka, he stops and talks with shop owners and street vendors. However, tonight, he has a scheduled appointment at a small touristy nightclub named Delphi Delight. He picks up his pace so that he will not be late.

The slope of the Acropolis inclines sharply as he approaches the area known as Anafiotika. His breathing becomes deeper and his heart beats faster as he uses more energy to accomplish the climb. The jaunt toward Anafiotika is not as easy as it once was. At forty-six, he is in good physical shape. His five feet and nine inch frame weighs 165 pounds, which is only ten pounds more than when he joined the navy twenty-nine years ago. The only other telltale signs of ageing are a few wrinkles around the eyes and a few patches of gray that intermix with his light brown hair.

As he approaches the Delphi Delight, he quickly scans the exterior of the building. Ray always attempts to calculate the age of buildings in Plaka. The building of the Delphi Delight appears ageless. Ray is often awed by the possibility that some of the buildings in Plaka can be anywhere from three hundred years old to three thousand years old.

He enters Delphi Delight. The small one-room nightclub seats fifty people. Young American tourists who mostly wear hippie-style clothes and hippie hairstyles pack the small club. Most of the men sport beards. Cigarette smoke hangs in the air like a low-lying cloud. On the small stage in the far corner, a young hippie-looking woman plays a guitar and sings folk songs in American accented English.

Ray scans the interior of the nightclub. A man seated in a secluded booth in a back corner waves, attracting Ray's attention. Ray approaches the man. They shake hands, and the man identifies himself as Andrei. The man does not provide a last name, and Ray does not ask.

"Please sit," Andrei offers as he points to the other side of the booth.

Ray sits and waits for Andrei to start the negotiation.

"Would you like something to drink?" Andrei asks.

"An Amstel, please."

Andrei raises his hand and snaps his finger. A waiter appears within seconds. Andrei holds up ninety drachmas. "My friend will have an Amstel, immediately. You may keep the change."

The waiter grabs the ninety drachmas, which is three times the price of an Amstel, and scurries to the bar. He is back in less than a minute with a dark-brown Amstel beer bottle and a chilled mug.

After the waiter departs, Andrei says, "Our mutual acquaintance tells me that you can provide large quantities of American goods like cigarettes, whiskey, and gasoline coupons."

"Yes, I can," Ray responds nonchalantly as he pours his beer into the glass.

"And firearms, pistols and rifles. You can provide those, also?"

"Yes, but only a few at a time, maybe two or three a month."

Ray takes a sip of his beer while he evaluates Andrei's physical features. Andrei's tall and solid frame projects confidence, and his short-cropped sandy-colored hair and gray eyes lend to his sophisticated and cultured manner. Facial features age him at early forties. An indiscernible accent tones a resonant, educated voice.

Ray speculates that Andrei comes from Northern European stock, maybe Dutch or maybe German. Ray wonders why their mutual acquaintance, a Greek national, arranged this meeting. Ray had been selling contraband to the Greek for two years. When the new enlisted club opened, Ray accepted the position of club manager. He gained access to large quantities of wholesale cigarettes, whiskey, and food, which he sold on the black market. The Greek could only afford to buy small amounts of what Ray could sell. *The Greek must know that if Andrei and I come to an agreement, the Greek is out of the picture.* Ray considers that Andrei must have paid off the Greek or maybe threatened him in someway.

"What quantities can you provide each month?" Andrei asks.

"One thousand cartons of cigarettes, three hundred bottles of various brands of whiskey, and five hundred beefsteaks. The quantity of gasoline coupons will vary, sometimes as much as eight hundred liters worth of coupons per month."

Andrei remains silent and calculates some numbers in his head.

After a few moments, Ray asks, "Are we going to do business? Can you buy those quantities from me?"

Andrei nods his head. He pulls out a small notebook and begins writing. One minute later, Andrei tears a page from the notebook and slides it across the table to Ray.

Ray looks at the paper. The amounts for each product, written in U.S. dollars, are three times what the Greek pays. Ray hopes his astonishment does not show.

"Are the amounts suitable?" Andrei asks.

"Yes, they are. Where and how often should I make deliveries?"

"I will have someone contact you. This is the last time that you and I will meet. I have many business arrangements, and I must depend on my associates to tend to the details."

Ray hesitates. He feels uncomfortable not dealing directly with the moneyman.

Andrei detects Ray's hesitance. He pulls an envelope from his pocket and slides it across the table to Ray.

Ray does not pick up the envelope but just stares at it.

"Take it, Ray. The envelope contains a $1,000.00 deposit on the first delivery."

Ray looks into Andrei's face and asks, "When and where will I be contacted? I need to make a delivery. My garage is full of goods I need to dump."

"By the end of next week," Andrei responds. "Continue to come to Plaka each night. Walk into Plaka from Syntagma Square, along Kydatheneon. When we are confident no one follows, my associate will approach you. Is that agreeable?"

Ray calculates how much money he will make each month and readily agrees with a nod of his head. He picks up the envelope and sticks it in his back pocket.

Andrei stands and says, "Now, I must go. Please do not leave immediately after me. Wait twenty minutes. Finish your beer and enjoy the entertainment."

Ray just nods his willingness to do as Andrei asks.

Andrei departs the club.

Ray looks around the room. He stopped patronizing this club several years ago when the club discontinued catering to locals and started catering to American tourists.

Ray shifts his attention to an American female singer on the stage. He does not recognize the song. Something about a magic dragon named Puff. Most of the audience sings along. Ray lost interest in American music decades ago.

Europe has been Ray's home for the last eleven years. He has not returned to the United States in six years, and he does not miss it.

Andrei exits the Delphi Delight and weaves through crowds of tourists as he walks across the narrow stone street. On the other side of the street, he approaches a man who leans against the corner of a building. The man's appearance and dress allows him to pass as a Northern European tourist, and he blends easily with the crowd.

Andrei stops in front of the man. Then, he looks back at the entrance of the Delphi Delight to ensure that Ray has not followed him out the door. Andrei turns back toward the man and asks, "Was he followed?"

"No," the man answers softly.

Both men shoot a glance back at the door of Delphi Delight.

Andrei orders, "Starting tomorrow night I want you to loiter along Kydatheneon. Our subject will enter Plaka each night for the next week by way of Kydatheneon. Find out if he is being followed. Report to me daily."

"As you wish, Andrei."

Chapter 2

Spring 1968 – Pacific Ocean

"Helm, ahead one-third," the OOD orders.

"Ahead one-third, aye," the helmsman repeats back.

The helmsman reaches forward and rotates the speed annunciator on the ship's control panel to one-third. Less than two seconds later, a bell sounds.

"Maneuvering answers ahead one-third."

The OOD orders, "Diving Officer, make your depth one-five-zero feet."

"Make my depth one-five-zero feet, aye," the diving-officer-of-the-watch repeats back. Then, he orders, "Helm, thirty-degree rise on the fairwater planes. Come to one-five-zero feet."

"Thirty-degree rise on fairwater planes, come to one-five-zero feet, aye," the helmsman repeats back; then, he pulls back on the fairwater planes control wheel.

The entire crew feels the gravitational impact as the 4400-ton, nuclear powered fast-attack submarine USS *Barb* rises.

When the USS *Barb* levels at 150 feet, the diving-officer-of-the-watch reports, "OOD, the boat is at one-five-zero feet."

The OOD reaches into the overhead, selects SONAR on the intercom, depresses the talk switch, and orders, "Sonar, Conn, report all contacts."

"Conn, Sonar, no contacts."

Then, the OOD selects the Radio Room on the intercom. "Radio, Conn, preparing to come to periscope depth."

No response from Radio.

The OOD waits for a few more seconds; then, he looks over at the chief-of-the-watch and queries, "Chief-of-the-Watch, who is the radioman-of-the-watch?"

"RM2 Page," the chief answers.

"Send the messenger to find Page and tell Page to report to me immediately."

"Send the messenger to find Page, aye, sir."

The chief-of-the-watch looks around the control room for the messenger-of-the-watch. The MOW has not yet returned from the coffee run to the crew's mess. The chief-of-the-watch operates the ballast control panel and cannot leave. The chief picks up a ship's phone handset, sets the switch to crew's mess, and cranks the call handle. The MOW answers. The chief orders, "Go find RM2 Page and tell him to report to the OOD."

The MOW knows where to find Page. He saw Page in the torpedo room five minutes ago working on basic submarine qualifications.

RM2 Page moves rapidly up ladders and along passageways. He makes the journey from the torpedo room to the control room in less than fifteen seconds.

"You wanted me, sir?" Page asks as he approaches the OOD.

"Yes, Page. We will finish clearing baffles in five minutes. Then, we are going to periscope depth." The OOD glances at the clock above the BCP; then, he says to Page, "You'll have about fifteen minutes to synch the broadcast and then copy the Twenty-two Hundred Zulu ZBO List. Let me know if you don't synch the broadcast on the first try, second try, and so on."

"Report each failure to synch, aye, sir." RM2 Page turns to walk away, but the OOD calls him back.

"Page, we are on a tight schedule. We need to copy that ZBO List on the first transmission. We need to know if there are any high precedence messages for us on the broadcast schedule. If not, we will go deep and continue our transit. We can't afford to miss the first ZBO List transmission."

RM2 Page cocks his head to the left and replies confidently, "Sir, every task gets my best effort—always. I don't need pep talks or external motivation to give it my best. I do my best, always, because it is my nature."

The OOD responds with a nod and turns his attention to clearing baffles. "Helm, come left to course three-four-two."

"Come left to course three-four-two, aye, sir."

Page walks the short distance from the control room to the Radio Room door. He enters the cipher code that unlocks the door.

The compact Radio Room contains teletypes, cryptographic equipment, and transmitters and receivers that provide radio coverage from the VLF to UHF frequency ranges.

Page must copy the very low frequency, VLF, submarine broadcast. All submarines at sea are required to copy this broadcast. He grabs a copy of the checklist for configuring the COMSUBPAC VLF Submarine Broadcast. He memorized the configuration when he worked on his qualifications for radioman-of-the-watch, but he must complete and sign the checklist per standard operating procedures.

In the control room, the OOD ponders his conversation with RM2 Page. He casts a glance at the chief radioman, RMC Tollman, who is the diving-officer-of-the-watch.

"Chief Tollman," the OOD calls.

"Chief Tollman aye, sir!" the chief responds with inflection and a grin on his face, but does not take his eyes off the depth gauge on the SCP.

"Chief, get a relief. I want you in Radio during this periscope depth period."

Chief Tollman wants to argue that he has full faith and confidence in RM2 Page, but then considers it wiser to just follow orders without question.

"Get myself a relief, aye, sir." Chief Tollman looks over his left shoulder toward the BCP and orders, "Chief-of-the-Watch, send the messenger to find me a relief."

In the Radio Room, RM2 Rigney Page checks the system configuration. He verifies all antenna systems are properly tuned and patched to the correct VLF receivers. Then, he verifies that crypto equipment and teletypes are correctly patched. He opens the Jason crypto key-card drawer and verifies the correct crypto card is inserted for the current crypto day.

With the configuration checklist complete, only synching the Jason crypto with the shore Jason crypto remains, but that cannot happen until the VLF receiver detects the shore transmitter signal. The synchronization requires a crypto code synch and a time synch. The synch clock on the Jason crypto device can be set in five-minute increments. Rigney looks at the cesium beam clock mounted above the VLF receiver. The cesium beam clock is set to Greenwich Mean Time, also called the ZULU time zone. All U.S. communications operates on ZULU time zone. He calculates that he will have three chances to obtain time synch—2145Z, 2150Z, and 2155Z. He sets the synch clock on the Jason crypto device to 2145Z.

The VLF receiver will detect the shore transmitter signal just before the VLF antenna breaks the surface, which is not unusual when considering the 480 thousand watt transmitter and the nature of VLF radiated signals hugging the curvature of the earth.

Although the cesium beam clock has always been accurate, he must verify the exact time transmitted from WWVH, Kauai, Hawaii. He dials 15 MHz into the HF receiver. He plugs an earphone headset into the audio output jack of the HF receiver and puts the headset over his ears. He hears the WWVH time signal. Now, he waits to feel the submarine rise.

In the control room, the OOD orders, "Diving-officer-of-the-Watch, make your depth five-nine feet."

"Make my depth five-nine feet, aye, sir," Chief Tollman repeats back.

"Raising number two scope," the OOD reports.

In the Radio Room, RM2 Rigney Page feels the submarine rise. He shifts his eyes back and forth between the signal decibel meters on the VLF and HF receivers. After fifteen seconds, he sees the decibel levels rise. He looks at the keying indicator lights on the Jason crypto; they flicker, indicating a teletype signal detected. He looks at the antenna indicator panel; the indicators for the VLF and HF verify *raised*.

The submarine pitches and rolls slightly due to wave action on the surface.

Page looks at the cesium beam clock—2143Z. The WWVH time signal sounds clear in his ears. Two minutes to spare; he sighs with relief. He has his right thumb poised over the Jason crypto START button.

When WWVH transmits the 2145Z tone, Page presses the START button on the Jason crypto device. Beeping noises from the Jason crypto device report that the synchronization process has started. Page crosses his fingers.

In the control room, the supply officer states, "Chief Tollman, messenger said you need a relief."

Chief Tollman looks over his right shoulder and sees the supply officer, who is a qualified diving-officer-of-the-watch.

In the Radio Room, RM2 Page stares at the SYNCH indicator on the Jason crypto device. The beeping becomes more annoying the longer the process takes. He becomes discouraged. *The signal is loud and clear. It should have synch'd by now.*

He looks at the MARK-SPACE indicator on the demodulator. Maybe the signal polarity is reversed. He wants to dismiss that possibility, because if he puts the switch to REVERSE, he will need to perform another RESTART at 2150Z, and he could be wrong. His experience with VLF signals is that the polarity never reverses. He shoots a glance at the cesium beam clock. He must make a decision. He cannot waste the 2150Z RESTART time. He knows from experience on this submarine that if he does not do something different for the next RESTART time, he will be scolded by the chain-of-command for lack of initiative, and the OOD's lack of confidence toward him becomes validated. He places his right hand on the demodulator's NORMAL-REVERSE switch with thoughts to switch it.

Then, the beeping stops, the Jason SYNCH indicator illuminates, and decrypted text prints to the teletype machine. He sighs with relief. He steps toward the intercom. "Conn, Radio, in synch on the broadcast." Page's clear, confident, and medium strength voice reports over the intercom.

The OOD's voice sounds over the intercom, *"Radio, Conn, aye."*

Page steps back from the intercom. He hears the door slide open.

Chief Tollman steps into the Radio Room.

Page stands bewildered for a few moments and stares at the medium-height, slight of build, blond-haired, and green-eyed chief. Page states, "Thought you are the diving-officer-of-the-watch."

"The OOD sent me in here to make sure everything is okay."

Page chuckles as he shakes his head, conveying amusement. He says, "Nothing but chaos and mayhem going on in here, Chief."

Chief Tollman steps over to the broadcast teletype and checks the print quality. Then, he performs a quick scan of the Radio Room. "Everything looks okay in here," he confirms and steps toward the door.

"Hey, Chief."

Tollman turns toward Page.

Page says, "I don't understand all this doubt. I never have any problems completing my assigned tasks."

Tollman smiles knowingly and responds, "You're a non-qual puke. Until you earn your dolphins, you will be treated that way. Every non-qual is—nothing personal about it."

"But I have qualified in all the watch stations that I am required to qualify and quicker than anyone else."

The chief counters, "That's expected of you, and you'll have six more watch stations to qualify in after you earn your dolphins. Don't take the disrespect personally and always remember that you're nothing special."

Tollman opens the door and steps out of Radio.

As the Radio Room door slides shut, Page ponders his place and situation aboard the USS *Barb*. Before coming aboard *Barb*, he completed a successful mission for ONI—the Office of Naval Intelligence, a mission that no one aboard *Barb* knows about. At the conclusion of that mission, he felt proud and patriotic regarding his participation. Nevertheless, he declined an offer to continue his service with ONI. Situations occurred during that mission that he does not want to experience again.

His initial navy training was at submarine radioman school. ONI accommodated his request by arranging assignment to a submarine in the Pacific.

At 2200Z, the ZBO List starts printing.

Page hears the cranking sound of the telephone. He picks up the handset. "Radio, RM2 Page speaking, sir."

"Page, this is the chief-of-the-watch. As soon as the ZBO List prints, bring it to the captain in control."

RM2 Page repeats back the order and cradles the handset. He returns to the printer and scans the ZBO List.

The ZBO List transmits at the top of every even hour and specifies the order of transmission of each message during the following two hours. The ZBO List, in line-item format, contains the precedence, addressees, and subject of each message.

COMSUBPAC removes messages from the ZBO List after twelve hours. Submarine captains use the ZBO List as a measure to manage periscope depth time.

Page tears the ZBO List from the teletype and places it on the message-routing clipboard. He writes the time-of-receipt in ZULU time in the top right corner. Then, he exits the Radio Room.

Page finds the captain, Commander Wittier, in the control room. The captain stands on the starboard side, next to the fire-control station. Page hands the message board to the captain.

While the captain reads the ZBO List, Page watches the activities in the control room. The OOD peers through the periscope. Every five seconds or so, the OOD rotates the periscope a few degrees. The helmsman, stern-planes operator, and diving-officer-of-the-watch have their eyes fixed on the *ships control panel*. RMC Tollman is back at the diving officer position. The quartermaster-of-the-watch stands at the chart table and rotates the dials of the LORAN receivers. The messenger-of-the-watch sits on a stool in the forward starboard corner—on the other side of the tracking table—looking bored.

Page looks into the overhead at the maze of pipes, valves, and cables. He performs a mental exercise of identifying each valve and its purpose.

The OOD reaches into the overhead and retrieves the microphone for the intercom and orders, "Sonar, Conn, report all contacts."

"Conn, Sonar, no contacts."

The OOD looks to the aft port corner where the electronics-technician-of-the-watch monitors the ECM equipment and queries, "ECM, report all search radar signals."

"No Search radars detected, sir."

These reports lead to the conclusion that USS *Barb* is the lone vessel in this area of the ocean.

The OOD looks at the QMOW and asks, "Quartermaster, did you get a LORAN fix?"

The QMOW turns toward the OOD and replies, "Yes, sir, and I plotted it on the chart."

"OOD," Captain Wittier calls.

The OOD turns his head away from the periscope and looks at the captain.

"We have a couple of messages on the ZBO List," the captain advises. "One priority OP Order change and a couple of routine messages at the end of the schedule. Stay at periscope depth to get the priority, but no longer. We'll copy the routines during the next watch."

The OOD responds, "Copy the priority. Then, go deep, aye, sir."

The captain hands the message board to RM2 Page and says, "I've circled the message I want copied. As soon as we get it, tell the OOD."

Page repeats back, "After we copy the message, tell the OOD, aye, sir."

The captain walks out of the control room.

Page follows the captain aft along the operations upper level passageway.

The captain enters his stateroom on the starboard side.

Page enters the Radio Room on the portside. He walks over to the broadcast teletype and checks print quality. Then, he compares the ZBO List with the message currently printing. He calculates the priority message the captain wants will print forty minutes from now.

He scans the ZBO List to see what type messages the other submarines are getting. Then, he sees a small garble in the right margin three lines below the line entry for the priority message the captain wants. The garble consists of a half-dozen uppercase characters. He knows part of the garble must be the insertion of an uppercase function. He writes in pencil below the garble the lowercase equivalents. He discovers that the third message under the priority message that the captain wants is for *Barb*, and it is a priority OP Order change also.

He must tell the OOD about the message. He goes to the control room. "Sir, this garble was hidden in a narrative description. When I fixed the garble, the text relocates to the address column. The captain probably didn't notice it."

"Alright, hold on a second," the OOD responds as he reaches for the ships phone handset. He rotates the switch to CO stateroom and cranks the handle. "Captain, RM2 Page discovered a garble in the ZBO List. He fixed it and the fix may change your mind about what messages to copy before we go deep." The OOD listens for a few moments; then, he says, "Send Page to your stateroom, aye, sir."

RM2 Rigney Page knocks on the captain's stateroom door.
"Enter."
Page enters.
The captain sits at his desk.
Page hands the message board to the captain.
Commander Wittier's eyes go immediately to the handwritten correction. He considers what to do. Then, he says. "We will stay at periscope depth to get this second priority. I will tell the OOD. Bring both priorities to me as soon as they print."

"Bring both priorities to you as soon as they print, aye, sir."

Commander Wittier studies RM2 Page for a moment. Then, he hands the message board to Page and asks, "Why didn't you find that garble earlier—before I looked at the ZBO List?"

"No valid reason, sir. I never encountered a garble like this before. I should have caught it, but I didn't. This experience shows me what else to check for in the future."

A contemplative expression appears on the captain's face. A few moments later, he nods acceptance of Page's answer; he advises, "I've never seen a garble like this before, either. You're dismissed."

In the control room, the OOD keeps his eyes glued to the periscope, except for occasional glances at the clock.

"Conn, Radio, both priority messages copied."

"Radio, Conn, aye," the OOD responds. Then, the OOD orders, "Chief-of-the-Watch, lower all antennas."

"Lower all antennas, aye, sir."

"Lowering number two scope," the OOD announces. Then, he orders, "Diving Officer, make your depth one-five-zero feet and get a one-third trim."

The pitch and roll dissipates as the submarine goes deep.

"Enter," Commander Wittier orders.

RM2 Page enters the captain's stateroom and hands the message board to the captain.

While reading the OP Order changes, the captain writes a few notes.

Page leans back against the stateroom door, waiting for the captain to finish.

The captain picks up the phone handset and calls the OOD. "Come to course 310. Then, increase speed to *full*."

Ten minutes later, the captain hands the message board back to Page and says, "That was a good catch you made on that garble. Your initiative to bring it to my attention saved us steaming in the wrong direction for the next ten hours."

"Thank you, Captain."

"Return to your duties."

At 1145 local time, RM2 Bennetto relieves RM2 Page as radioman-of-the-watch. Page goes to the crew's mess to partake in the midday meal. He stands at the aft end of the crew's mess for five minutes before a seat becomes available at one of the six booth-like tables.

Serving food on this submarine is much different from that on a surface ship or shore station. Instead of crewmembers walking with a tray down a steam line, plates and utensils are set at each table. A mess cook brings food to the tables in serving platters and serving bowls.

Page sits in an aisle seat of a table along the starboard bulkhead. He stares intently at the yellowish brown substance in a serving bowl. He considers what it might be. "Anyone know what that is?" he asks others at the table as he points at the bowl.

"It's gravy," one says.

"No, it's cream corn," another says.

Page's attention shifts to a tablemate who forks a circular slice of brown substance from a plate with many slices of circular brown substances. The tablemate takes a bite.

"What is it?" Page asks.

"Don't know for sure—definitely a mystery meat." He shakes salt and pepper on it; then, he spreads ketchup over it. "This submarine helper should give it some taste."

Page recognizes green beans in a bowl. After taking a scoopful, he takes a bite of the soft and soggy vegetable. *Yuk!*

A voice, rising above the medley of conversations and coming from the table next to Page, accuses, "Hey Page, hear ya fucked-up bad on the last watch."

Most conversations stop. Some heads turn and look at Page, and some turn to look at the accuser.

Page recognizes the whining accusatory tone and manner of RM2 Petroni, a fellow radioman who has a one-way conflict against Page. Petroni continually searches for ways to discredit Page. Petroni fabricates negative situations about Page and reports them to his seniors.

Petroni announces loudly, "Yeah, Chief Tollman had to get a relief from *the dive* so he could go to Radio and save yo' ass."

Petroni's attacks toward Page are well known by the crew. The majority of the crew knows that Petroni tells lies and half-truths. Some crewmembers find this conflict between Petroni and Page to be immature and ignore it, falsely believing that Page is somehow engaged in the conflict. Other crewmembers want to believe Petroni, and they collaborate with Petroni to discredit Page.

Another voice adds his opinion. "Yeah, Page, when ya gonna get qualified?"

One of the nukes orders, "Someone check the dink list. Make sure Page ain't on it."

"Fuckin' free air breather," says a softer, more serious voice.

Petroni's fabrications bewilder Page. To the best of his knowledge, he has never done anything to warrant Petroni's behavior.

Page does not respond to Petroni's accusations or to the negative comments of others. He knows they will stop soon, if he does not react. He concentrates on finding identifiable food.

Petroni demands, "Come on, Page, what did ya fuck up, man? No secrets with this crew, man."

Page remains quiet.

A nuke machinist mate across the table from Page says loudly for all to hear, "Hey, Page, can't ya hear Petroni, or have all those pushups and sit-ups made ya brain dead?"

Page remains quiet.

Most of the nonquals go through this hazing, but Petroni and his followers make it blatantly personal with Page.

A second-class torpedoman challenges, "Hey, Page, Petroni cut you, man. Are ya gonna let him get away with it?"

Page, weary of being the focus of attention, slides off his seat and stands. He picks up his plate and silverware. Then, he looks down at Petroni and says calmly, "Petroni, if you want to suck my dick again, I will be in the diesel room in ten minutes."

A loud and collective *wwwhhhhooooaaa* erupts from those in the crew's mess.

Page casts an amused expression when he sees several sailors look at their watches.

Page walks to the scullery.

"Arrogant asshole," someone behind Page hisses in a soft voice.

Page dumps his dinnerware in the scullery; then, he proceeds forward, toward the bow compartment.

"Hey, Page, wait up."

RM2 Page stops, turns, and faces the chief-of-the-boat.

"Yeah, COB, what's up?"

"I overheard the captain telling Chief Tollman what a good job you did during the last periscope depth. Why didn't you tell those guys in the crew's mess the truth?"

"They're not interested in the truth," Page declares matter-of-factly.

The COB scrutinizes Page's face for a few moments; then, he says, "I've seen a lot of hazin' and harassment during my years in submarines, but I've never encountered anyone who stays as calm and unmoved about it as you do. Don't those sailors ever get ta ya?"

A knowing grin appears on Page's face, and he reveals, "No."

"So what does get ta ya, then?"

"Shattered expectations."

"Like what?"

Page considers if he should reveal his thoughts to the chief-of-the-boat. He decides the COB is sincere in his interest. "Submarines and the navy in general are different from what I expected. I'm disappointed about that."

"That's common. What's not common is that ya never show your disappointment. Ya never take out your anger and frustration on anyone."

"I said disappointed. I seldom get angry or frustrated."

The master chief nods his head with understanding; then, he asks, "What has disappointed you lately?"

Page looks forward then aft to ensure no one hears; then, he replies, "Cancellation of the liberty port visits to Subic and Hong Kong, and two weeks from now we go into dry dock at Pearl for an eighteen-month overhaul. If I had known that beforehand, I would not have accepted orders to *Barb*."

"This is the navy, Page. You didn't have a choice."

"Well, believe it or not, I had a choice."

The COB expresses doubt. Then he advises, "The port visit cancellations were due to operational necessity and so is the overhaul."

"So I shouldn't be disappointed because it was for operational necessity? One of my major reasons for joining the navy was to travel to foreign lands and experience other cultures."

"Expect liberty ports to be cancelled at least eighty percent of the time."

"So I have heard since reporting aboard, but someone failed to include that information in the submarine recruiting program."

The COB looks quizzically at Page and says, "Being a submariner means a life of sacrifice and dedication to service."

"COB, just like everyone else, I volunteered for this. However, unlike others who are disappointed or feel cheated, I will still do my best. I would lose my self-respect if I let disappointments affect my performance."

The COB smiles appreciatively and declares, "You just defined dedication and service."

Page responds, "I define it as repetitive and tedious, and I am not looking forward to an eighteen-month overhaul in Pearl."

The COB shakes his head in dismissal and says, "Overhaul is like shore duty."

"For shore duty, I would have chosen somewhere other than Pearl."

"Thought you were into scuba diving and surfing. Hawaii is great for that."

"Right COB, but I've been surfing and scuba diving all my life. Being in Hawaii is like being in my hometown of Seal Beach, California. I want to experience other things."

The COB looks at his watch. "I must meet with the captain."

Page expresses anticipation as he queries, "COB, others have gotten orders to other boats because a full crew is not needed during overhaul. What are my chances of doing the same?"

"Those orders go to those who have earned their dolphins. I would say your chances are naught-to-none."

"Can I put in a request chit, anyway?"

"Sure, but expect not to get it."

Disappointment appears on Page's face.

The COB nods his understanding and says, "It will get better after you earn your dolphins. Now, I must go see the captain. Keep up the good work."

The COB walks aft and then climbs the ladder to operations upper level.

Page stares after the COB and considers, *shit, the ones who have the worst attitudes and worst performance already have their dolphins.*

Chapter 3

June 1968 - Headquarters, Office of Naval Intelligence

Commander Brad Watson enters the office of his immediate superior, Captain William Willcroft, Deputy Director for Counterespionage. The tall and slim gray-haired captain, dressed in his Tropical White Long uniform, stands facing the large window, which allows him a wide view of the Suitland complex.

Brad walks across the deep and plush sky-blue colored carpet toward his usual chair in front of the captain's large cherry wood desk. He remains standing until the captain gives permission to sit.

Captain Willcroft walks away from the window and sits behind his desk. He gestures for Brad to sit.

"Brad, CIA has sent us some intel on a situation developing in Greece. CIA has a KGB operative under surveillance. Last week, this KGB operative meets with a navy master chief at a nightclub in Athens. This master chief is stationed at the Nea Makri Naval Communications Station. CIA is asking us to investigate this master chief's activities and report back to them." Willcroft picks up a folder and hands it to Brad Watson.

Brad opens the folder and scans the contents. The folder contains only two items. One is a photograph of the master chief in Service Dress Blue uniform and identifies him as RMCM Raymond Rodgers. The other item is a report that includes the date and time of the Plaka meeting. The report also states that the CIA did not put a tail on Master Chief Rodgers, but CIA operatives on other assignments observed Rodgers in the Plaka every night for the following four nights. During those four nights, the report specifies, Rodgers acted as if he were looking for someone.

"Any timeline on this?" Brad asks.

"CIA didn't specify any, but ever since the USS *Columbus* incident, the director has been under intense pressure to quickly identify any naval personnel involved in espionage activities. Although we were eventually successful with the *Columbus* incident and with shutting down Lucifer's spy network, the director received criticism for how long it took us to do so. I want you to move this one to the top of your priority list."

"Aye, aye, sir. Any special instructions?"

"No, but we must know what this Master Chief Rodgers is up to, and we must know quickly. You are authorized to use whatever HUMINT and ELINT resources you need, and you are authorized to exceed your budget on this one. Provide me weekly, written reports on what resources you are using and how much you are spending. Include in the weekly report all the activities of our operatives and all the activities of Master Chief Rodgers."

"Aye, aye, sir."

Two days later, Commander Brad Watson completes his research of Master Chief Rodgers's background. He evaluates the ONI operatives available to him and which best suit a surveillance mission on Master Chief Rodgers. Brad pulls the files of six ONI operatives who currently work missions in Europe.

Two hours later, Brad calls the ONI travel section to arrange *Priority One* military transport to London and Berlin.

Chapter 4

June 1968 - Embassy of the Soviet Union - Athens, Greece

Andrei Yashin enters the office of his KGB superior, Eldar Khavanov. Andrei's supervisor obtained his current position in the Athens Embassy because of his political affiliations, and not his KGB experience, which is limited. Khavanov, a portly and balding man in his mid-fifties, rises from his desk chair to greet Andrei. The two men shake hands, and Khavanov offers Andrei the chair in front of his desk.

Khavanov sits behind his desk. He pulls out a large Cuban cigar from the humidor on his desk and lights it. Dense cigar smoke quickly fills the small enclosed room.

The foul-smelling acrid smoke burns Andrei's eyes and nostrils, but he does not complain nor does he indicate that the smoke bothers him.

Khavanov's office lacks decorative design and reflects his no-nonsense approach to his work. A print of Leonid Brezhnev hangs on the wall behind his desk. On the opposite wall hangs a print of Vladimir Lenin.

"Was your meeting with the American sailor successful?" Khavanov asks.

"Yes, it was. He agreed to sell his contraband to me."

"He believes you to be a black marketer, then?"

"Yes."

"And all the goods that you buy will be stored in our warehouse in Piraeus?"

"Yes. I have made the arrangements, and the large freezer has been installed."

"Freezer?" queries Khavanov with raised eyebrows.

"Pardon me, Eldar. I forgot to tell you that this Rodgers will sell us contraband American beef."

"Where will Rodgers deliver the goods?"

"I have rented a house with the proper facilities in Marathon. We will transfer the goods from Marathon to Piraeus once a month."

Khavanov stares at his desktop while he considers the situation with Rodgers. Then, he questions, "When will you ask Rodgers for classified material?"

"I think two months from now," Andrei responds with confidence. "By then, we should have enough evidence of his black market activities to blackmail him into cooperating with us."

"Andrei, Moscow Center continually presses me for more intelligence. Ever since Javier Ramirez disappeared and the Americans shut down his operation, our intelligence flow in the Mediterranean has slowed to a trickle. Our superiors in Moscow will never again allow such volume to filter through an independent. Javier was not a professional intelligence operative. He was a terrorist. The PLO controlled him. His objectives did not align with ours. I wonder how we ever let him have that much control."

Andrei did not know about Javier's PLO affiliation when the two of them frequently met to negotiate deals for NATO classified information. The fact that Javier was a terrorist surfaced after the KGB observed the NATO alliance closing down all of Javier's offices across Europe and across America. PLO operatives came looking for Javier, attempting to discover what happened to him. That is when the KGB discovered Javier's PLO affiliation.

"You knew Ramirez, didn't you, when you were posted in Rome?"

"Yes, I did. I was his Soviet contact."

"What was his failing? Why did he get caught?"

"You said it, Eldar. Javier was not a professional intelligence operative. He peddled information to support his terrorist cause. He never attended any of the advanced intelligence training that I offered him. He was not able to identify the clues that the Americans were setting a trap for him. I believe that his arrogant disregard for the competence of the Americans is what led to his capture. Javier was contemptuous of all Americans. The only Americans he knew well were the pathetic ones—the ones he blackmailed into espionage activities. He erroneously concluded that all Americans are of the same character. Instead of implementing standard evasion techniques when he sensed the American authorities were getting too close, he would act like a terrorist. He killed NATO intelligence operatives, thinking that would deter NATO from going after him. I suspect that he was going after one of those American operatives when he disappeared. Actually, I'm amazed he operated as long as he did."

"So am I," Eldar comments in a resigned tone and with a frown on his face.

Both men pause in thought.

"And now we must establish our own sources," Eldar states with a pointed stare at Andrei, indicating the urgency and importance of recruiting the American sailor.

"Do not worry, Eldar. This Rodgers fits the profile. He will turn. I guarantee it."

Chapter 5

June 1968 - U.S. NAVCOMMSTA - Nea Makri, Greece

Master Chief Radioman Raymond Rodgers sits behind his desk in the Club Zeus manager's office. He makes entries into two sets of accounting books. One set of books reflects the club's business. The other set contains an accounting of his black market enterprises.

After completing the entries, he sits back in his chair and ponders how easily he does it all. He started ten years ago with selling his excess gasoline rations and cigarette rations on the black market. He was stationed in Naples, Italy, at the time. One of Ray's neighbors, a fellow chief petty officer, came to Ray's apartment in need of some money. Knowing that Ray sold rationed items on the black market, the neighbor offered his entire monthly cigarette ration and half of his monthly gasoline rations. Ray paid the neighbor sixty percent of what Ray knew to be the current black market price. Within several months, all the American service members in his apartment complex were selling their excess rations to Ray. Within a year, Ray had over one hundred American service members selling their rations to him.

Ray had no illusions. He knew his activities were illegal. However, because the senior sergeant of the Naples American Military Police Detachment was one of his suppliers and because his black market contact was the local Carabineri Police Chief, Ray did not worry about being arrested.

Now, at Nea Makri, forty of the sailors sell their excess rations to Ray. As the manager of the Club Zeus, he buys large quantities of American cigarettes, whiskey, and beef at wholesale prices through the Armed Forces Exchange System. Only twenty percent is consumed through sales at Club Zeus, although the club's books report that 100 percent of inventory is sold through the club.

Additionally, the club's books account for three employees who do not exist. Ray pays the fake employees' salaries to himself.

Ray does not worry about an audit. Only the command special services committee would audit him, and he is the chair of that committee.

Ray smiles as he thinks about the payment he received on his first delivery to Andrei's associate in Marathon. Ray came away with over four thousand dollars.

A few more payments like that and I can pay off my retirement home on Skyros.

Five years ago, Ray spent a month on vacation in the villa that sits on the cliffs of the Island of Skyros. He fell in love with the large white-stucco house with a red tile roof. The spectacular view from the villa courtyard of the Aegean Sea and surrounding islands mesmerized him.

Ray faces mandatory retirement. He requested an extension on active duty, but the navy denied his request. Therefore, he figures he has ten months to maximize his illegal profits. Then, he will have no financial worries when he retires to Skyros.

Chapter 6

July 1968 - U.S. NAVCOMMSTA - Nea Makri, Greece

Two darkly clad Russian operatives step swiftly along the sandy beach. They move south toward the American base at Nea Makri.

Before they exited their vehicle, they applied black greasepaint to their faces and back of their hands. The quarter moon lessens the chance they will be detected.

The veteran Russian field operative leads the mission. The other Russian operative is a technician who carries tools and electronic components.

They arrive at the NAVCOMMSTA east perimeter which faces the Aegean Sea just yards away across a sandy beach. They easily straddle the four feet high fence and move westward toward the communications trailers compound. They follow the same route they followed four weeks earlier when they surveyed the area underneath the communications trailers.

They cross sand dunes of the base firing range. Then, they move through the antenna fields. Five minutes later, they arrive at the fifteen feet high chain-link fence that surrounds the communications trailers compound. The lead operative looks at his watch—2:18 AM.

Both operatives scan the compound through the fence. High-wattage lights mounted to the top of each trailer illuminate the area. No Americans move about. They verify no sentries and no roving patrols.

Each navy-gray colored trailer is the size of an eighteen-wheeler trailer. A total of ten trailers connect together. Each trailer stands raised on the tires originally used to put each trailer in place. The Russian operatives visualize American sailors scurrying about inside the trailers, performing their communications tasks. The Russians hear the sound of powerful generators.

The lead operative walks along the fence and finds the spot where they had dug under the fence four weeks ago. When they initially dug the two feet wide by three feet deep trench, they found the chain-link fence extended some depth into the ground. They had cut a two feet wide circular hole in the fence beneath ground level. After they had completed their survey under the trailers, they filled in the trench and covered the loose dirt with fallen dead branches from surrounding shrubs.

Tonight, digging-out the loose dirt from their trench takes only ten minutes. They belly their way into the trailer compound then rise on the other side. They walk quickly, crouched, to the closest trailer and duck into the underside. For close-in work under the trailers, their low-wattage flashlights cast a short blue-colored beam.

Their mission tonight includes modifying electrical ground configurations, attaching sensors to telephone and power cables, and installing a miniature one-quarter watt transmitter. A miniature parabolic dish antenna for the transmitter is positioned to radiate a concentrated ultrahigh frequency radio beam along bearing 90 degrees—due east. All the modifications they make and all the components they install are designed to collect electromagnetic signals and then transmit those signals on the one-quarter watt transmitter. They hide the modifications and installed transmitter inside fake junction boxes on the underside of trailers. Each fake junction box matches authentic junction boxes in size, color, and shape.

Their work consumes forty minutes. By 3:15 AM, they have filled in the trench and disguised it. At 3:40 AM, they walk north on the beach toward their vehicle.

Chapter 7

Late July 1968 - Pearl Harbor, Hawaii

Although the sun beats down from a partly cloudy sky, the heavy humidity keeps the pier wet from the heavy rain shower that passed through Pearl Harbor one hour ago. The high-altitude storm clouds now hover over the hills to the north.

Commander Brad Watson stands on the walkway above *dry dock #1* at Pearl Harbor. He looks into the dry dock and scans the length of the 278 feet long fast-attack submarine, USS *Barb*.

In his Tropical White Long uniform, Brad Watson looks out of place among yard birds who wear lightweight overalls, enlisted personnel wearing short-sleeve dungarees, and chiefs and officers who wear working khaki. All stare at the commander in whites and wonder about his purpose.

The submarine sits on large blocks. Dozens of cables and hoses hang between the dry dock and the submarine. Yard workers scurry about the bottom of the dry dock. The sound of whining motors and pneumatic tools drown conversation. Occasionally, a shouting voice overcomes the noise. Some yard birds stand on scaffolding and chip away at the hull. A crane lowers machinery through the Barb's aft hatch, guided by two yard birds. A continuous stream of sailors and yard birds walk to and fro across the gangway between the dry-dock wall and the submarine.

At first glance from a distance, the commander appears ordinary at five feet and seven inches. As you get closer to him, his thickly muscled frame becomes more noticeable. Muscle and veins bulge on his forearms and thick neck. His short cropped blond hair, dark blue eyes, and fair skin bare evidence to his Scandinavian ancestry. His stature and every movement disclose a man who is confident and self-assured.

The volume of sailors transiting the gangway lessens, and Brad Watson crosses the gangway. He renders proper honors and asks permission to come aboard. The topside watch grants permission.

"Commander Watson to see your commanding officer," Brad Watson tells the topside watch.

"Yes, sir," replies the topside watch, and he turns to call the captain's stateroom from the topside telephone.

"Captain, this is the topside watch. There is a Commander Watson here to see you."

The topside watch listens; then replies, "Yes sir. He's in uniform."

The topside watch listens; then, glances at Brad Watson. He says, "Yes, sir, I'll check that. Please wait." The topside watch turns and asks Brad Watson, "Commander, may I see your ID card, please?"

Brad reaches into his back pocket, retrieves his wallet, and hands over his Navy ID card.

The topside watch scans the front and back of the ID card and then asks, "What's your command, sir?"

"I can only discuss that with your captain," Brad replies with a pleasant smile.

"Yes sir. I will tell the captain that. Please wait."

The topside watch speaks into the handset, "Captain, I have checked Commander Watson's ID card. The commander says he can only discuss with you which command he belongs to." The topside watch listens; then says into the handset, "Yes, sir."

The topside watch replaces the handset and then informs Brad Watson, "The captain will send up an escort for you . . . should only take a few minutes, sir."

"Very well," Brad Watson replies.

Ten minutes later, a lanky lieutenant junior grade, dressed in working khakis, comes up through the weapons shipping hatch and introduces himself. "Commander Watson, I am Lieutenant Pollard."

The two officers shake hands.

"Please excuse the delay, sir," Pollard explains. "I will escort you to the captain's stateroom."

Lieutenant Pollard leads Commander Watson down the weapons shipping hatch ladder. At the bottom of the ladder, they walk aft along the operations upper level passageway. They pass the sonar room on the starboard side and the Radio Room on the portside. Just aft of sonar is the captain's stateroom. Several officers stand outside the captain's stateroom door and make reports regarding the progress of various overhaul projects. Pollard and Watson patiently wait their turn.

Several minutes later, Pollard announces, "You can see the captain now."

As Brad Watson enters the captain's stateroom, Commander Bartholomew Wittier, Captain of USS *Barb*, stands to greet Brad Watson and extends his hand. The two officers shake hands.

The *Barb's* captain informs, "I am Bart Wittier. Please excuse the delay topside. Squadron constantly tests our security procedures."

"No problem, Captain."

Bart Wittier motions Brad to a chair and says to Lieutenant Pollard, "Ben, I will escort the commander from here. You can return to your duties."

"Return to my duties, aye, sir." Pollard turns and walks forward along the operations upper level passageway.

As Brad Watson seats himself, Wittier asks, "What's all this secrecy about your command?"

Brad glances at the open door.

Captain Wittier looks in the direction of Brad's glance. He stands, closes the door, and returns to his seat.

"Captain, I am assigned to Headquarters, Office of Naval Intelligence in Washington. I am here to request that you release one of your crew for assignment to ONI."

Bart Wittier was not expecting this. He had expected that Commander Watson would advise that some sort of unscheduled inspection was about to take place. He studies Commander Watson, noticing the heavily muscled forearms and neck. He wants to ask what division of ONI, but he knows better. He inquires, "Who, why, and for how long?"

"RM2 Page. I cannot tell you why. I estimate six months, but I cannot guarantee it."

"Page is an ONI agent?!" Captain Wittier blurts. "Why did ONI put an agent on my boat?!" Captain Wittier's tone becomes irritated.

"No, Captain. Page is not an ONI agent, but he has done work for us in the past. We have a situation that fits his skills. ONI needs his help."

His irritability subsiding, Captain Wittier ponders Commander Watson's explanation. *Page, who would have thought.*

"If you wanted Page, why didn't you just issue official orders and transfer him? Why come to me and ask permission?"

"Deference to your command. ONI prefers to have the cooperation and understanding of commanding officers. Having commanding officers know why one of their crew is abruptly removed avoids inquires from the unit level. Also, knowing that we have a ready replacement available should, we hope, gain your cooperation. If you and Page agree to ONI's request, a replacement RM2 will be assigned to *Barb*. The replacement is qualified in submarines and currently serves on the same class submarine."

"You think that Page will turn you down?"

"He might."

Captain Wittier sits in thought. Then, he asks, "Does Page's replacement have ONI affiliations?"

"No. This replacement has requested an interfleet transfer from the East Coast to the West Coast as a reenlistment incentive. Currently, there are no billets on the West Coast. If you and Page agree to this ONI assignment, Page's replacement can be here within a week."

"Does squadron know about this?"

"Only the commodore, need-to-know is narrowly restricted."

"What does the commodore says about this?"

"He says it's your boat. It's totally up to you."

Captain Wittier considers the impact of losing Page. *RM2 Page's replacement is already qualified in submarines. That's a plus. On the other hand, Page is a rising superstar.* Captain Wittier's eyes go wide as a thought suddenly occurs to him. "If Page goes on this ONI assignment, will he be in danger?"

"There is risk of danger," Brad Watson replies. "Page has faced danger before. He deals with it well."

Captain Wittier stares wide-eyed at Commander Watson. *What has Page done in the past that instills so much confidence in this officer? When could Page have done this? Page is just a boy. Who would have thought.*

Captain Wittier says, "I have no objections, Commander. I will support whatever Page decides."

"Thank you, Captain. Is there somewhere private where I can speak with Page?"

"How long will it take?"

"Thirty to forty minutes."

"You can use my stateroom. I will go to the wardroom."

Captain Wittier picks up a sound-powered phone handset, turns the *select* knob to *radio*, and cranks the call handle.

"Chief, find Page and send him to my stateroom."

"Has Page done something wrong?"

"No, Chief. I just need him to clarify something that I read in his service record."

"Find Page and send him to your stateroom, aye, sir."

Five minutes later, RM2 Rigney Michael Page knocks on the captain's stateroom door.

"Enter," Captain Wittier orders.

The door opens. Page's broad-shouldered, six feet and one inch tall frame fills the doorway. When he sees Brad Watson, he beams a happy grin; his manner becomes excited. "Hey, Brad, great to see ya! How ya been?!"

Brad raises his brow in disapproval of the way Page greets him in the presence of another officer.

Rigney notices Brad's disapproving look. He glances at his captain who also expresses disapproval.

Rigney remembers Brad's instructions about military courtesy when they are both in uniform. Rigney glances at Brad Watson's shoulder boards and smiles.

"Excuse me, Commander Watson. I just got caught up with seeing you again." Then, he raises his eyebrows and in an inquisitively conspiring tone, he adds, "And so unexpectedly."

"It's okay, Page. I am glad to see you again, also."

"Congratulations on your promotion to commander," Rigney says sincerely. "As you can see I have been promoted to second class since I last saw you."

"Congratulations to you, also," Brad Watson says with a grin on his face.

"Thank you," Rigney responds.

All three men become silent. Rigney waits for Brad to state his business.

Captain Wittier, realizing the silence is his signal to leave, says, "I will be in the wardroom. Please let me know when you're finished."

"Yes, sir," Brad responds politely.

Captain Wittier shuts his stateroom door. He walks forward and goes down the ladder leading to operations compartment middle level. At the bottom of the ladder, He enters the ship's office. He opens the cabinet drawer that holds the service records of all those who serve in *Barb*. He pulls RM2 Page's record. Two minutes later, Captain Wittier sits at the wardroom table and thumbs through Page's service record.

Commander Brad Watson and RM2 Rigney Page stand facing each other. Brad gives Rigney a thorough head-to-toe appraisal. Brad is pleased to see that Rigney still looks physically fit. Brad frowns slightly when he notices that Rigney's reddish brown hair is longer than regulation allows.

"You look fit, Rig. You still exercise every day?"

"Not every day, but as much as I can. I'm working long hours six days a week."

"What kind of work are you doing in dry dock?"

"Mostly removing and installing electronics equipment. I have duty every four days as duty radioman." Rigney's tone and manner expresses resigned disappointment.

"Sounds like you're not liking it much."

"I'm not."

"Sorry, Rig. When I arranged your orders for this boat, she was on a WESTPAC cruise. It was the only opening for a nonqual radioman. I didn't know she was going in for overhaul. Maybe if I had dug deeper, I would have—"

"That's okay, Brad. I chose to leave ONI. Not your obligation to look out for me."

Brad nods his understanding and directs Rigney to sit in one of the two chairs in the stateroom. Brad sits in the other.

Brad explains, "A situation has developed that requires a combination of your youth, knowledge of electronics, and knowledge of naval communications. I am here to find out if you might do some work for ONI."

"Will it be dangerous?"

"All missions have an element of danger, some more than others."

Page bows his head in thought as he remembers the dangers of his previous mission with ONI.

"Rig, I wish that you would have taken my offer for counseling and therapy after the last mission. Barbara Gaile went through it, and she came through it okay."

A smile comes to Rigney's face at the mention of Barbara Gaile. They were friends and lovers.

"How is Barbara? Where is she?"

"She's well. She's in Panama and will return to Washington in a few months for graduation from the ONI counterespionage course."

"I'm glad she's getting what she wants," Rigney says with a pleasing smile and sincere tone.

"Are you interested in hearing about your possible mission?"

"Yes."

"You are familiar with the U.S. Naval Communications Station located at Nea Makri, Greece?"

"Yes. I have heard of it, never been there."

"Seven weeks ago, the CIA discovered a Soviet KGB operative working out of a fake import and export company in Athens. CIA put the KGB operative under surveillance. Two nights later, the KGB operative rendezvous at an Athens nightclub with a man who looks like an American. CIA puts a tail on the American, and they follow him to the NAVCOMMSTA at Nea Makri. When the American drove his car up to the gate, the sentry waved him through without so much as an ID check. CIA didn't follow into the NAVCOMMSTA for fear of revealing themselves. The CIA called us to investigate the American sailor."

Rigney contemplates Brad's explanation. Then, he comments, "So you think that the KGB is watching this American sailor to see if he has reported his meetings with the KGB to his superiors. That means the KGB will be evaluating all new arrivals to NAVCOMMSTA Greece as possible counterespionage operatives. Meaning, you need to send-in someone who would not be suspected of being an operative, someone who is too young, too brash, and too conspicuous to be suspected as a counterespionage operative, right?"

"That's it. We need you. Will you help us out?"

"I turned twenty-one a couple of weeks ago. I am not as young as I was on the last mission."

"You're still young enough not to be suspected. Will you help us out?"

Rigney does not say no, but he shakes his head slightly as he thinks about putting himself back into a dangerous situation. On the other hand, he feels an obligation to serve where he will do the most good. He learned on his first mission with ONI that successful enemy spies endanger the lives of American military men. If he can contribute to lessening that danger, he feels it his duty to do so. He is still shaking his head when he asks, "What would I need to do?"

An appreciative smile appears on Commander Brad Watson's face as he determines that Rigney may agree to do this. He advises, "I can't provide details unless you commit to the mission. You will get the rest of the details in Washington."

"If I do go to Nea Makri, how will I make my reports to ONI?"

"We set up an ONI Field Office in a villa in the town of Nea Makri. We have installed radio equipment in that villa so that we can keep in touch."

"Then you already anticipated that I would agree."

"No. The field office is for whomever we send."

"How long will I be in Washington?"

"About a week. In addition to your briefings, we need some time to modify your service record to match your cover."

"If I accept this mission, when will I leave Hawaii?"

"I'm scheduled on a military transport this afternoon to Clark Air Force Base. You must make up your mind now. I have travel vouchers for you. If you agree to this mission, you must be in Cheltenham five days from now."

Rigney evaluates what he should do. He comprehends that the Nea Makri mission is more important than his service on *Barb*. He asks, "Will the travel vouchers allow me a few days in Seal Beach?"

"Yes, as long as you're in Cheltenham five days from now. You cannot tell anyone at home what you are doing. They must think you are home on a few days leave and will come back to USS *Barb*."

Rigney hesitates a few seconds before he responds, "You can count on me, Brad. I'll go to the barracks and pack."

"Pack everything. No telling when you will be back."

"I have some scuba tanks and a surfboard that I must leave behind."

"No one you trust to keep them for you?"

"No."

Brad stares at Rigney for a few moments and states, "Still the lone wolf, huh?"

"Yes."

"Let's go to the wardroom. I need to talk to your captain about signing your orders."

They both stand.

"Oh, one more thing," Commander Watson adds. "Have a regulation haircut when you report into Cheltenham."

"Yes sir."

Chapter 8

Rigney's sister, Kate, meets him at the Los Angeles International Airport. She drove Rigney's 1951 Ford pickup to the airport. Kate has been taking care of the pickup and driving it since Rigney went into the navy.

"Want to drive it home?" she asks, knowing the answer.

When Rigney turned sixteen, his uncle gave him the pickup. The engine was in good working order, but the body required lots of work. He spent three months fixing the body, which ate all his part-time job savings. He could not raise enough money for a paint job. So, for the remaining two years of high school, he drove the pickup with only black primer. The pickup was perfect for hauling his surfboard and scuba gear. After that, what little money he made went to maintaining his pickup and infrequent low-cost dates he had with girlfriends.

After Rigney drives up the ramp to the interstate, he asks Kate, "How's mom and dad? How's Teri?"

Teri is their younger sister.

"Everyone is okay. Mom and dad had to work today. They didn't get your telegram until late last night. I'm still working part-time at the restaurant and going to community college. Teri starts her sophomore year at Saint Bartholomew High in September. Did you know that Terri works part-time as a teen model?"

"No. I didn't know. When did that start?"

"About six months ago."

"She must be excited about it."

"Yeah, she is, but she's not letting it go to her head."

Rigney nods and says, "I guess if I wrote more letters, I would get more letters telling me what's going on in the family."

"We all enjoyed those postcards you sent from . . . what's the name of that island you were at?"

"Guam."

"Guam? Wasn't there a big battle there during World War II?"

"Yes."

"Must be a lot of World War II relics there."

"There are."

They sit quiet for a few moments; then Rigney asks, "Are you still dating what's his name?"

"You mean Darrell?"

"Yes. Darrell."

"No. I dumped him. He was only interested in one thing. He didn't care about me."

Rigney nods understanding; then, he asks, "Anyone new in your life?"

With a sarcastic tone, Kate responds, "No. Men are pigs. I don't want anything to do with them."

"Am I a pig?"

"Of course not. You're different."

"Am I?" Rigney responds softly, questioning himself, not his sister.

"Believe me, brother. You're different."

Rigney asks, "Do you know if mom or dad contacted Diane Love? I asked them to do that in the telegram."

"Mom called Diane's parents. They said they would contact Diane and tell her about you coming home. Didn't you tell me when you were home last Christmas that Diane lived in a commune in Huntington Beach?"

"Yes, but she didn't answer my last two letters. She may not live there anymore."

The drive to Seal Beach takes one hour. Rigney parks his pickup on a sandy spot next to the garage. The garage is reserved for their father's car. The garage stands separate from the house. A small yard spreads between the house and the garage.

Rigney exits the pickup. The smell of the ocean fills his nostrils and the clean salty air fills his lungs. Boyhood memories flood his thoughts.

Rigney's home on Seal Way faces the fence of the Seal Beach Naval Weapons Station. A twenty feet wide cement walkway separates the front of Rigney's home from the chain-link fence of the naval station. The beach is a short walk southward on the cement walkway. The Page home is a small three-story structure. Counting the attic family room, the house is 1800 square feet. The exterior is stucco. A small 150 square feet courtyard outside the front door separates the house from the cement walkway. The interior of the house is a mismatch of furniture styles that Rigney's parents purchased at auctions and yard sales. All the floors are polished hardwood. Area rugs of different colors cover most of the hardwood floors throughout the three-story house.

Rigney's parents bought the house in 1948, when Seal Beach still had the remnants of a bad reputation. In the past, Seal Beach was called *sin city* and real estate prices where low. Rigney's father borrowed the down payment from his brothers. It takes all of James Page's effort and income to make mortgage payments and maintain the house. Rigney's mother, Margaret Page, works part-time at a personnel agency to help with the cost of living. All of their wealth is in their house. They have no savings.

All family gatherings, celebrations, and all entertaining occur in the third-floor family room. The family room is the most comfortable room in the house. The rug is thicker and softer. Overstuffed chairs and sofas stand strategically positioned throughout the room. The room has a wet bar, which is well stocked with scotch and bourbon. The Page's navy friends purchase the liquor at very low prices at the naval weapons station. Two walls have custom-installed bay windows, which provide a spectacular view of the naval weapons station and the Pacific Ocean.

Rigney enters the house. His sister, Teri, hugs him tightly. "Hi, big brother. Are you staying home this time?"

"No. I must return to Hawaii in a couple of days."

Teri says, "We wish you gave us more notice. So much is happening over the next two days. This afternoon, I must go to the photographer's studio. He will only be in town today, and he must take my picture."

"That's okay."

Kate adds, "And I have classes this afternoon. So you're gonna be here alone. Sorry."

"Oh. I forgot to tell you," Teri interjects. "Diane Love called. She said she couldn't meet you today. She said she will meet you for lunch at the Main Street Café tomorrow at noon."

Rigney takes a deep breath. He ponders about what to do with his day. He asks, "Is my surfboard still in the garage?"

"Sure is," Kate replies.

Rigney hauls his seabag and suitcase up to the third-floor family room. When Rigney entered the navy, his sister Kate took over his bedroom on the second floor. Whenever he visits home, he sleeps on the couch bed in the third-floor family room.

He drops his bags in the center of the room and goes directly to the bay windows. As a teenager, Rigney spent many hours at the bay windows with binoculars and scrutinized the ships and submarines that visited the Seal Beach Naval Weapons Station. Often, navy friends of his parents would describe the features of the vessels as Rigney analyzed them through the binoculars. Rigney would ask the sailors many questions; most of the time, they answered. Sometimes they would say, "Sorry, Rig, that's classified."

He picks up binoculars from the wide windowsill. He scans the naval weapons station. First, he views the beach area of the weapons station where as a young boy he and his family attended many beach barbeques as guests of their navy friends. The beach has one large gazebo with a cement floor and several picnic tables and barbeque pits. A ten-by-ten diving platform floats one hundred feet off the shore. An old PT boat anchor holds the diving platform in place. Rigney reminisces his numerous snorkeling and spear fishing experiences in the thirty feet deep water off that platform. Usually he speared yellowtail and halibut. He left the bonito and barracuda alone, because he did not like the taste. He remembers his excitement that afternoon when he speared a five feet long tiger shark, the largest shark he had ever seen in those waters. When he hauled that shark up to the beach on the end of his spear, his father and navy friends gathered around him. *Gosh, how old was I . . . eight?* He remembers his father's question. "What are you going to do with it, son?" Rig remembers saying something about mounting it as a trophy. Rigney was very proud, because he did not use spear guns; all his spear fishing was done with a ten feet long hand spear.

"Is that why you killed this magnificent creature of the sea— to put it on display?" his father had challenged. His father told him that no creature should be killed for display. "It's okay if you kill animals for food. All other reasons are nonsensical and meaningless."

Rigney shifts his scan southeast toward the naval station pier. The pier is empty. He remembers watching the weapons loading of surface ships and submarines. *Curiosity and wonder consumed me. How many hours did I watch ships come and go?*

Chapter 9

Rigney walks across the sand on the west side of the Seal Beach Pier. He carries his surfboard under his arm. The heat of the day warms his skin. Sunglasses protect his eyes from brightness and glare. No wind blows across the beach on this mild and sunny summer afternoon. Calm waves keep most surfers away. He appreciates that few sunbathe today. Wednesdays seldom attract crowds to the beach.

He wanted to wear his orange surfer baggies from his high school days, but he could not find them among his belongings stored in the garage. He dug out his bikini-style navy bathing suit from his seabag and put it on, but he thought it too revealing for a public beach. He finally settled on loose-fitting gym shorts and jockey underwear.

He drops his surfboard and lays down his beach blanket near the surf. After removing his t-shirt and sandals, he applies a think layer of sun block to his face, arms, and torso. He picks up his surfboard and walks into the water.

When he reaches knee-deep water, he climbs onto his surfboard. Lying belly down, he uses his hands to paddle seaward. Three other surfers paddle about, waiting for a deserving wave. Rigney paddles beyond the breaking surf.

He sits up and straddles his surfboard. He bobs up and down on the low rolling waves. He becomes aroused as he watches several bikini-clad females strolling along the waterline. He sighs deeply. Over six months has passed since his last sexual activity.

As soon as he knew he would visit Seal Beach, his first thoughts were of Diane. Her personality and outlook changed drastically since their high school days. When he and Diane dated in high school, Diane was conservative and a young republican. Their conversations were agreeable and reinforcing. But last December, their discussions turned to arguments. Diane's philosophy had changed. Now, she supports *leftist* solutions to America's problems.

Rigney usually professed the moderate right-wing view. In high school, she planned to earn a masters degree in finance and become a stockbroker. Then, during her first year at UCLA, she transitioned into what she describes as a social democrat. During high school, she groomed herself perfectly; now, she wears hippie-style clothes and wears her auburn hair long and stringy. When they dated in high school, their sexual activity was conventional and unimaginative. When they renewed their relationship last Christmas, Diane eagerly and lustfully engaged in oral sex and unconventional positions. In high school, she believed in God; now, she is an atheist. During high school, she never questioned the actions of government. Now, she leads protests against the Vietnam War, against institutional power, and against capitalism.

Her letters since Christmas promised that their political and social differences would not come between them. She promised that whenever he came home for a visit, their relationship would be the same as last Christmas. Her letters since last Christmas promised a continuation of sexual experimentation and hints of the most pleasurable blowjobs ever. Then, she stopped answering his letters.

Rigney thinks of what Kate said about her ex-boyfriend, that Darrel did not care about her, but only about sex. Kate called men *pigs*, but she said that Rigney was an exception. For the second time today, he wonders if he is an exception.

Rigney's penis enlarges as he remembers Diane's naked body and the sexual acts in which they engaged. He shakes his head in shame and says under his breath, "I must be a pig."

A random wave swell raises him abruptly, which brings him back to the present. He looks around and sees the few other surfers paddling furiously to catch the curl. He looks back to the open ocean to see if any more large waves are coming. None comes.

Rigney sits on his board for another thirty minutes. Then, he decides to go back to his blanket and sit so that he can get a closer look at the women in bathing suits.

After fifteen minutes of sitting on the beach and watching girls, his mind wanders toward his upcoming mission in Greece. He reflects on why he accepted Brad's offer. Duty aboard USS *Barb* did not meet his expectations. Since he was fifteen, the navy's submarine recruiting propaganda enticed him. The pictures of submarine crews in crisp navy-blue jumpsuits and operating impeccably clean equipment led him to believe in a shipboard environment that he subsequently discovered did not exist. Equally disappointing was that nuclear-powered submarines visited few liberty ports. Life aboard *Barb* bored him. Topping that, there was that incident in the *Barb* Radio Room with the weapons officer. Rigney went to the captain's mast over that incident. *Brad came along at just the right time.*

Chapter 10

When Rigney arrives back at the family home, his father meets him in the kitchen. The two men hug and exchange greetings.

At age forty-four, James Page's six-feet and four-inch tall, broad-shouldered, 220 pound frame still holds the powerful strength of his youth. However, the jacket of his summer-weight, blue pinstriped suit no longer buttons loosely across his belly.

James Page looks at his watch and says, "It's only 4:10. Your mom and sisters won't be home for several hours. What say we go to the VFW for a couple of drinks?"

"Dad, I told you before. I don't like going to the VFW. The cigarette and cigar smoke is thicker than water, and all those drunks cussing and cursing. Remember when you told that drunk his language was not suitable for women and children, and he told you, *Your fuckin' wife and fuckin' kids have no right to be here. This place is for fuckin' war veterans.*"

"That guy was banned from the VFW post."

"But the smoking and cursing still goes on . . . and the drunken arguments, right?"

"Not as bad as it used to be. C'mon Rig, just you and me. I want to show you off."

Rigney compromises. "Okay, but just for an hour."

"Good. Put on your uniform."

Rigney starts to protest, but complies with his father's wishes. He dons his Tropical White Long uniform.

James Page drives his five-year old Chevrolet Impala top-down convertible into a spot in the middle of the VFW Post parking lot.

Rigney observes that the one-story stucco building has not changed since his last visit more than three years ago.

As they walk through the front entrance of the VFW, the cold air-conditioned, dirty ashtray smell of the VFW smacks Rigney in the face. The ballroom area, which is the size of two side-by-side basketball courts, consists of a long bar at one end and a stage and dance floor at the other end. Dining tables circle the dance floor. Except for the wood floor having more worn spots, the ballroom looks the same.

Twenty men sit in the bar area. Boisterous arguing comes from several middle-aged men who present their opinions of which general officer or admiral was the winning factor for whichever war they are discussing. The constrained and dignified exchange includes such eloquent debating points as *moronic idiot* and *shit-for-brains*.

James Page selects a table near the bar and directs, "Let's sit here." He points to the bar and says, "I'll get the drinks. What do you want?"

"San Miguel."

"Never heard of it. What is it?"

"Beer."

"Oh."

While his father visits the bar, Rigney looks around the familiar barroom and dining area. He remembers the many times that his mother and father dragged him and his sisters to Sunday dinners and Christmas and Easter parties. The VFW post is a popular hangout for war veterans and their wives. Low-priced food and drinks and the promise of association with those of similar interests draws them in.

He also remembers how much he disliked his visits to the VFW post. He choked on the smoke and became annoyed by the loud, drunken, boisterous, and incessant arguing among the veterans. They argued everything from sports to politics to military policy and strategies; and because they always argued opinion instead of facts, no argument was ever won or lost, only reargued repeatedly.

Rigney's attention turns to the barroom door as two young men enter. They wear their hair in ponytails and wear full beards. They wear denim clothes with peace symbols sewn into their shirts and trousers. They are tanned, trim, and broad shouldered. Their short-sleeve denim shirts reveal heavily muscled arms. They walk the length of the bar and take two seats. Rigney notes that most veterans in the room stare disapprovingly at the two young men.

"No, San Miguel," James Page says as he places a Budweiser in front of Rigney and takes a seat across the table.

Rigney watches the bartender place two mugs of beer on the bar in front of the two young men.

"Get a haircut!" orders a middle-age man at the bar, his tone slurred with alcohol.

"Show some respect for your marine corps service!" another middle-aged veteran who sits at the bar demands loudly. "Cut off those traitorous pinko symbols!"

As a response to the verbal attacks, the two young men shake their heads and smile, amused. They raise their beers in salutes of defiance.

Rigney comments to his father, "Doesn't look like much has changed here. Those two guys at the end of the bar appear unconventional for these surroundings."

James Page looks toward the end of the bar and says, "Oh, yeah, Larry and Chuck. They are the first Vietnam vets to join the post. They served in the same unit. They did two tours back-to-back in Vietnam."

Rigney looks respectfully at the two; then, he comments, "That means they volunteered for the second year."

"Does it?" James Page responds. "I didn't know that."

Rigney nods his head and says, "Yeah, and I bet those older vets don't know that."

"You're right about that, son. The majority of war vets that come in here expect all vets to be like them. They feel that Larry and Chuck disrespect their marine corps service in Vietnam. They think that Chuck and Larry have joined the war protesters. So, every time they come in here, the older vets harass them."

"Are they war protesters?" Rigney asks.

"Don't know. They never talk about Vietnam. When they're in here, they talk about sports, cars, and their jobs as construction workers. If a conversation starts up about politics or Vietnam, they remain quiet."

"So why do the older vets think they are war protesters?"

"Because of their appearance."

"And what do you think, Dad?"

"Son, I've never been one to rush to judgment about anyone. As far as I'm concerned, they were born with a constitutional right to wear anything they want and to look any way they want, and four years as marines and two years fighting in the jungles of Vietnam reinforces their right."

"I'm surprised you feel that way, Dad. When I was home last Christmas, you told me you did not support the Vietnam War."

James Page nods with a solemn expression on his face and says, "I still feel the same way about the Vietnam War, but that does not diminish my gratitude and respect for their sacrifice and service and for the fear those young boys endured. They were not drafted. They enlisted, and they did their duty. They should be honored and respected by all."

Rigney chokes up, and his eyes mist over. "Dad, I am proud to be your son."

A look of appreciation spreads over James's face; then, he says, "Thanks, son. I am proud of you, too."

A heavyset middle-aged man with a flushed red face in a brown suit walks up to the table and asks, "Hey, Jimmy, this your son? How 'bout introducing me."

The man in the brown suit sits down at the table.

"Jack Carlucci this is my son, Rigney. He's been in the navy for three years and is a second class petty officer, an E-5."

Jack reaches across the table, shakes Rigney's hand, and says, "Nice to meet you Rigney."

James Page advises, "Rig, Jack is the post commander."

"You're in submarines, right?" Jack queries.

"Yes sir."

"Call me Jack. Where ya home-ported?"

"Pearl Harbor."

"How do you like Hawaii?" Jack asks.

"Island fever, I'm enjoying time away from it."

Another middle-age man sits down at the table. James Page performs the introductions again. The same questions are asked. After a few minutes, the conversation drifts to World War II and the experiences of the three older men.

Rigney's attention shifts toward the two Vietnam veterans sitting at the end of the bar. He wants to talk with them.

Frank lights up a cigar.

Rigney stands and says, "I'll get us some more drinks. What do you guys want?"

The older men tell Rigney what they want; then, Rigney goes to the bar. He gives the bartender the order, followed with, "And give Larry and Chuck a round of whatever they're drinking."

As Rigney delivers the drinks to the table, he hears a voice call, "Hey, sparks." He looks in the direction of the voice and sees Chuck and Larry motioning for him to join them. *Sparks* refers to the radioman emblem on Rigney's rating chevron.

"Please excuse me for a few moments," Rigney says to his father and the other two men, but they do not acknowledge; they are deeply engrossed in the discussion of World War II experiences. His father praises General Patton.

As Rigney approaches the two Vietnam vets, one of them sticks out his hand and says, "My name is Chuck Cramer. This is Larry Rockwell."

Rigney shakes each man's hand and says, "My name is Rigney Page. Most people call me Rig."

"Hope you don't mind me calling you sparks," Larry says apologetically. "We know you're Jimmy's son, but didn't know your name."

"Oh, my dad talks about me?"

Chuck says, "When he is not telling us about World War II, he is talking about his son who serves on a nuclear submarine."

"He must bore you to death," Rigney responds with a chuckle.

"Actually, he doesn't," Larry counters. "He's one of the few vets around here who talks with us. Most of the World War II and Korean vets don't respect us, but your dad respects everyone. He talks with everyone as equals."

Rigney looks admiringly toward his father. *He always has.* Then, he says, "My dad says you two guys spent two years in Vietnam."

"Yeah, we did," Larry responds. "But we don't talk about it. It's behind us."

Rigney nods understanding and says, "Where did you serve the rest of the time?"

Larry replies, "I spent my last eighteen months in the marine detachment on an aircraft carrier out of San Diego."

Chuck says, "My last eighteen months were spent at the Marine Gunnery School at Camp Pendleton."

Rigney asks, "Are you guys from this area?"

"Yeah," Chuck replies. "We were raised in Belmont Shore. We were next door neighbors when we were kids. Now, we both work for CDOT as heavy equipment operators."

"What do you do when you're not working?"

"We customize cars," Larry responds. "I have a '57 Chevy convertible that I am refurbishing and adding a 409 cubic inch engine. Chuck is doing the same thing to a 1960 Chevy. When we're not doing that, we workout at Vic Tanny's."

Chuck asks Rigney, "What do you do when you're not on your submarine?"

"Submarines are pretty much a twenty-four-hour a day job, but when I'm off I like to surf and scuba dive, also like to play basketball and lift weights. The gym at Pearl is the best equipped that I've seen in the navy."

Larry says, "Chuck and I go to Vic Tanny's four nights a week. How much can you bench press?"

Rigney looks thoughtful for a few moments; then, he says, "I don't know. I never thought about finding out."

Chuck says, "We will be at Vic Tanny's tomorrow night at seven. You're welcome to be our guest."

"I think I will have a date tomorrow night." Rigney hopes his time with Diane tomorrow will extend way beyond lunch.

"We're just goin' to workout," Larry says. "You don't have to show us anything. Join us if you're not busy."

James Page appears at Rigney's side. He nods to Larry and Chuck and says, "Excuse me, gentleman, I need to introduce Rigney to someone."

"Sure, Jimmy, no problem," Chuck responds. Then, he adds, "Like we said, Rig. You're welcome to join us tomorrow night."

Rigney nods; then, he asks, "Where's Vic Tanny's?"

Chuck provides the directions.

James Page looks questioningly Rigney and queries, "You gonna do some showing off, son?"

"No, Dad."

Chuck and Larry exchange amused glances.

Chapter 11

During the drive home from the VFW Post, James Page asks his son, "What were the three of you talking about?"

"We weren't talking about anything. We were discovering each other."

"Discovering?"

"Yeah. We were asking questions about each other . . . to determine our interests."

"Oh, I never thought of it that way before."

They remain quiet for several minutes. Then, James asks, "Are you meeting them tomorrow to lift weights?"

"I don't think so. I am meeting Diane Love tomorrow for lunch at the Main Street Café. I hope to spend the day with her."

"Oh," James Page responds while expressing an exaggerated grin.

Rigney and his father arrive home at 7:00 PM. Rigney's mother, Margaret Page, and his two sisters sit around the dining room table and eat pizza.

Margaret Page stands and throws her arms around her son. "About time you two got home," she chastises while throwing her husband a disapproving glance. "I haven't seen my son since Christmas, and you take him off to meet your cronies at the VFW."

Rigney hugs his mother tight. His eyes mist over, and his expression becomes loving as he says, "Hi, Mom. I'm really happy to see you."

Margaret pulls back from the hug and looks her son in the eye. She sighs deeply; a few tears flow from her eyes. She declares, "Rigney, no mother could be more proud than me. You look so good in that uniform."

"Thanks, Mom."

"Okay, let's eat up this pizza," James Page orders as he retrieves several bottles of beer from the fridge.

After they are all seated and wolfing-down pizza, Kate requests, "Tell us about your life on that submarine."

Rigney explains in detail his lifestyle aboard USS *Barb*. When he describes the long working hours to include more than forty-eight hours awake when equipment needs repair, Margaret Page exclaims, "Ouch!" Followed by James Page announcing, "Military hasn't changed."

When Rigney describes hot bunking, Kate and Teri utter a collective *eeeeuuuuuu*.

Rigney expresses disappointment when he explains the cancelled liberty ports.

At 8:00 PM, Kate stands and advises she must study for tomorrow's history test, and Terri stands and informs that she must make a telephone call.

After Kate and Terri depart the kitchen, James asks Rigney, "Now that you're twenty-one, will you register to vote?"

"Already have. I registered absentee last week."

"The Republican Party will nominate Richard Nixon for President at the convention next week," Margaret says. "Your father and I know him personally. We worked on all his campaigns."

"I know."

"Well, son, what do you think of Richard Nixon?"

"I think if elected president, he will continue to be part of the problem, and not part of the solution."

"You're not gonna vote for him?" Margaret snaps, surprised.

"Didn't say I wouldn't vote for him," Rigney counters.

"Then, what are you saying?" James Page challenges.

Rigney expresses thoughtfulness for a few moments; then, he answers, "I'm saying that I don't like his record, especially when he served with the *Committee on Un-American Activities*. However, I do not agree with the democrats, especially Eugene McCarthy. Nixon is a republican, and I believe more in what republicans believe than what democrats believe. The other thing

I favor about Nixon is that he promises to end the Vietnam War. The Democrats escalated the war and put five hundred thousand Americans soldiers there."

James Page questions with a surprised tone, "You're against the war? I thought you were for the war."

"Dad, I am for Nixon ending it."

James Page blinks his eyes a few times, not knowing for sure if his son answered the question.

Margaret Page interjects, "Yes, Nixon is for that and many other things we believe in."

The conversation pauses. Rigney yawns. He looks at his watch and says, "I've been up for almost twenty-four hours. I need to go to bed. See you in the morning."

Margaret Page says, "Good night, Rig."

"Sleep well, son."

After Rigney departs the kitchen, Margaret conveys concern and says, "I'm worried about him."

"Don't worry. I know you think about the submarine USS *Scorpion* sinking. Rigney is a strong young man. He will be okay."

"It's not the submarine. I don't think he tells us the truth about his work in the navy."

"What makes you say that?"

"He said that he must return to Hawaii the day after tomorrow."

"Yes. So what?"

"While you two were gone, I went through his things to see if he needed anything washed. I found an airplane ticket. He's flying to Washington DC the day after tomorrow."

"That doesn't make sense," James declares. "Let's ask him about it."

"No. We shouldn't do that. If he feels that he must hide it from us, we should not put him on the spot about it. I mean, well, it's all so strange."

James looks at his wife quizzically and asks, "What's all so strange?"

"Think about it, Jim. He spent two years at submarine school, but just before he graduated, they medically disqualified him from submarines. Then, he went to sea on that cruiser from Norfolk, which went on a six-month cruise to the Mediterranean, but three months into the cruise, the navy discovered they made a diagnosis error and declared Rigney medically qualified for submarines. Then, the navy sent him to that submarine in Hawaii . . . all the way from the Mediterranean. Now, he lies to us about where he is going next."

"Yes, that is strange," James agrees.

"I found something else disturbing in his belongings."

"What?"

"A marine corps training manual on hand-to-hand combat."

James sits thoughtful for a few moments; then he says, "I wonder what he's doing."

Margaret says, almost pleading, "Whatever the navy has him doing, I hope to God it's safe."

As Rigney enters the third floor family room, he notices all of his socks, boxer shorts, and t-shirts are neatly folded on the coffee table. His white uniforms are freshly pressed and on hangers.

Shit! Mom has been in my stuff! The tickets!

Rigney frantically digs to the bottom of his seabag. He pulls out his letter-writing kit and the hand-to-hand combat manual. He holds out the manual at arm's length. *I wonder what mom thought about this.*

He unzips the letter-writing kit and finds his airline tickets behind the envelopes. *She had no reason to look in here. Besides, if she had seen the tickets, she would have asked me about going to DC.*

Chapter 12

Rigney walks north along Main Street. He wears his best Tropical White Long uniform. His white hat rests cocked to the side. He enjoys the familiar sites and smells of Main Street. His boyhood memories flood his thoughts. He remembers frequenting all the sidewalk ice cream stands and hot dog stands with his boyhood friends.

He opens the door to the Main Street Café; he hears the familiar ring as the door nudges against the bell mounted on the doorjamb. Ten diners sit randomly around the café. He feels the old beach town décor of the café. Worn, wooden planks cover the aged floor. 1930s-style cabinets and counters line the walls. Old and worn wooden tables and chairs are located in no organized manner around the café. Six belt-driven ceiling fans stir the air. Nautical artifacts hang on the walls.

Like a city landmark, Fat Chad stands at the grill, flipping burgers. He wears the same old and worn grease-splattered white apron. Chad has owned the café since before Rigney can remember.

The best hamburgers in Seal Beach fry on the old grill. The aroma of frying onions fills the air. Greasy French fries drain in a basket over the deep fry.

"Hey, Rig, welcome home," Fat Chad calls out happily.

Rigney stops at the counter. He initiates a handshake.

"Your dad told me you serve in a nuclear submarine. I hear those nuke boats are luxurious hotels compared to the pig boats I served in."

Rigney thinks of his life aboard the USS *Barb*. "Probably are," Rigney answers with a nod and a smile.

Rigney has known Fat Chad most of his life. Rigney remembers his total astonishment last Christmas when Chad revealed for the fist time that he served in submarines during World War II. *Who'd have ever thought!*

"Are you waiting for Diane?" Fat Chad asks over his shoulder while flipping some hamburgers.

"Yes. Is she here yet?" Rigney queries as he attempts to look around the corner into the next room.

"Not yet."

"Okay. I will go into the back room and wait."

The back room is empty. Rigney selects his favorite chair at his favorite table.

He stares at the ceiling while reminiscing. Rigney hung out at the Main Street Café during his junior and senior high school days. He and his surfer friends gathered here. He often met his dates here. During his senior year of high school, he and Diane carried on deep philosophical conversations at this table. Diane proclaimed her future self-reliance at this table. She would become a republican activist, and she would follow her father's success and someday own her own stock brokerage firm. Rigney spoke of his quest to become an adventurer and world traveler. Someday, maybe, he would become an electronics engineer, but first, he must complete his military obligation.

At this table, Diane and Rigney pledged a life of conservative and free-market values. They declared self-accountability and rugged individualism as the principles on which America was founded, and they declared they would follow those principles. They felt optimistic about their futures.

They differed on the path to happiness. Diane believed accumulation of wealth to be the only path to happiness. Rigney believed searching for enlightenment and pursuing one's interests was the path to happiness.

They also differed on the nature and significance of God. Diane claimed the philosophies of the *Christian Right* to be her own. Rigney doubts God's power over man and over heaven and earth. Their sexual activity was a contradiction to Diane's Christian beliefs. She never justified that contradiction, and Rigney never challenged it.

After high school, Rigney went into the navy. Diane went to college. They exchanged letters, but Diane discontinued answering Rigney's letters after six months. Diane and Rigney did not see each other for more than two years. Then, Diane came to see Rigney when he visited Seal Beach last Christmas. During the two and one-half years they were apart, Diane completely changed in appearance and philosophies. She no longer cared for stylish clothes and a painted face. She tossed away her contact lenses for a pair of granny glasses perched precariously on the end of her nose. She wore hippie-style clothes and combed her auburn hair straight. Her whole being had become pessimistic, cynical, and socialist. She joined the Vietnam War protest movement. She cast aside the *Christian Right* values of her teenage years. Now, she denies the existence of God. She lived in a hippie commune when he was last home. He does not know where she currently resides.

The bell ringing caused by the opening of the door brings Rigney back to the present. He looks at his watch—12:13 PM. She's late. He hears Diane's voice say, "Hi, Chad." Five seconds later, Diane Love rounds the corner and enters the room.

She looks the same. She wears loose-fitting, faded blue jeans and a loose-fitting blue denim shirt. Peace symbols are sewn into the front thigh area of the jeans. An American flag is sewn into the shirt, just above the left breast pocket. Her nose still hosts the granny glasses. When she sees Rigney, she smiles. Her manner appears happy, but not joyous.

Rigney stands. He senses a reserved manner about her.

When she is a few feet away, she raises her arms for a hug.

They wrap their arms tightly around each other.

They kiss. Rigney attempts to put some passion into it, but Diane does not respond in kind. Diane pulls back from the kiss. She looks apologetic at Rigney and says, "Sorry, I must leave town in an hour. There is no time for us. I wish you would have given me more notice."

"I wish I could have," Rigney responds with a disappointed tone.

Diane holds Rigney at arm's length and looks him over; then, she comments, "That baggy uniform does nothing for you. You look better in tight jeans and t-shirt."

Rigney guides them to sit. Fat Chad enters to take their orders.

"Coffee and a slice of your famous apple pie," Rigney orders.

"I'll have the same," Diane says.

After Fat Chad departs the room, Rigney asks, "Leaving town. Where are you going? Uh, if it's okay for me to ask."

"It's okay. I'm going to the Republican Party Convention in Miami."

"As a delegate?"

"No, as a protester."

Rigney expresses bewilderment.

"You shouldn't be surprised, Rig. Surely you have been following the protest movement."

Rigney shakes his head and replies, "No, I haven't."

"You don't follow political events anymore?"

"I still do, but I usually skip over the reports of protests.

"Rig, students are protesting against the Vietnam War and against brainwashing education systems. Black people are rioting in the streets in protest against a racist society. A revolution is taking place in America. You need to understand it and accept it."

"Oh, I understand it," Rig counters. "But I have little time to read, and I must spend it on those things that are important."

"Rig!"

A smile spreads across his face as he admits, "Just kidding."

"That's not funny. You know I take these things seriously."

"To be fully truthful, I take the race riots seriously, but I don't take seriously privileged students protesting against a system that molded them. I suspect their motives are unwillingness to perform their military obligation."

Diane challenges, "You think they are cowards?"

"No, I don't think they are cowards. I think they are selfish. I think they don't want their lives interrupted with several years of military service. So they cover their true motives with protests against what they call an illegal and immoral war."

"You don't think we are sincere when we protest against the Vietnam War."

Rig looks contemplative; then, he says, "I think that if there were no military draft there would be no protests."

"You're not serious?" Diane responds in a sarcastic tone.

"Absolutely. If America had an all-volunteer military, Americans would not protest any war we fought. Well, not protest to the large scale we have now. There might be a few dissenting voices, but not many."

Diane declares, "The protest movement is not that shallow."

"I think it is. I think that if the American government announced today that the military draft has ended and from this date forward military service is voluntary, protests would slow to a trickle and die out within several months."

Diane's expression becomes defiant, and she shakes her head in disagreement, but she does not counter. She does not want this short visit with an old friend to turn into an argument about the Vietnam War.

"I just got home last night from protest organization meetings in Berkley. We will meet again two weeks from now to plan our protests at the Democrat Party Convention in Chicago."

"We?"

"The SDS," Diane replies.

Rigney shakes his head to indicate he does not recognize the abbreviation.

"Students for a Democratic Society! Damn, Rig, you are outta touch!"

"Oh, I have read about them, just didn't recognize the abbreviation."

Diane shakes her head with annoyance over what she perceives as Rig's dismissal of the SDS's importance.

"The SDS will change America," Diane proclaims. "We will pursue careers in teaching, law, and politics. We will gain political power and change America."

Rigney sits contemplative for a few moments; then, he asks, "Why? Is there something wrong with the one we have?"

Diane stares at Rigney for a few moments. Then, she expresses understanding and she says, "Your navy insulates you. You're not aware of what's going on in the real world."

Rigney thinks about the reality of his last ONI mission and the reality of the ONI mission on which he is about to embark. *Diane and I live in different worlds and definitely have different views as to what is real and what is important.*

He wants to avoid the same arguments he had with her last time he was home. He decides to let her do all the talking. "What changes will be made?" he asks.

"Everyone who resides in America will have health coverage. People will not be denied treatment because they cannot pay. The death penalty will be abolished. All education, through a four-year college degree, will be paid by the government. The government will control prices of all rents, utilities, food, and commodities. Corporate profits will be limited to a fair amount. We will dissolve the IRS and institute a two-level tax sufficient to pay for all of it. The rich will be taxed at fifty percent, and that's fifty percent of all income—earned income, dividends, capital gains. The rest of the people will be taxed at ten percent of earned income only."

An amused look appears on Rigney's face.

Diane misinterprets the look and asks, "Do you follow me? Do you understand what I am talking about?"

"Yes, I understand the society you describe." He expresses disapproval; then, he states in a negative tone. "It's called socialism enforced by totalitarianism."

"Rig, you are so outta touch!"

"The American public will not want it. You're naive to believe you can have a society as you describe without forcing it on the people. What you describe stifles individual achievement, because it stifles reward for individual achievement. You are describing a society that will eventually evolve into economic failure. America was built on rugged individualism, competition, and free enterprise. Your plan suppresses all that."

"You're wrong, Rig. Americans will embrace the equality."

"What you describe is not equality. It is not equality when you take property from those who have achieved and give it to those who have not achieved. What you describe is redistribution of wealth. What Americans want is equal opportunity to succeed, not the rewards of their success given to those who have chosen not to succeed."

"How would you know, Rig? What could you know about these things? You're only . . ." Diane pauses, looking for the right words.

Rigney interjects, "What? I'm only twenty-one? I only have a high school education? I don't have three years of college? You think three years of college makes you some kind of expert."

"No, I don't think that. I have friends, professors, much older and more experienced. They've enlightened me about the injustices in America. They enlightened me to how vulnerable most Americans are. I now understand that most Americans need a caring and compassionate government to take care of them."

Rigney dismissively shakes his head.

Their discourse pauses as Fat Chad delivers their food.

After Fat Chad departs, they remain silent as they drink their coffee and take a few bites of apple pie.

Rigney breaks the silence. "You're more focused and directed in your cause than last time. You're now leading and organizing, aren't you?"

"You can tell?"

"Yes. You've regained your confidence. Like the Diane I knew in high school."

Diane smiles appreciatively and says, "We are recruiting military people to join us. Don't suppose you're interested?"

"No. I think your plan for America is a plan that will fail. The American voter will not support it."

"You don't get it, Rig. When it's time, sixty percent of American voters will be convinced they are victims of a callous government that is controlled by big corporations. They'll vote for change."

"I'll tell you what I get, Diane. I get that the left-wingers in this country believe the American way of life is the enemy. I can tell you from experience that there are strong evil forces at work in this world that crusade to crush democracy and freedom . . . evil forces that would not allow you and your SDS colleagues to attempt what you're planning. Instead of fighting that evil, your SDS crusades to destroy those values that made America the greatest country that ever existed."

Diane takes Rigney's comments as a personnel attack. Her face flushes, and she becomes angry; she collects her thoughts and responds, "I don't understand the evil you describe. Has America really committed itself to fighting evil? Remember your history, Rig. America encouraged and supposedly supported Hungarian freedom fighters in 1956, but when the Hungarian freedom fighters took to the streets to overthrow a vicious dictatorship and almost succeeded, America did not come to their aid. Then, Soviet troops and tanks swept through Budapest and mercilessly slaughtered the freedom fighters. America did nothing."

Diane searches Rigney's eyes for understanding; then, she continues, "America encouraged Cuban exiles to return to Cuba and overthrow Castro. Our CIA provided logistic support and helped plan the invasion. We promised those exiles we would support their invasion. At the Bay of Pigs in 1961, America was absent, and the invasion failed. So tell me, Rig. How committed is America to fighting this so-called evil? There is no evil in South Vietnam other than its brutal dictator, but we have five hundred thousand troops there to keep him in power. None of it makes sense to me."

Rigney senses Diane's anger. He remains quiet, because he does not want to end this visit with anger.

To stop the argument from escalating, they return to their food.

Rigney understands the futility of this discussion. After several moments of thought, he asks, "What profession will you pursue—lawyer, teacher, politician?"

"I'm going into politics."

"American Communist Party?"

Diane rolls her eyes.

"Okay, democrat party, then."

"Yes."

A quizzical expression appears on Rigney's face, and he says, "The democrat party platform does not fit your SDS plan."

"It will."

"When?"

"Eventually."

They pause again and sip coffee. After several bites of pie, Diane says, "If I remember correctly, you just turned twenty-one. Did you register to vote?"

"Yes."

"Republican, right?"

"Right."

"Republicans only support the rich and big business. Republicans victimize the working class."

Rigney chuckles. Then, he asks, "What do you mean by working class? All the republicans I know work for a living, and they are not rich."

Diane shakes her head, an expression of futility deeply etched in her face. She sighs deeply and glances at her watch. "Sorry, Rig, I must go."

Rigney says, "I need a valid address for you."

"I'm living at home again. Write me there. I apologize for not telling you about the address change. Thanks for sending me those postcards and letters from Hawaii and Guam."

"You will answer my letters, then?"

"Yes. I don't want to lose contact with you. We must work hard to remain friends and not to let our philosophical differences separate us." Diane smiles as she remembers their previous times together; then, she adds, "You're my only friend left from high school. You have always accepted me as I am. Anyway, sorry I must leave. Give me more notice next time." She sighs deeply and adds, "You're still the sexiest man I know."

They get up from their chairs, move closer, and hug. They kiss. This time Diane puts more emotion into it.

She pulls back and grabs her canvas book bag from an adjacent chair. "When must you go back to Hawaii?" she asks.

"Tomorrow."

"Write me about your adventures."

"I will," he promises.

She turns to leave but stops and turns around to face Rigney; she requests, "Consider something for me, will you?"

"What is it?"

"During your life you will meet people who you judge to be despicable. Please remember that some of those people are victims of an unjust, uncaring, or unfair society not of their making. I ask that you try and understand them and help them when you can."

With this request, Rigney understands that Diane's goals are unenlightened, but her motivations are compassionate. With a nod and a serious expression, he responds, "Yes, I will do that."

"Thank you, Rig."

He watches her as she walks across the café and out the door. He feels deep concern for her. *Failure awaits her. I hope she survives it well.*

Two hours later, Rig sits on his surfboard near the Seal Beach Pier, one hundred yards seaward of the breaking surf and other surfers. He paddled to this calmness, not to wait for a good wave, but for solitude so he can think clearly.

Around the world, America fights both a hot and cold war against communism. Thousands of American teenagers die in Vietnam each year. Students violently protest on college campuses. Race riots rage in America's cities. The countries of the Middle East wage war against each other over ancient beliefs and ancient land rights. Many countries in South America suffer in anarchy while criminal, military, and political factions violently battle each other for control so they can plunder, as did the previous controlling faction. In the midst of all that, some American service men sell their country's secrets for money.

He easily concludes that if he wants to make a difference, he must succeed as a counterespionage operative for ONI.

The next morning, James Page drives his son to Los Angeles International Airport.

They are quiet for the first ten minutes. Then, James Page breaks the silence. "I heard you tell your mother you went to Vic Tanny's last night."

"Yeah, that's right. I worked out with Larry and Chuck."

"Did ya show them how strong you are?"

"No. I just matched them pound-for-pound as we kept adding weights. I got nowhere near my max."

They sit quiet for a few minutes; then, James asks, "So, your date with Diane didn't work out."

"No."

Rigney's lack of detail suggests he does not wish to discuss it.

When they are one mile from the airport, James asks, "Do you want me to help you with your luggage? Then, I will see you off at the gate."

"No, Dad, not necessary. Just drop me at departures."

With an inquiring tone, James Page says, "A full seabag of uniforms and a suitcase of civvies for three days. Seems like a lot."

Rigney turns his head and studies his father for a few moments; then, he asks, "Dad, do you have something you want to ask me?"

"Your mother and I are worried, son. We know you're going to Washington."

Rig bows his head in thought; then, he asks his father, "When you were in Europe during World War II, did you ever go on classified operations that you could not write home about?"

"Sure, all the time."

"Same applies to me. So, I can't talk about it."

"Is it dangerous?"

Rigney emphasizes with a stern voice, "Dad, I can't talk about it, and I must ask you not to say anything to anyone."

"Don't worry, son. I won't."

James Page stops his car in front of the doors to the departures terminal.

Rigney exits the car and retrieves his bags from the backseat. Then, he bends down and says through the passenger-side window, "Bye, Dad. As soon as I can write or call, I will."

With a concerned expression on his face, James Page looks into his son's eyes and says, "When I was fighting in Europe, the soldiers in my unit had a saying. *Watch your back and stay safe.* Promise me you'll do that, son."

"I promise."

Chapter 13

Brad Watson meets Rigney at the Washington National Airport. He drives south on the outer beltway through Virginia. Without air-conditioning in Brad's 1965 Mustang, the ninety-degree heat makes the ride uncomfortable. Sweat stains spread across their white uniforms.

They cross the Woodrow Wilson Memorial Bridge into Maryland. The landscape is much different from Rigney's previous visit last December when the woods were barren of leaves and the winter climate required a heavy overcoat. Now, the woods are thick with green foliage and the air hot and humid.

Brad exits the beltway and drives south on Route 5. Twenty minutes later, the gate sentry waves them through the main entrance of Naval Communications Station, Washington DC, at Cheltenham, Maryland. As they ride by the Cheltenham building with the small gym, Rigney thinks back to that night nine months ago when he spent the evening in the steam room with Cathy Gillard, followed by a week of sexual exercises in Cathy's apartment. Cathy is a young navy woman that he met during his first day in Cheltenham last December. He still has her telephone number, and he plans to call her this evening.

Brad parks his Mustang in the ONI building parking lot. Rigney retrieves his seabag and small suitcase from the trunk. They walk up the few stone stairs of the two-story rectangle-shaped brick building. As they stand outside the front door, Brad advises, "The cipher combinations have been changed since the last time you were here. I will give them to you later."

After passing through the front entrance, they stand in a small lobby. The air-conditioning provides comfortable relief from the sweltering heat outside. Brad enters the cipher lock combination for the inner security door. They both remove their hats and look up at the surveillance cameras. The motors for the locking slide bars churn, and the thick metal security door opens. They walk through the security door entrance and into the ONI working area. Just inside the security door, they step into a hallway that runs the length of the building. All offices are located in the first few rooms.

Rigney sees familiar faces. Those who work in the offices are a mixture of civilians and enlisted navy personnel. He hears the familiar clickity-clack of typewriters and the soft din of half a dozen conversions. The feel and sound of the place has not changed since his last stay.

As they walk down the hall, Brad advises Rigney, "You're in room number fifteen again. Take a shower and change into a jumpsuit, if you wish. Then, come to room 4."

"Yes sir."

Midway down the hallway, Brad opens the door to room 4 and enters.

Rigney walks to the end of the hallway. He opens the last door on the left and enters room fifteen. Inside the door, he drops his seabag and suitcase and looks around the BOQ-style accommodations that include a combination sitting room and kitchen. The room contains the same small couch and coffee table and television set. A refrigerator and a wet bar stand in the far corner. The same navy blue carpet covers the floor.

He checks the refrigerator. As usual, it is stocked with foreign beers, wines, and assorted sandwiches. A large plate of sliced turkey and sliced vegetables sits on the bottom shelf.

In the closet, he finds three short-sleeved, summer-weight navy blue jumpsuits. He checks the size label of each jumpsuit to verify they will fit. Three navy blue ball caps sit on the closet shelf. A pair of spit-shined work boots stands on the closet floor.

Rigney enters the bedroom and sees the same comfortable-looking double-size bed. Off the bedroom is the bathroom, which is luxurious by shipboard standards with a tiled floor and a large combination bathtub and shower.

Except for a couple weeks in Naples, Italy, last February, Rigney resided in the cramped and Spartan-like berthing compartments in the guided missile cruiser, USS *Columbus*, and the fast-attack submarine, USS *Barb*. He looks forward to a week of luxury in these quarters.

He remembers that it was in this room the focus of his life changed. Previously, he had been absorbed with self-serving goals. Then, Brad Watson recruited him for Operation Jupiter. At first, he participated reluctantly, because the operation would interfere with completion of his goals and would place him in physical danger. ONI taught him hand-to-hand combat and taught him how to use firearms. The prospect that he might need to kill someone made him even more reluctant. However, as he learned more and more about evil's quest to destroy America, the more he committed himself to fighting that evil. Eventually, he realized the danger to him was insignificant when compared to the danger to his fellow Americans. He discovered patriotism, and he committed to serve.

Rigney comes back to the present. He dumps the contents of his seabag on the bed. *I'll put it away later.* He strips off his sweat-soaked Tropical White Long uniform. He grabs his douche kit from the pile of items on the bed and enters the bathroom to shave and shower.

Fifteen minutes later, he stands naked in front of the full-length mirror mounted on the bedroom door. He takes this opportunity to inspect his body from head to toe. His most distinguishing physical feature is the matting of reddish brown hair that covers his body from his neck to his ankles. Thick reddish brown hair tops his ruggedly handsome face. His dark green eyes reflect intelligence and clarity of thought.

He flexes his muscles in a bodybuilder pose. Four months at sea on the USS *Barb* took its toll. His seventy-three-inch tall frame still looks trim. However, his broad shoulders and large biceps have lost some muscle tone. He has not gained any weight, but he detects some flab on his waist that was not there five months ago. The long and tough hours while underway allowed little time for exercise.

Except when the USS *Barb* was alongside the tender in Guam, fresh fruit and vegetables were not available. The *Barb* mess cooks did the best they could with what they had. Most of the time, the cooks served canned and frozen food high in fat and salt. Rigney ate little.

Rigney commits to spending his spare time at the Cheltenham base gym. He considers not seeing Cathy Gillard while he is here to allow more time for the gym. Then, he reconsiders. His last sex was with Sally Macfurson back in Naples last February—six months ago.

He enjoyed Cathy's company when he was in Cheltenham last December, and the thought of having sex with her again arouses him. *I have no time for this*, he reasons. *I must get to room 4.*

Rigney occupies his thoughts with getting dressed and planning his next workout. He plans on daily workouts when he gets to Nea Makri. He puts on a jumpsuit and boots.

As he stands at the door to room 4, he recollects his previous visits to this room. Nine months ago, this is where he had received his briefings for Operation Jupiter, and he was assigned the codename *Apollo*.

Chapter 14

"Enter," Brad Watson says loudly.

Rigney opens the door to room 4 and enters. He quickly surveys the room. The dark green tile floor and pea green colored walls with wood trim has not changed. The same 1940s style furniture decorates the room.

Dr. Williamson sits behind the desk.

Rigney smiles appreciatively. He walks over to the desk and vigorously shakes the doctor's hand from across the desk. "Hi, Doctor. Great to see you again."

Dr. Williamson responds, "Rigney, it's a pleasure to see you again, also." He gestures for Rigney to sit in the chair in front of the desk.

After Rigney sits, Dr. Williamson says, "I'm glad I finally have a chance to congratulate you on the success of your last mission."

"Thank you. I appreciate it," Rigney replies, blushing slightly. Rigney cannot help but think that Dr. Williamson with his shoulder-length pepper-colored hair and equally pepper-colored beard looks out of place in this military environment.

Brad Watson stands and says, "Well, you two have some talking to do. I will leave now. Rig, be here tomorrow morning at 0800. Bob Mater and I will brief you on mission details."

"Aye, aye, sir."

After Brad Watson departs, Rigney turns to face Dr. Williamson.

Dr. Williamson looks at Rigney over the top of his reading glasses and says, "The commander says you want to talk about some of those violent situations during your last mission."

"Yes. I want to try and understand my feelings about what I did."

"Okay, start talking."

Later, Rigney sits on the couch in his quarters—room fifteen of the Cheltenham ONI building. A few minutes ago, he finished his second three-hour therapy session of the day with Dr. Williamson. Rigney had told the doctor all the details regarding violent events during the last mission. During the therapy session, Dr. Williamson asked many questions and wrote many notes. The session concluded with Dr. Williamson scheduling two more sessions over the next four days.

Rigney looks at his watch—6:35 PM. *What now?* He thinks about going to the gym, but he is dead tired from his fourteen-hour trip from California. *I will start my workouts tomorrow.* He decides to eat some food from the refrigerator and drink a beer. But first, I will call Cathy.

"Hello," a female voice answers on the other end of the phone.

"Cathy?" Rigney questions because the voice does not sound like Cathy.

"No. Cathy is not here."

"Oh, uh, when will she be back?"

"Before I tell you that, I need to know who you are."

"My name is Rigney Page. Cathy knows me. We dated last December."

"Oh, yes. Cathy told me about you. She treasures the letters you sent from overseas. Oh, excuse me. My name is Claudia. I'm sorry, but Cathy is on leave. She is visiting her parents in Georgia and won't be back for another two weeks."

"I am only here for a week. Sorry I missed her. When she gets back, please tell her I called."

"She calls me every few days for messages. She will probably call tomorrow. I will give her your number if you wish."

Rigney provides his telephone number.

"Okay, I will give it to her."

"Thank you, Claudia. Good-bye."

"Good-bye, Rigney."

Chapter 15

RM2 Rigney Michael Page enters room 4. Commander Brad Watson sits on the couch along the wall. Bob Mater sits behind the desk.

Bob Mater's portly frame, thick white hair, white beard, reading glasses perched on the end of his nose, and his elbow-patched tweed jacket casts his image more as an aged college professor than the senior analyst for the Office of Naval Intelligence. Bob has been with ONI since World War II and is highly respected in the intelligence community.

When Mater sees Page, he stands, walks around the desk, stretches out his hand, and says warmly, "Apollo, nice to see you again. Great job you did on Operation Jupiter."

"Thank you, Bob, nice to see you again, also."

Bob motions for Rigney to sit in the chair in front of the desk. Bob returns to his chair behind the desk.

"Are you with ONI full-time, now?" Bob Mater asks with an enthusiastic expression on his face.

"Uh, well . . . I . . . I . . ."

Brad Watson interjects, "Apollo and I will discuss that later. For now, he has agreed to the Nea Makri mission. Proceed with your briefing."

Bob Mater nods. "I will bombard you with a lot of information today. Everything I tell you is also contained in these files." Bob points to a stack of files on the desk. "At the end of the briefing, you can take these files to your quarters and study them. You need to absorb as much of the detail in these files as possible. You will have plenty of time. Today's briefing will be the only briefing you will receive. The reason you are here for a week is so that we have time to modify your service record and have time for extended physical training." Bob looks over at Brad, indicating that Brad can now say his piece.

Brad briefs, "Tomorrow, we will spend the day at the Suitland Headquarters building. We will spend several hours at the firing range where you can practice with your favorite firearm, the 9 millimeter Beretta. I will also reacquaint you with the XM-21 sniper rifle. We will maximize your hand-to-hand training. You must really be rusty by now."

Rigney nods his understanding.

"Okay, Bob, continue," Brad directs.

Bob Mater begins his briefing. "The Naval Communications Station at Nea Makri, Greece maintains top secret inline cryptographic covered radio teletype circuits with aircraft carriers and other flagships in the Eastern Mediterranean. NAVCOMMSTA Greece is also connected to the worldwide defense communications network via similar top secret inline cryptographic covered radio and landline teletype circuits. High level Department of Defense staffs send top secret battle plans and top secret intelligence reports to NAVCOMMSTA Greece for relay to those ships at sea. Serious damage to America's national security will occur if the Soviets gain access to that top secret information. And it appears that could happen."

Bob riffles through a file folder, finds what he is looking for, and pushes a photograph across the desk toward Rigney.

Rigney picks up the five-by-seven black-and-white photograph of a man wearing the Service Dress Blue uniform of a U.S. Navy Master Chief Radioman. The master chief is slight of build, pointy noise, wide-set eyes, and light-colored hair with graying temples.

"That's Master Chief Radioman Raymond Rodgers," Bob advises. "He was observed meeting with a known Soviet KGB operative at a nightclub in Athens. Master Chief Rodgers is both the Top Secret Control Officer and the crypto custodian for NAVCOMMSTA Greece."

Brad Watson adds, "Master Chief Rodgers has been stationed at NAVCOMMSTA Greece for almost five years. He went there originally for a two-year tour. Then, he extended for a year. Then, he requested an additional two years as his twilight tour."

"Twilight tour?" Rigney asks as he glances up from the photo and looks at Brad Watson.

"The last tour of duty for an enlisted man who will serve thirty years is called a twilight tour. It's sort of a benefit for doing thirty. Since NACOMMSTA Greece is an isolated tour and considered sea duty for rotation purposes, he had no problem getting his request approved."

"Do we know why he met with a KGB operative?" Rigney asks.

"No," Bob Mater answers. "The master chief's name never surfaced in any espionage investigation before this meeting in Athens. However, Brad has a theory."

Rigney shifts his attention to Brad Watson.

"There are two interesting things in his record. His last two evaluations are lower than previous evaluations. He received lower marks in professional performance and military behavior. The other item is that he requested to remain on active duty past thirty years. The request was forwarded by his commanding officer recommending approval, but NAVPERS turned it down. The master chief appealed to the secretary of the navy and routed his appeal through Commander-in-Chief U.S. Naval Forces Europe for an endorsement. CINCUSNAVEUR forwarded recommending approval. The master chief and the CINC are old shipmates, but SECNAV turned him down also."

"Why was that?" Rigney asks.

"SECNAV echoed what NAVPERS originally said in their disapproval. Extensions past thirty years are approved only in cases of severe operational necessity. The navy brass wouldn't buy that the master chief was providing critical operational value as the alternate crypto custodian and as the enlisted club manager in a noncritical billet on his twilight tour.

"The navy's policy makes sense," Brad concludes. "Without a forced retirement policy, eventually there would be no open billets in the senior enlisted ranks. The advancement system would come to a choking halt."

"Well, I don't know much about these things," Rigney admits. "But I think I understand the reasoning of NAVPERS and SECNAV, and I agree with their disapproval."

Brad nods his head and continues, "So, I think the master chief has become bitter and disillusioned. He may feel the way so many sailors feel after serving for thirty years and then told they must retire, especially if you have made it all the way to master chief. Retirement for those sailors is going from a life where they are significant and everyone seeks their counsel to a life where they are anonymous. A year later, people are saying, *master chief who?* Rodgers might be looking for someway to get revenge. He might feel cheated. So, he wants the navy to pay."

"I don't understand that," Rigney responds. "Why would he want to take revenge on the navy? The navy made him what he is. The navy has been his life for thirty years."

"Because he lost confidence in the navy. The navy no longer wants him. As a result, he no longer trusts the navy. He now sees the navy as an adversary."

"Sounds deep," Rigney concludes aloud.

Brad nods his head in agreement and says, "Feelings of mistrust towards the navy near the end of a career is not uncommon. Forced retirement for a man in his forties is difficult for many to handle. Not just enlisted men, officers too. Most deal with it and get on with their lives after retirement. Rodgers might not be able to deal with it. He might have designed a revengeful plan. In any case, his last two performance evaluations show that something in him has changed."

Silence falls over the room while all three men think about Master Chief Rodgers's motives.

Rigney breaks the silence, "So what do you want me to do? I certainly don't move about in the same circles as master chiefs."

Bob Mater responds, "Get inside his circle. The intelligence gathered on the master chief reveals that he has a vice—poker.

Twice a week, he hosts a poker game at his house in Nea Makri. Usually, the other players are fellow chiefs. Sometimes, though, a junior enlisted man gets into the game."

Bob Mater focuses on Rigney's face, points a finger at him, and declares, "You must get into that poker game. Getting into that game gets you into his house. You need to search his house."

Rigney's eyes widen as his face reflects astonishment. "But I don't know anything about poker."

Bob Mater reaches into a leather satchel next to his chair. He pulls out a paperback book and hands it to Rigney.

Rigney peruses the book cover. The title, *Oswald Jacoby on Poker*, is unfamiliar to him.

Bob Mater directs, "You need to read and understand that book before you get to Nea Makri. Watch Rodgers carefully. He probably cheats."

"Will do," Rigney commits.

"Also, never follow or tail Rodgers off base. The KGB will be watching him, and watching for anyone who follows him. Off the base, either be with Rodgers, present in his circle, or stay away."

Rigney purses his lips and nods his understanding.

"Before you depart for Nea Makri, you will be given a wad of fifties and one-hundred dollar bills. Find an opportunity to flash that wad in Rodgers's presence."

"Okay, Bob. Will do."

"Good," Bob Mater declares. "Now, we are going to make some changes to your service record. The changes will remove any entry that you were ever on the USS *Columbus*. The word around the navy is that all those communications security changes several months ago were a result of security violations found on the *Columbus*. If someone in Nea Makri suspects you as a counterespionage operative, we don't want anyone discovering that you were on *Columbus* just prior to navy-wide security procedure changes. Your service record will show that you reported aboard USS *Barb* last December after graduating from submarine schools and that's where you've been since then. Your service record will also be changed to show that you were medically disqualified from submarines after developing an eardrum problem, and that is why you were transferred off the *Barb* and assigned to NAVCOMMSTA Greece. Any questions?"

"Not yet."

Bob Mater continues. "We're also changing your performance evaluations. The changes will make you look more like an average performer. At Nea Makri, you must demonstrate reluctant respect and courtesy toward your seniors. You need to be conspicuous. That is part of your cover. Typically, undercover operatives are not conspicuous. The Soviets think our operatives behave by the book and are quiet and subdued. Do you understand?"

"Yes, got it."

Bob looks down at his notes; then, he asks, "Tell us about this captain's mast in your service record. Says here that you called an officer a Rickover asshole."

Rigney shakes his head with frustration as he thinks about the events leading to the captain's mast. He explains, "From the day I reported aboard, the weapons officer, Lieutenant Wellington, was harassing me. I don't know what his problem was, but others in the crew told me that he was like that because he was a Rickover asshole. You know, he acts like Admiral Rickover—leads by intimidation—yells orders and demeans subordinates. All nuke officers must pass an interview by Admiral Rickover, and according to the crew, many of the nuke officers are the same way."

Brad rolls his eyes.

Bob comments, "I find that hard to believe."

"So did I, at first, but most of the time he was screaming at the enlisted men. He was always in radio demanding this and that. He screamed at my chief all the time. Mr. Wellington is a big man, towered over me. He would always get in your face when yelling at you. Very intimidating.

"Anyway, I was on watch in radio by myself. We were at periscope depth, and I was busy keeping the broadcast in synch and transmitting messages over ship-to-shore teletype. Mr. Wellington storms into radio and shouts at me to give him a message form. I was standing at the ship-to-shore circuit, working the teletype with the shore station. With my eyes still on the teletype, I told him to give me a minute. Suddenly, he grabs me by the shoulder and spins me around. He gets about six inches from my face and shouts, *'None of your attitude, Page. Get it now.'*

"I was stunned that he manhandled me. I just stood there thinking about what to do. Then, he places his hand on my chest, says *'now'* and pushes me backward. I stumbled back a few feet and fell into a sitting position on one of the chairs. Without thinking, I jumped to my feet and shouted, *'You are an absolute Rickover asshole.'* I seriously thought about pushing him back, but that's when Captain Wittier walked into the Radio Room. The only part of the whole scene that the captain heard or saw was hearing me calling Mr. Wellington an asshole, and I guess I looked like I was about to hit the son-of-a-bitch."

Brad cautions, "Easy, Rig. You don't have to respect the man, but you must respect the uniform."

Rigney looks sideways at Brad and responds, "I agree to an extent, but when obnoxious, overbearing, intimidating assholes use their uniform as part of their nature, then, I respect neither. Besides, officers are permitted to disrespect juniors all day long, but have an enlisted man supposedly disrespect an officer, the enlisted man is punished, and the officer goes unpunished."

Brad responds, "As you know, I had a talk with Captain Wittier. He seemed like a fair and levelheaded person. If Mr. Wellington acts as you say, Captain Wittier must have known it. He may have punished Mr. Wellington without you knowing about it."

Rigney raises his eyebrows and rolls his eyes, expressing his doubt.

Brad continues. "Think about it, Rig. You were awarded a suspended bust. Isn't that kinda light for the charges against you? No restriction and no extra duty. Doesn't it cause you to think that your captain knows Mr. Wellington may have instigated the incident?"

Rigney bows his head in thought; then, he says, "Lieutenant Wellington didn't change his behavior after the mast, and as I think back to the *Columbus*, there were officers and chiefs who led by intimidation, always shouting orders and using demeaning phrases towards juniors. I never encountered any of those while attending submarine schools in New London. It makes me wonder."

"I can shine some light on that," Brad advises. "Instructor duty is easy duty, no operational pressures. With no pressure, everyone is at their best. However, the pressures of shipboard operations bring out the best and bring out the worst in chiefs and officers. Just remember, they're all human beings who are subject to human weaknesses. Normally, those who are at their worst under pressure do not rise to the higher levels of leadership."

"What about Admiral Rickover?" Rigney counters.

"Admiral Rickover produced a nuclear submarine navy. He overcame impossible obstacles to do it. A person without his manner and style could not have done it."

Rigney sees no reason to continue what he interprets as an unsolvable disagreement. He remains silent.

After a short pause, Brad says, "Okay, Bob, let's continue."

Bob looks at Brad and responds, "I'm curious. I remember the term suspended bust from my navy days, but don't remember what it means."

Brad answers, "In Rigney's case, he got a suspended bust for six months. That means he stays an E-5, a second class petty officer, but if he goes to captain's mast during that six months, he will be reduced to E-4, a third class petty officer. Now, let's get on with the briefing."

Bob Mater continues with the briefing. "We have gone back and reviewed classified information leaks where the origin might have been the Nea Makri Communications Station. We turned up nothing. We conclude Rodgers probably hasn't done anything damaging yet."

Rigney interrupts, "I know that I am revealing my ignorance about intelligence strategy by asking this question, but here goes. Why doesn't ONI just arrest the master chief and interrogate him? You know, just ask him what he is up to."

"That's always an option," Brad replies. "But this situation provides us with an opportunity. By allowing Master Chief Rodgers to continue with whatever it is he is doing, we gain valuable information on how the KGB operates. We learn about how they go about recruiting American sailors. We, also, fine-tune our profile of American sailors that are susceptible to turning traitor. Python, from your last mission, is an excellent example. We gained valuable insight into what makes an American military man turn traitor.

"By not tipping our hand, we gain more in the long run. Again, I use your last mission as an example. By not stampeding onto the USS *Columbus* and shutting down Python's operation, we eventually uncovered an elaborate spy network that extended from Europe to the United States."

"I never knew that," Rigney comments. "I was not aware that a big spy network was uncovered."

"You would have known had you come to work for us full-time. You would have attended the debriefings last March. Anyway, while you're here, I will make all the Operation Jupiter files available to you. I want you to read all the files and remember the details. I will quiz you occasionally to ensure you know as much as you should know about Operation Jupiter."

Rigney nods his head several times and responds, "Will do."

"Good," Brad responds. "Now, getting back to your question, we may eventually bring Rodgers in for questioning, but, for now, we want to see what we can uncover."

Brad nods to Bob Mater to continue the briefing.

"There's a good chance that the KGB has Rodgers under surveillance, and I'm sure that they are investigating his background and history of assignments. Before the KGB gets too involved with Rodgers, they'll want to verify that he is truly turning traitor and that he is not an American agent. You can also be sure that the KGB is checking out any new arrivals at the Nea Makri NAVCOMMSTA. Once the KGB feels comfortable, they will make contact with Rodgers again."

Bob Mater pauses and looks back and forth between Brad and Rigney. Then, he asks, "Any questions?"

Rigney looks over at Brad and waits for Brad to ask any questions.

"I have no questions," Brad says.

Rigney turns toward Bob and asks, "How will the KGB investigate the master chief's assignment history, or that of any new arrivals? I mean, wouldn't they need access to service records to do that?"

Brad Watson answers, "Someone at Bureau of Naval Personnel works for the Soviets. During your last mission, we knew someone was investigating you, and your bureau service record turned up missing for two days. We haven't found out who it is yet, but we have a team working on it."

"I didn't know that. Doesn't that increase the chances that the KGB will identify me?"

Bob Mater replies, "The KGB is dangerous, but not efficient or effective. The KGB is a lumbering, mostly unproductive bureaucracy, just like most Soviet organizations. Yes, there is risk, but it's minimal."

Bob Mater flips through some folders. Then he says, "We established an ONI Field Office in a house on a hill overlooking the town of Nea Makri. We have a field operative staying there."

Bob hands Rigney a five-by-seven color photograph.

The photograph shows a woman standing in front of a white backdrop. She wears the standard ONI navy blue jumpsuit. Shoulder-length light-brown hair surrounds her thin and attractive face. He estimates her age as late twenties.

In the bottom-left corner of the photo are the woman's statistics.

Date: November 12, 1966
Name: Karen Drescher
Current undercover name: Anna Heisler
Height: 5' 11"
Weight: 115 lbs
Hair: light brown
Eyes: brown

"This photograph is two years old," Rigney observes. "That would make her age about thirty."

"She still looks the same as in the photo," Brad Watson informs.

Rigney stares at Brad, waiting for Brad to provide some more detail.

"We pulled Anna from her normal field assignment in Germany and sent her to operate the Nea Makri Field Office. She is your mission controller. You are to follow any orders she gives you. She and I will be in communications, and I will be feeding her instructions."

Rigney questions, "Won't she look out of place living in a house in Nea Makri, Greece?"

"Not really," Brad replies. "Greece is a vacation spot and retirement location for Northern Europeans. Nea Makri is a beach resort on the Aegean Sea. During the summer, vacationers from Germany, France, and Scandinavia migrate to Nea Makri. It's not uncommon for Northern Europeans to rent houses or cottages for the entire summer. Anna is third-generation German American. Her grandparents immigrated to the United States in 1914. She speaks fluent German. She blends-in with all the other German tourists.

"We have spent a month getting that field office set up, and it's operational. Anna has been there for five weeks. Her cover is that she is a German on vacation. She insures she is seen around town and on the beach. She reports that the sailors from the NAVCOMMSTA are constantly hitting on her, especially when she is at the beach. She remains aloof, waiting for Prince Charming. She waits for you to arrive and sweep her off her feet."

Rigney jerks back in his seat and blinks his eyes several times. Rigney looks at Anna's picture again and then looks back at Brad.

"So, our cover is that we are lovers, right? That's why I will spend so much time at her house, the field office, I mean."

"Correct," Brad confirms.

Rigney smiles devilishly. "Brad, you're always fixing me up with older women. Do I detect a trend here?" Rigney refers to his cover with Barbara Gaile during his last mission. Being lovers was their cover. Barbara is ten years older than Rigney.

A frown appears on Brad's face. "This is serious, Rig. Do not take your cover lightly. In public, you two must appear to be intimate."

Rigney looks at Anna's photograph again. He attempts to envision them looking like a couple, but the vision does not materialize.

"Okay, Brad, consider me advised and chastised."

Bob Mater patiently waits for the exchange between senior and junior to finish so that they can finish the briefing.

"May I continue?" Bob asks.

"Yes," Brad responds.

"Last night we received a report that NAVCOMMSTA Greece's crypto custodian was seriously injured in an automobile accident. He was transferred to a U.S. Air Force hospital in Germany. That means Rodgers will be the primary and the only crypto custodian for some time."

Rigney shakes his head with disgust. He utters a threat, "I will not allow evil to prevail."

Bob and Brad exchange raised eyebrow glances.

Brad nods at Bob and orders, "Continue."

Bob focuses his eyes on Rig and says, "You will have the same codename as your last mission, Apollo. Anna's codename will be Finback. The codename for your operation is Hammerhead. The message authentication computation is completely different from your last mission. The computation is specified in these files. Any questions?"

Rigney looks at Brad Watson and asks, "Will I take any weapons with me to Greece?"

"No," Brad replies. "Any weapons you might need are already at the Nea Makri field office." Brad reaches into a canvas gym bag and pulls-out a short-barrel automatic in a leather ankle holster. The holster has a silencer stored in a side pouch of the holster. Brad informs Rigney. "This is a new model 9 millimeter for field operatives. Take it with you to your room tonight and become familiar with it, and bring it with you to the firing range." Brad hands the holster to Rigney; then advises. "Return it to me before you leave for Greece. The same model will be available to you in the Nea Makri field office."

Rigney bows his head in thought for a few moments. Then, he asks, "Is Anna proficient with firearms?"

"Yes."

"I have no other questions, then."

"Okay, I'm done," Bob states as he stands and puts his hand out to Rigney.

Rigney takes Bob's hand and shakes it.

A large smiling grin appears on Bob's face as he says, "Good luck to you, Apollo. Be Careful. I will be looking forward to your intelligence reports from Nea Makri."

Bob Mater picks up his leather satchel, steps from behind the desk, walks across the room, waves good-bye to Brad Watson, and departs the room.

As the door closes behind Bob Mater, Rigney looks at Brad Watson and waits for further instructions.

"You will arrive at the Nea Makri NAVCOMMSTA next Saturday. On Sunday, go to the Nea Makri town beach. Find the small restaurant called Café Konstantina. The sailors at the base call it *The Blue Lights*. Make sure you are sitting at one of the outside tables at 1:00 PM and reading this book." Brad hands Rigney a large hard cover book, titled *The Reign of Charlemagne*. "Anna will make contact with you at that time. Just follow her lead and play along. Maps and directions are in the files. Any questions?"

"No sir. I understand everything so far."

They sit in silence for a few moments. Then, Brad states, "Knowing the direction that your mission will take is difficult to predict. The safety of our armed forces is at risk. Rodgers has unsupervised access to most Atlantic fleet and Pacific fleet key cards, codes, and cryptographic equipment technical manuals. Gathering intelligence on Rodgers's activities may lead to increasing the safety of our ships and sailors. You have two objectives. Your primary objective is to gather all the intelligence possible on Rodgers's activities. Your secondary objective is to safeguard your cover. You must apply all your ONI training to achieving those two objectives."

Both men sit in thought for a few moments. Then, Rigney asks, "Will I be required to use my sniper skills?"

"Rig, you don't have sniper skills. There is a hell of a lot more to being a sniper than being an expert shot with the XM-21. You would never be ordered on a sniper mission without going through the complete sniper course, and you must volunteer for that."

Rigney's face expresses confusion; he asks, "So what's with the training on the XM-21?"

"Because the XM-21 is an automatic rifle that can be used effectively in other situations."

Rigney nods understanding.

Brad stares intently into Apollo's eyes. Rigney looks back, with questioning, anticipating eyes.

Brad says, "Rig, you know that I originally recruited you because of your youth and technical knowledge. However, eventually, youth will no longer be an asset to you. If you want to stay with ONI after this mission, you must go through the full counterespionage course."

Rigney nods acknowledgement.

Brad continues, "You must make up your mind by the end of this mission. If you say no at that time, ONI will never contact you again."

Rigney sits thoughtful for a few moments; then, he asks, "If I decide to stay with ONI, what do you see me doing for the next ten years?"

"You would be a field operative. You're perfect for it."

"I will give it serious thought, Brad. Thanks for the time to think about it."

"Okay, that's all for today. I will pick you up tomorrow morning at 0800. Wear a jumpsuit."

"Yes sir."

Chapter 16

Rigney sits on the couch in his quarters. He studies the intelligence information in the Operation Hammerhead file folders that Bob Mater gave him. He looks at the topographic map of the Nea Makri area. He places on the coffee table several aerial photographs of NAVCOMMSTA Greece. He pulls several 100 Drachma notes from the file and places them on the coffee table.

His interest turns to the 9 millimeter automatic. He pulls the handgun from the holster and verifies the safety on. He removes the magazine and verifies it empty. As a safety procedure, he pulls back on the slide; no round ejects. He screws on the silencer which doubles the weight of the weapon. He studies the silencer and nods understanding as he observes that the silencer is the same length of the handgun's length.

A knock at the door causes Rigney to look at his watch—7:34 PM. He lays the weapon on the coffee table. Then, he stands, walks to the door, and opens it.

Rigney expresses surprise to see a hippie standing at his door. The man has Jesus-style hair, Jesus-style beard, wears hippie jeans, and a blue t-shirt with a peace sign printed on the front. Then, Rigney smiles as he recognizes John Smith.

John grins back.

During Rigney's last mission, John Smith guarded and mentored Rigney. John Smith's name is an alias, and Rigney knows that it would not be proper to ask John about his real name.

"John, great to see ya!" Rigney declares enthusiastically as he stretches out his arm and shakes John's hand. "Come in and sit down," Rigney invites.

John enters and sits on the soft, overstuffed chair. Rigney goes to the refrigerator and opens the door wide to display the contents to John.

"What would ya like . . . food, beer, what?"

"I'll have a Guinness. Thanks."

Rigney opens two bottles of Guinness and hands one to John.

Rigney sits on the couch, facing John.

John stares quizzically at the silencer equipped short-barreled handgun that lies on the coffee table.

"New field artillery," Rigney informs.

The two men raise their bottles at the same time in a toast to each other. They both take a sip.

Rigney stares at John and reaffirms that they being the same height and the same build and with similar facial features, they could pass for brothers, John being the older by ten years.

John smiles and says, "Still think you're looking into a mirror of the future when you look at me?"

"Yeah," Rigney replies softly with a nod of his head.

"Brad said you were back in town. Thought I would drop by and see ya. I've been wondering what you've been doing since Naples."

"I've been on a WESTPAC patrol in a submarine."

"I was on a submarine once," John Smith comments. "I went on a mission with a SEAL team."

"How long were you on that submarine?" Rigney asks.

"Long enough to know I don't want to spend a lot of time on one. I don't know how those submarine guys do it. No room to move around, submerged for months at a time . . . bad air, bad food, and no women."

"Well, you get used to it, I guess."

John's comments about the SEAL team and the submarine spark Rigney's desire to hear more, but he knows that John cannot say any more.

"So, why did you leave it?" John asks casually.

"Brad made me a better offer."

"I bet he did!" John blurts with a smile and a chuckle as he raises his bottle to signify another toast.

Rigney raises his bottle to match the toast.

"Are you here to stay this time?"

"I don't know. That decision will probably be made after this mission."

John advises, "I've been tailing your Master Chief Rodgers for the last month. That's why I look like this. Hippies and college students are all over Greece this time of year. Oh, I hear that you will be partnering with Anna Heisler on this mission."

"Yes. Do you know her?" Rigney asks, hoping to gain an understanding of what to expect.

"Sure do. I worked with her on a mission two years ago. She's all business, and she knows her stuff. You will learn a lot from her."

Rigney considers John's words then asks, "Is she an agreeable person. I mean, will we get along okay?"

"I think so, but you must be careful not to misinterpret her actions. Your cover will be that you two are lovers. In the presence of others, her role-playing is so convincing you'll think she has actually fallen for you. Don't make that mistake."

"I'll remember that," Rigney promises with a nod of his head.

Both men sit in silence for a few moments. Then John says, "One thing I always wondered about you is how you came to work for ONI. You're ONI's youngest operative. I know that Brad initiated some radical recruiting policy to get you for that mission on the USS *Columbus*."

Rigney spends a few moments to collect his thoughts; then, he responds, "Brad needed someone who would not act or look like a counterespionage operative and someone with technical skill in electronics and telecommunications systems."

John nods and asks, "You look in good shape. Have you kept up with running and weight lifting?"

"As much as I can."

John studies Rigney for a few moments; then, he says, "In this business you must stay in shape. You'll never know when you will need that extra bit of strength or extra measure of stamina to save your life."

"I know," Rigney acknowledges. "Before reporting to the *Columbus* last December, I was in the best shape of my life. Ever since I was a young teenager, I exercised and played basketball almost every day. But on that submarine, I had a grueling workload, very little time for anything except standing watches and working on qualifications. I'll get back to my exercise routine while I am here. Then, hit it real hard when I get to Nea Makri."

John nods his head with understanding. Then he advises, "Just to let ya know, Brad has assigned me as your hand-to-hand combat instructor while you're here. We'll do some laps around the gym first, just to see how many you can do before you pass out." John chuckles.

"Okay with me. I want to know myself."

John takes a sip of beer. Then, he looks at his watch. "Time for me to go."

They shake hands and again say how great it is to see each other again.

After John departs, Rigney resumes his study of the Nea Makri intelligence folders. Ten minutes later, the phone rings.

"Hello."

"Hello, Rig. It's Cathy Gillard."

"Hi, Cathy. I'm sorry that I missed you on this trip."

"Me too. I really enjoyed our time together. You should've let me know you were coming back. I would have rescheduled my leave."

"I only had several hours notice that I was leaving Pearl. Then, I was on a plane."

Cathy responds with a sexy tone, "Too bad. I would have made special plans for us."

Rigney visualizes the raven-haired beauty on the other end of the phone. He remembers her slim and trim naked body and milk-white skin. As he remembers some of their sexual activities, he feels his penis become warm and enlarged.

"Well, we still have our memories," Rigney responds wishfully.

"My new roommate, Claudia, wants to meet you. I told her all about you, and I showed her your picture. I also told her about your skillful tongue."

Rigney feels himself blush. He remembers Cathy's blunt approach to sex.

"Well, I don't know," Rigney hesitates. "I don't know her, and I will only be here for a few more days."

"It's up to you, Rig. You're under no obligation. I told Claudia that you would call her if you were interested."

"I'll think about it," Rigney responds.

"Where are you going after you leave Cheltenham?"

The question catches Rigney off guard, and he fumbles for an answer. "Uh . . . well . . . I don't . . ."

"Sorry, Rig. I forgot for a moment that you're a spy and can't tell me where you're going. Don't worry. I never told anyone about that and never will."

Rigney never told Cathy that he worked for ONI. She had figured it out last December after she discovered he was staying at the *spook building* on the Cheltenham base.

"Thank you for not saying anything to anyone. I hope to see you the next time I come to Cheltenham."

"Me too," Cathy coos over the phone. "Please remember to write. I truly enjoyed the letters and pictures you sent me from Guam."

"I'll remember," Rigney promises sincerely.

"Good. Now you take care, Rigney Page. I wish you well."

"I wish you well also," Rigney responds.

"Okay. Good-bye now." Cathy's voice has a measure of sadness.

"Good-bye, Cathy."

After hanging up the phone, Rigney sits silent and reflects. He sighs deeply. He glances at the intelligence folders and decides to take a break from them.

He eyes the Washington Post and decides to read a few stories.

(Israel) Gunfire across Jordan River between Arabs and Israelis. Israel says Jordan fired mortars and bazookas on three Israeli towns. Israel returns fire.

(Prague, Czechoslovakia) Three Soviet leaders: President Nikolai Podgorny, Premier Aleksei Kosygin, and Party Chief Leonid Brezhnev return from meeting with Czech Presidium. USSR agrees to let Czechoslovakia pursue its liberal internal reform and country will abide by Warsaw Pact. Last Soviet soldiers leave country. Country has democratic roots and its leaders, headed by Alexander Dubcek, want democratic communism.

(Vietnam) One hundred miles southwest of Saigon, American troops capture fifty Viet Cong suspects. Forty-four enemy combatants killed near Saigon. In Mekong Delta, Brigadier General Franklin Davis, Junior Commander, 199th Light Infantry Brigade, wounded. — Mekong Delta hard to patrol, tempting to infiltrate. Navy anchors floating base five miles from Cambodia.

Chapter 17

ONI Headquarters, Suitland, Maryland

Rigney Page and John Smith crouch toward each other on the martial arts mat. They sweat heavily after thirty minutes of continuous physical activity.

"You're either rusty or holding back," John Smith concludes.

"I never had a lot of training in this," Rigney responds with an apologetic tone.

"You're better than you think, Rig."

"I'm just not experienced enough."

"Rig, we don't have much time. I need to test you. I will do what's necessary to get you in a chokehold. Then, I want you to do everything in your power to free yourself."

"You're not going to hurt me, are you?" Concern fuels Rigney's tone and manner.

A serious look appears on John's face as he says, "You must stop me from hurting you."

"But I—"

John attacks Rigney with a flurry of arms and legs. Ten seconds later, Rigney is belly-down and his face buried into the mat; his arms are straight out.

John lies across Rigney's back and has Rigney locked-down in a half nelson. His left forearm presses against Rigney's larynx, and his right hand presses against the back of Rigney's head. John has his legs spread to use as levers to keep Rigney from rolling over.

Rigney rocks from side to side. He feels pain at the back of his neck and across his larynx.

John holds sufficient pressure on Rigney's neck to make Rigney's breathing difficult and cause pain. When Rigney does not move, he is free of pain and breathes easily.

"You're not going to get free that way, Rig. The more you twist from side to side the more pressure you put on your larynx and the point where your spine meets your brain stem."

Rigney lies still. After a few moments, he says into the mat. "What happens now? We could lie here all day."

"Hope not, Rig. You have five minutes to get out of this."

"Or what?" Rig challenges with a strained and frustrated voice.

"Or I let you go, and I record that you failed your hand-to-hand combat test."

"Bullshit," Rigney challenges. "You told me last time that there is no pass or fail." He struggles slightly to demonstrate his defiance.

John keeps steady pressure on his hold and responds, "Don't count on it."

Rigney flinches at John's verbal threat.

"You're wasting time, Rig. The clock's ticking. You've got to come clean with us. You're hiding something about your physical abilities. During your initial hand-to-hand training last December, you pretended that you were at the limit of your strength, but I detected that you had more to give. Brad sensed it also."

Rigney takes a deep breath and challenges, "Does Brad know about what you're doing here?" Rigney rolls slightly to the left to test John's hold.

John grips tight and warns, "Understand this. You're considering going full-time with ONI. A failing mark in hand-to-hand will go against you. If you keep playing your game, eventually your primary qualification, youth, will be gone. With no other ONI qualifications, you'll go back to the fleet and stay there. Consider this. You're a natural for undercover field OPS, and thirty years from now when you're too old for that, you could easily become a field communications officer, a very safe and comfortable job for sailing into retirement."

Rigney does not want to go back to USS *Barb*. Submarine duty is not to be what he expected. The lure of adventure with ONI attracts him. Retirement years have never entered his twenty-one year old mind, but it sounds appealing.

"You got two minutes, reveal yourself," John warns.

Rigney sighs deeply and says, "I'm stronger than most would calculate."

With a weary tone and deep sigh, John responds, "Talk, talk, talk, talk."

John feels Rigney's muscles become rock hard.

Rigney moves his arms and places his hands palm down to the mat. He slides his hands under his shoulders and then pushes himself up, like doing a pushup. John's weight equals Rigney's; John remains balanced on Rigney's back.

"What the hell!" John exclaims, astonished that Rigney can do the pushup with 190 pounds on his back. John presses his forearm tighter against Rigney's larynx, but Rigney appears unaffected.

Rigney brings his knees forward and raises his torso to a kneeling position.

Now, John kneels behind Rigney and still has the half nelson hold on Rigney's neck.

Rigney wraps his hands around each of John's wrists. Slowly, and with muscles flexing, Rigney pries John's arms away from his neck with as little effort as one peels a banana.

John attempts to pull his arms free from Rigney's grasp but finds himself powerless against Rigney's unbreakable strength.

Then, Rigney releases his grip on John's wrists and turns on his knees to face John.

John rubs his wrists as he stares at Rigney with an astonished expression. "Extraordinary. Far more than what you previously revealed. Why were you hiding it?"

"I want to be respected for my achievements and intellect, not feared because of my strength."

John considers Rigney's explanation; then, he asks, "So your motive is that you don't want people to know."

Rigney responds, "Growing up, I kept it hidden. It was my father who told me to keep it secret. He said every insecure strongman and bully in the county would challenge me. My dad said I would spend my life dodging such people. I guess it's just my habit to conceal it."

John responds, "There are martial arts moves that are best used by those without strength, and there are moves that are best for those with strength. During this week, we'll concentrate on those moves best suited for someone with strength."

Rigney nods and says, "Sounds good."

"But you need to remember what you're taught. You forgot the number one strategy of hand-to-hand."

"No, I haven't. The number one strategy is that when I'm attacked, I must become the aggressor—become the attacker. Never go on the defensive. Take out every attacker. Never give them a second chance to get you."

"Then why didn't you attack me before I got you into the half nelson? You could have stopped me."

"Oh . . . well . . . I . . . well . . . you will . . ."

"I will what, Rig? Live?"

Rigney bows his head in thought; then, he raises his head, looks John in the eyes, and says, "Like I said, I didn't want to reveal my strength."

John gently places his hands on Rigney's biceps, and he looks into Rigney's eyes; he pleads as a brother would plead, "Rig, you must promise me to never hold back. If you want to survive in this business, you must always exert 100 percent of your ability."

With a solemn expression, Rigney nods and responds, "Yes, of course. I promise."

After hand-to-hand combat training, John and Rigney go to the headquarters cafeteria for lunch. Their field OPS jumpsuits cause many to stare at them. John's hippie style hair and beard gets continuous stares.

After lunch, they proceed to the firing range located in the basement of the headquarters building. Brad Watson waits for them outside the firing range door.

"How did the hand-to-hand go?" Brad asks John.

"Rig did okay, but he needs to get into better shape."

Brad shifts his eyes to Rigney, indicating that he wants to hear what Rigney has to say about John's comment.

"I really got out of shape during those four months on that submarine. As soon as I get to Nea Makri, I will go back to my exercise regimen."

Brad acknowledges with a nod; then, he advises, "Our firing stall is ready."

As they enter the firing range, the sound of gunfire greets them. Brad leads them to a center stall.

A XM-21 automatic sniper rifle lies on the countertop; a silencer lies next to the rifle. Empty magazines and four boxes of ammunition sit on the far left of the countertop.

Brad glances at Rigney's gym bag and queries, "Did you bring that Beretta I gave you?"

Rigney nods affirmative.

Brad orders, "Your first task is to load the Beretta and make it ready for firing, including attaching the silencer. Then, fire one round at the target. Then, place the Beretta back on the table. Remember to keep the barrel pointed down range at all times."

For the remainder of the afternoon, Rigney practices with the Beretta automatic handgun and the XM-21 sniper rifle.

His last exercise of the day consists of loading the Beretta and XM-21 and making them ready to fire while blindfolded. The exercise includes loading the magazines, screwing on the silencers, setting the safety on and off, and setting the weapons to automatic and semiautomatic mode. For the XM-21 sniper rifle, Rigney also practices removing and attaching the scope while blindfolded.

Chapter 18

U.S. Naval Communications Station, Nea Makri, Greece

A sunny, hot, and humid eighty-eight degrees beats down from a cloudless Mediterranean sky onto the buildings and communications trailers that comprise the U.S. Naval Communications Station at Nea Makri, Greece. The administrative and support buildings and barracks stand on the west side of the small naval installation. The single-story prefabricated buildings are rectangular in shape and light green in color. The composite material assists with keeping the buildings warm in winter and cool in summer. The administration building houses the offices of commanding officer, executive officer, quarterdeck, personnel and admin office, library, and sickbay.

On this Saturday morning, the executive officer, Lieutenant Commander Mary Blakely, pounds on the side of the failing window air conditioner unit. She grunts in frustration as she returns to her desk and sits in the squeaky executive chair. She scans through the morning message traffic. Only two messages are relevant to her duties and responsibilities.

One message from the American Embassy in Athens warns of continuing, confrontational protest marches and rallies conducted by the Greek Social Democrat Party. The message advises U.S. military commanders in the Athens area to be on heightened alert. During several marches, protesters attempted to crash the fences of the U.S. Air Force base near Athens. The air force base security forces used tear gas and clubs to move the protesters away from the air force base security zone.

The other message from Bureau of Naval Personnel advises that a newly assigned sailor, RM2 Rigney Michael Page, will arrive at the Athens International Airport at 11:30 AM today. The message advises that Page transfers to NAVCOMMSTA after a medical board recently found him medically disqualified from submarines.

The XO looks at her watch. Then, she stands and walks around to the front of her desk and faces the full-length mirror mounted on the back of her office door. She inspects her image and straightens the skirt of her white summer uniform. She puts her hand to side of her head and pats back a few loose strands of her short auburn-colored hair. She takes a few moments to appreciate how attractive she looks in her uniform. At the age of thirty-two and a height of five feet and eight inches tall, she has the same slim and athletic figure as when she was a member of the University of Florida women's swim team.

To keep in shape, Mary swims forty laps every afternoon at the Olympic-size swimming pool at the Hotel Attica on the Nea Makri beach. She also hikes the rocky hills of Mount Penteli—the mountain that separates Athens from Nea Makri.

Still looking in the mirror, Mary twists her body to the side to verify her hips, buttocks, and thighs have not surrendered to the fat-producing activity of a desk job.

Satisfied with the look of her body in uniform, she moves her face closer to the mirror. She frowns at the few small lines that now spread around her brown eyes. With her face still close to the mirror, she checks her thinly and sparsely applied makeup.

She opens the door and walks into the narrow passageway of the administration building. She walks the short distance to the quarterdeck where she finds the duty master-at-arms sitting at the duty desk and asks him, "Karzack, who's the duty driver?"

Boatswain's Mate Second Class Victor Karzack looks up from the quarterdeck log in which he writes entries. "That would be Seaman Newman, ma'am," Karzack replies as he moves his six feet and two inches tall and wiry frame to a standing position.

"Where's he now?"

"He went to the galley to refill the quarterdeck coffee pot."

The XO glances at her wristwatch. She reaches to the top of the duty desk and tears a piece of notebook paper from a pad. She writes Page's name, arrival time, and flight number on the paper.

"Tell Newman to pick up this sailor at the airport this morning."

"Yes, ma'am."

The XO starts to turn away but then adds to her order. "Tell Newman he is to go directly to the airport and to come directly back here. Tell him he must go inside the terminal and meet Page at the gate. I don't want more of our new people getting lost and roaming the streets of Athens like last time, not knowing where to go. Tell Newman no detours to the air force base exchange and no stopping at cafés or bistros and no stops at all—not anywhere for any reason."

"Yes ma'am."

Lieutenant Commander Mary Blakely turns and walks back to her office.

Karzack walks the few steps to the rear doorway of the quarterdeck. He opens the door. Bright sunshine floods the quarterdeck. He squints his eyes against the sun. He looks around the small covered patio area. He spots the duty driver sitting on a bench, smoking a cigarette.

"Newman!" Karzack barks. "Get off your lazy ass! You gotta go to the airport!"

Seaman Newman, an antagonistic and disrespectful pudgy short nineteen-year-old black sailor takes a puff of his cigarette and replies in a sharp and disrespectful tone, "Yeah, man, in a *folkin'* minute, when I'm finished with my *folkin'* cigarette, man."

Karzack decides not to make an issue of the wisecracking and disrespectful tone. Correcting this unmilitary smartass for the hundredth time is not Karzack's priority right now.

Newman takes a final puff and stands. He ignores close-by ashtrays and tosses the smoldering butt to the patio cement floor. He crushes it out with the toe of his shoe. He brushes some ashes from the jumper of his Service Dress White uniform. He walks through the doorway and enters the quarterdeck. He allows the door to slam shut behind him. With an annoyed tone, he queries, "Who do I pick up, man?"

Karzack hands the piece of paper to Newman.

Newman glances quickly at the paper. He grabs the keys to the duty vehicle, turns, and walks toward the door.

"Hey, Newman, the XO said you are to—"

Newman closes the door behind him before Karzack can finish the instructions.

Karzack shakes his head disapprovingly. He enters Newman's departure time in the log.

Chapter 19

With his seabag slung over his left shoulder and carrying a small civilian suitcase in his right hand, Rigney exits the customs area of the Athens International Airport and enters the arrivals area. He feels exhausted and dirty. His bodily functions tell him that he needs to find a men's room.

The stifling August heat inside the airport has him sweating profusely. His Tropical White Long uniform sticks to his body. He decides to wash up, shave, and change into a clean uniform. He spots the men's water closet, WC, and he moves toward it.

As he enters the WC, he sees four sinks and several men holding shaving kits and hand towels in line for each sink. The Europeans turn their heads in Rigney's direction. Rigney nods a hello. Several men grin and nod back. They all look tired and are in dire need of a shave.

After Rigney visits one of the toilet stalls, he stands in line to use a sink. Three European men are ahead of him.

When Rigney finally gets to the sink, he strips off his uniform shirt and t-shirt, exposing his muscular and broad-shouldered torso. Rigney stands a full twelve inches above the other men in the room. They all steal glances at him and comment in Greek about the heavy matting of reddish brown hair that covers Rigney's body. "*A bear,*" as one Greek describes.

After shaving, Rigney gives his body a washcloth bath from the sink water. He pulls a clean set of short-sleeve whites from his seabag and slips it on. He looks in the mirror and checks his image. The uniform has a few wrinkles, but it looks fresh and clean. As he squares his white hat on his head, one of the Greek men points to the sparks on Rigney's second class rating badge and asks, "What mean this?"

"Radioman," Rigney responds with a smile.

The man does not understand and gives Rigney a questioning look.

Rigney puts his right hand on the metal shelf just below the mirror. He moves his fingers up and down as he would on a telegraph key and makes the sounds, "Dit-dah-dit dah-dit-dit."

Although most navy communications these days are accomplished via high frequency radio teletype, Rigney thought it easier to imitate a telegraph key.

"Ah! Morse!" the man responds gleefully, because he understands.

"Yes. You are correct, sir."

The other men in the room move closer to hear what Rigney and the Greek are saying. Rigney becomes apprehensive. He cannot judge their motives for moving closer.

Then, the Greek looks appreciatively into Rigney's eyes and says, "Many Greek people happy you Americans in Greece. Some no like Americans here. They not many. Greek peoples remember America help Greek peoples fight Nazi man. Nazi shoot my brother in war. He age you when Nazi kill him. All Greek people hate Nazi man. All Greek people remember American help."

Rigney does not know how to respond. This situation catches him totally off guard.

Some of the other men speak in Greek. The man who talked with Rigney responds. Then he says to Rigney, "Greek man here ask what we talk. I speak them. They much happy American in Greece. Much many communists here Greece. Many Greek think safe many American here Greece."

All the men nod their heads and smile at Rigney.

Rigney finds some kind words, "Me happy me in Greece. Greece people proud and democratic people. Greece start democracy thousands of years before."

"Yes! Yes! True! Many good you know this."

The man translates to the other men who nod their approval of Rigney's understanding of Greek history.

Rigney picks up his seabag and says good-bye to the Greeks. He shakes a few hands and waves good-bye to the others. They all smile and wave back.

Nea Makri

Rigney emerges from the men's room feeling good about his first encounter with Greek people. Holding his seabag by the handle in his left hand and holding the small suitcase in his right hand, he scans the arrival area. He observes the many posters advertising tours of Greece. He also searches for a sign that might direct U.S. military personnel what to do upon arrival. He does not find such a sign. He thinks that someone should be meeting him. He searches for someone dressed in a navy uniform.

He previously studied the maps and travel information that Bob Mater provided. He knows how to get to Nea Makri. He decides to go outside and check for a bus or taxi that can take him to Nea Makri. He slings his seabag over his left shoulder and looks for the exit.

The intense Mediterranean sun blinds him as he exits the airport building. He puts on sunglasses and looks around. He sees a U.S. Navy sedan in the parking lot, about one hundred feet away. A black sailor wearing sunglasses and with his white hat tilted forward slouches behind the wheel and smokes a cigarette.

Rigney walks toward the sedan.

Newman sees a sailor walking toward him. He feels intimidated by the confident stride of the tall broad-shouldered and rugged-looking sailor. He interprets the sailor's gait, swagger, and overall manner as arrogant.

Newman always attempts to present a tough, aggressive, and belligerent behavior when first meeting someone who may be a threat, which in Newman's mind is everyone except females. He wants people to know that just because he is black and just a seaman, he cannot be intimidated or be pushed around.

When Rigney comes to within twenty feet of the navy sedan, the pudgy short sailor exits the vehicle. When Rigney comes to within five feet, Newman throws the cigarette to the ground at Rigney's feet. As is the nature of those who litter the world with their cigarette butts, Newman discards the cigarette without any consideration for anything or for anybody. Newman did not intentionally throw the butt at Rigney's feet; he just tossed it absentmindedly as smokers do.

The force of the cigarette hitting the ground causes the fired tip of the cigarette to break away and to bounce off the ground and land on the bottom of Rigney's pant leg where it burns a hole in the cloth.

Rigney places his bags on the ground. He lifts his right foot to the car bumper and pats out the burning ash.

"Hey, man, tough break. Who'd-a-ever thought." As is the nature of rude and inconsiderate people everywhere, Newman takes no responsibility for his act.

As Rigney inspects the dime-size hole in his white bellbottom trousers, Newman smirks as he glances quickly back and fourth from Rigney's face to the burn in Rigney's trousers.

Rigney takes a quick look at Newman's face and sees the smirk. Rigney stands straight and glares at Newman.

"Hey, man, yo' Page?" Newman continues to smirk.

"Yeah, I am Page!" Rigney responds sharply and with an angry tone. More than thirty hours without sleep and the hassles of airline travel and sitting in the middle seat for fourteen hours has shortened Rigney's temper threshold.

"Hey, man! Don't get a case of the ass with me! T'wasn't my fault! T'was an accident, man!" Newman's manner is cocky and belligerent.

"What's your name, seaman?" Rigney asks in a stern tone.

"Leroy Newman!" the short and pudgy black sailor replies in a confrontational tone.

"Seaman Newman, you will not address me as *man*. You will address me as Page, or Petty Officer Page, and you will speak to me in a courteous and respectful manner. Do you understand?"

Anger overcomes Newman. His warped concept of military authority causes him to believe that RM2 Page has no authority over him.

Newman always interprets orders as being a racial insult and meant to belittle, because he is black. The idea that he has been corrected in accordance with navy regulations never occurs to him.

To Newman, all nonblack people are racists who hate him and try to take advantage of him. He learned these principles at an early age from Atlanta gang members who practically raised him.

Newman becomes antagonistic, not only because he is again being disciplined, but this time by a junior sailor. *This guy may be big and tough looking, but he can't talk to me like that! This asshole needs to know right now that I won't stand being insulted!*

Newman leans forward and presses his hand against Rigney's chest. In a menacing tone and with a menacing look on his face, he scolds, "Yo' just a second class, asshole! What are you—some kind of rank conscious *muthafolkar*?! Don't mess wid me, man! I know people who'll *folk* yo' up, man!"

Rigney looks down at Newman's right hand, which Newman pushes against Rigney's chest.

Rigney responds with lightning speed as he grabs the back of Newman's hand and twists it outward and downward.

This action causes a sharp pain to shoot up Newman's arm. Newman grunts in pain and instinctively slams his knees to the pavement in an effort to relieve the pain in his arm. Pain shoots through his knees.

Rigney applies just a little bit more pressure to keep Newman on his knees.

Pedestrians stop and stare at the spectacle of two American sailors in the airport parking lot. Greeks driving close by also stop and watch. The Greeks see a tall, tough-looking Caucasian sailor standing over a black sailor. The Caucasian sailor grips the black sailor's hand in a combative position that forces the black sailor to the ground. The tall Caucasian sailor holds the black sailor to the ground with one hand, like a marionette master controls a marionette with one hand. Both sailors wear white uniforms.

Rigney looks around expressionlessly at the gawking Greeks. He notices that he and Newman are blocking traffic in the parking lot.

"This will only take a minute," Rigney says calmly to the Greek in the nearest car. "Please be patient."

The Greek does not understand Rigney's words, but he understands the meaning. He would not miss this interesting scene for anything. He watched this scene develop since Rigney exited the terminal.

"Newman!" Rigney utters tersely. "You will speak to me and everyone else in a courteous and respectful manner. You will not call me or anyone else *man, bastard, asshole*, or any foul language name. You will address me as Petty Officer Page. If you violate my orders, I will break your nose and both your elbows. Do you understand me?"

"Yo' *muthafolkar*!" Newman shouts with his head now on the pavement. "Yo' *folkin*' dead, man! My brothers will kill your ass, man!"

Rigney twists Newman's hand slightly.

"*Aaaahhhhhhiiiiii!*" Newman screams in agony as sharp pain shoots through his wrist, elbow, and arm socket. He rolls to the ground onto his side.

"Newman, this is your last chance before I break your arm. Do you understand?"

Newman turns his head upward to look in Rigney's face and stutters with a painful expression on his face. "Yeah, yeah, man. I. . . I unerstan'. Please let ma go!"

"No, Newman. You do not have it correct. Say 'yes, Petty Officer Page. I understand.'"

Newman stutters it out, painfully, "Yes, I, I unerstan', Petty Officer Page."

Rigney releases his grip on Newman.

Newman stands up and starts rubbing his right arm. Dirt and grease cover his Service Dress White uniform.

Rigney orders, "Move over by the car so this traffic can get through. Open up the trunk so I can put my bags in there."

Newman goes to the driver's side of the sedan to retrieve the keys from the ignition. He continues to rub life back into his arm.

The Greek who watched from his car not more than twenty feet away drives past Rigney slowly. He grins, renders Rigney a casual salute, and then drives on. Rigney's face remains expressionless as he watches the Greek salute him.

Rigney picks up his bags and walks to the rear of the sedan.

Newman cannot get his right arm to function. He attempts to unlock the trunk with his left hand, but the pain in his right arm overwhelms his ability to focus on opening the trunk.

"I'll do it," Rigney directs mildly as he grabs the keys from Newman.

After putting his bags in the trunk, Rigney watches Newman massage his right arm. He becomes concerned that he may have injured Newman.

"Can you drive?" Rigney asks with a slight touch of concern in his voice.

"Yeah, man! I can drive!"

Rigney shoots a scornful expression at Newman.

"I mean, yes, Petty Officer Page. I can drive."

Newman finally notices the grease and dirt covering his uniform. "My uniform is trash. This is my only set of Service Dress Whites. The master chief's gonna be all over my ass, man."

Rigney becomes interested at the reference to master chief. "What master chief?" Rigney inquires casually.

"Master Chief Crimer, the chief-master-at-arms. He'll put me on report again."

"You'll get what's coming to you," Rigney responds flippantly. "You need to learn respect and courtesy towards others."

Newman's demeanor again turns hostile as he warns Rigney. "Yo' gonna be sorra fo' what you did. Ma bros will whip yo' up."

"How many brothers do you have at Nea Makri?" Rigney wants to calculate the threat against him.

"No. Not brothers like brothers and sisters. I'm saying like soul brothers, man. I mean, Petty Officer Page."

Rigney shakes his head, indicating he does not understand. "I don't follow you, Newman."

"Are yo' from outta space, man? I'm talkin' 'bout other blacks. We look out fo' each other. When I get back to the base, I'll tell them what yo' all did to me. They'll tear yo' ass up, man!"

Rigney now understands Newman's meaning. He explains, "I didn't nearly break your arm because you're black. I did it because you were pushing me." Then, with a more menacing tone, Rigney threatens, "And the next time you touch me I'll break your arm. And if your so-called brothers come after me, I will come after you and smash your face in. Do you understand?"

Newman smirks and confidently responds, "Yo' don' unerstan', Petty Officer Page! Yo' kung fu stuff won't work with dem. You won't see it comin'. So don't sleep tight, man."

Rigney shakes his head in dismissal of Newman's words.

Page orders, "Get in the car and drive us to the base."

Newman drives the southern outskirt of Athens and drives east over the mountain towards Nea Makri. During the drive up the mountain, Rigney absorbs the beauty of Athens. On a few occasion he catches glimpses of the Parthenon atop the Acropolis.

As they drive over the crest of the mountain. Rigney beholds a beautiful scene. The rocky and shrub-covered mountain declines steeply to a coastal plane that stretches approximately one kilometer to the dark blue of the Aegean Sea. Rigney sees the island of Euboea, which lays fifteen miles across the water. He scans the coastal plane. To the northeast, he sees an antenna field close to the shore. A small town borders the south end of the antenna field. Rigney assumes he sees Nea Makri.

He does not ask Newman about the antenna field and the town. Rigney and Newman have not exchanged a word since departing the Athens Airport. Newman rubs his arm less frequently now.

The steep and narrow road twists with sharp turns down the mountain. Newman rides the brake pedal to keep the car at a safe speed.

Rigney looks at his watch—1330. He asks, "How much longer until we get to the base?"

"Forty minutes," Newman responds flatly.

Two o'clock, Rigney says to himself as growls rumble through his stomach. *The galley will be closed.*

"Does the base have any place to eat in the middle of the afternoon?"

Newman shoots an irritating look at Rigney. He does not want to be of any help. "No."

Rigney suspects that Newman lies, but says nothing.

Twenty minutes later, the mountain road ends in the coastal town of Rafina. Newman makes a left onto the Marathon Road and drives north. The traffic slows to twenty miles per hour as they pass through the town of Nea Makri. Pedestrians who look like Northern Europeans intermingle with Greeks as they walk about in shorts and swimsuits. Roadside vendors, cafés, and restaurants line the street. At the town's main intersection, Rigney looks to the east and sees the beach and the Aegean one block away.

Rigney finds himself gawking at all the young women in bikinis. Most of them wear loosely woven, open-button shirts that satisfy some modesty rules, but conceals little skin.

Chapter 20

Five minutes later, Newman turns right and stops the vehicle at the NAVCOMMSTA Greece main gate. One American sailor and one Greek sailor serve as sentries. Each wear a shore patrol armband and guard belt. A .45 caliber automatic in black leather holster hangs from their guard belts.

Rigney looks for a sign that announces they are at NAVCOMMSTA Greece, but no sign is visible. The security fence that surrounds the base confounds him. The fence stands only four feet high and consists of four stands of barbed wire hanging from posts ten feet apart. *Anyone could easily step over it!*

He looks to the opposite side of the road from the NAVCOMMSTA and sees fields sparsely populated with olive trees and a few widely spaced houses. Sheep graze in the fields.

Rigney looks past the gate and into the base compound. He sees single-story light-green–colored prefabricated buildings. Just inside the gate on the right-hand side of the road is a large swimming pool. Men and women sit at tables around the pool. Others lie on patio lounge furniture. Several children splash and play in the pool. The pool patio connects to a single-story building. The sign above the entrance to the building reads Club Zeus.

The American sentry, a tall and lanky second class storekeeper in his Service Dress Whites, walks over to the driver's side window and bends over to look inside the car.

"Newman, what happened to you?" the sentry asks as he sees the dirt and grime all over Newman's uniform.

"I fell."

"Looks to me like you rolled around on the ground," the sentry opines as he shoots a glance at Rigney; he briefly glances at the rank on Rigney's sleeve.

"Go *folk* yo'self, man!" Newman growls. "Just raise the *folkin'* post and let us in!"

Rigney grabs Newman's arm at the elbow and with a viselike grip twists Newman's elbow outward.

Newman grunts in pain.

"Newman!" Rigney snaps. "I told you to show proper military respect. Now apologize to the shore patrol for swearing at him."

Newman, obviously frustrated, angry, and embarrassed, grits his teeth and inhales deeply. His mind screams silently, *I'm gonna kill this muthafolka!* He turns his head toward Rigney and glares. Then, he turns back toward the gate guard and says with a clinched jaw, "Petty Officer Simpson, I apologize for swearing at you."

Astonished by Newman's apology, SK2 Simpson says sarcastically, "Well, Newman, someone has taught you some manners." Simpson straightens up and walks around the front of the sedan to Rigney's side.

Rigney releases Newman's elbow.

Newman rubs his elbow.

"You reportin' aboard?" Simpson asks.

"Yes."

"Okay. Since I don't know you yet, I need to see your ID card and orders before I can let you pass."

Rigney reaches into his breast pocket, removes his ID card and copy of his orders, then he hands both items to Simpson.

Simpson scrutinizes Rigney's orders and ID Card. Then, Simpson studies Rigney's face and queries with a satisfied smile on his face, "Page, you responsible for what happened to Newman?"

"No," Rigney responds with a casual tone and with a carefree expression. "Newman is responsible for what happened to Newman."

"Well, don't mind Newman," Simpson advises. "He's just one of those annoying wiseass punks that the navy recruits these days. Everyone ignores him."

Simpson hands Rigney's ID card back to him. Then, he motions to the Greek guard to lift the post.

Newman slams his foot to the gas pedal. The sedan jumps forward, kicking up gravel and dust.

As they drive toward the administration building, Rigney wonders what kind of military command allows a seaman to be discourteous and disrespectful. *I guess I will find out.*

A Greek waiter walking out of Club Zeus and onto the pool patio catches Rigney's attention. The waiter wears a long-sleeve white shirt, black tie, and black pants, which is the typical wear of waiters in Southern European cafés and restaurants. The waiter carries a tray full of hamburgers, french fries, and several bottles of beer. The waiter delivers the tray to a table with three men in swimsuits. With a questioning expression, Rigney turns his head toward Newman.

Newman sees the waiter and the tray. Out of the corner of his eye, he sees Page looking at him. "Uh, well I . . . well I forgot about the club serving food," Newman responds with an intentional lack of sincerity in his voice.

Newman makes a left into a parking lot and pulls into the duty *vehicle* spot in front of the administration building.

"Quarterdeck's through that door," Newman says as he points to the door about twenty feet away.

Newman removes the car key, opens the car door, and steps out of the vehicle.

Rigney steps out of the vehicle and looks around. He sees a few sailors in Undress White uniform walking about. Children screeching and laughing causes him to look toward the pool where he notices the adults at the pool stand and look in his direction. Rigney waves.

Some of the adults turn away. An attractive and deeply tanned young woman with blondish hair enthusiastically waves back.

Newman opens the vehicle's trunk, turns, and darts off toward the barracks.

As he pulls his bags from the trunk, Rigney hears someone shouting Newman's name. He closes the trunk and looks in the direction of the shouting voice.

A medium-height and stocky master chief in Tropical White Long uniform stands at the doorway to the quarterdeck and stares toward Newman. The master chief shouts Newman's name again.

Rigney turns his head toward Newman, just as Newman turns around in response to the master chief's call.

The master chief orders loudly, "Newman, report to the quarterdeck. I have something for you to do."

Newman shouts back, "Can it wait ten minutes? I need to go to my locker."

"Come now!" the master chief commands.

Newman shrugs his shoulders and walks toward the master chief.

After slamming the vehicle trunk shut, Rigney falls in behind Newman and follows him toward the quarterdeck door.

When Newman is ten feet from the master chief, the master chief sees the dirt and grime on Newman's uniform and asks, "What happened to you?"

"I'll tell ya when I come back. I need to change my uniform. All I have clean are Tropical White Long uniforms."

"Then put one on and get back here."

Newman turns around and bumps into Rigney. As he pushes himself off Rigney, he mumbles obscenities.

"You Page?" the master chief asks.

"Yes, Master Chief."

"I'm Master Chief Crimer, the chief-master-at-arms. Welcome aboard."

"Thank you, Master Chief. I'm pleased to be aboard." Rigney notes the master chief's nametag reads Master Chief Boatswain's Mate.

"Come onto the quarterdeck. Karzack will get you logged in and assign you a rack."

Master Chief Crimer holds the door open as Rigney slides past him with bags in hand.

Chapter 21

On the quarterdeck, a tall and lanky sailor in Tropical White Long uniform stands behind a counter. The sailor's nametag identifies him as BM2 Karzack and a member of the master-at-arms force.

Rigney stops at the counter and sets down his bags.

"Hi, I'm Victor Karzack," the BM2 says as he reaches across the counter to shake hands.

"Rigney Page, pleasure to meet you."

The two sailors shake hands.

Rigney notes Karzack's strong grip and heavily calloused hand.

Karzack notes Rigney's strong grip and mostly uncalloused hands.

"I need your ID Card and the original of your orders," Karzack advises.

Rigney provides the items.

Master Chief Crimer enters the quarterdeck and sits at a large desk with radio equipment mounted on the desktop. He stares at Rigney, curiously. "Hey, Page, we ever met before? You look familiar."

Rigney takes a closer look at Master Chief Crimer. He does not recognize him. "I don't think so, Master Chief."

"I know I've seen you before," Crimer insists. "Where you been stationed?"

"Sub school and the USS *Barb*—fast attack out of Pearl. Never been anywhere else." Rigney lies. He omits the several months he spent on USS *Columbus* earlier in the year. Revealing he was on *Columbus* would be a security compromise to that ONI mission.

"Never been to 'Nam, then?" Crimer queries.

"No, Master Chief, never been there. How long you been here?"

"About a year."

Crimer's response assures Rigney that he and Crimer could not have been on *Columbus* at the same time."

"I was at sub school and on *Barb* during the last year. Don't think we ever crossed paths."

Crimer shakes his head in dismissal of Rigney's denial of previous contact. He picks up the radio microphone and speaks into it. "Nea Makri One this is Nea Makri Control, over."

"This is Nea Makri One, over."

The master chief recognizes the commanding officer's voice over the radio and says, "Captain, I will dispatch the duty driver to your residence in a few minutes. He will arrive at your residence in thirty minutes, over."

"Very well, Master Chief, Nea Makri One, out."

Rigney studies the radio equipment while he listens to the conversation between the master chief and the commanding officer. He attempts to recognize the model and frequency range, but the equipment is not familiar to him. *Probably commercial VHF*, he concludes.

Karzack waves his hand at Rigney to get his attention. "It will take about five minutes to get ya logged in. You'll be roomin' with me. All the other rooms already have two guys assigned."

As Karzack performs his work, Rigney roams around the quarterdeck.

The quarterdeck area is typical of most that he has experienced. Navy blue–colored tile covers the deck. White enamel paint covers the bulkheads. Prints of historic naval battles adorn the bulkheads. Highly polished shells from a battleship's twenty-inch guns cordon two sides of the quarterdeck. Decorative white-colored line connects the shells.

On the bulkhead next to the quarterdeck counter, a diagram displays the NAVCOMMSTA chain-of-command. A brass label under each picture identifies the officer's rank, name, and title. The picture of the executive officer captures Rigney's attention. *What a beauty!*

"Be careful," Karzack warns as he notices Rigney staring at the XO's picture. "Ya get in trouble 'round here for starin' at her . . . I mean in person."

Rigney evaluates Karzack's words. He turns his head and studies Karzack in an attempt to learn more about him. Rigney notices the master chief stirring.

The master chief shakes his head and smiles in response to Karzack's words.

Rigney turns away from the chain-of-command display and roams around the quarterdeck. He stops to study a print of the Battle of Trafalgar.

"Hey, Page," Karzack calls.

Rigney turns toward Karzack.

"I don't have enough keys for our room. I must go over to public works and make a key, should only take a few minutes." Karzack looks toward the master chief. The master chief nods his permission.

Rigney's perusal of the prints hanging on the bulkhead leads him off the quarterdeck and down a short hallway. Next to an office with a sign stating *Chief-master-at-Arms*, Rigney stops to study a print that shows three marines in battle fatigues walking along a Vietnamese jungle road. Each marine's rifle slings haphazardly around his torso. All three soldiers are bloodied and bandaged. A black soldier on the right and a white soldier on the left hold up a white soldier in the middle and assist him walk along the road. The caption on the bottom of the print asks, *"How hard did you work today?"*

Five minutes later, Karzack hands Rigney a key and advises, "Nothing more for ya to do today, weekend and nobody's here. Come back here Monday morning and report to the personnel office. The PN will give ya a check-in sheet, then."

Karzack issues Rigney some sheets, blankets, and pillowcases.

"The barracks is out the door and turn right. You'll see two long buildings. The one on the left is the junior enlisted barracks.

Go to the one on the right, just pass the galley. That's the petty officer barracks. Our room is number eight."

As Rigney steps outside into the ninety-degree heat, he glances left toward the swimming pool. No one looks his way. The attractive blond woman who waved to him earlier has her back to him.

Several minutes later, Rigney enters his new, hot, and stuffy accommodations. The room is ten feet by twenty feet. Dark green tiles cover the deck. The walls are composed of hard light-green-colored plastic. Four large wall lockers divide the room in half. The lockers are tall enough and wide enough to provide each occupant some privacy from the other. Two of the lockers face Karzack's area of the room, and the other two lockers face Rigney's area of the room. A single-size spring-frame bed with a bare four-inch mattress stands on Rigney's side of the room. The room has one window, which is on Karzack's side of the room.

Inadequate compared to my ONI quarters, but definitely superb compared to my matchbox-size patch of real estate on the USS Barb *that I had to share.*

He makes up his bunk. Then, he lays out the contents of his seabag and suitcase on his bunk. He puts all his navy-issue uniforms and navy gear in one locker and all his civilian clothes in the other locker.

He strips down to his underwear and puts on his shower shoes. He grabs a towel and his douche kit and departs the room. During his search for the showers, Rigney discovers a weight room. He decides to get back into a regular weight-lifting program tomorrow morning.

Chapter 22

Back in his room after showering, Rigney dresses in a loose-fitting light-blue cotton polo shirt and baggy tan-colored cotton slacks. Because of the heat, he decides on brown leather sandals, instead of sneakers or shoes.

As he steps out the doorway of the barracks, the bright sunlight causes him to put on his sunglasses. As he walks past the galley and the administration building, he has his eyes fixed on the pool area. He sees a man, a woman, and a small girl. Not seeing the pretty blond from earlier disappoints him.

As he walks through the main entrance of Club Zeus, cold air with a dirty ashtray smell blasts past him and cools his skin. He removes his sunglasses to get a better look at the interior of the basketball court sized club. A dance floor surrounded by tables and chairs and a stage take up the east half of the building. The bar and restaurant area occupy the west half of the building. Natural marble tiles cover the floor and rough stucco covers the walls. Paintings and fixtures with a Greek mythology theme hang on the walls.

As he walks up to the bar, he sees a three feet by three feet sign on the back of the bar that announces the following:

- Welcome to the Neptune Bar -
- He who enters covered here
will buy the bar a round of cheer -

A dozen young men in casual civilian clothes sit or stand around the bar. A half-dozen women sit around the bar and restaurant area. Rigney assumes the men to be off-duty sailors. He assumes the women are Greek girlfriends or dependent wives of the sailors.

He takes the nearest available barstool. He looks to the other end of the bar and sees the attractive blond from the pool; she sits next to a stunning brunette. Both women appear to be in their early twenties. Four men in casual beachwear form a semicircle in front of the two women, which pens the women against the bar.

A large plate-glass window permits viewing of the pool area. A wide glass door in the center of the wall allows access to the pool patio.

The Greek bartender approaches and asks, "Sir, what is your pleasure?"

"A very cold Amstel, please."

"Yes, sir, right away, sir." The Greek bartender speaks in understandable English, but with a deep accent.

Rigney starts to ask the bartender why the bar is named Neptune after the Roman god of the sea instead of Poseidon the Greek god of the sea, but the bartender departs too quickly. Rigney decides to ask the question later.

When the bartender delivers the Amstel, Rigney asks, "Bartender, what is your name?"

"All people call me Gus . . . nickname."

Rigney responds, "My name is Rig." He reaches across the bar to shake hands. "I just arrived today."

"Welcome aboard, Rig," Gus says sincerely and appreciatively. Rigney is one of the few sailors to introduce themselves. While shaking hands, Gus says, "I think you like Nea Makri."

Rigney responds, "I sure hope so." Then, he asks, "Can I get something to eat?"

Gus hands Rigney a menu. Rigney studies the menu while he sips his beer.

Occasionally, Rigney glances over the top of the menu to see if the blond still has her back to him. He wants to catch her eye to find out if she shows any interest.

Five minutes later, the bartender returns to take Rigney's order.

Rigney asks, "Please tell me more about the Greek steak sandwich?"

"The chef charbroils steak, then, cut thin, puts on toasted Greek bread, and spread feta cheese."

"What is feta cheese?"

"It Greek cheese—from milk of goat."

Rigney grimaces.

"Rig, you will like. I promise."

"Okay, I'll have the steak sandwich and cook the steak medium rare."

"Okay—fifteen minutes."

"Okay. Thank you, Gus."

The din of conversation rises as six more off-duty sailors enter the bar.

Occasionally someone stares at Rigney, wondering who he is. When Rigney catches one staring, he smiles and lifts his beer in a hello gesture, and the one staring nods back a hello.

Rigney does not see Master Chief Rodgers, so he tunes into some of the conversations. The conversations range from bitching about the way the base operates to sporting events to current political events. He cannot hear the conversation between the blond and the brunette and the four sailors.

From his seat at the bar, Rigney views past the dining area and through the west wall window into the pool area. He sees a man and woman in bathing suits lying on lounge chairs, and he sees a small girl playing in the pool. Rigney judges the adult's ages to be late twenties. Rigney assumes the man to be a sailor at the base, and he assumes the woman to be his wife.

Gus delivers the steak sandwich. Famished, Rigney takes a large bite and chews slowly to enjoy the flavor. *This is great!* He orders another Amstel.

Fifteen minutes later, Rigney has consumed half the sandwich. As he takes another bite, he feels a light hand on his shoulder and hears a female voice behind him ask, "How do you like Nea Makri so far?"

He rotates on his barstool and faces the attractive blonde-haired woman who waved to him from the pool. The slim blond woman with gray eyes arouses him. She wears a skintight light-blue t-shirt and skintight white cotton shorts. Her hair, still damp from swimming in the pool, hangs straight to her shoulders. She wears no makeup, which is a trait Rigney finds appealing.

"I waved to you from the pool. Remember?"

He quickly chews and swallows the bite of sandwich so he can answer before she walks off. "Yes, I remember. My name is Rigney Page."

Rigney puts his hand forward to shake her hand. She puts her hand in his. They do not shake hands. The contact is more like holding hands. Both feel a sexual magnetism at first touch.

"My name is Dottie Caldwell. Did you say Rigney is your first name?" A quizzical look appears on her face.

"Yes," he replies.

"That's an unusual name. I've never heard that name before."

"Rigney is my mother's maiden name. She wanted me to have a unique name. She taught me that each person should have something unique about them, so that people would remember them. Anyway, most people call me Rig."

Dottie tilts her head to a slight angle, smiles sensuously, and responds flirtatiously, "Well, Rig, you are certainly unique, unusual name or not."

Rigney's face flushes. The forward advance by this woman embarrasses him and pleases him at the some time.

They continue to hold hands.

Rigney then realizes that Dottie's last name matches the commanding officer's last name that he saw on the chain-of-command board on the quarterdeck. "Caldwell? The captain's name is Caldwell. Any relation?"

"He's my uncle. I am here with my cousin, Angie. The CO is Angie's father. We are spending the summer in Nea Makri."

Rigney looks across the bar to where Dottie previously sat. Angie is now alone with the four sailors. She appears nervous.

"I don't think your cousin is having a good time," Rigney comments to Dottie as he wraps his other hand around hers.

"She's okay. She pretends she is trapped, but she loves the attention as long as the sailors don't get physical."

Rigney looks around the bar. Some in the bar stare at him and Dottie. "Physical?" Rigney asks with raised eyebrows.

"Yes, physical, like they are always competing against each other, trying to seduce us. We don't mind them trying as long as they don't touch us. They would have better luck trying to make the European girls at the beach."

"Physical," Rigney whispers as he looks down at his hands holding Dottie's hand in his.

Rigney lets go of her hand, because he understands the implications of getting physical with the CO's niece.

Dottie reaches out both her hands and cups Rigney's hand in her hands.

"It's okay. I want to hold your hand," Dottie whispers with a sensual smile on her face.

They both chuckle lightly at Dottie's voicing the title of the famous *Beatles* song.

Rigney asks casually, "How long have you and your cousin been vacationing here?"

"Since early June. We must leave right after Labor Day and go back to San Diego."

"What's in San Diego?"

"We both attend UCSD, and my senior year starts at the same time that my dad comes back from his WESTPAC cruise."

"What does your dad do in the navy?"

"He's the captain of a guided missile cruiser."

Rigney ponders if he should pursue a relationship with this woman. The consequences of getting involved with an officer's daughter would draw attention, which would make him look less likely to be a counterespionage operative. *Pursue on! She obviously wants to get physical with me, and I haven't been laid in six months!*

"I'm an enlisted man," Rigney blurts out.

"Makes no difference to me," Dottie replies in a casual tone. "My father and my uncle care about those distinctions, but I certainly don't."

"I could get in trouble," Rigney responds as he lowers his voice.

"Rig, I have been around the navy all my life. There are no regulations against relationships between enlisted men and officers' daughters. You should not be concerned. Besides, no one like you has crossed my path in a long time."

Again, Rigney blushes at the woman's bold advance.

Dottie still holds Rigney's hand.

A tall sandy-haired, husky male that looks like a linebacker for a professional football team and who Rigney judges to be mid-twenties walks up behind Dottie and puts his hand lightly on her shoulder.

Dottie turns her head toward the linebacker.

"I thought we were going to Christina's party last night?" he challenges. "I waited two hours."

The linebacker then notices that Dottie holds Rigney's hand. An envious and angry look overcomes his face as he stares at Rigney.

"Eric, I told you I would not go to the party with you. Just because you kept insisting does not mean I agreed."

"May I speak to you, alone?" Eric urges as he shoots a glance at Rigney.

"No, Eric. I will not speak with you alone."

Rigney feels uncomfortable as a passive witness to the conversation between Dottie and Eric. He considers excusing himself and going to the head.

Rigney opens his mouth to state he is going to the head, when comments from down the bar catch his attention.

"He's hitting his kid again! Why doesn't the captain do something about that?"

Rigney looks in the direction that everyone else looks, which is through the glass window to the pool patio. A man stands over a little girl and holds her by the arm with one hand and slaps her repeatedly across the face with his other hand. The little girl cries and mouths words that cannot be heard inside the bar. The little girl fails to pull herself free from the man. Rigney estimates the little girl to be five or six years old.

Dottie and the linebacker stop their discussion and look through the glass window.

Even the bartender stops his work and shakes his head in disapproval of what he sees.

A slender dark-haired woman in a one-piece black swimsuit stands beside the man. Her actions show that she tries to stop the man from hitting the little girl.

"Someone should stop him," a male voice says from down the bar.

"Maybe we should go out there and stop him," says another male voice, sounding hesitant.

"Nothing happened the last time we reported it. Remember what the chief said, *we should not interfere with a man and his family.*"

The woman grabs the man's arm in another attempt to stop him from slapping the child.

The man stops slapping the little girl and backhands the woman across the face. The blow knocks her backward. She trips backward over a chair and falls hard to the cement.

"My god!" a female voice exclaims from down the bar.

"Somebody should do something!" another female voice pleads.

"Excuse me," Rigney says calmly to Dottie as he stands from the barstool.

Dottie drops Rigney's hand. Her eyes follow him, and so do the eyes of all others in the bar.

As he approaches the plate-glass doors to the pool, Rigney walks straight, tall, and purposeful. His stride does not slow as he pushes open the glass door and walks toward the man and the little girl.

As he approaches, he hears the little girl pleading, "No, daddy, please stop. I will do what you say!"

The man says angrily to the little girl, "When I tell you to do something, you do it!" He slaps her face again.

Just as the man raises his right hand for another slap, Rigney grabs the man's right hand and squeezes as hard as he can and bends the hand backward. The man grunts in pain, causing him to release his grip on the little girl.

The man turns his head to look at Rigney.

With his open right hand, Rigney slaps the man hard across the face. Then, he backhands the man across the face, breaking the man's nose. Both slaps are part of one fluid motion of Rigney's swinging right hand.

Rigney tightens his grip on the man's slapping hand.

Blood flows from the man's nose.

"Hurts, doesn't it?" Rigney barks menacingly as he looks directly into the man's eyes. "Now you know how the little girl feels. If you ever hit anyone again, I will find you, and I will break both your arms."

Stunned and seeing stars for a few moments and dazed by the pain in his nose, the man attempts to understand what just happened. Then, anger rises within him, and he clenches his left fist.

Rigney notices the man's clenched fist; he warns, "Swing at me, and I will knock you out." Rigney's tone is cold and threatening.

The man blinks his eyes. Anger and pain prevents clear thinking. He swings his fist at Rigney.

Rigney easily blocks the man's punch. Then, he grabs the man by the throat and pushes him backward and downward.

The man's knees buckle, and he falls backward. He puts out his left arm to brace his fall. As he lands on his back, Rigney pushes the man's head to the cement. A soft thud sounds. The man's head hits the cement hard enough to knock him unconscious.

Rigney stands and looks around. He sees the two sentries at the main gate staring wide-eyed at him. He sees the woman standing a few feet away looking down at her husband. She sobs heavily. Rigney looks for the little girl. He sees her standing behind a lounge chair.

Horrified by what the man did to her daddy, the little girl cowers lower behind the chair. She is now fearful of another adult—Rigney. She does not understand why the man did what he did. She was being a bad girl, and daddy hit her. That is the way it is. Daddies hit their little girls when they disobey. That is what daddies do.

"Is he your husband?" Rigney asks the women.

She nods yes.

"And the little girl . . . she's your child?"

The woman nods again.

Rigney closes the distance to the woman. He looks down into her face. She looks up at him, still crying.

With a consoling look on his face and with a compassionate tone of voice, he says to the woman, "Your husband will be in the hospital for a few days. I advise you to take your daughter and depart for the States—immediately. Distance yourself from this man. Brutality is his nature. He will never change. Someday he will kill you, not intentionally, but in anger, because that is his nature. Please do as I say."

The woman does not speak. She expresses fear as she realizes the truth of Rigney's words. She walks over to her daughter and takes her hand. She gathers up a few belongings. The woman and child depart the pool and walk into the parking lot.

Rigney looks down at the man. *Another bully taught a lesson!*

The woman starts a car and drives out the gate. Rigney notices the gate sentries gawking at him. They are the same sentries that were on duty when he came through the gate earlier. From their position at the gate, they saw everything.

While he walks across the pool patio toward the club, Rigney contemplates what will happen. *I'll be put on report. Surely, there will be an investigation into what happened. The gate sentries saw everything. That's in my favor.*

Just before entering the club through the glass doors, Rigney looks back at the man lying on the cement. *I wonder who he is.*

All eyes focus on Rigney as he walks into the club and walks toward his barstool. Dottie stands in the same place next to Rigney's barstool. Linebacker is gone. Her wide, open eyes and facial expression reveal her concern.

He sits on his barstool and grabs for his beer. The bottle is warm to the touch. Rigney sighs. He wanted a cold swig to quench his thirst from being out in the hot sun.

Suddenly, Gus appears and places an ice-cold Amstel on the bar.

"On the house," the bartender whispers with an approving smile on his face.

Rigney turns on the barstool to face Dottie.

She shakes her head and conveys concern. "Why did you do that? You should not have interfered."

"It needed done," Rigney replies softly and without emotion.

Rigney's casual manner regarding the incident puzzles Dottie. She expects that Rigney should be pumped up and emotional by what he did.

A voice from down the bar announces, "I'm going over to the quarterdeck and tell the duty master-at-arms that we need the doc here."

The sailor associated with the voice walks quickly past Rigney. He stares at Rigney in anticipation, thinking that Rigney may object.

For a brief moment, Rigney locks eyes with the sailor going to the quarterdeck. He does not object, even though he thinks the bully lying on the poolside patio deserves to lie on the hot cement and lick his wounds.

Dottie advises, "You're going to get in trouble. That man you hit is the supply officer. Doesn't that bother you?"

Rigney understands that he reacted instinctively, as he always does to take down bullies. He becomes concerned. *I could be ar-*

rested. Then, I miss my meeting with Anna tomorrow. Damn! I have put my mission at risk again!

He stares directly into Dottie's eyes and replies, "To some extent it does. I will probably be put on report, but the witnesses should back me up. I mean, well, if I hadn't stopped him, he could have severely injured or killed his wife and child."

"Well, maybe." Dottie's voice reflects doubt. "My uncle knows that Lieutenant Martin hits his wife and kid. I think my uncle has Lieutenant Martin going to counseling at the air force base."

"Counseling does not work for his kind. They only understand violence. Counseling will not change his nature."

Dottie shakes her head slightly in disagreement but does not argue. She does not want to end this relationship before it gets started.

Rigney notices movement outside on the pool deck.

Dottie looks in the same direction as Rigney looks.

Lieutenant Martin pushes himself off the cement and stands. He takes a few swerving steps and stops. He blinks his eyes and shakes his head slightly. He raises his right hand and stares at the swollen fingers. He tastes the blood flowing from his nose. He looks around the pool. Then, he looks into the parking lot. He moves his lips, and an angry expression comes over his face. He slips into a polo shirt. Then, he sits and puts on sneakers. After that, he stands and walks across the pool deck and enters the club. He does not look around for his assailant. He keeps his head straight and walks quickly through the club and out the front door.

"Well, maybe I won't be arrested. I guess I didn't hurt him as hard as I thought."

Dottie furrows her brow and appears thoughtful. Then, she says, "Angie and I fly to Corfu tomorrow afternoon. We are taking a two-week tour of the Greek Islands. When we get back, we only have a few days here until we fly back to the States."

"I'm sorry to hear that," Rigney responds with disappointment. "I wish we could spend some time together."

"Me, too." Dottie looks around to see if anyone is close enough to hear her words; no one appears to be. She smiles seductively and says, "I plan on swimming tonight at an isolated beach cove about three miles from here. Nobody goes there at night. Would you like to come along?"

"Definitely."

"Great!" Dottie beams and excited smile. "Tonight, about 9:45, go out the gate and turn right. Walk north along the Marathon Road for about a half of a mile. Wait for me there. I will pick you up at 10:00. It will be dark, then. No one should see us. I don't want anyone gossiping about me, or telling my uncle that I am sneaking around with anyone. If you're not there, then I assume you got restricted."

"Is that what we will do? Sneak around?"

"Hope you're not offended, are you?"

"No."

Dottie looks toward the door as she hears it open. She sees the chief-master-at-arms storm through the doorway, accompanied by the sailor who left the bar to notify the quarterdeck.

"Here comes Master Chief Crimer. I'm sure he's looking for you. I'm leaving now. Hope to see you tonight."

Dottie walks to the other end of the bar and joins her cousin.

Master Chief Crimer walks into the bar area and looks around. The sailor accompanying him, who is the sailor who said who would notify the quarterdeck, nods toward Rigney.

The chief-master-at-arms approaches Rigney. "Page, did you hit Lieutenant Martin?"

"I didn't know he was a lieutenant."

Master Chief Crimer shakes his head with disapproval and says in a scolding tone, "You've only been here a couple of hours, and you're already in trouble. Come with me to the quarterdeck. I need to hear your side of the story."

Rigney responds respectfully, "Aye, aye, Master Chief,"

The master chief nods toward the sailor who reported the incident and orders, "Vance, you come along as a witness."

"Okay, Master Chief."

Chapter 23

Master Chief Crimer sits behind the desk in his office. Rigney and the sailor named Vance sit in chairs in front of the master chief's desk.

"Okay, Vance, you're stating that Mr. Martin slapped his daughter several times and he backhanded his wife, which knocked her down. Correct?"

"Correct, Master Chief."

"You also stated that Page went out to the pool knocked Mr. Martin to the ground. Is that correct?"

"Yes, Master Chief, that's correct."

"What do you have to say about that, Page?"

"Master Chief, I don't think I should say anything."

Master Chief Crimer sits back in his chair. He spends a few moments considering what he should do next. Then, he says, "Vance, go wait in the passageway."

After Vance departs, Crimer stares Page directly in the eye and says, "Newman reported that you beat him up at the airport because he wouldn't carry your bags. He says you called him a lazy nigger. Do you have anything to say about that?"

"Newman lies," Page responds calmly.

"Why would Newman lie?"

"Beats me. Ask him."

Crimer attempts another approach. "What happened at the airport to cause Newman to think those things happened?"

"Don't know, Master Chief. I am not a mind reader." Page remains calm and unemotional.

Crimer sighs deeply; then, he orders Page, "Tell me what happened at the airport between you and Newman."

"I will not say anything about me and Newman at the airport."

Crimer assumes an angry and forceful manner. "Tell me what happened at the airport, that's an order!"

"Newman accuses me of a crime, correct?"

"That's correct."

"You can't order me to say anything about such accusations, and you know that, Master Chief."

Crimer relaxes, smiles, and sits back in his chair and asks, "You some kinda sea lawyer?"

Page says nothing. He casts a questioning expression at Crimer.

After a short pause, Crimer goes to the door and calls Vance back into the office.

"Page, you might be put on report for what you did, but not at this moment. I must speak with Mr. Martin and with the other witnesses."

Rigney bolts upright as he realizes the significance of Mr. Martin's quick departure.

"Master Chief, you must find Mr. Martin. I fear for the safety of his wife and daughter."

"A little melodramatic, don't you think?" Master Chief Crimer replies with a sarcastic grin on his face. "Aren't you just trying to reinforce your excuse for hitting him?"

Rigney pleads, "You don't understand. Mr. Martin is violent. He will beat his wife and daughter, because of what I did to him. He feels offended that someone had the balls to stop him, and humiliated because he was beat in front of others. He will blame his wife and daughter for what I did. He thinks that his wife and daughter will disrespect him now, because someone hit back for once. You must believe me, Master Chief. Please find him before he kills his wife and daughter."

"Page, you just got here. How could you possibly know what he will do?"

"Because I have seen men like him before. He's violent. It's his nature. He won't purposely kill them. In his warped mind, he believes that he must beat respect into women. He believes that the only way to keep women obedient is to beat them."

The chief-master-at-arms picks-up the radio handset behind his desk and speaks into it. "Front gate, this is Master Chief Crimer. Over."

"This is the front gate, go ahead, Master Chief."

"Have you seen Mr. Martin?"

"Yes, he left the base in a navy truck about thirty minutes ago. He looked angry as hell. Blood was runnin' from his nose and down his shirt. I think he's steamin' mad over what that new guy did to him."

Crimer slams down the radio handset, opens a desk drawer, and pulls out an address book. He picks up the telephone and dials a number.

"Air base police, main station," reports a voice on the other end.

"This is the chief-master-at-arms out in Nea Makri. I need assistance to quell a possible violent domestic situation."

"What's the address?"

Crimer looks down to the address book and reads the Kifissia address to the military policeman on the other end of the phone.

"Okay, Master Chief. We will have a team there in thirty minutes."

"I will meet you there," Crimer advises.

Crimer sets down the phone and walks over to a filing cabinet. He opens a drawer and pulls out a web belt with a nightstick inserted into a loop. He also retrieves handcuffs. As he wraps the belt around his waist and connects the buckle, he estimates that it will take him thirty minutes to get to Mr. Martin's house in Kifissia. The stocky square-jawed master chief casts a menacing image in his police gear. He starts for the door when he notices Page and Vance with questioning looks on their faces.

"You two can go for now. I will talk to you later." Crimer walks quickly out the door.

Rigney sighs in relief. Crimer did not order them to stay on the base.

Rigney and Vance stand at the same time to leave. They bump into each other. They both excuse themselves.

"It's okay," Rigney responds politely with a smile on his face.

"You're not mad at me?" Vance asks.

Rigney studies the sailor next to him. The thin, medium-height sailor, dressed in polo shirt and shorts, has a gangly frame with a narrow face and close-set eyes. Vance's black wavy hair is too long for regulation. He states, "No. I am not mad at you."

"Oh. Well, I thought that . . . well, that you—"

"Would be angry at you for reporting me," Rigney finishes the sentence for Vance.

"Yes. That's what I thought."

"You did what you were supposed to do, and you didn't lie about anything."

"It's not that I am on Mr. Martin's side, or anything. I thought he needed medical help. I mean, everybody has seen Mr. Martin hit is wife and kid before. You will probably get in trouble, but I'm glad someone finally decked that son-of-a-bitch. He's a mean bastard, he's always jumping on people, verbally I mean. Sometimes he gets in your face like he is gonna hit you."

"Like I said, you did the right thing."

"Okay. Good. My name is Bob Vance." He sticks out his hand.

"My name is Rigney Page."

The two sailors shake hands.

"May I buy you a beer?" Vance asks cordially.

"Sure can," Rigney replies, equally cordial. "I still have half a steak sandwich on the bar.

Chapter 24

Rigney and Vance enter the smoke-filled Club Zeus. Sailors in a semicircle-shaped booth invite them to sit.

Shortly after Rigney sits down, Gus delivers a fresh steak sandwich and cold Amstel. "I save for you," Gus says with an appreciative smile.

A tall and overweight sailor with thinning hair who everyone calls *The Professor* sits at the center of the semicircle booth and holds court. *The Professor* appears to be in his late twenties. Everyone else at the table are Rigney's age or younger. Except for Rigney, everyone drinks heavily. Except for Rigney, everyone talks excessively about the base. The captain's *chickenshit* regulations dominate the conversation. On a few occasions, Rigney's target, Master Chief Raymond Rodgers, becomes the topic of conversation as they discuss how Rodgers manages the club. Rigney contributes little. He listens intently.

Every time one of the drunks criticizes the base, criticizes the captain, or criticizes other officers, Rigney looks around the club to see if anyone appears to care about the conversation. Everyone in the bar appears Rigney's age. When someone at the table cracks a criticism, most around the club nod in agreement and take another swig of beer.

The Greek bartender appears to be the only one in the club who disapproves of the complaining.

The Professor does most of the talking.

During a head break, Vance tells Rigney, "We call him *The Professor*, because he graduated from Penn State, and he was in ROTC. He was a teacher at a small college in Pennsylvania. He knows a lot about everything. He seems to have all the answers. We all respect his opinion."

Rigney responds casually, "I'm more impressed with someone who has more questions than answers."

"I don't follow," Vance responds.

"Never mind. Anyway, you would think with his educational background, he would be an officer," Rigney speculates.

"We've all asked him that. He never gave a clear answer on that."

As Rigney and Vance return to the booth, *The Professor* continues to educate the unenlightened masses. "And the captain believed he had no choice. He is not a naval communicator. He is a washed-out pilot. Washington would not assign him to an aviation billet, so they made him CO here. He convinced himself that this is a special billet, and Washington sent him here to straighten out this mess of a command. He proved already that he has no clue how to run a NAVCOMMSTA. Just look at all the stupid regulations he made since coming here. Believe me. I know. My last command, NAVCOMMSTA Morocco, was great. It was nothing like this because it was commanded by a career naval communicator."

Sailors around the bar nod their heads and mumble agreement of *The Professor's* words.

A very young-looking member of *the court*, nicknamed *Big Louie*, adds, "And the XO's no better. She doesn't understand anything. What does a split-tail know about sailors? She's never served on a ship."

Such petty complaining, Rigney thinks to himself. *Don't these guys have anything better to do? It's Saturday in a sun-drenched and culture-rich country. They have all been here a while. Why aren't they out discovering Greece?*

The Professor asks Rigney, "Hey, new guy, the one that punched out Mr. Martin. What's your name?"

Rigney looks at *The Professor* and responds, "Rigney Page."

"Are you a radioman?"

"Yes."

"What was your previous command?"

"USS *Barb*."

"What kind of ship is that?"

"Fast attack submarine."

The Professor asks, "Okay, submariner, what do you think about this fucked-up command?"

All heads turn toward Rigney.

Rigney responds with an emotionless expression and looking directly in the eyes of *The Professor*, "I don't have an opinion. I haven't been here long enough to decide whether it's fucked-up or not."

With his arms outstretched, *The Professor* bellows a challenge. "Don't have an opinion! Haven't you been listening to us?!"

"I don't form opinions based on what others say. I base my opinions only on my own observances and experiences."

"For example?" *The Professor* queries.

Rigney looks at *Big Louie* and asks, "*Big Louie*, you claim the XO knows nothing about sailors, because she has never been to sea. Is that right?"

"Yeah. That's right," *Big Louie* responds with a smug expression.

"Okay, *Big Louie*, please tell us about your last sea command."

Big Louie looks around the table anxiously with his eyes darting from one person to the other. Then, he answers, "I've never been to sea, but I'm not the XO."

Rigney shifts his stare from *Big Louie* to *The Professor*. He says nothing.

"Well, I have been around," *The Professor* claims. "Have you been listening to what I say?"

"I have been listening. I will make up my own mind."

"You don't give detailed answers, do you?"

"Only when I want to," Rigney responds as he stares expressionless into the eyes of *The Professor*.

The discussion turns to religion.

Rigney tunes-out the discussion as he focuses on Master Chief Rodgers who just entered the bar. Rodgers spends a few minutes behind the bar talking with Gus the bartender. Then, Rodgers walks away from the bar and crosses the dance floor. He enters a door near the stage.

Rigney returns his attention to *The Professor* who is explaining Easter. ". . . and the Jews crucified Christ on Good Friday. Christ rose from the dead two days later on the day we now call Easter Sunday."

"That's not the way it was taught to me," announces a sailor with the nickname of Jake.

"Of course not," *The Professor* responds condescendingly. "If we waited for truth from Jews, we would wait to the end of time."

Rigney throws a scolding expression at *The Professor*, which is noticed by everyone. Rigney is not a religious person, but he becomes offended when others purposely insult those of another faith.

The others at the table are accustomed to *The Professor's* attacks on non-Christians.

The Professor frowns arrogantly at Rigney's scolding expression and asks, "The truth hurts, huh?"

"What truth is that?" Rigney challenges.

"That Jews killed Jesus and lie about Jesus's death and resurrection."

Rigney says with a challenging tone, "And what you said about Easter is the truth, I suppose."

"Of course it is."

Rigney explains, "Actually, Easter's origin has more to do with the ancient Jewish religious ritual of Passover and the ancient Pagan celebrations of the Spring Equinox. Scholars believe the word Easter comes from the Pagan goddess Ostare or Eastur, which is a derivative of the ancient German word for spring, *Eastre*.

"Some theologians reject Easter as the same period of the year that Jesus was crucified and resurrected. Some theologians believe that *John*, as in the *Gospel of John*, purposely changed the dates of the crucifixion and resurrection to coincide with Passover.

"Later, during the early Dark Ages, the Catholic Church linked together the most important days of Pagan spring celebrations, Passover, and the Crucifixion. They did this to make it easier to convert Pagans and Jews to Christianity. For example, the Easter Bunny and Easter eggs come from Pagan ritual."

Rigney stops his explanation, because he sees bewildering and doubting expressions on members of *the court*.

Except for *Hey Jude* by the Beatles playing softly on the jukebox, the bar is mostly quiet.

One of *the court* members with the nickname *Toot* breaks the silence. "Never heard any of that in catechism class," *Toot* challenges. "Where did you get that information?"

"From history books," Rigney answers.

"Never heard any of that in history class, either," *Toot* states, not a challenge this time.

Rigney studies *Toot's* appearance and manner. *Toot* has the same body frame as Rigney and the same size biceps, but *Toot* is not as muscled. *Toot* has a pretty boy face, unlike Rigney's rugged features. *Toot* appears mild mannered and friendly.

Rigney responds to *Toot's* challenge. "The history books I got that information from won't be found in high school history class . . . and probably not in standard history classes in college either. Isn't allowed by those in power."

"Why not?" *Toot* asks.

"Because those history books conflict with the traditional beliefs regarding the origins and growth of Christianity."

Big Louie interrupts, "What are you, some kind of atheist?"

Rigney contemplates his answer then replies, "I have said all I want to say on the subject."

The court is silent for about thirty seconds; then, *The Professor* turns the subject back to complaints about the commanding officer. "Then there was that order the captain issued that no one was allowed in the barracks during normal working hours. That's another action that shows he knows nothing about running a NAVCOMMSTA. And, then, he—"

Movement near the door causes Rigney's attention to focus on two tall black men dressed in civilian clothes who enter the club. The two men walk into the bar area and scan the patrons, as if they are searching for someone. One of the black men talks to a person at the bar. That person looks over at the table where Rigney sits and points in Rigney's direction.

The two black men strut with nonchalance across the bar toward Rigney's table. They both wear cream-colored pants and short-sleeve light-blue polo shirts, dressed like twins. Both men are broad shouldered and muscled.

The conversation at the table halts when both black men look directly at Rigney. One of the black men asks in a hostile tone, "You Page, man?"

Rigney looks directly into the questioner's eyes, but does not respond. Rigney concludes that these two sailors are two of *the bros* that Newman referenced.

"Hey, you Page, man?" the black sailor asks in a louder, menacing tone.

Rigney holds his stare on the black man and remains silent. All members of *the court* stare at Rigney.

Rigney sits on the far end of the booth and is out of reach of the two black men. On his third try, the black man points a finger at Rigney and elevates the volume of his voice and questions, "You, Page, man?"

Rigney shakes his head slowly and replies, "No."

Then, the other black sailor asks, "You're not RM2 Page?"

"Yes, I am RM2 Page."

The two black men exchange confused looks. Then, one challenges, "Hey, man, I asked if you're Page. You stupid or somethin'?"

The two black men now have defiant expressions on their faces.

All others at the table sit quietly and stare at Rigney, hoping that the two black men will not pick on them.

The bartender picks up the phone and calls the quarterdeck.

"You asked if I was *Page man*," Rigney responds sarcastically. "Please pardon my lack of understanding regarding your illiterate phrasing."

The others at the table shift nervously in their seats. Rigney understands from their actions that they expect trouble.

The manner of the two black men turns threatening.

The spokesman puts a sneer on his face and demands. "You come outside with us, Page. We want to talk to you about our man Newman."

Rigney smiles and in a dismissive manner replies, "I have no desire to discuss Newman with you or with anyone else."

Bewildered by Rigney's response, the two black sailors just stare with threatening expression.

Rigney stares unwaveringly at the two sailors. Rigney's body language indicates that the next move is up to them.

BM2 Karzack enters the club and walks over to the table. He faces the table and stands a safe four feet away from the two black sailors. Karzack wears a *duty master-at-arms* armband. He also wears a guard belt with a nightstick hanging from a belt loop.

Everyone looks at Karzack, waiting for him to state his business.

Karzack locks stares with the two black sailors and queries, "I got a report of a disturbance in the club. Any of you know about it."

No one says anything.

Karzack glances at each face around the table, looking for a response, but no one says anything. All at the table avoid looking at Karzack, except for Rigney.

"Page, you know anything about a disturbance?"

Rigney slowly shakes his head and responds, "Sure don't."

Karzack looks at the two black sailors and asks, "What are you two planning for this evening?"

"We're goin' into Athens," answers the taller of the two.

"The liberty bus will depart in a few minutes," Karzack advises as he looks at his watch.

"We'll be goin', then," the taller one says. The two black sailors turn and walk out of the club.

Karzack and all those at the table stare after the two as they depart. All at the table release a collective sigh. Rigney looks around at each person at the table and wonders why they were so tense.

"Anyone want to tell me what was going on?" Karzack requests with a demanding tone.

All eyes turn to Rigney, expecting him to answer.

In response to all looking to Rigney, Karzack asks, "Page, you have anything to say."

"Those guys wanted to talk to me about Newman."

"I got a call that trouble was happening in here."

"I didn't see any trouble," Rigney reports.

Karzack considers what he should do next. He got a call from the bartender who said he thought a fight was going to happen. Since he found no fighting or arguing in progress, he decides to let it go, but he will make a log entry that he was called.

Karzack turns away from the table and walks toward the exit.

"Hey, Victor, hold up a minute," Rigney requests as he rises from the table and walks over to Karzack.

Karzack stops and turns around.

Rigney says to Karzack, "Let's move out of hearing range of that table." Rigney nods back toward *the court* table.

They walk to a corner of the dance floor.

"Who are those two black guys?"

"Why do ya wanna know?" Victor asks suspiciously.

"I'm new here, just trying to find out about people."

"Newman reported that you beat him up at the airport. Is that true?"

"Do I look like the kind of guy that would beat up on someone smaller and weaker than myself?"

"Rig, you just got here and already you're in trouble for knocking out Mr. Martin. If this thing about Newman is true, you can really get into a lot of trouble."

"My evaluation of Newman is that he is a loudmouth and fabricator of stories, and he probably does not have a lot of credibility. Am I correct about that?"

"Yeah, ya got Newman pegged alright."

"Who are the two black guys? Newman's protectors, right?"

Victor sees no harm in telling Rigney about the two black men. "They are Patterson and Thompson. They're both electronics technicians, ETN2s. They work in the repair shop in the communications trailers compound. They and Newman and a couple other black sailors run in a group. They watch out for each other. No one ever messes with them. If Newman told them you beat-up on him, they were probably in here to find out if it was true."

"So they might not believe Newman, then."

"That's right. Newman's lied to them before about being beat-up."

"Victor, this makes no sense. I mean, this is the navy. There are no gangs or street warfare. The chain-of-command controls things."

"I don't know how to explain it. They don't never hurt no one, at least not that I know of. It's like everyone knows that ya just stay out of their way."

"What does the chief-master-at-arms think about it?"

"He don't know. This is somethin' that just the lower enlisted know 'bout."

Rigney puts his hand to his chin as he considers his situation. *Maybe I can convince Patterson and Thompson that Newman made it up. I can't get into a fight with those guys with this Mr. Martin incident hanging over my head. It would make me look bad. Wait a minute! Mr. Martin?*

Rigney asks anxiously, "Has the master chief returned from Mr. Martin's house?"

"No, but he called on the radio and said that he had to go to the air force base and would not be back until after midnight."

Rigney looks at his watch—7:10 PM.

"You think that Patterson and Thompson left on the liberty bus?" Rigney asks.

"Yeah. They go every night that they don't have duty. They're probably gone until Monday."

Rigney feels relief, because now there are no obstacles with him meeting Dottie at 10:00 PM.

"Thanks for the information, Victor."

"No problem."

"Okay, see ya later, then."

Instead of going back to the table and listening to *The Professor*, Rigney departs the club and returns to the barracks to get several hours rest before meeting Dottie.

Chapter 25

At 9:45 PM, Rigney exits the barracks. Cooler night air and a sea breeze replace the heat of the day. As he nears the gate, Karzack exits the guard-shack and walks toward him.

"You leavin' the base?" Karzack challenges.

"Just going for a short walk, such a nice night for one, don't ya think?"

Karzack hesitates. He considers, *the master chief didn't say anything about it, and Page is not on the restricted list.*

"Is there a problem?"

"No problem," Karzack replies in a cordial tone as he walks off.

Rigney nods to the sentries as he passes through the gate. He turns right and walks north along the Marathon Road. The moonlit night allows him to see clearly ahead for about one hundred feet.

A small café stands next to the road and just past the north perimeter fence of the base. Through the windows, Rigney sees what he assumes to be sailors from the base drinking beer and laughing. Their English and short haircuts give them away. Rigney thinks he smells frying hamburgers. *Hamburgers in a Greek café?*

He continues along the road for another fifteen minutes and stops.

Several cars pass him. One car comes too close, which causes him to stand back from the road about five feet. A few minutes later, a slow moving car approaches. He steps closer to the road so that Dottie can see him.

Dottie pulls up to him in a small white MGA convertible.

"Hmmm, I'm pleased you could make it," Dottie says in a husky, sexual voice.

Dottie wears an unbuttoned flimsy knee-length shirt. Underneath she wears a two-piece black-colored swimsuit.

Rigney runs his eyes over her body. Her legs are spread apart about eight inches to accommodate manipulations of clutch and brake. Rigney feels aroused as blood flows into his stiffening penis.

He opens the door and plops his butt into the passenger seat.

Dottie manipulates the clutch, gearshift, and gas pedal, and the convertible shoots down the road with the muffler uttering a low-pitch exhaust sound.

"Nice wheels," Rigney comments.

"It's my uncle's. It's part of his command fleet. Angie and I have this car to ourselves all summer."

Dottie drives north for another two kilometers. Then, she turns onto a solid-packed dirt road and drives east toward the beach. She parks the car next to some high rocks where the road ends and the beach begins.

Dottie explains, "This is a secluded and seldom used beach, because of the rocky shore. It's halfway between Nea Makri and the village of Agios Panteleimonas."

Dottie removes a large beach blanket and a picnic basket from the trunk.

The full moon makes navigating the beach easy. Dottie leads Rigney a short distance to a twelve feet high, horseshoe shaped rock formation. The open end of the horseshoe faces the water, which is ten feet away. Soft sand fills the floor of the horseshoe formation. They spread out a large ten feet by ten feet beach blanket. The rock formation hides them from view, and they have an excellent and romantic view of the Aegean.

Dottie removes her outerwear and reveals the skimpiness of the two-piece bathing suit. Her breasts swell over the top piece. The bottom piece does little to hide her curvaceous hips. She lies on her back. Rigney shucks his clothes down to his tight-fitting navy bathing suit.

Dotty stares at the rising bulge in the crotch of Rigney's bathing suit.

They hold hands while engaging in small talk. Dottie tells him, "Angie and me come here when we want to go to the beach. We avoid the crowded beaches, because the men, including the American sailors, do not leave us alone. We found out about this spot from some of the sailors' wives who also want a beach free of predatory males. According to the sailors' wives, European men on vacation pursue all women, good looking or not, married or not. Sailors from the base are the same way."

"You got something against American sailors?" Rigney asks with a chuckle.

"Uh, no. I just don't like pushy men. You're not pushy. Actually, I guess I pushed myself on you."

"That's okay," Rigney responds. "I like aggressive women. I don't want any doubt as to where I stand."

Dottie turns on her side and nuzzles her mouth against his ear. She slides her hand under his bathing suit and takes his penis in her hand. She strokes him slowly, and she says huskily, "You feel like you're standing steady."

Rigney pushes off his swimsuit and spreads his legs to add to the pleasure of Dottie stroking him. Then, he moves his hands behind her back, unties her top, and pulls it away. The sight of her firm and perfectly shaped breasts arouses him more.

"Take off my bottoms."

Rigney pushes on her bottoms with his right hand. She must raise her butt and let go of his penis to accomplish the removal of her bottoms.

She wraps her hand around his penis and resumes the slow stroking motions.

Rigney maneuvers to kiss her, but she avoids this kiss. She says, "No, just lay back and let me jack you off, so that you will last longer later."

Rigney lies on his back and spread-eagles his arms and legs. He relaxes his body. He releases full control of his pleasure to Dottie. He moans and breathes rapidly.

Dottie breathes heavily. Stroking Rigney's long, thick, and hard penis arouses her. "I love the size and shape of your cock," she rasps.

One minute later, he has not yet ejaculated. Dottie thinks he should have by now. She tightens her grip and strokes faster.

Rigney notices and says, "I might come faster if you suck on me." Rigney urges—begs.

"No," she says softly while staring at his penis, continuing her steady stroking.

Rigney senses that he is about to ejaculate, and he holds his pelvic muscles and penis tight to delay the ejaculation. He keeps his eyes open, alternately glancing between stars and her stroking.

Dottie feels his penis becoming harder and bigger, a sign that he is ready.

"I'm gonna come!" Rigney says tightly.

"Go ahead," Dottie responds, as if giving permission.

"Okay!" The pressure is more than he can stand. He relaxes his body. Semen spurts from his penis and lands on his chest and belly. He groans loudly as he ejaculates. Dottie continues to stroke him. The pleasurable, pulsating contractions of his penis and the stroking by Dottie cause his mind to shut out all other sensations. He balls his fists. Then, his whole body shudders with carnal ecstasy.

Ninety seconds later, Dottie squeezes out the last drop of semen from his softening penis. She releases her grip.

Rigney still pants rapidly and loudly.

She opens the picnic basket and retrieves a washcloth, a bottle of water, a bottle of skin-cleansing lotion, and four condoms. She wets the washcloth and cleans the semen from her hand and from Rigney's body. She applies the lotion to his penis, scrotum, and lower belly.

He comments, "Looks like you've planned this out."

Dottie responds, "I don't have sex that often, and it's been a long time since I had sex. I choose my lovers carefully, and I want the sex to be good in a certain way. I hope you don't mind."

Rigney quickly scans Dottie's naked body. "I don't mind. It's been good for me so far."

She lies down beside him and places her lips to his ear. "I think it will get better," she foretells. Then, she sticks her tongue into his ear.

During their five hours on the beach, they never let go of each other. They discovered every inch of each other's body with hand or tongue. Between each of their primitive, thrashing, fluid flowing acts, they lie in each other's arms and talk. They discover each other's past, interests, and life pursuits.

Dottie is also a surfer. Turns out, they both surfed Huntington Beach during their high school summers. No, they could not remember seeing each other. Dottie confided that she looked and acted like a tomboy then. Like Rigney, she had not done much surfing since graduating from high school.

Dottie studies marine biology at UCSD and will start her senior year next month. She does not protest against anything. "I don't understand why the other students protest. I don't associate with any of the student protesters. They're so smug and self-righteous, annoying, and clueless."

After she graduates, she wants to do research. "I think all this social and civil unrest has nothing to do with solving the world's problems. In the not too distant future, the world's most significant problems and solutions will be in the world's oceans."

"What about the race riots?" Rigney inquires.

"I think they were inevitable, and I think there will be more. I don't think racial equality will come without violent protests from black people. I believe equality will not come to them unless they protest, because I think most Americans do not understand the problem until they are slapped in the face with it. Racial equality is easier in the military. The regulations don't permit unequal treatment, but I think racial equality is coming faster in the enlisted ranks than in the officer ranks."

"Why faster in the enlisted ranks?" Rigney asks, his tone curious.

"Ten years ago, you never saw a black petty officer. Now, you see more black chiefs than ever. But I don't see an equal increase in the number of black officers. I'm not surprised, though. I have overheard the conversations of many officers who don't like this equal treatment policy. Anyway, that's my opinion after living in the navy for the past twenty-one years."

Later, as they lie intertwined in each other's arms, Dottie seductively whispers, "Did you enjoy the blow job?"

Dottie's blunt words startle him. He considers that Dottie seeks a compliment. *Enjoy it? Doesn't every man?*

"I never wanted to do that with any other guy before. Desire to do it just overcame me. I put all my physical and emotional strength into it. I feel an attachment to you. I want you to want more. I go away for two weeks tomorrow night, and I want to see more of you when I get back. You're the best sex I've ever had, especially the cunnilingus. I never came like that before."

Later, as Dottie drives south on Marathon Road toward the NAVCOMMSTA, Rigney considers Dottie's words. He reminisces about the five women he had sex with over the last year, including Dottie. With most of his partners, the sex focused on pleasure and reward. You pleasure me and I pleasure you, as if it were a matter of procedure. Sex with Sally Macfurson was pleasurable, but he also felt that they were sharing and caring. Sally was his last sexual partner, before Dottie; that was six months ago in Naples, a week after his last mission.

He senses that Dottie wants more from him than pleasure and reward. She said she feels attached to him. He understands that he was so caught up in the pleasure of the moment he had not considered his feelings for her. He concentrated on sex after being without it for six months.

Chapter 26

At the NAVCOMMSTA main gate, SK2 Simpson paces back and forth so that he keeps blood pumping through his tired body. Every six days, he catches duty and must stand four-hours-on and four-hours-off as the senior sentry on the main gate. His normal assignment is that of receiving petty officer at NAVCOMMSTA Supply Department.

Under the illumination of the guard-shack light, he looks at his watch—4:10 AM. Only ten minutes passed since he assumed the watch. He dreads the next three hours and fifty minutes of boredom. His dread increases as he considers that after his watch he must report to the supply department for a full day's work.

Simpson glances at his Greek counterpart, a Greek sailor who all the American sailors call Terry. The Greek sailor shows equal tiredness and just shrugs acceptance of the long hours ahead.

There are no streetlights on the Marathon Road. The illumination around the main gate comes from the powerful one thousand watt lights mounted on the twenty feet high lampposts on both sides of the gate and from the light over the doorway to the guard shack. Those approaching the main gate are not visible until they are within forty feet.

The sentries on the last watch closed the main gate at midnight. Simpson and Terry will open the main gate at sunrise. When anyone enters or departs the base between midnight and sunrise, the main gate sentries must open and close the gate manually and must log the names of those entering and departing. The sentries must also question those going through the gate as to where they have been or where they are going. Those sailors who refuse to say will endure an intimidating visit from the master-at-arms force the next day.

Closing the main gate at night makes no sense to the NAVCOMMSTA sailors, because the only fence protection around the base perimeter is a four feet high four-strand barbed-wire fence. No lights illuminate the perimeter of the base. If intruders want to gain access, all they need to do is step over the top strand of barbed wire.

Shortly after taking command, Commander Caldwell ordered the gate closing at midnight policy and the logging of those coming and going. He claimed the new procedure to be for security reasons. However, the NAVCOMMSTA sailors came to understand Commander Caldwell's character and know he ordered the new procedure so he could intimidate sailors who had no need to be carousing throughout the night.

The narrow two-lane Marathon Road provides the primary artery between Athens and Marathon. During the daytime, numerous private and commercial vehicles speed along the north-south road. During this quiet time of morning, however, the passing of any vehicle is a rare event. A few crickets and the shuffling feet of the two sentries are the only sounds that break the silence of night.

Simpson bends over and pulls a pack of cigarettes and matches from his sock. Smoking is prohibited while on watch, but Simpson knows that at this time of night no one will notice or care. He offers a cigarette to Terry, who gladly accepts to avoid smoking one of his own harsh Turkish brands.

While puffing on his cigarette, Simpson walks casually to the edge of the road and looks south for a few moments; then, he shifts his attention to the north. Headlights about one quarter of mile away catch his attention. *The vehicle is stopped*, he notes.

Terry, wondering what catches Simpson's attention, walks to the edge of the road and stares in the same direction as Simpson. Terry sees headlights approaching.

When she dropped-off Rigney, Dottie raised the top of the convertible. As the vehicle passes through the illumination of the main-gate lights at more than twenty miles over the speed limit, Dottie has her left hand to the side of her face, hoping the sentries are not paying attention or do not recognize her.

Both sentries recognize the captain's MGA and the driver as Dottie Caldwell.

"Too much late she be out night," Terry states.

As Simpson watches the taillights of the MGA fade southward, he responds, "Wonder where she's been."

"And what she do," Terry adds.

Fantasies about Dottie flash through the minds of both sailors.

Simpson attempts to flush from his mind images of him and Dottie Caldwell lying naked together. He paces along the edge of the road and forces into his mind thoughts of action in the supply department that need his attention. He lights another cigarette. His eyes shift to the north when he hears approaching footsteps.

Terry, who stands five feet back from Simpson, also hears the footsteps and looks north on the Marathon Road.

Rigney steps into the illumination of the main gate lights.

Both sentries grin widely. Both sentries shift their gaze south, the direction that Dottie's vehicle sped several minutes before.

Rigney stops to show his ID Card.

Knowing expressions appear on both sentries' faces.

Simpson glances perfunctorily at Rigney's ID Card. Then, with an admiring tone, Simpson says to Rigney, "I guess you've had a busy day. First, you mop up the airport parking lot with Newman. Then, within one hour of reporting aboard, you knock out the meanest officer that ever existed. Then, to top all that, you spend the night with Dottie. This place was boring before you got here. What's next?"

"I deny touching Newman, and will you keep quiet about Dottie?"

"Absolutely not!" Simpson declares with a friendly smile and friendly tone. "It's already all over the base about you two in the club yesterday, holding hands. Do you know how many squids have tried to get into her pants? Anyway, you've given us all something else to talk about other than how fucked-up the captain is."

Rigney sighs deeply and shakes his head slightly in resignation. He asks, "May I pass?"

"Yes, you can pass. Oh, I must log that you came through the gate at this time. Anyone coming through the gate between midnight and sunup must be logged, I must also log where you were."

"Nobody's business where I was," Rigney states evenly.

"Your funeral," Simpson responds.

Terry opens the gate.

Rigney shrugs and starts to walk away; then, he stops and turns around and asks, "Why is it my funeral?"

"Captain's orders. The master-at-arms investigates and reports back to the captain."

Rigney shakes his head, conveying his disagreement over such invasions of privacy. He asks Simpson, "Why would he want . . . I mean, I don't think—"

"I know," Simpson answers without the question being fully asked. "This captain pries into everyone's lives. He sets *boundaries* as he calls them. You'll have to answer-up for crossing this one."

"Oh, must I!" Rigney responds in a defiant tone. Then, he turns and walks away from the main gate toward the barracks.

Simpson stares after Rigney.

Terry walks to Simpson's side and stares after Rigney, also. Then Terry states, "Me think that sailor in much trouble these days here."

Simpson nods agreement.

As Rigney walks across the parking lot toward the barracks, he thinks about the events since arriving in Athens. *Was that only sixteen hours ago?* He thinks about Newman at the airport and about Lieutenant Martin at the pool. He thinks about the talk going around about him and Dottie. He wonders why sailors sit around the club on Saturday nights and gossip about other sailors. *This isn't a military command! This is a soap opera!*

Chapter 27

The barracks vibrates from violent and loud pounding on the thin walls.

A voice shouts, "Reveille! Everyone up for church!"

Rigney awakes.

The barracks walls vibrate again from more pounding.

The same voice shouts again, "Time to get up for church!"

Someone pounds on the room door. Rigney rises from his bunk to answer the door, but Karzack beats him to it.

Rigney looks past Victor and sees a first class petty officer with a DUTY MAA armband.

The DUTY MAA observes both Rigney and Karzack wearing only underwear and sleep still in their eyes. "Come on, Karzack. Get movin'. You know how pissed the captain gets when people are late for church, If you and Page are late or don't show up, I must put you on the list."

Karzack looks at his watch and says, "Okay. We'll be there on time."

The DUTY MAA turns and moves along the passageway; he continues his pounding on the walls and yelling his announcement.

Karzack closes the door and walks to his area of the room. He opens his locker and starts dressing.

Rigney stands in his area of the room. His sleep-drugged mind attempts to understand what just happened. *Did Karzack commit me to going to church?*

Rigney walks to Karzack's area of the room. Karzack dons his Service Dress White uniform.

"Wadda ya mean by *we'll be there on time*? Be where on time?"

Karzack slips on his neckerchief over his head; then, he looks questioningly at Rigney. He does not understand why Rigney would ask such a question. He responds, "Church—at 0900 in the galley."

Rigney looks at his watch—0840. "I don't wanna go to church. Why did you commit me to going to church?"

"Doesn't make any difference if you want to go or not. Captain expects everyone to attend. He closes the gate at 0830 and no one is allowed off station until services are over."

Rigney considers that Karzack exaggerates. He understands that Karzack is not a quick thinker. Therefore, he believes that Karzack did not clearly state the captain's expectation. "The captain can't order us to attend church," Rigney challenges.

Karzack frowns while he considers Rigney's words; then, he responds, "He's the cap'n. We must follow his orders."

Rigney and Karzack enter the galley at 0858. They remove their white hats as they step over the threshold.

The duty master-at-arms, Quartermaster First Class George Latham, the one who pounded on the walls in the barracks, stands inside the door and checks-off names on a list.

Latham stares disapprovingly at Page and challenges, "You didn't have enough time to shave?"

Rigney touches his cheek and chin. He feels the bristle of facial hair.

"No, I didn't."

Rigney and Karzack sit down at an empty table near the door.

Several dozen sailors, wearing Service Dress White uniforms, sit at tables. At the opposite end of the dinning area, several officers in Service Dress Whites sit with women adorned in light-colored summer dresses. At the table in front of the officers, a cleric in religious clothing sets a bible, some cards, and two candles on the table. At a table behind the officer's table, five chief petty officers in their Service Dress Whites chat casually. Several women, equally adorned in light-colored summer dresses, sit next to some of the chiefs.

Dottie and Angie Caldwell sit with a navy commander and a late-thirties looking woman at a table that is clearly set aside from the others.

Rigney recognizes Commander Caldwell, the commanding officer, from the pictures displayed at the quarterdeck.

Rigney assumes the older woman is Angie's mother, Dottie's aunt by marriage, Commander Caldwell's wife.

Dottie chats with Angie and did not notice Rigney enter the galley.

Most of the sailors and several officers, including Eric, steal lusty and longing stares at Dottie and Angie.

Rigney studies the cleric who converses with the officers. The cleric's pale complexion and short hair cause Rigney to conclude the cleric is a military chaplain.

Then, silence falls over the galley as the officers, the Caldwell women, and the chaplain look at Commander Caldwell.

"Just a moment, Chaplain," Commander Caldwell orders. He stands, crosses the galley, and confers with QM1 Latham.

All eyes follow the commander. Dottie now sees Rigney; she smiles at him, a smile that conveys recognition, remembrance, appreciation, devilishness, and a secret that only Dottie and Rigney share. Her dress is crisp and fresh. However, her appearance betrays a night of little sleep.

Commander Caldwell and Latham discuss the list of names.

Latham departs the galley.

Caldwell returns to his table. "Chaplain, please proceed," Commander Caldwell directs.

The chaplain opens the bible and advises, "I will start this morning's service with a quote from Luke, chapter 3, *'Every valley shall be filled, and every mountain and hill shall be brought low, and the crooked shall be made straight, and the rough ways shall be made smooth . . . And all flesh shall see the salvation of God' . . .* "

Rigney whispers to Karzack, "What's with the list?"

"Latham wrote down the names of those he saw in the barracks. He scratches their names off the list if they show-up here. Latham's goin' to the barracks to find those still on the list."

"What will he do when he finds them?"

"Question them on why they didn't go to church. Then, he'll report back to the captain."

Rigney stares out the window and watches the duty master-at-arms walk across the parking lot toward the enlisted barracks.

"... *'And the soldiers likewise demanded of him, saying, 'And what shall we do?' And he said unto them, 'Do violence to no man, neither accuse any falsely, and be content with your wages'*..."

Victor notices Rigney staring out the window. He looks out the window in the same direction. He leans toward Rigney, cups his hand to his mouth, and says in a low voice that only Rigney can hear, "I feel sorry for any sailors that Latham finds in the barracks."

Rigney turns his head away from the window and watches the chaplain.

"... *'and now also the axe is laid unto the root of the trees: every tree therefore which bringeth not forth good fruit is hewn down, and cast into the fire'*..."

Then, Rigney totally blocks out the chaplain's words and all other noises around him as he remembers the completely satisfying sex he had with Dottie last night. They had engaged in five separate sex acts. The last being a pleasurable surprise when Dottie gave him a blowjob. His penis enlarges as he visualizes his remembrance of her head bobbing up and down as she sucked on him.

Rigney returns to the present, and the chaplain's sermon penetrates his thoughts.

"Luke teaches us ... *'what we earn in life is by the grace of God, and we should be satisfied with that. We must earn honestly and betray no one during our quest to earn'*..."

Movement outside redirects Rigney's attention, and he looks out the window. Three sailors dash out the door of the enlisted barracks; they pull on shirts and pants as they dash across the parking lot. Rigney watches with amusement as they jump into a station wagon automobile and lower themselves beneath the windows.

Three seconds later, Latham rushes through the doorway; He stops on the sidewalk and scans the area. He shrugs his shoulders in bewilderment.

Rigney chuckles softly, shakes his head slightly, and glances over at Victor to see if Victor saw the comedy.

Victor stares, mesmerized, at the chaplain as the chaplain raises his voice to make a point.

" . . . *'I came not to call the righteous, but sinners to repentance . . . And they said unto him, 'Why do the disciples of John fast often, and make prayers, and likewise the disciples of the Pharisees, but thine eat and drink?' . . . And he said unto them, 'Can ye make the children of the bride chamber fast, while the bridegroom is with them? . . . But the days will come, when the bridegroom shall be taken away from them, and then shall they fast in those days' . . . And he spake also a parable unto them. No man putteth a piece of a new garment upon an old. If otherwise, then both the new maketh a rent, and the piece that was taken out of the new agreeth not with the old' . . .*"

Rigney watches Latham walk across the parking lot toward the galley. A few moments later, he hears the door open behind him and the shuffling of feet.

When church service ends, Rigney is the first out the galley door. He steps quickly along the sidewalk and stops where the sidewalk meets the parking lot. He knows that Dottie must walk past him, and he wants to chat.

Dottie exits the galley behind her uncle and aunt. She talks with Angie. She stares at Rigney.

Dottie whispers something to Angie; then, she stops next to Rigney. She glances sideways toward her aunt and uncle who walk away in the direction of the Caldwell's navy sedan.

When the CO and his wife are out of hearing range, Dottie speaks softly to Rigney, "I didn't expect to see you in church. Last night you said you don't go to church. Anyway, this gives me another chance to say how much I enjoyed last night. I thought about canceling my trip to the Greek Islands so I could spend more time with you, but the tour is all set, and I paid for it already. Sorry."

"No need to be sorry," Rigney replies with an understanding tone. "You may never get the chance again to tour the Greek Islands. I will do it myself once I get settled here."

"Okay. I am looking forward to spending some time with you when I get back," Dottie says with a seductive look in her eye. Then, she glances over to where the CO stands next to his vehicle, which is fifty feet away.

The CO gives Dottie a disapproving look and motions for her to come.

"I must go now." She walks off.

Rigney stares after her as she walks across the parking lot. Her walk has an emphasized swing to her hips, and Rigney knows it is for his benefit.

Rigney turns and walks toward the barracks; his meeting with his ONI contact is at 1:00 PM.

"Hey, Rig, hold up a minute."

Rigney stops and waits for Victor to catch up with him.

Victor stops less than six inches from Rigney and whispers, "Did ya see any guys runnin' out of the barracks durin' church?"

"No."

"Latham can't account for three of the guys on the list."

A quizzical expression crosses Rigney's face as he asks, "What is the captain trying to do?"

"The best way to explain it is to tell you what the captain and I did one Sunday when I had duty MAA. Do ya wanna hear it?"

Rigney glances at his watch, then, says, "Go ahead."

"The captain and me found about a dozen guys in the barracks. Some of the sailors were sleepin' and some were playing cards. Well, most of them are Jewish, and I think two of them are Muslims, ya know, that religion in Arabia. Anyway, the cap'n yelled at them for not goin' to church. A few of them tol' the captain that Sunday is not their holyday. Well, the captain got mad and called them heathens. The cap'n had me write down their names. A couple of guys who were in their racks heard the captain coming, and they grabbed their clothes and ran outta the barracks."

Rigney lowers his head and slightly shakes his head in disapproval. He chuckles.

"Not funny, Rig! Those guys are in real trouble if the cap'n ever finds out who they are."

Rigney prefers not to be one who voluntarily points out illogical thinking by others, but he has come to like Victor Karzack. Rigney wants Victor to understand that Commander Caldwell is the one who is in trouble should anyone file a complaint. "Victor, you do understand that Commander Caldwell violates his authority by pushing his personal philosophies on those he commands? He can be relieved of command for such behavior."

Victor stares seriously and confidently into Rigney's eyes as he explains. "He's the cap'n. We must do what he says. He leads us, and we are required to follow. Navy regs are clear on that. Besides, he's doin' the right thing by tryin' to get those sailors believin' in Jesus. If they don't start believin' in Jesus Christ, they'll all go to hell when they die. You know that, Rig. Everyone knows that."

Rigney remains silent and stares doubtfully at Karzack.

"Too bad about the weights, though," Karzack says.

"What about the weights?"

"QM1 Latham told me that when he told the captain he found some sailors lifting weights, the captain ordered all weights and exercise equipment removed from the barracks."

Rigney's expression changes to bewilderment.

"See ya later. Master chief wants to see me in his office." Victor turns and walks toward the administrative building.

Chapter 28

Karen Drescher, codename Anna Heisler, walks onto the Nea Makri beach; she scans the area for Rigney Page. She does not see him, but she is thirty minutes early for their 1300 rendezvous. She walks across a small strip of sand to the Café Konstantina. She steps up to the café's outside patio, and selects a table in a corner near the sand. Her location allows full view of the patio. She removes her sun hat to soak up the sun and feel the Aegean breeze. Somewhere close, traditional Greek music flows from a radio.

The café, known as *The Blue Lights* to the Nea Makri sailors, caters to both locals and tourists. Sailors from the NAVCOMMSTA frequent *The Blue Lights* daily. They call it *The Blue Lights* because at night the outside bright-blue neon lights are seen for miles on the beach.

As always happens when she comes to the beach, sailors from the base attempt to pick her up. She notices many young men from the navy base staring at her. Within a few minutes, they will approach her and start feeding her their lines.

The attention she gets from these young men bewilders her. *They are early twenties and I am thirty-one. There are plenty of pretty women on the beach more their age. Maybe they think I am an easier conquest. Maybe they think I am better in bed, because I am experienced.*

Anyway, Anna continues to turn them down, but they keep trying. During the last week, their seductive tactics became bolder. Therefore, her rejections were harshly rude. In some cases, she had to become insulting so they better understood rejection.

Anna recognizes Rigney as soon as he steps onto the café patio. She observes that he is much more rugged and good looking than his photograph portrays. *My god, look at all that body hair.*

Rigney wears tennis shorts and a tight t-shirt to show off his hard-muscled athletic build. A coat of reddish brown hair covers him from neck to ankles, which causes people to stare.

He notices Anna's location in the patio corner. He sits several tables away from her. He looks toward the blue water of the Aegean. The sun shines over a partially clouded sky. A light and humid breeze carrying the smells of the sea reminds him of his love for the beach.

Obeying his instructions, he pulls from his beach bag a book titled *The Reign of Charlemagne*; he opens it to the bookmarked page. Now, Anna must make the next move that causes them to meet accidentally.

A tall broad-shouldered man in a gray-colored boxer-style bathing suit and a gray-colored t-shirt approaches Anna's table. Rigney recognizes him as Eric, the linebacker, from yesterday at the Club Zeus, the one who bothered Dottie about not going to some person's party. He listens to their conversation.

"Hello, Anna."

"Hello, Eric," Anna responds unenthusiastically and with a thick German accent.

"Mind if I sit here?" requests Eric, eyes begging.

"If you wish, but I am leaving in a few minutes."

"Next Friday night, the American club in Kifissia is hosting a dance. Would you like to go with me?"

When Anna first arrived in Nea Makri and started visiting the beach, she overheard some European women talking about Eric. They would point him out. Eric spends a lot of time at the Nea Makri beach with the goal of picking up women. The European women advised her not to go out with him. They said, "The first time alone with him, he is all over you, physically." They said that Eric is full of himself, and he believes that all women want sex with him. They said Eric thought he could easily seduce women, because of his good looks and overwhelming strength. "Fortunately," they said, "He is civilized enough to back off after a woman issues a strong no, but not until you have put up a strong fight against his strength."

Anna sighs in resignation and responds, "No, Eric. I told you before I don't want to go out with you. I am not looking for a summer romance. I want a relaxing summer with no bothers and no obligations."

"But, Anna, I thought—"

"I must go now, Eric."

Anna stands and walks toward Rigney's table.

Eric watches after her with bewildered thoughts about how getting dates has become more difficult lately. He frowns with disapproval when he sees Anna stop by the table of the sailor that Dottie was with in the Club Zeus yesterday afternoon.

"Excuse me. You are interested in European history, yes?" Anna maintains her strong German accent.

"Yes, I am. Are you?" Rigney responds.

"Yes, I am German. You are American?"

"Yes, I am an American."

"I think it good that you want to know about European history. What do you find most interesting about Charlemagne?" Anna sits down next to Rigney.

Rigney read most of the book on the flight from the United States, so that he would be able to talk about the subject when Anna asked.

They exchange views on Charlemagne. They maintain a normal volume. Those tourists, Greeks, and American sailors who watch believe they have witnessed a chance meeting.

As they discuss Charlemagne, Anna stares with admiration at Rigney, and he returns admiring looks whenever Anna reveals a little-known historic fact. Those who watch believe they witness a budding romance.

Eric's ego gets the better of him. Recognizing Rigney from the day before, he becomes offended and envious. He is not jealous, because he feels nothing for the women he attempts to seduce. Anna pretended she must leave, but then goes to his table. Eric becomes angered as he notices the amused expressions on the faces of the sailors who stare at him. He stands and walks back to his blanket on the beach.

After fifteen minutes of discussion, Anna offers, "I have rare books on German history at my villa. Would you like to see them?"

"Yes, I would," Rigney replies enthusiastically.

Anna stands and walks toward the street. Rigney grabs his beach bag and follows Anna off the café patio.

At least a dozen sailors from the NAVCOMMSTA witnessed the exchange between Rigney and Anna. All of them believe it was a chance meeting.

Eric's blood boils. *Who is he?!*

Chapter 29

"How far is it?" Rigney asks Anna, referring to the distance to the field office—her villa.

"About half a kilometer up the hill on the other side of the Marathon Road." Anna points to the west.

Twenty minutes later, they stand at a large ornate wrought-iron driveway gate. As Anna searches her bag for keys, Rigney surveys the area. A ten feet high by three feet thick stone wall surrounds the grounds. The property sits on a thirty-degree grade. The multi story white stucco villa with red tiled roof cuts into the hillside. The ten feet high stone wall unevenly hugs the grade. The grade allows Rigney to see the top half of the villa and the grounds leading to the west wall. He can see beyond the west wall to the grade that leads up Mount Penteli.

He hears children laughing and speaking loud in English. Across the street, children run back and forth between two yards, playing. Adults sit in lounge chairs in both yards. The American automobiles parked in the carports reveal the residents to be NAVCOMMSTA sailors and their dependents.

Anna unlocks the gate, and they enter the courtyard. Inside the courtyard on a gravel driveway sits a red BMW convertible. They cross the gravel driveway and walk up several stone steps to the villa's front door.

Anna unlocks the heavy solid-wood front door, and they enter the villa. Just inside the front door, a light flashes on the alarm system. She flips several switches, and the light extinguishes. She advises, "I turned-off the windows and doors alarm so we can open them and allow a breeze to flow through. The front gate and wall alarms are still activated."

Anna walks through all rooms and opens all the floor-to-ceiling wood-frame, glass courtyard doors, allowing a humid breeze to flow throughout the villa.

Ceramic tile covers all floors, which aids in keeping the entire villa cool.

Anna leads Rigney to the end of the hallway where an eight feet high by four feet wide bookcase stands against the wall. Anna pulls on a book, and the right side of the bookcase swings toward them, like an opening door. The bookcase hides a door. Anna opens the door, and Rigney follows her through the doorway.

The narrow room is fifteen feet long by six feet wide. "It's a live-in maid's room," Anna advises. "Most large villas have them. The ONI installation team rigged all this to provide a hidden communications room." Anna loses her German accent.

Rigney looks around the room. Thick dark-blue colored carpet provides soundproofing for the floor. Two-inch thick soundproofing tiles cover the walls and ceiling. Portable communications equipment stands against one wall. He recognizes the radio equipment as the same he learned during his initial indoctrination in Washington. In addition to voice and CW Morse code capability, the equipment includes a radio teletype configuration with online Orestes cryptographic coverage. *I won't have any problems operating this equipment.*

She points to a small safe anchored to the side of the equipment rack. "The voice codebooks and the key lists for the Orestes are in there. I will give you the combination later."

A wardrobe cabinet stands against the wall farthest from the door. She opens the wardrobe doors, revealing two XM-21 sniper rifles, two .45 automatics, two 9 millimeter Beretta automatic pistols, and a dozen boxes of ammunition. Rigney also notices that two silencers for the Berettas and one silencer for the XM-21 rest on a cushion on the bottom shelf.

They exit the communications room. Anna shows Rigney how to operate the bookcase.

"I'll show you how to operate the security system."

Three control devices for the security system are mounted on the wall next to the front door. Anna explains, "The device on the left senses all the doors and windows. When activated, the alarm will sound when any of the windows or doors open. There is a fifteen-second delay on the front door alarm. When you enter the villa, always enter through the front door. You have fifteen seconds to reset the alarm before it sounds. The device in the middle senses motion at the courtyard gate, and only needs to be activated when we are in here. The device on the right senses motion on the top of the wall that surrounds the villa. There are alarm repeaters in the living room, all bedrooms, and in the communications room. Always have the security system activated."

Rigney nods his head to indicate his understanding.

"Go ahead and look around," Anna offers. "I will get us some ice water."

Rigney's technical curiosity sends him on a search for the radio antennas. He walks into the backyard. The inclined ground between the villa and the west wall allows him to stand level with the villa's roof. He stands higher than the east wall that runs in front of the villa. He looks down on the town of Nea Makri and beyond to the dark blue of the Aegean Sea. He easily views the receiver antenna fields of the NAVCOMMSTA that lay several miles to the north. He notes that nearly all buildings in town are white with a red-tiled roof.

He walks the perimeter of the stone wall that surrounds the villa grounds. He does not discover the antennas for the radio equipment. He walks to the west wall and looks to the roof of the villa. No antennas there.

As he steps through a tall patio doorway and into the villa's living room, Anna enters with a tray topped with a pitcher of ice water and two glasses.

She sets the tray on the coffee table and pours water into both glasses.

"I'm curious. Where are the antennas for the radio equipment?"

Anna moves to the center of the living room and points through the courtyard doors. Rigney comes to her side and looks to the direction her finger points.

"That's the antenna for the transmitter."

"The clothes line?"

"Yes. If you look closely, you can see the transmission line and the insulators."

"Now that you point them out, Yes, I see them . . . awesome camouflage."

"Standard configuration for field offices," Anna states flatly. "The antenna for the receiver is on the roof and is disguised as electrical wires and telephone lines."

"Ingenious," Rigney responds.

"We have a scheduled communications period at 1500," Anna advises. "I was directed to give you refresher training on the radio equipment. I was also told that you are to perform the communications procedures at 1500 today."

For the next hour, Anna steps Rigney through radio equipment setup and antenna tuning. Rigney remembers most of it from previous experience and has it memorized on the second go-through.

During the thirty minutes prior to the scheduled communications, Rigney reviews the communications procedure manual.

During the communications period, Rigney performs all functions flawlessly. Only one message is addressed to Apollo, and it is encoded. Rigney uses the ONI codebook and within a few minutes decodes the message.

"It's from Brad Watson," Rigney tells Anna. "He congratulates me on successfully communicating with ONI."

"That's it?" Anna questions.

"Yeah."

Anna shrugs her shoulders and orders, "Put all the equipment in standby. Then, come to the living room."

Rigney does as ordered. He finds Anna sitting on the couch, reading a book.

"Now what?" Rigney asks.

She looks up from her book and says, "You stay here through the night. I have made up the second bedroom for you. I will drive you to the base tomorrow morning to arrive at the gate at 0745. That time should give us maximum visibility to those going to work at the base."

Rigney comments, "To enhance our cover that we have become a couple, right?"

"That's correct," Anna confirms.

Rigney stands in the middle of the living room and looks around as he tries to decide how to occupy his time.

"You could actually read that book on Charlemagne," Anna suggests.

"I've read most of it already. I will finish it."

He retrieves the book from his beach bag and sits in an overstuffed chair on the other side of the room from Anna.

Anna returns to her book. After a few minutes, she pauses her reading and watches Rigney over the top of her book. She observes that he appears engrossed in the reading of the book. She wonders about Brad Watson's confidence in Rigney Page. She remembers her doubts when Brad Watson briefed her and told her Rigney's age and navy rank.

Chapter 30

Anna was a twenty-six year old navy lieutenant when ONI first attempted to recruit her. She had served four years as an intelligence officer on the staff of Commander-in-Chief Allied Forces Central Europe. Her quality assessments and predictions of East German Navy and Soviet Navy activities in the Baltic Sea and North Sea came to the attention of the DNI, Director of Naval Intelligence. Her fluency in English, German, and Dutch gave her an edge that her peers did not have. The DNI, a navy admiral, offered her a four-year tour on his staff.

At first, she declined the DNI's offer. She was at the end of her military obligation, and she had her fill of the sexually harassing environment that her commanders permitted. Her constant defense against the barrage of verbal and physical harassment drained her strength and enthusiasm for her work. The barrage came from American officers and officers of other NATO nations, many of them married. Her immediate superior, a married West German Navy captain, constantly pushed himself on her. She constantly refused him. Fortunately, he never physically touched her or threatened her because of her refusals. The crude jokes and pats on the butt from the male officers demonstrated complete disrespect for her as a woman and as a naval officer.

She complained to her U.S. Navy advisor, a U.S. Navy captain assigned to a different branch of the NATO staff. He advised Anna not to complain. He told her that she must adjust to the way men are. He told her that she did the correct thing by refusing their advances. He advised her, "That's the way it is with men and women. Men pursue and it's up to the women to say no."

She declined DNI's initial offer. She told him that she was leaving the navy, and she told him why. The DNI then offered her a position as a civilian analyst. She quickly informed the DNI that it made no difference if she were military or civilian. She advised him that sexual harassment exists in the military because senior officers allow it to exist. DNI assured her that the navy recently initiated programs to eliminate sexual harassment and that he had integrated those programs into his organization. He promised her that his door was open to her at anytime to report instances of sexual harassment.

She countered with a proposal that she would come to work as a field operative stationed in Europe and with the understanding that the first instance of sexual harassment toward her would result in harsh punishment by DNI to the offender, regardless of the offender's rank or position. The DNI agreed.

That was five year ago. During those five years, she never saw or heard of anyone as young as Rigney recruited as a field operative. She informed Brad Watson that she was concerned about Rigney's lack of training and lack of experience. Brad quelled her concerns by telling her that what Rigney lacks in training and experience he equalized with resourcefulness and with being physically picture-perfect for his cover. After meeting Rigney, Anna had to agree. If she were attempting to identify an American counterespionage operative, she would immediately dismiss Rigney because of his age and his conspicuous manner.

Chapter 31

Rigney closes the book titled *The Reign of Charlemagne*. He looks at the couch. Anna is not there. He had not noticed that she exited the room. He looks at his watch—1730. He stands and goes in search of the bathroom.

After using the hall bathroom, he searches each room for Anna. He finds her in the master bedroom, peaking through the curtains. Her back is to him. She has changed her clothes and now wears shorts and a tight halter, which shows off her perfectly formed body. The shape of her body arouses him. Until now, Rigney had not thought of her as a sexual partner.

Anna senses Rigney in the room. She looks over her shoulder and gestures for him to come to the window; then, she returns to staring out the window.

Rigney goes to the window and stands directly behind her. She turns abruptly, not expecting Rigney to be so close. She bumps up against him, face to face, both pushed off balance. They grab onto each other to steady themselves.

Rigney feels the firmness of her body and the scent of her perfume. He inhales sharply as sexual anticipation flows through his body.

Anna feels Rigney's large rock-hard biceps. She inhales sharply as sexual warmth flows through her body. She looks into his eyes and sees his desire.

He looks into her eyes and sees her desire.

Then, knowing that they should not continue, they release their hold on each other. They lower their hands and at the same time back away from each other. Both breathe heavily.

After a short awkward silence, Rigney says, "You called me over."

She still looks into his eyes. Sexual desire captures her senses. She knows that Rigney just spoke, and she understands his words, but she cannot respond. After a few seconds, the sexual hold on her senses dissipates, and she responds, "Yes, look out the window at the white sedan across the street."

Rigney steps to the window and slightly parts the curtains. He sees the white sedan and Eric sitting in the driver's seat. He closes the curtain and turns toward Anna. "That Eric, is he violent? I mean, do you think he wants to harm me?"

"I don't know. Why would he want to?"

"You're the second woman in two days that rejected him to be with me."

"Who is the other woman?"

"Dottie Caldwell. She's the niece of the NAVCOMMSTA commanding officer."

"I know who she is. Dottie and her cousin, Angie, frequent *The Blue Lights*. Eric is always bothering Dottie. He doesn't bother with Angie, because she is the CO's daughter."

"What's this Eric's problem?" Rigney asks.

"He's arrogant and full of himself. He was a football hero at the University of Ohio. He has no respect for anyone, especially women. He sees women only as sexual objects to conquer. Dottie and the other women at the beach know that."

"University of Ohio. I guess he's an officer, huh?"

"You didn't know that?"

"No. He doesn't act like one."

Anna Challenges, "You haven't been around the navy much, have you?"

Anna's challenge sparks Rigney's curiosity. "Are you an officer?" Rigney hopes not, because that would complicate the physical attraction they have for each other.

Anna looks into Rigney's face while she considers if she should tell him something about her background.

"No, not anymore. That part of my life is behind me."

Rigney feels the urge to press for clarification. "So, you're a civilian then?"

"Yes, of course. What do you . . ." She pauses as she attempts to grasp the purpose of his questions. Then, the purpose becomes clear to her. *He worries about going to bed with me and me being an officer. Well, he has some respect for navy regulations.* Anna is impressed. "No, Rigney," she responds with an understanding smile. "I am not an officer, not in the reserves, not in the military."

Rigney nods his head and expresses relief.

Anna parts the curtains slightly and looks out.

Rigney asks, "Do you think he might come in here?"

"He'd better not. I will shoot him if he does," Anna says flatly, without emotion.

Rigney wonders if Anna is serious.

"I think I will load the Berettas," Anna states as she turns from the window and departs the bedroom.

Rigney follows her into the communications room. He watches her open the wardrobe cabinet. She picks up a Beretta and verifies the magazine loaded. She pulls back the side and lets it slam forward. She verifies the safety is set. Then she screws on a silencer. Then, she performs the same actions on the other Beretta. Her actions are fluid and flawless. Rigney thinks that she must have done this many times before.

Anna turns and sees that Rigney watches her with fascination. She states, "I understand that the nine-millimeter Beretta is your weapon of choice."

Rigney wonders if she knows that he has killed with a Beretta. "Yes, I am experienced with the nine-millimeter Beretta."

"Good. Keep this one in your nightstand." She hands Rigney one of the Berettas. "I'll keep this one in my nightstand."

"Okay," Rigney responds.

Anna orders, "If Eric busts in here, shoot him."

"What!" Rigney spurts incredulously.

Anna looks questioningly at Rigney and says, "Now, neither one of us are going to invite him in here, are we?"

"Uh . . . no," Rigney responds, not certain of Anna's point.

"So, if he forces his way in here, just what do you think his intentions will be? Or, do you think you can have a manly fistfight with him and everything will be okay after that?"

Rigney nods his understanding. "No problem, Anna. If he gets in here, I will shoot him."

"I should hope so."

He does not know what to say. He stares at her.

"Don't be surprised that I know. Do you think Brad Watson would team you with me and not fully brief me on your capabilities, your strengths, and your weaknesses?"

He flinches, blinks his eyes, and asks in a meek tone, "What weaknesses?"

Anna rolls her eyes.

Rigney ponders all of what Anna has revealed. He understands the wisdom and necessity of Brad briefing Anna on everything. *Makes sense.*

"Did Brad tell you about my last mission?"

"Yes, and we should not discuss it."

"Agreed, should not be discussed."

"Any questions?"

Rigney stands thoughtfully for a few moments then responds, "Since you've been briefed on me, then you know I have not gone through the full ONI course. So, I don't know a lot about procedures and all."

"Like what?"

"Well, if we do shoot Eric, what do we do with the body?"

An amused smile appears on Anna's face as she answers, "I get on the radio and call in a disposal team."

Rigney has more questions, like, what if someone sees Eric come in the villa and then he comes up missing? He decides to stow his questions for a later time.

"I will show you frequencies and procedures for calling in a disposal team."

Eric sits in his car and stares at the gate to Anna's villa. *Now what?* He asks himself. He does not know why he drove to Anna's villa. *Frustration, maybe?*

After Anna and Rigney left the beach, Eric listened to the conversations of the other sailors. He learned Page's name. He also heard the roving rumor that Page and Dottie had a late-night rendezvous.

Eric thinks back to yesterday when he saw Page beat up on Jeff Martin. Instead of acting like an officer and taking charge of the situation, he departed the club quickly. He knew his duty was to take charge, but he was uncertain as to what he should do. He also worried that Page may turn on him, and he would be additionally embarrassed if he could not put Page down. Additionally, he did not want the CO to find out that he was in the club pursuing his niece. *Page is making me look bad.*

Women are rejecting me. The rejections have been in public, like with Dottie yesterday and Anna today. They both rejected me to be with Page! With his male pride damaged and his self-assurance lowered, he considers whom to blame and whom to punish.

If I go busting into Anna's house, then what? Is that what I want to do? This is crazy!

Eric starts up the car and drives off.

Chapter 32

Rigney and Anna sit in the living room, talk, and become more acquainted. He slouches on an overstuffed armchair. She sits across the room and sits upright on the couch. Rigney tells Anna about his life in Southern California. He speaks of his love for surfing and scuba diving. He informs her about his submarine training and his extensive training in electronics and radio communications. He skips over this ONI recruitment and subsequent mission aboard the USS *Columbus*. He does tell her about his five months aboard the USS *Barb*.

"Working and living aboard a nuclear-powered submarine was much different than I expected—no adventure and no glamour. It was all long hours and knuckle-busting, knee-scraping, elbow-bruising hard work. Liberty ports were cancelled most of the time."

"You object to hard work?" Anna asks.

"No, not at all. It's just that submarine duty was a disappointment after so many years of anxious anticipation. It was my quest for five years I think back to all those adventures told to me by submariners when I was a boy. I think a submariner's life changed drastically when nuclear-powered submarines came along."

"So you won't be going back to submarines," Anna concludes.

"I don't know. I sure would like to earn those dolphins."

"Dolphins?"

"It's a warfare pin that you wear over your medals to indicate that you have qualified in submarines."

"Yes, I have heard of it," Anna responds.

"Anyway, after this mission, I must decide to stay with ONI or go back to an ordinary navy life. If I turn-down Brad Watson's offer to join ONI full-time, he will never ask again."

"Appears to me you are looking for something other than a routine navy life."

"I am. I still have some time to make up my mind."

"What makes you hesitate? Seems to me that ONI provides you with what you are looking for."

Rigney wants to change the subject. "What did you do in the navy, and when was that?"

"I worked on a NATO staff as an intelligence officer. That was 1958 through 1962."

"Did you like it? Why didn't you stay in the navy?" Rigney is genuinely interested.

"I enjoyed the work, but not my working environment," Anna responds negatively with her eyes showing that her mind relives unpleasant experiences.

"What didn't you like about it?"

Anna does not want to share her navy experience with Rigney. "Like you, I was disappointed to discover that it was not what I expected. I do not like to talk about it."

A rumble comes from Rigney's stomach. He looks at his watch—1845. "I'm hungry. Shall we have dinner?"

"Sure," Anna says as she stands. "I'll bake the fish. You can make the salad."

"Do you drink wine?" Anna asks Rigney as she places several large filets of white fish on Rigney's plate.

"Yes, but I don't drink it often."

Anna retrieves a bottle of pale-colored wine from the refrigerator and sets it on the table. "This is the traditional Greek wine. It's called Retsina, should be served chilled."

Anna reaches for two wineglasses on a wine rack and sets one in front of each of them. Rigney pulls the cork and pours each of them half of a glass.

Later, Rigney falls asleep quickly. Three days of constant activity including travel and sporadic sleep, followed by several glasses of wine, provide a powerful sleeping agent.

Chapter 33

Anna stops her red colored BMW convertible directly across the road from the NAVCOMMSTA main gate.

At 0740 on a Monday morning, the main gate is busy with sailors and civilian workers going to work after the weekend. Whether they drive or walk, they all pause to get a good look at the couple sitting in the red convertible. Many of those entering the main gate recognize Anna from the beach. None of them recognizes the young man who sits with her.

"We're getting a lot of attention," Rigney comments.

"It's 0745. You need to get in there and change into your uniform and be wherever you're supposed to be at 0800."

"I just start my check-in this morning. No one gave me a specific time."

"Impress them by being there first thing like a good swabby should." Anna's tone conveys sarcasm.

"Okay, when do we meet again?"

"Next time that you can leave the base, walk to my villa. Use your keys and be obvious about it if people are watching. If I'm not there, make yourself at home."

"Okay, sounds good," Rigney says as he reaches for the door handle.

"Before you get out of the car, you must kiss me."

Rigney raises a brow as he turns toward her.

"For the audience," she clarifies.

Rigney leans toward Anna. She leans toward him. Over the gearshift, their lips meet. The kiss is lingering with their eyes closed, but the kiss is not passionate. Anna is the first to pull away.

Rigney enters the main gate and takes the short walk to his barracks where he changes into a fresh Tropical White Long uniform.

Several minutes later, he walks onto the quarterdeck in the administration building. BM2 Karzack sits at a back desk.

"Page. Where the hell have you been? The master chief has been lookin' for ya since yesterday."

"I've been off base since yesterday morning."

"The master chief wants to see ya in his office."

One minute later, Rigney knocks on Master Chief Crimer's door.

"Enter."

Rigney removes his white hat and enters.

"Page, who gave you authorization to leave the base?" Master Chief Crimer appears angry.

Rigney wonders what is wrong. No one, including Master Chief Crimer, ordered him to stay on the base. "No one said I couldn't," Rigney replies with an even tone.

Master Chief Crimer pauses and searches his memory. He attempts to remember when he ordered Page not to leave the base. He thinks back to when Page and Vance were in his office on Saturday afternoon. "Well, no matter now," Crimer advises with a calmer manner and tone.

"What happen with Mr. Martin and his wife?" Rigney asks.

A solemn manner overcomes the master chief as he explains, "You were right about that. The air force police got to the Martin residence fifteen minutes before I got there. They had him in handcuffs. According to their report, they found Mr. Martin beating his wife when they arrived. It took three air force policemen to subdue him. They had to beat him with nightsticks to get him to submit. Both Mr. Martin and his wife are in the hospital at the air base. There is a twenty-four hour watch on Mr. Martin."

"What about the little girl?"

The captain has her staying with them.

"I am not in trouble about all this, then?" Rigney asks with a concerned tone.

"I don't know about that, Page. I still have some investigating to do."

"What do I do now?"

"One more question. The main gate logged you coming back on base at 0420 Sunday morning. Where were you?"

"Not saying, no one's business but mine."

"You're wrong about that, Page. You're on overseas duty. Your commanding officer is responsible for your conduct, and, therefore, has the authority and responsibility to know your location at all times."

Page shakes his head and says, "Master Chief, you can ask me all day long where I was, and I won't tell you. So, is there anything else?"

"This is not the end of it, Page. For now, you can check in. Go see the personnelman. He will give you a check-in sheet. Check back with me this afternoon."

The personnelman tells Rigney to follow the order of the check-in sheet. "The order follows the chain-of-command. You get all the administrative stuff done first. Then, you see all the senior officers last. You must make an appointment to see the XO and CO. I'll make those appointments for you. Contact me later this morning, I'll tell ya when your appointments are."

Rigney makes his way around the administration building and checks in with personnel, disbursing, medical, and master-at-arms. Next on the list is his the communications officer.

"Where do I find the communications officer?" Rigney asks BM2 Karzack.

"Go out the front door of this building and take a left. Then turn left on the road and follow the road down to the communications trailers compound, about a quarter of a mile down that road, can't miss it. There's a small cinderblock building inside the compound. That's the communications office."

Chapter 34

The hot Mediterranean sun causes Rigney to sweat as he walks along the narrow roughly constructed macadam road. Dark patches of sweat appear under his arms. Several cars pass him in the opposite direction. All the drivers wear Tropical White Long uniforms and wave to Rigney as they pass.

As he walks along the road, Rigney studies the antennas. He recognizes rhombic, dipole, and log-periodic designs from his radioman 3 and 2 course book.

He approaches the communications trailer compound. A twelve feet high fence, topped with barbed wire, surrounds the compound, which includes the communications trailers and a small block building. A gate through the fence stands open. An unmanned guard shack sits just inside the gate.

He enters the compound and turns right toward the block building. He opens the door to the block building and steps inside. Cold air from a wall unit cools him. Rigney stands in a small outer office. A third class petty officer sits behind a battered old wooden desk. The nameplate on the desk reads CYN3 Hatcher. Rigney recognizes him as one of the bitchers and complainers on Saturday in the Club Zeus.

Hatcher looks up as Rigney enters. He expresses recognition and asks, "You checkin' in?"

Rigney nods in the affirmative and hands his check-in sheet to Hatcher.

"Lieutenant Lemont is in his office. Let me ask him if he will see you now."

CYN3 Hatcher walks to a door six feet behind his desk. He knocks and then enters.

Taking advantage of Hatcher's absence, Rigney scans the small office. The walls are rough cinderblock. A calendar and a communications department organization chart hang on the wall. Rigney notes the name and rank of the OIC Transmitter Site at Kato

Souli, which lay to the north. He also eyes a box with distribution slots, and he notes one slot labeled RMCM Rodgers.

"The lieutenant will see you now," CYN3 Hatcher informs.

Rigney removes his cover and steps through the doorway into the office of the communications officer. He quickly scans the office. The office looks neat and organized. A small six-chair conference table stands in the middle. Whiteboards full of writing hang on the walls around the room. The whiteboards contain dates and timelines for projects and priorities.

"Take a seat, Page," says the medium-height and medium-build officer who wears a Tropical White Long uniform.

Rigney notes that the officer's desk is as neat and organized as the rest of the office.

While Lieutenant Lemont reviews Rigney's check-in sheet, Rigney scans some of the lieutenant's memorabilia. Several items in the office reveal that Lieutenant Lemont is a limited duty officer—ex-enlisted, mustang.

Lemont looks up from the check-in sheet and asks, "What was your last command?"

"USS *Barb*, sir."

"That's a submarine, isn't it?"

"Yes."

Lieutenant Lemont bows his head and puts his hand to his chin. After a few moments of thought, he asks, "How long were you on the *Barb*?"

"Eight months, sir."

The officer's expression turns to one of confusion; he asks, "How is it that you transferred here after only eight months?"

"I was medically disqualified from submarines."

The lieutenant bows his head, puts his hand to his chin, and expresses thoughtfulness.

Rigney waits patiently for the officer's next action.

"Don't suppose you have any training or experience in crypto equipment repair?"

"Yes sir. I am qualified to repair Jason, Orestes, and Adonis cryptographic equipment."

"Any KW-26 repair experience?"

"No sir."

"Are you a technician of any other equipment?"

"Yes sir, antenna repair, radio repair, and teletype repair. I've graduated from all the schools."

"Well, I have plenty of teletype repairmen, and public works department takes care of antenna maintenance. What receivers can you repair?"

"R-1051 and R-390."

The COMMO stares at Page with doubtful eyes.

"Any other equipment you can repair?"

"URA-8 and URA-17."

Lieutenant Lemont gauges Rigney's age and wonders how a sailor with only three years in the navy could have attended so many repair courses. He asks, "What about operational experience . . . message processing or CW?"

"Yes, sir, I can do both of those, too."

Rigney sees doubt in the lieutenant's expression; he explains, "All those courses are part of the submarine radioman school. On submarines we must do it all."

The lieutenant's expression turns from doubt to understanding and then to appreciation. "Of all your skills, what are you best at?"

"I think electronic repair, especially crypto repair."

"We are shorthanded in crypto repair. I am considering assigning you to the repair division, instead of assigning you to the traffic division."

"What is traffic division?"

"They process all the messages—message center, tape relay, and fleet center. You know, message traffic."

Page nods understanding.

How would you feel about being assigned to repair division?"

"Repair division is fine with me, sir." Rigney reasons that where he works in the communications trailers has no impact on his mission.

"Good. I will take you over to the trailers and introduce you to your division officer, Mr. Linderhaus."

As Lieutenant Lemont leads them outside and toward the communications trailers, Rigney gets a better look at the construction of the trailers, which are full-size eighteen-wheeler trailers connected together.

They walk up a short set of steps and stand in front of a large metal door with a cipher lock. A sign on the door announces *Authorized Personnel Only*. Lieutenant Lemont punches-in the cipher lock code and opens the door. They step into a small security area; an armed guard stands behind a podium. The dirty ashtray smell of the air-conditioning soaks into Rigney's nostrils, skin, and clothes.

"You must sign-in until I can check your service record and add you to the access list."

The interior of the communications trailers reflects compactness and efficiency. Light-colored vinyl tiles cover the deck. Light-gray colored panels cover the walls.

Each trailer they walk through has dozens of sailors scurrying about performing communications duties. Half of the sailors have cigarettes in their hands or dangling from their lips. Some carry Coke cans and some carry coffee cups. Cigarette ashes, Coke stains, and coffee stains dirty the deck.

Page and Lemont come to a wall with two doors. A sign on the door to the left displays in large red block letters REPAIR OFFICER. The sign on the door to the right displays ELECTRONIC REPAIR.

They walk through the repair office door. Rigney stiffens with caution when he sees Eric, the linebacker, sitting behind the desk. The nameplate on the desk reads *LT(jg) Linderhaus*.

Eric stands to greet his boss. Recognition flashes across Linderhaus's face when he sees Rigney step through the doorway.

"Eric, I want to introduce you to RM2 Page. I am assigning him to repair division."

Linderhaus blinks his eyes in confusion as he stares at Rigney's RM2 rating chevron and then back into the Lemont's face.

"Yes, I know he's a radioman, but he's been to a lot of repair schools, including crypto repair and teletype repair, and he has some practical repair experience."

Eric slowly extends his hand to Rigney and says, "Welcome aboard, Page."

Eric stands four inches taller than Rigney and outweighs Rigney by thirty pounds. However, Eric carries no fat or flab on his body.

Rigney expects a bone-crushing handshake from Eric, but the officer's handshake is limp and lacks enthusiasm.

"Have you finished checking in?" Eric asks Rigney.

"I still have the XO and CO on my list. I won't know my appointment time with them until I get back to the personnel office."

Mr. Lemont advises, "Eric, I will leave Page in your care now."

"Yes, sir," Eric responds.

Lemont departs the office.

"Page, please sit," Eric directs, pointing to a chair next to his desk. "I will call the personnel office for your XO and CO appointment schedule."

Rigney sits while Eric dials the number to the personnel office.

Linderhaus asks into the phone, "This is Mr. Linderhaus. Do you have RM2 Page scheduled for his check-in appointments with the captain and the XO?"

Eric writes times on a paper pad in front of him.

"Okay. Thank you."

Eric hangs up the phone and looks at his watch. Then, he looks at Rigney and says, "Your appointment with the XO is at 1430, and your appointment with the captain is at 1500. I will give you a tour of the communications trailers. Then, you are free until 0800 tomorrow morning."

Mr. Linderhaus stands and motions for Rigney to stand and proceed out the door.

After exiting the repair office, they turn right and enter a trailer with six radiomen sitting at desks and teletype machines.

"This trailer is the message center," Eric advises. "All messages addressed to or originated by NAVCOMMSTA Greece are processed here. We also provide commercial refile services and refile services for NATO units."

They pass through the message center and stop in a small trailer where four radiomen sit CW positions and copy Morse code. One of the radiomen stands and tunes an R-390 radio receiver.

"This is the fleet center. We guard CW frequencies. Some navy ships still use CW to send their messages, but fewer and fewer as the years pass. Most navy ships now use radio teletype. We also guard the International Call and Distress frequency."

Mr. Linderhaus directs Rigney to cross into a trailer on their left.

"This is the technical control trailer."

Page watches three first class radioman scurry back and forth between radio receivers and racks of teletype machines. Each technical controller has several patch cords hanging around his neck.

Eric points to one of the first class radiomen who stops in front of a microphone and scans a piece of paper.

"Listen, he will talk over the CINCUSNAVEUR High Command Net and will order a ship to change transmit frequencies."

The technical controller steps on a pedal on the floor.

Eric informs, "That pedal keys the transmitter."

The technical controller speaks into the microphone while reading from a piece of paper, "Fast Charger this is Cactus Pete, over."

Rigney hears a response over a speaker. *"Cactus Pete this is Fast Charger, over."*

"Fast Charger this is Cactus Pete, Quebec Sierra Yankee NUCO Bravo Romeo . . ."

"Let's move on," Eric orders.

As they continue through the technical control trailer, Rigney notes that all the high frequency radio receivers are models R-390 and R-1051.

After exiting the technical control trailer, Mr. Linderhaus points to the right and informs, "That's the crypto vault."

The door to the crypto vault is open, and Rigney sees his target, Master Chief Radioman Raymond Rodgers sitting behind a desk. Stacks of key cards wrapped in cellophane clutter the desk. RMCM Rodgers busily writes on a pad of paper.

Rodgers senses that someone stares at him. He looks up from his writing pad and notices Mr. Linderhaus and a second class radioman passing the door to the crypto vault. Rodgers does not recognize the RM2 and wonders if the RM2 is the new radioman who punched out Lieutenant Martin at the Club Zeus on Saturday afternoon. *He looks tough enough.*

Linderhaus and Page pass through another doorway, crossing from one trailer to the other. Eric points to the right and advises, "This is the broadcast trailer. In here, the operator monitors the NAVCOMMSTA Greece Fleet Broadcast. He also operates the ship-to-shore termination with the auxiliary oiler USS *Neosho*." Eric points to a teletype printer and advises, "He's also responsible for keeping the news printing."

Rigney observes a single operator in the broadcast trailer who types on an AN/UGC-6 teletype machine. Above the teletype, a sign advises Ship-to-Shore Termination USS *Neosho*.

Rigney walks over to the news printer and reads a few lines.

California Governor Ronald Reagan candidate for Republican President nomination—California delegation asked him to become active candidate. Reagan declaration to try to stop first ballot nomination for Richard Nixon.

Stalin's daughter, Svetlana Alliluyeva, burns Soviet passport so no one will think she is going back. She may seek American citizenship.

Eight arrested in Los Angeles, California, after gunfight with police and group called Black Panthers.

Eric points to a door with a cipher lock and announces, "Through that door is the crypto operations center. That is where all the cryptographic devices are located."

"At the other end of this trailer is the general service torn-tape relay," Eric advises as he points. "We call it LO-COMM."

In the LO-COMM area, six radiomen process one-inch wide yellow tape that pours from dozens of teletype machines.

"The general service torn-tape relay has connections with all the other Naval Communications Stations in the Mediterranean and Northern Africa. LO-COMM also has connections with the American Embassy in Athens, the AUTODIN Switching Center in Spain, and the U.S. Air Base in Tripoli, Libya.

"It's called general service torn-tape relay, because it handles only secret classifications and below."

Eric points to a door with a cipher lock and advises, "On the other side of that door in the next trailer is the NAVCOMOPNET top secret message relay. We call it HI-COMM. In addition to having top secret cryptographic covered teletype circuits with other naval communications stations on the NAVCOMOPNET, they have top secret radio teletype circuits with aircraft carriers, cruisers, and other flagships."

Rigney and Eric drift back toward the repair office, but instead of entering the repair office, Eric leads them into the repair shop.

As Rigney walks through the repair shop door, ET2 Patterson and ET2 Thompson turn from their workbench and face the door. Both ETs express surprise when they see Rigney.

Rigney nods in acknowledgement toward the two black sailors who confronted him Saturday evening.

Eric notices the nods and smiles between Rigney and the two ETs. "Do you already know each other?" Eric asks Rigney.

"Yes sir," Rigney replies.

"Good," Eric responds. "The three of you and the LPO will share this shop. Page, you can have that spare workbench in the far corner."

Rigney looks around the repair shop for a few moments and then asks, "Sir, looks like everyone around here wears whites, except the repair division. Am I correct on that?"

"Yes," Eric Replies. "You can wear your dungarees to work."

"Okay, sir. What's next?"

"You're off until tomorrow morning. Just make sure you see the CO and XO this afternoon."

"Yes sir. Will do."

There is an awkward silence; then, Rigney says, "Sir, I believe I need to be escorted to the front door. Mr. Lemont signed me in."

"I will escort you," Eric responds. "And I will see the COMM department yeoman about getting you on the access list today."

Chapter 35

At 1420, Rigney enters the administration building and proceeds to the admin office. As he steps inside the door, he sees the yeoman speaking with a female lieutenant commander who Rigney recognizes from the quarterdeck chain-of-command board as the executive officer. The XO's back is to him. He waits just inside the door and waits for the yeoman and XO to finish their conversation.

The XO turns to leave the office. She walks toward him and stops three feet away.

Like a sponge, Rigney absorbs the sexuality of the woman. His heart pumps faster. Her lightly scented fragrance seeps into his senses. *She's prettier and sexier than her picture on the quarterdeck.*

Her figure reminds him of Barbara Gaile who was the thirty-year old navy woman he worked with on his last mission. Images of Barbara's naked body, but with the XO's face, flash through his mind. He pictures himself and the XO lying naked. Then, he visualizes her legs spreading and inviting him to move on top of her. *Easy, Rig! You do not want to show inappropriate behavior toward this officer. What is it with me, and older women, anyway!*

Lieutenant Commander Mary Blakely studies Rigney's face then glances at his RM2 rating chevron. "Are you RM2 Page?" she asks. Her gaze shows no emotion. She does not offer her hand to shake, nor does she welcome him aboard.

"Yes, ma'am," Rigney responds softly.

"Come to my office."

Rigney follows her along the passageway and into her office.

"Shut the door and sit there." She points to a chair in front of her desk.

Rigney does as ordered.

The XO sits behind her desk and leafs through Rigney's service record. After a full minute, she picks up some forms from her desk and studies them.

"Page, I have two reports of violent behavior by you since you arrived two days ago. The first report says that you assaulted Seaman Newman at the airport. What do you have to say about that?"

"I have nothing to say, ma'am."

The XO states with a serious tone, "Newman says you called him a lazy nigger and beat him up because he would not carry your seabag."

"Ma'am, my evaluation of Newman is that he is insolent and disrespectful. A person of his character has no credibility. It's his word against mine, and I say he's lying."

The XO stares at RM2 Page for a full thirty seconds; then, she comments, "Page, your performance evaluations indicate that you have been in trouble before, and that you have been in fights before. If this report about Newman were the only reference to violent behavior, your version of the incident would be more believable."

"Ma'am, I assure you that those incidents in my evaluations were occasions when I came to the aid of others who were being attacked."

"Your evaluations don't specify that."

"That's because my evaluations were written by officers who believe there are no justified circumstances under which one sailor should strike another."

"And you think there are such circumstances."

"Yes ma'am. Those officers are naïve and not in touch with what goes on in the enlisted ranks."

Lieutenant Commander Blakely stares curiously at RM2 Page. Then, she says, "Your actions against Lieutenant Martin show you are a violent person."

"Ma'am, I had to stop Lieutenant Martin from hurting his wife and child. I am sure that the chief-master-at-arms told you what happened at Mr. Martin's house, later."

"Yes, he has," the XO responds. "We are still gathering statements about what happened at the pool between you and Mr.

Martin." The XO pauses for a few moments; then she says, "You refused to provide a written statement. Why is that?"

"Before I make a final decision about making a statement, I want to know if I will be charged and what I will be charged with."

"What makes you think you can do that?"

"UCMJ."

"You're familiar with the UCMJ?"

"I completed the UCMJ correspondence course."

The XO thumbs through Page's service record, stops, reads a few lines, and says, "So you did." Her eyes go wide when she sees the dozens of navy correspondence courses that page has completed.

"Navy regulations correspondence course, too," Page declares.

Mary looks down at the service record and nods when she sees the entry for navy regulations correspondence course.

Rigney inquires, "What can I expect to happen regarding Newman's accusations?"

The XO advises, "I will recommend to the captain that we do nothing further regarding the Newman incident, because there are no witnesses to confirm either side of the story." The XO considers that Newman has been caught in lies before.

Mary notices that Page intently watches her every movement. When either of them speaks, he keeps his eyes riveted to her eyes. His unswerving gaze speaks his desire to absorb all information about her. She senses that his observations are more than sexual and that he seeks to understand her character and motivations. *I'm being evaluated by this sailor—this boy! Page searches beyond my sexual appeal. He wants to know if I am competent, and if I am honorable. Well, I am, and I don't need to prove it to him!* Mary does not consider that RM2 Page searches for competence and honor in all officers, men or women.

The XO stares back at Page. His reddish brown hair, green eyes, and muscled physique appeal to her. She fights the urge to give him the head-to-toe appraisal. When she first saw him in the admin office, she was stunned by his rugged good looks.

She ponders the accusations against Page. *Newman is a weasel, and Page's characterization of Newman is correct.*

Jeff Martin is an arrogant woman-beating son of a bitch. The captain has protected him for too long. Now, the whole thing is in the open. The captain can no longer cover it up.

Page is a hero in my book, but the captain wants a formal investigation into Page's actions. What about Jeff beating his wife and child? Many have witnessed that, several times. The captain never demanded an investigation into those events.

Unconsciously and giving into her urge to appraise his body, Mary stares at the thick bush of reddish brown chest hair that rolls over the top of his t-shirt. Then, her stare shifts to his muscled and hairy forearms.

Rigney notices the XO staring at this chest hair and arm hair. He pretends not to notice.

She is about to move her gaze lower on his body when Page speaks and stops her instinctive act. "Ma'am, I don't understand why there is a question about what I did to Lieutenant Martin. From what people tell me, his violent behavior is common knowledge."

Her eyes rise to meet his. "All incidents like this must be fully investigated. Nothing is taken for granted."

"Yes ma'am." Rigney waits for the XO to continue.

Mary lowers her eyes to study Page's service record. After flipping through several pages, she stops to study Rigney's history of assignments.

"You were on the USS *Barb* for only eight months before transferring here. Why is that?"

"I was medically disqualified from submarines."

The XO nods and continues her perusal of his service record.

"You spent more than two years attending schools prior to going to the USS *Barb*. Why were you in schools for so long?"

"I completed several of the submarine radioman courses in half the time and at the head of my class. Because of that, the director of submarine radioman school allowed me to take all courses."

Mary nods and looks back down to his service record and flips a few more pages. She reads with interest the report of a captain's mast.

"You're on a suspended bust. You went to captain's mast for disrespect toward an officer."

"Yes ma'am."

The XO looks seriously at Rigney and warns, "I won't tolerate any enlisted man speaking in a disrespectful manner to officers. If you repeat your insubordinate conduct, I can assure you that you will go to captain's mast and will be reduced in rank. Do you understand what I am saying?"

"Yes ma'am. Threats are not necessary. I learned a valuable lesson about the navy during that incident. I will not repeat it."

The XO studies Page's manner to determine if he really understands. She concludes from information in his service record that he is highly intelligent and resourceful. However, the record of the captain's mast and reports of his violent actions since reporting aboard tell her that she needs to monitor his activities.

"Have you checked in with Lieutenant Lemont?" she asks.

"Yes ma'am."

"Did he assign you to a division?"

"Yes ma'am. I will work in repair division."

"Okay, Petty Officer Page. I have nothing further for you at this time. I welcome you aboard and hope that your tour at Nea Makri is successful." Mary stands and offers her hand across the desk.

Rigney stands, takes her hand, shakes it firmly, and responds, "Thank you, ma'am. I also hope for a successful tour."

As they release their hands from the shake, the XO asks, "What does successful mean to you?"

Rigney must think about that, because his answer must be vague to hide his true purpose. "To me, successful means completing every task that the navy expects me to complete while I am here." Rigney finds his answer amusing, but his face does not show it.

The XO sits into her chair. She thinks Page's response to be unusual, because most of the other sailors had been more specific with responses like advancement to the next pay grade or acquiring certain skills.

"You are dismissed," Mary orders.

"Yes ma'am." Rigney turns and walks toward the office door.

Now, Mary succumbs to her urge to evaluate him, sexually. Viewing him from the back, she appreciates his broad shoulders and narrow waist and hips.

"Page, hold up."

Rigney turns to face the XO.

She can see the full length of him now. He wears a loose-fitting, untailored uniform. *So many lean and muscled sailors are full of themselves and have their uniforms tailored to a tight fit to show off their bodies. This sailor does not think it necessary to do so. That's a plus for him in my book.*

She cannot stop her eyes from moving to his crotch. She hopes for a bulge that she can evaluate. Rigney's trousers hang loose, and the bulge is slight. Visions of Page's hairy naked body and with an erect penis flash through her mind. Visualizing herself naked, she leads him to her bed and guides him to lie on his back. She straddles him. Her nipples harden as her fantasy causes a wave of warmth to flow from her thighs to lower belly. *Taboo!* She raises her eyes to his face.

Rigney pretends not to notice the XO's fantasy trip. He stands casually, waiting for her to state why she stopped him from departing.

"Oh, what time is your appointment with the captain?"

"1500, ma'am." Rigney understands she already knows that, but it is a good enough excuse so that she could appraise him.

"Okay, Page. You're dismissed."

"Yes ma'am."

Rigney turns and exits the XO's office.

Mary stares at the closed door. She ponders her meeting with RM2 Page. *So confident, so self assured, so sexy, his deep, resonant, and seductive voice, and totally untouchable. I must convince the CO not to proceed with any judicial action against him.*

Chapter 36

"The captain will see you now," advises the captain's yeoman. "Go through that door." The yeoman points to a door six feet away. "No need to knock. Just open the door and enter."

Rigney nods, walks the six feet to the door, opens it, and walks in.

Commander Oliver Caldwell stands near the far wall and studies writing on a whiteboard.

Rigney snaps to attention and states, "RM2 Page reporting as ordered, sir."

"Stand easy," the officer orders. "You may sit there."

The CO wears his Tropical White Long uniform. The pudgy officer stands six inches shorter than Rigney. Light-brown receding hair tops his round and flabby chinned face.

Rigney notices the gold wings of a naval aviator above four rows of ribbons. Rigney notes several Vietnam combat ribbons.

After both men are seated, the CO says, "Page, I have not had a chance to review your service record. Please tell me about yourself."

Rigney detects a lack of enthusiasm in the CO's tone.

"Sir, my home is Seal Beach, California. I joined the navy following high school graduation, which was June 1965. After boot camp, I attended basic radioman school. Then, I transferred to New London, and I attended submarine radioman schools in New London. After graduating from the submarine radioman school last December, I reported to the USS *Barb*. She's a fast-attack submarine home ported at Pearl Harbor. Last month I was medically disqualified from submarines, and I was sent here."

Commander Oliver Caldwell does not absorb the information he hears from RM2 Page. He looks toward Page, but not at Page. He detests these welcome aboard interviews. *I should be an air squadron commanding officer instead of babysitter to a bunch of sniveling and complaining communicators.* He endures these interviews at the insistence of his executive officer. *She says it's good for morale and portrays good leadership. What the hell does a split-tail know about leadership!*

Rigney purposely keeps his history short. He senses that this officer is not interested.

The CO, deep in his own thoughts, does not notice that Page has stopped talking.

Rigney sits silent, waiting for the CO to continue the interview.

After fifteen seconds of silence, the CO notices Page no longer speaks. He retrieves a perfunctory question. "What are your interests? What do you like to do during off time?"

"Mostly, I exercise with weights, play basketball, and I read a lot. While I am in Greece, I hope to tour as much of the country as I can. I also want to take up scuba diving again. I have a master certificate."

Again, the CO does not focus on Rigney's words. However, he hears the words master certificate and becomes curious.

"Master certificate in what?"

"Scuba diving, sir."

The CO nods his head slowly and blinks his eyes a few times.

Rigney wants to stand and leave. *This officer is not listening to me. He obviously does not care about any of this. So why is he doing it?*

"Huh . . . well . . . that's interesting," the CO responds without sincerity.

Rigney wants to give this officer a disapproving stare, but his navy training tells him to remain respectful.

The CO looks down at papers on his desk; then, he looks at Page and says, "Page, I have another matter that I must discuss with you. I have a report from the chief-master-at-arms regarding your attack on Mr. Martin. I must hear your side of the story."

"Sir, I think it best for me to say nothing."

"Page, you must understand that all acts of violence must be fully investigated. Also, I must inform you that if the facts show you acted without justification, you can be prosecuted."

Rigney nods and says, "Others tell me that Lieutenant Martin has beaten his family in public before."

Commander Caldwell flushes with anger. *How dare this enlisted man be so insolent! I am the judge of facts at my command! Who is this arrogant boy who judges the actions of an officer!* The CO prepares to scold Page when his phone rings. He picks up the phone. "Yes!" he spits tersely into the phone.

The XO says into his ear, *"I forgot to bring Page's service record to you. Should I bring it now?"*

"No!"

The CO slams down the handset.

Caldwell considers what he should do next about the insolent and insubordinate sailor who sits before him.

Rigney's eyes roam the CO's desk. A framed photograph of the CO and his family stands on the corner of the desk. Two full stripes on the uniform reveal that the CO was a lieutenant at the time. The photograph also reveals that the CO was forty pounds lighter at the time. His wife, an attractive brunette, stands next to him. Standing in front of the CO and his wife is a little girl about eight years old. Rigney recognizes the little girl as Angie Caldwell.

Commander Caldwell emerges from his thoughts and notices Rigney staring at the photograph. He says, "I have a memo here from Master Chief Crimer that reports that you refuse to explain where you were until 0420 Sunday morning. Do you still refuse to explain?"

"Yes sir."

"Page, are you aware that providing such information is my policy, not the master chief's."

"Yes sir. I understand that."

Caldwell expresses annoyance. He orders, "That's all for now. You're dismissed."

Rigney stands, snaps to attention, and responds, "Aye, aye, sir." He performs a smart about-face and departs the office.

Page's respectful and military-correct exit surprises Commander Oliver Caldwell. Since assuming command of Nea Makri, no sailor or officer has departed his office in such a manner.

After closing the door behind him, Rigney pauses in the passageway. He wants to be careful about not judging Caldwell too quickly. He looks at his watch—1520. He decides to change into civilian clothes and walk to Anna's villa.

Chapter 37

Anna returns to the villa after spending the day shopping in Athens. As she parks her BMW inside the courtyard wall, Anna sees Rigney standing on the grade next to the clothesline—antenna. He stares east toward the Aegean Sea.

He waves to Anna as she exits the red BMW convertible.

Anna waves back. Then, she reaches into the backseat of the top-down convertible and lifts several packages and grocery bags.

After placing her shopping items in the kitchen, she joins Rigney, who now stands facing the mountain behind the villa. She notices that he is deep in thought.

"What's on your mind?" she asks with a curious look on her face.

Rigney turns to face her. "This mountain behind the villa blocks high frequency transmissions to the west. Considering the radio frequency that we used yesterday afternoon, the construction of this antenna, which is directional, and that our transceiver has a maximum of one hundred watts of radiated power we must have been communicating with a radio station to the east of here."

An admiring expression appears on her face as she looks into his eyes. "Well, Rig, Brad said you know your radioman business. You are correct."

After a short pause, Rigney asks, "Are you allowed to tell me any details?"

"Sure. You need to know. I just never thought of explaining it yesterday." Anna turns and points to the east and says, "You see that large, mountainous landmass across the water about fifteen miles away?"

Rigney nods, then, replies, "Yes."

"Those mountains are on the island of Euboea. On top of the highest mountain is an ONI mobile radio relay station. From there, they relay our signals to Italy."

"Is it there all the time, or was it put in place to support this mission?"

"It was put in place to support this mission. When we are done here, it will be disestablished."

Rigney looks at his watch—1750; he asks, "Are we eating in or out tonight?"

"Eating here tonight. Tomorrow night, you are taking me to the Club Zeus for a steak dinner and drinks."

Rigney raises his eyebrows.

"We need to keep advertising our togetherness."

"Understood," Rigney responds with a nod.

"Do you know how to cook anything?" Anna asks with an amused look on her face.

"I can't even boil water," Rigney admits.

"Good, I will teach you how to make a lamb stew."

After dinner, Anna and Rigney sit in the villa's living room, reading. They sit in separate overstuffed chairs across the room from each other. Rigney reads *The Source* by James Michener. Anna reads a book written in German.

He glances over the top of his book and studies Anna. He admires this intelligent woman—a woman of language, history, and worldliness—a woman who lives a mysterious and dangerous undercover life in Germany.

Anna senses his stare. She looks up from her book and catches his eyes on her. "What's on your mind?" she asks.

"I was just thinking how easily you switch from speaking English with a German accent to English with no accent. You had a heavy accent yesterday when you talked with Eric and then with me on the beach. When we are alone, no accent."

"Years of practice," Anna explains with her face expressionless. Then, she lowers her eyes back to the page of her book.

Rigney returns his attention to *The Source*.

Chapter 38

At 0715 the next morning, Rigney and Anna sit in her BMW convertible across the road from the NAVCOMMSTA main gate. The top is down. Again, they draw stares from those entering the base.

Lieutenant Commander Mary Blakely drives north on Marathon Road. The drive each morning takes ten minutes from the small house she rents in Nea Makri. From a distance, she recognizes the red BMW convertible of the German woman she often sees on the beach and shopping the stores in Nea Makri. As she nears the gate, she recognizes RM2 Page sitting in the passenger seat. Just before turning into the gate, Mary observes the pair engaged in a lingering kiss. *Now that's interesting*, she says to herself. *Page didn't waste time finding a girlfriend. Older women attract him. They must have had sex.*

For the second time in two days, she fantasizes Page's hairy, naked body in her bed. Mary's heart pumps faster as warmth flows from her thighs to her belly. She sighs deeply as she passes through the gate.

Rigney exits the BMW, crosses the Marathon Road, walks through the gate, and goes to the barracks, where he changes into dungarees and dons his cleanest white hat.

Twenty minutes later, he presses the buzzer at the main door of the communications trailers. The inside security guard opens the door and allows Rigney to enter. Rigney recognizes the security guard as Bob Vance, the sailor who initially reported Rigney's decking of Lieutenant Martin to the master-at-arms. Bob wears his Tropical White Long uniform with guard belt and .45 automatic pistol. On his left sleeve, Bob wears the crow of signalman third class.

"Good morning, Bob."

"Hi Rig. Don't you know the combination to the door?"

"No. I'm not sure if my name is on the access list."

"Let me check." He runs his finger down a typed list. Then, he turns a few pages.

"Here it is. This memo from the communications officer authorizes you access to all spaces, including HI-COMM and crypto operations center."

"Good. I'll just go to the repair shop, then."

"Okay, Rig. See ya later."

As he enters the repair shop, three pairs of eyes turn to see who comes through the door. All are dressed in their dungaree uniform. Rigney recognizes ET2 Patterson and ET2 Thompson. The third sailor, a tall and lanky ET1, walks toward Rigney and offers his hand. The sailor stands three inches taller than Rigney. "You're Page, right?" the first class asks.

"Yes."

The two men shake hands. The twenty-seven-year-old ET1 has strong and calloused hands. "I'm Pete Straton, the leading petty officer, a pleasure to meet the guy who knocked Mr. Martin on his ass. He is one asshole who deserves to have the meanness punched out of him."

Rigney considers Straton's negative comments to be inappropriate for a senior petty officer to say in front of juniors. He does not want to respond incorrectly; he remains silent.

Straton continues his compliments of Mr. Martin. "Never known a meaner officer. Always yelling at people, talkin' down to them. Always puttin' sailors on report for no reason." Straton pauses; then, he smiles and says, "Well, anyway, welcome aboard. We're glad to have ya in repair. We're shorthanded and need all the techs we can get."

"I'm glad to be here," Rigney responds in a flat tone.

Straton says, "I must go. I got a repair in progress in the crypto center."

Patterson and Thompson remain quiet and just grin at the conversation between RM2 Page and ET1 Straton. As Rigney walks to the rear of the trailer to acquaint himself with this workbench, Patterson and Thompson follow him with their eyes.

Rigney sits on the swivel stool in front of his workbench and performs a quick scan of test equipment and tools. Then, he turns on the padded swivel cushion toward Patterson and Thompson. With knowing grins on their faces, they shake their heads in dismissal. They turn on their stools to face each other. They involve themselves in whispered conversation.

Straton grabs a tool bag from his workbench and exits the repair shop.

Patterson and Thompson slip off their stools and walk over to Page.

Rigney stands to face them. Patterson's height is equal to Rigney's. Thompson stands a few inches shorter.

"We want to explain to ya about the other night in the club," Thompson says. "We didn't come to hassle you, man. We just wanted to find out if Newman was telling the truth about what happen' at the airport. Before we can explain that, you're insultin' us."

"Your gestures were antagonistic," Rigney responds. "I just responded in kind."

"It's just the way we talk, man. We didn't mean anything by it. Look, Patterson and I have this rep about being tough and picking on people, but that's not us. People just read us wrong. We don't blindly go kicking ass just because Newman says something."

Rigney fully understands about others misperceiving one's actions. "Well, I can understand that," Rigney concedes. "We'll just forget about it, then?"

"We need to know if you knocked Newman down. We don't go looking for trouble, but we won't tolerate someone beatin' up on a brother."

Rigney stares into Patterson's face. Then, he shifts his stare to Thompson's face. He questions, "Why ask me? Don't you believe Newman? If I say I didn't do it, you will still have doubts, correct?"

The two black sailors just stare at Rigney. Their expressions convey they are waiting for an explanation.

Rigney declares defiantly, "I am not obligated to prove anything to you two."

Thompson and Patterson jerk their heads and blink their eyes at Rigney's strong and fearless response. They exchange glances.

A smile spreads over Thompson's face as he says, "What are ya gettin' so angry about, man? We just want to know. We believe you. This is not the first time that Newman lied to us, but he's a brother. We must look out for him."

Rigney shakes his head with disapproval.

"What?" Patterson asks.

Rigney continues to shake his head as he says, "Looks to me like you choose your friends based on the color of their skin, and not the content of their character."

The two black sailors stiffen at Rigney's blunt and brazen characterization.

"You sayin' we're racists?" Patterson challenges as anger flashes across his face.

Rigney answers evenly, without emotion, "Seems to me it's you two who are all concerned with race."

An awkward silence falls over the shop.

Rigney breaks the silence. "All this fuss over Newman annoys me. Doesn't it annoy you two?"

Patterson and Thompson look at each other and nod their agreement.

"I think we should put this Newman incident behind us. We need to get along if we are going to work together. My first name is Rigney."

Rigney stretches his hand toward Patterson.

Patterson glances at Thompson; then, he looks back at Rigney. He takes Rigney's hand and informs, "My first name is Larry."

"Very glad to meet you, Larry," Rigney says sincerely as they shake hands.

Rigney reaches his hand out to Thompson.

Thompson hesitates for a moment and then takes Rigney's hand. "Bill is my name. Never call me Willie!" William Thompson demands.

"Okay, Bill, no worries about that. It is a pleasure to meet you." Rigney has a pleasant smile on his face.

Bill Thompson stares intently at Rigney.

Rigney notices Thompson's stare, and he asks, "Where are you from?"

"Philadelphia."

"Rigney looks at Larry Patterson and asks, "What's your hometown?"

"Chicago."

Bill Thompson stares for a few more seconds; then, he asks, "Where do you come from?"

"Seal Beach, California."

"Big surprise," Thompson responds in a cynical expression and cynical tone while he looks Rigney up and down.

Chapter 39

Anna and Rigney stand in the villa's yard, near the clothesline—transmit antenna. They face the direction of the Aegean Sea and enjoy the spectacular view of Nea Makri and the shore. The sea reflects sparkles of sunlight back toward a cloudless sky.

Anna says, "Remember, you are taking me to the base club tonight for a steak dinner."

Rigney looks at his watch—5:45 PM. "I haven't forgotten," Rigney assures. "When can you be ready?"

"Thirty minutes."

"Okay, but first I need to talk to you about some things."

"What things?" she asks as she turns to face Rigney.

"I need detailed information on the background of some of the officers on the base."

"Which ones?" Anna's face dons a curious expression.

"Commander Caldwell and Lieutenant Commander Blakely. I think they will attempt to punish me for what I did to Lieutenant Martin."

"That doesn't make sense," Anna concludes. "You were defending two helpless people. I don't understand how they can fault you for that."

"I agree that it does not make sense, but I think they will try. I need some ammunition. Everyone has something in their past that they don't want revealed. I need some bargaining chips."

A conspiratorial smile spreads over Anna's face. "Tell me. How has such a young sailor learned such sophisticated strategies?"

"I read a lot," Rigney replies with a knowing smile. "And my experiences over the last year have enlightened me to the conniving, lying, and evil actions which humans are capable. I need an advantage. Can we get the information?"

"Yes," Anna responds. "I will request it during tomorrow's communication session. Is that soon enough?"

"Yes."

"Good. Now, let's go into the house and get dressed."

"What's wrong with what we're wearing? Casual dress is allowed in the club's restaurant."

"How casual?"

"Shorts and sandals, many just wear a bathing suit and a pullover top."

Anna's eyes look into the distance as she considers Rigney's words.

"I think that we will go casual in such a way that we are conspicuous."

Rigney shakes his head, indicating he does not understand.

"Come inside. I will select your clothes for this evening."

Several minutes later in Rigney's bedroom, Anna hands him a pair of dark gray tennis shorts.

"Why these?"

"Those are your tightest pair of tennis shorts, right?"

"Yes. How do you know that?"

Anna does not answer and busily tosses items in Rigney's clothing drawer. "Which of these short-sleeve pullovers fits you the tightest?"

"None of them fits me tight. I like loose-fitting clothes. Those shorts are reserved for when I have nothing else clean."

Anna stares at Rigney for a few moments; she glances back at the clothes drawer. "I think I may have just the shirt for you."

She walks out of the bedroom.

Rigney sees that Anna enters her bedroom across the hall.

Thirty seconds later, Anna comes back to Rigney's bedroom and hands him a folded black-colored t-shirt.

"I like to sleep in oversized t-shirts. This should fit you just like I want."

Rigney removes his loose-fitting polo shirt. He feels self-conscious as Anna stares at his hairy and muscled torso. He slips on the t-shirt. He looks at himself in the full-length mirror mounted on the inside of the wardrobe door. The t-shirt is skintight. The sleeves are extra short and expose most of his large muscled biceps.

"Yes. That's the effect I want. Here, put on the shorts."

Rigney waits for Anna to depart the bedroom, but she does not.

After fifteen seconds pass, Anna realizes why Rigney has not yet shucked his pants.

"Don't be bashful. I have seen men in their underwear before."

He shrugs his shoulders; then, he removes his pants.

She expresses doubt as she stares Rigney up and down. "Boxer shorts. They are longer than the tennis shorts. Don't you have any jockey shorts?"

"Yes, in the drawer." Rigney hesitates.

"Put them on."

"With you watching?"

"You worried about what I might see?"

"You may be awestruck by what you see," Rigney responds, arrogance edging his tone.

Anna smirks and shakes her head dismissively. "I'm sure that your dick is something special and spectacular. However, so that you remain masked in mystery, I will turn my back while you change your underwear and put on the tennis shorts."

Anna turns her back to Rigney.

Rigney quickly removes the boxer shorts and slips on jockey shorts and the tennis shorts.

"Okay. I've changed."

Anna turns and faces Rigney.

Rigney faces the mirror. He feels uncomfortable as he observes that the skintight clothes reveal every muscle. The abundant reddish-brown hair on his arms and legs contrasts against the color of the tennis shorts and the black t-shirt. He blushes as he notices the large bulge in the crotch of the shorts. In the mirror, Rigney notices Anna staring at his crotch.

"Anna, although my cover requires that I act like a showoff, I am not a showoff. If I wear theses clothes, I will feel like I'm on display. I know that dressing like this will draw stares."

"We will both be on display," Anna states. "I'm going to get dressed. We will leave in twenty minutes."

Twenty minutes later, Rigney sits in the villa's living room. He pages through a German magazine. He looks up as he hears Anna enter the room.

Astonished at what he sees, Rigney's eyes go wide and his mouth opens as he gapes at her.

Anna performs a 360-degree turn.

Anna wears light-green hip-hugger shorts that barely cover her butt cheeks. The hip-huggers are cut so low on her belly that Rigney thinks Anna must have shaved the top area of her pubic hair to keep it from showing.

She wears a matching light-green skintight halter that displays the shape and size of her beasts and nipples. Her taut stomach muscles show between the bottom of the halter and the top of the hip-huggers.

Anna's long tanned legs and her tanned midriff display no tan line. Rigney concludes that Anna's baiting suit must cover less skin that what she now wears or she sunbathes in the nude.

Rigney becomes aroused by Anna's sexual appearance. He feels his penis swell against his tight shorts. He hopes that Anna does not notice, but she does.

"Control yourself, Rigney. We will put on a performance tonight, but I don't want you to get the wrong idea."

"Please explain it to me, because I need to understand why I must do this." Rigney's arms are outstretched as a symbol that he will accept her explanation.

"Like I said the first night, you and I will never have sex. Do not let anything I do tonight make you think that I have changed my mind. Tonight, I will hang all over you. I will run my hands over your body. I want you to put your arms around me from time to time."

"What will we accomplish with such behavior? I believe we have convinced everyone we are a couple."

"To make us look less like counterespionage operatives. With tonight's performance, we will reinforce our image as frivolous lovers. We need to establish an image of being lighthearted and carefree. If the enemy is watching, they will dismiss us as any kind of threat. I have a responsibility to protect you. I might need to rescue you from dangerous situations. The less I look like a threat, the easier it will be for me to get close should you be in the hands of dangerous people." Anna pauses to gauge whether or not Rigney understands.

"Yes, of course. It all makes sense."

"Good. Let's go," Anna orders as she turns and leads them out the door.

Chapter 40

The top is down on the BMW. As they drive along the Marathon Road through the town of Nea Makri, they get the usual stares from the local populace and from the multinational tourists. Anna speeds ten miles over the speed limit—to draw attention. Anna brakes to a stop at the U.S. NAVCOMMSTA main gate.

This evening, BM2 Victor Karzack stands sentry watch on the gate. Victor wears his Tropical White Long uniform. A holstered .45 automatic pistol hangs from his guard belt.

"Hi Victor," Rigney says as he waves from the passenger seat.

Victor Karzack walks up to the driver's side and smiles at Rigney. Then, he stares curiously at Anna.

Anna looks up into Victor's face and smiles.

"May we enter?" Rigney asks.

Victor looks at Rigney and asks, "Are you going to *steak night* at the club?"

"Yes, we are."

"This car does not have a base sticker. You must park at the club and not drive anywhere else on the station. Hold on a second while I log you in and get you a visitor pass."

Victor walks the few short steps to the guard-shack. One minute later, he exits the guard-shack with a large red-colored card in his hand. Victor hands the card to Anna and says, "Put this visitor pass on the dash on the driver's side."

"Yes, sailor, I will," Anna responds with a deep German accent.

Karzack gestures for them to pass through the gate.

As they drive past the Club Zeus pool, Rigney smells steaks cooking on an open grill. He looks over to the pool area. He sees one of the club's Greek employees flipping steaks at a large barbeque grill.

Cars fill the few parking spots around the club.

Rigney says, "You can park in front of the administrative building."

As Rigney and Anna walk across the parking lot, they draw gawking stares from sailors who walk from the barracks to the Club Zeus.

After entering the club, they stand near the bar. They look into the restaurant area and search for an empty table. Anna slips her arm around Rigney's waist.

Rigney pretends not to notice that the diners stare. An empty table in the far corner appeals to Rigney, but Anna steers them to a center table. The diners are seventy percent male and thirty percent female.

Within a few seconds of seating themselves, one of the Greek waiters comes to the table. While taking their order, the waiter graciously avoids staring lustfully at Anna.

Rigney scans the restaurant. He notes with curiosity that Master Chief Rodgers tends bar with Gus.

He also sees Newman, Patterson, and Thompson sitting at a table with a black sailor that Rigney does not recognize. Thompson and Patterson stare at Anna for a few moments; then, they grin slyly at Rigney. Newman glares contemptuously. Rigney nods a greeting. Patterson and Thompson nod back.

At the bar, Raymond Rodgers notices the couple as they entered the club. He does not recognize them. As club manager, Ray considers advising the couple that they violate the club's dress code. However, on second thought, more of their bodies are covered than those who wear bathing suits in the club. As six other sailors enter the club, Ray overhears their conversation that mentions they came into the club to see the woman who accompanies the new guy. Ray realizes that the couple draws customers. Since he skims twenty percent of the club's profits, he decides that any situation that attracts more customers is good for business.

"Do you see who's behind the bar?" Rigney whispers to Anna.

"Yes. Have you flashed your bankroll at him yet?"

"No."

"This might be a good time. Think of a reason to pull out that bankroll in front of him."

"I think I have an idea. I will need to go to the bar."

"Go," Anna prompts.

Rigney approaches the end of the bar where Master Chief Rodgers tends.

"Bartender, may a talk with you a moment."

"Sure. What do you need?"

"Do you know Patterson, Thompson, and Newman over at that table?" Rigney nods toward the table.

"Yes, I know them."

Rigney pulls the two-thousand dollar wad from his pocket and holds it out in the palm of his hand.

Ray stares at the wad of fifties and hundreds.

Others sitting at the bar turn their heads to look at the wad of money.

Rigney pulls a one-hundred dollar bill from the wad, hands it to Ray, and says, "I want to pay for their dinner and drinks—their drinks for the entire night."

"This is way more than what it will cost," Rodgers advises.

"The remainder can be a tip to the waiters and bartenders. Will you see to that?"

"Sure."

"Thanks."

Rigney stuffs the wad of money back into his pocket.

"You stationed here at Nea Makri?" Ray asks. "I have not seen you before."

"I arrived last weekend."

"What's your name?"

"RM2 Rigney Page. What's yours?"

Rodgers nods acknowledgement as he recognizes the name of the sailor who hit Mr. Martin. "Ray Rodgers. I'm a master chief radioman. I'm the club manager."

With a quizzical look on his face, Rigney tilts his head to the side and asks, "Oh, should I call you Ray or master chief?"

"It's best that you call me master chief."

Rigney purposely opens his eyes wide and nods his head, "Okay, Master Chief, and thanks for taking care of Patterson, Thompson, and friends."

Ray stares at Rigney for a few moments; then, he says, "Page, that's a lot of money to be carrying around. If you don't mind me asking, where did you get it?"

"In a poker game, just before I left Pearl. First time I ever played the game. Everyone said it was beginner's luck." Rigney's manner displays joy and wonderment about his stoke of good luck.

Ray offers, "We get a game together once in a while at my place. Would you be interested?"

Rigney does not want to seem too eager. He purposely displays a doubtful look.

"Is that a no?" Ray queries.

"Master Chief, I'm just an RM2. I don't think I should gamble with chiefs."

"When we play poker, our ranks are in the closet with our uniforms. It's a friendly game, something to pass the time. I've never known anyone to lose any large amounts of money."

"What limit do you play?"

"Pot limit with a five-dollar ante."

Rigney puts a doubtful look on his face and replies, "I don't know, Master Chief."

"Think about it, Page. I will ask you again in a few days. Okay?"

"Sure, Master Chief. That's okay."

Rigney turns and walks back to the table and sits down.

Anna leans close to Rigney and whispers, "What were you and Rodgers talking about?"

"He invited me to a poker game."

Anna continues to whisper. "You did not accept, right, but left him thinking that you might?"

"Correct," Rigney whispers back. "He said he would ask me again in a couple of days."

Rigney observes one of the Greek waiters placing beers on the table with Newman, Patterson, and Thompson.

The waiter speaks to the men at the table and nods toward Rigney.

At the same instance, the four black sailors turn their heads toward Rigney.

Patterson and Thompson pick up their beer bottles and gesture a thank-you toast toward Rigney.

Newman sneers at Rigney and flips the bird in Rigney's direction.

Patterson and Thompson shoot a disapproving glance at Newman.

Thompson declares, "Newman, you're such an asshole. Sometimes, I'm ashamed to call you brother."

Newman sits back and feels shame and rejection. He glances at Page.

Page smiles at Newman and makes a motion with his hands, simulating snapping a twig.

Newman shifts his eyes to the others at his table and questions, "Did ya'll see that? Page's threaten' me."

Paterson responds, "Yeah, we saw it. Don' expect us to watch yo' back."

Chapter 41

Once each week, the commanding officer holds a department-head meeting. During these meetings, the department heads brief on the status of projects and any significant events that have occurred since their last meeting. They discuss any message traffic applicable to the command. The executive officer tracks completion of all action items.

On this Friday morning, the following people sit around the captain's conference table.

CDR Oliver Caldwell – Commanding Officer
LCDR Mary Blakely – XO and Admin Officer
LT Gerald Lemont – Communications Department Head
SKCS Johnson – Supply Department Head (Acting)
LT Mikel Polanski – Public Works Department Head
BMCM Lawrence Crimer – Chief-master-at-Arms
LT (jg) Tommy French – OIC Kato Souli Transmitter Site

The CO turns toward Lieutenant Lemont and orders, "Gerry, tell me about the three tracers in the message traffic this morning."

Lieutenant Lemont thumbs through his stack of message traffic and extracts the three tracer messages.

"COMSIXTHFLEET claimed late delivery of a priority precedence message from CINCUSNAVEUR. We researched our handling of the CINCUSNAVEUR message and confirmed our in-house handling time was twelve minutes. That's twelve minutes from the time we received the message from Naples tape relay to the time we transmitted the message over our fleet broadcast.

"Three days later, we receive a service message from COMSIXTHFLEET flagship that they missed thirty fleet broadcast messages three days prior and they specified the thirty broadcast sequence numbers they missed. That CINCUSNAVEUR message was one of those thirty. Then, we ZDK'd all thirty messages."

"ZDK'd?" Caldwell questions with raised eyebrows.

"Retransmitted, a ZDK is a retransmission," Lieutenant Lemont clarifies. "And COMSIXTHFLEET flagship eventually accepted responsibility for the delay, which complies with—"

"Wait a minute!" Commander Caldwell interrupts. "Why did COMSIXTHFLEET flagship accept responsibility? Didn't we verify they got the message the first time we sent it?"

Lieutenant Lemont casts a bewildered expression at the CO. Then, he remembers that the CO has been a pilot all his career and not a communicator. Otherwise, the CO would understand without question why COMSIXTHFLEET accepted responsibility.

"Sir, that's not the way a fleet broadcast works. Fleet broadcast is one-way, transmit only. Our responsibility is to transmit the message over the fleet broadcast. Each ship that copies the fleet broadcast has the responsibility to ensure they receive one discrete message for each discrete broadcast sequence number. Each ship has the responsibility for requesting retransmission of any message they did not receive. When COMSIXTHFLEET's flagship discovered that it was missing thirty numbers, their responsibility was to send us a service message and advise us. In this case, they waited three days before advising us."

"What's the flagship for COMSIXTHFLEET?" the captain asks.

All the officers at the table exchange glances of surprise that Commander Caldwell does not know the flagship for COMSIXTHFLEET, the senior fleet commander in the Mediterranean.

"USS *Little Rock*," the XO and COMMO respond in unison and with a not so well hidden tone of astonishment.

The XO expands, "The *Little Rock* is a guided missile cruiser home ported in Gaeta, Italy. She was at sea when this incident occurred."

Caldwell detects their tone and becomes irritated and embarrassed. His face flushes slightly. He stares sternly at the two officers for a few moments; then, he challenges, "This doesn't make sense. Two weeks ago, Mr. Pritchings gave me a tour of HI-COMM. He pointed out the ship-to-shore, two-way radio teletype circuit with USS *Little Rock*. Mr. Pritchings said that after we transmit each message, we obtain a Q . . . Q . . . what did he call it . . . means acknowledge receipt?"

"QSL," Lemont answers.

"Yes. That's it," Caldwell confirms. "Mr. Pritchings says we require a QSL from USS *Little Rock* after each message is transmitted."

"Sir, that circuit is different from the fleet broadcast. The fleet broadcast is one-way transmit. The ships do not QSL each message. On the fleet broadcast, delivery is assumed. All ships copying the fleet broadcast are responsible for requesting retransmission of any broadcast sequence numbers they missed."

Caldwell shakes his head defiantly. "Wait a second, Mr. Pritchings told me that flagships get their own ship-to-shore, two-way radio teletype circuit because of the volume of messages. He said that messages addressed to the flagship are transmitted over the ship-to-shore, two-way circuit to reduce the volume of messages sent over the fleet broadcast. That begs the question why was the message sent over the fleet broadcast and not over the two-way circuit?"

The COMMO, Lieutenant Lemont, glances quickly around the table. He takes a deep breath and says, "The ship-to-shore, two-way with USS *Little Rock* was out-of-service at the time and had been out for more than an hour. Standard operating procedure requires transmission of all flagship messages over the fleet broadcast when the two-way is out-of-service."

Commander Caldwell sits back in his chair. A curious look appears on his face; he asks the COMMO, "The *Little Rock* two-way was down at the same time they missed thirty messages on the broadcast. Was the fleet broadcast not working at the same time?"

"The fleet broadcast was up and operating normally."

"How do you know that?" the CO asks with a challenging tone.

"Our off-the-air teletype monitor shows continuous flow of messages during that time. Additionally, none of the other five ships copying the broadcast requested any missing messages."

The CO inquires, "What's an off-the-air teletype monitor?"

The COMMO and XO exchange glances. Their glance conveying that they spend too much time explaining basic communications configurations and concepts to Commander Caldwell.

Caldwell notices the glance between the COMMO and XO. He misperceives the glance as condescending. He expresses annoyance.

The COMMO explains, "We copy our fleet broadcast signal off the air with the same type equipment configuration as a ship does, provides us with real-time quality assurance."

Caldwell slumps back in his chair. He ponders all that he has been told. He does not understand any of the explanations. *I spent the last eighteen years piloting jet aircraft. They know I don't understand, and they take advantage of my lack of experience in naval communications. Their sneers are insulting, disrespectful, and insubordinate. They must spend hours talking and laughing about me behind my back. They are lying to me. They are hiding something. They need a stern lesson on who's in charge around here.* Caldwell looks at the COMMO and asks, "Gerry, the delayed message . . . what was its content?"

"It was a SECRET NOFORN INTEL. CINCUSNAVEUR wanted COMSIXTHFLEET's most recent accounting of Soviet Navy vessels in the Mediterranean. The message gave COMSIXTHFLEET a twenty-hour deadline to provide the information."

Caldwell shakes his head slightly. A look of disgust appears on his face. Then, he asks, "How long after COMSIXTHFLEET advised us of the missing thirty broadcast messages did it take us to retransmit those thirty messages?"

Lemont shuffles his papers. He reads a few pages; then, he reports, "I don't have that information. I'll need to research that."

The CO stares blankly at the COMMO for a few moments; then, he directs, "Okay. Let's take a ten minute break. Gerry, you call the trailers and get someone on finding out how long it took. I expect that information when we reconvene."

During the ten-minute break, Mary Blakely considers the conversation between Caldwell and Lemont. She knows where this situation is leading. She knows how this CO thinks and operates. She knows that the CO does not understand the technical details of navy and DOD telecommunications. Mary also knows Commander Caldwell's attitude regarding navy communicators. He continually shows disrespect and lack of confidence toward communicators. If a telecommunications concept or procedure does not make sense to him, he declares it invalid and orders that it be changed and done his way.

Since assuming command several months ago, CDR Caldwell has ordered a number of changes that go against long-standing navy authorized and navy accepted telecommunications concepts. All of the changes have negatively affected morale. The second day he was in command, he ordered that everyone on watch discontinue wearing dungarees and must wear the uniform of the day. Whites are the uniform of the day in the summertime. The CO declared, incorrectly, that message processing is not dirty work. "Aircraft maintenance is dirty work. Pushing messages is not!"

The radiomen chiefs and the communications officer explained that paper tape and teletype paper contained lubricating oil that is necessary to keep the tape punches and teletype print hammers in good working order. Additionally, all the teletype paper rolls are three-ply with carbon paper. They also explained that the radiomen frequently get oil and grease on their uniforms when removing teletype covers to clear paper jams, insert paper rolls, and when replacing ink ribbons. Additionally, they explained that ink, oil, and grease easily spreads and stains uniforms and does not wash out. The cost of purchasing more white uniforms and the upkeep of those uniforms will have an adverse impact on morale, especially since all radiomen understand the destructive nature of the oil and grease on cloth.

"Nonsense!" CDR Caldwell responded tersely. "You communicators are a complaining lot! Don't bring up the subject of uniforms again!"

Another of the CO's morale-damaging changes for the radiomen was to order the communications watch standers from a four-section, twenty-four hour rotating watch to a three-section rotating watch. This change extended the number of hours of each watch and lessened the downtime between watch strings. The CO ordered the schedule change after several visits to the communications trailers where he viewed what he misperceived as uncontrollable and voluminous message backlogs. The CO considered that Lieutenant Lemont was hiding the backlog condition from him, and he judged that the radiomen were slacking off. Instead of asking the COMMO to explain, Caldwell sent a memo to Lemont ordering that radiomen be placed in three-section watches to increase the number of radiomen per watch as a mechanism to lessen severe backlogs. The COMMO explained that severe backlogs did not exist. The COMMO provided the CO with statistics maintained by the traffic management section. The statistics revealed processing times to be within the parameters specified in DOD communications directives.

The XO was present when CDR Caldwell heaped his berating tirade on Lieutenant Lemont. "Don't bullshit me, Gerry," the captain had said condescendingly. "I see it with my own eyes—piles of message tapes all over the place. Teletype paper flowing over and spilling on the floor, and I see your radiomen standing in the middle of it all while smoking cigarettes and joking around."

"Captain, the statistics show we process messages within specified timeframes," Lemont argued again.

The CO had countered, "Aren't those statistics averages? Doesn't the data show some messages take longer than what is directed by publications?"

Lemont had justified, "Captain, the pubs say use averages to determine efficiency."

"Not good enough!" the CO had retorted. "In the air squadrons all actions are within specification. Pilots die and aircraft are lost otherwise!"

Lemont had advised, "Captain, experience has proven that when we increase the watch stander's working hours past ten hours a day and lessen their downtime, they make more errors."

Commander Caldwell shook his head with disapproval. Then, he informed, "Equal lack of attention to detail in air squadrons are not tolerated. Offenders are punished harshly for such mistakes and are banished from working with aircraft. What actions are taken to punish the incompetent acts of radiomen?"

"Sir, one or two mistakes by a radioman do not constitute incompetence."

Commander Caldwell again shook his head with disapproval and said, "In air squadrons, one minor mistake can cause the loss of an aircraft and death of a pilot. Gerry, I am disappointed with your minimization of such errors. I have concern that you communicators do not police these occurrences appropriately. I ask you again, what actions are taken against operators when they make such mistakes?"

With his face flushed with embarrassment from the CO's rebuke, Lieutenant Lemont responded, "Usually, counseling by the division officer. Repeated occurrences usually lead to lower performance evaluation marks."

Commander Caldwell was astonished. "That's it? No captain's mast? No Article 15 punishment?"

"Sir, during my sixteen years in naval communications, I have never encountered a situation where a radioman received Article 15 punishment for incorrect log entries."

"You communicators are an undisciplined lot!" Caldwell had accused. "I'm going to change that!"

The department head meeting reconvenes.

The CO asks, "What did you find out, Gerry?"

"Sir, we retransmitted those thirty messages two hours after receiving the service message from COMSIXTHFLEET."

"Two hours! What took your radiomen so long?!"

"Sir, we handle service messages first-in-first-out by precedence."

"What was the precedence of the service message?"

"Operational-immediate."

"This is outrageous! It took your radioman two hours to process an operational-immediate! Explain this criminal incompetence!"

"Sir, twenty percent of the messages in the DOD networks are operational-immediate. That means that fifteen percent are over prioritized. We are not allowed to make judgments as to the validity of precedence assignment. My radioman processed other operational-immediate messages in time-of-receipt order. The communications pubs are very clear on this."

"You always have a *by the book* answer, don't you?" Commander Caldwell challenges, irritation edging his tone.

As Lieutenant Commander Mary Blakely listens to the exchange between the CO and the COMMO, she questions the wisdom of Commander Naval Communications assigning an ex-pilot, instead of an experienced naval communicator, as commanding officer of a naval communications station. *This CO continues to show poor leadership. He continually compares air squadron operations to NAVCOMMSTA operation and criticizes naval communicators for not conducting operations the same as an air squadron. He shows no respect for anyone in his command, including me.*

Unless you are in the 'brown shoe navy,' you are not worthy of his respect.

The XO thinks about the CO's most recent exhibition of poor leadership. Commander Caldwell ordered the Club Zeus closed on Sundays. He was appalled to discover that Christians were drinking on Sundays instead of studying their Bibles.

The NAVCOMMSTA does not have a chapel. Religious services are held in the galley. The CO became irate when he discovered last Sunday morning that barracks residents were weight lifting instead of attending services. He ordered the weight lifting equipment removed. *Another morale-busting action.*

Commander Caldwell says, "Gerry, after this meeting, I want you and me and the XO to discuss methods for tightening up discipline in your department."

Following the department-head meeting, Lieutenant Lemont, Lieutenant Commander Blakely, and Commander Caldwell discuss motivation strategy for the radiomen.

Caldwell orders, "From this time forward, you will place on report all radiomen that make mistakes. In addition, you are to establish a watch position for a second traffic checker, a checker checking the checker concept. I want double checking on all logs. Also, I want a second off-the-air fleet broadcast teletype monitor, and a dedicated watch stander with no other duties glued to both off-the-air monitors."

Lieutenant Lemont sighs with resignation. "Captain, creating those watch stations will require the radiomen into a port-and-starboard watch rotation of twelve hours on and twelve hours off with no breaks."

"Enough of this whining!" The CO raises his voice as he hits the table with his fist. "You communicators need a lesson in commitment to mission. On the aircraft carriers off the coast of Vietnam, ship's crew and aircrews are always in port-and-starboard rotation. Do you think your radiomen are somehow privileged and above that?"

Gerry Lemont's last tour was on an aircraft carrier that made two WESTPAC cruises and performed combat missions off the coast of Vietnam. Gerry knows that he can argue against the CO's point with fact, truth, and logic. However, he knows that fact, truth, and logic have no place in the current discussion. He also understands that continuing to disagree with the CO will have no positive result. He responds, "No sir. I do not believe my radiomen are above those sacrificing in the Vietnam War."

"No wonder your radiomen are so undisciplined," the CO scolds with a loud voice. "You don't hold them accountable for anything. Put your radioman in port-and-starboard watches. If I see an increase in processing errors, I will demand report chits. If I must, I will establish waiting lines for captain's mast. Do you understand?"

Lieutenant Lemont, frustrated and disillusioned, decides to discontinue his efforts to make the CO understand. He knows that the number of mistakes will increase, because the radiomen will be exhausted and demoralized.

"Yes sir. I will do it today."

After Lemont departs, Mary Blakely voices her objections to Caldwell actions. "Sir, I can assure you that Mr. Lemont is correct. Putting the radioman in two sections as punishment and not for operational reasons will destroy morale and will increase errors."

"I didn't ask for your opinion," Caldwell chastises.

"Sir, as XO it is my duty to express alternative actions. My experience has taught me that a command culture of reward for good performance is more effective than a command culture of punishment. Reward motivates radiomen to do better. With no reward to achieve and only punishment to endure, morale suffers and feelings of victimization prevail."

Caldwell casts an expression of aloof disagreement; he responds, "XO, you have no understanding of the enlisted mind.

You lack leadership experience. You are not enlightened as to what motivates enlisted men. For the most part, they are aimless and lack self-motivation. They need strong direction by officers."

"Sir, I've managed and supervised radiomen for nearly ten years. This is my fourth NAVCOMMSTA. I know what works."

"XO, you are part of a communicator culture that excuses poor performance. Your experience is exactly the problem." Caldwell sits silent for a few moments; then, he reveals, "I have sent a letter to COMNAVCOM requesting that you be replaced. I have asked that a male non-communicator replace you. I specified in the letter that your lack of sea duty and your unwillingness to accept my direction reflect poor leadership and moral discipline. You are not qualified to serve as executive officer."

Astonishment overcomes her. After a few moments, she transits to a state of bewilderment. She realizes that COMNAVCOM will investigate before taking any action, because six previous commanding officers judged her performance and leadership as exemplary. However, she also considers that COMNAVCOM assigned Caldwell as commanding officer. Uncertainty about her future concerns her.

Chapter 42

"Lieutenant Martin, you have a visitor," advises the young military policeman.

Jeffrey Martin turns over in the narrow bed. He sits up and faces the guard through the bars of his jail cell.

"You must go to the visitor's room. Please put on your shoes."

Jeffrey slips on his shoes and stands. He feels dizzy, which is a condition he suffers since his head was slammed to the cement at the base pool. The detention center doctor had told Jeffrey that the bump on his head would be tender for a while but will shrink after a few days.

The doctor had asked Jeffrey yesterday, "Do you still feel dizzy?"

"No," Jeffrey had responded, although he felt dizzy every time he stood up. He did not want any medical situation to prolong his stay at the detention center.

"The bridge of your nose is fractured," the doctor had told him.

Jeffrey has difficulty remembering the incident at the pool. He remembers that he was disciplining his wife and daughter when a blur of a man, as he remembers it, hit him in the face. The next thing he remembers is that he was in his house in Kifissia beating his wife with a stick. Then, the military police placed him in handcuffs.

He has been in this cell at the U.S. Air Force base near Glifada for the last week and not understanding why. He thought Commander Caldwell would have contacted him by now.

The guard unlocks Jeffrey's cell door.

"Follow me," the guard orders.

Jeffrey steps in behind the guard and follows him. Another guard walks behind.

As he enters the visitor's room, Jeffrey recognizes his friend, Eric Linderhaus, sitting on the other side of the partitioned table.

"Hi Eric," Jeffrey says enthusiastically as he sits down.

"Hi, Jeff, how are you feeling?"

"I'm okay. Do you know what's happening with Constance and Laurie?"

Eric nods his head. "Constance has arranged for her and Laurie to fly back to the States tomorrow."

Jeffrey flinches in anger at the news. *My goddamn wife is disrespecting me again!* Constance had threatened to leave him before. His response was a cold threat to kill her if she ever did.

"Where is she going in the States?" Jeffrey asks.

"I don't know. Constance refuses to tell anyone."

Lieutenant Martin sits in thought for a few moments. Then, he asks, "Eric, do you know what happened at the pool? I just have a vague memory."

"Uh . . . hmmm . . . no. I just know what others are saying."

"What are they saying?"

"They say you took a swing at this new guy, a young sailor, and he hit you and knocked you down."

Jeffrey contemplates Eric's explanation. He attempts to remember, but he cannot.

"They say I took a swing at this guy? Why would I do that? What did he do that would make me do that?"

"I don't know," Eric lies.

"Who is he? Has he been arrested?"

"His name is RM2 Rigney Page. He just reported aboard the day all this happened. He has not been arrested."

"Why wasn't he arrested for striking an officer?"

Eric hesitates answering the question, because answering the question admits that Jeffrey was hitting his wife and child.

"Come on, Eric. If you know, tell me."

Eric sighs and says, "They say you were hitting Constance and Laurie, and this RM2 Page stepped in and stopped you."

Jeffrey jerks his head in anger and responds tersely, "What the fuck difference does that make?! How I discipline my family is my business! No one has the right to interfere!"

Eric glances at the guard standing in the corner. Then, he looks Jeffrey in the face and warns, "Calm down, Jeff. The angrier you become, the more the navy justifies keeping you here for counseling."

"Who says I'm staying here?"

"Commander Caldwell directed me to gather up all your military uniforms and gear and bring them here. You're goin' to stay here a while. The local JAG is investigating you for attempted murder of Constance."

Jeffrey sits quietly and ponders this situation. After a few minutes, he looks questioningly into Eric's face and concludes, "So I gather from all of this that I am the bad guy and this Page is the good guy."

Eric just shrugs.

"Where is this Page assigned?"

"Gerry assigned him to my division."

"What's he like?"

With a spiteful tone, Eric explains, "He's a real show-off, know-it-all type who believes he is something special."

Jeffrey focuses on Eric's words. *There must be some conflict between Eric and this RM2 Page.*

"This enlisted man bothers you, Eric. What has he done?"

"Nothing specific. It's his bearing and attitude."

Jeff smiles conspiratorially at Eric and asks, "Maybe he needs taken down a few notches. Maybe we can plan something for him when I get out of here."

Eric shakes his head as he ponders Jeff's words; then, he responds, "I don't think that's a good idea, Jeff. This Page is smart. He's wise beyond his years. He's no one's fool. I doubt we could get away with anything against him."

Jeff Martin slouches back in his chair, a resigned expression on his face as he says, "I've never seen you so impressed with an enlisted man. You won't help me get this sailor, then?"

"I can't, Jeff. I only have eighteen months left on my military obligation. I have a coaching job locked-up with the University of Ohio. I don't want to jeopardize an honorable military record, just too much to risk."

"I understand, Eric. I am being flushed down the toilet, and you don't want any part of me."

Eric doesn't answer. He stares at the floor.

Jeff Martin's expression turns dismissive; he says, "You can leave, Eric. You don't need to come back."

Chapter 43

Rigney Page and Anna Heisler sit in the villa's living room. They both wear shorts and loose fitting t-shirts. They enjoy the cool breeze flowing through the courtyard doors.

"Your file states that you have a masters diving certificate. Can you navigate underwater?"

"Yes."

"At night?"

"Yes."

"Good, because you and I need to make a dive."

"Why? What's up?" Rigney asks with a curious look on his face.

"You remember me telling you about that ONI mobile radio relay site on that Euboea mountaintop?"

Rigney nods.

"That radio relay site sent a message to the ONI Field Office in Naples reporting that high frequency encrypted radio teletype transmissions started coming from the direction of the Nea Makri base about four weeks ago. Because the Nea Makri location is the NAVCOMMSTA receiver site and Kato Souli is the NAVCOMMSTA transmitter site—located ten miles away—there should be no high frequency radio teletype signals transmitting from the Nea Makri receiver site. ONI dispatched an ELINT team to investigate. The ELINT team found a yacht anchoring itself every night three kilometers east of the Nea Makri site. Naples sent me the report with instructions to investigate further."

"Does the report say anything else?"

"Yes, it says the yacht arrives each evening about one hour after sunset and departs each morning about one hour before sunrise. The report also states that ELINT scans of the vessel reveal continuous encrypted radio teletype transmissions while it's anchored."

Rigney asks, "When do we make the dive and where do we get the diving equipment?"

"The military attaché office at the American Embassy in Athens will arrange for the equipment. We can't be seen renting diving equipment locally. We don't want any of the locals, including any of the sailors at the base, knowing that we are going scuba diving. We need to spec the equipment. I've only made a few scuba dives. I never took any lessons. You're the most experienced, so, you need to give me a list of what gear we will need."

Rigney advises, "I need to know everything we will do during the dive before I can put together a list of equipment."

During the next thirty minutes, Anna explains their mission.

Chapter 44

Anna and Rigney stand in the courtyard for a few minutes to allow their eyes to adjust to dark. Overcast skies block the moonlight. After their eyes adjust, Rigney unlocks and opens the courtyard gate. Anna passes through the gate, followed by Rigney. He shakes the gate gently to insure it is locked.

They wait at the edge of the road. As previously planned, they do not talk.

After five minutes, they hear a vehicle approaching. They see only two small parking lights coming toward them.

A battered, green and white colored Volkswagen bus stops in front of them. Anna enters through the passenger door. Rigney enters through the rear door.

In the bus, Anna sits in the passenger seat. Rigney sits in the seat behind the passenger seat. He discerns the shadow of a woman with long straight hair in the driver's seat.

Anna says, "Rigney, this is Pam. Pam, this is Rigney."

"Hi, Pam, nice to meet you," Rigney responds sincerely.

For the next few minutes, no one speaks while Pam navigates the Volkswagen bus through the dark streets of Nea Makri. When she comes to the Marathon Road intersection, she turns left onto the Marathon Road. Pam presses hard on the gas pedal to increase speed. The Volkswagen bus moves north at fifty kilometers per hour. Air funnels through the vehicle's open windows, cooling the three occupants.

Pam speaks into the dark, "I got all the equipment you requested."

"Excellent," Anna responds with a raised voice.

Before passing the NAVCOMMSTA main gate, Rigney ducks below the bus's window.

The eyes of the Greek sentry and the American sentry follow the Volkswagen bus as it passes under the illumination of the gate lights. Both sentries think they see Page's German girlfriend, but they are not sure. Neither sentry comments to the other about what they think they saw.

Five kilometers north of Nea Makri, Pam turns the bus to the right and onto a narrow potholed dirt road. They bounce up and down and shift side to side as the Volkswagen bus moves slowly across the rough surface.

At the end of the road, Pam stops the bus at a fifteen feet high chain-link gate, which connects to a chain-link fence that stretches into the darkness along the shore in both directions.

Beyond the gate, a short and narrow pier leads to a well-lit, dilapidated commercial fishing vessel.

Pam turns-off the lights and the engine.

They sit quietly for several minutes while their eyes adjust to the dark. The sounds of the night envelop them. A chorus of crickets mixes with the sound of the surf lapping at the rocky shore.

They exit the bus, walk to the gate, and stop.

Several minutes later, a man steps down a short gangway from the vessel to the pier. He walks a few feet; then, he bends over with his arm outstretched.

The gate opens.

They pass through the gate.

The gate closes behind them.

They walk along the pier toward the vessel. The man from the vessel waits for them near the gangway. The low rumble of the vessel's diesel engines vibrates the pier.

The man appears midthirties and typically Greek with a Greek fisherman's hat, black curly hair, and brushy mustache. Pam stretches out her hand and says, "Hi Bill, nice to work with you again."

"Hi, Pam, always happy to break the monotony of our normal ELINT missions to help our HUMINT brothers and sisters."

Pam turns to Anna and Rigney and performs the introductions, "Bill, this is Anna and Rigney. They'll do the dive."

Bill steps closer to Rigney and looks him directly in the face.

"You're Page?" Bill questions with a dubious expression.

"Without a doubt," Rigney quips as he grips Bill's hand. He knows that he is again under doubt because of his youthful looks, which leads veteran operatives to doubt Rigney's capabilities.

"Let's get underway," Anna urges.

Bill quickly shifts his attention from Rigney to Anna and then glances at Pam. "Yes, of course. Please step aboard the *Eleni*, and we'll get underway."

As Rigney steps from the gangway onto the deck of the *Eleni*, he observes the vessel's solid construction. Deceitful shades of paint portray the vessel as dilapidated from a distance.

Rigney also notices that the rigging for nets and fishing lines are not exactly what they appear to be at a distance. Evenly cut lengths of cable separated by ceramic insulators reveal a web of radio antennas.

Bill leads them through a hatch below the pilothouse and down a six-step ladder to a large compartment; racks of electronic equipment line the forward, port, and starboard bulkheads.

A middle-aged black man with close-cropped salt-and-pepper colored hair sits on a stool and tunes a radio receiver.

Rigney quickly scans the equipment racks. He recognizes radio receivers, radio transceivers, oscilloscopes, spectrum analyzers, and distortion analyzers.

The middle-aged man rotates on his stool and faces the group.

Bill says, "Eddie, this is Anna and Page. You know Pam."

Eddie nods and rotates on his stool back toward the equipment rack; he continues tuning the receiver.

"The galley, heads, and berthing compartment are through that hatch." Bill points to a door on the aft bulkhead.

Pam inquires, "Where is the rest of your crew?"

"I left them in Athens. They don't need to know about this."

"Where's our gear?" Anna asks.

Bill points at two canvas dive bags in a corner. Then, he announces, "I'm going to the pilothouse and get this bucket underway."

"Let's suit up," Anna orders.

Rigney unzips the two dive bags and pulls out a scuba air tank from each bag. He sets both air tanks in the corner. Then, he pulls two black-colored bodysuits with matching hoods and dive boots.

Anna quickly removes her blouse and shorts, revealing she wears a two-piece black bathing suit underneath.

Rigney shucks his clothes down to his boxer-style bathing suit. His near nakedness brings stares from Pam.

They slip into the thinly layered bodysuits, followed by pulling on the dive boots.

Rigney straps a twelve-inch diving knife to the outside of his right calf. Then he hands the other dive knife to Anna.

"I was wondering why those knives were on your list," Pam states. "I mean in addition to the automatic pistols on Anna's list."

"A dive knife is not a weapon," Rigney responds as he picks up one of the silencer-equipped automatics. "A dive knife is a tool needed for cutting your way out of discarded fishing nets or other snagging hazards that have found their way into your path."

"Oh," Pam mutters. She decides not to reveal that she always thought scuba divers strapped on the knives for some kind of adolescent macho image.

Rigney pulls a buoyancy compensator—BC—from one of the dive bags and hands it to Anna.

Anna slips the BC over her head and fastens the straps of the life-vest-like device.

The deck vibrates under their feet as the vessel moves away from the pier.

Rigney assists Anna with adjusting her facemask strap and with adjusting the snorkel attachment.

After he is satisfied that Anna's gear fits properly, he dons his own BC, mask, and snorkel.

Rigney stands still and cocks his head as if listening to something the others cannot hear. "No detectable swell," Rigney advises. "That'll make the swim easier."

He retrieves two dive compasses and hands one to Anna. They each strap a compass to their left wrist.

"How you gonna read those gauges and compasses in the dark?" Pam questions as she points to Rigney's gauge panel.

"Luminescent dials," Rigney responds. "But just in case, we will carry these." Rigney holds up two small watertight flashlights.

Bill's voice sounds over a speaker system. "We're coming close to the dive point. We have the target off the starboard side."

Rigney and Anna pick up their swim fins and start toward the portside hatch.

"Hey, aren't you taking the air tanks," Pam asks.

Anna turns and answers, "No. We're doing this swim all on the surface. After we analyzed the weather and tide forecasts and the lunar cycle, we figured we would not need them."

The vessel slows.

They exit the well-lit compartment, close the hatch behind them, and step onto the main deck portside. With swim fins in hand, they stand still and allow their eyes to adjust to the dark.

The only energized lights on the exterior of the vessel are the running lights.

Several minutes later, Eddie and Pam join Rigney and Anna.

The vessel has slowed to three knots and is barely making headway.

Eddie advises, "We're gonna drop you off here. That channel marker will be your point of reference to the target."

Anna and Rigney shift their attention to the channel marker buoy about one hundred feet away. The channel marker has a blinking light on top and sways slightly in the nearly motionless water. They put on their dive fins.

Eddie adds, "I just took a radio fix on your target. She bears 273 at 300 yards and is the only boat within forty degrees on either side of that bearing."

Rigney and Anna nod.

Pam asks, "There's more than one yacht out there?"

"Yes, nine others," Eddie replies. "That area is an overflow anchorage for the Nea Makri marina."

Eddie eyes Anna and says, "We'll pick you up at the channel marker buoy three hours from now."

Simultaneously, Anna and Rigney look at their watches; then, they nod their understanding of the pickup time.

Bill walks up to the group. He drags an eight feet long inflated rubber boat. Then, he tosses it over the side but holds the mooring line. Then, he hands the mooring line to Rigney.

"You must get into the water now," Bill advises. "We need to avoid drawing attention by staying here too long. The rest of your gear is in a rubber bag in the bow of the inflatable.

They slip their dive masks over their faces, insert their snorkels into their mouths, and jump into the water. Seawater fills the inside of their body suits. The taste of saltwater seeps onto their tongues.

After they surface, they blow air into their BCs. Then, they swim toward the channel marker buoy. Rigney drags the inflatable boat by the mooring line. When they reach the buoy, Rigney ties the inflatable's mooring line to it.

Anna removes the snorkel from her mouth and says, "Let's get the rest of the equipment."

Rigney reaches into the bow of the inflatable and unfastens the strap holding the gear bag to the bow. He opens the bag and pulls out a twenty feet length of line with snap fasteners on each end. He hooks one end of the line to a strap of his BC; he hooks the other end to a strap to Anna's BC. The connected line tethers them together and will prevent them from separating during their mission.

Rigney feels around inside the gear bag and removes the remaining items, which include one night vision monocular, one regular binocular, and an automatic pistol with silencer attached. All items are sealed in plastic bags. As they had previously planned, Anna will carry the automatic, and Rigney will carry both monocular and binocular. They put their items into pouches hanging from their buoyancy compensators.

"Ready?" Anna questions with a whisper.

Rigney removes the snorkel from his mouth and whispers his reply, "Ready when you are."

They whisper, because sound carries farther over water than over land.

"Let's take a bearing," Anna directs.

They both bring their compasses to eye level. They find 270 degrees and look down the bearing and locate the yacht. Lights on top of the yacht's cabin illuminate the forward and aft decks, and the illumination spreads out thirty feet in all directions over the water. The night provides no scale for distance, but they know from Eddie's previous report that the yacht is three hundred yards away.

Because the yacht's deck lights shine across the water, they will not be able to get as close as they previously planned. The positive side being that they will not need the night vision monocular to view activity on the decks. Additionally, deck sentries cannot use night vision goggles.

Anna modifies their plan. "We'll need to stop about twenty feet away from the illuminated area. We should have no problem watching any activity on deck."

They put their snorkels in their mouths and kick away from the channel marker buoy. They kick at a medium speed so as not to overexert themselves. As previously planned, Rigney takes the lead. During their swim to the yacht, Rigney stops twice to verify the bearing and their direction.

They quit kicking and stop in the dark about twenty feet from the illuminated area surrounding the yacht. Their inflated BCs keep their heads above water. Because of their excellent physical condition, the swim did not tire them; they breathe normally.

They bob up and down slightly in the mostly calm water. They can hear the low hum of the yacht's generator. As their plan specifies, Rigney watches the decks of the yacht, and Anna provides security.

Rigney removes his facemask and lets it fall to rest around his neck. Anna does the same. Then, he pulls the binocular from the pouch and scans the yacht. The binocular brings the yacht close enough to touch. A small radar antenna rotates on the roof of the forward cabin. He sees no one on deck.

Inside the aft cabin of the yacht, rack-mounted electronics equipment stand along all four bulkheads. A man with a dark complexion, curly black hair, thick mustache, and dark brown eyes sits in a swivel chair and watches a radarscope and a sonar screen. He wears a gray-colored cotton denim shirt and worn blue denim pants. A half-smoked cigarette smolders in an ashtray at his elbow. The acrid smoke from the Turkish cigarette fills the cabin.

The cabin hatch opens. A man of similar appearance and similar clothes steps down the short ladder. His manner conveys he is the mission leader. He speaks in Spanish, "Anything unusual to report? Any close contacts?"

"Nothing unusual, no contacts, except other yachts. No transmissions from them."

"Okay," the leader responds, "But we will follow procedure and turn off the deck lights anyway."

The subordinate reaches across several feet of consol and flips a switch. The exterior of the yacht goes dark except for the running lights.

After the deck lights extinguish, Rigney slips the regular binocular back in its pouch, and he pulls out the night vision monocular.

After several minutes of watching the yacht's decks, he feels Anna tapping on his shoulder. He reaches out and runs his hand up her arm; then, he taps her shoulder twice, which indicates nothing seen so far.

Several minutes later, Rigney observes a man exiting the aft cabin.

The man climbs to the top of the aft cabin. He removes a canvas cover from a deck-mounted device.

Through the green hue of the night vision monocular, Rigney recognizes the device as a parabolic dish antenna atop a four feet high pedestal.

The man steps down to the main deck and walks to the bow.

Rigney watches intently as the man loosens clamps on three metal poles.

The man screws the ends of the poles together. Then, he stands the pole vertically and screws the base into a deck-mounted connector.

Rigney estimates the whip antenna to be twenty feet in length.

The man walks back to the aft cabin and disappears below.

Rigney feels Anna tapping on his shoulder again.

He gives her one tap on her shoulder to indicate he is watching interesting activity.

Movement on top of the aft cabin causes Rigney to focus the night vision monocular on the parabolic dish antenna, which moves back and forth within a twenty-degree range.

Down in the yacht's aft cabin, the technician rotates a dial that controls the direction of the parabolic dish antenna. He watches the signal level meter on the radio receiver that connects to the parabolic dish antenna. After several moments, he finds the best bearing to get the best quality radio signal. Using a patch cord, he connects the output signal of the radio receiver to the input of a high frequency radio transmitter. Then, he flips a switch on the transmitter, and the transmitter's power output meter jumps to five hundred watts. He reports to the mission leader, "We are transmitting."

In the equipment room of the *Eleni*, Eddie wears an earphone set and tunes direction finding equipment. After several minutes, he hears the radio teletype signal from the yacht. Eddie leans toward the intercom, presses the lever, and reports, "Bill, the target is transmitting."

Anna and Rigney continue to bob up and down in the mild swell. Nothing has happened on deck for ten minutes.

Rigney considers taking a bearing on the direction the parabolic dish antenna is aimed. To do that, they must move twenty feet to the south. He nudges Anna to start her moving in the southerly direction.

They kick their legs four times to travel the necessary distance.

Rigney looks through the night vision monocular. The complete circular shape of the back of the parabolic dish antenna appears dead center in the night vision monocular. He knows that a straight line between him and the center of the antenna will give him the bearing that the parabolic dish points. He adjusts the compass control on the side of the monocular. The bearing display becomes clear. He memorizes the bearing.

Then, He turns and faces the direction of the channel marker buoy. Three hundred yards away, the light on the top of the buoy blinks repeatedly. He memorizes the bearing to the buoy.

He rotates in the water and continues his surveillance of the yacht.

Five minutes later, Anna taps the departure signal on his shoulder.

Rigney places the monocular in its pouch.

Anna had not removed the Beretta automatic from its pouch, but she kept her hand on the pouch most of the time.

They kick off in the direction of the channel marker buoy. After arriving at the buoy, they climb into the raft and wait.

Ten minutes later, they see the red, white, and green running lights of a vessel approaching from the south. Rigney retrieves the night vision monocular and raises it to his eyes. He easily identifies the shape of the *Eleni*. The vessel approaches slowly.

Rigney unties the raft mooring line.

As the *Eleni's* starboard side comes alongside of them, Rigney tosses the mooring line up to Eddie who stands near a low wattage light on the main deck.

The yacht is off the *Eleni's* portside, thereby hiding the boarding actions of Anna and Rigney.

Eddie ties the mooring line to the rail. The *Eleni* increases speed; she steams at six knots when Rigney and Anna climb the rope ladder and step up to the main deck.

They move forward quickly and enter the electronics compartment.

Rigney and Anna remove their bodysuits and towel off.

"What did you see?" Anna asks Rigney as she rubs the towel through her hair.

"I watched a guy set up a parabolic antenna on the aft end and a whip antenna near the bow."

"What does that mean to you?" Pam inquires.

"We know that the yacht transmits high frequency radio teletype. It makes sense they would do that on the whip antenna. I think they are picking up a signal on the parabolic dish and retransmitting on the whip."

Anna slips the wet towel around her neck and asks, "Did you take a bearing on the parabolic?"

"Sure did."

Anna looks around the compartment and spots the chart table. She asks, "Eddie, did you plot that yacht on the chart?"

"Yeah. Come over to the chart table, and I will show you."

Anna, Pam, and Rigney follow Eddie to the chart table.

"Yacht is here," Eddie points with the eraser end of a pencil.

Rigney informs, "The bearing I took on the channel marker buoy from the yacht was 098."

Using a chart device with compass gradients, Eddie draws a line from the yacht to the buoy; he confirms, "Right on."

"The parabolic dish was aimed on bearing 270 degrees—due west."

Using the chart ruler, Eddie draws a line from the yacht on bearing 270 degrees.

Everyone's eyes follow the pencil as Eddie draws the line. They exchange concerned looks as the pencil line crosses the shoreline.

Anna directs, "Please continue the line inland for one kilometer."

Again, they all exchange concerned looks. The chart has an outline of the land and buildings of the Nea Makri NAVCOMMSTA. The pencil line passes through the center of the communications trailers compound.

Pam inquires, "What do you think it means?"

Eddie responds, "Could mean a number of things. For example, the yacht might be jamming some frequencies crucial to operation of the NAVCOMMSTA."

Rigney runs his finger along the pencil line and expresses concentration. Then, he opines, "I don't think the yacht's parabolic dish antenna is transmitting. I think it is receiving a signal from the direction of the NAVCOMMSTA."

"Why do you say that?" Anna asks while focusing on Rigney's face.

"Because the parabolic dish was moving within a range of twenty degrees for nearly thirty seconds. Then, the range narrowed, as if the antenna operator were attempting to find the strongest signal and was narrowing in on it. Then, the dish stopped moving and pointed in the direction of 270 degrees. If it were a transmitting parabolic dish, the operator would have immediately pointed the dish to 270 degrees."

"So what does that mean?" Pam inquires, not totally understanding the technical aspects.

Eddie responds, "It means that the yacht is receiving a signal from the area of the NAVCOMMSTA and the yacht radio operator knows the radio frequency and the general bearing to find it. Also, it probably means that the yacht is taking the signal received on the parabolic and retransmitting that signal on the whip antenna."

Chapter 45

Rigney prepares for his first power walk since arriving in Nea Makri. He slips on a pair of lightweight black-colored cotton gym shorts and a gray-colored t-shirt. After several minutes of searching, he finds assorted dumbbells in the coat closet near the front door. He selects two eight-pounders.

After exiting the villa courtyard gate and locking it behind him, he turns left, which leads him up a steep incline. As he walks swiftly up the incline, he performs alternate curls with each eight-pound dumbbell.

As he walks, he absorbs the rugged beauty of the hilly terrain. Acres separate the villas on this road. Between the villas, sheep graze in small rocky pastures. Olive trees rise in no organized manner in open fields.

Twenty minutes later, the road comes to an end. He stops walking and stops curling the dumbbells while he decides which direction to go. He examines the landscape going west up the mountain and decides climbing that rough ground would require his hands to be free.

He observes a rock-laden dirt road to his left, leading southward. He sees cars parked about half a mile away at the end of the dirt road. The cars appear to be parked on a paved road. He concludes that if he walks the length of the dirt road and turns left on the paved road, he will be circling back toward the villa.

Rigney walks along the dirt road; he sweats profusely. His rapid pace kicks up the dirt, which cakes on his sneakers and socks. As he closes the distance to the end of the dirt road, he hears a loud barking dog. He also hears several people shouting in English; but the shouters have strong German accents, and one of the shouters has a strong British accent.

As he steps onto the paved road, turns to the left, and starts down the hill, he sees the source of the loud barking. A large

Doberman Pinscher barks ferociously as it runs rapidly back and forth behind a six feet high chain-link fence.

People stand in the yards of houses on each side of the house with the barking dog and in yards of houses across the street. A crowd of six people gathers on the far side of the street across from the Doberman house. The people in yards shout in English toward the house with the dog. The people have a mix of German and British accents.

"You ignorant Yank!" shouts a man from across the street. "Show some decency, you arrogant bugger! Tame that dog!"

Another man, who stands in the yard next to the Doberman house, shouts with a strong German accent, "You ugly American! We cannot rest our outside. Dog destroy quiet!"

Rigney stops in the middle of the street in front of the house with the Doberman. He continues to curl the dumbbells while he takes a long look at the dog.

The powerful and elegant black Doberman barks and bares its scissorlike teeth. The dog utters a deep growl. Then, the dog focuses its barking attack at Rigney. The dog runs rapidly back and forth along the fence and barks incessantly. Every twenty seconds or so, the dog attempts to climb the fence but cannot overcome the chain links and barbed wire strands across the top.

Rigney becomes fascinated with the menacing dog's behavior. He continues to curl his dumbbells and walk in place.

The Germans, Brits, and Greeks exit their yards and gather around Rigney.

The Doberman jumps to the top of a large marble table that sits seven feet back from the fence. Rigney and the other people around him take a few steps backward as the dog leaps from the table to jump over the fence. The dog's jump falls short, and the dog yelps as the barbs cut its skin. The dog falls back into the yard, shakes it off, and continues its barking attack.

One of the people behind Rigney speaks English with a British accent, "One of these days that dog will make it over that fence. Then, someone will be killed by that animal."

Others in the crowd voice their agreement with the Brit.

Rigney notices someone exiting the front door of the Doberman house.

A short, chubby man who wears a white undershirt, baggy shorts, and flip-flops steps into the yard; he carries a baseball bat in his right hand and holds a beer can in his left hand.

Rigney recognizes Mr. Pritchings, the warrant officer who is the traffic division officer.

Pritchings's flushed face tells of his afternoon of drinking. He started drinking at Club Zeus before driving home. Pritchings yells commands to the Doberman, "Quiet, Sparks! Sit!"

The Doberman stops barking and sits, but still bares its teeth and growls in a low tone.

The German, British, and Greek onlookers crowd around Rigney as they take a few steps closer toward the chain-link fence.

Pritchings scans the people staring at him. He sneers and shouts in an alcoholic slur, "What the fuck you people doing to scare my dog?! Get away from here, or I will let Sparks loose on you!"

One of the Brits steps forward and shouts, "That dog barks for hours—you rude American!"

For the first time, one of the Greek onlookers speaks, his English rich in Greek accent, "Our village peaceful before you ugly American come!"

Then, one of the Germans adds in almost-perfect English, "You Americans are not welcome here. You are arrogant and have no manners!"

Pritchings steps closer to the fence and shouts back, "Go to hell, you kraut and limey bastards! We saved your asses in World War II, and now you have no respect or appreciation! While Americans were dying to save your fucking asses, you were all hiding in your houses. Now, get the fuck away from me!"

Mr. Pritchings's curses and foul outburst astound Rigney. Until now, he had no opinion of the warrant officer. Now, he feels disrespect toward the officer. *Why did the navy ever promote such an unenlightened, rude, crude, and vulgar sailor to chief warrant officer? How did he pass his overseas screening?*

As the crowd moves toward the fence, Pritchings places the beer can on the marble table and brings the baseball bat to swinging position.

The crowd stops and steps back a few paces, which positions Rigney immediately ahead of the crowd of Europeans.

Rigney stops curling the dumbbells and stops walking in place as he notices Pritchings's gaze fall upon him.

For the first time, Pritchings notices the sailor accused of assaulting Jeff Martin. He does not remember the sailor's name. Pritchings casts an angry expression at Rigney, and queries in an angry tone, "Why are you here, sailor? Are you part of this mob?"

Until now, the crowd of Europeans did not recognize Rigney as an American. They had considered him a passerby who stopped to observe the commotion.

"No sir. I was just passing by," Rigney finally answers.

"Get the fuck outta here, then!" Pritchings orders in a threatening tone. "This is none of your business!"

Rigney's immediate reaction is to obey the officer's order. He considers walking away and putting this scene behind him. Then, he realizes he has all the right in the world to be here. *This is a public street. This officer has no right to order me away. Pritchings acts inappropriately.*

Rigney remains standing in the same spot. He decides not to obey the drunken officer's order.

"You are a sailor at the Nea Makri base, then?" asks one of the Brits.

"Yes," Rigney replies softly and with a nod of his head. Rigney feels embarrassed to be associated with Pritchings.

Pritchings's anger increases; he shouts, "I will take care of your insolence later. Report to my office at 0900 Monday morning!"

"Yes, sir," Rigney replies calmly and without emotion.

The Europeans shoot glances between Rigney and Pritchings. They nod their approval of Rigney's defiance. They all sense Rigney's embarrassment regarding Pritchings, and they appreciate Rigney's predicament.

The sound of sirens causes all to look down the hill. A Greek police car approaches rapidly up the hill.

"Schließlich!" announces one of the Germans with a sigh.

One of the Greeks comment, "All times happens this . . . police do nothing on dog and American."

Rigney backs his way through the crowd. Before he turns to leave, one of the Greek men says, "Young sailor, you be kind and understand person. Any times you want things come my house there." The Greek points to the house behind him.

"Yeah, Yank . . . same goes for me. You need help against that bastard. See me anytime. That's my house over there." The Brit points to a house with the fountain in the front yard."

In unison, the other Greeks, Brits, and Germans comment that Rigney is welcomed anytime.

"Thank you," Rigney responds shyly and with a smile. "I must go now."

He walks nonchalantly down the hill, hugging the side of the road. So that he does not bring attention to himself, he does not curl the dumbbells and hopes the police will not find him a person of interest.

When the police car passes him without slowing, Rigney sees the two policemen have their eyes glued to the crowd up the hill.

When the police are well behind him, he increases his pace and resumes curling the dumbbells.

Chapter 46

At 1930, Rigney begins the walk from Anna's villa to the house of Master Chief Raymond Rodgers. The walk is mostly downhill. The master chief's house is near the beach. The summer sun disappeared to the west side of Mount Penteli more than an hour ago. Nevertheless, enough sunlight remains for enjoying the view. White stucco structures with red-tile roofs cast against the blue of the Aegean. Locals and tourists sit in their front yards, and children jump and run in their fantasy games. Greeks and tourists pass him with cheerful greetings.

As he walks up to Rodgers's front door, he notices a large garage connected to the house. Rodgers's late-model Audi rests on the gravel driveway in front of the garage door.

Rodgers meets Rigney at the door and guides him inside. Rigney feels the blast of cool air-conditioning as he steps over the threshold. Air-conditioning is a rare convenience in Greek homes. *The villa isn't air-conditioned!*

"When you weren't here at 1800, I thought you might not come."

"Sorry about being late. I lost track of time."

Rodgers leads Rigney into a large room with a desk at the far end and plaques on the wall. Bookcases cover the wall to the right. In the center of the room, four sailors from the base sit around a professional-looking poker table. Rigney knows who they are, but has never met them formally.

Rodgers performs the introductions and advises, "Rigney, when we're playing poker, we are on a first-name basis. Are you okay with that?"

"I can call you Ray, then?" Rigney asks.

"Yes, away from the base you can call me Ray."

"Rigney Page, this is Bob Spaulding." Rodgers introduces the tall black sailor who is a first class radioman and a HI-COMM watch supervisor.

"Bob, please call me, Rig," Rigney says as he shakes Bob's hand.

"Hi, Rig, I'm Chuck Henry," the chief yeoman shakes Rigney's hand.

"I'm Steve Johnson," says the senior chief storekeeper.

Rigney shakes Johnson's hand.

"George Latham," the first class quartermaster stands and shakes Rigney's hand.

Rigney sits at the only empty seat. He looks around the room and decides it must be Rodgers's den. A sideboard of cold turkey, cold ham, rolls, and condiments stands on the opposite side of the room.

Rodgers offers, "Anytime you want a beer, you are welcome to go into the kitchen and get one from the fridge."

"Thanks," Rigney responds.

After an hour of play, Rigney is up $500.00 with a total stack of $2,200.00. Winning two months salary in one hour astonishes him. Each time he takes a pot, the other players speak of his beginner's luck.

The only other winner in the game is Master Chief Rodgers who now has $3,000.00.

"Seven-card stud," Rodgers announces as he deals.

Rigney watches the cards fall around the table as Rodgers deals.

Rigney's up card is the queen-of-hearts.

Spaulding checks to Rigney.

Rigney looks at his two hold cards and sees the queen-of-clubs and the queen-of-spades. *Three queens!* He looks around the table and sees no up card higher than his queen. He bets forty dollars.

Everyone folds, except for Rodgers, who calls.

Rigney looks at the master chief's up card, which is the ten-of-spades.

Rodgers deals the next card.

Rigney receives the ten-of-clubs.

Ray receives the eight-of-spades.

Rigney is first to bet, and he bets $150.00.

Without hesitation, Rodgers calls and deals the next card.

Rigney receives the queen-of-diamonds. Now, he holds four queens with two of the queens showing.

Rodgers receives the nine-of-spades. Rodgers shows the eight, nine, and ten-of-spades.

Rigney considers that Rodgers may have been drawing to a straight or a flush and may now have one of those hands. He decides to trap the master chief.

"Check," Rigney declares, hoping that Rodgers will make a big bet.

Rigney notices a slight expression of surprise on Rodgers's face.

Rodgers peaks at his hole cards.

Rigney evaluates the master chief's body language.

Rodgers portrays a stonelike poker face. He confirms the six and seven-of-spades in the hole. He holds a straight-flush to the ten.

Rodgers had previously put six stacked decks in the game this evening. All of the previous stacked decks were organized for Page to win from the other players. With the current stacked deck, Rodgers plans to break Page during the current hand.

The other players are ignorant pawns in Rodgers's devious and greedy plan. Rodgers gathers this group of navy men each week to play poker—sometimes twice a week. The navy men have rankings from lower enlisted to chiefs to junior officers. Rodgers entices these sailors into his poker game with promises of fun at games of chance and with a reputation that he does not allow the poker sharks from the base into his game. Enticements also include an air-conditioned playing environment and scrumptious feasts.

Rodgers has no scruples and no reservations regarding cheating his shipmates. He learned his cheating strategies ten years previous when he purchased several books on how to identify poker cheats. Rodgers carefully selects novice and naive players for his game.

Rodgers studies Rigney's face and attempts to understand Rigney's check. He knows that Page has four queens, because that is how he stacked the deck.

He's trying to trap me, Rodgers concludes. *Well, it can work both ways.*

"Check," Rodgers announces.

Because of his inexperience at poker, Rigney does not know that Rodgers's check makes no sense. He does not even consider that the master chief is attempting the trap in reverse.

Rodgers deals the fourth up card.

Rigney gets a ten-of-diamonds. His up cards shows two pair—queens and tens.

Rodgers gets the jack-of-spades and now holds a jack high straight-flush. His up cards show four cards to a jack high straight-flush.

Rigney considers what to do next. *The check didn't work. Master chief probably has the flush and he probably thinks I have a full house. If I check, he can't help but think I have the full house and trying to hide it. The pot has $700.00. If I bet $700.00, he will be sure that I have the full house, and he will fold.*

Rodgers stares at his sixth card, the jack-of-spades, and realizes the mistake he made. He did not stack the deck past the first five cards. He figured that Page would make a big bet on the fifth card . . . *and that's when I was to go all in on him.* Rodgers knows that he has destroyed his chances for breaking Page, because Page will never make a big bet now. Rodgers considers, *Page will make a small bet in an effort to confuse me. If I bet the pot after Page makes a small bet, he may realize that I have the straight-flush, especially now that I have four spades to a straight-flush showing. I must consider a new strategy to get as much as I can from this pot.*

Rigney bets $150.00, thinking that Rodgers will fold his flush.

Rodgers calls and deals the seventh card down.

Rigney stares at Rodgers's four up cards and evaluates what other hand that Rodgers could have. Then, he sees it. *Rodgers must have a straight-flush! What are the odds of me having four queens at the same time he has a straight-flush, unless Rodgers stacked the deck.*

Rigney read about stacked decks in the poker book that Bob Mater gave him. *They briefed me that Rodgers probably cheats, and Rodgers is dealing. Wait a minute . . . every time I won a big pot, Rodgers was dealing.*

The pot now has $1,000.00.

Rigney evaluates his position. His investment so far is less than half the pot. *If I bet and Rodgers raises, then, I lose more money. If I check, and Rodgers bets, and I call, I lose more money.*

"I check," Rigney says softly.

Frustration steams inside of Rodgers. *Damn my assumptions and not thinking past the fifth card. Page knows that I have the straight-flush. I can see it in his face.*

"I bet one thousand dollars," Rodgers declares confidently.

Rigney scoops up his cards and tosses them into the discards.

"You didn't have a full house?" Chuck Henry asks.

"No."

Rodgers stares intently at Page. He looks for a sign that Page did not know what he was doing and that Page's play was just amateurish. *He's too young to be a veteran poker player.*

"Think I'll get a beer," Rigney announces as he stands.

Just before exiting the den, Rigney glances over his shoulder to see if any of the players watch him. None look in his direction; they play the next hand.

Rigney finds the kitchen. He opens the door to the refrigerator and finds it stocked with Amstel and Budweiser. He removes an Amstel and opens it with a bottle opener from the counter top. He leans against the counter, takes a swig of his beer, and looks around the small kitchen. The appliances are small, but modern.

A narrow pantry draws his attention. He walks the length of the pantry and finds a door with a small window. The door leads to the backyard.

He returns to the kitchen and leans back against the counter. He studies a solid wood door on the opposite wall. He walks to the door and tries the knob—locked. He walks back to the counter on the opposite side of the kitchen and leans against it as he studies the door. He takes another swig of beer. He sees the keyhole in the middle of the knob. Then he notices a dead bolt with key lock at the top of the door. He searches his memory as to how the house appears from the outside. *Must be the door to the garage,* Rigney concludes. *Why would the inside door to the garage be locked? Why would you want to key-lock it from the inside when sliding-bolt locks or turn-bolt locks would work the same?*

Rigney hears steps, and he looks toward the doorway to the dinning room. Rodgers walks into the kitchen and says, "There you are. You've missed a couple of hands. What's taking you so long in here?"

Rigney thinks fast and says, "I am thinking that I am out of my league in this game. I worry that I will lose all my money before I gain an understanding of what's going on."

"Come on, Page. It's all a matter of luck. Sometimes you win and sometimes you lose. The goal is to just have a good time."

Spoken like a true manipulator. This master chief is despicable!

Rigney follows Rodgers back to the den and sits at the poker table. He stares at his stack and estimates he has just a little over $2,000.00. At that moment, he decides not to put much of it in jeopardy. He will be polite and still take hands, but will not play much or bet much.

For the last thirty minutes, Rigney has folded every hand after the initial deal.

Rodgers deals and announces, "The game is seven-card stud high-low split."

Chuck Henry, who sits on Rigney's right, bets $60.00.

Rigney's up card is the three-of-spades. He looks at his hole cards and sees the ace-of-spades and duce-of-spades. He sighs deeply and folds his hand.

Bob Spaulding declares, "Hey, Page, you're missing a great poker game." Spaulding calls the $60.00 bet.

"Not getting any hands," Rigney responds.

Rodgers stares at Page and wonders about Page's motivation for sitting in this game.

Chapter 47

Rigney enters the communications trailers. He waves to the security guard. He turns to the right and knocks on the door of Mr. Pritchings's office.

"Enter!" Pritchings orders from within.

Rigney removes his hat and opens the door.

Pritchings places his cup of coffee on his desktop. He glares at RM2 Page. Pritchings wears his Tropical White Long uniform. The gold and blue bars on his shoulder boards are those of a commissioned warrant officer—CWO2. Pritchings wrinkled white cotton uniform stretches tight across his chubby body. The uniform's yellowish shade betrays Pritchings's lackadaisical care of his uniforms.

"Well, Page, glad to see that you can follow orders and be here as I directed. After disobeying me on Saturday, I thought I would need to put you on report."

"Sir, ordering me off the street was an inappropriate order. I was on a public street and not doing anything wrong."

"You're too much of a boot camp to know such things. You'll do best by following all orders from your superiors."

"Mr. Pritchings, the chance of me ever obeying an order by you off this base is unlikely. You're a pathetic example of a naval officer. You're uncouth, unenlightened, and repulsive."

Pritchings's chubby face flushes red. "Watch it, Page. You continue with that kinda talk, I will place you on report for insubordination."

"You won't do that," Rigney declares.

Pritchings reaches into his desk and pulls out a pad of blank report chits. Pritchings calms and his face returns to a normal shade.

Rigney stares at the pad of report chits; then, he says unemotionally, "You have no witnesses. Your word against mine, and I suspect that you don't have a lot of credibility with your superiors.

If you place me on report, I will request court-martial. I will call your neighbors as witnesses. They will expose your true nature."

"True nature?! What the hell are you talking about?!"

"Mr. Pritchings, if you are not aware of your inappropriate nature, then, you're past redemption."

Rigney can tell from the expression on Pritchings's face that Pritchings is aware of his true nature.

"Is there anything else, sir?"

Pritchings stares at Page while considering how to handle this situation. On one hand, he wants to exert his authority over this disrespectful, boot camp know-it-all. On the other hand, he fears that Page will carry out his threat to request court-martial.

"Page, I will let you off with a warning this time. Stay off my street. If you continue to conspire against me with my neighbors, you will get that court-martial."

Rigney chuckles. He stands-up from the chair and replies, "I will walk any street I want, and I will socialize with any locals that I want. Now, sir, is there anything else?"

Pritchings becomes frustrated. He knows he cannot do anything against Page. He resorts to a threat. "Walk the straight and narrow, Page. Make a mistake with witnesses present, and I will be all over you. Now, get out of my office!"

Chapter 48

Rigney sits in the villa's living room. A humid breeze blows through the open patio doors. The natural marble floors cool Rigney's bare feet. Shorts and a t-shirt aid in cooling him. He turns to the comics section of the Stars and Stripes newspaper. He attempts to concentrate on his favorite comic strip, but his meeting with Pritchings this morning nags at his thoughts. He wonders about officers who act inappropriately and believe their subordinates must endure the results of those inappropriate acts.

Sailors in Pritchings's division continually bitch about Pritchings's behavior. They say he frequently snaps at sailors for no reason, constantly threatens to place them on report, and issues nonsensical orders.

Rigney wonders about his own stubborn and independent behavior. He considers that he engaged in several physical confrontations. He knows he could have avoided those confrontations, but being a submissive victim is not in his nature. *Have I acted inappropriately and put the mission in danger?*

The front gate alarm sounds. Rigney looks at his watch—5:15 PM. *Can't be Anna. She said she would not be back until 10:00 PM.*

He slips on sandals and steps out the front door and looks toward the gate. Through the wrought-iron bars, he sees some of Pritchings's neighbors.

They wave at him to come to the gate.

Rigney steps quickly to the gate, unlocks it, and steps to the outside of the gate.

The Englishman says, "Hi, Yank, remember us? I'm William and this is Nick."

"Yes, I remember. Nice to see you," Rigney responds with a smile and friendly manner. "What can I do for you?"

"We want you come road happy," Nick says.

Rigney smiles and turns to the Englishman for a translation.

"We are inviting you to a street party. All the neighbors along our street are bringing food and drink to Conrad's house for a party."

"Conrad?" Rigney questions.

"The German you met the other day."

"Oh . . . yes . . . sure," Rigney responds.

"You come? Yes?" Nick inquires.

Rigney worries about the warning he got from Pritchings this morning. Then, he dismisses it. *Pritchings has no authority to prohibit me from visiting with his neighbors.*

"Excuse me while I change my shirt and shoes. Then, I will go with you."

Chapter 49

The heat of the afternoon sun bakes Rigney's skin as he walks from the communications trailers compound toward the support area on the west side of the base. Every few minutes a light breeze blows inland from the Aegean and briefly cools him.

He looks at his watch—1243. He is on lunch break and decides to have a sandwich in the Club Zeus, instead of eating in the galley.

When he opens the door, a cooling blast of dirty ashtray-smelling air begins to dry the sweat from his face.

As he walks into the bar area, he observes *The Professor's court* assembled, but *The Professor* is not present.

Vance motions for Rigney to join them.

Rigney walks toward *the court* but is halted when he hears a female voice call him from the bar area. He stops and turns his head in the direction of the voice.

Nancy Bell motions for Rigney to sit on the stool next to her.

Rigney hesitates. He considers the propriety of sitting down at the bar next to the attractive brunette.

Rigney first met Nancy and Paul Bell while having dinner at *The Blue Lights* on Nea Makri beach. Paul, Nancy, and two other couples sat at the table next to him. He listened to their conversations on world events and their travels around Greece and other European countries. When they stood to go to the outside patio for after-dinner drinks, one of sailors asked Rigney to join them.

On the patio, the discussion turned to presidential campaigns. The three sailors and their wives impressed Rigney with their knowledge of the electoral process.

Rigney discovered that Nancy and Paul Bell formed this discussion group, which includes six sailors from the base and their wives. Members of the discussion group commit to reading assignments and report the details of what they read. Work schedules and family activities seldom allow all six couples to attend all meetings at the same time. They meet every Wednesday evening for dinner and drinks at *The Blue Lights*. Gossip is forbidden. Rigney became more impressed when he discovered they all attend Greek language classes at the U.S. Air Force base.

Since that evening at the beach, he noticed Nancy spends a lot of time in Club Zeus and the beach without her husband. She has approached him on several occasions to have a conversation. Their conversations were always about what they read recently in newspapers and weekly news magazines.

Bob Vance, who saw Rigney and Nancy conversing on a number of occasions in the club and at the beach, told Rigney about her rumored affairs with sailors at the base. Vance told him that Nancy prowled the haunts of single sailors when her husband was at work. Vance told Rigney that the sailor she last had an affair with transferred the week before Rigney arrived.

"Come on, Rigney," Nancy urges. "I researched what you said the other day, and I want to tell you about it."

Rigney glances toward *the court* table. All *court* members intently watch the exchange between Rigney and Nancy.

Rigney sits on the stool to Nancy's left "What did you find out?" he asks.

"I went to the central library in Athens. I looked up what you said about Pope Benedict VIII and Pope Urban II. You were right about them. I was totally flabbergasted."

Rigney grins at Nancy and says, "I'm impressed that you remembered the names of those popes."

"I wrote down their names when you talked about them. I was raised Catholic, but never heard in religion class about the history of priests being married."

Rigney reveals, "I never heard about it in religion class either."

"You attended religion classes?" Nancy says with raised brows.

"Yes, but not since I was eight years old."

"Can I buy you a drink?" Nancy asks with an inviting smile.

Rigney glances over his shoulder at *the court* table; all *court* members stare in his direction.

"No. Sorry. I'm just here for lunch. I must go back to work this afternoon." Rigney motions for Gus the bartender.

"I'll have a coke and a BLT," Rigney tells Gus.

Nancy continues. "I was surprised enough to find out that until the eleventh century it was common for priests to be married, but to find out many of them also practice polygamy was dumbfounding . . . and it was okay with popes . . . just knocked me off my feet."

Rigney nods then adds, "Yes, from ancient times it was common for clergy to practice polygamy and have mistresses. Early Christian clergy just continued the practice. During the dark ages in Central Europe, the sons of priests inherited church property. Eventually, so much church property was being lost, popes decreed all sons of priests to be illegitimate, banned marriages and mistresses for priests, and voided all marriages of priests. So, priestly celibacy is not about sanctity and sacrifice, it's about wealth and property rights. Anyway, not all priests complied. Later, one pope had priests' wives sold into slavery and forced priests to abandon their children."

Nancy shakes her head in disgust. She reaches for her pack of filter-tip cigarettes.

He studies Nancy while she lights up and takes a sip of beer. She wears tight-fitting clothes that accentuate her heavy bosom. She applies her makeup thinly. She carries ten pounds more than she should around her stomach and hips, but she still appears sexy and attractive. Her opinions are supported by logic and credible references. *I like her, but definitely hands-off!*

He wonders if the rumors about her sexual affairs are true. He understands how others misinterpret, connive, and lie. He knows innocent people relay rumors, because they lack self-respect, and they want others to be disrespected.

Nancy catches Rigney studying her. She blows smoke away from him. She knows he does not smoke. She says, "While I was researching popes, I discovered how much Catholic practices are based on papal decrees and not the Bible. Then, I read about paid indulgences."

"Thus, the Reformation," he interjects.

She nods her head and says, "Those revelations are enough to challenge my belief in God."

Rigney nods understanding. The same thing happened to him when he was a teenager and discovered the same information in the libraries of Orange County, California. "Why is your belief in God challenged?"

"Because I now believe that what I was taught as a child was taught by people who concealed the truth. Those priests and nuns must have known the truth. They were educated. How could they not know? Why did they never say anything? I feel cheated. I feel violated. What I believed, I learned from clergy who knew the truth about the church's past, but they never taught us about it. They are the ones who preached about God and God's will. Now, I find it impossible to believe them."

Gus sets a BLT in front of Rigney.

Rigney takes a bite.

Nancy looks at her watch; then, she looks toward the door.

"Waiting for someone?" Rigney asks.

"Yes, Paul is getting off early so he can take me to a doctor's appointment at the air force base. I should go outside and wait for him." She takes a final swig of beer; then, she slides off the stool. When she is a few feet away, she says cheerfully over her shoulder and loud enough for everyone in the bar to hear, "Thanks for the talk, Rig. It's always a pleasure."

Rigney stares at Nancy's swaying butt as she walks away. He glances over at *the court* table; they also stare after her butt.

Rigney picks up his sandwich plate and coke, walks over to *the court* table, and slides into the booth. Vance asks, "Did ya hear? They are putting the traffic division into port-and-starboard—indefinitely!"

"Who are *they*, and why are *they* doing it?" Rigney asks.

"Don't know who they are," Vance responds. "But the scuttlebutt is that the radiomen are being punished for making too many mistakes."

"What kind of mistakes?" Rigney asks.

"Message traffic processing errors."

"Why don't they just punish those making the mistakes, instead of punishing everyone?" Rigney asks.

Vance shrugs and admits, "Don't know."

Chapter 50

Rigney stands outside the main gate. He chats with the sentries. Occasionally, he glances southward along the Marathon Road, followed with looking at his watch.

He wears tennis shoes in case he must walk to Anna's villa. When she dropped him off this morning, Anna told him she had to go to the American Embassy in Athens and may not return by the normal pickup time.

Ten minutes later, Rigney decides to make the walk. He takes only a few steps when he hears the discernable guttural exhaust sound of Anna's BMW convertible.

Rigney swings himself over the passenger door, and he drops into the seat.

He starts to ask her what happened at the embassy.

"No talking now," Anna orders.

They sit silent during the drive to the villa.

Fifteen minutes later, they sit in the villa's living room.

"I must go away for a while," Anna informs Rigney.

"Can you tell me about it?"

"Yes, I have been ordered to Washington to brief on what we discovered about the yacht."

"Why will that take several weeks? We put all that we discovered in our report."

"I think ONI may have some strategies on what to do next. They will need to brief me on that."

Rigney nods his understanding and sits quietly.

"Stay here while I am gone, less chance of people knowing that I am not here."

"Should I totally move out of the barracks?"

"No. Don't do anything different than what you have been doing. Do you have an international driver's license?"

"Yes," Rigney answers as he nods his head.

"Good. You can drive me to the airport tomorrow evening."

Rigney returns to the villa after taking Anna to the airport. He goes directly to the communications room. As he enters, he hears the clickity-clack of the teletype machine. Yellow teletype paper spews from the equipment rack and spills to the floor. He estimates nine feet of teletype paper has printed. The teletype machine continues to spew paper as it prints.

Rigney reaches down to the floor and picks up the leading edge of the teletype paper roll. Five messages report intelligence regarding Soviet block espionage activities in Greece. Two messages contain background investigations on Commander Caldwell and Lieutenant Commander Blakely.

As he reads deeper, he whistles lightly, pulls up a chair, and sits in front of the teletype machine.

    201318Z AUG 68
    FM ONI WASHINGTON DC
    TO NEA MAKRI ONI FIELD OFFICE
    BT
    S E C R E T NOFORN INTEL – NOT AUTHORIZED FOR DISTRIBUTION OUTSIDE ONI CHANNELS.
        SUBJ: INTEL ANALYST BRIEF ON COMMANDER OLIVER CALDWELL, COMMANDING OFFICER NAVCOMMSTA GREECE(S)
        1947: ENTERED U.S. NAVAL ACADEMY
        1951: GRADUATED U.S. NAVAL ACADEMY
        1952: COMPLETED FIGHTER JET TRAINING AND EARNED WINGS
        1952–1961: SERVED WITH DISTINCTION. AWARDED MANY COMMENDATIONS AND CITATIONS.
        1961: NUMEROUS COMPLAINTS FROM ENLISTED MEN REGARDING LT CALDWELL'S

CHRISTIAN CRUSADING. CALDWELL ACCUSED OF NOT RECOMMENDING NONCHRISTIANS FOR ADVANCEMENT. CALDWELL'S COMMANDING OFFICER WRITES IN FITREP THAT CALDWELL TREATS TOO HARSHLY SUBORDINATES WHO ASK QUESTIONS ABOUT HIS ORDERS.

1962: CALDWELL'S WIFE ADMITS TO AFFAIR WITH CALDWELL'S COMMANDING OFFICER. COMMANDING OFFICER RELIEVED. CALDWELL IS TRANSFERRED TO SICILY. HIS WIFE ACCOMPANIES HIM. CALDWELL BECOMES DEPRESSED AND HE IS GROUNDED. HE TAKES UNPRESCRIBED PRESCRIPTION STRENGTH TRANQUILIZERS. HE ATTENDS PROFESSIONAL COUNSELING.

1963: FLIGHT STATUS REINSTATED. AFTER BEING PREVIOUSLY PASSED OVER FOR LIEUTENANT COMMANDER TWICE BEFORE, CALDWELL ADVANCED TO LIEUTENANT COMMANDER ON THIRD TRY. REAR ADMIRAL CALDWELL, COMMANDER CALDWELL'S UNCLE, ACCUSED OF ADMIRAL INFLUENCE WITH CALDWELL'S ADVANCEMENT TO LIEUTENANT COMMANDER. ACCUSATIONS DROPPED DUE LACK OF EVIDENCE.

1964: ASSIGNED AS EXECUTIVE OFFICER OF A FIGHTER SQUADRON AGAINST PROTESTS OF SQUADRON COMMANDER. AGAIN, ADMIRAL INFLUENCE SUSPECTED, BUT NOT PROVED.

1964-1965: RECEIVES AVERAGE FITREPS AS EXECUTIVE OFFICER. CALDWELL COUNSELED ON SEVERAL OCCASIONS FOR QUOTING BIBLICAL VERSE TO SUBORDINATES, ORDERING SUBORDINATES TO CHURCH, AND PUNISHING

HARSHLY THOSE WHO QUESTION HIS ORDERS. STILL FLYING.

1966: NOT RECOMMEND FOR COMMAND BECAUSE OF HIS POOR LEADERSHIP QUALITIES. AGAIN CAUGHT TAKING UNPRESCRIBED TRANQUILLIZERS. LOSES FLIGHT STATUS BECAUSE OF TRANQUILLIZERS AND WEIGHT GAIN. PASSED OVER FOR COMMANDER. MORE PROFESSIONAL COUNSELING.

1967: FITREPS IMPROVE, RECOMMENDED FOR ADVANCEMENT TO COMMANDER, BUT HIS OCCASIONAL EMOTIONAL OUTBURSTS DISQUALIFY HIM FOR COMMAND. HE IS RECOMMENDED FOR STAFF DUTY AND OTHER NONFLYING POSITIONS. TEMPORARILY ASSIGNED TO COMFAIRMED WHILE AWAITING ORDERS. ADVANCED TO COMMANDER DURING NOVEMBER.

1968: VICE ADMIRAL CALDWELL INTERVENES AND PULLS STRINGS FOR CALDWELL TO ASSUME COMMAND OF NAVCOMMSTA GREECE OVER PROTESTS OF COMNAVCOM.

OTHER: MORE INTEL TO FOLLOW.
//BOB MATER SENDS//
BT

201318Z AUG 68
FM ONI WASHINGTON DC
TO NEA MAKRI ONI FIELD OFFICE
BT
S E C R E T NOFORN INTEL – NOT AUTHORIZED FOR DISTRIBUTION OUTSIDE ONI CHANNELS.

SUBJ: INTEL ANALYST BRIEF ON LIEUTENANT COMMANDER MARY BLAKELY, EXECUTIVE OFFICER NAVCOMMSTA GREECE(S)

1958: GRADUATED FROM FLORIDA STATE UNIVERSITY. ATTENDED OCS. COMMISSIONED ENSIGN.

1959: GRADUATED FROM NAVY COMMUNICATIONS COURSE

1959: ASSIGNED TO NAVCOMMSTA SAN DIEGO. EXCELLENT FITREPS. ADVANCED TO LTJG.

1961–1964: ASSIGNED TO NAVCOMMSTA WASHINGTON DC. EXCELLENT FITREPS. ADVANCED TO LIEUTENANT.

1964–1967: ASSIGNED TO NAVCOMMSTA NORFOLK VA AS ASSISTANT COMM OFFICER. EXCELLENT FITREPS. DEEP SELECTED FOR LIEUTENANT COMMANDER AND LATER ASSUMED DUTIES AS COMMUNICATIONS OFFICER. SELECTED FOR EXPLORATORY PROGRAM TO ASSIGN WAVES TO REMOTE OVERSEAS NAVCOMMSTAS.

1967: ASSIGNED AS EXECUTIVE OFFICER NAVCOMMSTA GREECE. EXCELLENT FIRST FITREP BY PREVIOUS COMMANDING OFFICER. NEXT FITREP WRITTEN BY COMMANDER CALDWELL - ALL MARKS LOWERED AND NEGATIVE LEADERSHIP REMARKS.

OTHER: MORE INTEL TO FOLLOW
//BOB MATER SENDS//
BT

Chapter 51

"Sir, this is my report on the investigation into the cause of late delivery of the CINCUSNAVEUR message to COMSIXTHFLEET."

With an irritable tone, Commander Caldwell challenges, "What took so long, XO?"

"Took me a week to interview all the radiomen."

"Didn't the logs provide you with all you needed? If not, why not?"

"Eventually, yes. The event happened so long ago, that the radiomen I interviewed couldn't remember the details. The logs and written standard operating procedures provided all the details I have."

"Are you telling me that the on-watch radiomen could not remember a three-hour outage with the COMSIXTHFLEET flagship?"

"It's not uncommon to have hours of outages on any high frequency, crypto covered, radio teletype circuit. Weeks later, radiomen cannot remember back to any specific outage and identify it."

Caldwell shakes his head with disapproval. He looks at the typewritten pages in the XO's hand. "Looks like a thick report, XO. Please give me a verbal overview."

"Yes sir," Mary Blakely responds. "On the night when the initial transmission was sent, the two-way radio circuit with the COMSIXTHFLEET flagship was down. SOP required the supervisor to reroute the message over our fleet broadcast. COMSIXTHFLEET flagship copies our broadcast."

"How long was the outage on the two-way radio circuit?"

"Three hours."

"Three hours! What the hell was the problem?!"

"I searched all the applicable logs. The logs revealed the circuit was restored after we changed the Orestes cryptographic equipment."

"It took three hours to swap out the crypto equipment!" The Captain's voice rises with an incredulous tone.

"They swapped the crypto equipment three times. The circuit came up after the third Orestes device was put in place."

The CO blinks his eyes, shakes his head in disgust, and sits back in his chair.

"Sir, please let me explain the whole sequence of events. After that, we can discuss it."

Commander Caldwell frowns; then, he relents, "Okay, go ahead."

"As previous messages conveyed, COMSIXTHFLEET did not report the missing broadcast sequence numbers until three days later. Which was the cause of the—"

"Yes! Yes! I already know about that!" Caldwell interrupts impatiently. "Get on with the cause of the outage!"

Mary inhales deeply, nods her head, and replies, "Yes sir." She looks down at her written report and continues, "The technical controllers logged the reason for outage as failed crypto equipment."

Caldwell inquires, "What did the technical control log say was wrong with the equipment?"

"Nothing."

"What about the maintenance and repair logs?"

"Nothing . . . until last week. The crypto repair technicians had been troubleshooting all three pieces of equipment since the outage and could not find anything wrong. Bench diagnostics resulted with nothing found wrong with the equipment. The techs continued—"

"Damn it, XO! What happened last week?"

"I was getting to that, sir."

"Okay. Continue."

"Because of repair backlog, the technicians abandoned troubleshooting the three Orestes devices. They dumped them on an empty workbench.

"A few days after RM2 Page reported aboard, he was assigned to troubleshoot the devices. He found the problem in less than an hour. He discovered that all three devices did not have the most recent field changes installed—Field Changes 4 and 5. Page said that Field Change 3 inserted a problem that causes the Orestes equipment to fail after about an hour in use. Anyway, Page initiated—"

"How come the other techs did not discover the missing field changes?" Caldwell shakes his head in disgust.

"They didn't know about them. Until Page discovered the problem, no one in the repair division knew that Field Changes 4 and 5 existed."

A questioning look appears on the CO's face as he asks, "How is it that Page knew?"

"Page was the crypto repair technician at his last command. He said he installed Field Changes 4 and 5 during early July."

Commander Caldwell sits in thought; then, he asks, "Why are all the other Orestes devices working? If I remember correctly, we have a lot of them, right?"

"The others are working because they only have Field Changes 1 and 2 installed. Field Change 3 inserted a problem into the three Orestes devices in question, which cause the equipment to fail after about an hour of operation. Page also said that Field Change 4 fixes the problem inserted into the equipment by Field Change 3, and Field Change 5 enhances performance of Field change 4." The XO pauses as she looks down at her written report.

The CO asks, "Why did only three of the Orestes equipment have Field Change 3 installed?"

She turns a few pages of her written report; then, she looks at the CO and continues her report. "Because the person who scheduled the field change installations was moved out of his job and was not replaced."

"Who was that?" asks the CO.

"YN3 Grandville. He was the repair department yeoman."

"But he's my yeoman." Caldwell shakes his head slightly to exhibit his bewilderment.

"Sir, you remember the second day you were here? You ordered that we find a yeoman somewhere in the command and put him in the administrative office to serve as the captain's yeoman."

Commander Caldwell remembers his order. There were only two yeoman assigned to the admin office, and they were working eighteen hours a day because of heavy workload. Caldwell wanted his own yeoman, primarily to type his memoirs and serve as his driver. He remembers the outrageous protests from the communications officer. Lemont had threatened reduced performance from the repair department, because one of the technicians would be required to pick up Grandville's duties. *Damn complaining communicators!* "Yes, I remember," the CO admits.

"Grandville was the only yeoman in the command not assigned to the administrative building. You may remember that the COMMO strongly protested."

"Okay, XO. So you are saying that those three crypto equipments did not have Field Changes 4 and 5 installed because Grandville left his position in the repair division?"

"If you remember, sir, you ordered the COMMO to release Grandville immediately. There was no time for a turnover."

"You're saying it's my fault?!" Caldwell challenges with an incredulous expression and tone.

"No, sir, but it is a contributing factor. The same day that Page discovered the field changes were not installed, he went searching for the field change packages. He found the packages on Grandville's old desk. The date-of-receipt stamp on the outside of those packages was the day after Grandville left his repair division position."

"Who put the packages on the desk?"

"We believe it was CYN3 Hatcher. He is the one who distributes all the mail in the communications trailers. He said that he always puts the repair division mail on that desk."

"Where is that desk located?" the CO asks.

"In a small cubicle just outside the repair office door."

"That means that those field change packages sat on Grandville's old desk for months," Caldwell concludes. "Why didn't anyone process the field changes?"

"No one was assigned to schedule field changes," the XO advises.

"What?!"

"Sir, when Grandville departed, Mr. Linderhaus divided up Grandville's duties among all the members of the repair division. Mr. Linderhaus did not know that Grandville scheduled the field changes, so no one was assigned."

"Wasn't anyone curious about the packages that sat on the desk for months?" Commander Caldwell shakes his head in bewildered disbelief.

"No sir. The desk stands behind a cubicle wall and is not visible by those passing by. I talked to everyone in the repair division. No one was assigned to process any items on the desk, and Mr. Linderhaus said he never thought to assign anyone."

"This is disturbing, XO. There must have been other items that sat on the desk that were important."

"Sir, Mr. Linderhaus told me that Grandville had been the repair division yeoman since before he was assigned as repair officer. Grandville was the key to the repair division operation. Mr. Linderhaus admitted that he was not aware of many of the tasks that Grandville performed until after Grandville departed."

"Didn't Linderhaus ask Grandville about his duties?"

"I doubt it, sir. Mr. Linderhaus and Grandville did not get along. Grandville's lack of respect for Mr. Linderhaus is obvious, and Linderhaus knows it. I think Mr. Linderhaus did not ask Grandville about his duties, because he was embarrassed about not knowing."

Commander Caldwell bows his head in thought.

Lieutenant Commander Blakely sits quietly and waits for the CO to speak.

Caldwell raises his head and shakes it slightly; then, he comments, "XO, if there ever was a situation that defines the classic navy SNAFU, this is it!"

Mary Blakely stares at the CO. She does not agree. She knows that constantly changing operations and sudden personnel transfers often result in such situations. She experienced many of such situations. She understands that her responsibility as a naval officer is to anticipate situations like this and implement policies and procedures to minimize adverse impact before they happen. It's a matter of officer accountability and leadership.

"SNAFU, sir?" Mary stares at the CO questioningly.

"Yes, XO . . . SNAFU! The communications department is negligent and culpable. I am bewildered by the logic of the communications environment. The communications department caused the nondelivery of that message through their incompetence, but COMSIXTHFLEET must take responsibility for the nondelivery because of a regulation in a communications publication that places the burden of accountability on the receiving station. It makes no sense. Has anyone ever officially challenged the writers of these publications?"

Mary ponders for a moment; then, she responds, "Sir, communications publications are written and issued by the Joint Chiefs of Staff. I suppose the JCS knows what its doing."

"Come on, XO! We both know how staffs work. Communicators wrote the pubs and the pubs are approved and issued by some flag officer who doesn't understand what he is signing."

Fed up with Commander Caldwell's continuing criticism and mistrust of navy communicators, Mary blurts, "If the communications pubs had been written by pilots, you probably wouldn't criticize, correct?!"

Surprised by the XO's outburst, Caldwell flinches and blinks his eyes. The XO's words convey that she believes his negative opinion of naval communicators offends her. Yes, he has a low opinion of naval communicators, but his opinion is justified. Throughout his naval career, he has experienced only negative situations—too many mishandled and corrupted messages and too many messages taking too long to get from one command to another. Wherever he went, officers were always expressing their dissatisfaction.

With a condescending expression on his face, he responds, "XO, why do you think I was assigned as commanding officer and not a career navy communicator?"

Mary sits quietly.

"When I had my command briefing at the Pentagon, I was advised that Nea Makri had performance and discipline problems. COMNAVCOM tasked me to improve the situation to a level that would be noticed at the Pentagon. I was told that the preventive maintenance program was mismanaged and the 2-Kilo maintenance form submissions are erratic and incomplete. COMNAVCOM wants to know why they have not received any 2-kilos for five months." Caldwell pauses; then, casts a challenging expression at the XO and asks, "Have you discovered why COMNAVCOM no longer receives NAVCOMMSTA Greece 2-kilos?"

Mary replies, "I am still investigating."

"Get it done XO. Solving that problem is why I was assigned as CO and why another incompetent career communicator was not assigned."

Chapter 52

Rigney slips out of his uniform and slips into shorts, t-shirt, and running shoes. He retrieves the eight-pound iron dumbbells from the closet.

Several minutes later, he stands in the late afternoon sun outside the villa. He considers the best route for the best workout in the shortest time. He calculates the best route will take him up the hill and past Mr. Pritchings's house. He hesitates to take that route. Then, he justifies to himself, *I have the right to take any route I want.*

Rigney curls the dumbbells as he walks. When he reaches the corner, he turns right and starts up the hill. As he ascends the hill, he hears Pritchings's barking dog. He hopes he will not have another encounter with Pritchings.

The barking pulls residents from their homes.

When Rigney comes abreast of Pritchings's house, the neighbors are shouting for Pritchings to silence his dog.

As he stands and chats with the neighbors, Rigney continues to curl the dumbbells

Sparks concentrates his ferocious barking and growling in Rigney's direction.

"Hey, Yank. I think lifting those weights angers the dog."

Rigney had not considered that. He turns his head to look at Pritchings's dog. As he focuses on the dog, the dog makes another leap from the marble table. At the same time, Pritchings exits the house with softball bat in hand.

This time, Sparks successfully leaps the fence.

The neighbors begin shouting for everyone to retreat to their houses.

Sparks runs toward Rigney.

Rigney turns and runs down the hill.

Pritchings runs after his dog and shouts, "Stop, Sparks! Stop, Sparks!" As Pritchings runs, his flabby belly flops up and down under his t-shirt; his poor physical condition slowing his pace.

Rigney looks back and sees Sparks only twenty feet behind him. He knows he cannot outrun the dog. Thinking quickly, he stops and turns to face the approaching canine. He releases the dumbbell in his left hand, and it drops to the ground. He allows the dumbbell in his right hand to slip slightly, and he grips it like a club. He knows Sparks will go for his throat. Rigney plants his feet and judges the direction and height that he will swing the dumbbell.

Pritchings yells, "Page, what are you doing?! Run, you idiot!"

Sparks springs at Rigney with mouth wide open and baring pointed sharp teeth.

Rigney swings the dumbbell and hits the Doberman solidly in the side of the head. Rigney hears a loud cracking noise at the same time that Sparks lets out a sharp yelp.

Sparks falls limply to the ground.

Rigney stoops to check the dog's condition. Blood flows from a crack in the dog's skull. Sparks stops breathing.

Rigney hears running feet. He sees Pritchings about fifteen feet away, running toward him with a bat raised over his head.

Neighbors run behind Pritchings, and they are pleading with Pritchings to stop.

"Danger, Rig!" Nick yells.

Pritchings closes the distance in three seconds. He shouts, "You son of a bitch!" and swings the bat at Rigney.

Rigney falls to his side and ducks the bat swing.

Pritchings brings the bat over his head.

Rigney grabs one of the dumbbells and throws it at Pritchings.

The dumbbell slams into Pritchings belly, which knocks the wind out of him. He drops the bat and doubles over, holding his belly.

Rigney stands and picks up the bat.

Sparks lies dead at their feet.

Anger flares within Rigney. He wants to slam the bat into Pritchings's face. He suppresses his anger.

Pritchings regains his breath and looks wildly into Page's face. "You fuckin' asshole!" Pritchings spits at Rigney. "You killed Sparks! You could have run away!"

Rigney grabs Pritchings's bicep with a viselike grip and swings him around.

"No! Mr. Pritchings!" Rigney responds angrily. "You killed your dog with your flagrant narrow-mindedness, imbecilic arrogance, and total disregard for others! You have no one to blame but yourself! If you don't understand that, then, there is no hope for you ever becoming a valuable human being!"

Pritchings's eyes go wide at Page's rebuke. "How dare you speak to me that way! You will pay for this, Page! You will regret the day you crossed my path!"

"No worry, Rig," Nick consoles. "We know this man. We know him ugly man. We see here today."

"Don't worry, Yank. All of us will back you up. We will talk to your commander, if you want."

Rigney nods his head and smiles with appreciation toward the neighbors. All of them, the Greeks, Germans, and Brits, nod their heads in affirmation.

Conrad says, "We move dog from road."

"You leave you' fuckin' hands off Sparks!" Pritchings yells, tears streaming down his face. While crying deeply, Pritchings bends over, picks up Sparks, and cradles the dog lovingly against his chest. He walks back to his yard.

Rigney drops the bat, picks up his dumbbells, and walks down the hill toward the villa.

Chapter 53

Rigney walks through the villa and opens all the doors to the patios and courtyard. A soft breeze with the salty aroma of the sea flows throughout the villa interior. To aid the cooling effect of the breeze, he wears only t-shirt and jockey-style underwear.

He locates his paperback copy of Harold Robbins's *The Adventurers* on the coffee table. He flops on the couch and turns to the bookmarked page. He engrosses himself into the lives of international playboys and the intrigue and violence of Latin American politics.

The soft beep of the courtyard gate alarm sounds several times.

Rigney lifts himself from the couch and goes to the master bedroom. He peeks through the curtain. He sees Dottie Caldwell shaking the gate. Her white-colored MG blocks the gate.

He slips on gym shorts and sandals. He deactivates all security systems, exits through the front door, and dashes across the courtyard.

Dottie steps back from the gate as she hears footsteps crunching gravel on the other side of the gate.

As he opens the gate, he becomes aroused as he appraises her slim body in halter top and hip-hugger shorts.

Dottie jumps toward him. She throws her arms around his neck, and she gives him a passionate, open-mouthed, wet kiss.

Rigney wraps his arms around her and matches her passion. Tongues intertwine. Both become sexually aroused. Rigney's penis gorges with blood and becomes erect.

Dottie feels Rigney's erect penis pressing against her belly. She moves her right hand from around his neck and rubs his penis through his gym shorts.

Rigney pulls away from the kiss but keeps his arms around her. He glances over her shoulder through the gate and quickly scans several houses across the street. He counts four of his neighbors standing in their front yards; they stare at Dottie and Rigney. Some of those neighbors are American sailors whom he works with in the communications trailers.

"People are staring at us," Rigney says to Dottie.

She drops her hand from his penis and turns her head toward the houses across the street. "I didn't know they were there. I didn't see them before."

"Let's go inside," Rigney urges.

"What about my MG?"

"Drive it into the courtyard."

Rigney locks the gate. Then, he walks toward Dottie who stands by her MG.

Dottie stares at Rigney's crotch; she appears hypnotized as she sees the outline of his erect penis.

Rigney's face expresses a resigned smile. He leads Dottie up the seven stone steps to the front door.

After closing and locking the front door, Rigney engages all the security systems.

Dottie's sexual desire dissipates as she watches on Rigney's complex button pushing on the three security controllers. Curious as to what the villa contains to warrant such a security system, she investigates the interior of the villa's foyer and living room. Then, she wanders around the three levels of the villa and explores every room.

"Not a lot of furniture," she comments.

Rigney walks closely behind her to ensure she does not discover the communications room, their sexual arousal at the gate, now, mostly forgotten.

"Do you have any cold beer?" Dottie asks as they return to the living room.

"I'll get us a couple bottles of Amstel."

When Rigney returns with beer bottles and beer glasses, Dottie asks, "When did you move in here?"

"Several days after you left When did you get back?"

"Last night. Earlier today, I went to the base looking for you. Everyone said you moved in with your girlfriend."

"No, I moved in here."

"With your girlfriend?"

"Anna is not my girlfriend."

"Everyone says she is."

"You asked people about me? Won't that raise suspicions about us? Your uncle might find out."

"No. I didn't ask about you. All I had to do was sit in Club Zeus and listen. You are the focus of many conversations. Some of the sailors really like you, and some really hate you."

"I'm not surprised."

"Some of the sailors who hate you say that you—"

Rigney interrupts with a wave of his hand. "I really don't want to hear about it."

"Don't you want to know what people say about you?"

"No."

Dottie looks puzzled. "Don't you want to know who your friends and enemies are?"

"I already know who my friends are."

"Aren't you the odd one?"

"Yes. I am," Rigney confirms with a nod of his head. "Do you think you can adjust to all my oddities?"

"I don't know. What are they?"

"My friends are few, and my enemies are many."

"That's cryptic. Do you care to explain?"

"No, but as we get to know each other, I think you'll find out."

Dottie explains, "Well, I don't think I am odd. I think I am ordinary."

"I can't believe that," Rigney challenges. "You don't care that I am an enlisted man. You're the first officer's daughter I have met.

I know that I am stereotyping by what I have heard, but I thought enlisted men are taboo to officers' daughters."

"Yes, that's true, but in high school I rebelled against such social rules. It all started when my best friend wanted to go to the junior prom with the son of an army sergeant. In the DOD schools, the officers' kids ran in cliques and the kids of enlisted men had their own cliques. It was like an unwritten rule. The classes were mixed, of course, but anytime something social happened, there was no mixing."

"Excuse me," Rigney interrupts, "What are DOD schools?"

"In places overseas where there are lots of American military, the Department of Defense established grammar schools and high schools for military dependents. It's DOD's way of allowing dependent children to live with their parents overseas. The schools are in Japan, Philippines, Spain, Italy, Germany, and the United Kingdom. Probably other places, too."

"Sounds like a great benefit for career military people."

"It is. Anyway, my girlfriends and I turned down every officer's son who asked us to the prom. Word got around and eventually, the sons of enlisted men started asking, and we accepted."

"How did your parents respond to that?"

"They prohibited me from going to the prom . . . same with my girlfriends' parents."

"You didn't go to the junior prom?"

"No and neither did any of my girlfriends. Then, when I turned twenty, my parents expected me to participate in this debutant ritual at the officers' club. I refused. I fought with my parents for weeks. They wanted me to follow the traditional path of other Annapolis alumni daughters and marry a young, career-oriented officer."

Rigney remains thoughtful for a few moments; then, he reveals, "When I went to high school, it was the rich kids who ran in cliques. I knew a girl like you. She defied her parents and dated an economically deprived Irish beach bum—me! Actually, the last half of our senior year we were boyfriend and girlfriend."

"But not anymore?"

"No."

"What happened?"

"We grew apart. We no longer believe in the same things."

"What things?"

Rigney responds with a reluctant tone, "I'm breaking my rule about not discussing other women with you."

Dottie sighs deeply; then she asks, "What about you and Anna?"

"She lets me stay here. I take care of the place, like a security guard. This place is a palace. The barracks suck."

"People said they saw you kissing her."

"It didn't click. We found we really didn't have an attraction to each other."

"Where is she?"

"I don't know. She left several days ago. She didn't say when she's coming back."

"We have this place to ourselves, then?"

"Yes."

"Rig, I need to talk to you about something. Can we talk seriously?"

"You can talk anyway you want."

"Did you have sex with Anna?"

"No. You are the only one I had sex with since arriving here."

Dottie stares doubtfully into Rigney's face, and she says, "That is hard to believe, Rig. I mean, you're so sexy. She didn't find you sexy?"

"I don't know."

Dottie moves closer to Rigney and says sexily, "She doesn't know what she missed." She leans toward Rigney.

He puts his arms around her and pulls her close.

During the middle of the night, they both awake. The patio door in Rigney's bedroom stands wide open. The breeze from the Aegean cools them. Moonlight floods through the wide-open patio doors. They easily see the other's naked body.

"I am not going back to the States tomorrow as I originally planned. Classes don't start until late September. I want to stay with you longer."

Lengthening her stay concerns Rigney. He thought they would have a couple days—and a couple of nights—together. Then, she would go back to California. *She's falling for me. This can get complicated.*

Rigney asks, "What are your plans for the next five years?"

"What?"

"I was just wondering about your plans for the next five years," Rigney explains. "Do those plans include me?"

"I hope to see you when you rotate back to the States, but I want to earn my bachelor's in marine biology. Then, somewhere in the Pacific Ocean, I do research for the following two years while I work on my masters. I hope that doesn't insult you. I mean, you're unlike any guy I have ever met. I want to spend more time with you, but I don't plan on anything serious with anyone until after I earn my doctorate."

"What would your parents say if I showed-up in uniform on your doorstep in San Diego?"

"Like I said before, my father and Uncle Oliver care about this separation of enlisted and officer, not me. I guess those separations are necessary in the military, but I am a civilian. I date whom I want."

"Ever date an enlisted man before?"

"No, and you're the first military man I've had sex with. Great sex, too!"

Rigney smiles and says, "So it's all sexual?"

"Anything wrong with that?"

"I thought, maybe, you find my superior intellect to be irresistible." Rigney chuckles.

"I admit your broad shoulders and good looks are what first attracted me. This is only our second date, and we haven't done a lot of talking. But what about you?" Dottie challenges. "I suppose you were first attracted to my 3.75 grade point average and not my body?"

"Guilty," Rigney replies as he casts a sideways sly expression. "Now, it's about getting to know each other, but, like you, I do not want any serious relationships. My immediate plans are travel, discovery, and adventure."

"What about college when you get out of the navy?"

"I am not looking that far ahead."

"How were your high school grades?"

"A's and B's."

"Come on . . . I'm serious."

"I am serious."

Dottie turns on her side and faces Rigney; then, she queries, "So you're smart, too?"

He turns on his side and faces her then asks, "Define smart."

"Smart means knowing a lot of stuff."

"There are some subjects I know a lot about, but I think smart means something else. I think smart means the ability to reason logically."

"Well, yes. That makes sense," Dottie admits. "But you need to know a lot to reason logically."

"Agreed, but just because a person knows a lot or is well educated does not mean that person reasons logically. History has taught us that."

"That's for sure," Dottie agrees.

They become silent. Their eyes roam over the other's body.

Dottie asks, "What are your plans for the next five years?"

"I still have three years on my enlistment. That's all I am focusing on, now."

"What do you do in the navy?"

"Well, I was a submariner, served in a submarine out of Pearl. Now, I repair crypto equipment."

"Crypto equipment? That's top-secret electronics equipment, right?"

"Yes."

"Do you like it?"

"It's a living."

"How do you plan on experiencing the travel and adventure you want?"

"I find ways to experience it."

"What do you do that is adventurous?"

"Scuba diving, surfing, exploring new places, and meeting new people. When exploring new places, I walk through the place, instead of driving through it. That way I meet the people."

With an admiring look on her face, Dottie scans Rigney's body; then, she asks, "How did you get all those muscles? Were you a laborer?"

"No. I exercise regularly and workout with weights."

"Do you think it is important to have hard muscles?"

"Yes."

"Why?"

"Gives me an edge in physically dangerous situations. My strength has saved my life."

"Physically dangerous? What are you talking about?"

Rigney hesitates to answer; then, he says, "Dottie, we're getting to know each other here, but there are some episodes in my past that I wish to keep secret . . . maybe when we know each other better."

"My god, Rigney, you lick and suck on my clit until I scream in ecstasy. I suck your cock until you come in my mouth. How much closer must we get?"

Rigney flinches at Dottie's crude honesty. "That's not the type of closeness I mean. This is only our second time together."

Dottie's face expresses defiance, followed with her face expressing understanding. "Yes, of course, I understand. I guess I am used to men doing whatever I want. I want you to know I have never given myself to a man the way I give myself to you. I want to please you so that you will stay in my life."

Rigney places his hand gently on her cheek and says, "Please understand this about me. I want to stay in your life, not just because of the sex, but because I like what I know about you. I can be stubborn when someone attempts to manipulate me. I will always be honest with you. If I don't want to do something, I'll be honest with you about it. I hope you will do the same. That is the only way we can discover the realities about each other. I want to experience as much as I can in my youth, which means no committed relationships. How do you feel about all that?"

Dottie beams an understanding smile and says, "No commitments, Rig. I totally agree, which means I can have the same sex with other men as I have with you. Do you agree with that?" Dottie expects to get a jealous reaction from Rigney.

"Absolutely. When it comes to sexual activity, I don't set different standards between men and women."

Dottie looks dubiously at Rigney and says, "Not the response I expected."

"Yes. I know."

"What about people who are engaged or married?" Dottie inquires.

"Well, those are committed relationships. Those relationships should be monogamous."

Dottie evaluates Rigney's words; then, she asks, "Are there other women in your life?"

"Dottie, when I am with you I do not want to talk about other women in my life, and I hope you will not tell me about the other men in your life."

"You are an unusual man, Rigney Page."

Rigney wants to change the subject. He finds interesting Dottie's commitment to become a marine biologist. He asks Dottie, "Tell me about what you want to do as a marine biologist."

"I want to save the whales."

"What whales?"

"All of them. Saving the whales is a saying meaning to stop man's slaughter of sea mammals."

"You mean like whales, dolphins, and seals?"

"Yes."

"Why do you need a doctorate in marine biology to do that?"

"Because governments pay more attention to those with credentials. As a doctor of marine biology, I can get the ear of influential people who will help my cause."

Rigney does not know much about this topic. Magazine articles report the conflict between those in the whaling industry and those who endeavor to stop the eventual extinction of certain sea mammals. He knows that whaling and seal hunting are essential to the economy and culture of some people.

He changes the subject again. "Tell me about your travels to the Greek Islands."

"Interesting enough . . . saw some beautiful places and learned a lot about Greek history, but our enjoyment was less because of guys trying to pick us up all the time. Angie and I could not go anywhere without a dozen men hovering . . . Greeks, Italians, Spaniards, Germans, Turks . . . and Iranians!"

"When we first came to Europe, we were flattered by all the attention, but it got old—fast. I must have said no a thousand times."

"Was it just you and Angie, or did all the women suffer that much attention?"

"All women traveling without men . . . it really got annoying. I enjoyed the peace last night at Uncle Oli's."

"Won't your Uncle Oli wonder where you are tonight?"

"Probably not. He goes to bed early. Mornings, he always leaves the house before Angie and I get up. His driver always picks him up at seven."

They lie silent with their eyes closed.

Dottie feels sleepy. She moves closer to Rigney and cuddles against him.

Rigney wraps his arms around her. Within a few minutes, they are asleep.

Chapter 54

Lieutenant Commander Blakely scans the NAVPERS 1626, report chit, completed by Mr. Pritchings regarding the killing of his dog by RM2 Page. Then, she looks up from the report chit and stares expressionlessly at Commander Caldwell.

"See what I mean, XO. This Page is violent and needs tamed. I want to bring him to mast on Friday and award maximum punishment under Article 15."

Mary scans the repot chit again. "Pritchings did not list the UCMJ Articles in violation, and Page has not signed the chit."

"You're the command legal officer, XO. Look up the applicable articles and write them in. I want you to include the assault on Mr. Martin. Then, have Master Chief Crimer present the chit to Page for signature."

"Sir, I think Page will request court-martial."

"Don't tell him that he has that option," the CO orders as he looks directly into the XO's eyes.

"Sir, the option is on the report chit. He will know he has that option."

"Tell Page that court-martial does not apply to his case," the CO says sternly. He searches the XO's eyes to see if she knows he exceeds his authority.

"Sir, Page will know court-martial is open to him. We cannot lie to him about that."

Commander Caldwell sits in anger. His face flushes red, and his nostrils flare. His anger based on the XO challenging him, and the XO being correct. He wants to punish the arrogant, brash, sacrilegious, unconventional, and overconfident RM2 Rigney Page. He attempts another strategy. "Mary, the book does not apply to every case. Page needs the arrogance knocked out of him."

"Sir, with all due respect, arrogance is not punishable under the UCMJ."

"XO, as a female, you have never led men in battle. You do not understand how the subtle manner of some enlisted men can be detrimental to good order and discipline."

Mary had wondered how long it would take Commander Caldwell to resort to his sexist philosophy to justify his actions.

"Sir, I investigated the incident where Page struck Lieutenant Martin. Too many witnesses specify that Page acted in a defensive manner to protect Martin's wife and daughter."

"True, XO, but we know more about Page, now."

"Sir, please let me investigate the killing of Pritchings's dog before we proceed with nonjudicial punishment. If we decide to take Page to mast, we need to know all the facts first. Your judgment as a commanding officer could come under question should he stand before a court-martial and be found innocent."

"Why do you think Page will request court-martial?"

"Because he's an intelligent boy. He has completed the correspondence courses for the UCMJ and for navy regulations. He will know that rules of evidence do not apply at captain's mast, but do apply at court-martial. He will know that you can punish him at captain's mast regardless of the facts and witnesses in his favor. He will know that a court-martial must consider facts and witness testimony and must find him guilty before he can be punished."

Commander Caldwell does not believe that any enlisted man could be so well informed regarding military law. Nevertheless, he knows that the XO reasons logically and has excellent judgment, which irritates the hell out of him. He relents, "Okay, XO, investigate, but get it done within a few days."

"Yes sir."

Mary stands and exits Caldwell's office. She waits until she enters her own office to let out a deep sigh. *How did Commander Caldwell ever get command? His actions border on criminal.*

Chapter 55

RM2 Rigney Page sits in the XO's office and faces Lieutenant Commander Mary Blakely across her desk. He just completed explaining the events and circumstances surrounding his killing of Pritchings's dog.

"And you are sure that these locals will substantiate your version of what happened."

"Ma'am, it's not a version. It's the truth. Any statements contrary to mine are not the truth."

"Mr. Pritchings tells a different story. He says that you had a previous confrontation with him in front of his house and again in his office."

"Ma'am, I am truthful when I tell you that in all instances he was angry and confrontational. I was a passive victim of his behavior."

"Passive victim?" responds the XO with eyebrows raised.

"Yes ma'am."

The XO looks down at the written statements. She considers what her next step should be. She decides to interview the locals herself.

"That's all for now, Page. I will talk to you tomorrow."

"Yes ma'am."

Rigney stands and exits the XO's office.

Mary Blakely stops her car across the street from Pritchings's house. She exits her vehicle and looks around. She sees a gathering of local men and women standing in the front yard of the house next door to Pritchings's house.

The attractive woman in the U.S. Navy white uniform creates interested stares from the locals.

Mary waves at the gathering. Several of the locals smile and wave back, which motivates her to walk over to the gathering.

"Hello, I am Commander Blakely."

Bill Clarke steps forward and asks, "Are you the commander of the U.S. Navy base?"

"No. I am the executive officer."

Bill Clarke sticks out his hand and says, "Pleasure to make your acquaintance. I'm Nobby Clarke, formally of the Royal Navy. Of course, that was long ago."

"Nice to meet you, Mr. Clarke," Mary responds; then, she looks at the others.

"My name Conrad Borman," the German national says in broken English.

"My name Nikandros Papadopoulos. We all friends neighbors this place."

Mary smiles and nods. "A pleasure to meet all of you."

Everyone in the crowd smiles back.

"Do any of you know Mr. Pritchings . . . the American who lives in that house?" Mary points to Pritchings's house.

"Yes, we all know ugly American," Conrad answers with a scowl on his face.

Nobby Clarke declares, "Yes, Commander. That Pritchings is one bad Yank."

Nikandros translates the conversation for the other Greeks in the crowd. They all nod their agreement.

"May I speak with any of you regarding the killing of Mr. Pritchings's dog?"

Everyone nods agreement to talk.

Nobby Clarke informs, "Most of us saw it happen."

"The young sailor Rig much polite and courtesy boy," Nikandros praises. "Much sad Rig must kill dog . . . Pritchings problem."

Mary listens to Pritchings's neighbors as they confirm RM2 Page's statement.

Chapter 56

Newman finds Maximos on the south side of the public works building.

The lanky, solidly built, aged olive-skinned Greek pours engine oil into the block of a base pickup truck.

Newman looks around and verifies no one else present.

"Hey, Maximos," Newman whispers.

Maximos looks up from the engine well and eyes the short and pudgy young black sailor. He says nothing; he waits for Newman to state his business.

"You know me?" Newman asks.

Maximos replies with a thick Greek accent. "Yes, you Newman. You work in barracks and driver sometimes."

"That's right," Newman responds as he nods his head.

Newman looks around again to ensure no one listens.

With an impatient tone, Maximos demands, "What you want, Newman?"

Newman focuses on Maximos's face and says, "They tell me yo' know people who'll do thin's for money."

Maximos's expression turns curious. He does not admit to anything. He waits for Newman to clarify.

"Ya know, I want ya ta beat-up someone . . . break som' bones."

"Me no harm American sailors . . . never."

"Yeah! Right! How much money to beat-up Page? Ya know him?"

"Everyone know Page."

"How much to beat him up . . . break an arm and a leg?"

Maximos remembers hearing the talk about Page hurting Newman at the airport and about Mr. Martin.

"Page tough man, I hear. Not easy hurt him, maybe."

"Can yo' do it, man?" Newman becomes antsy.

"No me . . . friends do . . . two hundred dollars."

The low amount stuns Newman. It would cost two thousand back in Atlanta. "I don' have that much." Newman attempts to haggle. "One hundred dollars."

"No haggle . . . no do less dollars . . . half before . . . half after."

"Okay. Give me a few days to get the money. Oh, I wan' ta be der when Page get it."

"No, no," Maximos objects. "No possibles. You must not see my friends."

"No do then," Newman counters. "If I no there. I no want Page hurt. No money, then."

Maximos takes a few minutes to consider; then, he says, "Much dangers many peoples watch. You there . . . see my friends . . . two hundred dollars more."

"Total three hundred dollars," Newman counters.

"No! Four hundred . . . no less. Half before, half after."

Newman responds, "Okay, get it started. I'll come back with the money."

Newman knows only two sources to borrow money. He goes to the galley and finds Commissaryman Second Class Gordon Benedict.

Between meal times, only the cook and a few Greek dishwashers are present in the galley.

As Newman approaches, he sees Benedict icing a cake.

Benedict turns his head toward the sound of footsteps. When he sees Newman, a disgruntled expression appears on his face. He grunts disapproval. "Whatta ya want, Newman?" Benedict challenges with a disapproving tone.

Newman declares, "I need ta borra two hundred dollars."

Benedict lends money to help people who need emergency funds for personal or family needs. He feels fortunate that his grandfather bequeathed him thirty-two thousand dollars. He does not charge interest, and he does not lend more than one hundred dollars to any one person. He will not lend money to those who gamble or those of questionable character.

"Lose your paycheck in last night's crap game?" Benedict questions with a sneer.

"Look, man, I jus' wanna borra some money. Yo' lend ta ever'one else."

"No way, Newman."

"Why? 'Cause I'm a nigger, and no nigger can be trusted, can he?"

Newman always accuses white people of being racist when they will not give him what he wants. He hopes they will feel guilty about it and submit to him.

"You're pathetic, Newman. I don't trust you because you're an obnoxious and conniving asshole. You cheat and lie and accuse everyone of being a racist. Get out of my galley . . . now!"

Newman stands in the hot August sun on the sidewalk leading to the petty officers' barracks. He reluctantly accepts that the only remaining source of funds is Steward First Class Cassius Jackson.

Newman finds Jackson sitting in the X-division office, located at the north end of the petty officer's barracks.

"Hey, Newman, yo' got the one hundred and fifty dollars yo' owe ma?"

"No, man. I need to borra some mo," Newman pleads.

"Look, Newman, 'cause yo' a brother, I cut yo' a break on the vig. I can't lend yo' no mo 'til yo' pay off what yo' owe ma."

"Yo' my last hope, man. I need two hundred real bad . . . fast."

Jackson sits thoughtfully for a few moments; then, he asks, "What 'bout yo' friends Patterson and Thompson?"

"They're no longer my friends, man. They took Page's side. They did nuttin 'bout Page knocking me 'round at the airport."

Jackson stares into space for a few moments; then, he says, "Tell yo' what, Newman. Yo' sign over that car of your'in, and that settles yo' debt. Then, I will thin' about lendin' yo' mo money."

Newman thinks about his fifteen-year-old Renault coupe rusting away in the parking lot. The car runs, but burns oil by the gallon. The tires are bald and the brake shoes worn away. He drives the vehicle occasionally but is embarrassed by the annoying looks he gets when he presses the screeching brakes and when idling at an intersection with oil smoke billowing around him. He originally paid a transferring radioman two hundred dollars for the Renault. The radioman was honest with Newman. He told Newman the car was in need of repair; that's why he asked only two hundred dollars. Newman was aware of the Renault's bad condition, but he wanted a car, and the Renault was the only one he could get for two hundred dollars, which was all he could borrow from others. Later, when other sailors ridiculed him and his car, Newman claimed the racist white radioman took advantage of him.

"Title is in my locker," Newman responds gleefully. "Be back shortly."

While he walks to the enlisted barracks, Newman feels elated that he got over on Jackson. *I can't believe he take that piece of junk to clear my one-hundred-fifty-dollar debt.*

Later Newman returns to the base motor pool. He hands Maximos two hundred dollars.

"When you want do?"

Newman explains his plan.

After his meeting with Maximos, Newman heads for the barracks. He feels satisfaction and superiority now that he has planned the attack on Page. He struts along the sidewalk in front of the administration building, exaggerating the swing of his right arm. His white hat tilts forward, and it rests on the rim of his sunglasses. As he walks across the barracks parking lot, he sees Jackson supervising the towing of the Renault.

"Whatta ya goin' to do with my old car?" Newman asks Jackson.

"I sold it to a Greek junk yard fo' its parts," Jackson replies nonchalantly.

"Oh, fo how much?"

"Fo a profit," Jackson replies flippantly.

Newman walks off wondering how much profit Jackson made.

Chapter 57

Lieutenant Commander Mary Blakely sits at her desk and studies the written statements regarding the killing of Pritchings's dog. Mary wrote a report on the statements made by Pritchings's neighbors. She also went to the Nea Makri police station and obtained reports regarding three occasions when the police investigated complaints by Pritchings's neighbors. The command contract interpreter translated the police reports.

After reviewing Pritchings's service record, she wonders how a four-oh chief radioman five years ago turned into such degradation as a warrant officer.

Mary rereads Pritchings's statement regarding the death of his dog. Afterwards, she sits back in her chair with a bewildered expression on her face. *He's lying. Why?*

Several hours later, Pritchings sits in front of the XO's desk. He has just finished reading all the statements from Page and his neighbors and the police reports. He comprehended early in the reading that the XO gathered a lot of evidence that contradicts his version.

"Mr. Pritchings, all the witnesses to the events contradict your version of what happened. Your neighbors substantiate Page's statement. How do you account for that?"

Pritchings understands that he cannot claim Page and the local neighbors are conspiring against him, because the police reports make negative statements about his drunken behavior and lack of control of his dog.

Pritchings shakes his head and states, "I can't. All I can say is what my neighbors say and what Page say is not what I recall happening."

The XO looks doubtfully at Pritchings. She studies him for a few moments; then, she states, "The police reports are not on your side. I conclude that you have acted inappropriately in your relationship with your neighbors."

"Look, XO. These people don't appreciate American bases in their country. They want to embarrass us. They exaggerate and conspire to make Americans look bad."

The XO shakes her head to convey her lack of acceptance of such a point of view.

"Mr. Pritchings, your opinions regarding the motivations of local nationals are not relevant to the events regarding your dog. I recommend you rescind your report chit. At executive officer's prescreening mast, I would judge the evidence insufficient to forward to captain's mast. Your credibility with your subordinates will be damaged when they hear that one of your report chits was dismissed at XO's prescreening. If you rescind now, there will be no record. If it goes to XO's prescreening, there will be a formal record of the results."

Pritchings stares at the XO's desktop while he considers her words.

"Who all knows about the report chit?" Pritchings asks.

The XO replies, "You and I and the CO and Master Chief Crimer, unless you have told someone else."

"No ma'am. I gave the report chit to the master chief. I told no one else about it."

"Well, Mr. Pritchings, what is your decision?"

Chapter 58

"Mr. Pritchings rescinded the report chit on Page," Lieutenant Commander Blakely tells Commander Caldwell.

The CO becomes angry. "Why did he do that?"

"Too much evidence against his story."

"What evidence?"

"Statements from Pritchings's neighbors and police reports."

"What do the neighbors and police say?"

"It's all quite voluminous. The bottom line is that Page is not at fault for what happened. Pritchings's neighbors confirm Page's statement. The police reports reveal that Pritchings is the essence of an *Ugly American*."

Commander Caldwell stares contemptuously at his XO. "How did you come into possession of these documents?"

Mary detects Caldwell's confrontational manner. "I interviewed the neighbors and got their written statements. Then, I went to the police station and got copies of the reports on Pritchings."

The CO angrily chastises the XO. "When I gave permission for you to investigate, I did not tell you to gather evidence against Mr. Pritchings!"

Mary stares at her commanding officer. Again, she questions COMNAVCOM judgment in assigning Oliver Caldwell as commanding officer. *What does Caldwell have against Page? He is making this personal.* "Sir, I thought you wanted all the details."

Caldwell fumes over the XO's lack of understanding. "Damn it, XO! This Page needs a knockdown. Don't you understand that?"

Mary sits silent.

After a few moments, Commander Caldwell calms down and states, "As my XO, you are required to carry out my policies."

"I understand that, sir. My responsibilities also include providing sound and logical alternative actions."

Caldwell sits quietly as he considers how to proceed. *This Page needs punished for his confidence and his arrogance!* "Okay XO. Let's proceed with prescreening mast on the Mr. Martin assault charge."

"Captain, no charges have been filed against Page."

"What about the report chit?"

"No one has placed Page on report for assault against Mr. Martin."

Commander Caldwell shakes his head in disgust and declares, "I truly do not understand how you communicators consider yourselves a valuable asset to the navy. You communicators have no discipline! In the air squadrons, Page would have been in the brig by now. Have the chief-master-at-arms place Page on report . . . and let's get on with it!"

"But, sir, I suggest—"

"That's an order, XO! Your objections on this issue border on insubordination! No more arguments!"

Mary Blakely stares wide-eyed at Commander Caldwell. *There is something wrong with this man.* "Aye, aye, Captain. I will get it done."

Chapter 59

Lieutenant Junior Grade Eric Linderhaus enters the repair shop. He sees ET1 Straton and RM2 Page sitting at their benches and repairing cryptographic equipment.

"Hey, Page," Linderhaus calls from the doorway.

Rigney cradles his soldering iron, swivels on the stool, and faces his division officer.

"XO wants you and me in her office."

"Right now?"

"Yes, Right now."

Straton looks over at the disassembled KWR-37 crypto equipment on Rigney's workbench. Then, he looks at the officer and asks, "Sir, can it wait? We only have one operational KWR-37."

"I told the XO that," Eric advises; then he looks at Page and asks, "How much longer before you have it repaired?"

"Two hours, sir," Rigney replies. "That does not include putting it back in its operating position and testing it."

"That's too long. The XO said immediately. Let's go."

Rigney lowers himself off the stool, retrieves his white hat from the hat rack, and follows Mr. Linderhaus out the door.

The XO, Mr. Linderhaus, and Master Chief Crimer sit quietly and watch Page.

Page rereads the report chit. This time he takes more time to analyze each word.

The XO is satisfied that Page does not become emotional. She expected him to remain the cool and calm person he always portrays.

Mr. Linderhaus is displeased that Page has not become emotional.

Master Chief Crimer is displeased that the CO ordered the report chit initiated.

Page looks up from the report chit and scans the XO's desk for a pen. He sees one in a leather cup. He plucks the pen from the cup. He looks into the faces of the other three people in the room.

The two officers and the master chief stare questioningly at RM2 Page.

"I'm requesting court-martial," Rigney states while shifting his eyes to each person. Rigney looks back down at the form. Then, he signs the report chit and circles the box that *demands court-martial*. He hands the report chit to the XO.

"You're making a mistake," Mr. Linderhaus declares. "You should accept Article 15 punishment. That will be less punishment than awarded at a court-martial."

Rigney does not respond to Mr. Linderhaus.

The XO inspects the report chit to ensure the form is complete and correct.

Master Chief Crimer stands knowing that the meeting is over.

The XO advises, "Okay, Page. You're dismissed."

Rigney stands and turns to leave. Then, he turns back to face the XO and asks, "Ma'am, what happens next?"

"The paperwork will be sent to CINCUSNAVEUR in London. The legal staff in London will arrange for the investigation."

"So I can't be punished by the CO, correct?"

"That's correct," the XO replies calmly.

"Will CINCUSNAVEUR send investigators here?"

"Yes."

Rigney wants to ask the XO if she thinks there is enough evidence to convict him, but he decides against it. He does not believe there is.

Rigney returns to the repair shop and continues repairs on the Jason cryptographic equipment. The possibility of being found guilty at a court-martial preoccupies his thoughts. Because of his lack of concentration, he takes longer than his initial prediction to make the repairs. However, he earns praise from the crypto center operator and from his fellow technicians when he restores all Jason equipment to full operation.

Before departing the communications trailers for the day, he stops by the news printer in the broadcast trailer. He scans the headlines. One Associated Press story catches his eye. *Democrats selected Julian Bond as candidate for vice president, but at age twenty-eight, he is too young to accept.*

At 2000, Rigney exits the communications trailers. He goes to the barracks and changes into civvies. He walks to the administrative compound where he earlier parked the BMW.

As Rigney drives toward the main gate, Commander Caldwell watches from his office window. Caldwell still fumes from the XO's briefing that Page demanded court-martial. He admits to himself that a UCMJ investigation may result in dismissed charges against Page. Now, he becomes enraged as he realizes that the brash, arrogant, and irreverent Page has freedom to leave the base. He returns to his desk and looks at the report chit. *That bitch split-tail XO marked NO RESTRICTION!*

The CO picks up his phone and dials the XO's extension. When the XO answers, he yells into the phone loud enough for everyone in the administrative building to hear. "Come to my office—now!"

All those in the administrative building turn their heads toward the direction of the CO's office.

Chapter 60

Rigney parks the BMW along on the road near the villa's courtyard gate. He leaves the BMW's engine running and headlights on while he gets out of the car to open the gate. The sound of running feet turns his attention to the road. In the illumination of the BMW headlights, he identifies two tall lean and hardened Greek men running toward him. One has eighteen inches of heavy chain-link in his right hand; the other has a three feet long iron pipe in his right hand. The one with the pipe leads the other by four feet. *They're attacking me! They're right-handed! I must counterattack!*

Rigney dashes toward the two Greek men.

The two Greeks look disconcerted. They slow their pace so not to run past Page.

Rigney charges the lead Greek. At a distance of six feet from the lead attacker, Rigney jumps, makes his body horizontal, and thrusts his feet into the attacker. His left foot hammers into Mihalis's chest; his right foot slams into Mihalis's larynx.

Mihalis expels a loud groan as the force of the blow crushes all air from his lungs. The force of Rigney's thrust knocks Mihalis forcefully backward and into Ioannis. All three tumble to the ground, tangled in each other's limbs. Mihalis drops the pipe when his elbow smacks the pavement.

While still prone, Rigney grabs the iron pipe.

Mihalis is out of breath and out of action. He lies on his side gasping for air.

Ioannis, still lying on the ground, sees Rigney grab the iron pipe and rise to his knees. Ioannis knows he must do something now, or he will not have a chance several seconds from now. Still lying on his back, Ioannis swings the length of heavy chain at Rigney's head.

Rigney, just coming to his knees and off balance, sees the swinging chain. He raises the iron pipe and ducks to the right.

The pipe blocks most of the chain and most of the power swung by Ioannis, but a few inches catch him across his left temple and left side of his nose. The knock to his head stuns him for a moment, giving Ioannis enough time to stand and jump toward Rigney. Ioannis swings the chain with all his power.

Rigney, still on his knees, becomes alert. He ducks the chain.

When the chain hits nothing but air, Ioannis's own swinging power twists his body to where his back is toward Rigney. Ioannis must spread his legs to regain balance.

Rigney, thinking quickly, takes advantage. He swings the iron pipe in an upward motion and hammers the pipe into Ioannis's crotch.

Ioannis yells in pain, doubles over, grabs his crotch, and falls to the ground. On the ground, he continues to yell in pain.

Rigney jumps to his feet and stands over the two Greeks. Only thirty seconds have passed since Rigney first saw the two Greeks.

With the iron pipe in hand, Rigney considers how to kill the two men. *Never give an attacker a second chance to eliminate you.*

Forty seconds have passed.

Smash the end of the pipe into an eye socket; that will kill them.

Forty-five seconds have passed.

Rigney raises the pipe like a knife, ready to stab down.

"Did you see that, Pete?" a voice says from the dark of the neighbor's yard directly across from the villa.

"Yeah, I saw it," another voice affirms from the dark.

Rigney lowers the pipe to his side and looks around—cautious. He hears footsteps coming from the dark. He realizes the fight took place within the illumination of the BMW's headlights. Obviously, some of his neighbors saw it.

Three people step into the light—two men and one woman.

Rigney recognizes his neighbors. He does not know their names. He recognizes the two men as first class radiomen who work shifts in technical control. The woman is the wife of one of them.

The three neighbors look down at the two moaning Greeks lying on the road. "I saw you jump at those two. Why did you do that?" one of the first class radiomen asks.

"They attacked me."

"Oh, I didn't see that part. I just saw you running at them and then jump on them. Why did they attack you?"

"I don't know," Rigney responds. "Did any of you see them attack me?"

All three neighbors shake their heads.

"What happens now?" the woman asks.

"I guess we should call the police station," another neighbor says.

Rigney hears footsteps. He looks around the illuminated area cast by the headlights of the running BMW. More neighbors, Greeks and Americans, step into the light.

Then, Mihalis stands. He helps Ioannis to his feet. The two men look around the crowd; their eyes stop on Rigney.

Rigney still holds the pipe in his hand.

Mihalis and Ioannis exchange whispers; then, they limp off. When they reach the corner, they are shadows. They appear to talk with someone who stands, hidden, behind a high bush.

Then, the headlights of an automobile rounding the corner catch Mihalis and Ioannis in the headlights. The two men dash behind the bush. The automobile approaches the group standing in the road in front of the villa's gate.

Rigney recognizes Dottie's MG convertible.

Dottie sees Rigney standing with a group of people. Everyone looks in her direction. She parks her car to the side of the road. She climbs out of the MG and walks over to Rigney. "What's going on?" she asks Rigney.

"Let's go inside?" he directs.

Rigney opens the gate, and they both park their cars in the courtyard. They enter the front door of the villa. Rigney turns on the lights and resets the alarm system.

Dottie expresses concern and says, "Rig, your face is cut and your eye is swollen. Come into the bathroom, and I will clean those cuts."

In the bathroom, Dottie dabs hydrogen peroxide on Rigney's wounds. "What happened out there?" she asks.

"A couple of Greeks attacked me."

"Why?"

"I don't know."

"Who were they? Do you know?"

"No, I don't know, but you saw them . . . at the corner. They were in your headlights."

"You mean the two Greeks who got in the car with that black sailor from the base?"

"Which black sailor?"

"I don't remember his name. The short pudgy one . . . the one with the foul mouth."

"Newman?"

"Yes. Newman."

"That conniving asshole!" Rigney blurts angrily.

Dottie looks fearfully at Rigney and says, "What are you gonna do to Newman?"

Rigney ponders Newman's fate. Then, he calmly says, "For now, nothing."

"You won't hurt him, will you?"

"No."

Dottie sighs with relief.

Rigney requests, "Please don't tell anyone about what happened."

"I won't. You didn't need to ask."

Chapter 61

RM2 Rigney Page, Mr. Linderhaus, and Master Chief Crimer sit in front of the XO's desk. The XO sits behind her desk.

"Have you been fighting?" Mary Blakely asks RM2 Page as she looks at his black eye.

"I wouldn't call it fighting," Rigney responses with a dismissive tone.

"I received a report this morning from Senior Chief Hilton. He said that your neighbors reported to him that you were in a fight last night with two Greeks, in front of Anna's villa."

"It was nothing, ma'am. They attacked me. I disarmed them, and it was over. No big deal."

"They were armed? Senior Chief Hilton didn't say anything about that."

"I'm not surprised, ma'am."

"Not surprised at what?" the XO queries.

"That the report did not include I was defending myself against two armed men who attacked me."

"Who were they?"

"Don't know, ma'am."

"Why didn't you report the incident?"

"Didn't think it important enough, ma'am. Sailors are always getting into fights with Greeks and don't report it. Didn't think my situation was significant."

Mary looks at the chief-master-at-arms.

Master Chief Crimer shakes his head and shrugs, indicating he does not get reports of frequent fighting between sailors and Greeks.

Mary returns her eyes to Page and orders, "Before you leave this building, you are to provide a complete written report to Master Chief Crimer regarding the fight last night."

"Yes ma'am."

"There is another matter, Page," the XO advises. "There has been a development regarding the Mr. Martin assault charges against you. The CO has placed you on pretrial restriction. Effective immediately, you are restricted to the base. You may not leave the base without my permission or the CO's permission. Master Chief Crimer will advise you of the times of day you are to muster with the master-at-arms force."

Rigney bows his head and shakes his head slightly, indicating resigned disappointment. He remembers that the report chit he saw yesterday did not list restriction. He senses mission failure. "Ma'am, you told me yesterday that the CO cannot punish me."

"Pretrial restriction is not punishment."

"Ma'am, I would like to talk to the CO about this restriction."

"Why?"

"I want to change his mind."

Master Chief Crimer snorts and shakes his head.

Mary had advised Caldwell against the restriction, but he imposed the restriction anyway. The XO responds, "The CO is firm on this, Page. You will not change his mind."

"Ma'am, may I speak with you privately."

Mr. Linderhaus and Master Chief Crimer look disapprovingly at RM2 Page.

Rigney urges, "It will just take a few minutes, ma'am."

Mary spends a few moments considering Page's request. Page's request is unusual and probably inappropriate, but, then, Caldwell's behavior on this matter is completely inappropriate.

"Okay, Page. I will give you five minutes. Mr. Linderhaus, Master Chief, please excuse us."

When he hears the door click shut, Rigney looks at the XO.

With an expressionless stare, Blakely says, "Okay, Page. What is it?"

"Ma'am, I can change the captain's mind about the restriction. Would you please arrange I meet with him privately?"

"Listen, Page, I think such a request will make him angry. The CINCUSNAVEUR legal team will probably be here within two weeks. Why not just let it go until then?"

"Ma'am, I can't be restricted to the base. I promise not to run away."

"No one thinks you will run away."

"Then why am I restricted?"

Mary does not answer.

"Ma'am, I think Commander Caldwell has something against me. There is no chance that I will run away. Deserting is much more serious than assault. You know that. Commander Caldwell knows that."

Yes, I know that, Mary affirms to herself. However, she does not want to anger Oliver Caldwell. "Page, I am going to tell you something and you must not tell anyone what I am about to tell you."

Rigney contemplates how to respond. After a few moments, he responds. "XO, if I go to court-martial, I will tell my lawyer anything I think beneficial for me. That may include what you are about to tell me. Except for the possibility that I may tell my lawyer, I promise not to tell anyone else."

"I'm agreeable to that," Blakely responds. "What you tell your lawyer is privileged. You understand that?"

"Yes ma'am."

"Okay. I argued against restricting you. Unless you have some special power to sway people, you should not talk to the CO about this."

"Why did you argue against it, ma'am?"

"Because you are no risk to run," Mary responds. "And I think the results of the UCMJ investigation will clear you."

Rigney nods his agreement and says, "I must talk with the CO."

"What will be your defense with the CO? It needs to be something unique."

Rigney sits in thought for a few moments. Then, he says, "Ma'am, tell him it's an important family matter."

"Okay," Mary responds. "I will advise the CO of your request."

"One more thing, ma'am."

"What is it?"

"I want to talk to him today."

"Okay, Page. I will see what I can do. You are dismissed."

Later in the day, Page enters Commander Caldwell's office.

"Sit down, Page," Commander Caldwell snarls as he points to the chair in front of his desk.

Rigney sits and stares directly into Caldwell's eyes. He wants the CO to know that he is not intimidated.

Oliver Caldwell has encountered many like Page—arrogant and disrespectful. *I have knocked the arrogance out of these types before. Page will be no different.*

Ten minutes after RM2 Page exits Commander Caldwell's officer, Caldwell steps into the XO's office and states, "I am lifting the restriction on Page." Then, he turns abruptly and exits the XO's office.

Mary blinks her eyes several times and expresses astonishment.

Chapter 62

Andrei sits at his desk and shifts through the dozens of photographs of Nea Makri sailors. One of his field operatives took the pictures over the last several weeks. The field operative took pictures of people entering and leaving the Nea Makri main gate. He also took pictures of people visiting Master Chief Rodgers's house.

He has viewed two-thirds of the photographs when he recognizes the picture of a young American sailor who enters Rodgers's house. *Where have I seen him before, or did I see his photograph somewhere before?*

Andrei decides to review his files for the last three years. He judges the age of the American sailor to be early twenties. *If I have a previous picture of him, it cannot be more than several years old.*

He glances at the twelve filing cabinets sitting against the wall. The cabinets contain all the operation files he has accumulated during his KGB career. Fortunately, they are in date order, and he has a cross-reference index by operation, code words, and codenames. He estimates the task will take him a week to complete.

Andrei makes a mental note to assess the value of his field operatives going undercover to put names with the photographs.

Chapter 63

RM2 Page works on a common problem with the Orestes KW-7 crypto device. Broken contacts on the plug-wire module cause the crypto device to malfunction.

His repair action is simple. He will replace the entire module. Then, he will put the damaged module in a bin for items destined to the crypto repair facility in Naples. However, he expects Mr. Linderhaus will soon order the techs to repair the modules, because the Nea Makri supply of operational modules dwindles.

Two days ago, Straton discovered two dozen broken modules in the bottom drawer of Grandville's old desk. Another one of Grandville's task was to ship damaged modules to the repair facility. Since no one knew were Grandville stored the damaged modules prior to shipment, everyone thought the modules were at the Naples crypto repair facility.

Rigney hears the door open and close. He has his back to the door and does not turn around. The door opens and closes hundreds of times per day.

Senior Chief Radioman Ralph Hilton walks to Page's workbench.

Rigney senses someone standing behind him. He lays his tools on the workbench, turns on his stool, and recognizes Hilton—the technical control chief. Hilton is the second senior enlisted man working in the trailers; Master Chief Rodgers is the most senior enlisted man.

"Hi Senior Chief, what's up?"

"Come with me to the tech control office."

Rigney shoots a glance at the two KW-7 devices on his workbench.

"Those repairs can wait. You and I must talk."

"Okay."

Rigney follows Senior Chief Hilton to the technical control office located on the south end of the technical control trailer.

As Rigney follows Hilton into the office, Hilton orders, "Close the door behind you."

Rigney sits in front of Hilton's desk and waits for Hilton to begin the conversation.

"Page, we need to discuss your inappropriate behavior. There will be no record of this meeting if you commit to changing your behavior. However, if you continue along the same path, negative comments will be entered into your service record."

Rigney chuckles and says, "Senior Chief, I am not aware of any inappropriate behavior on my part."

Hilton shakes his head, indicating his disbelief. He warns with a harsh tone, "Page, if you don't take this seriously, I will report the content of this meeting to the COMMO."

"Senior Chief, I think it important to advise you that I cannot be intimidated. Report whatever you want to whomever you want. I have no problem with that as long as you report facts and not misperceptions."

Hilton stares curiously at Page; he does not understand Page's point.

"What do you want to talk about?" Rigney asks impatiently.

Hilton pulls a pad of lined paper from his desk and writes several lines.

"What are you writing, Senior Chief?"

"I made a note that your attitude is hostile."

"So, you're starting your report with a misrepresentation. Stating that I am hostile is a judgment, not a fact, and, by the way, I don't feel hostile."

"My report . . . my judgments," Hilton declares.

"I'm not surprised," Rigney responds with resignation.

"Dispense with the attitude, Page. You're not making any points."

"Senior Chief, I would say we are making a lot of progress here. We haven't even started on the subject of this meeting, and you have already and incorrectly judged me as hostile with an attitude. So why don't we move onto the false accusations that are the subject of this meeting."

Hilton shakes his head in dismissal of Page's logic. He writes a few more lines; then, he demands, "You must stop beating up people. The navy does not tolerate bullies."

"Calling me a bully is another incorrect judgment. As for the navy not tolerating it . . . well . . . there sure are a lot of them around for the navy not to tolerate it."

"Denying your actions will not help you. You must commit to changing your behavior."

Rigney shakes his head, sighs in frustration, and counters, "What actions? What behavior? All you have done so far is misjudged me as a hostile bully with an attitude and with no facts to back up your judgment."

"I am not going to argue the details," Hilton declares. "Our purpose here is for you to commit to changing your behavior."

"Senior Chief, I don't believe I have done anything that would classify me as a hostile bully with an attitude and who is in denial. If you want me to commit to changing my behavior, you must give me examples of my behavior that you believe needs changing."

"You must stop hitting people."

"Senior Chief, I will be judged under processes specified in the UCMJ regarding guilt or innocence of assaulting Mr. Martin. Until found guilty, I am presumed innocent."

"It's not just that, Page. There are several instances where you beat-up others."

"Senior Chief, I have not been charged with beating-up anyone."

"Just because you have not been put on report, does not mean you have not bullied others. Your actions show a general physical aggressiveness toward others."

"You're judging again and incorrectly again. I think that unless you can specify the facts of some event, we are not going anywhere with this, and I should get back to my crypto repairs." Rigney rises from his chair.

"Sit down!" Senior Chief Hilton orders.

Rigney sits.

"Your shipmates know about you calling Newman a lazy nigger and beating him up at the airport because he would not carry your seabag. That makes your shipmates think you are a bully. As a result, they are afraid of you—afraid to work with you—afraid to include you."

"Senior Chief, I am not responsible or accountable for Newman's lies or the misperceptions other have of me because of those lies. Others are reacting to what Newman said and not to anything I did."

"What about killing Mr. Pritchings's dog? That was a brutal act and says a lot about your character and has an adverse effect on how people perceive you."

"The correct word is misperceive. I was defending myself."

"That's not how your shipmates see it."

"What shipmates are you talking about, Senior Chief? Except for Mr. Pritchings, no one from the base was there. I have friends here who know me. Not everyone believes the lies spread by Newman and Mr. Pritchings."

"Page, if others think badly of you, it is up to you to make them think otherwise."

"This is unbelievable, Senior Chief. Your reasoning is illogical. Again, you are saying that I am accountable for how others react to the lies spread about me. How can I be accountable for the actions of liars and for the misperceptions resulting from those liars? I have no obligation to change the misperceptions that people have of me."

"Yes, you do!" Hilton declares in a raised voice. "How people perceive you affects how they interact with you."

Page responds, "Well, I perceive those shipmates to be liars. So, why don't you go to them and tell them they are responsible for changing my perception of them."

Hilton blinks his eyes and expresses confusion. Then, an understanding expression crosses Hilton's face. He finally understands Page's logic.

Rigney states, "My friends believe me and not the lies."

Hilton sits thoughtfully for a full minute. He writes a few more lines. Then, he asks, "What about that incident in the front of your house last night, when you attacked those two Greeks?"

"Another misperception. Those two Greeks attacked me."

"Page, your neighbors work for me, here in technical control. They said you attacked the Greeks."

"My neighbors did not see the whole incident."

"Your chain-of-command is concerned that you didn't report the incident and that we had to hear it from your neighbors."

Rigney shakes his head in dismissal and says, "I am not aware of any regulation that requires me to report such an incident."

Hilton states, "The command SOP requires it. You were told about it during command indoctrination. Those Greeks could file charges against you with the local police."

"I never attended any command indoctrination. Besides, those two Greeks attacked me with weapons in their hands. I disarmed them, and I wasn't hurt that bad. It never occurred to me to report it to anyone."

Hilton stares at Page's black eye as he challenges, "Page, your behavior is unconventional. We've had no violence at this command until you got here. How do you explain that?"

"I don't explain it, and I have no obligation or qualifications to explain it."

"You are at the center of those violent events."

"Again, incorrect judgments and misconception. Just because I'm involved does not mean I am guilty of anything. Don't you understand that, Senior Chief?"

"What you must understand, Page, is that you are an American serviceman overseas. American bases are in Greece at the courtesy of the Greek government. The mere perception of impropriety, real or not, may adversely affect the relationship between Greece and America. Dealing with adverse perceptions is high priority with the chain-of-command. So, you—"

"I don't think they are high priority," Rigney interrupts. "I find it difficult to take this propriety argument seriously. The chain-of-command allows Newman to roam the streets of Athens, allowed Mr. Martin to beat his wife and child in front of Greeks, and allows Mr. Pritchings who is a disgrace to his uniform to live among the locals. Did you know that Mr. Pritchings's neighbors call him the Ugly American?"

"This meeting isn't about your shipmates."

"Maybe it should be," Rigney counters. "Had the chain-of-command previously reigned in Newman, Mr. Martin, and Mr. Pritchings, the incidents with me would never have happened."

"We're not changing the subject. It's about you, and fighting isn't the only thing we need to talk about."

Rigney stares curiously at Senior Chief Hilton.

Hilton continues, "Your moral character is in question. Your overt advances toward Nancy Bell are outrageous and you are to discontinue."

"This is unbelievable!" Rigney declares. "There is no truth in that."

"Witnesses, some of your shipmates, say they have seen you two together."

Rigney considers walking out of this meeting, but first he asks, "Senior Chief, may I ask your age and how long you've been in the navy?"

"Irrelevant."

Rigney attempts another approach. "Do you think your life and navy experiences enable you to tell the difference between facts and judgments?"

"Yes, of course."

"Have you ever seen me with Nancy Bell?"

"No."

"Then how can you possibly accuse me of making overt advances toward her?"

"Like I've been telling you, Page, it makes no difference if it's true or not. You must take action to change the negative perceptions that other have about you."

"Like what?"

"Well . . . uh . . . you can stop pursuing Nancy Bell."

Rigney smirks as he responds, "Well, that's easy. I wasn't doing that in the first place. So, I need not change my behavior."

"Page, you must have done something to make people think you made advances toward her."

"I did nothing. What others misperceive about Nancy Bell and me are fabrications in their own minds. My only interactions with Nancy have been a few, short conversations."

"Then stop having conversations with her. All this womanizing and fighting casts a bad image."

"Womanizing?"

"Yes. Shacking up with that German woman and while she is away carrying on an inappropriate romance with Dottie Caldwell and chasing after Nancy Bell."

Rigney sits contemplative for a few moments; then, he says, "Please understand this about me. I will not go around being paranoid about how others might misperceive my actions. I will not consider how others might judge me prior to doing anything. You can report that to the chain-of-command. I'm going back to work now."

Hilton's eyes and mouth go wide in disbelief as Page stands and turns toward the door.

"Page, you can't just walk—"

The slamming door cuts off the remainder of Hilton's sentence.

As Rigney walks back to the repair shop, he mumbles to himself, "All this prying into my private life by chiefs and officers. This isn't a military command. It's a fucking soap opera!"

Chapter 64

ET1 Straton, ET2 Patterson, ET2 Thompson, and RM2 Page huddle around Page's workbench. They team on troubleshooting and repairing two Adonis crypto machines. Both machines broke down during the midnight watch.

Page, Patterson, and Thompson work together rebuilding one of the Adonis machines. Straton spreads-out the pages of the KL-47 technical manual on the adjacent workbench; he provides technical specifications on each part.

The phone rings, and Straton answers it.

"Hey, Page, the communications officer wants to see you in his office," ET1 Straton says as he hangs up the phone.

"What's he want?"

"Didn't say. He wants to see you now."

Rigney looks at the pair of broken Adonis crypto machines. He sighs and hopes the one remaining operational Adonis machine outlives his trip to the communications office.

The reason for delay in starting repairs was the requirement for everyone to attend this morning's all-hands personnel inspection. Only those currently on-watch were excused from the inspection—Commander Caldwell's orders. All day-workers were required to attend—absolutely no exceptions per Commander Caldwell's orders. Also required to attend were all watch-standers who were off-watch between their twelve-hours-on and twelve-hours-off watch schedule.

Gerry Lemont sits in his office and reflects on the events earlier today. This morning, Lieutenant Lemont asked Commander Caldwell to exempt the crypto technicians from the personnel inspection. "Sir, we have several, essential cryptographic machines that need repair. We have one remaining—"

"Get your complaining communicator ass out of my office!" Commander Caldwell's shouting voice was heard by everyone in the administration building.

Lemont worries over the six radiomen that went to captain's mast yesterday and received nonjudicial punishment for message processing errors that resulted in late delivery. They each received suspended reduction in rank and loss of one month of pay. He scans the report on his desk of seven more reports of processing errors. He slouches in his chair, bows his head, and worries how this unprecedented punishment will affect the morale of his radiomen.

Page still sits at his workbench and estimates five hours of troubleshooting and repair time were wasted for the personnel inspection. The officers and crew of NAVCOMMSTA stood in ranks in Full Dress White uniform for three hours while Commander Caldwell read extracts from U.S. Navy Regulations and then inspected each sailor to the minutest detail. YN3 Grandville followed behind Caldwell with a clipboard and recorded discrepancies. Commander Caldwell found a uniform or grooming discrepancy for every sailor. Rigney was hit for an improperly tied neckerchief, a scuff on his shoes, and nonregulation haircut.

At the end of the inspection, Caldwell stood at the podium and announced that there would be a reinspection same time next week.

Rigney steps down from his workbench stool; he walks toward the door and opens it. He finds Master Chief Rodgers standing on the other side. Rodgers carries the one remaining Adonis device.

"Broke dick," Rodgers advises. "Some of the keys are jammed and the rotors will not rotate."

Rigney takes the heavy typewriter-like machine from Rodgers and places it on the nearest workbench. Then, he turns toward the door.

"Where are you going?" Rodgers asks.

"COMM office."

"You should stay here and work on the Adonis equipment. You're the only one here who's been to Adonis repair school."

"I agree, but the COMMO has ordered me to his office."

Rodgers shakes his head in disgust.

Rigney advises, "I don't think I will make the poker game tonight."

Rodgers nods and walks off.

On his way to the communications trailer's front door, Rigney must pass through the fleet center. RM1 Burgess, the fleet center leading petty officer, puts up his hand to stop Rigney. A lit cigarette dangles from the mouth of the slim, medium-height sailor. The cigarette bounces up and down as he speaks.

"Hey, Page, what's the estimated time of repair on those Adonis machines? I have over twenty messages needing encryption before sending over the Alpha CW Net. Some of those messages are priority precedence."

"Don't know for sure," Rigney replies. "We're finding lots of worn gears with broken teeth and worn switches. We are replacing those parts, but we are running low. Those machines are clogged with paper dust and require detailed cleaning. We will probably cannibalize one or two of the machines just to get one machine operational."

Burgess removes the cigarette from between his lips. "Unsat!" he sputters with a frustrated tone. "What could cause all three Adonis machines to go down within twelve hours of each other?"

Rigney replies, "I think it a coincidence they all went down within twelve hours of each other, but I am not surprised they went down. I don't think preventive maintenance has been performed on those machines for a long time."

"No shit, Sherlock!" Burgess utters sarcastically. "Come with me, I want to show you something."

Rigney hesitates, because he should be going to Lieutenant Lemont's office.

"Come on," Burgess demands. "I think you will find this interesting."

Burgess leads Rigney to the NATO Message Refile Center that is located in a vault on the north end of the fleet center trailer. He dials the combination and opens the heavy steel door.

Rigney follows Burgess into the vault.

"These are the three Adonis operating positions for the NATO Refile Center."

Rigney quickly scans the ten feet by six feet room. A ten feet long custom made table runs the length of the room. Three chairs stand equally spaced along the table. Pens, pencils, rubber stamps, inkpads, file folders, overflowing ashtrays, and partially filled coffee cups clutter the tabletop. The clutter surrounds three empty square footprints where the three Adonis machines previously sat. Approximately forty message paper copies with attached paper tapes hang from a wire that stretches the length of the vault over the operating positions.

Burgess explains, "When I became the fleet center LPO a year ago, we only had two Adonis operating positions, but volume increased so much, we had to install the Adonis spare. Three operators encrypt and decrypt messages twenty-four hours a day, seven days a week. There's always a backlog."

Rigney expresses thoughtfulness for a few moments then asks, "When was the last time any of the machines were taken out of operation for preventive maintenance?"

"Not for six months," Burgess replies. "Not since ET1 Lyndell transferred. He was the Adonis tech. He wasn't replaced."

Rigney shakes his head with bewilderment.

"That's not all," Burgess advises. "Let's go to the repair office. I will show you something you won't believe."

"Look, Burgess, I must go to the COMMO's office. You can show me later."

"You need to see this. Mr. Lemont probably wants a status report on the repair of the Adonis equipment, and he will probably ask you the cause of the failures. You need to know this other piece of the problem . . . only take a few minutes."

Rigney responds, "I don't think we should go in there. Mr. Linderhaus will chase us out. He doesn't like people going in there uninvited."

"He's not on base," Burgess informs. "I saw him leave the base with the captain right after the inspection."

Rigney shrugs and sighs and relents. "Okay."

Rigney and Burgess enter the repair office. Burgess leads Rigney to the preventive maintenance schedule hanging on the wall.

Burgess asks, "Do you know what scheduled PMs the Adonis equipment requires?"

"Yeah," Rigney replies. "There are monthlies, quarterlies, and annuals."

Burgess points to the preventive maintenance schedule and orders, "Find 'em."

Rigney runs his finger down the far-left column, which lists all equipment in the communications department that requires scheduled preventive maintenance. He does not find the Adonis machines on the first pass of his finger. He repeats the search to confirm the absence of the Adonis machines from the schedule.

"Not there," Rigney confirms.

"No shit, Sherlock!"

Lieutenant Lemont looks anxiously at RM2 Page and asks, "What's your estimate on getting those three Adonis machines repaired?"

"Sir, we are rebuilding one of the machines. I think we will run out of parts and will need to cannibalize at least one of the others. Master Chief Rodgers delivered the third Adonis to the shop just a few minutes ago. The message backlog is growing—fast. Some of them are priority precedence."

"Yes, I know. Master Chief Rodgers called me about it."

"By the way, sir, I discovered that none of the Adonis machines are on the preventive maintenance schedule."

An expression of disbelief appears on Mr. Lemont's face.

Rigney has nothing more to report, so he sits—silent—waiting.

The COMMO says, "Page, we are in a serious situation here. Without the Adonis machines we must find another way to deliver those messages, probably by courier. That could take weeks for some of the addressees, because they are foreign NATO ships at sea. Sometime today, we must make a decision regarding using the courier service. The closest courier station is in Naples. An officer or chief from this command would need to take those messages to Naples."

Rigney nods and reports, "Sir, when you called the repair shop, we were about seventy-five percent complete with rebuilding the first machine. We only had a few key levers and switches left. We have no spares for any of the vacuum tubes. So if any of the tubes are bad we must take them from another machine."

"Page, all three Adonis machines must be operational."

"We'll do our best, but at best, I think we will have two and at worst we will have one."

"I can't tell the CO that. You must find a way to make all three machines operational—soon—today. None of the crypto techs can secure until all three Adonis machines are operational."

"Sir, I estimate five hours before we know how many machines we will have operational and what parts we will need to make the remaining machine or machines operational."

"Time is of the essence, Page. You must find a way to do it faster."

Rigney shakes his head as he dismisses Lemont's threats and concern for an unrealistic timeline. He comments, "Sorry, sir . . . difficult to convince me time is critical when all of us spent three hours in ranks this morning while those Adonis machines sat on my workbench."

"Not your place to judge the best use of your time, Page."

"Yes, sir," Rigney replies with a tone revealing his lack of agreement. "Is that all, sir? I should get back to working on those Adonis machines."

"Okay, Page, you can return to those Adonis machines. I want you to report to me personally every four hours. I won't be leaving the base until you have all those machines repaired." Lemont gestures toward a cot in the corner of his office.

After Page departs, Lieutenant Lemont pulls a copy of the Command Equipment Allocation List. He searches the document three times and confirms that the Adonis crypto devices are not listed.

Chapter 65

Master Chief Rodgers sits at his desk in the crypto vault and reviews the Adonis file. The file contains letters, notes, memos, and transcriptions of conversations regarding the Adonis equipment over the last three years. He started the file after the meeting of the NATO Southern Region Communications Committee three years ago in Naples. He attended the meeting with Commander Franks, who was the NAVACOMMSTA Greece commanding officer at the time—two commanding officers ago—and Lieutenant Dunbar, who was COMMO at the time.

During the meeting, the Greek Navy and the Turkish Navy representatives advised they could not comply with the unfunded reporting requirements of the NATO Southern Region Commander-in-Chief. They advised that they did not have the funding to establish NATO Message Refile Centers.

The NATO staff advised funding would come, but not for several years. The committee brainstormed ways for the Greek Navy and Turkish Navy to comply with reporting requirements while waiting for funding. Then, the NAVCOMMSTA Greece commanding officer, Commander Franks, declared he would establish a NATO Message Refile Center at NAVCOMMSTA Greece.

Rodgers and Dunbar were astonished at Commander Franks's declaration, because they both knew that NAVCOMMSTA Greece did not have funding, manning, or equipment resources either. During the next break, Dunbar and Rodgers advised Commander Franks of lack of resources.

Commander Franks exhibited no concern and stated, "I am confident that you two can get it done."

That's when Rodgers told Commander Franks that a NATO Message Refile Center would require the use of Adonis crypto machines. Rodgers further advised that COMNAVCOM had ordered transfer of all three of the NAVCOMMSTA Greece

Adonis crypto machines to NAVCOMMSTA Washington DC. Rodgers also advised that all the paperwork to transfer the Adonis machines had been processed. All that remained was for public works to complete construction of the shipping containers and the Adonis machines would be shipped.

"Don't ship the Adonis machines," Commander Franks ordered. "I will resolve all that with COMNAVCOM." Then, Commander Franks ordered, "I want our refile center up and operating within fifteen days of our return. Get started on it right away."

Master Chief Rodgers was the operations chief at the time, and it was his project to establish the NATO Message Refile Center. He scrounged teletype equipment, CW equipment, and radio receivers. He built a vault on the north end of the fleet center to house operating positions for two Adonis crypto machines. He complied with the CO's order and had the refile center up and operating by the end of fifteen days.

Commander Franks was happy, but the radiomen were not. In order to man the refile center, the radiomen went from a four section watch rotation to a three section watch rotation. They became demoralized and their performance suffered.

Over the next few months several letters were received from COMNAVCOM and NAVCOMMSTA Washington DC regarding the disposition of the three Adonis machines. Rodgers sent copies of the letters to the CO with a note asking the CO how he should respond. The CO told Rodgers not to answer the letters. The CO advised he would answer the letters. The CO did not provide Rodgers with copies of the response letters.

Several months later while reviewing the Command Equipment Authorization List, Rodgers noticed that all three Adonis machines were no longer listed. That meant that the Adonis machines would no longer receive maintenance and parts support, and if NAVCOMMSTA Greece ordered spares, the navy supply system would deny the order with justification that NAVCOMMSTA Greece was not authorized to have Adonis machines. Rodgers approached Lieutenant Dunbar and asked for guidance. Dunbar advised he would talk to the CO about it.

Dunbar never advised Rodgers of the CO's response to the Equipment Authorization List problem. Rodgers, then being a master chief not to let problems ferment, approached the CO regarding loss of maintenance and parts support for the Adonis machines.

The CO responded, "Never again bring me problems regarding the Adonis equipment. If you can't handle problems associated with the refile center, I will replace you with a more resourceful and less negative master chief."

After six months of operation, the increasing message load in the refile center required the third Adonis machine to be placed in operation. Rodgers and Dunbar were too fearful to inform Commander Franks about placing the third machine in operation.

Inquiry letters regarding transfer of the Adonis machines continued to be received. Complying with Commander Franks's order, all letters were filed without taking any action. Neither Dunbar nor Rodgers ever informed Commander Franks of the continuing inquires.

Commander Franks often spoke of anticipated advancement to the rank of captain and becoming commanding officer of a larger command. Instead, he abruptly retired at the end of his tour as commanding officer of NAVCOMMSTA Greece. Rumors ran rampant that he had fallen into disfavor with COMNAVCOM.

After Commander Franks retired, the inquiries into the Adonis equipment transfer stopped. The three Adonis machines were never placed back on the Equipment Allowance List.

Rodgers closes the file folder. He leans back in his chair and stairs at the ceiling. *I knew this would eventually bite us in the ass!*

Chapter 66

Once each month, NAVCOMMSTA Greece chief petty officers meet to discuss command events. They meet in the ballroom area of the Club Zeus before it opens at 1030. During these meetings, the chiefs develop strategies to solve leadership problems and morale problems. Master Chief Crimer allows no one but chief petty officers in the club during the monthly meeting.

Master Chief Crimer chairs these monthly meetings because he serves as the most senior of the chief petty officers and serves as the senior enlisted advisor to the commanding officer. Master Chief Radioman Raymond Rodgers is actually the most senior enlisted man. However, six months ago he resigned his role as senior enlisted advisor. Rodgers had told Crimer, "The navy has rejected me. Now, I reject the navy. I'm just serving my time to retirement date." Rodgers no longer attends any of the chief petty officer meetings.

Crimer stands at the podium on the slightly elevated stage and performs a head count. Sixteen chief petty officers are present. The only chiefs missing are the ones on watch in the communications trailers. As the chiefs take their seats, the murmur of conversation softens.

Crimer pounds the gavel on the podium and declares, "The monthly meeting of chief petty officers is now in session. The captain has asked that we focus on formulating a plan to improve the first-term reenlistment rate. The CO told me to relay to all of you that he holds chief petty officers accountable for the good morale and good discipline of junior sailors. The CO also told me that he believes reenlistment rates are directly proportional to chiefs' leadership abilities. During the last several months, the first-term reenlistment rate has dropped to eighteen percent. Before the drop, first-term reenlistment rates held steady at eighty-five percent for the previous two years. Every month, our reenlistment rates are reported to COMNAVCOM. Yesterday, the

CO received a message stating that the COMNAVCOM Admin Inspection Team arrives in two weeks determine the reason for the drop in reenlistment rates. Our CO directs us to reverse the downward trend."

The room is silent. Most of the chiefs are looking at each other and shaking their heads in bewildered astonishment.

Crimer points a thick-point ink marker at chart paper on an easel and explains, "We will brainstorm about five ideas. Then we will discuss implementation strategy."

All the chiefs sit silent. Crimer knows what they are thinking. None of them want to utter negative comments regarding Commander Caldwell's morale-busting initiatives. Crimer knows that chief petty officers must support their commanding officer's initiatives. However, he knows that the chiefs are not doing that. He knows that the chiefs are not openly criticizing Commander Caldwell, but they are not openly supporting him either. As a group, the chiefs are telling their sailors that being in the navy is all about service and sacrifice, and they will not always understand the actions of commanding officers. However, sailors are not stupid. Sailors comprehend that what the previous CO allowed, the current CO disallows. Sailors question how could what the previous CO allowed be okay, but not okay with the current CO. Sailors are also aware of the CO's contempt for communicators. They believe they are victims of the current CO's whims. Commander Caldwell reversed policies that were good for morale. The inconsistency makes no sense.

Within the first thirty days of Commander Caldwell's command, five first-term enlisted men who planned to reenlist changed their minds. They feared encountering future commanding officers who have no regard for morale and who change logical policies to illogical policies at whim.

Master Chief Crimer knows the results of this meeting will have no influence on Commander Caldwell, and he knows what initiatives the chiefs will propose. They will propose to reverse Commander Caldwell's morale-busting actions. Crimer questions in his own mind, *does Commander Caldwell really believe chiefs are at fault for the decrease in reenlistment rates? If he does, he is more disturbed that I suspect. Caldwell must realize that the COMNAVCOM Inspection Team will discover the truth.* "Anyone have any ideas?" Crimer asks.

Senior Chief Bullock raises his hand and proposes several actions. After thirty minutes, the chiefs have proposed eight action items.

Master Chief Crimer shakes his head as he studies the list of actions. The action items on the list would reverse all of Commander Caldwell's morale-busting policies.

Chapter 67

Commissaryman Second Class Gordon Benedict enters the Club Zeus bar area and sights RM2 Page. He walks to the empty stool next to Page and sits.

Rigney offers, "Hey, Gordon, may I buy you a beer?"

"Amstel . . . thanks."

"My pleasure," Rigney responds. Rigney likes the amicable cook. Gordon speaks ill of no one. His benevolent acts help those in need. Everyone on base likes Gordon.

The Greek bartender places a cold Amstel in front of Gordon.

Benedict takes a deep gulp, then, sets the bottle on the bar top. He says to Rigney, "I'm glad you're here. I came in here looking for you."

Rigney gives Gordon a quick, quizzical glance and asks, "What can I do for you?"

"Can you teach me how to defend myself? Everyone says you are tough when it comes to fighting. I heard what you did to those two Greeks outside your house."

Rigney reacts jokingly. "Why do you need to defend yourself? Someone choke on your meatloaf?"

"No," Gordon responds with a smile and light chuckle, politely conveying Rigney's comment was funny. Then, his expression turns serious. "I think someone will beat me up. I need to know how to fight back."

"Gordon, you're the nicest guy on base. Why would anyone want to beat you up?"

"You know Jackson, the first class steward?"

"Yeah, he's in charge of the barracks . . . runs X-division . . . big black guy . . . looks like a pro football tackle. Is he the guy you're afraid of?"

"He said that if I don't stop lending money to people, he will beat me up. Ya see, Jackson runs a slush fund, and I lend people money at no interest."

"What's a slush fund?" Rigney asks.

"Jackson lends people money at thirty percent interest per payday. Like if he lends you twenty dollars, you must pay him twenty-six on payday. If you don't pay back on payday, then it's a total of thirty-two dollars the next payday. Six dollars is added every payday until the money is paid back."

"That's against navy regulations," Rigney declares.

"So it is, but you can find someone running a slush fund on every ship and shore station. Anyway, I'm not married, and I inherited some money. I want to help people out. I don't lend money to gamblers, but to those who really need it. I don't want to take advantage of them by charging interest."

"Does everyone pay you back?"

"Yes. If someone is late, I tell his shipmates. Then, his shipmates put the squeeze on him to pay me back . . . doesn't happen that often, though."

"I see," Rigney responds with a nod of his head. "You're cuttin' in on Jackson's business."

"That's the way Jackson sees it."

"And he threatened you with bodily harm if you don't stop."

"'Knock yo' upside yo' head' were his exact words."

"And you're not going to stop lending—right?"

"Why should I stop? Jackson shouldn't bully people. I want to stand up to him, but I need to learn how to fight first."

"Have you thought of reporting Jackson's threat to the chain-of-command?"

"Come on, Page, where you been?"

Rigney evaluates the medium-height, scrawny sailor before him; then, he says, "Do you have any experience with fighting?"

"No."

"Do you think Jackson has any experience fighting?"

"Yeah, he's from South Philly. People say he carries a switchblade."

"I recommend you avoid Jackson, don't fight him."

"But what if he comes after me?"

"Kick him in the balls. Then, find something to club him in the head."

"That's dirty fighting. It's not honorable. I couldn't do that."

"You want to face Jackson using Queensbury rules? I doubt he will. If you're not willing to do what's necessary to put Jackson down, then stay away from him."

"What if he comes after me?"

"We're in the navy. You could always report him to the chief-master-at-arms."

Benedict expresses disagreement. "That's not the way it works, Page. Never get the chiefs and officers involved. You lose the respect of your shipmates if you can't handle these things on your own. It's a bad thing to be known as a snitch."

Rigney nods his head several times to portray his understanding. Ever since he first went aboard the USS *Columbus* last December, he continually receives lessons on the *real navy* versus what the navy formally teaches. He remembers the words of his friend Larry Johnson on the USS *Columbus* eight months ago. *"You're in the fleet now, the real navy. You can throw out what you learned in boot camp and from navy training manuals."*

Rigney advises Benedict, "He might not come after you. He could be bluffing."

"Maybe, but I still think I should learn to fight. They say you know martial arts. Can you teach me a few things?"

Rigney bows his head in thought. After a few moments, he says, "I am not a martial arts expert. All I could teach you is the most damaging moves, but you need to be in top shape to pull them off. I would teach you kicking balls as soon as he walks up to you. Then, I would teach you how to kick him in the head to do the most damage. You see, Gordon, you don't stop someone like Jackson with Queensbury rules. To come out on top, you must become the attacker. You must be fast and you must be merciless. You must be so brutal that Jackson would never want to come after you again. Do you think you could do that?"

Benedict stares at Page with a horrified expression.

Rigney anticipated Benedict's response. Rigney wants to scare the fight out of Gordon.

With a doubtful look, Benedict replies, "I guess I need to think more about this." He takes the final gulp of his beer and slips off his barstool. "I appreciate your advice," he says. Then, he exits the club.

Chapter 68

RM2 Page enters the petty officer barracks and walks directly to the barracks office where he expects to find Steward First Class Cassius Jackson. He opens the office door and walks in.

Jackson sits at his desk, poking on a typewriter. A cigarette smolders in the ashtray. He looks up as Page enters.

Page notes that Jackson is right-handed.

"What the *folk* yo' wan', man?"

"Benedict told me about you threatening him. I'm asking you to back off."

"*Folk* yo'! Get out!"

Page had previously decided to discuss the issue in a civil manner, but Jackson's rough greeting irritates him. With the most threatening tone he can muster, Page warns, "Leave Gordon Benedict alone or I'll rip out your balls and stuff them down your throat."

Jackson cannot believe what he hears. *No one threatens me. Everyone fears me.* He stands and comes around to the other side of the desk, knowing he will tower over Page, intimidating him. He feels no fear.

Page smiles knowingly at Jackson's intimidation tactic.

Jackson flexes his arm muscles to cause veins to stand out on his muscular forearms and biceps, but his bulging belly betrays his weakness.

"I'm not Newman. I'll bust yo' up, man!" Jackson steps closer to Rigney.

"I warn you, Jackson, don't come any closer."

"*Folk* yo'," Jackson slurs in a dismissive tone. He steps closer to Page.

Page kicks Jackson in the shin, hard.

"Aahhhh!" Jackson utters sharply in pain. Jackson bends over to rub his shin.

While Jackson bends over, Page considers hitting him in the face with an uppercut, but he decides to use restraint. *Maybe I can resolve this without hurting him more.*

Jackson stands straight. His fearlessness fades, his confidence lessened.

Page watches Jackson's body language so that he can predict any aggressive action. Rigney knows the right-cross punch is coming before Jackson decides to throw it. Rigney already knows his own counteraction.

Jackson steps forward with his left foot as he brings back his right arm to put force behind a punch.

Jackson's movements are slow and lumbering.

Page easily blocks the punch with his left forearm. Then, he locks his left forearm under Jackson's elbow and jerks up sharply.

Jackson yelps as he feels pain in his elbow and shoulder. He stands on tiptoes to avoid more pain and avoid his arm from being broken.

"Alright, Page! Let up! I'll do what you want!"

He lessens the pressure against Jackson's elbow enough to stop the pain, but he does not release his grasp. He expects Jackson to swing at him with his left fist. Then, Page releases his grasp on Jackson's right arm.

Jackson throws a left cross, another slow and lumbering swing.

Rigney grabs Jackson's left wrist, applies a viselike grip and turns Jackson's wrist outward and down.

Jackson yells out as he lowers his body to the floor, attempting to relieve the sharp pain that he feels from his wrist to arm socket.

Rigney twists just a hair more to ensure Jackson stays down. Then, he places his right foot on the area between Jackson's left armpit and left shoulder blade. "Tell me when to stop," he says to Jackson.

Jackson lies belly down on the floor. He yelps and groans in pain. His twisted left arm is vertical and held at the wrist by Page.

"What's going on in here?"

Rigney turns his head toward the voice.

Seaman Cussack, X-division sailor, stands in the doorway, holding the door open. He quickly scans the scene. He backs out of the doorway and announces, "I'm gonna get the MAA."

The door slams shut.

Jackson squirms under Rigney's foot. The grime on the floor dirties his white uniform.

"Stop!" Jackson pleads.

Rigney allows Jackson's arm to come back two inches toward its normal position.

Jackson lets out a sigh and says, "Okay, man, I'll give up my slush fund and leave Benedict alone."

"You misunderstand me, "Rigney responds, "I don't give a shit if you continue your slush fund or not. I only demand that you let Benedict continue his lending and that you do nothing to harm him."

"Okay! Okay! Let go a ma arm, man!"

"Before I let you go, you must agree to a few other things. You must apologize to Benedict for threatening him and tell him that he can continue his no-interest lending. Tell him today. And you must not report this incident to anyone."

"Okay! Okay!"

"One more thing . . . don't underestimate me. If you ever try to ambush me, I will cripple you. If anyone else tries to harm me, I will assume you're behind it, and I will cripple you. Your life as you know it with four functioning limbs will be over. Do you understand?"

"Yes! I understand. I'll do nuttin' ta yo'. Please let me go, man!"

Rigney drops Jackson's arm and takes his foot off Jackson's back.

Jackson stands. He brushes dirt from his uniform. He rubs his arm to jumpstart blood flow. He looks at Page out of the corner of his eye.

Rigney turns to leave.

Jackson says, "Dat's som' talent yo' got der, Page. Ever thin' a makin' som' money wid it?"

Page turns back to Jackson and questions, "What?"

Jackson looks conspiringly at Rigney and says, "Som' of the toughes' guys on dis base are behin' in payments ta me. I thin' yo' cud make 'em to pay me. I wud pay yo' 25 percen' of everythin' yo' collect."

Page shakes his head in disgust. "Where do sailors like you come from? How do you get so far in the navy without the navy discovering what you are?"

Jackson shakes his head in dismissal. "What boy scout camp yo' com' from, man? Yo' got lots to learn 'bout the realities of dis man's navy." Jackson continues to rub life back into his arm.

The door opens, and QM1 Latham, the duty master-at-arms, steps into the office. He carries his nightstick in his hand. Seaman Cussack follows close behind.

Latham looks Page and Jackson up and down. Latham notices the dirt and grime on Jackson's uniform. Then, he says, "Cussack said a fight was goin' on in here."

"We weren't fightin', man. Page was showin' me som' his kung fu moves. Dat's all. Cussack misunner'stood."

Latham looks questioningly at Cussack.

Cussack shrugs his shoulders, but he knows the truth.

Page says, "I must be going now." He turns and walks toward the door.

"Hey, Page," Jackson calls.

Page looks over his shoulder at Jackson.

"Thin' 'bout ma offer," Jackson says with a wink of his eye and continuing to rub his arm.

As he departs the office, Page shakes his head and expresses disgusted dismissal.

Within several hours, the news of Page's confrontation with Jackson spreads over the entire base. Cussack spared no creativity explaining what he saw. As each person retells the story, the confrontation becomes bloodier and bloodier.

Later in the day, SD1 Jackson enters the galley in search of CS2 Benedict. He finds Benedict in the kitchen preparing the evening meal.

Benedict has been in the galley all afternoon and has not heard about the fight between Page and Jackson. Benedict looks up from making potato patties and becomes alarmed when he sees Jackson walking toward him. Benedict back steps to put distance between them. He grabs a fry pan by the handle and raises it over his head.

"No, No," Jackson says softly as he waves his hands in front of him to indicate Benedict misreads the situation. "I hav' com' to 'pologize fo what I say ta yo' da utter day. I was wron' to ask yo' ta stop lendin' money. Go 'head an len' yo' money. You'll get no mo' shit from me, man."

At first, Benedict does not believe Jackson. He keeps the frying pan raised.

"I'm serious, man. Take back ever'thin' I said. Yo' frien', Page, made it mos' clear, man."

This time, Benedict believes Jackson. He lowers the frying pan and puts it back on the pan rack.

Jackson puts a friendly smile on this face and says, "Good. Ever'thin' is okay, now. See yo' latta, ma man." Jackson turns and departs the galley.

Benedict stands dumfounded.

Thirty minutes latter, Jackson sits in his office.

Seaman Newman enters.

Jackson turns in his chair and stares at Newman.

Newman expresses surprise and states, "Man, I thought yo' be all busted up."

"Why's dat?"

"I heard Page beat da shit out of yo'. I heard he knock yo' all around da office."

"What the *folk* yo' talkin' 'bout, man? Page and ma did not fight."

"It's all over the base, man."

"Page was showin' me som' of his martial arts stuff, dats all."

Jackson needs to quell the perception that Page beat him and disrespected him. He cannot afford for those who owe him money to think he was physically beaten. Then, he thinks of a way out of this. He decides to tell Newman a lie that he knows Newman will spread around the base. "Page agree ta be ma enforcer. I ask' him to show ma how he get dose deadbeats to pay ma. He was showin' me som' thins' he will do when Cussack cum in. Cussack misunner'stood and looks like ever'one else have it wrong."

Newman greedily accepts this negative information about Page. He never considers that Jackson lies to him. Jackson is Newman's mentor and role model.

During the following twenty-four hours, Newman spreads the word about Page becoming Jackson's enforcer. No exaggeration is too large as the story passes from sailor to sailor. The most accepted version is that Page beat Jackson to a pulp, took all Jackson's money, and has taken over Jackson's loan-sharking business.

Page goes about his duties unaware of the swelling sea of lies spread about him.

Chapter 69

Rigney exits the small market in Nea Makri's business district. He carries two bags of fruits and vegetables. He committed to providing a large bowl of green salad and a similar size bowl of fresh fruit salad for tonight's patio dinner with Pritchings's neighbors.

The glaring sun in a cloudless sky causes him to nearly close his eyes. He places the two bags on a small outside table while he puts on sunglasses.

The top is down on the BMW, and he places the bags on the backseat. He turns the ignition key. The sound of soft, balanced rumbling from the exhaust reveals a smooth running engine. He steps on the clutch peddle and places his hand on the gearshift. He looks over his right shoulder to check traffic. A woman in tight light-red colored shorts and tight, low-cut white tank top walking on the opposite side of the street catches his eye. He recognizes Nancy Bell. She struggles with shopping bags.

He waves at her.

She steps off the sidewalk and steps across the street toward Rigney. When she arrives at the car, she asks, "Can you give me a lift? I will never make it home without dropping these and breaking something."

"Sure. Get in," Rigney replies.

Nancy places her shopping bags in the backseat, opens the passenger door, and sits in the bucket seat.

Rigney performs the necessary manipulations of clutch pedal, brake pedal, gas pedal, and gearshift; he drives the BMW out of the parking space. As he drives the BMW through the market district, Nea Makri sailors and their wives take notice. Some of them shake their heads in disgust at Rigney and Nancy's open and flagrant disregard for proper behavior.

"Where do you live?" Rigney asks.

"Near Mary Blakely. Do you know where that is?"

"No."

"Take a left on Marathon Road. Then, I'll guide you."

As Rigney drives, they start up another of their social-political discussions. When he turns the car onto Nancy's street, she is questioning Rigney's opinion. "And you believe that if there were no draft, there would not have been riots at the Democrat Convention in Chicago?"

"That's right," Rigney replies.

"Why?"

"Because without a military draft, our generation would have little interest in the war. How many Americans beyond draft age do you see throwing rocks and bottles at the police?"

Nancy considers Rigney's words and responds, "Interesting thought. I would like to see your opinion proven someday."

"Me, too," Rigney responds. Then, he asks Nancy, "Who do you think will win the presidential race, Nixon or Humphrey?"

"Nixon."

"Why?" Rigney questions.

"Eight years of warmongering democrats and the negative effect of eight years of liberal legislation."

"War mongering?"

"Yes," Nancy replies. "The democrats took American involvement in Vietnam from a small military assistance group to a five-hundred-thousand-man army."

"Yes . . . makes sense," Rigney concurs. Then, he asks, "What do you mean by negative effects of liberal legislation?"

"Eight years of liberals controlling both the White House and the U.S. Congress. You know, liberals have controlled congress for most of the last thirty-five years, and except for eight years of Eisenhower, the liberals have had the White House for the past thirty-five years. Taxes are the highest they have ever been. Government is the largest it has ever been. The so-called Great Society has not emerged. Liberal legislation holds everyone responsible except criminal perpetrators for crime in the streets. The poor are still poor. The feelings of victimization by inner-city blacks led to the riots after Martin Luther King's assassination.

The Great Society liberals feed those feelings of victimization by continuing to blame conservatives. The American public is awakening to the lies of liberalism. The democrats don't have a chance to take the White House." Nancy glances to the side of the road and directs, "Park in front of the house on the left with the orange lawn furniture."

No curb or sidewalk exists, just patches of sand and dead grass. He parks the BMW on a patch of dead grass at the edge of the road.

Rigney asks, "Do you think the liberals will lose the majority in congress?"

"I hope so, but I think it will take a long time for grassroots voters to understand their liberal government slowly erodes American liberty and the American economy. The democrats have not achieved one thing they promised to do."

"What about Medicare?"

With a negative tone, Nancy responds, "Well, yes. They delivered on that."

"You don't approve of Medicare?"

Nancy expresses thoughtfulness for a few moments; then she comments, "I don't think the government will manage Medicare properly. The government will renege on their promises, just like it did with social security. Mark my words."

Nancy exits the car. After slamming the door shut, she reaches into the backseat for her shopping bags. Her bending across the car accentuates her cleavage.

Rigney stares at her breasts.

Nancy notices, and she says, "I would ask you in for a cold drink, but Paul is at work, and I don't want any more rumors spread about me." She quickly glances around at the other houses. "Most of my neighbors are watching and most of them are Americans from the base."

Rigney looks around and sees about half a dozen people in their yards, pretending not to stare at Rigney and Nancy.

Nancy walks around to the driver's side so that she can talk to Rigney in a low voice. "Paul told me that Ralph Hilton told you to stay away from me. Ralph did that without Paul knowing. Ralph is always getting into other people's business. He tells the sailors he is investigating for the chain-of-command or for good discipline. He's just prying and interfering for his own interest. We were stationed with Ralph in Morocco. He was the same way there. If you ask me, Ralph Hilton causes problems the way he pokes into other people's business. Paul knows there's nothing going on between you and me. Just like there was nothing between Dave Elders and me. Dave transferred just before you came to Nea Makri. Did you hear the rumors about Dave and me?"

Rigney nods affirmative.

"Like you, Dave is an interesting person. Paul and I enjoyed Dave's company. There was nothing more to it than that. People are mean and deceitful. I don't know why people are like that. I wish I understood it all."

Rigney sighs deeply; then reveals, "So do I."

"Ralph told Paul that I should not be seen alone with you. Ralph said we must be cautious not to give others the wrong idea."

For the thousandth time in his life, Rigney declares, "I am not accountable for what others think. I am only accountable for what I think. I won't consider the misconceptions of others before I act."

"Exactly!" Nancy affirms. Then, she asks, "You will disobey Ralph's order, then?"

"Yes."

"Even if he puts you on report?"

"He won't put me on report. I told him if he did, I would request court-martial. He knows his charges would not survive the scrutiny of a UCMJ investigation."

Nancy cocks her head to the side. With a curious expression, she asks, "What is a UCMJ investigation?"

"It's a process with the purpose of separating facts from the bullshit to see if there is enough evidence to proceed to court-martial."

"I never knew that. You know a lot about how the navy works for such a junior sailor."

"I'm only seven years younger than you."

"Thanks for reminding me."

They both chuckle.

Nancy says, "We're having a barbeque tomorrow afternoon. Some of our friends are coming over. Please come. Bring Dottie . . . or the German lady . . . or both, if you want."

"What time?"

"Four."

"I'll be here."

"Great." Nancy retrieves the remainder of her shopping bags from the backseat and walks toward the house.

Rigney watches her and notices the exaggerated sway of her hips. He concludes, *she just wants to look sexy and attractive, like all women . . . nothing wrong with that. It's not a come-on. She's okay. She does not cheat on her husband.*

He drives away. When he reaches the intersection, Mary Blakely jogs around the corner toward him. She wears exercise clothes and a headband. Sweat soaks her t-shirt.

Rigney waves.

Mary waves back and keeps jogging.

Rigney drives north through the intersection.

Mary stops, turns, and stares after the BMW. *Wonder what he's doing in this neighborhood?*

Nancy answers the knock at her kitchen door. Her friend and neighbor, Marge Straton, stands in the doorway with a conspiratorial smirk on her face.

"Come in," Nancy invites.

Marge sits at the kitchen table and says jokingly, "Couldn't help but see your secret lover bring you home."

Nancy casts a disapproving stare at Marge.

"But since the whole base is talking about it, I guess he's not a secret anymore, is he?"

"Come on, Marge. You know I'm not having an affair with Rigney Page, just like I didn't have an affair with Dave Elders."

"Yes. Of course, I know you're not and I know you didn't, but you fan the fires of scandal, a fire that needs feeding by the intellectually deficient who suffer withdrawal from lack of the afternoon TV soaps."

They both chuckle.

"Seriously, if you want the rumors to stop, you must stop being seen with Rigney Page when Paul isn't around."

"Paul loves me, and I love him. He knows that rumors about Dave and Rigney are not true."

"How does Paul feel about it?"

"Paul thinks like I do. We will not let our actions be controlled by how others might misjudge those actions. We stimulate our lives by continuing education, by travel, and by having interesting friends."

"You and Paul consider yourselves above it all, don't you?"

"If you mean above those who can only infuse excitement in their lives by gossip and lies, then, yes, we believe we are above that. We choose friends, like you and Pete, who we believe are also above it."

"I'll take that as a compliment," Marge responds with an appreciative smile.

The two women are silent while Nancy puts away the items from the shopping bags.

Marge queries, "What about Rigney Page? Do you believe what you hear about him?"

"I only consider what I know about him firsthand. I won't judge him on what I hear about him."

"Does he ever talk about what people say about him?"

"No. Our conversations are about current events and politics and interesting places we have been in Europe."

"He doesn't come-on to you, then."

"No."

"And you don't flirt with him?"

"No."

Marge nods acceptance of Nancy's response. They are close friends who tell each other the truth. Marge advises, "Pete talks about Rigney Page. Rigney works for Pete, ya know. Pete says Rigney doesn't conform like most sailors. Pete says Rigney is a good technician, but an unconventional sailor. Pete says Rigney is . . ." Marge pauses while searching for the correct words.

"Is what?" Nancy questions.

"Pete used the word *fearless*. Not sure what that means."

Nancy responds, "Probably means Rigney is unemotional."

A curious look appears on Marge's face as she asks, "Unemotional? Is that how you see him?"

"Yeah."

Marge pauses while calculating how to form the words of her next question. Then, with a mock suspicious tone, she accuses, "But you fantasize about him, don't you?"

Nancy does not answer. She stares into space and sighs deeply. She visualizes Rigney and herself lying naked in bed with their arms and legs intertwined and kissing passionately. A few moments later, the visualization dissipates as she thinks about the many times she masturbated while fantasizing sex with Rigney. A guilty expression appears on her face. She glances toward Marge.

"No need to feel guilty about it," Marge consoles. "Fantasizing is healthy. I fantasize about him, too. Just like our husbands fantasize about sexy women we know."

Nancy nods agreement.

With raised eyebrows and an inquisitive expression, Marge asks, "Do you think Rigney fantasizes about you when he jacks off?"

"We're gossiping!" Nancy declares.

"Yes, we are," Marge agrees with a smile on her face.

Chapter 70

The midmorning sun heats the outside tables of Papaspyros Café. The café, located on the bottom floor of the Athens American Express office building, spreads to an outside patio with tables that face Syntagma Square. The café is widely known as a meeting place for travelers and is known as a favorite haunt of the Nea Makri sailors for picking up women. A favorite saying of those who frequent the café is that *"if you sit there long enough, you will eventually see everyone you have ever known."*

On this Sunday morning, Rigney sits alone at a small two-chair table in the center of the some forty tables on the café's patio. American tourists who wired home for money crowd the tables. Waves of Athenians and tourists move along the streets. Young American tourists and young Western European tourists are the most noticeable in their casual and hippie-style clothing.

Rigney looks toward Syntagma Square. Beyond Syntagma Square, he sees the Parliament Building, formerly the King's Palace.

Although Rigney wears sneakers, faded denim jeans, and a plain black t-shirt, he stands out among the other young men because of his white-sidewalls haircut and clean-shaven face.

He scans the faces of all those who walk toward the Papaspyros Café. He glances at his watch—10:35 AM. The message he received over the villa's communications equipment said that John Smith would contact him at 10:30 AM. Rigney continues to search the faces of those who approach the café. He sees John Smith emerge from the crowd in Syntagma Square and stand at the curb. John wears worn denim jeans and a short-sleeve denim shirt. John's long brown hair is pulled back into a ponytail, and he sprouts a bushy brown beard. A canvas bag hangs from John's shoulder.

John Smith dodges vehicles as he steps quickly through the traffic toward the Papaspyros Café. When he steps onto the patio area, he looks around as if searching for an open seat. Few seats are available. His eyes pass over Rigney several times to disguise his objective of sitting at Rigney's table. Then, he fixes his eyes on the open chair next to Rigney. A gym bag occupies the chair. John shifts his gaze to Rigney.

Rigney stares in a different direction, as if not paying any attention to John.

John weaves his way through the maze of tables and asks, "Excuse me, sir. May I sit in that chair? There are no other available seats."

Rigney turns in his chair and looks at John and replies, "Yes. Please do." Rigney removes his gym bag from the chair and places it under the table.

John slips the canvas bag from his shoulder, sits down, and places his shoulder bag under the table next to Rigney's gym bag.

"Thanks for the seat," John says. "I'm meeting my girlfriend here. She's shopping, and she's always late."

"No problem," Rigney responds. "This is a great place to wait, and there are always interesting people to meet."

The casual conversation is for the benefit of anyone who might have interest in Rigney's activities.

"Do you spend a lot of time here?" John asks.

"I'm stationed at a U.S. Navy base near hear. Some of the sailors at the base told me about this place. During my off days, I stay in a hotel here in Athens, and I always spend a couple of hours at this café."

"So you're a military man, then?"

A beautiful woman with flowing blond hair wearing tight shorts and a tight top stops at the table, focuses on John, and says in a louder than necessary voice, "Here you are. I need some more traveler's checks."

"They're in my bag." John leans from the waist, reaches under the table, and unzips the canvas bag.

All male eyes stare transfixed on the beautiful and sexy woman. She distracts others from John's actions under the table.

John pulls a cigarette-pack-sized device from his bag and slips it into Rigney's gym bag. Then, he reaches back into his bag. He sits up in his chair and hands some traveler's checks to the woman.

"You need to come with me," the woman says. "I need your help with mailing a flakati rug back home."

John rises and says to Rigney, "Good-bye, sir. Thanks for the seat."

Rigney smiles and responds, "Anytime. Enjoy your visit to Greece."

John nods, and he and his female companion disappear around the corner of the American Express building.

Rigney reaches under the table, sticks his hand into his gym bag, and pulls out the novel *The Source* by James Michener. He opens the book to the bookmark, which is halfway through the one-thousand-page novel.

He leans back in his chair and crosses his legs, exhibiting that he plans to sit there for a while.

Chapter 71

With all their crypto repairs complete and their preventative maintenance up-to-date, ET1 Straton, ET2 Thompson, ET2 Patterson, and RM2 Page sit at their workbenches studying technical manuals.

When the repair shop door opens, they all turn to see who enters.

Mr. Lemont enters, followed by Mr. Linderhaus. The two officers walk to the center of the shop.

Mr. Lemont advises, "I want to commend all of you on a job well done during the Adonis crisis. Page briefed me on how the four of you teamed up to bring the crisis to resolution.

Mr. Lemont looks at Pete Straton and says, "Straton, Page told me that you solved a major problem by manufacturing levers, using public works equipment."

Straton glances at Page.

Page nods.

Lemont faces ET2 Patterson and says, "Page tells me it was your idea to transfer Adonis parts and equipment from the aircraft carrier USS *Shangri-la* while she was in port Athens. Good thinking! *Shangri-la* was more than agreeable and cooperative."

Patterson flinches, blinks his eyes, and expresses surprise while he stares at Page.

Page smiles.

"I am putting all of you in for letters of commendation."

Lemont walks toward the door, followed by Linderhaus.

After the officers have gone, Thompson and Patterson slip off their stools and gather around Page's workbench.

Thompson purses his lips together and nods. With respectful tone and expression, he says, "You're okay, Page."

"I agree," Patterson chimes in.

"Thanks," Rigney responds. "I think you guys are okay, too."

Straton says from his stool as he hangs up the phone, "If you guys are finished with your meeting of the local mutual admiration society, one of you needs to go to the crypto trailer and perform a miracle on a sick KW-7."

"I'll go," Patterson declares. He grabs his toolkit and steps toward the door.

Straton says, "Page, you mind the shop while Thompson and I go to chow. When we get back, you and Patterson can go."

Rigney nods and then returns to reading the technical manual.

Later, prior to departing the trailers for lunch, Rigney stops by the broadcast trailer to check the news printer.

Vice President Humphrey campaigns in Pennsylvania. He attempts to disassociate himself from the Johnson Administration.

French President Charles de Gaulle holds first news conference in ten months. Condemns communists and says his no-compromise approach saved France from totalitarian regime after students and workers riot during summer.

Soviet press says antisocialists and right-wing forces in Czechoslovakia must be protected from anti-Soviet propaganda. Communist Party leader Alexander Dubcek calls meeting of full-party central committee.

Israel and Egypt have five-hour artillery duel at Suez Canal. Casualties reported. United Nations Security Council to debate Israeli charges of Egyptian aggression along Canal. Terrorists plant mine in Gaza and Israeli truck blown up. South of Sea of Galilee, Israel and Jordan gunners exchange fire.

Chapter 72

Andrei Yashin sits in his office at the Russian Embassy near Athens city center. In his right hand, he holds a photograph of Rigney Page entering Rodgers's house in Nea Makri. In his left hand, he holds a photograph of Rigney Page standing in the berthing compartment of a warship. In the Nea Makri photograph, Page sports a dark tan, wears lightweight summer clothing, and wears disguising sunglasses. In the warship photograph, Page wears only a towel around his waist, and his skin is pale from lack of exposure to sunlight. Because of the radical difference in Page's apparel and skin tone between the two photographs, Andrei nearly missed the match. The subject's abundant reddish-brown body hair caught Andrei's attention.

Rigney Page. Yes. Now I remember. That American sailor Javier worried about. Javier had me investigate Page's background.

Javier, codename Lucifer by American intelligence agencies, formed an anti-American espionage ring that operated successfully for more than ten years. Andrei was Javier's KGB contact.

The background report I gave Javier revealed nothing suspicious about Page, and I told Javier that. Nevertheless, Javier read more into the report than what was there. Then, several weeks later, Javier disappeared.

Andrei rereads the background report on Page. Again, he sees nothing suspicious. However, the current situation stirs suspicion. *Page had reported aboard that cruiser last December. Nine months later, he arrives in Nea Makri shortly after I recruit Rodgers. I don't believe in coincidences. Javier was right about Page.*

Later in the day, Andrei briefs his supervisor. "I believe the American authorities discovered our association with Rodgers."

Andrei's supervisor at the embassy, Eldar Khavanov, looks up from the open file folder before him. As he points to the open folder, he asks, "You say this Page is an American operative sent to Nea Makri to investigate?"

"Yes."

Eldar picks up the two photographs of Page and holds them side by side. "This boy can't be more that twenty-two, twenty-four at the most. Are you sure about this?"

"About as sure as I can be."

"I have enjoyed the American products you purchased from Rodgers," Eldar states with a satisfied smile on his face. "That ends now, yes?"

"European products are equally enjoyable," Andrei advises. "Some are more enjoyable."

"Yes, that is true," Eldar admits. Then, he asks, "How much American products do we have?"

"We have a one-year supply in the Piraeus warehouse." Andrei glances at the pack of American-brand cigarettes on Eldar's desktop. "It's ours as long as we do not inform Moscow."

"You know the policy, Andrei. Eventually, we must send an inventory to Moscow Center."

Andrei nods acknowledgement of the policy.

Eldar asks, "Can we salvage anything from our Rodgers operation?"

Andrei sits contemplative for a few moments; then, he explains, "Rodgers provided only one packet of cryptographic material before Rigney Page arrived. I think Page's role is to track Rodgers's movements and report those movements to his superiors. We will schedule the next drop when Page has duty."

Eldar speculates, "Page may not be the only operative."

"I have Rodgers followed continuously. No one follows Rodgers outside the Nea Makri base."

Eldar nods his acceptance. Then, he asks, "How is the operation with the yacht progressing?"

"The yacht has operated successfully for more than a month."

"And Rodgers knows nothing about the yacht operation?" Eldar seeks assurance.

"No, he doesn't. Each operation is separate from the other. No resource is shared between the two."

"Where did you get the crew for they yacht?"

"You remember that Javier disguised his espionage operation as an import and export office here in Athens?"

Eldar nods his remembrance.

"Sanchez Imports and Exports was raided by American agents who were disguised as local policeman. They closed the office and abducted everyone on the books. Some of Javier's undocumented employees, associates as Javier called them, stayed around hoping Javier would show up. They are all Spanish citizens. KGB knows who they are. I contacted them and offered them jobs. One of them has yachting experience. I made him captain. He recruited other crewmembers from Spain. Several are good with electronics and I had them trained on the signals collection equipment. They all have criminal backgrounds and think their work aboard the yacht is all about smuggling, which is a continuation of what they think they were doing for Javier. They believe I am a criminal kingpin."

"Has Moscow Center reported anything regarding what we send them from the yacht?"

"Moscow Center reports the signal collections provide valuable information."

Eldar shakes his head in bewilderment and comments, "Incredible that our operatives so easily penetrated the U.S. Base at Nea Makri—twice."

"Yes. Both times at 2:00 AM," Andrei adds. "They entered from the beach on the east boundary of the base. They stepped over a four feet high fence and proceeded to the communications complex, which they accessed easily. There are no posted sentries or roving security patrols."

"And what did our operatives do there?" Eldar asks. "I didn't understand the descriptions in the reports."

"The operatives modified the electronic ground cables, installed electromagnetic sensors, and a miniature transmitter."

"Yes, I read that," Eldar claims. "But I don't understand how that increased the strength of the classified signals so that we can detect them with the yacht's equipment."

"Yes, I don't understand the technical aspects, either," Andrei admits. "The engineer provided a layman's explanation at the debriefing. He said that without specifically designed electronic grounding, echoes of classified signals find their way onto other radiating devices. For example, classified signals piggyback on the normal radiated signals of power lines, phone lines, and radio waves. The engineer explained that the sensitive receivers aboard the yacht detect and capture those radiated signals. Then, equipment at Moscow Center can filter the piggyback classified signals through electronic processing systems and produce printed versions."

"Well, yes, that explanation is understandable," Eldar acknowledges. "But, certainly, the Americans must have inspections and must monitor the radiated signals of power lines and phone lines around their communications stations."

"They do," Andrei informs, "But not on a continuous basis. They have inspectors called Tempest Teams, based in Washington, that travel to bases around the world and conduct the inspections. Sometimes, two years may elapse between inspections. Between inspections, the American military relies on their communications operators to comply with all cryptographic regulations, which they do not, and that makes it easier for us to collect their classified signals."

"That is bewildering," Eldar declares. "What do you mean they do not comply with all their cryptographic regulations?"

"Yes, it is bewildering," Andrei agrees. "The American military have concentrated their forces to the Western Pacific and the Vietnam War. As a result, American military installations like the one in Nea Makri are undermanned, which imposes a heavy workload. They are overworked and overtired, resulting in increased mistakes and many occurrences where they do not think clearly. They cannot keep up with all they are required to do by official directives. For example, there are scheduled maintenance inspections to verify electrical grounds and cryptographic radiation shields are in good repair. If the equipment appears to be operating, they will not take the time to properly inspect for damage, fraying, or wear. They will signoff on the maintenance check, even though the check was not done. The sailors have a name for falsifying records . . . *gun-decking*. Another *gun-decking* practice is to falsify daily inventories of classified material. Communications operators will sign-off on the inventories without verifying the presence of the material. The heavier the workload, the more often the inventories are *gun-decked*."

Eldar raises his hand slightly to indicate he wants to ask a question.

Andrei pauses.

Eldar asks, "This term, *gun-decked* or *gun-decking*, where does it come from?"

Andrei answers, "I asked the same question many years ago. The word comes from some nautical source in history."

Eldar shrugs and says, "Okay, continue."

"One common violation that benefits our Nea Makri operation is the Americans' practice of operating cryptographic equipment with the tempest radiation shields removed. That allows more classified signals to find their way onto unsecured transmission media such as power lines and phone lines."

"That is absolutely criminal!" Eldar interjects with an incredulous tone and expression.

"It certainly is," Andrei concurs. "Operating cryptographic equipment with the radiation shields removed is a security violation and must be reported to their National Security Agency every time such a situation occurs."

"Are the occurrences reported?"

"Rarely," Andrei answers sarcastically. "No commanding officer wants to report to higher authority that he has allowed security violations in his command."

"Why do they violate their operating rules, then?"

"These American Naval Communications Stations have operational requirements that stretch their resources to the breaking point. If those sailors complied with every procedure and regulation in all their manuals, there would be no time to operate their radio circuits. Career-minded officers know that their future depends on keeping those radio circuits operational. Therefore, when a situation arises where officers must decide to comply with a security regulation at the expense of down radio circuits, they choose to keep the radio circuits operational.

"For example, when crypto equipment overheats and fails, American officers will order radiation shields removed to aid in cooling the equipment."

"Scandalous, unethical, and shameful behavior!" Eldar declares.

Andrei adds, "Yes, such behavior is the product of a corrupt capitalist system."

Eldar sits thoughtfully for several moments; then, he asks, "I assume, Andrei, that from time to time you sabotage the Nea Makri climate control equipment."

"Not necessary for us to collect sufficient signals. Nevertheless, a climate control equipment failure at Nea Makri would provide an abundant harvest, because the American radio operators will remove many tempest radiation covers to aid in cooling their cryptographic systems. I have scheduled a team to sabotage the air-conditioning equipment in the NAVCOMMSTA communication trailers."

Chapter 73

Senior Chief Radioman Ralph Hilton holds his fellow chief petty officers in contempt. His early military years as a combat marine in Korea justify his opinion that his fellow navy chiefs are inferior military men. After Korea, he discharged from the Marine Corps and joined the navy. His six years' experience as an E-7, and five years experience as an E-8 have convinced him that as a group, his fellow chiefs lack leadership skills and lack skills in their technical specialties. His contempt stems from his judgment that most first-enlistment sailors are undisciplined, which is a sure sign of poor leadership by chief petty officers. He perceives that most sailors are inept and incompetent in their job specialties, which is a sure sign that the chiefs who supervise those sailors are inept and incompetent.

Since his early days in the navy, Hilton shined as a technical superstar. His superstar status always earned him praise and the halo effect in performance evaluations. The halo effect caused his supervisors to award performance marks in leadership and military bearing to be much higher than they should have been. He has become a victim of his own halo effect. Because he performs superiorly as a radioman, he misperceives he possesses superior skills in all behaviors required of him as a petty officer. He became so confident in his own judgments that he always reacts without much thought. He believes that his way is always the best way, and he ignores anyone who questions his way. Because he sees others as incapable of correct conduct and judgment, he often steps in and interferes in areas that are none of his business. Hilton exhibits the textbook model of one who is seldom correct, but who is never in doubt. Hilton's primary co-conspirators in his corrupt judgment processes are his past and current superiors who always awarded him the highest marks in his performance evaluations when he should have received substandard marks in most, especially in leadership.

Except for his radioman specialty of technical control, Hilton has no credibility with his fellow chiefs. The chiefs avoid conversations in Hilton's presence, because they know Hilton will arrogantly interrupt, dominate the discussion, and utter illogical judgments and advice.

Hilton sits behind his desk. He motions for RM2 Page to take a seat.

"You disobeyed my order to stay away from Nancy Bell. Explain yourself."

Rigney shakes his head, a dismissive smile on his face. "I am not obligated to explain my relationship with Nancy Bell."

"So you admit you're having an affair with Nancy Bell."

Rigney shakes his head, a defiant expression on his face, conveying he will not answer the question.

"Your silence is a confession of your guilt. People have seen you coming and going from Nancy's house."

"Paul and Nancy's house," Rigney specifies.

"So you admit you were in their house."

"Only when Paul was there. They have invited me to gatherings of friends and cookouts at their house."

"That's not what others say," Hilton challenges. "I have witnesses that say you have been at their house when Paul was at work."

"I am not responsible for what people think based on what others say." Rigney's tone is defiant.

"Page, if you continue this inappropriate behavior you will be officially counseled. Negative comments will be entered in your next performance evaluation."

Rigney shrugs, indicating his lack of concern and replies, "Won't be the first time incorrect judgments of my actions have been placed in my evaluations."

"You could be placed on report."

Rigney shrugs again.

Hilton sits back in his chair while he contemplates a different approach.

"Living with that German woman and having an affair with Dottie Caldwell at the same time you are having an affair with Nancy Bell can be viewed as behavior negative to the image of the U.S. Military in Greece."

Rigney starts laughing, which develops into extended chest-heaving laughs.

Hilton's face turns red, and his manner expresses anger.

"Stop laughing, Page! This is a serious situation!"

"Only in your mind, Senior Chief," Rigney spurts between laughs.

One minute later, Rigney's laughing spell subsides. He breathes deeply. Then, he asks, "Senior Chief, why do you talk to me about these things. You are not in my chain-of-command."

"Because you have no chief in your division."

"Pete Straton is my LPO, and his boss is Mr. Linderhaus. They never seem concerned about these things. It makes me wonder why you involve yourself."

"Because it's a chief petty officer's responsibility to correct bad conduct when he sees it, regardless of the chain-of-command."

Rigney nods his understanding and says, "I guess I understand that, but too bad you got it all wrong. You're just a slave to innuendo and gossip who ignores facts and logic. Makes you look foolish."

Hilton shudders with astonishment at Page's egregious disrespect. His face flushes and reflects anger.

Rigney adds, "And, because of your conduct, your shipmates judge you foolish." Rigney pauses for effect, then adds, "And since you place so much significance in the judgment of others, you should consider modifying your behavior."

Rigney watches Hilton's facial expression. *I must have hit a sore point.* He considers walking out.

Hilton states, "Okay, Page, if that's the way you want it. I'm placing you on report for disobedience of an order and for unethical conduct."

"Whatever, Senior Chief. Anything else?"

"Yes, you must close down your slush fund."

"Uh, Senior Chief, I don't have a slush fund."

"Don't lie about it. The whole base knows you beat up Jackson and took his slush fund."

Rigney chuckles as he shakes his head. He says, "You are unredeemable." He stands and turns toward the door.

"Page, if you go, you leave me no choice but to place you on report for operating a slush fund."

Rigney does not respond. He opens the door and exits Hilton's office. He lets the door slam shut behind him.

As he walks back to the repair shop, he mutters to himself, "Yep! Just one big fuckin' soap opera!"

Chapter 74

The *Eleni* steams a northerly course eight thousand yards east of Rafina. In the aft section of the *Eleni's* electronics compartment, Page readies his dive gear. He donned a wetsuit and slipped his air tank over his shoulders. Now, he checks the pressure gauge of his air tank. He looks at his dive watch—0145.

Eddie sits on his stool and studies a radarscope. Then, he swivels on the stool and plugs his headset into the audio jack of a high frequency radio receiver. After listening in the headset for a few moments, he turns toward Page and says, "The yacht is at anchor two thousand yards off the Nea Makri Communications Station, and she's transmitting an FSK signal as usual."

Page wears the standard navy dive gear. Everything, including the buoyancy compensator, is black in color. Weights and air tank are rubber coated for noise reduction. He makes a final check of all his gear. He ensures the beacon transmitter that John passed to him is secure in a pouch attached to his BC. As he straps a dive knife to his right leg, he says to Eddie, "I'm ready."

Eddie presses the talk lever of an interior communications device and says to Bill who is at the helm, "Page is ready."

Bill's voice sounds over the intercom, *"Okay. I'll be right down."*

A few seconds later, Bill enters the compartment. He walks over to Page and says, "You will deploy the same way as last time. I have the inflatable ready. We will return to get you three hours after you enter the water."

"Okay," Page acknowledges as he adjusts the buckle on his weight belt.

Bill briefs, "There are several boats at anchor in the vicinity of our friend. Since you have seen the target before, you should not have any trouble identifying it. You can verify the bearing at the buoy. It will be 300 yards on a bearing of 274 from the buoy. None of the other boats are within twenty degrees of that."

When he hits the water, Page feels the cold seawater streaming into the area between his skin and wetsuit. He tastes saltwater at the corners of his mouth. Several minutes later, his body temperature has warmed the seawater between his skin and wetsuit.

After tying the small inflatable boat to the buoy, he brings his luminescent compass to his eye. He finds 274 degrees and positions himself to look along that bearing. He only sees lights from the NAVCOMMSTA, which is some two miles away. The yacht sits between him and the NAVCOMMSTA.

He puts the snorkel in his mouth, and he kicks away from the buoy. He wears oversized fins for maximum thrust, and he keeps his arms to his sides to minimize drag. He kicks steady at a medium pace. He keeps his head down in the water and breathes through the snorkel. Every thirty seconds, he looks at his compass.

He allows forty-five minutes of swim time each way. After twenty minutes, he stops kicking and raises his head from the water. He cannot discern the shape of a boat, but he believes he sees the target's running lights mixed with lights from the NAVCOMMSTA in the background.

He continues his swim toward the target. He raises his head more often to insure he does not come too close while still on the surface. He does not see the full shape of the target until he is within forty yards.

Rigney removes the snorkel from his mouth and inserts the air tank regulator. Then, he releases air from the buoyancy compensator. He sinks slowly.

After sinking twenty feet, he shoots a short blast of air into the buoyancy compensator.

Page hovers at twenty-five feet. He looks at the compass, finds his bearing, and swims toward the target.

Ten minutes later, he surfaces at the yacht's stern. He shoots a blast of air into his buoyancy compensator, and he becomes positively buoyant. He pulls the air-tank regulator from his mouth, and he pulls his dive mask down around his neck. Then, he pulls back on his wetsuit hood and exposes his ears. He feels and hears the yacht's engines.

After waiting several minutes for his eyes to adjust, he scans the yacht's stern. He observes a makeshift anchor line tied to the rail. He inspects the line to the point where it enters the water. He scans the aft decks for any movement. He does not see or hear anyone moving about.

As he swims toward the bow, he searches the hull for any metal plating. The beacon transmitter has a magnet to hold it in place.

As he rounds the flared bow, the deck lights come on and cast illumination thirty feet across the surface in all directions. Page hugs the hull under the flared bow. He hears footsteps on deck.

He glances up and looks through the hawsepipe. The bow anchor chain fills only half of the hawsepipe. He sees the movement of feet. He notices that the person wears worn and tattered red canvas deck shoes.

Red . . . Odd!

The illumination of the deck lights allows Page to inspect the area around the hawsepipe. The hawsepipe is metal plated. The bottom of the hawsepipe forms a lip. Behind the lip, there is a notched area large enough for the beacon transmitter.

The color of the beacon transmitter matches the color of the hull. Page reasons the notch will hide the beacon transmitter from view of a casual observer.

After several minutes, the deck walker moves aft. Page stretches his right arm toward the notch behind the lip of the hawsepipe. His reach is short by ten inches. He ponders ways to gain the distance. He considers climbing up the anchor chain, but that would cause the bow to dip too much that someone would surely come to investigate.

Page places his mask over his face and puts the regulator in his mouth. He opens the valve to his BC and squeezes the BC to force out the air. He sinks. At forty feet, he blasts air from his tank into his BC. He kicks hard as he shoots for the surface. He has his right arm raised with the beacon transmitter in his right hand. He shoots through the surface and rises to the height of the anchor hawsepipe. He reaches his right hand toward the metal lip below the anchor hawsepipe. An almost inaudible metal clank confirms the magnet on the beacon transmitter takes hold. Page's body lowers. The inflated BC keeps him surfaced.

Page forces air from his BC and sinks to thirty feet. Then, he inflates the BC to a point where he is neutrally buoyant. At this depth, the darkness causes his gauges and compass dial to illuminate. He finds the bearing of 094 and kicks off in that direction.

Chapter 75

Following his normal workday routine, Rigney enters the Nea Makri main gate at 0730. He parks the car outside the barracks and pulls up the top. He latches the top shut then locks the car doors. In his barracks room, he changes from civilian clothes to dungarees. He exits the barracks and begins the twelve-minute walk to the communications trailers compound.

As he approaches the communications trailers compound, he sees all the emergency exit doors wide open. An armed sailor stands at the bottom of the steps leading to each emergency exit.

Lieutenant Lemont, Mr. Pritchings, Senior Chief Hilton, and Master Chief Rodgers stand on the cement pad outside the message center emergency exit. They appear to be arguing. Rigney passes them by forty feet and cannot hear the subject of their argument.

The normal blast of cool, ashtray-smelling air is absent as he steps through the main door.

"Hey, good morning, Rig," Bob Vance says cheerfully.

"Back at ya," Rigney says enthusiastically as he stares at the shirtless Bob Vance who stands his watch in white uniform trousers and white t-shirt. Then, he asks, "What's going on?"

"Air-conditioning went out about 0200."

As he walks through the trailers, he sees all the radiomen stripped down to t-shirts. All equipment not in use is powered off. Although an Aegean breeze flows through the open doors and circulates the air, the temperature inside the trailers hovers at ninety-five degrees.

Page enters the repair shop, expecting to see ET2 Patterson who had duty last night, but the shop is empty.

Curious as to the effect of high temperatures on electronic cryptographic equipment and quality of message traffic, he hurries to the LO-COMM message relay trailer. He spends several minutes watching the teletype printers and verifies that most secret and confidential messages have few garbles. Confidential classified messages include U.S. Navy warship movement reports, warship locations, and warship destinations. Most of the messages classified as secret are intelligence reports from various U. S. military staffs located in Southern European countries and destined to U. S. ships at sea.

Rigney steps toward the HI-COMM NAVCOMOPNET trailer door. A first class petty officer that Rigney recognizes as a sailor who normally works at the transmitter site stands guard at the open door to the NAVCOMOPNET trailer. The guard checks the access list, verifies that Rigney's name is on the list, and allows Rigney to enter.

The NAVCOMOPNET trailer functions as the last relay point in the DOD communications network for top secret messages destined to U.S. warships at sea in the Eastern Mediterranean. The NAVCOMOPNET trailer is also the keying point for the U.S. Navy top secret fleet broadcast for the U.S Sixth Fleet.

Rigney walks slowly along the teletype banks. He observes four radiomen fully engaged with message processing. All messages relaying through the NAVCOMOPNET trailer are classified top secret. Most messages contain changes and amendments to battle plans for a possible attack on Czechoslovakia, which was invaded by the Soviets several weeks before.

Rigney exits the NAVCOMOPNET trailer and proceeds to the crypto trailer. He stops at the crypto trailer door, which is wide open, and QM1 Latham stands guard.

As Rigney stands at the door, he realizes why the door is wide open. The emergency exit on the opposite end of the trailer is also open. A wind tunnel of air blows through the doorway and carries away heat from the crypto trailer.

Latham checks the crypto trailer access list and allows Page to enter.

As he enters the crypto trailer, Rigney sees Patterson leaning against the wall at the far end—near the wide-open emergency exit door. The crypto operator types furiously on the order wire teletype—the communications device with technical control. As Rigney walks the length of the trailer, he notices many of the crypto equipment components powered down. All other crypto components are racked-out to their stops, but powered up, which means the power-off interlocks are defeated. As a method to cool the crypto components, tempest shields have been removed and are stacked in piles around the trailer. Rigney shakes his head with disapproval at what he sees.

He stops in front of the patch panel. As he runs his fingers across several patch cords, he glances at various racked-out crypto components. Astonishment knocks him back a few feet when he realizes that those racked-out crypto components with tempest shields removed are patched to operational radio teletype circuits in the LO-COMM message relay trailer and the top secret NAVCOMOPNET trailer.

Rigney shoots an incredulous glance at ET2 Patterson.

Patterson stares at Page and shakes his head with resigned disbelief as he mouths, "That's right."

Rigney wants to question the crypto operator, but the crypto operator still types furiously on the order wire with technical control. He walks to the end of the trailer and stops within a few feet of Patterson.

Rigney declares the obvious to Patterson. "There's a major security violation going on here."

Patterson responds with a resigned shrug. "I told them last night when the crypto equipment started going down. After half the equipment went down, they started racking out the equipment, removing the tempest shields, defeating the power interlocks, and opening the emergency exits. The crypto equipment came back up. The communications watch officer told me it is standard procedure when crypto malfunctions because of ambient temperature problems. I protested for hours. Then, Mr. Lemont came in here and told me to back off."

"What time was that?"

"About 0500. Mr. Lemont told me he would take full responsibility. So, I shut up about it."

Rigney shakes his head and expresses disapproval. He moves to the open emergency exit door to receive a blast of cooling air. As he stands in the doorway, he looks to the east, over the sand dunes on the station's eastside and toward the blue Aegean, He notices a few yachts anchored in the Nea Makri Anchorage area. Then, his eyes go wide open, and he mutters, "Oh my god!"

"What's a matter?" Patterson inquires in a cavalier tone. "Ya see the Soviet hordes storming the base."

Rigney does not respond, his mind busily formulating tonight's intel report to ONI.

Chapter 76

Rigney enters the administration building and walks into the head. He places his white hat on the hook behind the door. He wets a wad of paper towels with cold water. He wipes the sweat from his face and forearms. He spends a few minutes cooling down. Then, he combs his hair.

Feeling refreshed, he exits the head and walks to the small library. The library door is closed. A sign taped to the door says, "IN USE – DO NOT ENTER."

Rigney leans against the opposite wall and waits.

Ten minutes later, Bob Vance exits the library door and closes the door behind him.

"Hi, Bob," Rigney greets cheerfully.

"Oh. Hi, Rig. Uh . . . uh . . . I had to give a statement on what I saw that day you hit Mr. Martin. I had to give a written statement. Uh . . . I had to say exactly what I saw."

Rigney smiles and says, "I wouldn't want you to do anything else. The truth will prevail, eventually."

"I hope so!" Vance responds then lets out a big sigh.

"Good luck," Vance offers as he walks off.

Five minutes later, the library door opens and a first class yeoman who wears Service Dress Whites sticks his head out the door. He looks at Rigney and asks, "You Page?"

Rigney nods his head.

"Come in."

Rigney enters the library.

Two male officers sit at the reading table. One is a lieutenant and the other is a lieutenant junior grade. Both wear white uniforms.

The first class yeoman takes a seat behind a stenograph.

Rigney observes that both officers have the stars of line officers on their shoulder boards, instead of JAG corps insignias.

Two stacks of file folders sit on the table before them.

Rigney snaps to attention and announces, "RM2 Page reporting as ordered, sir."

The senior officer responds, "Stand easy, Page. Sit there." The officer gestures to a chair directly across the table from both officers.

Rigney sits and waits for the officers to speak.

The senior lieutenant says, "I'm Lieutenant Boyington, and this is Lieutenant Farmer." Boyington nods toward the junior officer. "We are from the naval investigative service office in Naples."

"Pleasure to meet you both," Rigney says enthusiastically and with a smile on his face.

The two officers spend a few moments shuffling file folders.

Rigney studies the two NIS officers. Both officers are of average height and weight. Both wear navy-issue eyeglasses. Neither have any distinguishing physical features. Their manner is nonthreatening and nonintimidating; therefore, Rigney knows he must be on his guard.

Lieutenant Farmer finds the folder he wants and opens it; then, he informs, "Page, we are conducting interviews with the intent of collecting signed statements regarding your assault on Lieutenant Martin. Gathering these statements is a prerequisite to the commencement of the UCMJ investigation. The yeoman will record your words, then, he will type a statement for you to sign. Before you can make a statement, you must sign this on all four pages." The officer pushes stapled papers toward Rigney.

The soft clicking of the stenograph keys emphasizes the official status of this interview.

Assault? These two officers are already convinced that I am guilty of assault. Why wasn't Lieutenant Martin placed on report for assaulting his wife and child?

Rigney pulls the stapled papers toward him and begins reading. The papers advise him that he has the right not to provide a written statement and not to say anything at all. Halfway through reading the papers, Rigney looks at the two officers. They appear annoyed and impatient regarding Rigney's choice to read thoroughly what he must sign.

Boyington and Farmer glance at their watches several times. Their minds are not on gathering statements, but on whether they will have enough time to club hop in Plaka before their flight departs.

Rigney signs the *Advisement of Rights* paperwork and pushes it back to Lieutenant Farmer.

The two officers verify Rigney has signed all pages.

Boyington, the senior lieutenant orders, "Okay, Page. Tell us why you assaulted Mr. Martin. Then, tell us exactly, blow by blow, what happened on the pool patio."

This is not what Rigney expected. He becomes more guarded. He shifts his eyes back and forth between the two officers. He senses that these two officers are attempting to trap him. He searches his memory back to the time when he studied the UCMJ correspondence course. *That was two years ago!* He feels disappointed with himself that he did not study the UCMJ prior to attending this interview. Rigney also searches his memory for all the *Perry Mason* novels he read as a teenager. *What would Perry advise me to do?*

Both officers detect Rigney's hesitancy.

Lieutenant Boyington orders, "Respond, Page. Tell us what you did."

Lieutenant Farmer warns, "Page, your reluctance to make a statement will be recorded in the official transcripts. That would not look good before a judge who may decide your punishment."

Rigney becomes irritated at the manipulating threats.

"Tell us what you did!" Boyington demands in a raised tone.

Rigney again glances at the yeoman.

The yeoman stares at Rigney; the yeoman's fingers hover over the stenograph keys.

Rigney responds, "I don't think I should say anything until after I have spoken with my defense counsel."

Lieutenant Boyington says in a threatening tone, "Your stubbornness will look bad for you during the court-martial."

The yeoman's fingers dance over the stenograph keys.

Rigney recognizes the manipulative attempt. He smiles with amusement at the officers as he says light heartedly, "I will take my chances, sir."

The two officers glance at each other; then, the senior orders, "You are dismissed."

As Rigney closes the library door behind him, he sees Seaman Newman leaning on the wall directly across from the library door.

In his normal insubordinate manner, Newman whispers a threat, "Its payback time, asshole."

Rigney expresses an amused smile; then, he walks away from Newman. Rigney hears the library door open behind him and hears the yeoman's voice asking, "Are you Newman?"

Chapter 77

The U.S. Naval Support Activity for all U.S. Naval Forces in the Naples area resides in the valley known as Agnano. The Agnano valley, an ancient—now defunct—volcano sprouts a lush green landscape and a growing economy of small businesses and hotels. The headquarters area of the naval support activity houses many different command elements. The second floor of the administration building contains regional offices for the navy judge advocate general.

Commander Isaac Justin serves as the senior JAG officer in the Naples office. In addition to his legal duties, he administers the office and assigns cases. He writes the performance evaluations for all navy lawyers assigned to the office.

Justin looks up from his desk as he hears a knock on his office door. "Enter!" he orders loudly.

Lieutenant Michael Maston enters. He carries a file folder in his right hand. He lays the folder on the desk as he sits down.

Commander Justin recognizes the folder and asks, "Have you read the Nea Makri statements?"

"Yes, sir."

"Any first impressions?"

"Yes sir. The name Rigney Page is familiar to me. It's an odd name and easy to remember."

"Familiar to me, also, but I cannot remember why."

"Page was mentioned in some classified messages regarding the homicides in Licola about six months ago. I reviewed the Licola files."

"Yes. I remember now," Commander Justin recollects. "NIS had just gotten us involved when we got a message from CINCUSNAVEUR to discontinue our investigation, because the investigation would be handled by NIS and JAG headquarters in Washington."

"That's right," Maston confirms. "And now Page is in Nea Makri and charged with assault and battery on an officer."

Justin asks, "What is your opinion? Is he guilty of the charge?"

Maston fingers the file folder and says, "There is no doubt that Page hit Lieutenant Martin, but I am not sure he is guilty of assault or battery. Some of the witness statements refer to previous incidents when Martin hit his wife and daughter. The witnesses say Page hit Martin to stop Martin from hitting his wife and daughter."

"What does Page's statement say about the incident?"

"The packet doesn't contain a statement from Page. According to NIS, Page refused to provide a statement."

Justin nods his head to indicate his acknowledgement of Maston's opinion. Then, he says, "Looks like you must go to Nea Makri and sort it all out. You are assigned as Page's defense counsel. The XO in Nea Makri has made reservations for you at a small hotel on the Nea Makri beach."

"Who's trial counsel?"

"Not sure. It will be someone from the JAG office in London."

"Who's the hearing officer?"

"No message traffic on that either."

Chapter 78

Master Chief Radioman Clayton Spyke enters the office of Rear Admiral Vernier, Commander Naval Communications. Spyke serves as the Command Master Chief for COMNAVCOM. The rear admiral and the master chief have been close shipmates for over twenty-five years. Whenever they are not around others, they are informal and friendly. They are honest with each other. They respect each other and trust each other's judgment.

The admiral opens the conversation. "How was your leave, Clayton?"

"Great, Admiral! Thirty days on my sailboat in the Bahamas was exactly what I needed."

"Well, it's time to get back to business."

"Do you have something interesting for me?"

"You're familiar with the NAVCOMMSTA Greece at Nea Makri."

"Yes sir. Some of the chiefs there are old shipmates. We still correspond."

"I want you to go there and spend a week talking with the crew. Find out how they feel about things."

"Things?"

The admiral picks up a letter from his desk and hands it to Spyke. "I received this several days ago from the Nea Makri COMMO, Gerry Lemont. Gerry was the fleet center division officer at NAVCOMMSTA Norfolk when I was commanding officer there."

Spyke reads the letter—twice. Then, he looks at the admiral and comments, "Looks serious, but isn't he jumping the chain-of-command?"

"Yeah, he is. I know Gerry. He wouldn't jump the chain-of-command unless he thought it absolutely necessary. Taking five or so radioman to mast every week is unprecedented. You said you correspond with some of the chiefs there. Any of them confirm this?"

"None of them wrote anything about it. Most of them just write about their lives on the Greek economy. Chiefs don't complain about their commanding officers, even when a commanding officer deserves such complaints."

Admiral Vernier raises his eyebrows.

Chapter 79

"Rodgers did not make his drop of cryptographic material last night," Andrei tells Eldar. "He delivered only his black market goods."

"What do you think it means?" Eldar asks.

"Rodgers is lost as a source. He plans to flee. However, I think Rodgers and some other sailors from the Nea Makri base can be of value to us."

"The December spy exchange?" Eldar queries with raised eyebrows.

"Yes. We should capture Rodgers and Page and hold them as bargaining chips."

"We have no resources here for such an operation. By the time we do, Rodgers and Page could be gone."

"I will use the Spaniards. With them, we can complete the operation quickly."

"They are not trained operatives, Andrei. Too much can go wrong."

"A risk we must make, Eldar. If anything does go wrong, the authorities will consider the kidnapping as a criminal offense, not affiliated with any government."

Eldar bows his head in thought. Then, he stands and paces his office. After several minutes he asks, "Why do you think Rodgers and Page are valuable enough to risk our yacht operation?"

"The Americans will not want any of their spies held hostage . . . too much bad press during a time when the North Vietnamese parade prisoners of war to the world. Additionally, Rodgers has expert knowledge of crypto systems, and Page knows the identification of American operatives. The Americans will want them back."

Eldar nods his head; then, he asks, "What about this woman who owns the house where Page lives?"

"She is West German, resides in Bremerhaven, and works as a financial analyst for an investment company. She rents the house in Nea Makri for the tourist season."

"Is she in the game?"

"Nothing indicates that. Moscow Center continues their investigation."

Eldar nods his head again; then asks, "When will you get Rodgers and Page?"

"I am waiting for approval from Moscow Center. I should receive it within a few days."

Chapter 80

Lieutenant Maston stands alone in the NAVCOMMSTA Greece library. He studies the titles of several books as he waits for his client.

A knock on the closed door causes Maston to turn toward the closed door. "Enter!" he orders.

Rigney enters, stands at attention, and states, "RM2 Page reporting as ordered, sir." Rigney quickly evaluates the tall and trim lieutenant. The officer's wide set gray eyes and closely cropped blond hair remind him of Commander Watson.

Maston takes a few moments to evaluate Page's manner. Although Page stands at attention in ceremonial respect, Page exudes power and confidence. Maston feels slightly intimidated by the young sailor before him.

"At ease, Page. Sit there."

As Rigney sits, he scrutinizes the officer. The officer's nametag reveals he is Lieutenant Maston from the JAG office in Naples. The gold braid on his shoulder boards gleams and shows no sign of tarnish. The lieutenant's tanned and taut skin tells of his frequent outside exercise.

"Page, I am Lieutenant Maston from the JAG office in Naples. I am your defense counsel. We don't have much time to prepare, so you need to be completely open and honest with me. Do you understand?"

"Yes sir."

"Tell me about your background."

Rigney glances quizzically at his service record, which sits in front of the officer.

"Uh . . . yes, Page, I have read your service record, but I want you to tell me anyway."

Rigney provides a brief history of his life in Seal Beach, California. Then, he briefly describes his military history.

Maston looks Rigney directly in the eyes and queries, "You were on the USS *Barb* from January to just recently, prior to coming here?"

Rigney looks intently at Lieutenant Maston. He wonders why the only question about his past applies to the only period misrepresented in his service record.

Maston, sensing Rigney's hesitancy, advises, "Page, anything you tell me falls under attorney-client privilege. I cannot tell anyone what you tell me."

Rigney unconsciously shakes his head slightly in refusal while considering if he should continue lying.

"Page, I know you were in Naples last February. Your presence in Naples conflicts with your service record, which says you were on a WESTPAC cruise. Your name was in messages regarding two murders in Licola. So that I can provide you with the best defense—"

"No," Rigney interrupts.

Maston flinches, blinks his eyes, and sits back in his chair. After a few moments, he asks, "No, what?"

"No, I can't talk about any of that."

Maston spends a full minute considering the significance of Page's response. Then, he asks, "What are you, Petty Officer Page? You are not what your service record represents you to be, are you?"

"Like I said, sir, I can't talk about it."

"Which means you cannot tell me why you are here in Nea Makri."

"That's correct, sir."

Maston suspects that Page is undercover and is involved in a classified operation.

"I have statements from over twenty Nea Makri crewmembers regarding your actions since you have been here. Some statements portray you as aggressive, antagonistic, and violent."

"Sir, I am not that kind of person. None of those traits are part of my character."

Maston responds, "During the UCMJ hearing, trial counsel will put those people on the stand. Trial counsel will attempt to portray you as such a person."

"People have lied about me before. I've become accustomed to it."

Maston pulls a written statement from the stack, looks it over, and asks, "Tell me what happened at the airport with Seaman Newman."

Rigney details the sequence of events with Newman at the Airport.

"Newman tells a different story," Maston advises.

"I'm not surprised. May I read Newman's statement?"

Maston hands the statement to Rigney.

Rigney reads the statement, twice. He shakes his head in dismissal as he hands the statement back to Maston.

Maston appraises Rigney's physique; then, he asks, "You forced Newman to the ground with a . . . a . . . what did you call it?"

"A reverse wristlock."

"And you used only your left hand to apply this reverse wristlock?"

"Yes sir."

"Have you studied martial arts?"

"Yes."

Maston nods his head as his speculation of Page's background is substantiated.

"You said that Newman was pushing you in the chest with his fingers. Was he hurting you?"

"No sir."

"Did you think he might hurt you?"

"I didn't consider that."

"Anyone can tell by looking at Newman that he is not a physical threat to you. What were you thinking?"

"I didn't think. My actions were instinctive, automatic reaction, I guess. I don't like people physically handling me. No one has the right to lay a hand on me."

"Have you always reacted that way?"

"Well . . . yes . . . ever since my first year of high school."

"But not as a young boy?"

"No sir."

"What happened from the time you were a young boy and when you started high school?"

"I became more confident in my ability to knock the *bully* out of bullies."

Maston again appraises Rigney's physical manner. He cannot picture bullies going after Page.

"You don't look like the typical target of bullies."

"I was as a young boy."

"But not when you were in high school?"

"Not as much."

Maston sits silent in thought for a few moments; then, he says, "I'm confused. I thought you said that as a teenager you became more confident to fight bullies."

Rigney contemplates if he should reveal this side of himself to this officer.

"Page, for me to provide the best defense, I need to understand your motivations."

"In high school, bullies did not usually come after me. When I saw bullies beating-up on someone, I would step in and knock the fight out of them."

"When you did that, was it an instinctive reaction?"

"Yes sir. I become angered when I see bullies seek out and hurt the defenseless. I see red, as the saying goes."

"And that's what happened to you when you saw Lieutenant Martin hitting his wife and daughter?"

"I saw him hitting defenseless human beings. He deserved it."

Maston looks quizzically at Rigney and says, "You are a paradox, Rigney Page. You are an uncover agent for some government agency, so, someone must have judged you to have control over your actions. Yet, you act impulsively in some situations. Are your superiors aware of your instinctive violent side?"

"Yes sir. I think they consider it an asset."

Maston again sits in thought for a few moments; then, he asks, "Were you involved in those homicides in Licola last February?"

"Sir, you've obviously figured out what I am. You should understand that I'm not permitted to talk about any mission. That whole mission is top secret."

"Okay, Page. Your commitment to security is commendable."

"Thank you, sir. I appreciate your understanding."

Lieutenant Maston shuffles more of the statements; then, he says, "Now, regarding the day you hit Mr. Martin, tell me everything you remember in time-sequence order from the time you entered the Club Zeus to the time you departed the club."

Rigney relates the events of that afternoon.

Maston takes notes.

"So you did hit Mr. Martin before he took a swing at you."

"That's correct," Rigney confirms.

"Why?"

"Because he deserved it. I wanted him to feel the pain that others feel when he hits them."

Maston lets out a deep sigh and says, "You cannot take the stand in your own defense. Trial counsel will chew you up and spit you out."

"No problem, sir. I never intended to tell my side of the story. That's why I didn't provide a verbal or a written statement."

"Then you must have anticipated immediately after the incident that you might be court-martialed."

"Yes, sir, I anticipated that."

"And without advice from counsel, you already knew that you should not say anything."

"That's right."

"Have you been in this kind of trouble before?"

"Yes sir. In my service record . . . that incident on the USS *Barb*. That actually happened."

"But you went to mast on that one and awarded punishment."

"I learn quickly."

"What did that mast teach you?"

"I learned that at captain's mast, instead of being judged impartially on the evidence, you are judged on misperception, whim, innuendo, lies, discriminate thought, a bad day, or any other unjust reason."

"Your record says you were punished for insubordination and open disrespect towards an officer."

"Yes, and that officer was disrespectful towards me, but he never went to captain's mast."

"Were there any witness to the incident between you and the officer aboard *Barb*?"

"No. I was punished solely on the word of the officer."

"On a submarine, no one else saw what happened?"

"It happened in the Radio Room at 0330."

"At captain's mast, did the officer lie?"

"He didn't lie. He just did not tell everything that happened in the Radio Room. He omitted his own improper behavior. He shoved me."

"He shoved you, and you did not react physically? How far did he shove you?"

"A couple of feet. I tripped back over a chair and ended up sitting upright. The amount of time it took me to stand allowed me to gain control my actions, but I did yell at him. I called him a Rickover asshole."

"Did you tell your captain that the officer shoved you?"

"Yes, I did."

"But he didn't believe you."

"Actually, I think he did believe me. I think that's why my punishment was not severe."

"What's a Rickover asshole?"

"Well, it's when an officer acts in the same manner as Admiral Rickover."

"Acting like Admiral Rickover is a bad thing?"

Rigney thinks for a moment then responds, "I think you need to serve in submarines for a while to understand it."

Maston shakes his head with bewilderment. Then, he reaches for another statement. Then, he directs, "Tell me all events leading up to and including the actions of everyone you remember when you killed Mr. Pritchings's dog."

Rigney relates the events to Mr. Maston.

"Mr. Pritchings statement tells a different story."

"I am not surprised."

Maston stacks all his papers and puts them in a black leather briefcase. Then, he tells Page, "I need some time to review all my notes and go over all the statements again. We will meet tomorrow to discuss our defense strategy. The UCMJ hearing starts the day after tomorrow."

Chapter 81

Lieutenant Commander Mary Blakely sits in her office. Lieutenant Maston of the navy judge advocate general corps sits in the chair across the desk from the XO.

The XO advises, "I thought you should know that I have another report chit here on RM2 Page. He is charged with disobeying orders, engaging in adultery with the wife of another sailor, and operation of a slush fund."

Maston asks, "Did Senior Chief Hilton initiate the report chit?"

"Yes."

Maston advises, "Page told me about Senior Chief Hilton and that a report chit might be initiated. Have you talked to Page about the chit?"

"Yes," Mary replies. "Page says it's all nonsense that exists only in the mind of Hilton."

"What do you think, XO?"

"I don't know what to think. Since Page has arrived here, he has been involved in more unusual situations than any other sailor I have encountered. Rumors about him are waist deep on this base. I have investigated most of the rumors and find them to be just that—rumors. I don't believe Senior Chief Hilton's charges to be valid."

"What will you do with the report chit?"

"I'm sitting on it for a while. I will wait until after this UCMJ hearing is over."

Maston nods his agreement and asks, "Anything else, XO?"

"No. I just wanted you to know about the report chit."

"Okay. Thank you, XO." Maston does not get up.

After thirty seconds, the XO asks, "Is there something else?"

Maston raises his eyebrows and smiles, "I was wondering if you are free for dinner . . . to give us more time to discuss your testimony."

Mary glances quickly at Maston's left hand to see if he wears a wedding ring or for indications that a wedding ring was recently removed. She notes no wedding ring and no markings. She considered Mike Maston to be intelligent, charming, and attractive.

"Sure, Mike. When and where?"

"I have no vehicle of my own," Mike Maston advises. "I am riding with Captain Jack. Can you meet me at the restaurant in my hotel . . . say seven o'clock . . . casual civilian attire?"

"I'll be there," Mary states with a gleeful smile on her face.

Chapter 82

Mary Blakely stands outside Commander Caldwell's closed office door. She completed the investigation into why COMNAVCOM has not received NAVCOMMSTA Greece 2-Kilo maintenance forms during the last five months. She does not look forward to briefing the CO, because she knows he will become angered and will release his anger on her. She knocks on the door and enters.

Mary carries a leather portfolio, a thick file folder, and a five-inch wide three-ring binder. She sits into a chair in front of Caldwell's desk. She places the leather portfolio and the three-ring binder on a side table.

Commander Caldwell says, "Before you start, XO, I need to tell you that I had a meeting with the COMNAVCOM Master Chief late yesterday afternoon. Master Chief Spyke is here to measure enlisted morale. We also discussed this 2-Kilo issue. Spyke advised that COMNAVCOM ordered him to hand-carry our investigation report back to Washington."

Mary nods and adds, "I met with Spyke earlier today. He advised me of the same. He reminded me that an accurate and up-to-date COMNAVCOM 2-Kilo database is crucial to rapid equipment improvements, legitimate manpower authorization levels, parts and maintenance support, and assignment of trained technicians."

Caldwell questions, "Did he think we don't know that?"

"He portrayed his comments as a friendly reminder."

"Did you tell Spyke what you uncovered regarding our 2-Kilos?"

"No," Mary responds as she shakes her head. "He asked, but I advised him I could not reveal anything regarding the matter until I reported to you."

The CO expresses approval. Then, he focuses on the thick file folder and asks, "Is that your investigation folder?"

"Yes, sir, and on top is the investigation report that I prepared for your signature."

The CO focuses on the thick three-ring binder that the XO set on his side table. He points to the binder and asks, "What's in the binder?"

"The last five months of 2-Kilos which I verified were never sent to COMNAVCOM."

Caldwell purses his lips, shakes his head, and expresses a mix of anger and bewildered disgust. Then, he orders, "Tell me what you discovered."

Mary retrieves the six page investigation report from the file folder and suggests, "Sir, I recommend you read the report in private. Then, we should discuss it."

Caldwell shakes his head and conveys impatient annoyance. "Just give me the highlights, XO, and tell me the names of those responsible."

Mary hesitates.

"C'mon, XO. I'll find out, anyway. Tell me who they are, so I can schedule mast and punish them. I want their names in the investigation report, including the punishment I award them."

Mary responds cautiously, "Sir, I think you should read my report in private. Then, we can—"

"Damn it, XO!" Caldwell interrupts with shouting that can be heard throughout the admin building. "Enough with protecting incompetent communicators! Who is responsible?!"

Mary inhales deeply, casts an apprehensive expression, and says, "Appears that you are responsible, sir."

Caldwell stares, incredulous at the XO. His face flushes red. First he is angered; then, he expresses concern, because he knows the XO would not have accused him if she did not have overwhelming evidence. With a distressed, tight lipped, and cautious tone; he orders, "Give me all the details."

Mary shows relief. She thought Caldwell would become wildly angry and strike her. Feeling less fearful, she explains, "I think it best to explain how the process worked before you took command. Then, I will explain what happened when you ordered the process changed."

"What change?" Caldwell interrupts in a challenging manner.

"Sir, I think you will understand after I explain."

"Okay! Explain!" he orders tersely.

"Before you took command, the process was as follows. All 2-Kilos funneled up from work centers through the Command 3-M Manager, Mr. Linderhaus. As 3-M manager, Mr. Linderhaus verified all 2-Kilos were complete and accurate before forwarding to the CO for signature.

"After the CO signed 2-Kilos, the CO placed them into his outbox. The admin yeomen collected all paperwork from the CO's outbox and processed it. The yeoman sent the 2-Kilos back to the Command 3-M Manager for final processing. Then, the 3-M Manager verified the CO's signature on the 2-Kilos, updated *equipment status list*, mailed a copy to COMNAVCOM, and filed remaining copies in the 2-Kilo master binder. That entire process is written in the NAVCOMMSTA Greece instruction for processing 2-Kilos."

Caldwell holds up his hand to direct the XO to pause. He queries, "How do we know they were mailed?"

Mary replies, "Every 2-Kilo copy has a date-mailed stamp. The stamp was applied to all copies just before one copy was placed into an envelope addressed to COMNAVCOM."

Caldwell inquires, "Then why did COMNAVCOM tell me during my command brief that 2-Kilo submissions were erratic?"

Mary shrugs and responds, "I don't know, sir. All 2-Kilos prior to five months ago have the stamp."

"Continue," Caldwell directs.

"According to Mr. Lemont, Mr. Linderhaus, and Senior Chief Hilton, you ordered Mr. Linderhaus to discontinue mailing the 2-Kilos. They report that during a meeting with them just after you took command, you told them you did not trust the process of 2-Kilos going back to the 3-M Manager for mailing. They told me that you said you believed that process *'dropped 2-Kilos through the cracks'* and that in the future you would take care of mailing 2-Kilos to COMNAVCOM."

Caldwell now remembers ordering the change in the mailing process during that meeting. He shrugs and expresses curiosity. He says mildly, "Okay. That's correct."

Mary braces for an attack and asks, "Did you mail them, sir?"

Caldwell conveys arrogant superiority as he specifies, "Of course not. I leave such minor administration chores to the admin staff. The staff you supervise as admin officer." Caldwell smiles confidently and feels joyful that he can pin all this on the XO.

"Sir, please let me continue. There is more clarifying information."

Caldwell sits back in his chair with a satisfied smile on his face. "Continue," he orders.

"Mr. Lemont and Mr. Linderhaus advised me they came away from that meeting with the understanding that you would mail 2-Kilos, so they stopped."

"Yes, XO . . . makes sense. Are you saying you never informed your admin staff to mail them?"

"Sir, you never told me that you ordered the mailing process changed."

Caldwell utters a sinister chuckle and declares, "After I sign 2-Kilos, I put them in the outbox on my desk to be mailed."

With a blank expression, Mary informs in a soft and even tone, "Sir, placing the signed 2-Kilos in your outbox is what the previous CO did. When the yeomen cleared the outbox, they did with the 2-Kilos what they had always done. They sent them to the 3-M manager, Mr. Linderhaus."

Caldwell objects, "But that's not what I wanted. I wanted the yeomen to send one signed copy to COMNAVCOM, and the other copies to Mr. Linderhaus."

"That may have been your intention, sir, but you never advised me or any of my staff."

"But outbox means mail the items!"

"Sir, without instructions from you to do otherwise, the yeoman processed the outbox paperwork as they always have."

Caldwell's lips quiver. He blinks rapidly. He feels totally embarrassed as he admits to himself that he failed to follow-up on his order to change the process. Then, he feebly attempts an out. "Didn't Mr. Linderhaus wonder why he received my signed copies back?"

"He always received signed copies back, but after your order, he only updated his files and did not mail a copy to COMNAVCOM."

Caldwell's mind races while searching for another out. Then, he blurts, "Didn't Mr. Linderhaus wonder why he got three copies back instead of two?"

"He did not. Actually, he never handled 2-Kilos. His yeoman handled all the paperwork."

"Didn't his yeoman wonder about getting three copies back instead of two?"

"If you remember, sir, that was around the time you ordered YN3 Grandville, who was the repair division yeoman, to become your personal yeoman—here in the admin building. When Grandville left the repair department, signed 2-Kilos just piled-up on Grandville's old desk. Months later, RM2 Page discovered the stack of unprocessed 2-Kilos, and Mr. Linderhaus assigned RM2 Page to process them."

"What did Page say?"

"Page states that when he processed the first batch of signed 2-Kilos he asked Mr. Linderhaus what to do with them. Mr. Linderhaus told him to update the *equipment status list* and file the copies."

"Page never questioned it?"

"No sir."

Caldwell sighs deeply and spends several minutes considering how to recover.

Mary sits silent waiting for Caldwell to say something.

Finally, Caldwell asks, "What do you recommend, XO?"

"We mail one copy of all 2-Kilos without a date stamp to COMNAVCOM. I instruct the admin staff to mail one copy of all future 2-Kilos, and I will change the command instruction to reflect that the admin office mails one copy to COMNAVCOM."

Caldwell knows that COMNAVCOM receiving a large stack of five-month old 2-Kilos will draw a lot of attention and many questions. Nevertheless, there is no better option. Caldwell agrees, "Yes. That's the correct action." Then, he directs, "Give me your investigation file and the investigation report. I'll insure Master Chief Spyke gets a copy of the report before he departs."

Mary hands the file to Caldwell.

Without looking Mary in the eye, Caldwell takes the file and orders, "You can return to your duties, XO."

Mary retrieves the leather portfolio and 2-Kilo binder and exits the office.

Just outside the CO's door, Mary reaches into the leather portfolio and turns-off the small tape recorder. As she walks back to her office, she expresses amusement. She shakes her head and utters a soft chuckle. She knows that the investigation file and investigation report she gave Caldwell will never be seen again. *Good thing I made copies!*

Chapter 83

The master-at-arms force converted the ballroom area of the Club Zeus into a courtroom. The club ballroom is the only space large enough to accommodate the hearing. The XO modified the club's operating hours to open at 1600, instead of the normal 1030.

Neal Jack, the judge—hearing officer–and a navy captain, sits at a desk on the stage. The stage stands eighteen inches higher than the dance floor. The witness chair stands on the edge of the stage close to the judge's desk. The trial counsel—prosecutor, Lieutenant Commander Powers—sits at a table on the dance floor facing the judge. Rigney and Lieutenant Maston sit at a second table facing the judge. The same yeoman that operated the stenograph during the taking of statements sits at a small stenograph table. A marine sergeant who serves as bailiff sits at a small table off to the side of the stage. The witnesses and fourteen spectators sit randomly around the ballroom. The COMNAVCOM Master Chief, RMCM Clayton Spyke, sits among the spectators.

Captain Jack ordered the hearing open to spectators over the protests of Commander Caldwell. Captain Jack specified, "The navy's legal process has nothing to hide from the rank and file."

Most of the sailors have never experienced navy legal proceedings beyond the numerous UCMJ Article 15 captain's masts held by Commander Caldwell.

Captain Jack states, "The Uniform Code of Military Justice requires a thorough and impartial investigation of charges and specifications before they may be referred to a general court-martial. The purpose of this pretrial investigation is to inquire into the truth of the matter set forth in the charges, to consider the form of the charges, and to secure information to determine what disposition should be made of the case in the interest of justice and discipline. The investigation also serves as a means of pretrial discovery for the accused in that those copies of the criminal investigation and witness statements are provided, and witnesses who testify may be cross-examined.

"This proceeding is a hearing, not a trial. Therefore, strict rules of evidence do not apply. However, I will only allow relevant facts submitted into evidence. Because this is a hearing, I will also allow evidence of mitigating circumstances that relate to the charges against the accused."

Captain Jack looks at counsel for the United States and asks, "Commander Powers, has the accused been advised of his Article 31 rights?"

The lean, medium height, short cropped brown-haired lieutenant commander in summer white uniform looks over the half-lenses of his reading glasses and responds, "Your honor, the accused has been informed of his Article 31 rights."

Captain Jack nods his head and asks Powers, "Is counsel for the United States ready to proceed with this hearing?"

"Yes, your honor."

Captain Jack looks at Lieutenant Maston and asks, "Is defense counsel ready to proceed?"

"Yes, your honor."

Captain Jack orders, "Counsel for the United States shall read the charges."

Powers pulls a sheet of paper from the tabletop. He scans the paper then reads aloud, "Petty Officer Rigney Michael Page, you are charged with the willful unprovoked assault and battery on Lieutenant Jeffrey Martin. Specification . . . In that Radioman Second Class Rigney Michael Page did onboard NAVCOMMSTA Greece on August 10, 1968 at approximately 1500 hours strike his superior commissioned officer, Lieutenant Jeffery Martin."

Captain Jack orders, "Mr. Powers, call your first witness."

"I call Petty Officer Robert Vance."

Vance rises from his chair in the spectator area. He walks to the stage, steps up, walks to the witness chair and sits.

Lieutenant Commander Powers walks half the distance to the witness chair and asks, "Do you affirm that the evidence you give in the case shall be the truth, the whole truth, and nothing but the truth?"

"Yes, sir," Vance responds.

All heads turn toward the club door as it opens. Commander Caldwell enters and sits in the chair reserved for him in the front row in the spectators' section.

The prosecutor directs Vance, "Please state your name, grade, command, and branch of service."

"Robert Vance, Signalman Third Class, United States Navy, NAVCOMMSTA Greece."

Powers asks, "Do you know the accused?"

"Yes sir."

"Please point to the accused and state his name."

Vance points at Rigney and says, "Radioman Second Class Rigney Page."

Powers says, "Let the record show that the witness pointed to the accused when stating his name."

Powers starts his direct examination. Powers asks, "You are familiar with the layout of the Club Zeus and the adjacent pool?"

"Yes sir. I have been in there many times."

"Describe the view of the pool from inside the club and from the bar area."

"The whole side of the club on the pool side is plate-glass windows from floor to ceiling and for the whole width of the bar area. There is a double plate-glass door in the middle which goes out to the pool."

"Would you say that there is a total, unobstructed view of the pool and patio from the bar?"

"Yes sir."

"Petty Officer Vance, describe what you saw when Petty Officer Page attacked Lieutenant Martin."

"Objection," Lieutenant Maston says casually, without emotion, and almost yawns. "No evidence introduced that proves Petty Officer Page attacked anyone."

"Sustained," the judge rules.

Powers turns to Vance and directs, "Tell us where you were and what you saw during the encounter between the accused and Lieutenant Martin."

"I was in the Club Zeus, near the bar, with about ten other sailors. RM3 Spencer said, 'He is hitting his kid, again.' We all turned to look at the pool. That's when I saw Mr. Martin hit his wife and kid. Then, Rigney, I mean Petty Officer Page, went out to the pool. He grabbed Mr. Martin with his left hand and slapped Mr. Martin across the face—twice. Then, he pushed Mr. Martin to the cement. Then, Petty Officer Page said something to Mr. Martin's wife. Then, Page came back in the bar and started talking with Dottie Caldwell again."

Powers queries, "Did Petty Officer Page speak to Mr. Martin before grabbing him?"

"I don't know."

"So, your testimony is that the accused grabbed Mr. Martin, slapped him twice, and pushed him to the cement?"

"Sir, he didn't push him to the cement immediately after the two slaps. There was some time between."

"How much time?"

"I think about twenty or thirty seconds."

"Describe what happened during those twenty or thirty seconds."

"I think Page said something to Mr. Martin. I don't know for sure. Some of the guys say that Mr. Martin took a swing at Page, before Page pushed him to the cement."

Powers turns to the judge and asks, "Your honor, I request the comments about Mr. Martin swinging at the accused be removed from the record, because the testimony is hearsay."

"Granted," Captain Jack responds. "The reporter will strike the witness's total response to the last question."

The yeoman lifts a section of the stenograph tape and reviews it; then, he uses a pen to mark the stricken testimony.

Captain Jack advises, "Petty Officer Vance, what others tell you, but you did not personally experience is considered hearsay and is not permitted as evidence. Do you understand?"

"Yes sir," Vance responds.

Captain Jack orders, "Reporter, repeat trial counsel's last question."

The yeoman looks at the tape and says, "Describe what happened during those twenty or thirty seconds."

Vance says, "I'm not sure. I think Page said something to Mr. Martin."

Powers pauses as if deeply pondering his next question; then, he directs, "Describe how Petty Officer Page pushed Mr. Martin to the cement."

"Page put his hand around Mr. Martin's throat and pushed him down and backwards."

"Page used only one hand around Mr. Martin's throat?"

"Yes sir."

"Which hand?"

"His right hand."

"What was Page doing with his left hand?"

Vance pauses as he remembers the positioning of the two men; then, he responds, "Page had a hold of Mr. Martin's right wrist."

Powers asks, "Then, what happened?"

"Page came back in the club, sat at the same barstool, and talked with Dottie Caldwell again."

Commander Caldwell flinches at the second mention of his niece.

"No further questions," Powers advises.

Lieutenant Maston rises from his chair and walks half the distance toward the witness chair.

All eyes follow Maston as he approaches the witness.

"Petty Officer Vance, you testified that your attention was drawn to the pool after you heard RM3 Spencer say, 'He is hitting his kid, again.' Did RM3 Spencer say anything immediately following those words?"

Vance squirms in his chair, and he shoots a furtive glance at Commander Caldwell. Their eyes meet for a few seconds; then, Vance looks away.

Commander Caldwell wonders why Vance looked at him; then, he fears he will hear something detrimental.

"Objection," Powers says, staying seated at the trial counsel's table. "Irrelevant?"

The judge looks at Maston and queries, "Response?"

"Your honor, during direct examination, the witness said he turned to look out to the pool because of the words of RM3 Spencer. I think we should know if it was those words, or if there were more words that may have caused Petty Officer Vance to look at the pool."

"Objection overruled."

Maston turns toward Vance and asks, "Did RM3 Spencer say anything in addition to what you previously testified?"

"Yes sir. He actually said, 'He's hitting his kid again. Why doesn't the captain do something about that?'" Vance shoots a glance at Commander Caldwell.

Commander Caldwell feels insulted. Anger flashes across his face.

Both the judge and Maston notice Vance's glances toward Commander Caldwell.

Maston looks at Commander Caldwell; then, he turns toward Vance and asks, "Where were you looking before RM3 Spencer spoke those words?"

"I was facing toward the bar."

"What were you doing?"

Vance shoots another glance at Commander Caldwell; then he looks Maston in the eye and says, "I was talking with Angie Caldwell."

Commander Caldwell stiffens. He becomes angrier. He fears that his family will be drawn into this.

Maston queries, "Angie Caldwell is the commanding officer's daughter?"

"Yes sir."

Maston spends a few moments considering Vance's testimony; then, he asks, "Why did RM3 Spencer's words cause you to look toward the pool?"

"Because I knew Mr. Martin and his family were by the pool. I knew Spencer was talking about Mr. Martin."

"How did you know that Spencer was talking about Mr. Martin?"

"I saw Mr. Martin hit his wife and kid before, and everyone on the base knows Mr. Martin is a kid beater."

"Objection!" Powers almost shouts as he jumps up. "Speculation! Hearsay! Facts not in evidence!"

"Sustained," the judge rules. "Petty Officer Vance, you may only testify on what you have observed, not what you think others know or have observed."

"Yes sir," Vance responds. He spends a few moments to form his answer to Maston's question. "At the Fourth of July picnic, on Nea Makri beach, I saw Mr. Martin slap his kid across the face several times, and I saw him push his wife, hard."

"Objection, your honor. Irrelevant to the charges against the accused."

The judge looks toward Maston for argument. "Counsel?"

Maston directs his eyes toward the judge and says, "Your honor, the defense's position on the matter before this hearing is that the accused reacted to Lieutenant Martin's violent behavior, because no one else in the command, including the commanding officer, took any action in the past to protect Mr. Martin's wife and child. The accused was compelled to protect Mr. Martin's wife and child, because he knew that no one else would. Words spoken in the Club Zeus during the minutes prior to the alleged assault and battery conveyed to the accused Mr. Martin's violent manner, and conveyed to the accused that no one in authority would take action to safeguard Mr. Martin's family. Therefore, Mr. Martin's past violent behavior is relevant."

Commander Caldwell stands and departs the club.

All eyes in the club follow Caldwell until the door closes behind him.

The judge looks at Powers and prompts a response, "Trial counsel?"

Powers responds, "Your honor, I will prove during this hearing that the accused has a history of violent behavior, and it is his violent manner and not his concern for Mr. Martin's family that prompted him to hit Mr. Martin."

The judge sits in thought for a full minute; then, he rules. "I will allow all factual evidence that substantiates past violent behavior on the part of Lieutenant Martin and the accused."

Maston asks the witness, "Petty Officer Vance, when is the first time you ever saw the accused?"

"When I saw him talking with Dottie Caldwell at the bar, just before he went out to the pool and had the fight with Mr. Martin. I never saw him before that."

"Petty Officer Vance, during the time you were aware that the accused was in the club and prior to the accused going out to the pool, did anyone make reference that Jeffrey Martin is an officer?"

"Not to my knowledge, sir."

"When did you discover that Petty Officer Page arrived in Nea Makri?"

"Later in the day. Page told me he arrived at NAVCOMMSTA about one hour prior to entering the club."

"Did the accused ever reveal to you when he discovered that Jeffrey Martin was an officer?"

"Yes sir. He told me that he did not know Mr. Martin was an officer at the time of the incident at the pool."

"Petty Officer Vance, were there any other officers in the club or pool prior to and during the incident at the pool?"

"Yes sir. Mr. Linderhaus was talking with Dottie Caldwell and Page, just before Page went out to the pool."

"I have no further questions," Maston advises.

Powers stands and asks questions on redirect. "Petty Officer Vance, has the accused revealed to you that he would not have confronted or hit Lieutenant Martin had he known Lieutenant Martin was an officer?"

Vance bows his head in thought for a few moments; then, he raises his head, looks at Powers, and says, "No."

For dramatic effect, Powers stares dubiously at Vance during the next question. "Petty Officer Vance, are you and the accused friends?"

Vance shifts his gaze to Rigney and declares, "Yes. I am proud to call Rigney Page my friend."

Rigney nods agreement and casts a smile of appreciation.

"Petty Officer Vance, would you lie to protect the accused?"

"No!" Vance responds. "I would not lie. Rigney told me to tell the truth, because the truth will eventually prevail. That's one of the reasons I call him friend."

"No more questions," Powers advises in a resigned tone.

During the next two hours, Powers calls to the stand four additional witnesses, including RM3 Spencer, who were in the Club Zeus during the altercation between Rigney and Mr. Martin. Direct examination and cross-examination of all four witnesses substantiates most of Vance's testimony. The only difference being that two witnesses testified that Mr. Martin threw a punch at Page just before Page slammed Mr. Martin to the cement.

Powers declares, "I call Seaman Newman to the stand."

Maston stands and declares, "Objection, Seaman Newman did not witness the incident between the accused and Mr. Martin."

A hostile glare crosses Newman's face as he believes he may not have his say against Page.

Powers counters, "Your honor ruled that all testimony regarding the physical aggressiveness of the accused may be presented. Seaman Newman will testify to that aggressiveness."

"Objection overruled," Captain Jack declares.

With an arrogant smirk on his face, Seaman Newman struts across the courtroom and sits in the witness chair. Newman's Service Dress Whites are impeccable, his shoes shine like mirrors, and his recent haircut shortened his hair by three inches. The short and chubby sailor sits in the witness chair and crosses his legs. A superior expression crosses his face, an expression that conveys he will enlighten the crowd regarding RM2 Rigney *'King Shit'* Page.

After Newman swears-in and identifies the accused, Powers begins his direct examination.

"Seaman Newman, tell us what happened when you picked-up Petty Officer Page at the airport."

"I was waitin' fo' Page in the airport parkin' lot, jus' outside the terminal. When I saw him come outta da terminal, I got outta the car and waved at him. He dropped his seabag at ma feet, and start' yellin' at me fo' not comin' inside to meet him. He say he wasted an hour inside lookin' fo' someone to meet him. I tol' him that I look inside, but don' find him. He yelled and shouted that I was insubordinate, and, if I keep lyin', he would put me on report. Then, he order' me to pick-up his seabag and put it in the trunk. When I didn' he come closer and act like he gonna hit me. Page much bigger dan me, and I was afraid he would hit me. When I didn' pick-up his seabag, he grab ma jumper with both his hands and pulled ma over the seabag, I tripped and fell. He called me a lazy nigger. Then, he kick me around some while I on da ground. It really hurt when he kick me. When he finally let me up, I saw ma uniform was ruined. I was 'fraid he would kick ma again, so I picked-up his seabag and put it in the trunk. Den, I drove Page here to the NAVCOMMSTA."

"Was there any other time when you feared Petty Officer Page would hurt you?"

"Yes, sir, when da NIS officers were here gettin' everyone's statements. Page saw ma standing outside da library where da NIS officers were workin'. Page said he would break my arms if I told 'em what happened at da airport."

Rigney sits in his chair and shakes his head in disbelief. He heard people lie about him before, but never so creatively and so believably.

"No more questions."

Lieutenant Maston rises and says, "Seaman Newman, your testimony is a complete fabrication, correct?"

"Sur, I don' know what fabrication mean."

"In this case, it means you made it all up. Nothing you said is true, correct?"

"Everythin' I say be true."

"Can anyone verify your testimony? Was anyone else present during the events you described?"

"No sur."

"You don't like Petty Officer Page do you?"

"No sur."

"Why don't you like him?"

"He's a bully. He push people 'round. Ever'one's 'fraid of him, 'cept ma brothers and me."

"Seaman Newman, you don't like Page because he is big, powerful, confident, and Caucasian, correct?"

"No sur! Dat's not true!"

Everyone in the courtroom notices that Newman's word inflection has degraded.

"Who has Page bullied? Name someone, and we will bring him into this hearing to substantiate your claims."

"Der was Jackson. Page beat him up bad and stole his slush fund. And Page beat up two Greek guys in front of his house for no reason."

Maston smiles and asks, "Were you present when Page allegedly beat-up Jackson?"

Newman is about to blurt out yes, hoping that lying will improve is testimony. Then, he realizes he could be trapped again. He responds, "No, but ever'one know about dat."

Maston challenges, "Were you present during the alleged beating of two Greeks by Page in front of his house in Nea Makri?"

"No, but ever'one know 'bout dat, too."

Captain Jack interrupts, "Mr. Maston, do you object? If you don't, I will."

"Yes, your honor, I move to strike the witness's testimony regarding Jackson and two Greeks. The testimony is hearsay."

"Agreed. Reporter, strike the testimony."

Newman glances back and forth between the judge, Maston, and the court reporter. An anxious expression appears on his face, and he asks, "Does dat mean Page ain't gonna be punish' for dose thin's?"

Maston is about to respond, when Newman blurts out, "It's not dat he hit anyone else dat I know of. He strut 'round dis base as if he own it. Yo' know da type. He don' step outta nobody's way. Ever'body step outta his way, like he be king a da place. Ever'one kiss his ass. He thin' he better dan ever'one. Yo' know wut I mean. But my brothers and me don' step outta his way. No sur. He ain't gonna mess with us no mo'."

All in the courtroom stare at Newman—stunned by Newman's words and astonished how easily Lieutenant Maston turned Newman's testimony.

Newman smiles. He believes that he has pulled off the deception.

Maston expresses doubt as he stares at the grinning Newman; then, he says in a medium tone, "Objection. Conclusions. Hearsay. Request to strike."

"Sustained."

Newman frowns and does not understand what just happened.

"No further questions," Maston announces.

Captain Jack orders, "The witness is excused."

With a sneer of successful deception on his face, Newman swaggers slowly back to his chair.

Lieutenant Commander Powers stands and calls, "Chief Warrant Officer Donald Pritchings to the stand."

Pritchings walks toward the witness chair. He wears a wrinkled white uniform. The gold on his hat and shoulder boards look tarnished. His manner lacks confidence, and his expression cautious.

After Pritchings swears-in and acknowledges Page as the accused, trial counsel begins his direct examination.

"Mr. Pritchings, explain your position in the chain-of-command and how it relates to the accused."

"I'm traffic division officer. Message center, HI-COMM relay, LO-COMM relay, and fleet center come under my direction. My immediate superior is the communications officer. Page works in repair division, which comes under direction of the repair division officer, Lieutenant Linderhaus."

"So, Petty Officer Page does not work directly for you?"

"That's correct, sir."

Powers directs, "Mr. Pritchings, tell us what happened during your first encounter with Petty Officer Page in front of your house in Nea Makri."

"Page was leading a group of my neighbors to harass me about my dog. Page incited them into making a commotion in front of my house. When I came out of the house, Page made aggressive motions toward me. My dog attempted to protect me from Page. My dog tried to jump the fence. The barbed wire cut him across the belly. He didn't make it over the fence. I had to take him to a vet."

Astounded by how easily the officer lies, Rigney shakes his head and expresses disbelief.

Pritchings observes Page's reaction and diverts his eyes from the defense table.

Maston stands and says, "Objection. Mr. Pritchings is not an expert in dog behavior. He cannot know why his dog attempted to jump the fence. Request witness testimony as to the dog's intentions or motivations be stricken from the record."

"Sustained."

Powers asks, "Mr. Pritchings, did you later have a conversation with the accused regarding the incident in front of your home?"

"Yes, a day or so later. I called him into my office in the communications trailers."

"Please relate to the court what was said during that conversation."

"I counseled Page as to his inappropriate behavior. I told him that if it happened again, I would place him on report. Page accused me of harassing him. He said that if I didn't back off, he would find an opportunity off base to beat me up like he did Mr. Martin."

"The accused threatened he would beat you up like he did Mr. Martin?"

"Yes."

Powers continues, "Tell us the details of the second encounter with the accused in front of your house."

"He incited my neighbors to gather in the street in front of my house to do things to scare my dog. I was inside my house when I heard my dog barking. When I went outside, my neighbors shouted at me. Page stood in front of them. He was moving those metal bars up and down, again, to scare my dog, like he did before."

"Objection," Maston declares. "The witness speculates as to why the accused was moving those bars up and down."

"Sustained."

"Continue," Powers orders his witness.

"Page made threatening moves toward Sparks. That was my dog's name. Sparks was excited. He jumped the fence this time and went after Page. That's when Page hit sparks in the head with a dumbbell and killed him."

"No more questions. Your witness."

Lieutenant Maston stands and smiles knowingly at CWO2 Pritchings.

Pritchings squirms in his chair. His portly body stretches the buttons on his uniform. His face expresses caution. Sweat seeps through the cloth of his uniform.

"Mr. Pritchings, why did the accused and your neighbors want to scare your dog?"

"Objection!" Powers speaks loudly from his chair. Calls for a conclusion, argumentative. The witness is not qualified to answer the question."

"Sustained."

Maston inquires, "Mr. Pritchings, how many complaints have your neighbors filed against you with the local police?"

"Objection," Powers declares. "Facts not in evidence, irrelevant, and calls for speculation."

"Sustained."

Maston attempts another approach. "Mr. Pritchings, during the five minutes following your dog being killed, what were your actions?"

"Objection! Irrelevant! Not covered during direct examination."

"Sustained."

Maston continues, "Mr. Pritchings, you said you were inside your house when you heard your dog barking. Isn't it true that your dog had been barking for hours prior to you going outside and seeing the accused and your neighbors?"

Pritchings squirms in the witness chair. He realizes that Maston exposes each lie one detail at a time. "I don't recall that, sir."

"Mr. Pritchings, you said when you came outside you saw the accused and your neighbors standing in the street in front of your house. Is that correct?"

"Yes sir."

"Mr. Pritchings, how can you know the accused was inciting your neighbors? On both occasions, you claim you were in your house when you heard your dog start barking. How could you know what Page was doing outside when you were inside?"

Pritchings blinks his eyes rapidly, and his chin twitches. He searches for an answer and cannot find one.

Maston shifts his attention between Pritchings and the judge several times. Then, he requests, "Your honor, please instruct the witness to answer."

The judge commands, "Answer the question, Mr. Pritchings."

Pritchings responds, "Page admitted it to me in my office. During that conversation when he threatened me."

"Did Page tell you why he incited your neighbors against you and your dog?"

"No sir. He didn't say."

Maston smirks and looks around the courtroom.

Pritchings looks around the courtroom. He glances at the judge; then, he looks at Powers. He sees men of his division as spectators. Pritchings sees the look of doubt in all faces. *They know I am lying.*

Maston queries, "Mr. Pritchings, why did you have a barbed wire fence constructed around your yard?"

Powers interrupts, "Objection, irrelevant, your honor?"

The judge looks at Maston.

Maston explains, "Your honor, my question relates to culpability. The defense's position is that the accused was merely protecting himself against an attacking dog. Had Mr. Pritchings erected an adequate fence to keep his dog penned-in, the attack would not have taken place. In other words, your honor, Mr. Pritchings was solely responsible for his dog's actions, not Page."

Powers objects, "Mr. Pritchings is not the accused."

Maston looks into the judge's eyes and specifies, "Your honor, you authorized all facts regarding Page's alleged violent manner to be entered into evidence. The defense has legal right to challenge such evidence."

"Objection overruled. The witness will answer the question."

Pritchings's face displays apprehension. Sweat pours from his body. His wet uniform clings to his body. He says with a quivering voice, "I don't remember the question."

The judge directs, "Counselor, repeat your question."

"Mr. Pritchings, why did you have a barbed wire fence constructed around your yard?"

Pritchings frantically considers answers that do not sound like lies. He responds, "To keep people out."

"To keep people out of where?"

"Out of my property."

"Not to keep your dog in?"

"Uh . . . no sir."

"You didn't think it necessary to keep your dog penned in?"

"No sir. Sparks was a mild-mannered and loving dog. There was no reason to pen him in. I just wanted to keep people out."

A chuckle rises from the spectators.

Captain Jack slams the gavel to the desktop.

Maston continues. "You did not consider Sparks as a threat or a danger to others, then?"

"No sir."

"You claim Sparks did not act aggressively and did not bark viciously when others came close to your property, is that correct?"

Pritchings hesitates; then, he declares, "No, sir, only when Page scared him."

"Mr. Pritchings, I will bring to the witness stand some of your neighbors. I will submit into evidence reports from the local police chief. Do you want to change your testimony?"

"No sir. You can't trust anything they say. They all hate Americans."

Loud gasps rise in the spectator area.

"Do you want to change your testimony, Mr. Pritchings?"

"No sir," Pritchings responds defensively.

"Mr. Pritchings, you said the accused killed Sparks by hitting him in the head with a dumbbell?"

"That's correct, sir."

"Where did Page do that?"

"In the street."

"In the street in front of your house?"

Pritchings hesitates; then, he responds, "No, sir, about half a block down the hill."

"Did Page run down the hill away from your dog?"

"Uh . . . I don't know."

Chuckles come from the spectators, verbalizing that Pritchings has lost all credibility with the spectators.

Maston walks back to the defense table and looks down at his notes. "Mr. Pritchings, did you see the accused hit your dog with the dumbbell?"

"Yes sir."

"How many times did Page hit Sparks?"

"One time, but very hard."

"What did you do after Page hit your dog?"

"Objection! Not covered in direct examination."

"Sustained."

Maston sighs deeply; then he asks Pritchings, "Mr. Pritchings, later today you will be called as a hostile witness for the defense. At that time, under direct examination, you will be required to answer all my questions. Do you want to take this opportunity to change any of your testimony given so far?"

"Objection! Defense counsel harasses the witness."

"Sustained."

"No further questions," Maston states.

"No redirect," Powers declares.

Captain Jack advises, "You are excused, Mr. Pritchings."

Powers orders, "Radioman First Class Melvin Beaucamp take the stand."

The tall and lanky sailor stands and walks toward the witness chair. His slim stature and tailor-made Service Dress Whites pose a recruiting poster image. He sits in the witness chair. Powers swears him in. Beaucamp identifies the accused.

"Petty Officer Beaucamp, where do you live?"

"I live in Nea Makri, across the street from where Page lives with the German woman, Anna. I don't know her last name."

"Were you home on the evening of August 29?"

"Yes. I was."

"Explain what you saw."

"I was sitting in my front yard with my next-door neighbor. I went inside to get a couple of beers. When I returned to the yard, just outside the door, I heard people running. I looked at the street. I saw Page running toward two Greek men. It was shortly after sunset, not real dark, yet. I could see everything in the headlights of Page's car. I mean Anna's car. Page drives it all the time. Anyway, Page jumped into the air and kicked the two Greeks in the chest and face. They fell, and Page landed on top of them. Page was sitting on top of one of the Greeks when he picked up a metal bar, a piece of pipe I think. Then, the other Greek swings at Page with a chain. Page used the pipe to block the chain, but some of the chain hit him in the face. Then, the Greek with the chain stood up and swung at Page's head with the chain. Page ducked. Then, Page swung the pipe and hit the Greek in the crotch. The Greek yelled out, fell down, and laid in the street, moaning. Then, Page got to his feet. That's when my wife and I and my neighbor went to the street to find out what was happening. Page didn't know we were there. I saw him raise the pipe, as if he was going to hit one of them, but when I called his name, Page lowered the pipe. A few minutes later, the Greeks stood up. They looked dazed. Then, they limped away into the dark."

Powers asks, "What was your impression of the accused's willingness to fight those two Greeks?"

"Objection. Irrelevant and calls for an opinion," Maston says from his chair.

"Sustained."

Powers rephrases, "How would you describe the accused's manner during the encounter?"

"Objection. Irrelevant."

"Sustained."

Powers says, "No further questions. Your witness."

Rigney leans toward Maston and whispers, "Even I, with my meager and inadequate knowledge of court procedure, knew those questions were objectionable. Mr. Powers must have known that. Why did he even try?"

Maston whispers back, "To reinforce images of your frequent violent encounters in the mind of the judge."

Rigney flinches. He exhibits worrisome surprise as he understands the damage of trial counsel's tactic. Concern for his future deepens.

Maston stands and asks the witness, "Petty Officer Beaucamp, you stated that you came out your door and saw the accused running toward the two Greek men. What were the two Greek men doing?"

"They were moving toward Page. I think they had been running. They were slowing down as Page ran toward them."

"Have you ever seen those two Greek men before?"

"No sir."

"Did those Greeks carry weapons?"

"I didn't see any."

Maston raises an eyebrow at Beaucamp and asks, "What about the length of pipe and length of chain?"

"Yes, one Greek had the pipe in his hand and the other Greek had the length of chain, if that's what you mean by weapons."

Maston asks, "Did the Greek with the pipe attempt to hit the accused with the Pipe at anytime?"

"Yes sir. When Page got a few feet a way, the Greek raised the pipe as if he were going to hit Page."

"Did the Greek swing the pipe at the accused?"

"No."

"No further questions."

Powers stands and says, "Redirect your honor."

Captain Jack says, "Proceed."

"Petty Officer Beaucamp, did the Greek raise the pipe in defense or in aggression?"

"Objection," Maston says from his chair. "Argumentative and calls for a conclusion."

"Sustained," Captain Jack rules.

Powers takes a moment to rephrase the question in his head; then, he asks, "Did it look to you as if the Greek raised the pipe in defense?"

"Objection. Calls for conclusion," Maston says loudly from his chair.

"Sustained," Captain Jack rules impatiently.

Powers nods acceptance of the ruling. Then, he asks, "Petty Officer Beaucamp, considering your life experiences, knowledge of your own physical ability, and what you have observed of the accused's physical ability, if you had a pipe in your hand, and you saw Page running toward you in the same manner you observed that night, would you have hit Page with the pipe in defense."

Maston jumps to his feet. "Objection! Irrelevant! Improper direct! Calls for an opinion. Speculation—"

Captain Jack raises his palm toward Maston, indicating Maston need not continue his objection.

"Sustained. Trial counsel, this is a hearing, not a court-martial. Members are not present, and you cannot affect my judgment with such maneuvers. I will only allow facts entered into evidence. Move on!"

"No further questions," Powers announces.

"No recross," Maston declares.

Captain Jack says, "The witness may step down."

Powers announces, "I call Seaman Samuel Cussack to the witness stand."

Cussack, who also wears Service Dress Whites, sits in the witness chair, swears in, and he identifies RM2 Page.

Powers asks, "Seaman Cussack, tell us what you saw during the morning of September 4 regarding the accused and Petty Officer Jackson."

"I was swabbin' the main passageway in the barracks, when I heard a scream coming from Jackson's office. I dropped the swab and ran to Jackson's office, I opened the door, and I saw Jackson pinned to the floor by Page."

"Tell the court exactly how the accused had Jackson pinned to the floor."

"Page held Jackson's wrist and twisted his arm, like it was totally twisted around. Page had his foot on Jackson's back, holding him down like."

"Did Jackson appear to be in pain?"

"Yes sir."

"Then what happened?" Powers asks.

"I told Page I was gonna get the master-at-arms, and I did."

"No more questions. Your witness."

Rigney leans toward Lieutenant Maston and whispers, "Why didn't Mr. Powers ask Cussack what happened next? I mean, what happened next exonerates me from the so-called Jackson beating. I don't understand why Cussack was even called."

Mr. Maston whispers back, "Cussack was called because of the remote chance I did not investigate or question the entire incident."

"Mr. Powers must know you're smarter than that."

"He does," Lieutenant Maston reveals. "It's his duty to try."

"Defense counsel," Captain Jack calls. "Do you have any questions of this witness?"

"Yes, your honor, I do."

Maston stands, "Seaman Cussack, did you find the master-at-arms?"

"Yes."

"And then what happened?"

"Objection," Powers states from his chair. "Not covered in direct."

"Sustained."

"No more questions."

Powers stands and declares, "The prosecution has presented sufficient evidence to take this case to court-martial and requests that your honor so recommend."

Captain Jack asks Maston, "Will the defense present a case at this time?"

Maston stands and says, "Yes, your honor. The defense will present a case at this time."

Captain Jack announces, "This hearing will recess and reconvene at 1330."

Captain Jack hits the gavel against the desk.

"All rise!"

After the judge departs, Rigney looks at his watch—1209.

The club empties, except for Rigney and Lieutenant Maston.

Rigney looks curiously at Maston and asks, "How come Mr. Powers never called Mr. Martin as a witness?"

"Because Mr. Powers knows that during cross-examination I would have made Mr. Martin look like Satan incarnate."

For the first time in a long time, Rigney worries about how someone may judge him. He understands that the direction of his life is at stake. He worries he will not have the option to join ONI. He wonders why no one from ONI has contacted him regarding these legal proceedings. He includes status of the investigation in his daily intelligence reports to ONI.

"What now?" Rigney asks.

"We go to lunch."

Rigney and Lieutenant Maston are side by side going through the galley steam line.

At the end of the steam line, Maston tells Rigney, "We must separate now. I must sit with the other officers of the court." He nods toward the table where Captain Jack and Lieutenant Commander Powers sit. "I will see you back in the courtroom."

Rigney finds an empty seat at a table with sailors who were spectators and witnesses in the club. The table falls silent as Rigney sits.

RM3 Spencer breaks the silence. "Hey, Rig, your lawyer kicks ass, man!"

The others at the table look at Rigney, nod their heads, and mumble their agreement.

Rigney smiles, but does not respond verbally. He understands that Mr. Maston could shatter everyone's testimony. Nevertheless, Rigney's experience in the navy leads him to believe that the truth will not necessarily set him free.

Chapter 84

Rigney enters the Club Zeus—courtroom—at 1320. Spectators crowd the room—standing room only. The reputation of *Maston the Witness Slayer* quickly circulated around the base.

After he sits at the defense table, Rigney looks around the room. He sees his local friends who are Pritchings's neighbors. He recognizes a Greek in khaki uniform as the local police chief. Commander Caldwell sits in his reserved chair in the front row. Lieutenant Commander Blakely sits next to Commander Caldwell. Next to the XO is the master chief from COMNAVCOM. Rigney looks at Dottie Caldwell; she gives him a thumbs-up. He smiles at Nancy and Paul Bell, who smile back and give him thumbs-up. Senior Chief Hilton stands in the back. Also present are Jackson, Pritchings, Newman, Vance, *The Professor*, Grandville, Mr. Linderhaus, and everyone from repair division, including Patterson and Thompson.

At 1330, Captain Jack brings the court to order and tells Lieutenant Maston to present the defense.

"I call Dorothea Caldwell to the witness stand."

Murmurs of surprise rise in the courtroom.

Captain Jack taps the gavel to the desk.

Fantasies dance through the heads of the young sailors as Dottie swishes her hips to the witness stand; her sexual appeal enhanced with pixie-style blond hair, deep-blue eyes, and wearing tight hip-hugger slacks and waist-clinging white sleeveless blouse.

Dottie swears to tell the truth and acknowledges she knows the accused.

Maston begins direct examination. "Miss Caldwell, on the afternoon of August 10, did you witness a physical confrontation between Lieutenant Martin and the accused?"

"Yes, I did."

"What drew your attention to Lieutenant Martin and his family out by the pool?"

"One of the sailors commented that Jeff was hitting his daughter."

"Were there any other comments prior to the accused going out to the pool?"

"Yes. Some of the sailors questioned why Uncle Oli, excuse me, Commander Caldwell never did anything about Jeff hitting his family."

"Were these comments loud enough for everyone in the bar to hear?"

"Yes."

"Describe the sequence of events."

"Rigney and I and Eric Linderhaus were standing at the bar, talking, when someone said loudly something about someone hitting someone. We all looked out at the pool. I saw Jeff hitting Laurie, and then he hit Constance and knocked her down. Then, Rigney went out to the pool, hit Jeff, and pushed him to the ground. Then, Rigney came back inside and sat down at the bar."

"Did the accused say anything as to why he went out to the pool to stop Lieutenant Martin?"

Dottie shoots a glance at Rigney and says, "No."

"You stated that Lieutenant Linderhaus was with you and the accused. Was Lieutenant Linderhaus the only officer in the club at the time?"

"Yes."

"Was Lieutenant Linderhaus in uniform?"

"No."

"Did Mr. Linderhaus take any actions to stop Lieutenant Martin from hitting Laurie?"

"No."

Powers stands and says, "Objection, your honor. Irrelevant."

Captain Jack looks to Maston for argument.

"Your honor, the basis of the defense's case is that the accused went out to the pool to stop Lieutenant Martin from inflicting additional injury, and the accused did so when he realized that there was a history to Martin's brutality and no one from the command had ever done anything about it. Our case is that the accused acted as a brave and valiant knight and not the villain as portrayed by the prosecution."

Some of the spectators burst into cheers and applauses.

Captain Jack slams the gavel on the table and declares, "Order in the court. Outbursts by spectators will not be tolerated."

Commander Caldwell exchanges glances with Captain Jack. Caldwell's expression communicates his objection to an open courtroom has just been validated.

The judge looks toward Powers and states, "Objection overruled."

Maston continues, "Did Mr. Linderhaus say or do anything with the accused when Page returned to the bar?"

"Eric left before Rigney returned."

"Did Mr. Linderhaus depart before, during, or after the confrontation?"

"Eric left as Rigney walked back to the bar."

Maston questions, "Previous to the event you just described, did you ever witness Lieutenant Martin hit his wife and daughter?"

"Yes."

"When and where?"

Commander Caldwell stiffens and stares intently at his niece.

"Several times at family gatherings," Dottie replies.

"Are you and Lieutenant Martin related?"

"Yes. Jeff is my first cousin. He is the son of my father's older sister."

"That would make Jeff Martin the nephew of Commander Caldwell, the commanding officer of NAVCOMMSTA Greece, correct?"

"Yes."

Again, the spectators gasp sharply and loudly. Spontaneous comments rise from the spectators.

Commander Caldwell looks disapprovingly at his niece.

Dottie returns an apologetic stare toward Commander Caldwell and says, "I'm sorry, Uncle Oli, but I must tell the truth. Don't you think it best that all this finally comes out?"

Loud chattering breaks-out in the courtroom among the spectators.

Captain Jack hits the gavel to the tabletop and declares, "Order in the court. The spectators are ordered to remain silent."

Maston continues, "Miss Caldwell, were the injuries inflicted by Lieutenant Martin on his wife and daughter ever severe enough to require treatment by a doctor?"

"Yes."

"No more questions."

Lieutenant Commander Powers stands and asks, "Miss Caldwell, did the accused tell you why he hit Lieutenant Martin?"

"Objection!" Maston declares. "Asked and answered during direct examination."

"Sustained."

Powers attempts another track. "Miss Caldwell, did the accused ever boast about his confrontation with Lieutenant Martin?"

"No."

"Miss Caldwell, describe your relationship with the accused."

"We are friends."

"Do you and the accused have a romantic relationship?"

"Yes."

Commander Caldwell presses his lips tightly together and shakes his head with disapproval.

Mary Blakely smiles as she thinks about Page's success with women.

"Miss Caldwell, are you in love with the accused?"

Dottie smiles appreciatively at Rigney and responds, "No, but with time I might be."

Rigney nods with an understanding smile on his face.

Dottie's answer to the last question leaves Powers nowhere to go.

"No more questions."

Dottie casts a perky smile at Rigney as she walks back to her chair. More self-conscious of her appearance as she notices everyone watching her, she swishes less.

"The defense calls Lieutenant Commander Blakely."

The XO stands and walks to the witness chair. Today, Mary wears loose-fitting whites. She attempts to look official, but this slim, red headed, brown-eyed beauty distracts all.

Powers swears in the XO. She identifies the accused.

Maston commences his direct examination. "Commander Blakely, what is your current assignment?"

"I am the executive officer of NAVCOMMSTA Greece."

"How many times did you witness Lieutenant Martin hitting his wife or his child?"

"Three occasions . . . all occurred at social events. Actually, he only hit his daughter during the first event. The other two times, he grabbed Constance and shook her violently."

"Please describe these social events."

"All three were gatherings for Sunday tea at Commander Caldwell's house in Kifissia. All the Nea Makri officers and their families attended."

"Commander Blakely, were you at the command Fourth of July picnic?"

"Yes."

"Commander, previous witnesses testified that they saw Lieutenant Martin hit his daughter at that picnic. Did you witness that?"

"No. I left the picnic early."

"What were your actions, if any, regarding these incidents when Lieutenant Martin physically handled his wife and daughter?"

Powers wants to object to relevancy, but he knows he will be overruled.

"On the first occasion at Commander Caldwell's house, I started toward Lieutenant Martin to stop him. Commander Caldwell stopped me and told me not to interfere. Commander Caldwell said he would take care of it. Commander Caldwell stopped Lieutenant Martin on all three occasions."

"How did Commander Caldwell stop Lieutenant Martin on these occasions?"

"Commander Caldwell ordered Lieutenant Martin to stop."

"And did Lieutenant Martin stop."

"Yes, on each occasion."

"But Lieutenant Martin did not stop his violent attacks on his family, correct?"

"Yes."

"Are you aware of other occasions when Lieutenant Martin acted violently against his wife and child?"

"Yes. I received reports from the Greek Police of times they were called to Mr. Martin's residence by Greek neighbors. The neighbors reported shouting and screaming coming from the Martin house."

Powers stands and declares, "Objection. No evidence of such reports involving the local populace has been submitted."

The judge asks, "Will defense counsel submit the reports into evidence?"

Maston responds, "Yes, your honor." Maston hands copies of the police reports to Captain Jack. "English translations are attached."

Captain Jack scans the pages then declares, "These reports are accepted as evidence. Objection overruled."

Caldwell glares at Commander Blakely. She obtained the reports without his approval.

Maston continues. "Commander Blakely, have you taken any actions regarding Lieutenant Martin's conduct? If you have, please explain your actions."

"I counseled Mr. Martin after each incident. For the last two incidents, I put the counseling in writing, and I had Mr. Martin sign the counseling sheets. Those counseling sheets were made a permanent part of his service record.

"I also discussed Mr. Martin's behavior with Commander Caldwell. I recommended to Commander Caldwell that Mr. Martin's overseas suitability status be terminated and that Mr. Martin be returned to CONUS for long-term professional counseling."

"When did you make those recommendations to Commander Caldwell?"

"Several months ago."

Maston picks up a brown folder from the defense table. "Commander Blakely, this is Lieutenant Martin's service record. Please locate the counseling sheets that you previously mentioned."

Maston hands the service record to Blakely.

Without looking inside Martin's service record, Mary reports, "The counseling sheets are no longer included in Mr. Martin's service record."

Trial counsel jumps to his feet and says loudly, "Objection! Irrelevant!"

Captain Jack stares intently at Mary Blakely, and his mind is riveted to Mary Blakely's testimony. He begins to suspect inappropriate command influence. Without even looking at Powers, he commands evenly, "Overruled."

Maston continues his direct examination, "Commander Blakely, when were the counseling sheets removed?"

"I do not know."

"Where is the current location of those counseling sheets?"

"I don't know."

"Are you saying that you did not remove them?"

"That is correct."

Maston pauses and does not ask the obvious question as to whom has the authority. He does not need to.

All eyes in the courtroom fall on Commander Caldwell.

Oliver Caldwell's eyes go wide, and his body stiffens as he realizes that he is accused and that he is becoming the focus of the defense's strategy.

Powers realizes the defense strategy at the same time.

"Commander, when did you discover that Lieutenant Martin is Commander Caldwell's nephew?"

"Today, when Dottie Caldwell testified."

Maston asks, "Commander Blakely, who at Nea Makri writes officers' fitness reports?"

"I write the drafts, and Commander Caldwell finalizes and signs them."

"Commander Blakely, please look inside Mr. Martin's service record and read Mr. Martin's last fitness report."

Mary scans the fitness report. Just yesterday, she spent time reading every word in the fitness report.

"Commander Blakely, what is the date on the fitness report."

"July 15."

"Does Mr. Martin's fitness report contain all that you wrote?"

"No."

"What's missing?"

"Specifics of Mr. Martin's violence on his family, including references to the police reports and to my counseling sessions."

"Are there any other differences?"

"Yes. Some of the performance marks are higher than I assigned."

Powers finally stands and objects, "Your honor, defense counsel rambles with irrelevance. What does this line of questioning have to do with the charges against the accused? Commanding officers have every right to modify the records and evaluation drafts of those under their commands. The commanding officer's judgment is final."

Captain Jack looks at Maston for argument.

All eyes in the courtroom focus on Maston.

"Your honor, I am not challenging the rights and authority of commanding officers. As I declared before, the defense asserts that the accused went to the aid of two defenseless victims, because the accused sensed, correctly, that no one in the chain-of-command had done anything to defend Constance and Laurie Martin, and that no one else in the club at that time were going to aid Constance and Laurie Martin. To that concept, I solicit testimony that confirms there was no command involvement to stop the violence. I solicit testimony that there was command influence exerted to suppress any official record of Mr. Martin's brutality."

The spectators cannot hold back their verbal expressions of what was just revealed. The chatter in the courtroom spreads out of control.

Captain Jack slams the gavel rapidly three times. The spectators become quiet. Captain Jacks declares, "Order in the court, or I will clear the courtroom of all spectators." Captain Jack has no intention to clear the courtroom.

"Your honor," Powers interrupts. "What might have happened to official records of Mr. Martin is irrelevant to the charges. By regulation and by tradition, the accused is forbidden to strike another individual under any circumstance."

Maston contests, "With that reasoning, Martin could have beaten both his wife and child to death and the correct action by all present was to do nothing."

"Nothing physical," Powers contests.

"Hold on," Captain Jack inserts. "Prosecution and defense are delivering final arguments. This is not a court-martial. We are here to gather relevant facts. I will allow testimony on both sides as to the accused's motivations."

Maston turns to face the witness and asks, "Commander Blakely, if you were to write a performance evaluation on the accused today, would you write a positive or negative account of his performance?"

"Objection!" Powers says loudly as he stands. "The witness is not qualified to judge the innocence or guilt of the accused."

Maston responds, "Your honor, I did not ask the witness to judge innocence or guilt, I asked her if she would write a positive or negative account of his performance. The witness is the accused's executive officer. The navy has officially placed trust and confidence in her judgment by assigning her as NAVCOMMSTA executive officer."

"Objection overruled. The witness will answer the question."

Mary responds confidently, "I would write positive comments regarding his professional performance. He has proved to be a superior technician. As far as his military conduct goes, he is only accused of criminal actions. Page has not been found guilty of anything. If I wrote the evaluation today, Page would not receive negative marks regarding his military conduct."

Maston smiles.

Powers sighs deeply.

Commander Caldwell shakes his head in disapproval.

Rigney nods his head with appreciation that the XO answered fairly.

"Commander Blakely, you are the command legal officer, correct?"

"Yes. That is correct."

"Commander, witnesses alleged that the accused knocked Seaman Newman to the ground, assaulted Lieutenant Martin, killed Mr. Pritchings's dog, fought two Greeks in front of his house, and beat up Petty Officer Jackson. Did you investigate any or all of these allegations?"

"I investigated them all."

"After you completed your investigations, did you consider that the evidence was sufficient to place the accused on report for any of those alleged acts?"

"I found no evidence that he violated any order, regulation, or the UCMJ. I judged that Article 15 punishment or court-martial was not warranted."

"No further questions," Maston states.

Powers stands and walks half the distance to the witness chair. He asks, "Commander Blakely, how many years have you been in the navy?"

"Ten years."

"How many different commands have you served?"

"Counting Nea Makri—four—all NAVCOMMSTAs."

"Would you say that you have had significant experience in leading and supervising enlisted personnel?"

"Yes. I am proud to say that my leadership marks have always been the highest."

Powers nods; he asks, "How long has the accused been assigned to Nea Makri?"

"Five or six weeks, I believe."

"Commander Blakely, in all your naval experiences have you ever before encountered a sailor who was the focus in five powerful acts of violence in as many weeks."

Mary sits thoughtfully for a few moments; then, she responds, "No."

"Don't you find that unusual?"

Maston says from his chair, "Objection. Calls for an opinion. Argumentative."

"Sustained."

"No more questions," Powers announces.

Maston looks down at a sheet of paper lying on the defense table.

"I call Master Chief Crimer to the witness stand."

Master Chief Crimer weaves his way through the spectators; then, sits in the witness chair. Today, he wears a crisp and immaculate Tropical White Long uniform. He goes through the swearing-in process.

Maston asks, "Master Chief, were you on base during the afternoon when the accused allegedly committed assault and battery against Lieutenant Martin?"

"Yes."

"You interviewed witnesses to the alleged battery?"

"Yes."

"How many witnesses did you interview?"

"Fourteen over the course of several days."

"After interviewing those fourteen witnesses, did you find cause to place Petty Officer Page on report?"

"I found no cause to place him on report."

Maston pulls a sheet of paper from a file folder. "Master Chief, I have here a NAVPERS 1626, also known as a report chit. This form charges Petty officer Page with assault consummating with a battery against Mr. Martin. Your name and signature are on the form as the submitter. This report chit conflicts with your testimony that after interviewing fourteen witnesses, you did not find cause to place Petty Officer Page on report. However, you placed Petty Officer Page on report. Why?"

Master Chief Crimer breathes deeply and shifts in the witness chair. He glances at Commander Caldwell and replies, "Commander Caldwell ordered me to."

"Master Chief, did any officer in your chain-of-command ever order you to place Lieutenant Martin on report for assault and battery on his wife and daughter?"

"No."

"Master Chief, when did you discover that Commander Caldwell is Lieutenant Martin's uncle?"

"Today, when Dottie Caldwell testified."

"Master Chief, I take you back to the afternoon of Page's alleged assault and battery on Mr. Martin. Did you have reason to call the air force base police and request they send the U.S. Military Police to the Martin residence?"

"Yes."

"Did you also go to the Martin residence?"

"Yes."

"Explain what happened when you arrived at the Martin residence."

"When I got there, the air force military police were already there, and they had Mr. Martin in handcuffs."

"Master Chief, how much time elapsed from the time of the accused's alleged assault and battery on Lieutenant Martin at the base pool and the time you arrived at the Martin residence?"

"About ninety minutes—two hours, maybe."

"Did you later discover why the military police handcuffed Lieutenant Martin?"

"Yes."

"How did you discover it?"

"The military police informed me verbally, and later, they provided me with a written report as to what happened."

Maston pulls a paper from another file folder, hands it to the judge, and says, "Your honor, the defense submits into evidence a copy of the report to which the witness refers."

Captain Jack scans the report and declares, "The report is accepted into evidence."

"Master Chief, what does the report say?"

"When the military police arrived at the Martin residence, they found Mr. Martin beating his wife with a broken broom handle. When the MPs attempted to stop Mr. Martin, he swung the broom handle at the MPs. They subdued him and put him in handcuffs. The MPs administered a sobriety test to Mr. Martin while still at the Martin residence. Mr. Martin failed the sobriety test."

"Master Chief Crimer, what was the eventual result of the incident at the Martin residence?"

"The air force base provost martial charged Mr. Martin with attempted murder on his wife."

Chatter breaks-out in the courtroom. Except for the Caldwells, Blakely, Linderhaus, and Crimer, no one else on the base knew that Mr. Martin was charged with attempted murder.

Captain Jack slams the gavel and orders, "The spectators will remain quiet."

Maston produces another piece of paper with the charges against Lieutenant Martin and submits them into evidence.

"Master Chief, based on the evidence submitted, would you say that your actions to call the military police to the Martin home saved Constance Martin's life?"

"Yes."

For dramatic effect, Maston stands to the side of the witness chair and faces the spectators. Then, he asks, "Master Chief, during your previous testimony, you said you found reason to call the air force military police to the Martin residence. What was that reason?"

"Petty Officer Page told me that Mr. Martin would violently attack his wife and child. Petty Officer Page convinced me that Mr. Martin would take out his beating from Page on his wife and child."

Loud gasps sound from the spectators. The gasps are accompanied with softly uttered 'oh my gods' and 'thank gods' and a few 'way to go, Rig!'

Captain Jack hits the table with his gavel. He does not issue a warning this time, because he understands the deep effect of the witness's last statement.

Maston sighs deeply and declares, "No more questions."

Powers sits wide-eyed and shakes his head bewilderingly at the turn of events. Then, he stands, and inquires, "Master Chief, how long have you been the Chief-master-at-Arms?"

"Since I arrived more than a year ago."

"Before coming to NAVCOMMSTA Greece had you ever served in a law enforcement capacity?"

"Yes. Ten years ago, I served as watch supervisor for the Norfolk Naval Station Shore Patrol Department, and many years before that I was a Shore Patrolman for several years at Mayport Naval Station."

Powers casts a challenging stare and inquires, "Master Chief, you obviously had a lot of experience. Are you saying that it never crossed your mind that Mr. Martin might go home and beat his wife until the accused, a junior and inexperienced sailor, mentioned it?"

"No sir. I am not saying that. I did seriously consider that Mr. Martin would go home and hurt his wife and child."

Surprise flashes across Powers's face. Impulsively, he starts his next question, "Then, why . . ." Powers pauses as revelation flashes across his face. "No more questions," Powers announces.

Spectators mumble as they wonder why Powers stopped.

Rigney leans close to Maston and asks, "What's going on? Why did Mr. Powers stop in mid-question?"

Maston answers in a whisper, "Mr. Powers realized that I trapped him into asking an obvious question, a question when answered would have had more meaning if he had asked the question. Now, I must ask it." He stands and declares, "Redirect, your honor."

"Proceed."

"Master Chief, if you considered that Mr. Martin might go home and beat his wife, why didn't you call the military police earlier and go to the Martin residence immediately after Mr. Martin left the base?"

Crimer shifts uncomfortably in his seat. He avoids eye contact with Commander Caldwell. He answers, "Shortly after Commander Caldwell took command, he ordered me not to interfere between Mr. Martin and his family, and he ordered me to instruct the master-at-arms force of the same."

Chatter erupts among the spectators.

Captain jack slams the gavel.

Powers cannot veil his astonishment and embarrassment. He realizes the lesser of the two damaging options would have been for him to have asked that question. Now, he appears to be someone attempting to hide the truth.

After the spectators quiet down, Maston asks, "Master Chief, why did Rigney Page's advisement of the obvious cause you to take action?"

"Hearing it from Page categorized and emphasized the danger to Constance and Laurie Martin. I just couldn't stand on the sidelines any longer."

Clapping and cheering erupt throughout the club. Some yell out, "Good for you, Master Chief."

Captain Jack slams the gavel repeatedly.

Commander Caldwell fumes. He is angered and offended by the cheers and applause from his crew. He wants to order all spectators from the club, but knows that such action would further alienate his crew, because it would convey he attempts to hide the truth.

Captain Jack warns, "One more outburst and I will clear the court." Again, Captain Jack knows he won't do that. *This is too much of a learning experience in the legal process. These sailors need to experience military justice in action. Seldom does such an opportunity arise.*

"No more questions," Maston states.

"No recross," Powers says while slumped in his chair and with his head bowed.

The judge orders, "Step down, Master Chief."

Crimer avoids eye contact with anyone as he returns to his seat.

Rigney again leans close to Maston and whispers, "Sir, this is disturbing. Revealing the truth should not need to depend on the cleverness of the officers of the court. I mean, if you were not as smart as you are, many lies would not be exposed and the truth never revealed. I mean, what if the roles of you and Mr. Powers in this proceeding were reversed?"

"Don't underestimate Mr. Powers's ability as defense counsel. I have seen him in action."

"Mr. Maston," Captain Jack calls from the bench. "Call your next witness."

Maston says, "I call Nikandros Papadopoulos."

Nikandros stands in the spectator's area and walks to the witness chair. A slim middle-aged Greek woman follows Nikandros to the stand.

Many in the courtroom wonder how a Greek national fits into all of this.

Maston explains, "Your honor, although Mr. Papadopoulos speaks English, we will use the NAVCOMMSTA contract linguist, Professor Callidora Tzathas, when needed."

Captain Jack says, "Proceed."

As Nikandros swears in, he smiles at Rigney.

When Maston asks Nikandros to identify the accused, Nikandros nods enthusiastically and replies, "Oh yes, Rig much friend."

"Mr. Papadopoulos, are you a lifetime resident of Nea Makri?"

Professor Tzathas translates.

"Yes," Nikandros replies in English.

"Mr. Papadopoulos, how long have you lived at your current residence?"

"Eleven years."

"Does U.S. Navy Warrant Officer Pritchings live directly across the street from you?"

Nikandros looks to the linguist for a Greek translation.

"Yes. Pritchings lives over road from me."

"When did Mr. Pritchings move into the house across from you?"

"Eight months before."

"Eight months ago," the linguist clarifies.

"When did Mr. Pritchings build the fence around his house?"

"Three months ago when he bring dog."

"Mr. Papadopoulos, we must be clear on this. You are saying that Pritchings built his fence just a few days prior to bringing his dog, Sparks, to his house."

Nikandros listens to the linguist's translation; then, he responds, "No fence before dog come."

"Mr. Papadopoulos, please tell us what happened on the afternoon when you met the accused."

Nikandros explains in Greek, and Professor Tzathas provides the English translation. "Sparks was barking for many hours when my neighbors and I finally came out of our houses to protest. Pritchings was not home. We were talking about calling police again when Pritchings came home. He wore his U.S. Navy white uniform. Sparks continued to bark and growl. Pritchings saw us gathering in the street in front of his house. Before going into his house, he waved the American finger at us. We all went back to our yards. Sparks continued to bark.

"About twenty minutes later. We all saw Rig jogging from top of the hill. He was pumping dumbbells as he jogged. He stopped in front of Pritchings's house and watched Sparks.

"Then Pritchings comes out of his house. He carries beer can and baseball bat. Then, he puts down beer and raises bat motioning he will swing bat at us. Then, he yells at my friend Rig, and Rig walks away downhill. Then, police come. Sparks attack police, and police give Pritchings another citation."

"Mr. Papadopoulos, tell us about the next few times you saw the accused."

Professor Tzathas translates the question and translates the testimony to English. "Several times my friend Rig exercises past my house. I stopped him one day and offered him tea. He fixed my radio and my player record. For my neighbor, Nobby, Rig help Nobby when automobile broke. He took Nobby and wife to store, and Rig helped repair automobile. My neighbor, Conrad, have broken electrical on water heater. Rig fixed. We have neighbor dinners outside and Rig comes. He tells us about his life in California, we tell him about Greece. We teach him Greek and Deutsch. Rig very nice American. We call him our friend."

Maston responds, "Thank you, Mr. Papadopoulos. Now, tell the court how often Mr. Pritchings's dog created disturbance in your neighborhood."

"Every day, all day. Only when Sparks inside Sparks quiet. Mr. Pritchings destroyed our neighborhood. Pritchings disrespects all people."

"Mr. Papadopoulos, describe the events of the afternoon when the accused killed Sparks."

Nikandros describes the sequence of events, including Pritchings's attack on Page with a baseball bat, and Page's defensive actions by throwing a dumbbell at Pritchings.

"No more questions," Maston announces.

Powers remains seated and studies the witness list. He sees that the next two witnesses are Pritchings's neighbors. Powers knows that the two witnesses will corroborate Papadopoulos's testimony. He knows the prosecution case will weaken if he attempts to discredit Papadopoulos and then the following two witnesses substantiate Papadopoulos's testimony.

"No questions," Powers advises.

Maston calls Nobby Clarke to the witness stand, and Nobby verifies Nikandros's testimony.

Powers cross examines Nobby. "How long have you and Mr. Papadopoulos been neighbors?"

"More than ten years."

"Are you friends?"

"Yes."

"No more questions."

Maston calls Conrad Borman to the witness stand, and Conrad substantiates the testimony of his neighbors.

"No questions," Powers informs.

Conrad returns to his seat in the spectators section.

Maston says, "Your honor, at this time I submit into testimony a statement signed by the captain of police for the town of Nea Makri. The entire statement and the attachments are translated into English. The translations have been verified as accurate by two separate professional linguists." Maston hands a copy to Captain Jack. "Your honor, the Nea Makri Captain of Police declined to appear as a defense witness. I request to describe in open court what his statement and attachments say."

Captain Jack looks at Powers and questions, "Does trial counsel have any objections?"

Powers stands and states, "Your honor, I have thoroughly read the statement and attachments. I have no objection to defense counsel describing the contents. I do reserve the right to object should I disagree with defense counsels description."

"The statement is accepted as evidence. Defense counsel may describe the contents of the statement and attachments."

Maston explains the police document. "Attached to the statement are citizen complaints against Chief Warrant Officer Pritchings. Please note that there are eighteen complaints. Some complaints regard Mr. Pritchings's disturbances of the peace through drunken acts of yelling and threats of physical violence against citizens of Nea Makri. Please note that some of the complaints are signed by the prior three witnesses. Also, please note half of the complaints report the day-and-night incessant barking of Mr. Pritchings's dog. The complaints state that residents within three blocks could not sleep at night. Note that two sailors stationed here at NAVCOMMSTA made two of the complaints and specify continuous barking and who are residents in Mr. Pritchings's neighborhood. On attachment pages four, eight, twelve, and sixteen, the police report they went to Mr. Pritchings's house to investigate. On two of those occasions, the police arrested Mr. Pritchings, because Mr. Pritchings was drunk and disorderly and because Mr. Pritchings threatened the police officers with a baseball bat. The report on those incidents includes results of sobriety tests, which show Mr. Pritchings was inebriated by the measurements dictated by Greek law. The police captain's written statement, which is the first page, describes three occasions when he came here to the NAVCOMMSTA to talk to the commanding officer about Mr. Pritchings's conduct. Please note that on the first occasion, the police captain talked with the previous commanding officer. During the two later visits, he talked with the current commanding officer, Commander Caldwell. That concludes my description."

"I have no objections," Powers declares.

Maston looks down at his witness list then calls, "Steward First Class Cassius Jackson to the stand."

The six-feet and four-inch tall, 280 pound, bulging belly, former all-city high school football tackle struts to the witness chair. The scars on his face and hands tell of brutal history of tough physical battles. He wears Service Dress Whites tailored-made to fit his tall and wide body.

After the preliminaries are complete, Maston asks Jackson, "Have you or Petty Officer Page ever engaged in a physical fight against each other?"

"No sur."

"Has Petty Officer Page ever beaten you up?"

"No sur, and he should never try."

Chuckles utter from the spectators.

"Did you hear Seaman Cussack's testimony this morning?"

"Yes sur."

Maston stands beside the witness chair and faces the spectators, and he asks, "What were you and Page doing when Cussack said that he would get the master-at-arms?"

"I ask Page to show ma som kung fu."

"So the hold Page had on you was at your request?"

"Sure was. He couldn' o done it if I didn' let him."

More chuckles from the spectators.

Captain Jack slams the gavel.

Maston continues his direct. "Petty Officer Jackson, have you ever operated a slush fund here at Nea Makri?"

Jackson hesitates. He shifts in his chair. He looks uncomfortable.

Maston orders, "Answer the question."

"I did, but no mo'. XO tol' me to stop."

"Did Petty Officer Page ever beat you up and take away your slush fund?"

"Page never beat me up and never take away my slush fund."

Rigney looks to the back of the room and expresses an *'I told you so'* smile to Senior Chief Hilton.

Hilton's expression remains stone-faced.

The XO concludes to herself, *settles that report chit charge.*

"No more questions," Maston declares.

"No cross," Powers announces.

Maston looks out at the spectators and says, "I recall Dorothea Caldwell to the witness stand."

Dottie stands from her chair in the spectator area and walks to the witness stand. She knows everyone stares at her. She conscientiously avoids too much sway of her hips.

"You are still under oath, Miss Caldwell," Captain Jack advises.

Maston stands close to the witness stand. He glances at a clipboard of papers he holds in his right hand. Then, he asks, "Miss Caldwell, you heard the testimony of Petty Officer Beaucamp this morning regarding that altercation between the accused and two Greek men?"

"Yes, I heard it."

"Tell the court what you observed the same evening."

"I was driving up the hill toward where Rigney lives. As I approached the corner of the street where he lives, I saw in my headlights two Greek men walk around the corner. Actually, they were more limping than walking. One was helping the other to walk. I thought it odd, because one of them was holding a length of chain in his hand. Then, they entered the backseat of a parked car. A sailor from the NAVCOMMSTA helped the Greeks into the car. Then, the sailor got in the driver's seat and drove off. I turned the corner and I saw Rigney and some of his neighbors standing in the street. Rigney held a pipe in his hand. Rigney later told me what happened."

Shameless! Powers says to himself. Maston is staging this.

The grin on Captain Jack's face reveals he thinks the same.

Mary Blakely also recognizes Mike Maston's strategy. She smiles at him with amused disapproval.

Newman fears exposure. He knows only a few moments remain before Dottie identifies him. He begins to stand and run, but realizes he has nowhere to run.

Again, to add drama to the proceedings, Maston stands by the witness chair and faces the spectators. He asks, "You said the two Greek men were helped and driven by a sailor from NAVCOMMSTA. Is that sailor in the courtroom? If he is, please identify him."

"Yes, he is in the courtroom." Dottie points to the spectator section and says, "The sailor sitting in the fourth row, the one everyone calls Newman."

Comments and chatter erupt in the courtroom. Everyone in the courtroom turns their heads toward the fourth row and focuses their eyes on Newman.

Captain Jack slams the gavel and orders sternly, "Order in the court. Spectators are ordered silent!"

Newman sits lower in his chair, thinking he can disappear from the disapproving stares cast toward him.

Silence falls over the courtroom.

Maston turns his eyes toward Powers and says, "Your witness."

Powers stands and approaches the witness chair; he asks in a challenging tone, "Miss Caldwell, would you characterize your relationship with the accused as intimate?"

"Objection! Irrelevant!" Maston says in a loud voice.

Powers explains, "Your honor, my question goes to motivations regarding the witness's testimony."

Captain Jack responds. "Objection overruled. The witness will answer."

Dottie feels embarrassed. She must reveal to all in the courtroom her sexual relationship with Rigney; she asks, "Would you repeat the question, please?"

"Miss Caldwell, would you characterize your relationship with the accused as intimate?"

"Yes," Dottie replies with her eyes on Rigney.

A few unintelligible comments raise from the spectators—not loud enough or numerous to cause Captain Jack to use the gavel.

Rigney nods slightly and smiles appreciatively, acknowledging the significance of what Dottie just revealed to her family.

"Miss Caldwell, you testified the accused later told you what happened. When and where did he tell you about it?"

"About thirty minutes after I arrived. In his bathroom when I was treating the cuts and bruises around his eye."

"When you say in his bathroom, do you mean his bathroom in the house known as Anna's Villa?"

"Yes."

"Is that when you and the accused invented a plan to frame Seaman Newman for the incident?"

Dottie expected the question. Lieutenant Maston briefed her that trial counsel would probably ask it.

Maston could object, but he doesn't. An objection would appear as trying to hide possible connivance. Maston briefed Dottie on how to respond.

A quizzical look appears on Captain Jack's face. He wonders why Maston does not object; then, it hits him. He smiles.

Powers demands, "Answer the question."

Dottie declares, "Sir, you did not ask a question. You made an accusation."

A few low-volume chuckles rise from the spectators.

"Rephrase," Captain Jack orders.

"Miss Caldwell, did you and the accused invent a plan to frame Seaman Newman?"

"No," Dottie answers firmly and confidently.

Powers stares directly into Dottie's eyes and advises, "Miss Caldwell, are you aware of the punishment for perjury?"

"Yes. I could be fined or sent to jail or both."

"Good that you understand that, Miss Caldwell. I ask you again, did you and the accused invent the story you told about Seaman Newman?"

Maston stands and says loudly, "Objection! Already asked and answered!"

"Sustained," Captain Jack rules. "Move on, Mr. Powers."

Powers nods and asks, "Miss Caldwell, prior to your testimony here today, did you report Newman's alleged involvement to anyone besides the accused?"

"No."

"Why not?"

"Rigney asked me not to."

"Did the accused tell you why he did not want you to tell anyone?"

"No."

"You were not curious as to why he wanted you to hide Seaman Newman's alleged involvement?"

"Objection," Maston declares with a resigned tone. "The question assumes facts not in evidence. No evidence has been submitted that the accused and the witness conspired to hide anything."

"Sustained."

Powers refers to his notes; then, he asks, "Miss Caldwell, how many times did you spend the night at the residence known as Anna's Villa."

"Objection. Irrelevant."

Captain Jack looks at Powers to prompt argument.

"I withdraw the question."

"Miss Caldwell, what is the relationship between this Anna and the accused?"

"Objection. Irrelevant and calls for an opinion."

"Sustained. Mr. Powers, move on."

"No more questions," Powers advises.

"Any redirect?" Captain Jack asks Maston.

"No redirect."

"The witness may step down."

As Dottie walks back to her seat, she avoids looking at Newman.

Newman eyes shoot lightning bolts at Dottie. He formulates revenge.

Chapter 85

Maston dramatically delays announcement of his next witness. He stands at the defense table and shuffles a stack of papers. Then, he pulls a sheet from the stack and studies it.

Powers shakes his head at the shameful display.

Captain Jack looks disapprovingly at Maston.

Rigney looks at Maston questioningly. He knows Pritchings is up next.

The spectators audibly shift in their seats, and a soft mumbling rises.

Captain Jack hits the gavel on the desk and orders, "Defense counsel, call your next witness."

"I call Chief Warrant Officer Donald Pritchings."

Pritchings walks from the spectator section to the witness stand. Unlike earlier in the day, Pritchings's white uniform is pressed and immaculate. This uniform better fits his obese stature. His shoes are spit-shined. His shoulder boards look new, and the gold shines bright.

Captain Jack advises, "Mr. Pritchings, you are still under oath."

Pritchings nods and responds, "I understand, your honor."

Maston says, "Your honor, I request that Mr. Pritchings be declared a hostile witness."

"So recorded."

Pritchings looks up at Captain Jack and says, "Your honor, I will not be hostile. I will not lie, anymore—too many—too many lies." Pritchings chokes up, and his eyes mist over. His chest heaves up and down rapidly. He shakes, and he is on the verge of crying. "It's not Page's fault. We conspired against him. I am so sorry. Captain Caldwell forced me to do it. I thought—"

Commander Caldwell jumps to his feet and commands, "Mr. Pritchings—silence!"

Powers stands. "Objection, immaterial, irrelevant, accusatory, facts not in evidence, improper direct, and—"

"Sustained."

Captain Jack orders, "The reporter shall strike all the witness's statement." Then, he says to Pritchings, "Mr. Pritchings, you must follow court procedure. Respond only to the questions you are asked."

Pritchings cannot catch his breath. He grips the arms of the chair so tight that his knuckles are white. His face is beet red. His chest heaves. His uniform becomes drenched in sweat.

Maston moves quickly toward Pritchings. "What's wrong?" he asks.

Pritchings lips move rapidly, but he cannot speak.

Captain Jack scans the spectators, and his eyes land on Mary Blakely; he orders, "Commander Blakely, get the corpsman over here!"

The XO nods to the judge. She turns to a chief who stands a few feet from her. She speaks a few words, and the chief jogs from the building.

Captain Jack slams the gavel to the table. "The court is in recess until further notice."

No one moves—no one dares leave and risk missing the most intriguing military courtroom drama since the Caine Mutiny.

The XO goes to the witness stand and checks Pritchings's pulse. She places her hand on his chest. His heart beats fast but beats steady.

Conversations burst out all over the club. No one moves more than a few inches for concern over losing their chairs.

Several minutes later, the command corpsman, with stethoscope around his neck and medical bag in hand, moves swiftly through the spectators.

The XO and Lieutenant Maston stand aside to allow the corpsman access to Pritchings.

"I think he is breathing easier, now," the XO tells doc.

Doc checks Pritchings's vitals. Pritchings heart rate is fast, but the rate is steady.

"Lay your head back, Mr. Pritchings, and try to take regular breaths."

Fifteen minutes later, Pritchings's breathing and heart rate are back to normal.

Doc says to Commander Blakely, "XO, Mr. Pritchings is okay. I think he had an anxiety attack."

Captain Jack asks, "Mr. Pritchings, are you ready to resume your testimony?"

Pritchings sighs deeply and replies, "Yes sir. I am ready to tell the truth."

Maston asks, "Mr. Pritchings, tell us what you want to change in your previous testimony."

"Everything, except that Page killed Sparks. That part is true, but I lied about everything else. They hated me from the beginning, always complaining about Sparks and loud music. They never invited me to any of their gatherings. Neither did any of my shipmates who lived on the next block. Page did not lead my neighbors against me. I bought Sparks to annoy my neighbors. I put up the fence, because I knew Sparks was dangerous, not to me, but to my neighbors. Sparks loved me. The farmer I bought Sparks from told me Sparks was vicious and that Sparks killed some of his sheep."

Maston asks, "Mr. Pritchings, do you blame the accused for the death of your dog?"

"No sir. Page was protecting himself. Sparks would have ripped him apart. I've had time to think about it. Page did what he had to do."

Rigney lets out a big sigh.

Maston turns to the spectator section; he notices that Commander Caldwell is no longer in the courtroom.

Maston turns and faces the witness; then, he asks, "Why did you change your testimony?"

Powers says from his chair at the prosecution table, "Objection, Irrelevant?"

Maston responds, "Your honor, I believe this witness will provide the key evidence that will cause your honor to recommend dismissal of the charges against my client. I beg your honor's indulgence to continue this line of questioning."

Captain Jack says, "Objection overruled."

"Mr. Pritchings, why did you change your testimony?"

Pritchings shifts in his chair; he cannot look Maston in the eye. He chokes back a sob. "Life has been miserable since my wife and boy were killed. I am jealous of those who have happy family lives. I wanted to make everyone else miserable, too. That's why I acted the way I did against my neighbors and my shipmates.

"This morning when you made it so obvious that I was lying, it was like the final blow to my diminishing existence." Tears seep from Pritchings's eyes. He takes two rapid breaths. "When I looked around the courtroom and saw stares of disgust and contempt from my shipmates, I concluded my only redemption was to tell the truth."

Pritchings wipes his hand against his cheek to remove tears.

Maston stares intently at Pritchings, wondering if Pritchings will truthfully answer the next question.

"Mr. Pritchings, you have just explained why you changed your testimony. Now, why did you lie when you gave direct testimony as a prosecution witness?"

"I was trying to save my career. I only have two more years to qualify for retirement. I know that is not possible now." Pritchings glances apologetically at the prosecutor.

Maston asks, "How would that have saved your military career?"

"I was going to tell you," Pritchings insists. "My last two fitness reports are the worst ever. When I was a chief radioman, I had four-oh across the board. Then, my wife and my son were killed. I understand, now, how their deaths changed me. My life disintegrated and my navy career went down the toilet. I feared that my next evaluation would lead to me being busted out of the navy. Then, last week, Commander Caldwell called me into his office. He told me that it was important that Petty Officer Page be found guilty of the assault and battery charges. He told me that Page is part of that new breed of enlisted who are arrogant, too confident, and who too easily challenge authority. He told me that my testimony could convict Page. Commander Caldwell promised that if Page was convicted based on my testimony, he would write a special fitness report on me that would carry me to retirement."

Maston asks, "For clarification, Mr. Pritchings. When Page was in your office after the first incident, did he threaten to beat you up like he did Mr. Martin?"

Pritchings takes a deep breath and replies, "Page did not threaten me. Commander Caldwell told me to say that."

A deafening silence falls over the courtroom. The spectators sit absolutely still and hold their breath in reaction to Pritchings's revelation. Then, they all exhale at the same time.

"No more questions," Maston states.

"No questions," Powers states.

"The defense has no more witnesses or evidence to submit."

Captain Jack looks at his watch; then, he announces, "Court will recess until 10:00 AM tomorrow. At that time, I will hear summations." He slams the gavel to the table.

"All rise."

After Captain Jack departs the club, Rigney turns to Lieutenant Maston and asks, "How did you know about Commander Caldwell?"

Maston smiles knowingly at Rigney and replies, "I didn't know for sure. I sensed it."

Rigney shakes his head in bewilderment. He glances at the spectator section and sees Dottie smiling at him. *The Professor* and Vance give him thumbs-up.

Maston busies himself with stuffing folders into his briefcase; then, he looks at Rigney and says, "See you tomorrow morning."

Rigney asks, "Sir, you don't think I'm off the hook. Do you?"

With a serious expression on his face, Maston replies, "I destroyed Newman's credibility, and I forced Mr. Pritchings to reverse his testimony. Just because they lied, does not mean you are innocent of assault and battery."

"What do you think the judge will decide?"

"I don't know. During summation, I must convince him that your actions against Martin were not because you are violent and aggressive, but because you wanted to save two helpless females."

Rigney nods understanding.

Lieutenant Maston departs the club.

Rigney walks over to Dottie Caldwell. Dottie throws her arms around Rigney and hugs him.

While they hug, Rigney watches ET2 Patterson walk up to Master Chief Spyke, who stands a few feet away. Rigney hears the conversation between Patterson and Spyke.

"Master Chief, I am ET2 Patterson. May I speak with you for a few minutes?"

"Sure Patterson, what's it about."

"I heard you were talking to the sailors. Anyone tell you about the air-conditioning failure and the security violations?"

Spyke glances around quickly, determining if anyone heard Patterson. Spyke's eyes land on Page for a few moments, understanding Page heard Patterson's words.

Patterson notices Spyke's stare at Page and confides, "Page already knows about it, Master Chief. He can verify everything I tell you."

"Let's find some privacy," Spyke advises.

Dottie and Rigney continue hugging as Patterson and Spyke depart the club.

Chapter 86

Donald Pritchings does not bother to turn on the lights in his house. He sits, limply in the dark and holds to his breast a picture of his wife and child. He weeps uncontrollably. His emotions tortured by the memories of that night in Norfolk five years ago.

After spending the day at the beach, they were covered with sand, were irritable, and tired. Donald drove the family station wagon along the expressway, not looking forward to the forty-five-minute drive to their home in Norfolk. His wife, Sharon, sat on the passenger side of the front seat. His little boy, Ronnie, sat between them.

Ronnie fidgeted and fussed. Sharon attempted to quiet him.

Donald lit a cigarette and tried to relax. He had smoked half the cigarette and held it in the fingers of his right hand. While fidgeting, Ronnie bumped his father's arm. Donald accidentally dropped the cigarette on the seat between his legs. He took his eyes off the road and stared at his lap as he searched for the burning cigarette.

"Look out!" Sharon had yelled.

Donald looked up and panicked when he saw that he was speeding on the shoulder and headed for a deep ditch. He slammed his right foot on the brake, but his foot slipped off the brake pedal and hit the gas peddle. He could not recover. The rapid acceleration launched the vehicle off the shoulder and into the ditch. The station wagon hit the far bank of the ditch head-on.

Ronnie and Sharon went through the windshield and were killed. The steering wheel held Donald in the vehicle, and he came away with a collapsed lung and some broken ribs.

He later told the police that some joyriding kids forced his station wagon off the road. The police accepted the lie, and Pritchings was free to live his life.

Several weeks later, He found his name on the warrant officer selection list. That event triggered feelings of guilt. He caused the deaths of his wife and child, lied about it, and then the navy rewards him with significant advancement in his naval career.

Eventually, guilt led to self-loathing. Self-loathing led to poor performance. Poor evaluations led to anger toward his shipmates and himself. He gradually became mean and spiteful. Misery controlled his existence, and he sought to initiate misery in others.

As time passed, he found himself frequently weeping, sorrowfully in the dark. He ached from the absence of his wife and child and from the absence of the man he once was.

A milestone in his path to self-destruction came in the form of a special fitness report written five months ago by the departing commanding officer. The fitness report specified that Pritchings had six months to improve his performance to the level of an officer and a gentleman, or Pritchings should be reduced in rank back to chief petty officer or possibly petty officer first class or should be dismissed from the navy.

With only two years remaining until he qualified for retirement, Pritchings feared loss of retirement benefits. Then, earlier this week, Commander Caldwell offered salvation.

"That Page is part of a growing cancer eating away at the good order and discipline of the navy," Caldwell had told Pritchings. "Donald, you can help stop that cancer. If Page's case goes to court-martial, it will scare others like him. You just need to testify to his true nature during the UCMJ hearing."

"I'm not sure I know how to do that," Pritchings had told Caldwell.

"I will coach you," Caldwell said. "Testify as I say, and I will write a special fitness report that will carry you to retirement."

I prostituted myself today—like a whore. For what? Nothing! Lieutenant Maston so easily revealed my lying. I looked foolish. I saw the look of disgust on all their faces. My God! I have fallen so far! I cannot cope in this pit! I cannot survive!

Does anyone remember that spit-and-polish, squared-away chief? Do they remember that lean and confident sailor who all held in high regard? Officers came to me for advice! No, those days are over. I am in that void where my essence has no value. I no longer exist, and no one cares. I am a coward, and I must commit one more cowardly act.

Pritchings raises the .44 magnum revolver and nestles the barrel just above his right ear. The pistol shakes in his hand. He lowers the pistol to his lap.

His weeping turns to chest-heaving sobs. "I must to this!" he cries out. "I am not worthy to survive!"

With no more thoughts, he raises the pistol to his right temple and pulls the trigger.

Earlier, about 5:00 PM, Pritchings's neighbors had gathered on Nikandros Papadopoulos's front patio. Rigney's trial was the topic of conversation.

About an hour later, Pritchings parked his car in his driveway. He still wore his white uniform. After exiting his car, Pritchings stood in the driveway and looked across the road at his neighbors who all sat on Nik's patio. Pritchings cast an expression that begged for their forgiveness. No one understood Pritchings's expression; they remained silent. Feeling rejected, Pritchings entered his house.

Nik cooked up a batch of souvlaki meat, vegetables, and pita bread on his outside grill. They ate heartily. By sundown, they were starting on their second case of Amstel.

The conversation on Nik's patio again turns to Pritchings. Nobby Clarke makes a point as he nods toward Pritchings's house. Someone comments that Pritchings's house is dark. No lights shine from any window. All turned their heads toward Pritchings's house. A few seconds later, a flash of light appears through the living room window, followed almost instantaneously by a loud blast. All know it was a gunshot.

Several stand and take a few steps toward Pritchings's house but do not step off Nik's patio.

Nik says solemnly, "I phone police and American base."

Chapter 87

Pritchings's suicide is the talk of the base. Rigney first hears about it from Bob Vance shortly after entering Club Zeus. Rigney's eyes go wide in disbelief as Vance explains what he knows. As he walks to his seat at the defense table, Rigney considers his role in Pritchings's suicide.

Last night, he and Dottie ate dinner at their favorite Nea Makri restaurant. Wine flowed freely as they celebrated the turn in Pritchings's testimony. They enjoyed their evening, and Dottie spent the night in the villa.

Powers begins. "Your honor, this is a simple case of the accused assaulting and committing a battery against a commissioned officer. The accused reacted impulsively and did not stop to consider what was happening and who was involved.

"Regulations and procedures exist for military members to report acts of violence. The accused chose not to follow those regulations.

"Defense counsel has submitted voluminous mitigating evidence, but defense does not address that the accused exceeded that force necessary to stop Lieutenant Martin. Witnesses have testified that Lieutenant Martin was forced to stop hitting his daughter when the accused grabbed Lieutenant Martin's wrist. Then, the accused willfully and without provocation and without threats toward himself did strike down Lieutenant Martin.

"Exceeding that force necessary to protect others is a violation of military law under the UCMJ. The accused is guilty of violating the excessive force code, and is, thereby, guilty of assault and battery and he should be punished as a court-martial may direct."

Powers sits down and lets out a deep sigh.

Maston stands and begins. "Your honor, Petty Officer Page is unjustly accused, and he is the victim of selective prosecution. He is unjustly accused because he has not violated the law. Military law allows a military person to defend others from assault and battery. In this case, Petty Officer Page intervened to protect Constance and Laurie Martin when no one else would. Petty Officer Page's actions were not criminal. The UCMJ permits his actions.

"There are no facts that prove Page exceeded that force necessary provisions of the UCMJ. Some witnesses testified that the accused hit Lieutenant Martin before Lieutenant Martin took a swing at the accused. An equal number of witnesses testified that the accused hit Lieutenant Martin only after Martin threw a punch at the accused. Therefore, there is conflicting testimony as to the sequence of events.

"The accused is not an aggressive and violent person as counsel for the United States charges. Seaman Newman's testimony must be discarded as the testimony of a prejudiced person.

"Regarding the accused's actions toward Lieutenant Martin, Petty Officer Page was not the aggressor. Page reacted to the aggressive and violent actions of Lieutenant Martin, and Page reacted within the legal parameters of navy regulations and the UCMJ. Additionally, both the NAVCOMMSTA Chief-master-at-Arms and the NAVCOMMSTA Executive Officer thoroughly investigated, and they did not find evidence sufficient to charge Petty Officer Page. Yet, Commander Caldwell, the uncle of Lieutenant Martin, ordered the NAVCOMMSTA Chief-master-at-Arms to charge Page with assault and battery.

"Regarding the death of the dog named Sparks. Killing sparks was the tragic result of Chief Warrant Officer Pritchings's irresponsible actions. In the end, Mr. Pritchings did the right thing by claiming responsibility for his dog's death. Again, Petty Officer Page was not the violent aggressor. He reacted to violent aggression against him.

"The fight with the two Greeks in front of Page's residence was initiated by Seaman Newman as substantiated by the witness

Dorothea Caldwell. Again, the accused was not an aggressor. He acted in self-defense. I recommend that your honor order an investigation into Seaman Newman's culpability.

"Chief Warrant Officer Pritchings testified that he and Commander Caldwell conspired to lie about Page's actions. I recommend that your honor order an investigation into that alleged conspiracy, and the possible criminal actions of improper command influence by Commander Caldwell.

"The defense argues that had Commander Caldwell exercised reasonable command judgment in the first place, he would have shipped Lieutenant Martin back to the states months ago and the encounter with the accused would never have occurred. It was just a matter of time before some courageous person finally came forward to stop Lieutenant Martin during one of his vicious attack on his family.

"Petty Officer Page is the victim of selective prosecution. Witnesses have testified to the continuous assault and battery committed by Lieutenant Martin against Constance and Laurie Martin. However, no charges of assault and battery were ever initiated by the Nea Makri chain-of-command. Yet, Commander Caldwell ordered charges against the accused after the accused acted chivalrously and honorably to protect the safety of Constance and Laurie Martin.

"Based on the evidence collected during this hearing, I respectfully ask your honor to forward to the convening authority a recommendation that the charges against Petty Officer Page be dismissed. That concludes the defense summation, your honor."

Captain Jack looks at his watch; then, he states, "We will reconvene at 1500. At that time, I will announce my recommendations."

Captain Jack slams the gavel to the tabletop.

"All rise!"

"Be back here at 1450," Maston tells Rigney. Then Maston walks over to Powers, and the two engage in conversation. Powers busily writes notes.

Rigney stands alone at the defense table, not sure what he should do next. Then, he notices Lieutenant Linderhaus walking toward him.

"Page, I need you to come to the communications trailers. Straton is having a tough time troubleshooting a problem on one of the T-37s, need your assistance on it."

"Yes, sir, will do. I must be back here at 1450."

"No problem. I have my car outside. I will drive you to the trailers compound."

At 1500, Captain Jack settles in his chair and brings the court to order. Spectators jam the courtroom beyond its safe capacity.

"I have reviewed all evidence, and I find the evidence lacking to support the charges against Petty Officer Page. I will recommend to the convening authority to dismiss all charges."

Spectators jump to their feet. Applause and cheering erupt throughout the club.

No one hears Captain Jack say, "This hearing is adjourned."

Captain Jack slams the gavel, which no one hears.

"All rise." No one hears.

Chapter 88

The top is down on the BMW. Rigney sits in the driver seat. He glances at the air terminal exit of the Athens Hellinikon International Airport. He waits for Anna. A cool Aegean breeze wafts across him. The night air refreshes him after the life-sucking heat of the afternoon. He smells the Aegean Sea that lay a short distance to the west. He wonders what kept Anna away these many weeks.

Every several minutes, he looks to the northeast and enjoys the view of Athenian lights sloping up the mountains that he drove over just two hours before.

As he sits in the BMW, he continually scans the parking lot for any unusual activity. His senses sharpen each time someone comes close.

A crowd of people exits the terminal. Anna is one of them. She wears rumpled khaki-colored pants and a wrinkled pink blouse. Her appearance reveals the long, tiring TWA flight from New York.

Rigney steps out of the BMW and waves toward her.

She sees him and quickens her step. She throws her suitcase in the backseat, opens the passenger side door, and drops herself into the seat. She lets out a loud and long sigh and pushes her hair away from her face.

"Let's get home," she pleads. "I need a shower and a good night's sleep." She wraps a scarf around her head and ties it under her chin.

"Damn, it's so hot and humid," Anna complains. "I thought the summer climate would be over by now."

"Do you have anything to brief me on?" Rigney asks casually.

"Yes, but it can wait 'til morning."

The drive through Athens traffic and over the mountain to Nea Makri takes nearly two hours. After Rigney parks the BMW in the villa's courtyard and locks the villa's gate, he jerks Anna's suitcase from the backseat. He follows her into the villa.

She passes Rigney's open bedroom door on the way to her bedroom. She stops, turns, and steps a few feet into Rigney's bedroom.

She sniffs the air. "You've had a woman in here." She states with a disapproving tone.

Rigney remains silent.

"Well, I didn't order you not to. Nothing in this house was compromised, was it?"

Rigney smiles.

"I mean other than the woman." Anna smiles and shakes her head slightly.

"No. Dottie knows nothing about the purpose of this place."

"Dottie Caldwell?"

"Yes."

"She hasn't returned to the States, yet?"

"No."

Anna turns and exits Rigney's bedroom.

When they reach the door to her bedroom, she takes her suitcase from Rigney and says, "Tomorrow morning . . . wake me at seven and have breakfast ready. I want yogurt, dates, strawberries, and that Turkish coffee I like. If we don't have any of those items, go get them."

Anna turns, walks through the doorway, then closes the door behind her.

Rigney stares at the closed door. He says to himself, *we don't have any of those things.*

While Anna was gone, he ate most of his meals at the base or at restaurants in Athens and Nea Makri. The villa's cupboards and refrigerator are bare.

He looks at his watch—11:30 PM. *Where am I gonna get that stuff this time of night?*

Chapter 89

Rigney knocks on Anna's bedroom door. "Seven o'clock," he says loudly.

"Alright, I'm up," Anna responds from behind the door.

Fifteen minutes later, Anna enters the kitchen. She wears a lightweight midthigh bathrobe. The low fold across her breasts reveals more cleavage than she wants, but she is too weary to be modest.

Rigney pours rich dark Turkish coffee into small white cups.

Anna sits down to a buffet of yogurt, strawberries, dates, toast, and poached eggs.

"Looks like you have kept the kitchen well stocked," Anna says with an appreciative smile on her face.

"Yes ma'am."

Rigney does not tell her that he was up at 0430, went to the base chow hall, and collected on a favor from MS2 Benedict; then, he made several stops at roadside fruit stands.

Anna and Rigney sit silent for ten minutes while they eat.

After finishing her first cup of Turkish coffee, she begins her briefing. "CIA and NSA have uncovered a massive espionage attack against NAVCOMMSTA Greece. Master Chief Rodgers's involvement is only a segment of the total espionage effort. The discovery of that yacht and your later action of attaching that beacon transmitter has led CIA along a path rich in foreign intelligence operatives. The Russians are bombarding NAVCOMMSTA Greece with COMINT, ELINT, and HUMINT."

Anna takes another sip of coffee; then, she continues, "Your intel report on the air-conditioning failure has moved up our counterespionage timeline. The Russians are running their operation out of a house in Marathon. It's the same house where Rodgers delivers his black market goods. The yacht operation and the Rodgers operation appear separate and not connected.

"CIA and ONI are pooling resources on this one. Your role is expanding. In addition to watching Rodgers on base, you must listen for any talk about top secret operations at the NAVCOMMSTA transmitter site at Kato Souli and report what you hear to me."

"I've already heard about that," Rigney advises.

Anna raises her eyebrows and asks, "What have you heard?"

"Just pieces of conversations and some observations."

"Where?"

"In the communications trailers . . . I heard several technical controllers talking about the delta trailer at the Kato Souli transmitter site. When I asked them about it, they told me that if I didn't already know, then, I was not supposed to know. While tracing some cabling, I discovered a black patch on the technical control patch panel that carries signals from the U.S. Embassy in Athens and routes those signals to the delta trailer."

"What's a black patch?"

"That's when NAVCOMMSTA is used only as a relay point for signals originated and encrypted elsewhere and destined for some distant location."

"What have you concluded?"

"I think there is a secret U.S. Government organization operating some transmitter assets at Kato Souli, and the U.S. Embassy in Athens has something to do with it. I think the embassy originates a classified signal that is used to key transmitters at Kato Souli."

Anna stares wide-eyed and astounded at Rigney as he describes exactly what is happening. She wonders why this young sailor hesitates at becoming a full-time counterespionage operative. *He's a natural!*

Rigney understands Anna's stare, and he says, "I guess I nailed it, huh?"

She nods affirmative a few times. Then, she says, "Yes, and it's that secret operation in the delta trailer that must be protected above all others. My orders from director ONI are to assist CIA operatives with shutting down the enemy's espionage activities. Director ONI also ordered me to involve you with any actions to shut down the enemy's operation."

"What kind of things must I do?"

"A CIA field operative will guide you. You know John Smith. He will direct you."

Confused, Rigney blinks his eyes several times. "When did John leave ONI and join CIA?"

"He's always been CIA."

Rigney takes a few moments and reflects on his experiences with John Smith; then, he says, "Well, that explains a lot."

They continue eating breakfast. After several minutes, Anna advises, "Starting today, we will receive CIA intelligence reports and orders for this mission."

"Anything else you want me to do right now?"

"Well, don't you have a poker game at Rodgers's house tonight?"

"Yes, but plan on not going."

"You must go. What time does the game start?"

"It starts at six, but I always arrive at eight, to make Rodgers anxious about separating me from my money."

"You must go to the poker game, and you must find out what's in Rodgers's garage."

"That could be risky. He keeps the garage locked, and there are bars over the windows. I don't know where he keeps the keys."

"Then, break-in."

He looks questioningly at Anna and considers how he could break-in without those in the poker game hearing him.

Anna reads his mind and says, "Do it when no one is there, then."

"That would be during normal working hours, during daylight. With our workload in the repair shop, I don't think I could get permission to get away. It would draw attention."

"Rig, this mission is coming to a climax. Chances are we will destroy the enemy's operations by the end of the week. Now is not the time to be concerned with navy propriety. Just pick a time today and go to Rodgers's house."

"Okay. Will do."

"Starting today, you must carry a weapon. I recommend the smallest of the automatic pistols. I have ankle holsters for all of them."

Chapter 90

Master Chief Raymond Rodgers sits in the executive officer's office and faces the XO across her desk.

"Master Chief, this directive from CINCUSNAVEUR directs immediate audits of all morale, welfare, and recreation activities."

Rodgers easily hides his apprehension. He had read about the MWR scandals at bases in Vietnam and other WESTPAC commands. The first news of military personnel skimming money off the top of revenue from enlisted clubs and other MWR activities surfaced about one year ago. Other activities included selling U.S. products on the black market. The press labeled the guilty army personnel as the Khaki Mafia.

Anticipating that his books for Club Zeus would be examined someday, he created another set of official books. However, his apprehension stems from uncertainty as to how well his official books hide his criminal activity. His only accounting education came from reading the procedures in the MWR manuals.

"The audit is not necessary, XO. I can assure you that all Club Zeus activities are properly handled."

"This is a theater-wide directive, Master Chief. Your operation is not under suspicion or a target. The CINC wants no question or doubt regarding the ethical operation of activities under his command. Until recently, all MWR activities were controlled by the local command and without oversight from higher commands. This message states that eventually all MWR oversight will be with theater commanders. The purpose of the theater-wide audit is to establish a baseline for MWR operations. There are no exceptions to this audit."

"Who will perform the audit?" Rodgers asks.

"The captain has directed that I perform the audit," Mary Blakely replies. "He feels that I am the most qualified, because I have degrees in finance and accounting."

Rodgers nods nonchalantly, but he becomes mentally agitated. His mind races through the pages of the official books and worries about what might look suspicious.

"When will the audit begin?"

"Immediately."

"Okay, I will go to the club and lay out the books for you, and I will be available for opening the safe."

"Your assistance won't be necessary, Master Chief. The direction from CINCUSNAVEUR states that all MWR activities must be closed during the audit and must be guarded by the master-at-arms force. Master Chief Crimer is at the club now. He is closing it down and installing locks on all doors. As of this moment, you and club employees are not allowed access to the club until the audit is over. You must give me the combinations and keys to all safes and storage spaces."

Rodgers had not anticipated this maneuver. Both sets of books are in his office safe in Club Zeus. He thinks of ways to get into the club office. He instinctively considers appealing to his fellow master chief. *No. That won't work. Crimer is squeaky-clean ethical. He will become suspicious at any attempt of me trying to get into Club Zeus, and he will report that attempt to the XO.*

"I will let you know when you can reopen the club," the XO advises Rodgers. She stands to indicate the meeting is over.

Rodgers stands and says, "Let me know if there is anything I can do to assist."

As Rodgers drives to the communications trailers compound, he evaluates how long it will take the XO to discover his illegal activities. He considers that she may not understand the discrepancies she finds, and she will ask him for clarification. *I won't have convincing answers, and the XO is too smart to buy a load of bullshit.*

Rodgers decides not to make a rash decision about what he must do, but he comprehends that he must make the decision by tomorrow morning. I can't panic or do anything out of the ordinary. I must go ahead with the tonight's poker game.

Chapter 91

Rigney parks the BMW one block away from Rodgers's house. The heat, humidity, and bright sun of the afternoon drains his energy as he walks across the street and enters the dirt alley that leads to the back of Rodgers's house. He wears an army-green-colored cotton t-shirt and olive green-colored trousers. He hopes to blend into the tall shrubbery that borders the backyards on both sides of the alley.

Usually he wears shorts, but now he must wear long pants to hide the compact 9 millimeter caliber Beretta and silencer in the holster strapped to his right ankle. He wears low-cut sneakers, instead of his usual sandals so that he can effectively run when needed. Work gloves and an eighteen-inch crowbar are tucked into his belt. A bosun's knife in a leather case and a small flashlight in a leather case are clipped to his belt.

As he walks along the alley, Rigney sees no one. Siesta and the heat of the day keep most people indoors. He must count the houses from the corner. All the houses are white stucco with red-tiled roofs. When he reaches the fifth house, he looks between the shrubs and into Rodgers's backyard. He does not expect to see anyone, because Rodgers is still at work at the NAVCOMMSTA.

He slips between two shrubs and enters the backyard. Two feet high weeds blanket the ground. The house, garage, and tall shrubs enclose the backyard and hide him from the prying eyes of neighbors.

He discovers a back door to the house. He tests the door and finds it locked.

Typically, garages in the town of Nea Makri are white stucco with red-tiled roofs and stand separated from the house, but Rodgers's garage connects to the house where the kitchen door should be. Rigney moves closer to that part of the house that connects to the garage. He observes that the connection to the house is an add-on construction of white stucco with red-tiled roof.

He walks around the outside of the garage and inspects the structure for weak points. There are two windows; both painted black on the inside, and both have bars. One window faces the driveway, to the front of Rodgers's house. The other faces the backyard. He determines that the security for the garage is only strong enough to prevent the casual trespasser from entering. He decides to pull several bars from the window facing the backyard; the location of that window hides him from the neighbors.

He puts on the work gloves and uses the chisel end of the crowbar to remove stucco around the bars. Forty-five minutes later, he has chiseled out three bars. He uses the crowbar to break the black-painted window glass. On the other side of the window, stacked boxes block access through the window. The boxes have logos of brand-name American cigarettes. He reaches through the broken window and pushes one of the stacked boxes. He receives heavy resistance.

He grabs the top of the window frame with both hands as if it is a curl bar; then, he swings his body, feet first, into the garage. His feet hit the stacked cigarette boxes; the stack of boxes collapse and cushion him as he lands on his back.

He stands and looks around the small one-car garage. The sweltering, hot, and humid interior of the garage causes his t-shirt and trousers to become drenched in sweat, and sweat flows from his forehead into his eyes. He looks around for something to wear as a sweatband. The sunlight penetrating through the broken window does not provide sufficient illumination. He uses his flashlight to investigate the interior of the garage.

He finds an old dark green towel hanging on a nail. He tears a strip of cloth from the towel and ties the strip around his forehead to serve as a sweatband.

He tests the lock on the door that leads to the house—locked from the other side.

He circles the interior of the garage. He finds the window that faces the street. Using the bosun's knife, he scrapes away a two-inch square of black paint. He looks through the square and easily views the street that runs past the front of the house.

Using his small flashlight, he quickly checks the labels on boxes. He estimates the garage contains forty boxes of cigarettes, twenty boxes of quality liquor and brandy, and thirty cases of American beer. He also finds cases of American soft drinks and mixers. Stenciled across all the boxes are the words FOR SALE IN THE ARMY & AIR FORCE EXCHANGE SERVICE ONLY.

The hum of a motor causes him to slide aside some boxes. He discovers a freezer unit six feet long and four feet deep. He opens the lid. The freezing cold air rolls out of the freezer and cools his skin. The freezer contains cases of steaks, ribs, and hamburger. He holds the freezer lid open for several minutes to aid cooling his body.

He searches for goods he might have missed during the first round. He finds a large footlocker wedged into a corner. The words on the locker read Athens Rod and Gun Club. The lid is locked. He breaks the lock hinge with the crowbar. Inside the footlocker, he finds four bolt-action Remington rifles. Also in the footlocker are twenty assorted pistols—automatics and revolvers. He recognizes the Smith & Wesson .357 magnum revolvers and the Colt .45 automatics. He also recognizes several Berettas. Drawers inside the footlocker contain boxes of ammunition.

After twenty minutes searching the garage, he thinks about what he has found. *There's no classified material here, but Master Chief Rodgers must be selling this stuff on the black market.*

He looks at his watch—4:35 PM. He feels uncomfortable in his sweat-soaked, clinging clothes. He walks over to the freezer. He opens the lid to cool himself while he decides what to do next.

Several minutes later, he hears vehicles in the alley. The vehicles' engines idle next to the garage. He moves to the broken window and looks toward the alley. Through the shrubbery, he can see two white-colored sedans. He sees at least two people in each vehicle. Only one face is fully visible to Rigney. The face is dark and leathery with thick black eyebrows and thick black mustache.

He moves back from the window. *What do I do now? I can't go out the window. They will see me.*

Knowing that he may need to stay in the garage for an undetermined amount of time, he opens a case of tonic water and places some bottles in the freezer. He opens a case of frozen steaks and wraps the remainder of the green towel around a couple of steaks. He presses the towel-wrapped frozen steaks to his face and arms to cool his body.

After thirty minutes, the two cars are still in the alley. He has downed three bottles of tonic water and placed another six in the freezer. Five steaks lie thawing on the garage floor.

Rigney hears car doors open and close. Then, he hears footsteps in the alley. He looks around a stack of boxes and peers out the broken window. Someone stands at the side of the closest car and speaks Spanish.

Car doors open on both vehicles. Rigney stands back but keeps a view of the backyard. Then, he sees four men emerge through the shrubbery that borders the alley. They all have the same features—medium builds, dark leathery skin, mustaches—two have beards. They carry large automatic pistols with twelve-inch long magazines. Using a tire iron, one of them pries the back door open. Then, they step through the back door and into the house.

Rigney moves to the front window and peers through the small viewing square he scraped earlier. The street in front of Rodgers's house appears deserted. Then, Rodgers parks his car in front of the house. Rodgers exits his car with two of the regular poker players, RM1 Bob Spaulding and YNC Chuck Henry. They are laughing and joking as they enter the house. Rigney looks at his watch—5:10 PM.

Rigney hears shouting in accented English. A voice orders excitedly, "Down on floor!"

Rigney's mind races as to what he should do. Again, he is alone during a crisis on a mission, and he has no one to turn to for guidance. He curses himself for not going with ONI full-time and taking advantage of the training that would tell him what to do now. *But would that training tell me. Could this event be anticipated?*

He decides to wait and watch the events unfold. He downs two more bottles of tonic water. He wraps another frozen steak in the towel and presses it to his neck.

The back door of the house opens. One of the dark strangers exits first with automatic pistol in hand. Then, Rodgers, Spaulding, and Henry exit; they are bound and gagged. One of the dark strangers follows with his weapon pointed at the three navy men.

Rigney pulls his Beretta and silencer from his ankle holster. He quickly screws-on the silencer to the short-barreled automatic. He stands back from the window, cocks the weapon, and aims at the trailing stranger. *Can I shoot both of them before they shoot me, or will they kill Rodgers first? What about the other two strangers still in the house?* Rigney lowers his weapon as he realizes he must report what happens. He cannot risk being killed. Otherwise, no one will know. He believes his superiors would want him to survive to tell what happened. He remembers Brad Watson telling him during a training session, *"Never risk sacrificing yourself in a heroic act that will put successful completion of an operation in jeopardy."*

As the five men walk across the backyard, the shrubbery and garage hide them from the eyes of neighbors. The dark strangers use the barrels of their weapons to force the three navy men into the backseat of the front vehicle. The two strangers get in the front seat, and the car drives away.

Rigney goes to the freezer, raises the lid, and takes out a cold bottle of tonic water. He downs the tonic water in two gulps. For several minutes, he allows the freezer to cool him. Then, he shuts the lid.

He goes to the window that faces the street. While looking through the small, two-inch peephole, he wonders why two strangers stayed behind in the house. They're probably searching for classified material.

He hears the vehicle before he sees it. Then, the vehicle comes to a stop at the curb in front of the house. Rigney recognizes Master Chief Crimer's personal vehicle. Crimer and Lieutenant Commander Blakely exit the vehicle and walk toward the house. Rigney loses sight of them as they walk to the front door. Several seconds later, he hears knocking on the front door. Then, silence.

After fifteen minutes, Crimer and the XO do not return to the car.

I must to do something! I can't let those kidnappers take more people, especially a woman!

Rigney climbs through the broken window and steps into the backyard. The breeze off the Aegean begins to cool him, but his sweat-stained clothes still cling to his body. He moves quickly to the back door of the house.

He tests the door. *Unlocked!*

The door makes no sound as he pushes it open.

Rigney hears two men arguing in Spanish. He steps into the pantry and moves quickly to the kitchen. He tiptoes across the kitchen floor. He holds his weapon out in front of him in the conventional two-handed firing grip.

As long as they keep arguing, I know they don't hear me.

The Mediterranean construction of cement floor covered with ceramic tile prevents the creaking associated with wood floors.

He pokes his head around the kitchen door and looks into the dining room. A struggling body on the floor in the living room catches his attention. He double-checks the dining room for any danger and finds none. He walks slowly across the dining room and into the living room. The kidnappers still argue elsewhere in the house.

Master Chief Crimer lies bound and gagged on the floor. Duct tape covers his mouth. His arms and legs tied together behind his back. He stretches and twitches in futile attempts to loosen his bonds. Crimer looks up as he notices someone approaching him. He expresses astonishment as he sees RM2 Page approaching with a silencer-equipped pistol in hand and wearing dark sweat-soaked clothing.

Crimer's wonders, *How the hell is Page involved in this? Then, he quickly realizes that Page is not a threat, but a rescuer.*

Rigney quickly scans the living room, looking for Mary Blakely; he does not see her. Then, he stoops. His thoughts are to free Crimer.

Crimer interprets Page's intentions, and he shakes his head. He jerks his head toward the direction of the arguing Spanish voices.

Rigney reads Crimer's motions as orders to find the XO, and rescue her. He nods his head to indicate his understanding.

The foreign voices become more excited.

Rigney stands and moves rapidly but quietly toward the direction of the voices. Then, he steps cautiously along a short hallway as the voices become louder.

He peeks around a doorway and views a large bedroom.

The XO lies on the bed, naked. Her hands and feet are tied, spread-eagled, to the bed frame. Duct tape seals her mouth. She twists and turns to free herself and to exhibit her defiance. Her face expresses fear and horror.

Two dark-skinned men with thick mustaches stand naked at the side of the bed. They both have erections. They argue and point at the XO as each makes his point. Their desires to take her deepen as she twists and turns her shapely body.

The men's clothes drape across chairs; their automatic weapons lie on the dresser.

Mary's ripped and torn uniform lies at the foot of the bed, her bra and panties torn to shreds.

Rigney knows that when he enters the bedroom he must enter firing his weapon, because he knows when they see him, they will go for their weapons. *No unrealistic words like "hands up" or "freeze!"*

First, the guy on the right, then, they guy on the left.

He turns into the doorway and enters the bedroom.

Mary sees Page enter the room with a gun raised in firing position. Her eyes go wide with amazement.

The two men do not notice Mary's actions, but they turn toward Rigney as they detect motion out of the corner of their eyes.

Rigney fires a round into the chest of the man on the right.

The man on the left dives toward Rigney's gun hand and successfully grabs Rigney's wrist, pushing the gun upward. Rigney pulls the trigger, but the round hits the far wall. The man is forty pounds lighter than Rigney, but hard and wiry. Using the same maneuver Rigney has used, the man twists Rigney's wrist, forcing Rigney toward the floor. The pain in his arm causes him to drop the Beretta.

Mary watches the battle before her; first with hope when the first man is shot, then fear again when she sees the second man getting the best of Page.

Rigney instinctively employs the countermove to the wristlock. Instead of allowing the maneuver to press his belly to the floor, Rigney performs a gymnast forward roll, which relieves the pain in his arm. Rigney jerks his right arm; the power of the jerk frees his wrist from the man's grip. Rigney jumps to his feet.

The man moves his eyes around the room, looking for the nearest weapon. He sees Rigney's Beretta a few feet away; he steps toward it, but Rigney is too fast. The man realizing he cannot reach the gun before the large American reaches him, the man turns and attacks Rigney. Big mistake—he should have chanced for the gun.

When the man comes within Rigney's reach, Rigney throws an uppercut that catches the man squarely under the chin. The man's head snaps back as the punch lifts him off the floor.

Mary expresses shock at the blur and power of the punch that Page delivers to the naked man.

The man falls limply to the floor—on his belly—near the doorway.

Page moves quickly to the unconscious man. He places his right hand on the man's chin and his left hand on the side of the man's head. He violently jerks the man's head. A crunching noise reports the man's brain stem breaks free from his spine.

Mary's eyes express horror, then, relief.

Rigney retrieves his Beretta. He steps quickly to his first victim and fires one round into the back of the man's head. Then, he takes the few steps toward his second victim near the doorway and fires a round into his head.

He takes a few moments and stares at the two men. He fiercely kicks each on the side to see if either reacts; they do not.

He tucks his weapon into his belt. He moves to the bed and sits beside Mary. He slowly peals off the duct tape from her mouth.

"Are you okay ma'am?" he asks.

"Yes," Mary responds softly and inhales through her mouth.

Rigney removes the bosun's knife from its leather case and begins cutting her bonds.

Mary's face and skin turn red with embarrassment as she realizes her nakedness in Page's view. She whispers, "Page, put that blanket over me. Then, you can cut me loose." She nods toward a blanket on a chair in the corner of the room.

"Yes ma'am."

Rigney steps over his first victim on his way to the chair. He picks up the blanket, unfolds it, and spreads it out over Mary's body.

He continues cutting her bonds.

Mary remains quiet as she watches Page cut the ropes with the bosun's knife. She runs the actions of the last half hour through her mind. She remembers her stunned fear as one of her would-be rapists answered the door and pointed a gun at her and Crimer.

In the bedroom, they tore and ripped her uniform from her body. They cut the straps to her bra and tore away her panties. They forced her to the bed and ran their hands over her as they tied her down. Then, she watched with horror as they removed their clothing. When she saw their erections, she shuddered with revulsion. She knew she could survive the rape. She nearly vomited when she visualized all that they may do to her.

She feared they would kill her when they finished. She decided to resist and fight them with all her strength. She twisted and jerked her body in futile attempts to break her bonds.

Then, she detected the two men were arguing. A few moments later, she sees Page come through the doorway firing a gun—*with a silencer!*

She comes back to the present as Page cuts the last rope around her left ankle.

Mary sits upright on the bed with the blanket tucked around her. She orders, "Look in that closet. Find me something to wear."

Rigney stands and opens the door to the large wardrobe. The wardrobe contains civilian clothes and uniforms belonging to Master Chief Rodgers.

As Rigney goes through the clothing, Mary stares at the dead men on the floor. She shivers as she thinks about how close she came to death.

"Just hand me a set of Rodgers's whites and one of his t-shirts," Mary says impatiently.

Rigney offers her a 100 percent cotton white summer uniform.

Mary stands with the blanket still wrapped around her. She takes the uniform and says, "I will dress in the bathroom, but first, move that body away from the door. I don't want to step over it."

"Yes ma'am. While you dress, I will free Master Chief Crimer."

Mary lets out a sigh and expresses relief. "He's still alive." The words are more a statement than a question.

"Yes ma'am."

"Okay," she replies. "Then, you have a lot of explaining to do."

"Yes ma'am."

Mary enters the bathroom and shuts the door behind her.

Rigney goes to the living room. He stoops and removes the duct tape from Crimer's mouth.

"Is the XO okay?" Crimer asks urgently.

"Yes."

"Did they harm her . . . you know?"

"No. I don't think so. She appears okay."

Rigney uses the bosun's knife to cut away the ropes around Crimer's hands and feet.

Crimer stands and asks, "Did you kill them?"

"Yes."

Crimer starts to ask another question when Mary comes into the living room. Rodgers's uniform fits her loosely, but the length is right. She did not bother to go back to the bedroom to get her rank devices.

Mary demands with stern authority in her tone, "Okay, Page, what the hell is going on?!" The fragile and frightened woman from the bedroom has transformed to the confident executive officer who is now in charge.

"I don't think I can tell you anything."

Crimer says as he stares at the Beretta stuffed inside Page's belt, "I had better take that weapon until this is all straightened out."

Rigney places his hand on the weapon's grip and responds firmly and forcefully, "No. I am trained on how to use this, and I have been trained not to relinquish it. While we stand here, the others could return, and I might need to use it again."

Page's defiance irritates Crimer, but he does not attempt to take the weapon.

"What others?" Mary questions with a raised tone as she looks around the room, an inquisitive expression on her face.

"Tell us what's going on," Crimer orders.

"I don't know how much I can tell you. Now that my cover is blown, I think Anna will want to talk to you. We must go—now!"

"Hold on, Page," the XO demands. "First things first—what others?"

"Two others, like the two in the bedroom. they kidnapped Master Chief Rodgers, Spaulding, and Chief Henry."

"When did that happen?" Crimer asks.

"Just before you two got here."

"You saw them kidnapped and didn't do anything to stop it?" Mary challenges.

Rigney shifts his eyes several times between Crimer and the XO; then, he explains, "Ma'am, I can't tell you more."

Both look questioningly at Page, indicating he should continue his explanation.

Rigney urges, "Ma'am, we must go before they come back. You must speak to Anna."

Mary shakes her head in disagreement. "What does a German national have to do with this?"

"Anna is not German. She's American, and she's my mission controller."

Crimer looks at the XO and advises, "XO, we have stumbled on more than Rodgers's books not balancing."

"We sure have," Mary agrees. Then, she asks Page, "Are you undercover NIS?"

"No ma'am."

Page's response surprises and confuses Mary. She expected him to say yes. Then, after a few moments, the realization of Page's possible identify comes to her.

"Alright," she agrees. "Let's go talk with Anna."

Rigney sighs in relief. Then, he removes his Beretta from his belt, unscrews the silencer, and stores both items in his ankle holster. He pulls his pant leg down to cover the holster.

The XO and Crimer exchange glances as they wonder how long Page has been carrying that weapon.

Chapter 92

Anna looks out the window of her bedroom and watches Master Chief Crimer drive his vehicle into the courtyard.

Rigney closes and locks the courtyard gate.

Anna thinks about her weapon; then, she observes Rigney displaying their prearranged okay signal.

Anna shakes her head in disapproval. *Something went wrong.*

Several minutes later, they all sit in the living room. Rigney briefs Anna on everything he did, starting with his breaking into the garage and finishing with bringing the XO and the master chief to the villa.

Anna looks sympathetically at Mary as Rigney describes what he saw in the bedroom.

When Rigney stops talking, Anna asks, "Mary, please tell me everything you remember from the time you walked up to Rodgers's front door."

"Before I do that, I must know who you are and your purpose. Your heavy German accent is gone. I know you are not what you have been portraying."

Anna sits in thought for a moment; then she says, "My real name is Karen Drescher. Please continue to call me Anna. I am a counterespionage operative with the Office of Navy Intelligence. My current assignment is Nea Makri mission controller for Operation Hammerhead."

Mary states, "Karen Drescher? That name is familiar to me."

Anna smiles and says, "I was two classes ahead of you at OCS."

Mary's face expresses recognition. She did not know Karen Drescher well, but she remembers several short conversations. She leans closer to Anna and studies her face. "You don't look as I remember you."

"I've had several cosmetic surgeries, different nose, different cheeks and chin, different hair color. All needed to preserve my undercover identity."

Mary nods acceptance of the information; then, she asks, "Are you still in the navy?"

"No."

Mary sits back in the chair and says, "I need something to drink before I tell you what happened."

Anna says to Rigney, "Get some ice water."

"And something stronger," Mary urges.

Rigney says, "We have some Jack Daniel's whiskey. I'll get you some." Rigney looks at Crimer and asks, "Master Chief, can I get you anything."

"A couple of cold beers, if you have them. Otherwise, ice water is fine."

All sit silent in the living room while Rigney gets drinks.

Several minutes later, Rigney returns with a tray of ice water, three cold Heinekens, a couple of empty shot glasses, and a half-full bottle of Jack Daniel's.

Mary grabs a glass of ice water and downs it in one long drink.

Rigney hands two bottles of beer to Crimer. He consumes half of one bottle straight down.

Rigney pours a triple shot of Jack Daniel's and hands it to the XO.

Mary takes a hearty sip. She sighs deeply. Then, she relates the sequence of events in Rodgers's house as she remembers them. She does not relate her fears and horror in the bedroom. She tells only the sequence of events.

Anna asks, "What language were your abductors speaking?"

"Spanish."

Anna looks at Crimer and asks, "Anything to add, Master Chief?"

"No. Page and the XO covered it all."

Anna turns her head toward Mary and asks, "Why did you go to Rodgers's house?"

"We are conducting an audit of the Club Zeus. We found no cash in the safe. The books say there is $8,000.00 ready for deposit. We went to Rodgers's house to ask him about the money. We found some other irregularities we wanted to ask him about."

Rigney's curiosity gets the better of him, and he asks, "So Rodgers is a thief, not a traitor?"

"Traitor?" the XO and Crimer question in unison as they swing their heads toward Rigney.

Rigney looks as Anna for an answer.

"He's both," Anna responds. "And we must find him and the other two before they are tortured and interrogated."

They all sit quietly for a few moments, considering Anna's revelation about Rodgers.

Mary breaks the silence. "Why didn't ONI tell us about Operation Hammerhead? Shouldn't the Nea Makri command structure know about it?"

Anna responds, "ONI does not trust Commander Caldwell. His performance over the last few years has brought doubt on his character. His assignment as commanding officer was a result of inappropriate admiral level influence. Commander Caldwell was assigned as commanding officer against the protests of COMNAVCOM. Caldwell's conspiracy with Pritchings to convict Page rattled the navy's command structure. The COMNAVCOM Chief-of-Staff will arrive unannounced the day after tomorrow and immediately relieve Caldwell as commanding officer. The chief-of-staff will serve as temporary CO until COMNAVCOM can assign a suitable replacement. Caldwell will be sent back to Washington to explain his illegal actions against Page. A UCMJ investigation into Caldwell's actions was initiated two days ago."

Mary's face expresses concern. She worries how this will affect her.

Anna assures, "Don't worry, Mary. Your integrity and leadership are not in question. You will remain as executive officer."

Mary looks questioningly at Anna and asks, "How do you know all this? How did COMNAVCOM have enough time to act? Page's UCMJ hearing was concluded only four days ago."

Anna responds, "I get daily intelligence messages that tell me everything of significance regarding NAVCOMMSTA Greece."

The communicator within Mary causes her to survey her surroundings and causes her to ask, "How do you get—"

"You'll find out, because you and the master chief will assist Page and me with putting together an intel report on what happened today. But before we prepare the message, we must erase all evidence that you and Master Chief Crimer were ever at Rodgers's house, and we must get all the belongings of the two dead men."

Anna turns to Rigney and says, "Go to Rodgers's house and get all the clothes, weapons, and everything else that looks like it belongs to those two men. Search their car for any belongings and anything that could identify them. Also, bring back all remnants of the XO's uniform. We don't want anyone discovering she was there."

Anna pauses; then, she asks, "Mary, Master Chief, can you think of anything you left behind?"

"Other than my uniform and underwear, I can't think of anything else that could be there."

Crimer says, "No. I left nothing behind, but what about the ropes and duct tape that bound us? Shouldn't Page bring that back, also?"

Anna looks at Rigney and says, "Get the ropes and duct tape."

"What about the bodies?" Rigney asks.

"I need to think about that. We'll just leave them there for the time being."

Rigney nods understanding.

"And drive my car back here," Anna orders.

Rigney calculates how long it will take him to get to Rodgers's house on foot. *If I run the whole way, I can make it there in less than ten minutes.*

"Anything else?" Rigney asks Anna.

"No, but as you approach Rodgers's house, have your weapon ready, just in case the other kidnappers have returned."

Rigney nods. Then, he stands. He reaches to his ankle and pulls the Beretta from its ankle holster; he ejects the magazine and counts the number of rounds. He slips the partially loaded magazine into his back pocket and then pulls a fully loaded magazine from the same back pocket.

The XO and Crimer stare with fascination at Page as they watch the reloading process. They think how deadly Page appears in dark clothing and gun in hand.

Rigney slams the magazine into the butt of the pistol. He bends down, pulls up his trouser cuff, and holsters the Beretta. Then, he lifts the cuff of his other leg and verifies that the six-inch dagger in its sheath is securely strapped to his ankle. He straightens, turns, and walks quickly out the front door.

Master Chief Crimer stares at the front door. He expresses astonishment as he comments, "I would never have guessed that Page is a . . . a . . . I mean he is so young and brash . . . not what you would think a . . . a . . ." He turns to Anna and asks, "What is he?"

Anna smiles at Crimer's bewilderment.

Mary asks, "Yes, what is he? Who is he?"

Anna replies, "It's good that you never thought him to be what he is. That's why ONI deploys him and why he is so effective. As to what he is . . . he has no job title or permanent status with ONI. He is a cross between a counterespionage specialist, specializing in navy communications systems, and a counterespionage field operative. As to whom he is. He is a young patriotic sailor who has committed himself to fight evil."

"So he is active duty navy, then?" Crimer asks.

"Yes," Anna replies. "He actually is a second class radioman."

Mary stares dubiously at Anna and says, "Where did he learn to be a ruthless killer? He certainly didn't learn that in Radioman A School. I mean, he didn't tell them to put their hands up or didn't try to tie them up. He calmly stepped into the bedroom, didn't say a word, and killed them."

"*Put your hands up* is only in the movies. Page stated that he saw their weapons on the dresser. His training told him they would go for their weapons."

"But he did it so matter-of-factly, so emotionless, like he was making log entries."

"It's instinctive within him, but he is in self-denial about it. He demonstrates his denial by declining to work with ONI full-time. And he is only brutal and ruthless when fighting those who victimize the innocent."

"Well, whether he denies it or not, I am one person who is alive because of his instinctive skill. I will always be grateful." Mary lets out a deep sigh of relief.

They remain silent for a few moments to adjust to a new subject.

Mary asks Anna, "Are you going to tell us about Operation Hammerhead?"

Anna responds, "Mary, I know you have a final top secret clearance. Master Chief, what is your clearance?"

"Final Secret."

A look of hesitancy appears on Anna's face.

Mary announces, "Master Chief, you now have an interim top secret. We will get the paperwork started tomorrow."

Anna spends the next thirty minutes explaining the details and purpose of Operation Hammerhead.

Mary adds, "As CMS Custodian, Master Chief Rodgers has single access to all the NAVCOMMSTA's crypto key cards and code books. Do you know if he gave any of it to the Russians?"

"We believe he has."

Master Chief Crimer shakes his head and says emphatically, "My god! Ray is a traitor! What happened to him?!"

Chapter 93

Rigney enters Rodgers's house. The sun sank below the horizon just before he entered the house. He flips on the lights as he moves from room to room. He walks directly to the bedroom.

He scans the bedroom for items to retrieve. Blood spreads over the tile floor from the two bodies. The XO's torn clothes lie on the floor at the foot of the bed. Her clothes are soaked in blood.

He steps around the blood and removes a pillowcase from a pillow on the bed. With his thumb and forefinger, he picks up the XO's uniform, shoes, hat, torn bra, and shredded panties and drops them into the pillowcase.

The dead men's clothes are draped over chairs. He checks the pockets and finds car keys. He removes another pillowcase and stuffs the dead men's clothes into it. He picks up their pistols and stuffs them into the pillowcase.

He looks around the room and locates the duct tape that was over the XO's mouth and the pieces of rope that tied her to the bed frame. He stuffs those items into the pillowcase holding the XO's uniform.

He moves to the doorway, turns, and surveys the room one more time. Satisfied that he has everything, he turns and proceeds to the living room where Crimer was bound and gagged. He finds the rope and duct tape; he stuffs those items into the pillowcase with the XO's uniform.

Rigney starts toward the back door but stops short. He stands, thoughtful, for a few moments. Then, he returns to the bedroom.

He stands just inside the bedroom door. Looking down at his two victims, he wonders how he was capable of such brutality. When he had seen the XO lying on the bed bound and gagged and tied to the bed frame and the two naked men standing over her, he took only five seconds to decide he must kill the two men. *They would have reached for their weapons. Killing them is justified.*

The two men lie facedown. Rigney stares intently at each body. He sees the holes made by the bullets. He uses the toe of his shoe to flip each man on his back. Rigney sighs deeply as he looks at the lifeless faces. Their eyes are open. Dried blood coagulates around their open mouths. Splotches of dark blue skin show where blood settled in their bodies after their hearts stopped pumping. In life, their bodies were solid with good muscle tone. *They could have overpowered me had I made a mistake. I got lucky with the second man. I was overconfident.*

An object around one man's neck draws Rigney's attention. He bends over for a closer look. A crucifix hangs from a chain around the man's neck. Rigney yanks and breaks the crucifix chain and stuffs it into his pocket.

He steps quickly from the bedroom through the dining room and into the kitchen, turning off lights as he exits each room. In the kitchen, he picks up the two pillowcases and exits through the back door. He dashes across the backyard. The doors of the dead men's car are unlocked. He uses his flashlight to search the interior. He finds no objects in the front or back of the car. He opens the glove box and finds registration papers, which show the car is a rental from an Athens agency. Rigney stuffs the papers into the pillowcase holding the dead men's belongings. Then, he searches the trunk, which is empty.

Rigney walks the one block to the BMW. Clouds block the moonlight, and he walks unnoticed by others. A breeze off the Aegean cools him. His sweaty skin begins to dry. When he reaches the BMW, he tosses the pillowcases into the trunk. He starts the car and drives off slowly. He glances around to see if anyone watches; he sees no one.

Chapter 94

All heads turn toward Page as he comes through the front door of the villa, carrying two pillowcases. Bloodstains show through one of the pillowcases.

Rigney raises his right hand and says, "This one has the belongings of the dead men." He holds up the other pillow case and says, "This one has the XO's stuff in it."

Mary Blakely stares at the bloodstained pillowcase. Her fear of the enemy returns. She shudders.

Anna takes the pillowcase with the dead men's belongings and spills the contents on newspaper spread on the floor. She stoops and goes through the pockets. She finds drachma currency and one small Swiss knife.

"No identification," Anna comments. Then, she checks the clothing labels. "Their clothes have Greek labels."

Anna stands and looks thoughtful; then, she asks Rigney, "Are you sure this is everything?"

Rigney is about to say yes when he remembers the crucifix. He pulls the religious item from his pocket and hands it to Anna. "One of them had this around his neck."

Anna scrutinizes the crucifix; then, she speaks the words on the back, "Fabricación en España."

"Made in Spain," Rigney translates.

Mary stands and walks over to Anna and requests, "May I see the crucifix?"

Anna hands over the crucifix.

Mary studies the crucifix and becomes bewildered as to how a man wearing a crucifix would be motivated to rape and murder her.

After spending several moments studying the crucifix, Mary says, "They spoke Spanish, they wore Greek clothes, they were Catholics, they stayed at Rodgers's house after Rodgers and the other two sailors were kidnapped. What does it all mean?"

Rigney adds, "And none of the kidnappers went to the garage to see what is there."

Anna stoops and examines the dead men's shoes. She looks for brand names and trademarks, but finds none. Both pairs of shoes are severely worn. She stands and says, "I must sit down and think about all this."

While Anna sits quietly in thought, Rigney downs four glasses of ice water. Crimer downs another beer. The XO pours herself another voluminous portion of Jack Daniel's whiskey, but sips it slowly.

Anna reasons aloud. "Maybe Rodgers wasn't their only target, or Spaulding or Chief Henry. They didn't get everyone they came to get. That's why two kidnappers were left behind. They were expecting someone else to come to Rodgers's house."

"Who?" Mary asks.

"Me," Rigney states, startled by his own sudden revelation.

The XO and Crimer turn their heads and stare at Rigney; their eyes reflect their astonishment.

"You knew?" Anna challenges.

"Not 'til just now," Rigney reveals. "The logic of it just hit me."

"Yes. It makes sense," Anna concludes.

"Please explain it to us?" Crimer asks.

"Yes, please do," the XO demands.

Anna knows that what she is about to say will reveal additional classified information. She needs the XO's confidence, because she will need the XO's help.

"These kidnappers are from Spain. These characters have all the markings of an espionage organization that was uncovered during Page's last mission. Page was instrumental in the capture of the organization's leader—a sinister PLO operative. That PLO operative, codename Lucifer, operated a spy organization that gathered volumes of U.S. and NATO classified information for more than ten years, including crypto codes and keys.

"Lucifer's home base was Madrid. To help hide his true objectives, he owned and operated an import-export business. He hired local Madrid thugs and criminals of varying ethnic and religious backgrounds to do his dirty work. Many of those he hired originated from the Madrid Palestinian community. They spoke Arabic and Spanish fluently, but some were Christians, some were Moslems, and some were Jewish. The criminal element Lucifer hired did not know their leader's true identity as a PLO operative. They all thought he was just a high-class criminal.

"In reality, he had a network of NATO military personnel who sold him NATO military secrets, including several Americans. Lucifer paid his network of NATO servicemen a monthly sum for any classified information they could pass to him. Then, Lucifer sold the classified information to the Soviets. Whatever Soviet money was left after he deducted expenses and his commission, he gave to the PLO.

"While on an ONI mission, Page uncovered one of Lucifer's American traitors. ONI detected Lucifer's plan to come after Page. We trapped Lucifer, who now resides in a prisonlike classified location somewhere in the States.

"Then, a few months ago, Rodgers is seen meeting in Athens with a Soviet KGB operative. I just got back from ONI in Washington. While I was there, ONI identified Lucifer's Soviet contact as the same KGB operative that met with Rodgers.

"I think this KGB operative has identified Page, and, therefore, knows that Page's presence here in Nea Makri is no coincidence. I think this KGB operative has hired Lucifer's men to abduct Page.

"I think the Soviets plan to hold hostages and demand release of Lucifer. There is a spy exchange scheduled for December. The Soviets thought they would get several Americans to exchange, including Page, but then you two showed up." Anna gestures toward the XO and the master chief.

Rigney adds, "I never arrived for the poker games until several minutes after 8:00. If the kidnappers had Rodgers and me under surveillance, they know that." Rigney looks at his watch—08:15 PM. "It's only quarter past eight. We have some maneuvering time before the other kidnappers start worrying about the two left behind at Rodgers's house."

"Yes, we do," Anna agrees. "Give me a moment to think about this. Anna paces the living room.

After several minutes have passed, Anna asks Mary, "Do you have any association with the local police?"

"Sure do," Mary advises. "The local police chief comes to the base at least once a week to meet with me. I am on several committees with the locals including the police chief to promote cooperation between the locals and American sailors. The police chief has an attraction to me. He is always asking me out. I went a few times as his date to some local gatherings."

"Perfect!" Anna declares as she looks at the clock on the wall. "Where do you think the police chief is now?"

Mary responds, "He is single and married to his job. I bet he's at the police station."

"Mary, you need to go there. Tell him there are dead bodies at Rodgers's house. Tell him he needs to seal-off Rodgers's house as a crime scene, but he is to tell reporters that the police captured two burglars who are foreign nationals whose identity is not yet known. Tell him that it is a matter of Greek and NATO security and that he must deceive the press and the public for several days. That will give us time to prepare for tomorrow."

"What's gonna happen tomorrow?" Crimer asks.

"The other Spaniards will come after Page tomorrow—here. When they discover their comrades have been arrested, but their nationalities not known, they will feel secure that their operation has not been compromised, and they will try again to get Page."

A worried look appears on Rigney's face. He sighs deeply as he realizes that once again he is the target of evil men and realizes what he must do to combat them.

Mary asks, "Why do you conclude they will come here?"

Anna explains, "This is the only place they can do it and not draw the attention of locals. They won't do it at the beach or in town with the chance of innocent civilians looking on who can later identify them. They will want to break into the villa while we are not here.

"Tomorrow, Page and I will go to the Nea Makri beach. We will frolic and play and put ourselves on display. We will act as if we know nothing about the crime at Rodgers's house. Knowing that we are away at the beach, they will break in here. They will probably come over the west wall, which is the back wall and the least visible to other houses on this hill."

Anna pauses; then, she says, "Mary, you must go find the police chief, now. After you are confident the police chief will do as you ask, come back here. We must prepare our report of what happened tonight. I will include my analysis and predictions of what will happen, and I will ask for more people. We need to capture as many of these scum as we can."

Rigney asks, "Won't they suspect we are setting a trap for them?"

"I don't think they are sophisticated operatives," Anna responds. "Wearing that crucifix and carelessly speaking Spanish in front of others shows they are not well trained."

"But trying to capture them is too dangerous," Rigney objects. "They won't give up when surrounded. They'll shoot it out. When they come over the outside wall, we must shoot to kill. That's what my training tells me to do."

Anna, the XO, and Crimer fall silent and stare at Page for a few moments.

Anna explains, "You won't be involved with their capture. You and I will be at the beach. They will break in while we are at the beach. We will have a team of operatives already here, waiting for them."

"I'll help," Crimer offers.

Anna studies Crimer for a few moments; then, she asks, "Do you have any weapons training?"

"I served in swift boats in Vietnam for a year, lots of combat experience, and I am trained and skilled at how to capture enemy combatants alive."

"Are you qualified on the M14?"

"I have some experience with it."

Anna looks at Mary and asks, "I could use him, any objections, XO?"

"No objections. Anything else I can do?"

"Yes, but I will explain it to you later. Now, go to the police station." Anna hands Mary the BMW keys and offers, "Take my car."

The XO stands and states, "I must go to my house and change clothes first." Then, she exits the villa.

Rigney announces, "I need a shower."

"Make it quick," Anna orders. "We need to get started on the daily report."

Chapter 95

Fifteen minutes later, Rigney exits his room; he is freshly showered and wears t-shirt, gym shorts, and sandals. He enters the communications room where he finds Anna and Master Chief Crimer. Rigney sits down in front of the teletype machine.

Anna and Crimer gather behind Rigney's chair.

Crimer gives the communications configuration a quick scrutiny. He was in the communications trailers many times. Except for the KW-7 Orestes crypto device, he recognizes the individual pieces of equipment, but does not know the function of each. A boatswain's mate by trade, he is lost in this communications environment, just as Page would be lost in his environment of deck operations, deck maintenance, deck equipment, deck machines, swift boats, and jungle survival.

Anna explains, "I will dictate the report to Page. He will type a page copy and a paper-tape copy. Then, we will edit as necessary, but we need to get this out within a few hours."

Anna dictates. Page's fingers dance expertly over the teletype keyboard.

While he waits his turn to dictate, Master Chief Crimer roams the small communications room. The cabinet against the far wall of the communications room draws his attention. He views the weapons inside. He stares at several silencer-equipped XM-21 sniper rifles. *Now I know why she wanted to know if I was qualified on the M14.* During his year in swift boats, his vessels transported many warriors who carried this model of sniper rifle.

One hour later, a flashing indicator on the security repeater catches Rigney's eye.

Anna sees it at the same time and says, "That's the courtyard gate. Must be Mary."

Rigney stops typing and stands. He glances at the wall clock—10:33 PM.

"I'll open the gate for her," Crimer offers.

"No, Master Chief," Anna directs. "Page knows all the security settings."

Page is back to the communications room with the XO in less than ten minutes. The XO now wears a fresh, loose fitting summer blouse and summer slacks.

Rigney sits down at the teletype and continues typing the edits specified by Anna.

"How did it go with the police chief?" Anna asks Mary.

"He did everything I asked of him. Before I left his office he pinched me on the butt, smiled sensually at me, and stated I owe him a romantic weekend on Corfu."

Rigney shakes his head. Without looking away from the teletype, he declares in a disgusted tone, "Men are pigs!"

Mary, Anna, and Crimer turn their heads toward Page at the same time, chuckle, and smile at Rigney.

Mary says appreciatively, "Well, such an enlightened male for your age."

Rigney does not respond; he just keeps typing.

Forty-five minutes later Anna declares, "Okay, this report is good enough. We must transmit now. Rig, go ahead and send it."

Rigney places the beginning of the paper tape in the tape reader. He reaches up with his right hand and presses-in and holds the *send* button on the KW-7 Orestes crypto device. The P&I indicator illuminates. This action causes a synchronization signal to transmit to the Orestes crypto device in the ONI European Message Relay center in Naples.

Because of her naval communications background, Mary understands all the steps Page performs.

After twenty seconds, Rigney releases the *send* button. Several seconds later, the P&I indicator extinguishes, indicating that the phasing signal has completed and the message can be transmitted.

Rigney glances at the clock on the wall that is set to ZULU Time Zone, which is two hours earlier than the current time. He types the time and Julian date on the teletype keyboard. Then, he toggles the tape-reader send switch, and the paper tape advances through the tape reader, and the message transmits Baudot code bytes. At seventy-five baud, roughly 100 words a minute, the message takes twelve-minutes to send.

After the last character transmits, Rigney patiently waits for the operator on the other end to acknowledge receipt of the message. Thirty seconds later the following prints below the message:

2149Z NM DE ONI QSL NM 01/264 AR //MRE

Rigney looks over his shoulder at Anna and says, "They got it."

Anna looks at her watch—11:49 PM.

Mary looks at Anna and asks, "Who got it?"

"The ONI message relay center in Naples. They will send it to ONI HQ and to the CIA office in the Athens Embassy."

"CIA is involved in this?" Crimer asks.

"Yeah," Anna replies. "This is a combined ONI CIA operation. CIA will send us some field operatives to help capture Lucifer's men."

"When will they get here?" the XO asks.

"Before daylight," Anna answers. "I will call Pam and give her a heads-up on my manpower request. The embassy communications center should notify her within the next thirty minutes.

"I anticipate that Lucifer's men will start watching this place sometime between sunrise and noon. Everyone needs to be here before sunrise. Master Chief, you should stay here. Mary, you should go home, now. Go through your normal routine for the next forty-eight hours. You will need to cover for all the missing sailors for the next two days."

Chapter 96

Anna, Rigney, and Master Chief Crimer doze in the living room. The courtyard gate alarm sounds. They all come awake as the constant, high-pitch, and low-volume alarm penetrates their senses.

Anna looks at her watch—0410. She stands up the couch and goes to the window. She sees John Smith standing outside the gate. A green and white Volkswagen bus is behind him.

"Rig, go let them in."

Rigney jumps up from the overstuffed chair and moves quickly out the front door.

Rigney unlocks and opens the front gate.

John and Rigney exchange handshakes and greetings. Then, John climbs into the driver's seat of the Volkswagen bus and drives it into the courtyard.

John Smith and three other men exit the Volkswagen bus with two footlockers in hand.

Rigney locks the gate and leads the four men up the steps and through the front door of the villa.

Anna and Crimer stand as Rigney and the four men enter the living room. The men set the lockers down on the tile floor.

Everyone introduces themselves. John and his colleagues use first names only.

When the one named Greg shakes hands with Rigney, Greg says, "Actually, we worked together before, but did not meet face to face. I was a member of Brad Watson's command center team in Naples last February . . . good job in that Licola beach house."

Rigney's memories of Licola flash through his mind. "Uh . . . yes . . . thanks," Rigney sputters; his face flushes.

Greg smiles at Rigney's embarrassment.

When John shakes Master Chief Crimer's hand, the two smile at each other in recognition.

Crimer glances at Page and says to John, "When I first met Page, I thought I had met him in *The 'Nam*, but it is you I remember. Even with that long hair and beard, you and Page could pass as brothers."

Rigney concentrates on the conversation between John Smith and Master Chief Crimer. He finally learns something about John's background.

"Yeah, I remember you, Senior Chief. You and your crew extracted me from a riverbank where I was pinned down by a hail of Vietcong gunfire. Your crew gave me covering fire while I swam out to your boat. I remember you manning the fifties and cutting down everything standing within fifty yards of the riverbank."

"All in a day's work, and it's master chief, now."

John looks at Crimer's collar devices then looks back to Crimer's face and says, "Congratulations on your promotion. Well deserved."

Crimer smiles appreciatively at the compliment from a valiant warrior.

John, as team leader, turns to Anna and says, "Give us a brief on what happened at Rodgers's house and what you expect to happen here, today."

Anna briefs the ONI Team. When she describes Rigney's actions to save Lieutenant Commander Blakely and Master Chief Crimer, the ONI Team turns their heads toward Rigney and smile in appreciation of his abilities.

Rigney raises one eyebrow in a cavalier manner, indicating he did what any of them would have done.

"What time will you and Rig leave for the beach?" John asks.

"10:00 AM. They should be watching the house by then."

John nods his agreement with Anna's evaluation.

"Okay. Let's suit up," John orders.

John opens one footlocker, and Greg opens the other.

John pulls sets of black-colored body armor from the footlocker and hands the items to Crimer and the other team members.

Rigney watches with fascination as the men don their body armor. The vest stretches from shoulders to midsection, covering most of the torso. A protective flap snaps to the front of the jacket and protects from midsection to midthigh. Rigney asks, "How reliable is that bulletproof vest?"

"Not bulletproof," John responds as he tightens the straps of his vest. "Bullet resistant."

"How resistant?"

"Should stop an AK-47 slug . . . from a distance."

Rigney informs, "The guys at Rodgers's house carried machine pistols, looked like .38 caliber, or close to it."

"Don't worry about it, Rig. We'll take care of them."

John pulls helmets from the locker and hands them out. Fully outfitted, the five men look like members of a SWAT unit.

From the other footlocker, Greg pulls two XM-21 sniper rifles and four 9 millimeter Beretta automatics. Then, he screws silencers on each XM-21 and each Beretta. The silencers for the XM-21s are twelve inches long.

Rigney notes that the XM-21s do not have scopes, which are not needed for close-in work.

"What are those?" Rigney asks as he points at folded rubber items with zippers at the bottom of one of the footlockers.

Greg glances to where Rigney points and replies, "Body bags."

John looks over his team and concludes they are properly suited and equipped. "Let's go over the plan," he directs as he pulls a sheet of paper from his pocket. He looks for a place to lay it. "Let's go into the kitchen and gather around the table." Then, he walks toward the hallway; everyone follows.

John lays out the sheet of paper on the kitchen table. The paper has an illustration of the villa, courtyard, and courtyard wall. "They will probably come over the west wall. That area of the wall is the least visible to other houses, and all the trees back there will give them good cover."

Everyone nods agreement.

John continues, "I think the living room gives us the best cover to hide as they enter. The living room is the largest room in the villa, and we can hide behind the couches and overstuffed chairs. We will lower and lock all shutters, except the double glass doors that lead from the patio into the living room, and we will open the window in the front bedroom. That way it will look like the patio door and front bedroom window are open to allow a breeze to air the house while the residents are away."

As they study the drawing, all nod their heads in agreement.

"Master Chief and Larry will carry rifles. The rest of us will carry automatic handguns.

"As far as positioning goes, Larry will be at the window in the back bedroom, Master Chief, I want you on the stair landing that goes up to the bedrooms. Greg, you must hide on the other side of the west wall. They may leave a driver in a car. If they do, abduct him and bring him into the villa. Jeff and I will conceal ourselves behind the couch and chairs in the living room.

"Larry, when you see them come over the north wall, go to the bedroom door and sign with your fingers to the master chief the number of intruders coming toward the house. They will probably leave one or two lookouts just inside the north wall. Then, go back to the window. When you hear us shouting at the intruders that enter the living room, you are to take out the lookouts by the wall. Shoot to kill, we cannot let those lookouts either get back over the wall, or come to the aid of their associates."

Larry nods his understanding.

Rigney looks curiously at Larry. He wonders how easy it will be for Larry to kill. Larry does not look sinister or brutal; his manner appears mild.

John continues. "Master Chief, on the landing, you will have clear line of fire into the living room. When the intruders come into the living room, Jeff and I will attempt to get the drop on them. We will have our weapons raised on them. If they are as amateurish as I think they are, they won't have their weapons raised in firing position, and they will give up when they know our weapons are aimed at them. If they raise their weapons, take them out. We will catch them in crossfire."

"You got it, John," Master Chief Crimer responds confidently.

John adds, "Then, we will put the bodies and our captives in the wine cellar. After dark tonight, we will load ourselves, our captives, and the bodies into the Volkswagen bus and take them to our interrogation center, where we hope our captives will reveal the location of Rodgers and the other two sailors."

Quiet comes over the room, giving Rigney a chance to ask a question. "When should Anna and I come back from the beach?"

John responds, "Greg will come to the beach and stand around where you can see him. That will be your signal to return."

Anna says, "Put the alarm sensors on silent mode. So only the blinking indicators on the command unit will warn you when they come over the wall. Those indicators can be seen from anywhere in the living room."

"Good idea," John responds.

Rigney looks at John and asks, "What now?"

"We relax until you and Anna leave for the beach. Then, the rest of us will take our positions."

Chapter 97

Anna lies stretched out on a beach blanket in the skimpiest bikini ever designed.

At Anna's insistence, Rigney spends thirty minutes spreading suntan lotion over her entire slender, taut-skin body. His erection stretches his skimpy bikini bathing suit to its limits. *Why did I let her talk me into this swim suit!*

When Anna sees off-watch sailors from the base staring, Anna tells Rigney to run his hands under the bottom of her bikini to lotion all of her butt.

"Do it," Anna orders.

"Okay. You asked for it." Rigney spends five minutes rubbing her butt under her bathing suit. Every now and then, he moans, "Oh, baby, oh, baby."

"Do it for five more minutes," she orders.

"Come on, Anna," Rigney whispers. "Everyone is staring at us. I have such a hard-on, I can't stand for fear of embarrassment."

Anna grins and says, "See those two men standing at the edge of the parking lot who stare at us?"

Rigney casually looks around and sees the men on the edge of the parking lot. "Yes, I see them. They are the two I saw leading Rodgers, Spaulding, and Chief Henry out of Rodgers's house."

Anna comments, "I bet they have hard-ons, too. They have been watching you run your hands over me for the last twenty minutes. Let's make sure they have a difficult time walking away, and we can give a show to your shipmates."

Anna turns over on her back and spreads her legs, not too wide.

Anna whispers, "Okay, Rig, put some more lotion on your hand. Then, run your hand under the front part of my bottoms. Then, run your hand under my top. You may linger slightly as you enjoy yourself feeling me up. Make sure everyone on the beach sees pleasure on your face. I will fake pleasure, also."

"Who the hell is faking pleasure," Rigney says with a sigh. He rubs lotion on his hands. Then, he runs his right hand inside the front of her bottoms and lingers for a moment while he fingers her pubic hair, then, removes his hand."

"Such a gentlemanly feel, Rig. Now, the breasts, linger a little longer."

"Anna, don't you think this is inappropriate for the beach?"

"You're in Southern Europe, Rig. Nudity on beaches is considered appropriate. At least we are still clothed."

He runs both his hands under her top. He lingers for a few moments as he cups her breasts and feels her hard nipples. "I guess you are enjoying this, too," Rigney comments with a devilish smile."

"Don't get the wrong idea."

"Yeah, Yeah, I understand."

"Okay, it's your turn to be felt up," Anna says matter-of-factly, as she rises and kneels on the blanket. "Lie on your back."

"I can't lie on my back. It will be like a flagpole marking my spot."

Anna hands Rigney a towel. "Lay this somewhat bunched over your hard-on. That way you will hide it."

She pours suntan lotion over her palms and begins massaging Rigney's shoulders. The firmness of Rigney's muscles arouses her, against her own resistance to be aroused. As she slowly moves her hands over his hard belly, she glances up and looks around. The crowd of American sailors has grown. She snickers to herself. Then, she runs her right hand under the towel and under his suit. She strokes his penis twice before removing her hand. She giggles.

The suddenness of Anna's actions causes Rigney to jerk. Fantasies dance through his head as he is pleasured by the stroking of his penis.

Anna's actions cause every staring male to skip a breath and skip a heartbeat. What Anna did was obvious to everyone.

"Oh my god!" Rigney moans.

A demure look appears on Anna's face, and she says, "The thought to do that just popped in my head, to substantiate everyone's opinion that we are playful and carefree."

Rigney gulps and breathes heavily; then, he asks in a husky whisper, "Ever consider finishing that task?"

As she moves her hands to his legs, she replies, "Exorcise ideas of hand jobs and blow jobs from your mind. It will never happen."

"Never?" he challenges. "You trying to convince me it never crossed your mind? I suppose discovering the length and width of my dick never crossed your mind before. Now, you know." Rigney smiles arrogantly.

"Don't you get enough hand jobs and blow jobs from Dottie?"

"No confirmations. Are you jealous?"

Anna feels a hint of jealously but controls not showing it to Rigney. "Do you know how to treat a woman romantically and how to tenderly make love to her?" Anna challenges, jealousy getting the better of her. "A loving sexual relationship with a woman is more than hand jobs and blow jobs."

"And cunnilingus," Rigney adds. "Don't you agree?"

Anna inhales sharply as she visualizes Rigney's head between her thighs, sucking and licking her clitoris. She sighs deeply.

"Uh hah! Got ya thinking about it, huh?"

"This is getting too hot," Anna scolds.

"This act was your idea. You're the one who jerked my dick."

"This is going too far. Let's get off it."

"Okay, but when you're ready to act out your fantasies, I will be ready."

"Stop!"

Rigney nods his head and sits up; he looks toward the parking lot. "Our bad guys are leaving."

Anna does not look toward the parking lot. "Let's get into the water."

"We just put on suntan lotion," Rigney objects.

"We need to stop petting each other and cool down."

Chapter 98

John sits on the tile floor behind the couch, concealed from the view of the patio doors. He has a clear view of the movement sensor control panel. He also has a clear view of Master Chief Crimer who stands elevated from the living room on the stairs landing. Jeff hides behind an overstuffed chair that sits away from the wall and on the edge of the area rug.

Although a strong breeze moves through the villa, John sweats under the heavy body armor. He looks at his watch—1300. Page and Anna have been gone for three hours. *What's keeping these guys?* Then, John chastises himself. *Come on, John. Lack of patience is an enemy in these situations.* He remembers the days and nights he spent in one spot on a hill or edge of a field while he waited for his target. *If I could lie in the same spot in a jungle for three days, I can easily endure this.*

For the thousandth time, John glances at the sensor panel. The alarm light is flashing. He snaps his fingers twice.

Crimer and Jeff become alert. They double-check safety-off on their weapons.

John and Jeff look up at Crimer who crouches on the landing.

Crimer stares up and to his left, waiting for Larry who stands at the upstairs bedroom window and watches the west wall. Larry will step outside the bedroom door and signal to Crimer the number of intruders entering the villa.

Thirty seconds later, Larry appears at the bedroom door and signals. Master Chief Crimer turns his head toward the living room and raises two fingers. Then, he brings the XM-21 to firing position.

A few seconds later, the intruders' footsteps sound on the patio, followed by a moving shadow. Whispering in Spanish is heard. The first intruder steps through the patio doors and into the living room.

John peers around the corner of the couch. He sees the first intruder motioning to the other to follow.

Jeff keeps his eyes fixed on John. He will jump to his feet when John gives the signal.

Crimer who now hides behind the wall of the staircase peers over the banister. He sees the two intruders. His eyes open wider when he observes that the intruders have their automatic pistols tucked into their waistbands.

The two intruders face each other. They discuss where in the villa they should hide and the best way to capture Page and the German woman.

John and Jeff jump to their feet with their weapons aimed at the intruders. John shouts, "Poner a pavimento!"

Crimer steps down to the landing with the XM-21 aimed at the closest intruder.

Each intruder stiffens and exhibits fear. They look around. One of them whispers something in Spanish. They bend as if they are following John's order to lie on the floor. Then, each intruder reaches for his weapon.

Crimer fires the XM-21 in semi-automatic mode. John and Jeff fire their Berettas in semi-automatic mode.

The patio glass doors shatter; glass splinters and shards splatter the floor.

Chips of stucco fly from the walls.

The two intruders fall to the floor. Multiple spurts of blood shoot from their bodies.

Crimer pulls the trigger nine times.

John pulls his trigger nine times.

Jeff pulls his trigger ten times.

Some of the bullets exit through the patio doorway and kick up clouds of dirt. The Spaniard standing at the west wall knows something is wrong. He takes a few steps toward the house, stops, and turns around. He runs toward the west wall.

In the upstairs bedroom, Larry hears the barrage of dampened gunfire. He hears some shouts in a foreign language. His aim on the man near the west wall does not waiver. When the intruder turns toward the west wall, Larry fires three shots into the intruder's back. The intruder falls facedown into the dirt.

The lower level of the villa fills with a haze of gun smoke.

Chapter 99

Anna stands and walks toward the water. She sexily sways her hips as she walks. Rigney follows close behind.

"Is that hip movement for me or for the audience?"

Not sure whom it's for, she minimizes her swish. She busies her thoughts with self-rebuke as she realizes Rigney has brought her to sexual revelation. She seriously considers having sex with him—not the tender lovemaking she talked about, but pure hardcore sex with lots of pawing, fingering, sucking, and licking.

They splash around in the water. Occasionally, they wrap their arms around each other and kiss. Anna puts some feeling and passion into the kisses, unlike previous times when they kissed for the benefit of the audience.

After a too-long and too-passionate kiss, Anna pulls back, looks into Rigney's eyes, and says softly, "You're getting too much into character. Let's get out of the water."

"I can't. I got another hard-on."

"Okay. We will wait a few minutes."

As they exit the water, they see Greg standing at the edge of the parking lot.

When Greg is sure that Rigney and Anna see him, he gets back in the Volkswagen bus and drives off.

"We will wait thirty minutes before we leave."

Rigney nods.

With their sexual familiarity from earlier subdued and no longer necessary, they sit quietly on their beach blanket and stare at the water.

Sailors from the base watch Anna and Rigney. After ten minutes, they realize the erotic show is over. Some leave, and some stay and scan the beach for women in skimpy bathing suits. One sailor scans the beach for men in skimpy bathing suits.

After several minutes, a curious expression appears on Anna's face, and she asks in a whisper, "You killed two men yesterday, less than twenty-four hours ago. It doesn't seem to bother you."

"I have killed evil men before. I don't feel guilt or remorse about it."

"But that bothers you, right? That you don't feel guilt or remorse, right?"

"It did once, but not anymore. Killing evil men in the act of being evil no longer bothers me."

"Have you made your decision about joining ONI? Brad Watson told me that if you say no after this mission, your days with ONI are over."

"I don't see that as a bad thing."

"You want to go back to just being a sailor?"

"Nothing wrong with just being a sailor."

"Yes . . . of course . . . that's not what I mean. I don't think you will be satisfied with living a sailor's normal life. You crave the danger of the mission. You thrive on the thrill. You seek to fight evil and overcome it."

Rigney nods his head in agreement with Anna's words. Then, he asks, "Did Brad tell you to talk to me about this?"

"Yes, and Brad and John think you're an ONI rising star. They say that you need go through ONI's counterespionage course."

"That course takes six months. I don't want to be dry-docked for six months—back in school."

Anna chuckles and responds, "It's not like being in school. You can't imagine any training like what that course involves."

Rigney glances around the beach and sees two people walking nearby. He asks in a lowered voice, "Did you go through the training?"

"Yes, and I almost failed. I became very ill during survival training."

"Survival training?"

"Yes, six weeks in the Panama Jungle."

Rigney stares out to the water and considers his future. Then, he asks, "If you would have failed the course, would you still have worked for ONI?"

"Yes, as an analyst sitting in an office, not a field operative."

"Analyst sounds safer."

Anna smiles knowingly, chuckles, and says, "Like you, Rig, an office job is not what I am."

Rigney nods agreement. He wonders about the difficulty of survival training in Panama. *Panama!* "Panama—survival training—that must be what Barbara Gaile is doing now."

"Actually, she just finished survival training. I met her at ONI headquarters when I was back in DC. She passed the survival training and has moved into the final weeks of her training. She said a lot of nice things about you."

"Barbara and I are close friends. ONI is what she wants. I wish her success."

"You left submarine duty to come on this mission. Seems this is what you want, also."

"I still have time to decide."

Anna sighs deeply and cautions, "Well, we are only a few days away from concluding this mission. Then, you must advise Brad of your decision." Anna stands and directs, "Let's go back to the villa."

CHAPTER 100

Anna and Rigney express astonishment as they look around the villa's living room. Bullet holes splatter the walls. The wall paintings hang torn and tattered from violating bullets. The patio doors hang limply on one hinge with all the glass shot away.

Greg and Larry sweep up and mop up plaster, glass, and blood.

"Any survivors?" Anna asks John.

"No."

"Where are the bodies?" Anna asks.

"The wine cellar," John replies.

"How many?"

"Three."

Anna stands, thoughtful, for a few moments; then, she asks John, "Where's their car?"

"Still parked on the other side of the west wall."

Anna nods; then asks, "Have you prepped the bodies for shipment?"

"Not yet. I want Rig to look at them to see if he recognizes them."

Rigney follows John and Anna through the kitchen and down the stairs to the wine cellar. John and Anna discuss plans as to how they will discover Rodgers's location, now that the intruders are dead.

Rigney studies the faces of the three dead men and advises, "I can't recognize the two on the left, too many bullet holes in their faces. The third one is one of the kidnappers who took Rodgers, Spaulding, and Chief Henry. Anna and I saw him at the beach."

John advises, "Still leaves us nowhere to go."

Anna and John huddle and resume their planning of what to do next.

The footwear of one of the dead men catches Rigney's eye. He walks around to the other side of the three bodies to get a better look. His eyes go wide with recognition. "I think I know where they have Rodgers!" Rigney says with confidence as he stares at the dead man's tattered and threadbare red-colored boat shoes.

Chapter 101

Commander Caldwell orders Lieutenant Commander Blakely into his office.

"What's going on around here, XO? We got Master Chief Rodgers, Master Chief Crimer, Chief Henry, RM1 Spaulding, and RM2 Page missing muster this morning."

Mary replies, "I don't know, sir. I have two of the master-at-arms investigating. They haven't reported back, yet."

Caldwell stares suspiciously at the XO. He does not trust her. He knows he lost credibility with his officers, because of the Page incident. *She knows where they are. She lies to me.*

"Okay, XO. That's all." Caldwell dismisses her with an annoyed look on his face and a backward motion of his hand, as if he were swatting away an annoying fly.

After the XO exits, Caldwell slumps in his chair. He ponders his fate. *I will I not survive the fallout of Pritchings's testimony. Now that Pritchings is dead, I can claim Pritchings was lying, but Captain Jack was swayed by Pritchings's testimony. Pritchings practically gave a deathbed confession, and now I am being investigated. The COMNAVCOM master chief watched the whole thing. Pritchings was too believable as a defense witness!*

Caldwell picks up the COMMANDING OFFICER EYES ONLY message from COMNAVCOM and reads the text for the third time.

BT
C O N F I D E N T I A L COMMANDING OFFICER EYES ONLY
SUBJ: RELIEF OF COMMANDING OFFICER (C)
1. (C) CAPT RONALD RAYBURN WILL RELIEVE COMMANDER OLIVER CALDWELL AS COMMANDING OFFICER NAVCOMMSTA GREECE EFFECTIVE CAPT RAYBURN ARRIVAL

NAVCOMMSTA GREECE. CAPT RAYBURN WILL ARRIVE NAVCOMMSTA GREECE WITHIN 48 HOURS.
2. (C) MESSAGE ORDERS FOR COMMANDER CALDWELL TO FOLLOW.
BT

Caldwell sits back and slumps in his chair; he shakes his head in denial as he contemplates Page's impact. *What has the navy come to? An insignificant, arrogant, and disrespectful enlisted man reports aboard, then, destroys the lives and careers of two officers, and causes the death of another.*

Chapter 102

Rigney and John stoop, hidden, in a mound of jagged rocks on the elevated shoreline at the north end of the Nea Makri Marina. The hot, late afternoon sun glares in their eyes. The scent of the sea lingers heavy in their nostrils. Waves crash on the rocks thirty feet below them. The rocks provide few flat surfaces, and they must carefully choose where they step.

They arrived at the marina thirty minutes after Page identified one of the dead Spaniards as yacht crewman. They parked the Volkswagen bus on an olive orchard's dirt road one hundred meters to the north of where they currently stand. Dottie showed Rigney this spot several weeks ago as a place to snap some great pictures. *"It's a difficult place to get to,"* she had said, *"because of the jagged rocks you must climb."*

John hands Rigney a set of binoculars. They rise and stand straight and peer over the rocks. A breeze blows in from the sea and evaporates the sweat from their faces.

Rigney brings the binoculars to his eyes. Along the shoreline of the marina, shops and cafés are open. Dozens sit on patios of cafés. Others walk about from one shop to the other. Boats of all sizes lay moored to the floating docks of the marina. He focuses on the yacht tied to the dock most distant from the shore. "That's her," Rigney tells John. "The one tied to the farthest dock. There's a man topside, scanning the approach road with binoculars. He keeps checking his watch. He's got a sidearm."

John nods and comments, "We need to get aboard before she sails. Once she's on the open sea, we'll never get close to her." John shifts his binoculars to the approach road. "Uh oh," John utters. "They have a lookout on the road . . . in that red van. There is an automatic rifle on the seat next to him."

Rigney lowers the binoculars, shakes his head, and responds, "How we going to get aboard her while she's still tied up? Anyone topside will see us coming. If we try to swim to her, they'll feel us climbing aboard."

John looks thoughtful as he considers what they can do. Then, his eyes go wide as it hits him. "We must get them to move off that yacht."

"How we gonna do that?"

"We must disable the yacht so that it cannot get underway, but we must do it in a way that it doesn't look like sabotage."

"Like what?" Rigney questions with a furrowed brow.

"You're the sailor, Rig. What would you do?"

Rigney tosses around a few ideas in his mind; then, he says, "We could clog seawater intakes and exhausts. Ya know, cooling systems and flushing systems."

John looks curiously at Rigney and queries, "What would be the result of that?"

"Engines would overheat and air-conditioning would stop working . . . toilets would back up."

"Would all that happen while the yacht is still at the pier?"

"Yeah. The engines and air-conditioning within a few minutes and the toilets depending on use."

John looks doubtful and asks, "You think the engines are running?"

"Must be," Rigney replies. "No shore power cable connected to the yacht."

John raises his binoculars to his eyes. He sees single ropes on the bow and stern tied to cleats on the dock. He does not see any power cables.

John lowers his binoculars and asks, "We only have a few hours before they give up on their associates. What's your plan for clogging up those pipes?"

"Me?!"

"You must do it. You're the expert swimmer. Only one person can approach that yacht."

Rigney blinks his eyes; he exhibits concern; he evaluates the physical difficulties of the task ahead. The dive gear is in the bus parked in the orchard. He makes a mental list of the items he will need. "Give me ten minutes to get what I need from the bus."

Rigney returns fifteen minutes later; he dons his gear. He removes his ankle holster and hands it to John. Then, he straps a dive knife to his right leg. His facemask hangs around his neck. He will not use air tanks, because the lookout on the yacht might see air bubbles.

"What are you going to use to clog those pipes?"

"I've dived around docks before. All sorts of trash lie on the bottom."

John directs, "As soon as you clog those pipes, get back here. I will need you perched on these rocks when the rest of us go to free the hostages."

"Why here?"

"We must free the hostages somewhere between the yacht and their van. This spot provides an unobstructed view of the entire marina. If something goes wrong, I need you up here with the XM-21 to neutralize the enemy. You can do that, correct?"

"Yes, I can do that."

"Good, because I need to rely on you."

Rigney looks through the binoculars and estimates the distance from the docks to the van to be approximately fifty yards. "How will you rescue the hostages?"

"I haven't figured that out, yet," John admits. "But I will have a plan by the time you get back."

Chapter 103

Rigney steps down the rocks to the water's edge. He carries his dive fins in his right hand. His facemask hangs around his neck. The rocky shoreline hides him from the marina. He wears cotton pants and a cotton t-shirt. He wears sneakers as protection against sharp objects he is sure to find on the bottom under the docks.

He enters the water, straps on his fins, and secures the dive mask to his face. He swims southward for thirty feet. Then, he sees the marina and estimates the closest dock to be one hundred feet away. He raises his dive watch to his eyes and takes a bearing on the dock. Then, he submerges to six feet and begins his underwater swim. The extra weight of his water-soaked clothes makes the swim more strenuous than he estimated.

When he reaches the pilings of the nearest dock, he swims upward; then, he surfaces under the dock's wooden planks. He checks his compass and moves southward under the docks. When he must cross a separation in the docks, he swims underwater to the next dock. He can see the bottom and estimates the water to be twenty feet deep. Patches of tall sea grass sprout from the sandy bottom. As he predicted, small appliances, fishing rods, newspapers, plastic containers, engine parts, and dinnerware litter the bottom.

He slows as he approaches the yacht. Only a few people walk the docks; he does not worry about detection. He looks between the gaps in the dock's wooden planks and sees the topside lookout. Rigney hears the sounds of a two-way radio. The topside watch pulls a small radio from its holster on his belt.

It's a radio—not a sidearm.

The topside watch speaks Spanish into the radio and looks toward the approach road.

As he listens to the talk on the radio, Rigney employs his two years of high school Spanish to interpret the conversation. The voice on the other end of the radio reports in an impatient voice that their socios—partners—have not yet returned.

Rigney dives to the bottom and quickly gathers waterlogged newspapers and places those newspapers on the bottom under the yacht's hull. Then, he springs from the bottom and surfaces next to the hull near the stern. He hears the hum and feels the vibration of the yacht's engines. He takes a deep breath. Then, he dives to the bottom in search of an adequately sized fishing pole. He finds the size pole he needs, and he lays it next to the accumulated pile of newspapers. Then, he surfaces for another breath of air.

During his next dive, he grabs a handful of newspaper and picks up the fishing pole. He rises to the keel and finds the nearest water-intake pipe. Using the handle end of the fishing pole like a ramrod, he packs the newspaper into the pipe.

During the next ten minutes, he rams newspaper into all the intake and exhaust pipes. During the last two dives, he cuts away clumps of sea grass and releases the grass near the surface; the grass floats to the surface. Then, he surfaces under the dock next to the yacht. Looking through a space between the wood planks, he watches the topside lookout for any reactions. After several minutes, no change occurs in the lookout's behavior. Rigney swims off.

Fifteen minutes later, Rigney climbs the rocks where his swim began. At the top, he finds John and Master Chief Crimer waiting, impatiently. John holds a XM-21 sniper rifle.

"How'd it go?" John asks.

"It's done. The topside watch has a radio on his belt not a weapon."

"Yeah. We figured that out."

"They're speaking Spanish over that radio."

John nods and says, "We have settled on a plan. We will take out the driver of their van. We will hide in the van. When the kidnappers from the yacht open the door of the van we capture them.

A worried look appears on Rigney's face as he visualizes a thousand things that could go wrong with John's plan.

"Something's going on down there," Crimer reports while looking through binoculars. "Another guy has come topside and both of 'em are looking over the side."

"They must be experiencing seawater system failures," Rigney advises. "They're looking at sea grass floating around the yacht. Shouldn't take long for them to conclude that sea grass has clogged the yacht's intake systems."

John hands Rigney the sniper rifle and says, "Not much time left. You will cover us. Master Chief is your spotter."

Rigney nods. He worries about what will happen if he fails. Images flash through his mind of John and the others laying dead on the docks and shore.

"Come on, Rig. We got a rapidly changing situation here. It's show time. I can depend on you, right?"

Rigney nods and replies emphatically, "Yes!"

"After we take the van, you must decide on your targets and when to shoot."

"How will I know when to shoot? I don't—"

"God damn it, Rig! You'll never be trained to cover every situation. You must use your own judgment. I trust your judgment, and I trust your ability!"

Rigney takes a deep breath, sighs, and nods acceptance of John's counsel.

Master Chief Crimer evaluates the exchange between Page and Smith. He doubts Page's ability, but he trusts John's judgment.

"When making your decisions as to whom and when to kill, you must consider these facts. The U.S. Government will never negotiate with kidnappers. Because of that, those hostages will never survive their captivity. This is their only chance for freedom. We want Rodgers alive. We would like Henry and

Spaulding alive, also, but not at the expense of Rodgers's life. Do you understand?"

Rigney comprehends the cold reality of John's explanation. Then, he says softly, "Yes, John. I understand."

Crimer bows his head slightly in sorrowful acceptance of John's logic.

"One more thing," John announces.

Rigney raises his eyes to meet John's eyes.

"You must remain undercover. You cannot expose who you are. No matter what happens down there, you cannot come down there. Stay up here until either I or Anna says its okay."

"Yes, John. I understand."

"What about me?" Crimer asks.

"You must stay up here, too. We don't want more people knowing that you are part of this. It's all compartmented. We can't risk it."

John turns and makes his way down the rocks and jogs back to the Volkswagen bus where he meets up with Greg, Jeff, Larry, and Anna.

Rigney looks through the sniper rifle's scope at the kidnappers' van. The view through the scope provides a close-up of the driver and several feet on each side of him. A short automatic rifle with a curved magazine lies on the passenger seat. A handheld radio sits on the dash.

The crosshairs divide the van driver's nose. The powerful scope provides a crystal-clear image of the driver's face. The driver's shifting dark eyes, blowing black hair, and twitching nose above a thick mustache adds humanity to Rigney's target. Rigney cannot pinpoint the man's age, but with no gray hair, Rigney estimates thirty-five to forty. Jagged holes in the man's skin tell of former teenage acne.

Rigney reflects on his training with the sniper rifle. Previously, he shot motorized mannequins, and he shot expertly. This is the first time he has aimed a sniper rifle at a living human being. His stomach churns as the driver's eyes shift from the road to the yacht to the rearview mirror. At one point, the driver looks directly in Rigney's direction, as if he sees Rigney aiming the rifle. Then, the man's eyes shift to the rearview mirror. Rigney shudders slightly as he understands the life within this man and the result of a bullet piercing the man's brain.

The van driver keeps his eyes moving. As lookout, he must report the arrival of his compadres with the hostages Page and the German woman. He must also report any suspicious activities.

What suspicious activities? The driver thinks to himself. *The Americans do not know of our existence. How could they?*

The van driver scans the marina again. This time he takes a few extra moments to study the rocky hill at the north end of the marina. *Excellent place for an ambush . . . but the Americans do not know we are in Greece. We have hidden our identities and movements so well. The local police could not possibly know who we are from whatever was found in Rodgers's house. A simple burglary gone wrong they will think. Hmmm . . . but won't they wonder about what happened to Rodgers? Still, the authorities have no knowledge of our presence.*

Chapter 104

Up on the rocks, Master Chief Crimer alternately scans the yacht and the kidnappers' van with binoculars.

Rigney keeps the sniper rifle aimed at the van driver.

Crimer reports, "They are getting anxious on the yacht, and the chatter over their radio has increased. One of the crew on the yacht has raised the access doors to the engines."

Crimer shifts the binoculars to the van. "Oh my god!"

"What is it?" Rigney asks, not taking his aim off the van driver.

"Anna is walking . . . approaching the van from the rear. She's wearing a skimpy two-piece bathing suit."

"Won't the driver recognize her?"

"She's wearing a large sun hat—hides her face."

"How do you know it's her?" Rigney asks as he holds his aim on the driver.

"She's wearing the same two-piece she had on earlier today when you went to the beach, but she's done something to it . . . to reveal more of her. If that doesn't distract the van driver, he ain't human."

Anna stops in the middle of the road about fifteen feet from the van's passenger side window.

The van driver has his head turned to the right and stares, mesmerized, at the bikini-clad woman.

Anna turns around several times and makes actions as if she is looking for someone of something. The sun hat hides her face from the van driver.

The driver's heart pumps faster, and his penis swells. He moves his eyes over the body of the woman standing in the road. The tight, low-cut bikini top leaves nothing to the imagination as to the size and shape of her breasts and nipples.

The van driver leans across the driver's seat to get a better look. He has lost focus of his mission.

Then, the driver focuses his gaze on her tiny bikini bottom, which reveals half her butt and a half inch of her pubic hair.

Rigney keeps the scope aimed at the van driver's head.

A gust of wind rises from the water and blows Anna's hat from her head.

The van driver takes about five seconds to recognize Anna and to understand her purpose for such an erotic display.

Crimer reports, "The driver recognizes Anna—he's reaching for the radio."

Through the scope, Rigney sees the van driver reach for the radio. He applies pressure to the trigger.

"Wait!" Crimer chirps. "John's got 'em."

Rigney eases up on the trigger as he hears Crimer's words and sees a 9 millimeter automatic with silencer pressed against the van driver's head.

John threatens the van driver in a menacing tone, "Pare—si usted respectar tu existencia!"

The van driver recognizes the American accent of the grammatically incorrectly spoken Spanish, but the words convey the American's intentions. He pulls his hand back from the radio.

On the rocky hill, Crimer shifts the binoculars to the yacht. The two men topside pay attention to what happens at the van; they stare and point into the engine well.

Anna walks away from the scene and back to the bus in the orchard.

Greg and Larry climb into the back of the van. Greg moves to the front of the van, pulls his silencer-equipped 9 millimeter Beretta, and places the barrel against the driver's head, relieving John.

John lowers his weapon and tucks it into his belt. He climbs into the back of the van with the others. They remain quiet, waiting for the next unpredictable action to occur.

Up in the rocks, Rigney's trigger finger rests against the XM-21 trigger guard. He still has the scope aimed at the van, but only for viewing what is happening in the van.

Crimer reports, "One of the guys on the yacht is calling the van on the radio."

John moves forward in the van and kneels next to Greg. John asks the driver, "Do you speak English?"

"Yes, I speak English good," the Spaniard responds nervously; sweat flows down his face.

John responds, "And I speak Spanish good. Say only what I tell you to say on the radio, and you will live through the day."

The van driver nods nervously and says, "Boss speak on radio he want me drive van more close to docks."

"Just tell your boss okay. Then drive to the docks."

The driver picks up the radio, keys it, and responds with a "Si."

Up on the rocks, Crimer tells Rigney, "The bad guys are bringing the hostages topside. Wait—what the—they have Dottie Caldwell!"

Rigney swings the sniper rifle around to the direction of the yacht. He sees the hostages standing in a single line on the bow; their hands tied behind their backs. All the hostages have bruised and swollen faces. An abductor stands in front of the hostages, and another abductor stands behind. Rigney has a clear shot on both.

Rigney's heart skips a beat when he sees Dottie's bruised, swollen, and cut face. He becomes angered. He places his finger around the trigger. He says in a whisper to Master Chief Crimer, "I can pick them off. Then, it's all over."

Rigney hopes for confirmation from Crimer, but Crimer remains silent. Rigney knows the decision to kill is his. Rigney places the crosshairs over the right ear of one of the kidnappers; he applies slight pressure to the trigger. Then, he stops abruptly as he sees his target talking down a ladder. All the hostages stand in the line of fire to the ladder.

Rigney lets off the trigger. "Fuck! There must be more kidnappers below decks!"

Knowing that there might be more kidnapers onboard, Crimer agrees with Rigney's decision not to shoot, but he does not voice his agreement.

Rigney takes a deep breath. He waits for the kidnappers to make their next move.

The van parks several feet from the entrance to the docks.

"They're coming off the yacht," Crimer reports.

Rigney refocuses the sniper scope on those disembarking. He sees one kidnapper following Dottie and Rodgers off the yacht. Their bonds have been removed, obviously so as not to attract attention of others around the marina. The kidnapper has his hand inside his shirt. Rigney assumes the kidnapper grips a weapon.

The distance from the yacht to the van is fifty yards. Rigney estimates five-to-six minutes for Dottie, Rodgers, and the kidnapper to make their way to the van. He takes his eye off the scope and looks toward the docks. He scans the area between the yacht and van and verifies no innocent bystanders in the way.

"I need to kill the kidnapper with Dottie and Rodgers before they get to the van." Rigney glances at Crimer for agreement.

"That's what I would do," Crimer agrees.

"But when I do that, Spaulding and Chief Henry will probably be killed by the kidnappers on the yacht."

"Probably," Crimer responds flatly. Crimer wishes they had brought another sniper rifle.

Rigney sighs deeply and declares, "I will do my best to protect them." He looks through the scope and places the crosshairs above the ear of his target.

Crimer provides Rigney with reports of happenings near the target. "No one within sixty feet . . . target follows hostages at four feet . . . van thirty feet away."

John kneels behind the van driver and peers over the driver's shoulder. He waits anxiously as Dottie, Rodgers, and the kidnapper approach the van. "Okay," John says softly. "It's time Rig. You must kill him before they reach the end of the dock."

The kidnapper walking behind Dottie and Rodgers shifts his focus back and forth from the van to his hostages. As he walks toward the van, he scans the outside cafés. He is on alert for a trap. Then, he looks at the driver in the van. He sees shadows of others in the van. He stops walking. A look of fear appears on his face. He pulls his weapon.

"Now Rig!" John pleads.

"He's pulling his weapon," Crimer reports.

Rigney pulls the trigger. The wind carries away the slapping noise of the suppressed firing noise.

The kidnapper's head explodes, and a red mist of blood, brains, and skull drifts away in the wind. He falls off the dock and into the water.

The van driver inhales sharply as he watches his compadre fall. He realizes his own fate if he does not cooperate with the Americans.

Rigney shifts his aim to the kidnapper on the yacht. He cannot find the topside kidnapper.

"He went below," Crimer reports.

John jumps from the back of the van and runs toward Dottie and Rodgers. John holds a .45 automatic in his right hand.

Bystanders who sit at the outside cafés stare out at the docks, seeing and sensing unusual activities. Those bystanders who saw the kidnapper shot and fall into the water point in the direction where the man fell.

Dottie and Rodgers stand on the dock; they look around, confused. Their backs were to the kidnapper. They did not see why the kidnapper fell into the water.

"This way—quickly!" John says loudly has he beckons Dottie and Rodgers to the van.

Dottie and Rodgers bolt toward the van. No one follows them.

John guides them into the rear of the van; he tucks his .45 automatic in his waistband.

On the yacht, Chief Henry and Spaulding, with their hands still bound, shuffle toward the gangway, escape in their minds.

"Henry and Spaulding are moving toward the gangway," Crimer reports.

Rigney focuses the sniper rifle scope on the topside hatch, hoping the kidnapper reappears.

"Page, he came up through the aft hatch! Uh oh—he's got an automatic rifle!"

Rigney shifts his aim aft.

"He's shooting at the van!" Crimer's voice pitches high with alarm.

Chief Henry and Spaulding throw themselves to the deck to avoid the line of fire.

The sound of automatic weapon fire causes shoppers and café patrons to flatten on the ground or scurry into shops.

The crosshairs of Rigney's sniper rifle finds his target near the aft hatch. He pulls the trigger three times. The first two bullets enter the kidnapper's chest. The third bullet passes the kidnapper and harmlessly hits the water. The topside kidnapper drops the automatic rifle, staggers backward, and falls over the rail and into the water.

Crimer announces loudly, "Who's that at the forward hatch? He's diving overboard."

Rigney shifts his aim to the forward hatch and sees no one. Then, he moves his aim to where he estimates the man entered the water. He flips the switch to full automatic and fires a burst of bullets into the water. He takes his eye off the scope so that he can get a wide area view of the yacht and immediate vicinity. Then, he considers that the man who dove into the water might be hiding under the dock. He puts his eye back to the scope and aims at the dock area alongside the yacht. He fires a six-shot burst into the dock. Wood chips and water spout in a mixed spray.

In the kidnappers' van, John has bound, gagged, and blindfolded the Spanish driver who now sits behind the driver seat and is tied to a cargo stay.

John exits the van. He quickly scans the marina; then, he glances toward the rocky mound. Then, he stares at the yacht some fifty yards away. He sees to men he believes to be Spaulding and Henry lying on the deck near the gangway.

Believing the shooting is over, some bystanders stand and look around. Some stare at John, knowing he is a central figure in this drama.

Greg drives the van away from the marina and disappears around a curve.

Chapter 105

"Do you think that's it, Master Chief?" Rigney asks as he lowers the sniper rifle.

"Don't know. Looks like John is going to the yacht. Henry and Spaulding are getting up. I guess—"

A loud explosion interrupts Crimer. The earth shakes and the air shockwave pounds against their ears. The blast blows apart Henry and Spaulding, and their remains incinerate in the fireball. Windows shatter. The air shockwave knocks diners off their chairs. Some on their feet who are closer to the yacht, including John, are knocked to the ground. The surface shockwave pushes water over the docks. Thousands of burning pieces of the yacht and dock rise with the fireball two hundred feet into the air. The explosion and fireball consumes one hundred feet of dock. The fireball quickly devours all fuel within its reach and subsides just as quickly.

Rigney keeps the sniper rifle aimed in the marina's general direction, but he scans the area with his eyes looking over the top of the scope. He sees people rising from café patios and running away, putting distance between themselves and the docks. Understanding replaces his initial astonishment. *Make's sense . . . must have been a lot of intel data on that yacht that they wouldn't want us to find.*

Now, only floating smoldering debris remains.

Rigney glances at Crimer and asks, "Do you think the guy who dove overboard survived?"

"Don't know . . . could have."

"We can't let him get away, Master Chief. If he gets away and gets to Spain, I still have a threat over my head."

"Don't think he was part of that gang—fair skinned and blondish-colored hair. He didn't wear dark clothes like the others. He wore light-colored pants and a white shirt."

Rigney ponders Crimer's description; then, he comments, "Could have been another hostage."

"Unlikely. He was not tied up."

Crimer looks toward the marina and watches John's actions. "John is going back to the bus. He must think it's over. He needs to know about the man who might have escaped. I'll meet him at the bus. You stay here. I will come back and get you when John says its okay."

Rigney nods acceptance of Crimer's order.

"Keep an eye on the marina. That blond-haired guy could surface anywhere."

Rigney lays the sniper rifle on a rock next to him. He picks up the binoculars and scans the marina. The binoculars give him a wider view than the scope on the sniper rifle. He feels confident that if the blond man comes ashore, he will see him.

Crimer lowers himself down from the rocks. He grunts softly as some of his unexercised leg muscles stretch more than they are accustomed.

An understanding smile crosses Rigney's face as he hears Crimer's grunts. His smile fades as he focuses the binoculars on the smoky area where the yacht previously existed. Pieces of smoldering wood float on the surface. His manner becomes reflective and sympathetic as he thinks about the death of Chief Henry and Spaulding.

He shifts the binoculars to search the shoreline around the marina and continues to think about Chief Henry and Spaulding. *They were ordinary sailors who worked hard at their jobs. I don't know their motives for being in the navy. I did not know them well, but they served, which reveals a level of dedication. They were innocent victims of circumstances they did not create. I had more to do with creating those circumstances than they did.*

His sympathetic mood fades as he thinks about the cruel and evil men responsible for innocent deaths. Then, his thoughts turn to anger and revenge. He thinks back to last February when he stood less than five feet from Lucifer—Javier Ramirez. Rigney clearly remembers Lucifer's threat. *"You successfully deceived me, but my associates and I have long memories. You will sleep well for a while, but not for long."*

Rigney worries about a life of looking over his shoulder, wondering if Lucifer's men will one day be successful and kill him. He also worries about Lucifer's men killing more innocent people in the future. *I must finish this. I cannot let this organization survive. I must do all that I can to destroy them.*

Andrei crawls onto the rocks. Blood seeps from his nose—a result of the concussion his body took from the underwater shockwave. He looks southward and verifies that the mound of rocks hide him from the marina. He stares at the top of the rocky mound and estimates the height of the rocky mound to be about thirty feet. He concludes that he can view the entire marina from the crest of the mound. *I will verify the American operatives are gone before I sneak away.*

Anger and fear regarding Lucifer's gang wells within him. He considers actions he can take to insure his lifelong safety. His thoughts are interrupted by the sound of movement behind him.

Andrei comes around the corner of a rock. His eyes look down, watching where he puts his feet. He senses someone a few feet away; he quickly looks up.

Rigney turns his head and sees a man with sandy-colored hair, light-colored pants, and white shirt. Water dripping from the man's hair and clothes discloses he swam from the marina. *The man who dove off the yacht!* He picks up the sniper rifle with one hand and turns swiftly to face the man; but as he swings around, the silencer and barrel slam into a rock. The force of the sudden resistance knocks the rifle from his hand. The rifle bounces on the rocks and falls into a crevice outside of Rigney's reach.

Andrei stops, fearful as he sees the young man pick up a rifle; then, he feels relief as he sees the rifle fall into the rocks. He quickly surveys the immediate vicinity for an escape path. The young man blocks the only way down from the rocks to the landward side. Then, Andrei recognizes the young man from many pictures. *Rigney Page!*

Rigney looks around frantically for his Beretta.

Andrei follows Rigney's eye search.

Rigney's eyes land on the pile of dive gear at Andrei's feet.

Andrei stoops quickly, picks up the dive knife, and jumps back to a standing position. He unsheathes the knife and holds the knife in his right hand. The two-inch wide by ten-inch long blade gleams in the sunlight. Andrei points the knife at Rigney.

Fear flows through Rigney's body. A moment ago, he was the hunter. Now, he is the prey.

"Out of my way—let me pass—you will live."

Rigney notes the man's slight accent. He evaluates the threat before him. The man is middle aged, but his trim, broad-shouldered physique conveys the man probably knows how to handle himself. *I can't let this murderer go. He killed Chief Henry and Spaulding and probably many others.* Commitment for revenge and stubbornness for justice forces fear from his mind. Rigney centers himself in front of the gap in the rocks that allows access to the landward side. He spreads his feet to allow quick jumping in any direction.

"Do not be foolish, Rigney Page. I have no reason to kill you, even though you killed my associates. I have no cause to harm you. I do not take it personally."

Andrei has no experience with a knife, but the boy before him does not know that. Andrei believes he has the upper hand. Andrei feels concern, but no fear.

Rigney stands his ground and shakes his head, indicating he will not stand aside. *He called me by name. How much does he know about me?*

Andrei jabs forward with the knife.

Rigney jumps to his right and at the same time throws a lightning-fast left hook, which lands squarely on the man's mouth.

The impact of the powerful punch knocks Andrei back three feet, and his back slams against a rock.

Rigney quickly steps forward, preparing to throw a right hook.

Andrei jabs forward again.

Rigney attempts to sidestep the jab. The knife cuts him across the forearm. He steps back and puts five feet between himself and the stranger. The cut on his forearm is only two inches long and one-eighth inch deep.

Andrei leans forward off the rock and resets his feet. He stares menacingly into Rigney's eyes. He raises his left hand to his mouth and feels the flowing blood. He spits out four teeth. He realizes the boy before him will fight and fight hard. He says, "Javier was right. You are dangerous. I should have listened to him." Andrei attempts to gain psychological advantage. *I can reveal my identity to Page, now, because he will not survive this fight.*

Andrei's revelation about Lucifer causes Rigney to pause as he attempts to understand why the man before him made this revelation.

"Did you kill Javier?" Andrei questions.

Rigney remains silent and calculates his next move.

"Or maybe he resides in one of your prisons?" Andrei, the relentless intelligence operative, attempts to gain information.

Rigney takes two steps toward Andrei.

Andrei jabs the knife toward Rigney.

Rigney successfully dodges the jab. His hands move at dazzling speed; he clamps his hands around Andrei's right wrist.

Andrei, startled by Rigney's speed, tries to push the knife toward Rigney, but Rigney's strength pushes Andrei's arm back. Andrei balls his left hand into a fist and slams his fist repeatedly into the side of Rigney's head.

Rigney feels pain from the man's punches, but he shakes them off. He puts all his energy and strength into pushing Andrei back against the rock.

Andrei continues to punch Rigney in the side of the head until he realizes he must use his left hand to push his right hand, the knife hand, toward Rigney. He shifts his left hand to the top of the knife's handle and pushes, but pushes futilely. He attempts to kick Rigney in the groin, but he cannot get any power behind a kick.

Rigney's strength defeats Andrei's efforts. Rigney twists Andrei's wrist clockwise.

Andrei screams in pain as the ulna and radius bones break free from his elbow. He pushes his left hand against his right hand, but his right hand and forearm no longer have power. He only feels the excruciating pain in his right elbow. He screams in pain. He yells, "Page, please stop! I beg you to stop!"

Rigney ignores Andrei's pleading. Rigney thinks about a threat-free future as he twists Andrei's knife hand 180 degrees. The knife, still in Andrei's hand, now points at Andrei's throat.

Andrei can no longer resist Rigney's strength. He yells, "Please stop! I surrender!"

The knifepoint cuts one-half inch into the pocket just below Andrei's larynx.

Their faces are just six inches apart. Andrei's face expresses fear and horror. Rigney's face expresses no emotion, but his mind calculates a reckoning.

Then, with the anger of a thousand victims, Rigney hisses, "You did not give Chief Henry and Spaulding a chance to surrender!"

Tears flow from Andrei's eyes. He knows he will die. He closes his eyes to the inevitable.

With a final powerful push, Rigney drives the knife to the hilt into Andrei's neck. Several inches of the knife's point punch through the back of Andrei's neck. Rigney purposely keeps his face close to Andrei's so that he does not miss any of the man's agony.

Blood spurts from Andrei's neck.

Blood sprays over Rigney's face. He tastes Andrei's blood on his lips.

Andrei shakes and shudders as he fights death, but death comes.

Rigney releases his grip on Andrei's arm and steps back.

Andrei's lifeless body falls to Rigney's feet.

Rigney turns, startled, to find John Smith and Master Chief Crimer ten feet away, staring at him.

"How long you been standing there? I could've used some help."

John responds, "We just got here."

"We thought we heard someone yelling surrender," Crimer adds.

Rigney shrugs and says, "Must have been the wind whistling through the rocks."

John stares knowingly at Rigney and says, "You have blood on your face, and your arm is cut."

Rigney nods, stoops, and searches through the dive bag. He finds a towel and the first-aid kit. He rises, hands the first-aid kit to John, and asks, "Will you bandage my arm?"

"Sure. Sit on that rock."

John studies the wound and declares, "You need some knife-fight training so you don't cut yourself next time."

Rigney's face becomes confused at John's words then states, "I didn't have the knife. He did."

John turns his head toward Andrei's body and stares at the protruding dive knife. He expresses revelation regarding Rigney's actions. Then, he says, "Your abilities continue to impress me."

While John sterilizes and bandages Rigney's wound, Rigney wipes the blood from his face. He asks, "Master Chief, where's the canteen?"

"I left it on a rock. Oh, here it is." Crimer hands the canteen to Rigney.

Rigney wets the towel and rubs the remaining blood from his face. The right side of his head throbs with pain from the multiple hits he took from the man's fist.

Crimer busies himself with gathering up their gear. "Where's the rifle?"

Rigney points to a crevice on the seaward side of the rocks. "It fell down there."

Crimer grunts as he works his way down the crevice.

John and Rigney engage in a private conversation. "You had to kill him?" John challenges.

"He would have killed me."

"You're sure of that?"

Rigney reflects for a few moments; then he answers, "His death increases my chances of a safe future."

"We could have arrested him," John proposes.

"If he killed me, he would have escaped."

"You're sure he would have killed you?"

Rigney stares curiously at John, wondering about John's obvious doubts.

"John, he killed Chief Henry and Spaulding. He would have killed me, too. I applied my ONI training, which is to never give an attacker a second chance to come after you."

"This guy was important. We didn't expect him to be here." John stands and walks over to Andrei's body. Rigney follows.

John stares at the knife protruding from Andrei's neck.

Rigney comments, "He knew Lucifer, but he doesn't look Spanish. Who is he?"

"His name is Andrei Yashin. He was a KGB operative. He was Rodgers's Russian contact. CIA believes Yashin contacted some people from Lucifer's organization. CIA thinks that Yashin resurrected Lucifer's organization after he discovered you were in Nea Makri."

"What could be the benefit in that?"

Crimer climbs out of the crevice with the sniper rifle in hand.

John whispers to Rigney, "We'll talk about this later."

Crimer scans the area; then, he looks at John and asks, "What now?"

"We go back to the villa," John replies.

"What about him?" Rigney asks as he nods toward the body.

"We take him with us and store him in the cellar with the others."

With a serious look on his face, Crimer shakes his head and says, "The body count is high on this mission."

Rigney looks at Crimer and responds, "Look at it this way, Master Chief. We rid the world of some evil men today."

Chapter 106

The van moves just under the speed limit. Greg drives the van up the slope of Mount Penteli, away from Nea Makri and toward Athens. Larry, Dottie, the captured Spaniard, and Rodgers sit on the floor in the back of the van. Larry holds a handgun on their Spanish prisoner. The Spaniard is near unconsciousness from the tranquilizer injection applied by Larry ten minutes ago.

Rodgers looks through the windshield and notices they are driving up the mountain away from Nea Makri.

"Where we goin'?" Rodgers asks Larry.

"We're goin' to get you and Miss Caldwell medical attention."

"Where?" Dottie asks. "I should call my uncle and tell him I'm okay."

"You can call him when we get there."

"Get where?" Rodgers questions, his voice becoming agitated. He leans forward toward Larry. "I'm okay. You can take me home or take me to the base."

"That's not an option, Master Chief." Larry's tone becomes domineering.

"Why not?" Rodgers believes he already knows the answer.

"Because you are under arrest for black marketeering and for espionage against the United States."

Dottie inhales sharply, and her eyes go wide as she stares at Rodgers.

Rodgers glances toward the rear door.

Larry points the handgun toward Rodgers and warns, "You have nowhere to run, Master Chief. We have seized your bank accounts, and we know about your villa on Skyros."

Rodgers sits back against the side of the van. His body goes limp with resignation.

Dottie glances around the van. She turns back to Larry and asks, "What's this all about? Who are you? Why did they kidnap me?"

Larry responds, "I can't tell you anything now. I will tell you as much as permitted, later. You can be assured that you are safe now."

Dottie asks, "What was that explosion? Did you guys blow up that boat?"

"Can't tell you anything about that." Larry has been in the game long enough to speculate accurately on what blew up and who did it.

Night falls as the Volkswagen bus approaches the villa. The outside security lights are off.

After driving into the courtyard, Crimer exits the car and closes the gate. Anna unlocks the door. John and Rigney carry Andrei Yashin's body to the wine cellar.

Rigney, Anna, and John enter the communications room.

Master Chief Crimer goes to the refrigerator. He finds cold bottles of Heineken; he grabs one and downs it in one gulp. Then, he grabs a couple more bottles and puts them on a tray. He makes a pitcher of ice water and puts it and four glasses on the tray. He takes the tray to the communications room.

"That's a nasty bruise on the side of your face," Anna says to Rigney. "How'd you get it?"

"I got into a fight. I will make an ice pack after we're done in here."

"It's swelling," Anna argues. "You need an ice pack now."

"I'll make you one," Crimer offers. "And I will find something to tie it to your head."

"Thanks, Master Chief."

"No problem."

Chapter 107

Rigney stands at the side of Dottie's hospital bed. He holds her hand.

"They're releasing me this afternoon," Dottie tells him.

"So you're not hurt bad?"

"No. The doctors just wanted me to stay overnight while they ran tests."

"You have a black eye," Rigney observes sympathetically.

She responds, "That bruise on the side of your head looks worse. What happened?"

"Stupid thing, there was some radio equipment racked out. I didn't see it and turned right into it."

"Does it hurt?"

"Only when I breathe."

Dottie smiles and shakes her head slightly at Rigney's cavalier manner.

Rigney asks, "How did you get that black eye and those cuts and bruises on your face? Some sailors at the base said they saw you come off a boat with Master Chief Rodgers and a civilian that got shot. Then, a man who looked like an American with a gun in his hand jumped out of a van and ushered you and Rodgers into the van. Then, the boat you were on blew up."

A serious look overcomes Dottie's expression as she says, "Rig, I was kidnapped several days ago by Spanish criminals. They took me aboard that boat. The next day they brought Master Chief Rodgers and Chief Henry and that black first class . . . I never knew his name. Then, this blond-haired man came aboard, and they all started speaking English with each other. Then, the blond-haired man, named Andrei, questioned Master Chief Rodgers and the others. When they wouldn't answer, he would hit them across the face—"

"Hold on," Rigney interrupts. "This Andrei was the one doing the hitting?"

"Yeah, he wore thin black gloves when he hit us."

"This Andrei hit you, too?"

"Yes, three times. He didn't hit me as hard as he could, but it still hurt. He would put a mirror up to my face to show me the damage he was doing."

Dottie's explanation reinforces Rigney's initial opinion of Andrei as an evil person.

Rigney asks, "Did they hurt you in any other way?"

"No. They did not rape me. Some of the Spaniards felt me up, and they kept threatening to rape me."

Rigney's face expresses relief. Then, he says, "I will wait here until they release you. I will drive you home."

"Rig, that man, Andrei, questioned me about you."

"What did he ask?"

"He wanted to know what you did at the base. I told him I didn't know. That's when he hit me the first time. He questioned me about you and Anna and about Anna's house. He knew I had been there and wanted to know if I saw anything unusual. When I said no, he hit me again. Then he asked me about the layout of the house. He wanted to know about security systems. Why would he want to know about you and Anna and the house?"

"I don't know."

Dottie removes her hand from Rigney's hand and accuses, "Yes, you do know, Rig. I am not stupid. I have been around the navy all my life. I know about people like you . . . secret agents working undercover."

"No, Dottie, I don't—"

"Please don't lie to me! Everyone's lying to me!" Dottie starts to sob. "God damn it, Rig, I feared for my life for three days. I cried all the time. I could have been raped and murdered, and it's your fault. Those criminals saw me with you and they kidnapped me . . . to use me as hostage so you would do what they told you to do . . . right?"

Rigney's expression and manner become regretful and apologetic as he explains, "I didn't know you had been taken hostage until I saw you come topside on their yacht, just before you and Rodgers and one of the kidnappers left the yacht to go to the van."

"You were there! I didn't see you. Why didn't you come to me in the van when we were rescued?" Dottie's tone becomes demanding and confrontational.

"My boss told me not to do anything to blow my cover. I couldn't come out into the open. I didn't know you had figured it out . . . who I am, I mean."

Dottie regains composure. She stops crying. "I hadn't figured it out, then. Who would have ever suspected that you are some kind of secret agent. I put it all together when the agent in the van arrested Master Chief Rodgers . . . all those poker games at Rodgers's house and those questions about you from that Andrei."

Rigney reflects on Dottie's emotional condition; then, he says, "I couldn't tell you about me. I hope you understand that."

"Of course I understand. You're the one who doesn't understand." Dottie's eyes mist over, and her words are strained. "I gave more of myself to you than I ever gave to any man, and you put me in danger. Don't you understand that the people around you are in danger?"

Rigney realizes that he had never considered how his work endangered Dottie. *Am I so selfish—so self-centered?*

"Don't wait for me to be discharged. I want you to go. My aunt will come and get me. I'm going back to the States. I need to put distance between me and that Andrei and his gang. I leave in two days. I don't want you to contact me again, unless you quit your line of work. You know where to find me."

Rigney attempts to lift Dottie's spirits. "You don't need to worry about Andrei and his gang. They're all dead."

"Dead? John didn't say anything about that."

"John?"

"Come on, Rig. Don't tell me you don't know John, the American agent who took me and Rodgers to the van. John came to see me this morning. He asked me a lot of questions about what happened on the boat, but he didn't say anything about Andrei and his gang being dead. What about the van driver? I saw the MPs take him off in handcuffs."

"The van driver will never see the outside of a prison. I assure you, Andrei and the rest of his gang are dead."

"I am more afraid of that Andrei than I am of those who followed his orders. Did you see him dead? I must know so that I can sleep at night."

"Yes. I saw his dead body."

"Where did you see him dead? I must ask you this, because I have come to doubt you."

"I saw him dead at the marina."

"Did he blow up with the boat?"

Rigney hesitates to answer. He believes that if he lies, he has no chance with Dottie in the future. "No, not on the boat." Rigney hesitates, takes a deep breath, and reveals, "I killed him . . . after he attacked me with a knife."

Dottie inhales sharply. She expresses shock. She stammers, "God, Rig, I thought I knew you!"

"You can never tell anyone," Rigney cautions. "What I did at the marina is top secret."

"So why did you tell me?"

"Because I want you to feel safe from Andrei, and maybe someday you will trust me again, and we can be close again."

Dottie shakes her head slowly as she says, "I don't think you will ever be close to anyone."

In the hospital parking lot, Rigney lowers the top on the BMW. He needs the warm, humid air blowing against his face as he drives through Athens and over the mountain back to Nea Makri.

During the drive, he stresses over Dottie's feelings toward him. Dottie made clear to him what he should have understood himself. *If I stay with ONI, I cannot become close to anyone.*

Chapter 108

Captain Rayburn stands on the small stage in the ballroom of Club Zeus. He faces the chiefs and officers of NAVCOMMSTA Greece. His trim six feet and five inches tall build, coupled with his squared jawed tanned face, wavy gray hair, and impeccable white summer uniform commands respect from the men before him.

"When I assumed command last week, my first order was that all current command instructions and standard operating procedures remain in effect. During the last seven days, I have talked with all of you and many junior members of the NAVCOMMSTA crew. I gained valuable information as to command operations and command morale. I believe that the information I gained now allows me to make some sound decisions and accurate judgments.

"Today's meeting is one-way. I will tell you what I want done and by when I want it done. I will not consider questions or objections at this meeting. If you wish to discuss my orders, please use the chain-of-command to arrange a meeting with me. YN3 Grandville attends this meeting to record orders I issue and required deadlines."

Captain Rayburn steps over to the podium and looks at a stack of papers. Then, he looks at the COMMO and says, "Lieutenant Lemont, I will trust your judgment as to how many watch sections and watch positions are needed to meet our communications commitments. You may establish the structure as you see fit without permission from the XO or from me. You may also specify uniforms best suited for watch standers in the communications department."

Gerry Lemont writes notes and smiles with relief.

"Master Chief Crimer, I want your recommendations for establishing additional sentries and roving patrols twenty-four-seven for both here at Nea Makri and for the transmitter site at Kato Souli. Submit your recommendations to the XO within four days from now."

Crimer nods and responds, "Aye, Aye, Captain."

"XO," Rayburn calls.

Mary looks up at Rayburn.

"Return all report chits with specifications of message processing errors back to the COMMO. Those report chits do not exist, and I do not want to see any more of them, except for those unusual occurrences of numerous or continuous errors judged so egregious by Lieutenant Lemont that he believes captain's mast or court-martial is warranted."

Mary Blakely and Lieutenant Lemont respond in unison, "Aye, aye, Captain."

"XO, who is the new Club Zeus Manager?"

"CWO3 Yearling. He was the assistant OIC at Kato Souli. He will also be the new CMS Custodian."

A murmur of conversation erupts among the chief petty officers. They wonder what happened to Master Chief Rodgers.

Captain Rayburn hears the name of Rodgers. He explains, "Master Chief Rodgers has been transferred. He will not return."

That revelation causes more talk. Captain Rayburn stops the talk with a question. "Is Mr. Yearling in the room?"

Mary answers, "No, sir. He is with the COMNAVCOM CMS inspectors. They are performing an inventory of the crypto account."

"XO, have you completed the audit of Club Zeus?"

"Yes, sir, and the report is complete."

"Can we reopen the club?" Rayburn asks.

"Yes, sir, we can."

"Today?"

"Yes sir."

"Let's open it at noon. Oh, and I want all the Greek employees of the club paid as if they were at work all along."

"Yes, sir, will do."

"And the club shall be open seven days a week," Rayburn orders.

"Yes, sir," Mary responds with a smile.

"Mr. Lemont, I want a report by this time next week as to why we have three Adonis machines that are not on the authorized equipment list."

"Aye, aye, sir," Lemont responds.

"Mr. Linderhaus," Rayburn calls as he looks over the crowd.

Eric steps out of a shadow, raises his hand, and says, "Here, sir."

"Mr. Linderhaus, mailing 2-Kilo maintenance forms to COMNAVCOM is again your responsibility."

"Aye, aye, sir," Eric responds; then, he steps back into the shadow.

Captain Rayburn looks at his list. Then, he calls, "Master Chief Crimer, from this time forward the barracks is open to all residents twenty-four hours a day and reinstall the weight machines."

"Aye, aye, captain!" Crimer replies, jubilant and cheerful.

"And, Master Chief, no more reveilles in the barracks for church or for any other reason."

"Yes sir."

"XO, for security purposes, I still want the main gate closed at midnight and the names recorded of anyone who enters or departs the base after midnight. However, investigation of those entering or departing will be discontinued unless some security condition warrants."

Marry nods and takes more notes.

"To relieve overcrowding in the petty officer barracks, single E5 and above may request to move off base and receive single BAQ and COMRATS. I will consider each request on a case-by-case basis."

As Captain Rayburn looks at his notes, low-volume comments of approval rise from the chief petty officers.

"And the final item," Captain Rayburn announces, "no more weekly, Saturday morning personnel inspections. Weekend liberty is automatically authorized for all hands, except for those in the duty section and those on the restricted list."

Smiles and enthusiasm return to the faces of the NAVCOMMSTA officers and chiefs. They revel in the anticipation of good morale returning to the base.

CHAPTER 109

"Page, we need to talk to ya about Newman."

Rigney lays the probe leads of the multimeter on his workbench. He turns and faces Patterson and Thompson.

"What about Newman?" Rigney responds with an uncaring tone.

Patterson says, "Master Chief Crimer is on Newman's ass to tell who the two Greeks are that attacked you. If Newman tells, he puts his life in danger. He stepped into some deep local criminal shit when he hired those Greeks."

Rigney shrugs and responds, "His problem. He must suffer the consequences of his actions."

Thompson's manner becomes agitated; he says, "Look, man, Newman ain't all that bad. He's had some tough times. No father . . . no good role models when he growin' up. His mother was an addict. He grew up on the streets of Atlanta. First person to give a shit about him was a gang leader. He dropped outta high school after his junior year. On his first try to sell drugs, he was arrested. The judge told him to join the military or go to jail. Navy almost didn't take him, 'cause he was a high school dropout, but his high GCT-ARI scores earned him a waiver for a two-year enlistment. But a two year hitch don't get a school. Now, he faces Leavenworth. If he goes there, his life is ruined. After Leavenworth, he'll go back to gangbanging on the streets of Atlanta, and he becomes another black man who is destined to life in prison." Thomas pauses and stares into Page's eyes, searching for some sign of sympathy toward Newman. "So whatta ya say, Page? Newman can be salvaged, but not if he goes to Leavenworth."

Patterson and Thompson's concern for Newman confounds Rigney. He responds, "I don't think there is anything I can do. The navy is chargin' him, not me."

"Yeah, but you could stand up for Newman," Patterson declares. "You're in tight with the chief-master-at-arms. Maybe ya could do sum'thin'."

"Like what?" Rigney challenges.

"I dunno! Go talk to him and see!" Patterson challenges back with a loud voice and exasperated tone.

With a furrowed brow, Rigney sits in thought for a few moments. Then, he asks, "Let's say that we can prevent Newman from going to Leavenworth. Won't he just go back to Atlanta and join the gangs anyway when his enlistment is up?"

"We're trying to talk him outta that," Patterson says. "He says he will change his ways. He says he learned his lesson."

Rigney responds, "Newman must commit to a concrete goal. Something that sets his future on a path other than going home to Atlanta and rejoining the gangs."

"Like what?" Patterson asks.

Rigney responds, "Will Newman talk with me? Will you two set up a meeting and the four of us sit down and talk?"

"I'll ask him," Thompson advises. "I'll get back to ya."

Chapter 110

Master Chief Crimer and RM2 Rigney Page sit across the desk from the XO in her office.

Lieutenant Commander Mary Blakely asks, "Master Chief, what did you two want to talk about?"

"Ma'am, Page wanted me to arrange this meeting. He wants to talk with us about Newman."

"Okay, Page, you have the floor."

"I want to know if we can prevent Newman from being court-martialed for hiring those two Greeks to attack me."

The XO expresses surprise. Then, she orders, "Explain."

"Ma'am, if Newman goes to Leavenworth, I believe an injustice will be done. I think that if he goes to prison, he will be another life destined to live at the bottom of American society. I think Newman's actions against me were the result of a lifetime of hate rammed down his throat from the time he was born. I think Newman is redeemable. I think that if we prevent him from going to prison, we can mold him into a respectable sailor who can be of value."

"How would that be done?" the XO asks.

"First, we will tutor Newman on the GED exam. Then, when he has earned his GED, he applies for a navy school, and he obligates the necessary active duty time to get that school."

"Who are *we*?" Crimer asks.

"Me, Patterson, and Thompson."

The XO sits silent for several minutes while she considers Page's proposal; then, she asks, "Why are you doing this?"

Page remembers the promise he made to Diane Love when they last met at the Main Street Café in his hometown of Seal Beach, California. Newman's situation is exactly what Diane was talking about. "Ma'am, I think it's our duty and obligation to salvage Newman. He needs a break. Otherwise, he is destined to a valueless life."

Mary stares at Page. She visualizes that day when Page saved her from abduction, rape, and death. She remembers how easily he brutally and without emotion killed her abductors. Now, he reveals compassion. "His actions against you cannot go unpunished," the XO declares.

Page offers, "What about Article 15 punishment instead of court-martial?"

Mary looks at Crimer and asks, "What do you think, Master Chief?"

"I've seen sailors worse than Newman turn around when seniors showed interest and provided guidance. I think we should try."

The XO nods acceptance of the master chief's evaluation. "I will talk to Captain Rayburn. I will let you know."

Chapter 111

ET1 Straton enters the repair shop. He carries mail in each hand. He lays mail on his workbench and the workbenches of Thompson and Patterson. An inquisitive expression crosses his face when he finds one envelope for RM2 Page.

"Hey, Page." Straton calls. "You got a letter."

Straton hands the envelope to Page and asks, "How come you never get mail? Since you arrived here, this is your first letter. Nobody loves ya, eh?"

Rigney studies the envelope. No return address—postmarked Norfolk, Virginia.

Dear Petty Officer Page,

I heard the assault charges against you for hitting Jeffrey were dismissed. I support that dismissal, and I am happy for you.

I also heard you are responsible for having the police come to my house in Kifissia that night when Jeffrey was arrested. You saved my life that night.

I thank you, because your actions that day forced me to do what I wanted to do and should have done seven years ago. Laurie and I are safe now. Jeffrey does not know our location, and I have restraining orders against him.

Jeffery's court-martial for attempted murder against me starts next week, and I think he will be convicted.

I wish you well, Petty Officer Page. Laurie and I owe you our lives. We are forever in your debt.

Warmest regards,
Constance Martin

Rigney sighs. His eyes mist over. *If that does not vindicate me, nothing does.*

A loud bang and strong vibration comes through the floor. Thompson jumps to his feet, looks down, and questions to no one in particular, "What was that?"

ET1 Straton responds, "Oh, I forgot to tell ya. NAVELEX Tempest Team arrived this morning. They're working under the trailers."

Chapter 112

Patterson, Thompson, Page, and Newman sit around the table in the small library in the administration building. They meet three nights a week for two-hour study sessions. At the end of each session, they assign Newman chapters to review from the GED study guides. They quiz Newman on the material during the next study session.

Patterson holds up a study guide to an open page. Newman looks at the picture and reports, "Stonehenge."

"Location?" Thompson asks.

"England," Newman responds.

"Function?" Page asks.

"Uncertain," Newman replies. "Historians say everything from a temple to a burial site."

Page holds up an open study guide.

"Isosceles triangle," Newman reports.

"Specifications?"

"Two equal sides and two equal angles."

Thompson does not hold up a study guide but asks a question.

"Magna Charta?"

Newman spends a few moments thinking; then, he responds, "One of the first democratic documents . . . gave liberty to the English during the 1200s."

Thompson looks at his watch and says, "It's almost 2000."

Everyone sighs and leans back in their chairs. The grueling session tires them, but they smile knowing they have been successful.

Thompson says to Newman, "You're doing well with the geography, history, and math, but you need lots more study in grammar and syntax."

"Don't we all," Page admits. "I wonder if I could pass the English part of this GED Test."

"Understand that," Patterson adds.

Thompson directs Newman, "Read section eight in all guides for next time."

Newman nods his acceptance of the assignment and says, "No problem. Wid all this restriction the captain give me at mast, I can't go nowhere, plenty of time to study."

They all stand and prepare to depart the library.

"Wait a minute," Newman says. "I want to thank yo' all for what you're doin' to help me. Page, you stood up for me with the master chief and XO so I didn't have to tell who I hired to beat you. That saved my life, man. Don't know why yo' helping me. After what I did to yo', I mean. Nobody ever help me like this before. Gettin' me a chance for a navy school."

Patterson says, "Just pass the GED tests. That's what ya need to focus on now."

"I'll pass that test," Newman promises. "Then, I apply for Fire Control Technician School."

Thompson tells Newman, "Your GCT and ARI scores are high enough for that, but you'll need to obligate six years for that school."

"I'm ready to do it," Newman replies.

RM2 Page stares intently at Newman.

Newman asks Page, "Why you lookin' at me like that?"

Page responds, "I was just wondering why you no longer talk like . . . like . . . I don't what to call it other than black-man talk."

Thompson and Patterson chuckle.

Newman smiles and says, "That black-man talk as yo' call it is how we learn to talk on the streets. Thompson and Patterson tol' me that if I want to advance, I must talk clearly and distinctly. They never talk that way 'cause they raised in the white man's world. Their parents are teachers and engineers. Black-man talk as you call it not allowed in their homes. I can talk like ya all, but I must concentrate. It's comin' easier."

Rigney nods; then, he says, "You also look like ya lost some weight."

"Yeah. Thanks for noticin'. With all this restriction and loss of pay, exercise and weight liftin' is about all a can afford. Don't know iffin ya all noticed, but I quit smokin' too."

"Way to go, Newman!" Patterson applauds.

Newman nods and responds, "Thanks, man. From now on, self-improvement is what I'm all about."

Chapter 113

John Smith and Master Chief Crimer sit on the couch in the villa's living room.

Anna enters the living room.

John and Master Chief Crimer stand.

Anna wears a black evening gown. She wears her hair up. Her earrings sparkle and so does the matching necklace. Her appearance is one of modesty, elegance, and grace.

John wears a black tuxedo with black bowtie, which contrast against his ponytail and beard.

Master Chief Crimer wears Full Dress Blues.

John takes Anna's hands and says, "You're gorgeous."

Anna smiles, looks into John's eyes, and says, "Thank you, sir, and you are looking very handsome." Anna bats her eyelashes.

Crimer bows his head slightly and smiles at the shameless show of affection.

Rigney walks into the living room. He wears Full Dress Blues. His white hat sits squarely on his head. His neckerchief expertly rolled and tied. For Rigney's uniform, the only difference between Service Dress Blues and the Full Dress Blues is that on his breast he wears the National Defense Medal instead of the National Defense Ribbon. Rigney, not one to always be prepared with correct uniform items, had to borrow Master Chief Crimer's National Defense Medal.

Master Chief Crimer's six rows of medals hide that fact that his National Defense Medal is missing.

Crimer walks over to Rigney, looks Rigney up and down, and says, "Sailor, your shoes need some work and your hairline could be trimmed better."

Rigney looks down at his black leather shoes. The brilliance from the spit-shine that took him two hours to create could not possibly be improved. Then he looks at the master chief's shoes and says, "As if you could do any better, Master Chief."

Crimer nods and chuckles, followed by smiles and chuckles from Rigney, John, and Anna.

Two beeps from a car horn sound from outside. John looks at his watch and reports, "Right on time."

They file through the front door. Anna sets the timer on the security systems.

They walk through the courtyard gate toward the awaiting Mercedes limousine. Rigney is the last through the gate and verifies it locked.

The limousine moves through the dusk of the evening. The darkly tinted windows and Greek license plate conceal the purpose of the limousine and conceal those who ride inside.

Rigney looks at John and asks, "Did you ever get clarification as to what this is all about?"

"Nope. All I know is what the ONI message said, which specified what to wear and what time we would be picked up."

"It's obviously some kind of formal affair," Anna offers. "And must have something to do with Hammerhead, because we are all going to this . . . this . . . whatever this is."

They all sit quiet for ten minutes; then, Rigney asks, "Anna, any word from Brad on where I'm going from here—been a while since the mission ended?"

"No. Brad's last message said orders are coming."

The limousine approaches a side gate of the American Embassy. A marine sentry opens the gate and waves the limousine through without a security check. The limousine parks under a canopy. Two marine sentries open the limousine doors.

A marine sentry guides them through darkly tinted double glass doors and into a small lobby.

Commander Bradley Watson who wears Full Dress Blues greets the Operation Hammerhead team. John introduces Brad to Master Chief Crimer.

Brad smiles with appreciation and says, "Master Chief, an honor to finally meet you. ONI is forever in your debt."

Crimer responds, "It's an honor to serve, Commander."

Brad smiles and announces, "You are all invited to a military awards ceremony, followed by a reception."

"Who's being awarded?" Anna asks.

"Master Chief Crimer and Petty Officer Page."

Crimer and Rigney exchange surprised glances.

The marine sentry leads everyone up a set of stairs, down a hallway, and into a large dark-paneled meeting room. A mixture of twenty civilians in formal wear and military officers in full dress uniform mingle around inside the meeting room. The murmur of conversations halt and all eyes turn toward the Hammerhead team and curiously appraise them.

The meeting room has no windows. A podium stands at one end of the room. At the same end of the room as the podium, a United States flag hangs from a pole in one corner and the flag of the Department of State hangs from a pole in the other corner. A table buffet loaded with food stands along another wall. A drink bar stands at the far end of the buffet table; a bartender serves drinks. Six white tablecloth-tables with chairs stand on the other side of the bar. Silverware sparkles on the tabletops. The Hammerhead team walks over to the bar.

The din of conversations resume, and the volume rises.

Radioman Second Class Rigney Page and Master Chief Boatswain's Mate Lawrence Crimer have a few minutes alone at the bar while Brad, John, and Anna mingle with some of the military and civilians. Rigney sips a cocktail of unknown mixture; he trusted John's recommendation. Crimer sips a draft beer.

During a pause in sipping, Crimer queries Page, "Something I've wanted to know . . . just curious."

"What, Master Chief?"

"I'm curious as to what you said to Commander Caldwell that caused him to lift your pretrial restriction to base. I've never seen that happen before. He restricts you to the base in the morning. Then, you talk to him during the afternoon, and he lifts the restriction. Can you tell me what you said to him?"

"Oh, that. I told him I knew he was Mr. Martin's uncle. I warned him that if he didn't lift the restriction, I would expose the relationship. I told him that I would never tell anyone if he lifted the restriction."

"How did you find out he was Martin's uncle? Dottie?"

"No. She never said anything. First time I heard it from her was when she testified. I found out through an ONI intelligence report."

"But you told your lawyer?"

"No, I never told anyone. My lawyer said he found out during reading Mr. Martin's service record. He said that a copy of Mr. Martin's security clearance application listed 'Caldwell' as Mr. Martin's mother's maiden name."

"So you kept the secret, even when Commander Caldwell was plotting and conspiring against you?"

"Yes, that's right."

Master Chief Crimer sighs deeply and wonders what corrupted Oliver Caldwell. He must have been a respected officer at one time.

Several minutes later, after they refresh their drinks, Crimer tells to Page, "I envy you."

"Envy me. Why?"

"Because you have your whole navy career ahead of you . . . to discover all that I discovered . . . experience all that I experienced. I have less than six months before mandatory retirement. I would give anything to do it all over again."

"I don't think I have a navy career ahead of me. Officers like Mr. Martin and like Commander Caldwell cause me to doubt the navy's wisdom as to whom they put in leadership positions. Those types of officers destroy morale and make sailors' lives miserable."

Crimer counters, "Regarding Martin and Caldwell, the navy corrected itself. Justice was done."

"But not until they did a lot of damage. Had I not bucked the system, they would still be destroying morale. The navy took too long."

"No, Page, you did not buck the system. You used the system. You employed those legal procedures available to you to avoid miscarriages of justice."

Rigney admits to himself that he sees some logic in Crimer's reasoning.

"Page, you're putting too much significance on the impact of some poor leaders. The value of your work in the navy and with ONI far outweighs some of the navy's personnel problems."

A doubtful look appears on Rigney's face. He attempts to calculate his importance in such a large organization.

"I am no gung-ho, spit-and-polish sailor, Master Chief."

"Few are," Crimer reveals. "Look, Page, let's say you stop working with ONI and work in the navy only as a radioman. I want you to think about this. Working in rate for twenty to thirty years is more important and provides more of a contribution to America than any job you can have in civilian life. Why trade a life of adventure for the dull routine of some civilian job? Add to that continuing service with ONI and at the end of your life you can proudly say that you served and made a difference. How many civilians can say that?"

"You make a powerful argument, Master Chief."

"John told me that you must make a decision about continuing to work with ONI, or you will be sent back to normal radioman duties. I hope you make the choice that best serves your country."

Rigney sighs deeply as he realizes he must make a decision soon and realizes his decision will determine the direction of the rest of his life.

Commander Brad Watson comes back to the bar to refresh his drink. He glances at Rigney and asks, "You're in deep thought. Anything I can help you with?"

"No sir." Rigney responds. "Master Chief gave me a lot to think about."

Rigney looks around the room and notices two admirals talking with two distinguished-looking civilians near the podium.

"Who are the admirals?" Rigney asks Commander Watson.

"The one on the left is Rear Admiral Vernier. He is Commander Naval Communications, COMNAVCOM. The one on the right is Rear Admiral Yarns. He is director of naval intelligence. The civilian on the left is the United States ambassador to Greece. The civilian on the right is the undersecretary of State, European division."

"Oh," Rigney responds. He stares admiringly at the four powerful men.

Admiral Yarns notices Brad, Crimer, and Page looking in his direction. The admiral turns to a navy lieutenant behind him and speaks a few words.

The lieutenant steps smartly across the room to the Hammerhead team. He says to Brad Watson, "Admiral Yarns wants you all to come over. He wants to introduce you to some dignitaries."

Admiral Yarns performs all the introductions. Rigney and Crimer are honored that Admiral Yarns knows their names.

After the introductions are complete, Admiral Yarns says to Master Chief Crimer, "Master Chief, I read the reports of your actions during Operation Hammerhead. Your voluntary actions provided valuable resources when we badly needed them. I read your record. You are an outstanding example of senior enlisted leadership. It is my honor to serve with you."

Crimer's face flushes red with embarrassment. He stutters, "Uh . . . well . . . thank you, Admiral."

Admiral Vernier adds, "Master Chief, your performance during Hammerhead was courageous. I am proud to have you as a member of my command."

"Thank you, Admiral." An appreciative smile appears on Crimer's face.

Admiral Yarns asks Crimer, "I understand you reach maximum time-in-service within the next six months. Then, you must retire. Is that correct?"

"Yes Admiral."

"How do you feel about that?"

"Admiral, I would stay for another ten years if the navy permitted. My request for continued service past thirty was denied, just as it is for most of my peers when they ask for continuance. I understand the policy. We must make room for those who follow us, like Page here."

All eyes glance at Page.

Then, the director of ONI advises, "Master Chief, if you want to continue serving after you retire, I have something for you. ONI maintains boat operations around the globe, for ELINT and for quick deployment and retrieval of operatives and others. We constantly search for qualified and experienced veterans." Admiral Yarns hands a business card to Crimer, "After you retire, contact my staff at the number on the card. Give my staff the codeword on the back, and they will make an immediate appointment for you to see me."

"Thank you, Admiral. I will contact you."

Admiral Yarns nods then turns his attention to Page. "Petty Officer Page, you have demonstrated initiative, resourcefulness, and courage during Operation Jupiter and Operation Hammerhead. You have proven yourself as a competent field operative. You need some tempering, which I believe ONI's training will provide. Now, you are at a pivotal point in your life. It's time for you to make an important decision. I sincerely hope you choose wisely."

There is a pause in the conversation; then, the American ambassador says, "Rigney, because of the classified nature of your mission, I have not been provided all the details. I know that the Operation Hammerhead team shut down a spy ring that was also involved in kidnapping and black marketeering and your team did not damage American-Greek relations while doing it. Greek authorities report the deaths and explosions in Nea Makri as the actions of foreign criminals."

Rigney responds, "Ambassador, I just did what I was ordered to do. I don't know who took care of the political maneuvering."

The ambassador smiles knowingly and says, "Rigney, knowing that it took political maneuvering reveals that you're less naive than you convey."

Commander Watson tells Admiral Yarns, "It's time, Admiral."

Admiral Yarns walks to the podium.

Commander Watson stands beside Admiral Yarns.

All civilians and military gather loosely to the left and right of the podium.

Commander Watson orders, "Master Chief Crimer . . . front and center!"

Crimer marches stiffly and stops six feet in front of the podium; he stands at attention and salutes. Admiral Yarns returns the salute. Crimer conveys confident experience with this type of ceremony.

Admiral Yarns lifts a thick navy-blue colored folder and opens it. He reads, "To all who shall see these presents, greeting. This is to certify that the President of the United States of America has awarded the Bronze Star Medal, third award, to Master Chief Boatswain's Mate Lawrence Charles Crimer, United States Navy, for courageous actions while engaged in classified operations during September 1968. Signed, Lyndon B. Johnson, President of the United States."

Admiral Yarns comes around the podium and walks to Master Chief Crimer. The admiral pins the medal on Crimer's chest. Then, the admiral steps back a few steps and orders, "Dismissed."

Crimer salutes. The admiral returns the salute. Crimer performs an about-face and marches back to the crowd and stands next to John Smith.

Rigney stands on the other side of John Smith. Grateful that the master chief went first, Rigney now knows how to act when called to the podium.

Commander Watson orders, "Radioman Second Class Page . . . front and center!"

Rigney marches to the podium and stops on the same spot were Crimer stood. Page comes to attention; then, he salutes.

Admiral Yarns returns the salute. Admiral Yarns lifts a thick navy-blue colored folder and opens it. He reads, "To all who shall see these presents, greeting. This is to certify that the President of the United States of America has awarded the Bronze Star Medal, first award, to Radioman Second Class Rigney Michael Page, United States Navy, for courageous actions while engaged in classified operations from December 1967 through September 1968. Signed, Lyndon B. Johnson, President of the United States."

The admiral comes around the podium and stands facing Page. He pins the Bronze Star Medal just above the National Defense Medal.

The admiral stands back a few feet and orders, "Dismissed."

Rigney forgets to salute. He relaxes and walks back to stand beside John Smith.

Rigney's incorrect protocol draws amused smiles from the military members in the crowd.

John whispers, "You forgot to salute at the end and march back."

"Shit!" Rigney whispers to himself—audible to John, but inaudible to others.

"That concludes the awards ceremony," Admiral Yarns announces from behind the podium. "You are all invited to enjoy the refreshments and the bar."

Several minutes later, Crimer, Page, and John Smith stand together and chat.

Rigney asks John, "Where are you going from here?"

"Back to what I was doing before Hammerhead."

"What's that?" Rigney asks.

"Back to my hippie cover and lots of beach."

"Where?"

John shakes his head emphatically.

"Okay, then, when do you leave?"

Tomorrow morning. I have a 6:30 flight. I have a room at the King George for tonight."

Rigney responds, "Oh, I thought you might stay at the villa—spend some time with Anna."

"You got it all wrong, Rig. Anna and I are just friends."

"Oh."

Commander Watson joins the group. He congratulates Crimer and Page. Then he says to Rigney, "You must give me your Bronze Star before leaving tonight. You cannot wear it. Your file at ONI will be the only record of this award. Someday, it will be returned to you."

"Okay sir." Rigney's tone conveys understanding.

"I depart for Washington tomorrow morning," Brad advises. "When I get there, I must reassign the members of Team Hammerhead. Should I order you to ONI for permanent duty, or should I send your name to the submarine radioman detailer, or do you want to stay in Nea Makri for the remainder of your enlistment?"

Rigney glances around to see who is listening. Only John Smith and Master Chief Crimer listen.

"Sir, if I come to ONI, will I stay in the navy, or must I become a civilian." Rigney glances at John, wondering if his career will match John's career.

"Your country would be best served if you stayed in the navy."

Rigney glances at John Smith. Then, he glances and smiles at Master Chief Crimer. He looks to Brad Watson and says, "I would like to work for ONI."

Brad Watson smiles and says, "Good, you will receive orders in two weeks. Meanwhile, go back to Nea Makri and stay out of trouble—for once."

"Yes sir."

Commander Brad Watson turns, walks off, and joins the admirals.

Master Chief Crimer stares appreciatively into Rigney's face and declares, "Rigney Page, I am proud to call you shipmate."

Glossary of Navy Terms

1MC - Ship's announcing system; ship-wide reports and announcements made over this sound system; announcing general quarters, chow time, ship's time by bells, flight quarters, reveille, taps, commence ship's work, liberty call.

2-Kilo - A 3-M form used for reporting technical problems and repair actions for all navy equipment by serial number. Also used as a work order. The information on the form is entered into central computer databases. An accurate, up-to-date, and centralized 2-Kilo database is crucial to rapid equipment improvements, legitimate manpower authorization levels, parts and maintenance support, and assignment of trained technicians.

3-M (Maintenance, Material, Management) - The U.S. Navy system for managing maintenance and maintenance support in a manner that will ensure maximum equipment operational readiness. The 3-M system standardizes preventive maintenance requirements, procedures, and reports on a fleet-wide basis.

4.0; four-oh - 4.0 was the highest numerical value a sailor could be assigned in a performance evaluation.

96 - The number of hours between watch strings. For most navy watch standing [shift work] organizations, watches are organized as two day watches, two mid watches, and two eve watches; then 96 hours off until the next watch string.

Adonis Crypto Machine / device - An electromechanical typewriter style machine used for offline encryption and decryption of military messages of all classifications and accesses. Codes changed daily.

ARI / GCT - Scores resulting from navy enlistment tests for math, knowledge, and reasoning skills.

ASC - AUTODIN Switching Center; Communications complexes located throughout the world that provide interface with tributary stations to AUTODIN and perform computerized relay of messages from one ASC to the other and to distant tributaries.

ASW - Anti Submarine Warfare; systems and processes used to combat enemy submarines

BAQ - Basic Allowance for Quarters; Expense paid by navy when sailor authorized to live off base.

Baudot code - A character set predating EBCDIC and ASCII and the root predecessor to International Telegraph Alphabet No 2 (ITA2), the teletype code in use until the advent of ASCII. Each character in the alphabet is represented by a series of five intelligence bits; sent over a communication channel such as a telegraph wire or a radio signal. Example: Baudot code for the alphabet character "A" = 11000; for "E" = 10000

BCP - Ballast Control Panel; located in submarine's control home contains controls for adjusting submarine's ballast / weight. Underway, BCP manned by the Chief of the Watch.

Blue Jacket - navy slang for a U.S. Navy sailor; a junior enlisted sailor

BOQ - Bachelor Officer Quarters.

Brown shoe navy - Navy jargon for those who work in naval aviation; based on a uniform that was unique to naval aviators that required wearing of brown shoes.

BUPERS - Bureau of Naval Personal; assigns personnel to ships and shore stations; establishes manpower requirements; maintains central personnel records

burn bag - A paper bag used for storing discarded classified paper.

burn run - Communicator jargon for the action of destroying classified material – normally paper bags full of classified paper.

butterfly wrapped - A method of wrapping teletype tape around fingers of the hand to produce compact product on long paper tape messages.

Captain's Mast - Navy terminology for Uniform Code of Military Justice (UCMJ) Article 15 punishment. Process by which commanding officers punish sailors for minor infractions.

CASREP; casualty report - Report of un repairable equipment onboard; tells the senior chain-of-command that ships personnel unable to fix equipment. Report will request outside technical help and / or parts.

CDO - Command Duty Officer – 24 hour duty. Represents Commanding Officer after normal working hours

CINCEUR - Commander in Chief of all U.S. military forces in Europe

CINCUSNAVEUR - Commander in Chief U.S. Navy forces in Europe

CINCLANT - Commander in Chief U.S. military forces Atlantic area

CINCLANTFLEET - Commander in Chief of U.S. Navy forces Atlantic area

CINCPAC - Commander in Chief of all U.S. military forces Pacific area

CINCPACFLT - Commander in Chief of U.S. Navy forces Pacific area

cleaning bill - Specifies what is to be cleaned, when it is to be cleaned, and who is assigned to clean it.

CMS - COMSEC (cryptographic) Materials Systems – manages distribution and accountability of crypto devices, codes, key-lists, and ciphers for both online and offline communications security systems.

CO - Commanding Officer

commercial re-file - A telecommunications activity that serves as interface between military and civilian communications channels.

COMMO - Communications Officer; Communications Department Head

CWO2; CWO3; CWO4; Chief Warrant Officer - Officer ranks between chief petty officer and ensign. Officers in these ranks are selected from the senior enlisted ranks, and selected because of their technical expertise and demonstrated leadership.

Communications Watch Officer; CWO - The person who supervises all command-wide communications operations during the shift. Originally, junior officers were assigned. As navy manpower lessened, the position was assigned to chiefs and, then, to first class petty officers.

Communications Watch Supervisor; CWS - The senior enlisted technical advisor to the Communications Watch Officer. Originally, chiefs were assigned. As navy manpower lessened, the position was assigned to first class petty officers and below.

COMNAVCOM - Commander Naval Communications; all Naval Communications Stations are under authority of COMNAVCOM Washington D.C.

COMRATS - Commuter Rations; expense paid by navy for food when sailor authorized to live off base.

COMSIXTHFLEET - Commander Sixth Fleet; operational commander of U.S. Navy ships in the Mediterranean

COMSUBPAC - Commander Submarines Pacific

COMSUBRON - Commander Submarine Squadron

CONUS - Continental United States

crow - navy slang for rating chevron.

CW - continuous wave; a mode of radio communications using Morse code.

Chief Warrant Officer; CWO2; CWO3; CWO4 - Officer rank between chief petty officer and ensign. Sailors in this rank are selected from the senior enlisted ranks.

DCA - Defense Communications Agency

Deck and Conn - Deck: At sea, in charge of ship navigation and safety; Conn: control of ship's engines and rudder.

dink list; Delinquent in Qualifications list - A list published weekly aboard submarines reporting who in the crew is behind schedule in submarine qualifications a program.

DNI - Director, Naval Intelligence

dungarees - U.S. Navy working uniform; denim fabric shirt and trousers; phased out during the 1990s

ECM - Electronic Counter Measures; electronic equipment used to detect and combat radiated signals from the enemy.

ELINT; Electronic Intelligence - ELINT is the collection of electronics intelligence, typically the collection of the target's electronic countermeasures capabilities, including areas such as jamming capability, electronic deception capability and other electronic emanations. Specifically, intelligence is derived from non-communications electromagnetic radiations from foreign sources (other than radioactive sources). ELINT covers operations including RADINT (Radar Intelligence), COMINT (Communications Intelligence), and TELINT (Telemetry Intelligence, i.e. interception of space vehicle telemetry during launch, in orbit, or during terminal stages) since these areas are also concerned primarily with electronic emissions. ELINT can be gathered by means of airborne platforms, ships on or below the sea, and in rising numbers via satellites.

EMI - Extra Military Instruction; a process used by midlevel leadership to punish sailors for minor infractions. Called "instruction" to get around the legalities that only a commanding officer can award punishment. Usually a dirty job loosely related to the infraction.

EMO - Electronics Material Officer; officer responsible for maintenance, repair, allocation of electronic equipment

ET - Rating designator for navy electronics technician

ETOW - Electronics Technician of the Watch; submarine control room watch position

eve watch - Navy communicator jargon for the swing shift

Exclusion Area - a Security Area defined by physical barriers and subject to access control; where mere presence in the area would result in access to classified material.

field day - Organized and scheduled activity to clean decks and spaces

FITREP - Annual report of officer performance

five by five; fivers - A radio communications term meaning loud and clear, high quality radio signals.

fleet broadcast - Shore based teletype, one-way transmit system that ships at sea are required to copy.

frock; frocked - The process by which a sailor who has been selected for advancement is allowed to wear the uniform and rank of the next pay grade before the official advancement date.

galley - chow hall; dining facility;

Galley Master at Arms - A navy petty officer who enforces regulations and provides crowd control in the navy dining facility.

GCT / ARI - Scores resulting from navy enlistment tests for math, knowledge, and reasoning skills

GMG / GMM - Rating designator for navy gunners mate; GMG – guns; GMM - missiles.

GMT - Greenwich Mean Time; Zulu time zone.

gut; the gut - The area of a port city with a heavy concentration of bars and brothels catering mostly to visiting sailors.

Helmsman - Mans the steering control on the bridge of ships

HF; High Frequency - Radio frequency range 3 – 30 Megahertz

HM - Rating designator for navy hospital corpsman

HUMINT - Human Intelligence; method of gathering intelligence using people watch, listen, and interact with other people.

IFF - Radio system that receives interrogation signals from air, surface and land IFF-equipped units and automatically replies with a coded response signal that provides own ship identification.

JASON Crypto – An electronic inline crypto device used for encrypting and decrypting teletype signals. Primarily used for fleet broadcasts.

KGB - The security agency of the Soviet Union government, which was involved in nearly all aspects of life in the Soviet Union since March 1954. Yet its roots stretch back to the Bolshevik Revolution of 1917 when the newly-formed Communist government organized Cheka, a Russian acronym for "All-Russian Extraordinary Commission for Combating Counter-Revolution and Sabotage. Headquartered at dom dva (House Number Two) on Dzerzhinsky Street in Moscow, the KGB had numerous tasks and goals, from suppressing religion to infiltrating the highest levels of government in the United States. They had five main directorates into which their operations were divided:

- Intelligence in other nations
- Counterespionage and the secret police
- The KGB military corps and the Border Guards
- Suppression of internal resistance
- Electronic espionage

LDO - Limited Duty Officer; previous first class petty officers and chief petty officers advanced to officer rank; duties normally involve managing departments related to previous enlisted specialty

LF; Low Frequency - Radio frequency range 30 – 300 kilohertz

MED – Mediterranean

Message minimize - A period of time when non-essential messages are prohibited from entering the military communications networks; usually initiated during periods of high-level defense alerts.

mid watch - Navy communicator jargon for the graveyard shift

MS - Rating designator for navy Mess Management Specialists; cook

mustang - A sailor who was advanced to officer rank from senior enlisted rank.

MWR - Morale, Welfare, and Recreation (department); a non-appropriated fund activity on military bases used to provide recreational services that is directed to improve the morale and welfare of personnel; usually includes baseball fields, basket ball courts, swimming pools, sports equipment check-out, gymnasiums, bowling alleys, enlisted clubs.

NATO - North Atlantic Treaty Organization; multinational coalition of mostly European countries.

NATO Message Re-file Center - A message center operated by U.S. Military communications facilities that receives messages from NATO in NATO message format and converts to U.S. message format and for converting U.S formatted messages destined for NATO into NATO message format.

NAVCAMSMED - Naval Communications Area Master Station; located in Naples Italy.

NAVCOMMSTA - Naval Communications Station

NAVCOMOPNET – A navy tape relay network that processed top secret message between operational units ashore and afloat.

NEC - Navy Enlisted Code; Code assigned to navy enlisted personnel that defines technical specialties and skills

NESTOR – Mythological designator for KY-8 encrypted voice devices

NOFORN - No foreign dissemination

ONI - Office of Naval Intelligence; Located near Washington DC

OOD (underway) - Officer of the Deck; captain's on watch representative; in charge of ship's maneuvering and operations during watch (shift); The OOD underway is designated in writing by the commanding officer and is primarily responsible, under the commanding officer, for the safe and proper operation of the ship. The OOD under way will: 1. Keep continually informed concerning the tactical situation and geographic factors that may affect the safe navigation of the ship, and take appropriate action to avoid the danger of grounding or collision according to tactical doctrine, the Rules of the Road, and the orders of the commanding officer or other proper authority.

OOD (in port) – Officer in charge of quarterdeck; controls access to ship in port

orderwire - A channel within a multichannel radio teletype configuration used to facilitate radio circuit management. Usually channel 1 of the multichannel configuration; normally operated from the technical control facility at the shore station and technical control room on the ship.

Orestes crypto - An electronic inline crypto device for encrypting and decrypting teletype signals. Usually used for ship-to-shore two way communications circuits.

peak loader - Additional operators assigned during busiest message volume periods.

PMs - Preventive Maintenance actions; part of the 3-M system

port-and-starboard watches - A situation when those who work shifts are required to stand watches for 12 hours on and 12 hours off.

Quartermaster of the Watch (QMOW) – Bridge watch position; primarily assists with ship's navigation while on watch; enters deck log entries

quarters - An event when divisions gather prior to start of working hours for muster, reading of the plan-of-the-day, and to here other announcements.

Restricted Area - Access controlled to specifically authorized personnel only.

RM - Rating designator for navy radioman.

RMSN - Navy rate *radioman seaman*; E-3 Radioman

Romulus crypto - An electronic inline crypto device (KW-26) for encrypting and decrypting teletype signals.

Routing Indicator - A four to seven alphabet character sequence; every military unit is assigned a routing indicator; similar in function to a email address.

SACEUR - Supreme Allied Commander European NATO forces

SCP - Ship's Control Panel; located in submarine control room; a panel containing controls and displays for steering and driving the submarine.

Seabee - A person in the navy construction ratings

SEA; Senior Enlisted Advisor - Advises commanding officer on enlisted matters. Usually, the senior enlisted man in the command, and usually a collateral duty. SEA was the predecessor to the Command Master Chief position / program.

ship over - navy jargon for reenlisting

ship to shore circuit - A radio teletype or radio Morse Code circuit in the high frequency range between a U.S. Navy ship and U.S. Naval Communications Station. Used to transmit and receive messages to and from the ship.

SOP - Standing Operating Procedure

Sound-Powered Phone – Intercommunications device aboard ships; normally used during battle stations; powered by the sound of human voice. Consists of earphones and microphone that rests on a chest plate.

squared away - Navy terminology for situations or people that significantly exceed minimum performance and uniform requirements.

SSN - Submersible Ship Nuclear; fast attack nuclear powered submarine

SSBN - Submersible Ship Ballistic Nuclear; nuclear powered submarine carrying intercontinental ballistic missiles; boomer.

suspended bust - A reduction in rank, but suspend for the specified period of time. Any misconduct during the specified time will result in actual reduction in rank.

synching - Military telecommunications slang for cryptographic synchronization between transmit and receive electronic cryptographic machines

TAD - Temporary Assigned Duty

Tape Relay - A teletype message relay system in which the paper tape punched by a re-perforator is torn off after each message is received and manually transferred by an operator, who examines the tape for the destination address and feeds it to a transmitter-distributor connected to a teletype line leading to that destination.

Technical Control - Facility within Naval Communications Stations responsible for radio circuit management and quality control

Tempest - Electronic specifications for minimizing classified information riding on electromagnetic waves.

The East - Cold War term referring to the communist countries; primarily, Eastern Europe and the Soviet Union

The West - Cold War term referring to the democracies and republics of Europe and North America

tracer(s) messages(s) - Official messages that request information regarding processing, handling, and disposition of other official messages. Usually initiated after or non-delivery or delayed delivery of important official messages.

traffic channels - Channels within a multichannel radio teletype configuration that are used to transmit and receive specifically formatted military message.

UCMJ - Uniform Code of Military Justice; The foundation of military law in the United States; established by U.S. Congress in accordance with U.S. Constitution, Art I, Section 8.

VLF; Very Low Frequency - Radio frequency range 3 – 30 kilohertz

Watch - Shifts to cover 24 / 7 work schedule

watch bill - Document, usually updated monthly, that lists who is in which watch section, specific watch positions by name, and the dates and times watches are stood.

WESTPAC - Western Pacific

WILCO - Radio telephone abbreviation for "will comply"

WWVH - The call-sign of the U.S. National Institute of Standards and Technology's shortwave radio time signal station in Kekaha, on the island of Kauai in the state of Hawaii.

XO - Executive Officer (second in command)

Yard bird - Navy jargon; refers to civilians who work in shipyards.

ZBO - Communications signal; list of messages by precedence

ZULU - Military communications operates on the same time worldwide. All communications clocks are set to ZULU (GMT) time zone.

Example of Naval Message

(destination routing indicator)

RTTCZNYW RUWPSAA0123 1651915-CCCC--RULYSUU.
ZNY CCCCC
P 150346Z JUN 67
FM NAVCOMMSTA PHILIPINNES
TO CINCUSNAVEUR
BT
C O N F I D E N T I A L
A. YOUR 141631Z JUN 67
B. JCS 072230Z JUN 67
C. JCS 080110Z JUN 67
D. NAVCOMMSTA PHIL 130041Z JUN 67
1. REF B TOR 133E/08 FROM NAVRELSTA KUNIA
   TOD 1700Z/08 TO DCS RELSTA DAGIS.
2. REF C TOR 0400Z/08 FROM NAVRELSTA KUNIA
   TOD 0449Z/08 TO NAVCOMMSTA GUAM.
3. REF D TRACER ACTION BY NAVCOMMSTA PHIL
   PERTAINING TO REF C.
GP-4
BT

NAVY RANK

Pay Grade	Rank	Abb.
E-1	Seaman Recruit	SR
E-2	Seaman Apprentice	SA
E-3	Seaman	SN
E-4	Petty Officer Third Class	PO3
E-5	Petty Officer Second Class	PO2
E-6	Petty Officer First Class	PO1
E-7	Chief Petty Officer	CPO
E-8	Senior Chief Petty Officer	SCPO
E-9	Master Chief Petty Officer	MCPO
W-1	Warrant Officer	WO1
W-2	Chief Warrant Officer	CWO2
W-3	Chief Warrant Officer	CWO3
W-4	Chief Warrant Officer	CWO4
O-1	Ensign	ENS
O-2	Lieutenant Junior Grade	LTJG
O-3	Lieutenant	LT
O-4	Lieutenant Commander	LCDR
O-5	Commander	CDR
O-6	Captain	CAPT
O-7	Rear Admiral (one star)	RDML
O-8	Rear Admiral (two stars)	RADM
O-9	Vice Admiral (three stars)	VADM
O-10	Admiral (four stars)	ADM